Beverly!
Best Wish
Kevin E. La
9. 3. 21

Bigfoot Sasquatch Files

Anthology 1

Volumes 1 through 10

Kevin E Lake

Copyright Kevin E Lake 2021

*No part of this work, in part or its entirety, may be reproduced or distributed, for sale or for free, without the express written permission of the author or the author's representative(s)

These stories are true…

...potentially.

The following stories are from Bigfoot Sasquatch Files
Volume 1:

We Never Asked For This Nightmare

Our dream, nay, our *unbelievable fantasy*, had come true!

My beautiful bride, Dearly, our son, Daniel, and I had made the huge move from the Philippine Islands, where we'd been, at most times, living like near starving third world peasants, to the United States!

And not just anywhere in the United States.

Albemarle County, Virginia! Right outside of Charlottesville, home of the University of Virginia and its founder and former U.S. President, Thomas Jefferson!

Charlottesville is one of the most beautiful and notably historic cities in America. It's the spot of both the beginning and the ending of the Lewis and Clark Expedition, sanctioned, of course, by Jefferson. Economically, Albemarle County is ranked one of the wealthiest counties, per capita, in the country- Charlottesville, of course, being the county seat. U.S.A. Today has consistently ranked Charlottesville as America's favorite small city in America to live in, and this, based upon polls from actual residents, showing just how happy and content the people who live here truly are.

And we didn't just come here, all the way from South East Asia, as serfs, but as proud, Virginia landowners, having bought approximately six acres of pristine land on the outskirts of Albemarle County, only a twenty five minute drive from Charlottesville, shortly after having arrived.

We'd made this miraculous transition in our life status by way of what I'm doing right now as I write this; writing! After many years of often living off of the equivalent of two U.S. dollars a day in the Philippines, my wife's native country, and the country in which our son was born, we'd finally hit paydirt due to what *you* are doing right now as you read this; reading what I write!

I'd expatriated to the Philippines for nearly six long years after coming home from the war in Iraq and spending six months in an Army hospital- having surgery and going through rehab- and summarily losing everything of earthly value, including but not limited to my first family, any hopes of a civilian career, any money or items of material value, and not by any means lastly, my sanity.

Written off for dead, and with good riddance, by anyone who'd known me in my previous life, I found myself in the islands, drinking myself to death, and every now and then, writing a word or two in a simple notebook with a cheap ballpoint pen that might write a hundred words or so before running out of ink. But hey, what can you expect to get for the equivalent of two U.S. cents, right? One quickly learns after expatriating to any third world country that there's a price to pay for that currency conversion being in your favor. The old saying, 'you get what you pay for,' holds true whether you're paying in dollars or pesos, and you quickly find that when true value *does* lie in the conversion and in your favor, the 'skin tax' will quickly take that away.

For those of you who've never been to Asia, and who can't quite read between the lines, the 'skin tax' is the *huge* price increase added to anything being purchased by a white foreigner when travelling through or living in Asia. No, this cold hard fact I share with you is not politically correct (one of the reasons these stories are being written down and shared in book form- all the social media platforms would punish us, if not outright delete our accounts for sharing such truths of the world with our followers), but it is a fact. It's only terrible to talk about such facts in the year this book is written, 2020. You see, when Pearl S. Buck discussed this truth by way of her Nobel prize winning novel, "The Good Earth" back in 1931, no one batted an eye. Such matters were enough to allow for the first female in history to win a Nobel prize in literature, but today? Well, no one wants to get locked under the social media jail, so here we are with the written word.

Oh, how I regress...

...and ramble.

Anyway, along came Dearly, the most beautiful woman, then and now, that I've ever seen in my life. Of course, upon seeing her, I asked her out, and surprisingly, she said no.

Here I was, in a country where women were throwing themselves at me, the underlying reason being that I was a white foreigner, and therefore, in their minds, a rich American (boy, were *they* wrong), and this young beauty was refusing my advances. When I asked her why, she simply said, in her somewhat limited and extremely cute broken English, "You talk too much! About nothing. Ramble, ramble, ramble…"

This, or course, made me want her even more.

After more than a month of courting her- taking her food at the end of her work shifts (she worked in her uncle's billiard hall, serving food and drinks at the counter), having birthday parties for her friends and co-workers so they would invite her and she'd actually show up, and trying my damndest to talk less (quite the challenge for me, being that I can turn a three minute long story into a twenty minute saga)- she finally agreed to a date, and not soon after that first date, we fell in love. Rather, I should say, she did. I was already there.

Ten months later, our son, Daniel was born.

I'll skip the intervening years between the birth of our son and our long struggle to make it to America. All that's more than enough fodder for a dozen other books, some of which have already been written. I'll skip right to the part where we moved into our old farmhouse, originally built as a sharecropper's house in 1903, ironically, the first year the Philippines experienced independence in nearly five centuries after 433 years of Spanish occupation, and then half a dozen or so years of being occupied by the U.S. after having been liberated from Spain by the U.S. in the Spanish American War.

All we ever wanted was a simple life. In the Philippines, we'd tried raising and growing our own food, but it was always a struggle, mostly due to all those "friendly" Filipino neighbors stealing everything we ever grew or raised. Or anything else that wasn't locked down and guarded with a gun. (Have I mentioned all the wonderful facts of life I'm not allowed to mention on social media?)

We thought for sure our gardens would grow well and our animals would do well here in Virginia, and we had no worries about "friendly" neighbors taking what didn't belong to them, due to the massive cultural differences in this regard. But we soon discovered we had different kinds of neighbors that were just as 'help themselves' minded as our former Filipino neighbors. They included, but were not limited to foxes, hawks, raccoons, black bears, minks, and, potentially...

Bigfoot Sasquatch!

Yes, I just said Bigfoot Sasquatch, and I kid you not.

Potentially!

***

So here's the story. Not as elegantly as Pearl S. Buck could have written it, but just as openly honest, and without sugar coating any of it to appease our modern times, and the thin skinned folks that live in them.

From the time we first moved in, we began having problems with a man who lives a couple miles away, but whose parents live across the road. It seems that the near ninety year old woman we bought our house from (maybe she'd met Ms. Buck?), who'd used it as a rental property for nearly thirty years, is this man's great aunt. She'd allowed him to take the hay from the property for years, and upon us purchasing the property, the man quickly rolled up our driveway, introduced himself, and let us know that the house was ours, but the hay was his. He said he'd been getting it for the last one thousand years, and he was going to *by God* get it for the next one thousand years, and there was nothing we could do about it. He further stated that we could put up a gate, and it wouldn't keep him out.

For our first two months here, the man harassed us relentlessly. He's the perfect example of a non-working, welfare, entitlement minded bum, who has nothing better to do all day but drive up and down the road in the small, rural community where he was born and raised, and never left, and harass anyone and everyone he sees out and about, because he simply has no purpose in life, or, as some observers might say, a life itself.

I guess that's the long way of calling him a 'busybody.'

I could go much further into detail about this loser and our nightmarish interactions with him at this point, but I will not, because we have Bigfoot Sasquatch, potentially, to get to, so if you're interested in how I got rid of this completely annoying neighbor, post haste, I'll refer you at this point to our YouTube channel, (something I've alluded to earlier with the social media jabs) "Homesteading Off The Grid." Go to the search box on YouTube and type in "How To Get Rid Of An Annoying Neighbor With A Crayon." This will bring you to the video on our channel that tells you the tale of the tape. The clean, polite version. You see, I'm not allowed to call people 'entitlement minded welfare bums' or 'losers' on YouTube, because it's a violation of their platform policies, hence, I've come back to my formerly successful medium of writing to do it.

But hey, look at all the other goodies I've been able to disclose, like the skin tax in Asia, because of it.

The reason I bring this dirtbag up in the first place (I do love being able to call a dirtbag a dirtbag here, and not have to worry about a community guideline strike), is because shortly after we ran him off with our crayon, we began noticing odd things. These odd things, no doubt, were going on before, but we'd been so engrossed with trying to figure out how to get this local dirtbag to leave us alone, we simply weren't noticing them.

However, one strange event occured that could not easily be overlooked. Dearly and I were in our large front field test flying a small remote control drone that one of our friends had bought for our son, Daniel. We were actually making a video of the test flight, in order to upload it to our YouTube channel.

Unfortunately, the thing wasn't so user friendly to fly, and we got it stuck in the top of a very tall white pine tree. I would estimate the tree to be eighty feet tall. There was no way we were climbing up there to get the drone down, and there was no way we were uploading a video of us losing our son's drone in a tree on YouTube, so we scrapped it.

Early the next morning, I'd say around 6:00 a.m., I stepped out the back door to go feed the chickens, and there, only feet away from the door, lay the drone!

Now, there is an awning on our back porch, which extends out at least twenty feet in all directions from the door. There is *no way* physically possible that the drone could have fallen from the top of the tree and landed only feet from our door. Also, the tree was a good fifty feet away from the porch. Someone, or some*thing*, had climbed to the top of that tree and retrieved that drone and placed it, ever so perfectly, at our backdoor.

When I saw the drone, I felt the hair on my arms and the back of my neck stand up.

Now, here's where things take an even *stranger* turn.

After this happened, I took to our YouTube channel, which you could probably assume by its name, featured mostly horticultural and agricultural videos at the time. We used our channel to showcase our gardens, the trees that I've become obsessed with in a borderline unhealthy way (is it possible to hord trees and shrubs? Am I lying to myself, justifying my addiction by claiming to simply be planting new forests everywhere I see open pastures?) Dearly regularly showed how to cook various Filipino dishes on our channel. We often made videos of our family out hiking in nature. But one thing is for sure, of all the content we'd uploaded and had planned to publish in the future, cryptozoology and paranormal activities and experiences were not on the list.

But this time, I shared a very true story by way of a video about a similarly strange event Dearly and I had had in the Philippines, when, I am convinced beyond doubt, that we were visited by the Filipino Kapre, that nation's version of the North American Bigfoot Sasquatch. The experience we had was so nerve wracking and real that it inspired an entire novel I wrote, titled "Isle of Kapre," which is available on Amazon, by the way, and of course I'll include the link to that book at the end of this one. (Hey, a guy's gotta make all the fifty cent royalties he can, right?)

I spoke, during the video, of how I felt it might be possible that a Bigfoot, or Sasquatch (I didn't know which name to use in reference to the creature at the time, so I ended up using both, 'Bigfoot Sasquatch,' and man, did that *then*, and does it *now* piss a lot of people off for some reason), visited our family. I took it a step farther in asking the question of whether or not this thing, or these things were already here, and if *we* were the ones visiting *their* home. Were we, like the lifelong losing dirtbag from down the road was to us, trespassing on their land?

Here's where the 'nightmare we didn't ask for' begins, and it has nothing to do with our friendly (so far), furry forest friend, or friends, as much as it does our fellow bipedaled mankind friends who had been watching our YouTube channel up to this point.

People flipped their freaking lids and totally lost their shit!

Ah, the first *bad* word or our book, the real language I *do* use sparingly in my daily life, but *not at all* on social media. God, how I truly *have* missed storytelling by way of the written word.

Shortly after publishing the video, I began scrolling through comments left in the comment section below the video, curious to see what people thought, and anxious to respond to their comments and communicate with them in the comment section as I'd always done since we'd started our YouTube channel nearly two years before.

All of a sudden, these seemingly sweet little old ladies and mild mannered retired men who'd always been so supportive of my family and me, and any video we'd ever posted in the past, no matter how boring the content (there's only so much you can do with the planting of corn and green beans) were outraged. How *dare* I discuss the idea of Bigfoot Sasquatch! What did I take them for? Idiots? How stupid did I think they were?

But it went further than that!

Many of our viewers who'd always been supportive accused me of making a Bigfoot Sasquatch video for the sole purpose of inflating our views, and thereby inflating our Google Adsense revenues. (I'd *NEVER* thought of that, honestly, but it seemed like a pretty good idea. How had I missed it?)

Folks screamed, "mental illness," from the rooftops! They demanded I seek mental health professionals immediately. They claimed I'd "gone off my meds." Others, who knew I'd struggled with addiction in the past, accused me of having relapsed. And lastly, but not leastly, many of our tried and true followers let me know in no uncertain terms that if I made any other Bigfoot Sasquatch videos, they'd unsubscribe to my channel immediately!

I'm ashamed to say this now, but at the time, I cowared to my audience and went back to making videos about corn and green beans, and lessons I've learned in life as part of my regular "morning ramble" episodes, and I made no more Bigfoot Sasquatch videos.

For a time...

Odd events kept taking place on our homestead, and I decided that I was no longer going to stay in the box into which people wanted me to remain. Sure, we have a homesteading channel, by title, but it's *our* channel, and we have *every right* to produce any kind of content we want, as long as we adhere to YouTube's very stringent (and to a very strong degree, pinkish) community guidelines and corporate policies. People could simply choose to not watch those videos or unsubscribe to our channel all together. Many, if not most of those crybaby assholes did, and my only regret is that they didn't leave sooner.

Okay, so here's how I went about it, at first. I didn't want to influence people into seeing what I wanted them to see, which would have been, of course, what I thought I was seeing. I wanted to present open ended evidence and allow people to make their own judgement calls. Would they end up seeing and hearing what I felt I was seeing and hearing? Or would I be proven insane?

One of the first videos I made, I did so, because as I was simply trying to walk a piece of outgoing mail to the mailbox a couple of hundred yards away from our backdoor, down by the road, I got the *distinct feeling* of being watched. I'd stop in the field, and I'd scan my surroundings, yet I could see no one or nothing around me, watching. But I *knew* something was there.

I ran back inside, grabbed the camera, and I set it up on the back porch and pushed the record button. I didn't speak, or anything. It was officially my first *silent film*, so to say. I simply took the mail to the box, and walked back, though I took my time in doing so, and I paused and visually scouted my surroundings the whole while. It took about seven minutes for me to make the trip down to the mailbox and back, and I think I titled the video, something to the effect of "When You See It Type The Word Blue." It was not clickbait, though I was accused of creating such ever popular yet ever hated drivel by making the video.

A few days later, I recorded the same type of video when I experienced the same feelings of being watched while attempting to feed the chickens. I actually spoke in that video, titled, "When You See It Type The Sum Of Four And Three."

I got blasted even harder by our followers, many of whom, for months had been loving loyalists, mind you. People who we'd given shoutouts to without requiring superchat payments or monthly subscription fees. The very people who "loved me and my family" the previous summer when we'd made videos of ourselves picking blackberries while out on a family hike now hated my soul for making videos that might have had something to do with that which cannot be scientifically and reasonably explained, and certainly wasn't mentioned in the Bible.

Good mother fucking riddance!

After a slew of, "That's it! I'm unsubscribing!" comments, I started pinning such comments to the top of the comment section under the videos, and then replying with, "Don't let the gate hit ya, where the good Lord split ya!"

I was making my point that I did not care, nor do I care now, about what any of our viewers thought of our content. It was the same process I had to go through with my writing, years ago, when I spent years writing crap not worth reading, because I left the truth out of all of it, because I feared what people who read it might think.

Soon after this, I stopped responding to comments entirely, re-learning a lesson, once again, that I'd obviously not paid enough attention to all the other times I'd sat in this particular classroom in life. Sadly, most of the support you'll ever receive in life is conditional. As long as you do what people want you to do, or as long as they agree with what you're doing, you'll have their support. But the minute you veer from doing things their way, they'll retract their conditional support.

You'd be amazed how many people have commented something to the effect of, "...when I saw that you were a veteran, I fell in love with you. Then, when I found out you married an immigrant, I instantly hated you..."

Dear reader, I kid you *not*. How these types of comments even make it through YouTube's policy filters is beyond me. If I were to make a statement like that, as a content creator, I would have my account shutdown. But as a content creature, I get the pleasure of being subjected to such hatred and ignorance daily, and it's only a problem if I'm dumb enough to respond to it (which I don't) which, again, would only result in me losing my YouTube account. You see, the community guidelines and policies, at least at YouTube, only seem to work one way. Content creators must abide by them, but the slew of crazy and hateful bastards who watch and comment on content on YouTube do not.

Now, this having been said, I'll point out that those two test videos (erroneously alleged 'clickbait' videos) had another type of result as well. A much more pleasant result.

People watching the videos were actually sensing, seeing and hearing what I believed I'd been sensing, seeing and hearing myself. Some folks, long time viewers of better temperament, even started commenting that they'd been watching my videos for months because they kept spotting Bigfoot Sasquatch in the forest behind my home where I made most of the videos. Further, they commented that they didn't know if I knew they were there and was choosing not to acknowledge them, so as not to draw unsafe attention to them, or if I hadn't yet spotted them, and they wanted to see if I would, eventually. As one commenter put it, "I came for the green beans, but stayed for the Bigfoot." As a group, me as the onscreen guide, and our viewers as our tagalong distant, virtual followers, have been out to find this Bigfoot Sasquatch ever since!

As many of our previous subscribers left the channel (did I say good mother fucking riddance?), we gained more *new* subscribers, three to one, it seemed, in their wake. And, I'll point any, a good many of our original subscribers stuck around for the ride, because… wait for it… they actually gave and continue to give my family and me unconditional support. They like us as people, they enjoy our videos, and they are not a bunch of small and close minded judgemental hypocrites who only know about conditional love and support. They are, in fact, the salt of the earth. They're my kind of people, and they're my kind of crazy.

If you feel you can fit that mold, we'd love to have you subscribe to our channel and watch our videos over at "Homesteading Off The Grid" on YouTube as well.

If you're offended by all things paranormal, Bigfoot Sasquatch, and inside out beanies (it's how I happen to like to wear mine), and it's all just too much for ya?

Don't forget to shut the gate on your way out, and for God's sake, please remember, don't let it hit ya where the good Lord split ya!

2

Forbidden Love

It's impossible not to be intrigued by individuals we meet who've claimed to have had some quite interesting experiences, especially in regard to all things Bigfoot Sasquatch. The most interesting of these people, however, are the folks who do *not* want their stories shared. Not because they fear that people won't believe them, but because they fear that people *will* believe them.

These are not the folks you hear about who claim that their lives were ruined because they saw a Bigfoot Sasquatch and were dumb enough to tell others, resulting in being labelled a nutcase and then having been ostricized. Oh, come on! Cry me a river and give me a break. Anyone singing this sad song simply suffers from a classic case of martyr syndrome, and they've obviously reached the point in life, not where they realized they've not accomplished much of anything of note, but that their excuses for not having accomplished much or anything of note have run out. People aren't buying their tired lies anymore. So hey, why not claim that you were on the up and up, getting ready to join the Forbes Fortune list, but, oops! You screwed up and went and told someone about the time you were fishing in the Pacific Northwest and saw a Bigfoot Sasquatch, so everyone wrote you off as a cook, and they took away the patent for cancer you'd just discover.

Bullshit!

What's truly intriguing is when people don't want to tell of their Bigfoot Sasquatch encounters, not because they worry whether or not they'll be believed, but because there are certain details *within* their stories that could ruin them or others, and it has nothing to do with being thought of as a cook. It has to do with disclosing certain facts about themselves- their lifestyles, their whereabouts on certain dates, etc.- that could be more damaging than their claim of having seen a creature that may or may not exist.

Such is the case of a man we'll call Dave.

I was in my front yard, several hundred yards away from my house and by the main road, mulching the hundreds of trees we transferred from the forest behind our home several years ago. We'd done so, because we wanted to build a privacy blind to shelter our view and block the noise from cars passing on the road.

We'd planted the first row with strictly eastern red cedars, which are evergreens, and will grow thick and tall, and create the perfect screen. Behind that row, we planted leyland cypress trees. We staggered each tree so that they would be in between the cedars in front of them, for even greater privacy. This row is about ten feet back from the first row. And then, behind that row, we planted five more rows of randomly mixed hardwoods, made up of poplars, maples, oaks, mulberry, black cherry and a couple of weeping willows strategically placed.

While hauling yet another pull-behind trailer load of mulch into our 'man made forest' as we call it, named after such a place on the island of Bohol in the Philippines, where the Philippine Government, in one of their rare and probably only eco-friendly gestures planted approximately two kilomters worth of road frontage with mahogany trees years ago (the rest of the area being populated by tropical trees, of course) I noticed a car pulling into my drive. At first I assumed it was merely a lost driver turning around, as this happens often, but then the driver, a man in his late seventies, parked and got out of the car and began walking into my yard.

Again assuming he was lost, I approached him, prepared to give him directions. I soon realized I was wrong. He was exactly where he'd intended to go.

"This is a lot of work for one person," he said, looking around at all my trees, about eighty percent of them now mulched.

"I've got another shovel," I said, a head nod toward my other shovel leaning against one of the trees. It was half in jest, but half serious, because he was right. It was a lot of work.

Dave, as we're calling him, actually walked over to the other shovel and picked it up. He came up to me, rolling his sleeves up to work as he did, and said, "And I've got a story for you."

"What kind of story?" I asked, my curiosity now piqued by this complete stranger who'd stopped by my place to help me mulch my man made forest. I've had others stop by, unannounced and uninvited, who I summarily ran off quickly, some of whom I had to start dialing the police to report. Typical freaks who can't draw the line of appropriateness between the difference of 'it's okay to watch a family on YouTube, but it's not okay to actually seek them out and go to their home like a creepy ass, ax murdering stalker!' (*Please* don't be that guy, or creepy ass girl!)

But Dave was different. He had an aura of peace and tranquility like I've rarely encountered in anyone, and I in no way felt threatened or creeped out in his presence.

"A story about your Bigfoot Sasquatch," of course, he said, and then dug in, quite forcefully for a man of his age, to the mulch in the back of my trailer. "A story I haven't told anyone in forty years," he said, as he began placing the mulch around the tree closest him.

"Why have you not told anyone your story for so long?" I asked him, now somewhat skeptical. Could this actually be one of those creepy ass stalker types who watched me on YouTube here to pull my leg? To see if I'd mention him in one of my next videos?

"I'm gay," Dave said, having stopped working, looking me square in the eyes.

"So?" I said. "I don't care."

"And that's *exactly* why I came to you to tell you this story," he said. "I've been watching your show for more than a year, and I know that you don't judge people based upon such things as sexuality or ethnicity. You were a hard nut to crack, because I can tell you have a conservative nature, but I was able to figure out pretty quick you're not a racist, or a homophobe, or any of those other types."

"Of *course* not," I said, almost laughing, not just because I found what he said humorous, but because I know I've driven others batshit crazy in the past due to my 'all over the board' beliefs. People have a tendency to pigeonhole others. They want to place them in these little boxes, and they find me very difficult to place into their boxes. They assume since I'm post middle aged, white, male and straight that I must be all these evil things. Zenophobic, homophobic, racist, etc. They get to know me and find out that I'm not. Those mindsets disgust me, and I'll have nothing to do with anyone who harbors them.

Many others see that I'm married to an Asian woman, have a bi-racial child, speak multiple languages, and, having lived around the world, that I am quite cultured, especially for a post middle aged straight white male with a southern accent, and they assume I lean quite the other way. Then they get to know me and they realize I don't.

For the love of God, people. Can we all just be ourselves, and throw out these God forsaken boxes everyone wants to place each other in? Can we kill our televisions and think for ourselves?

Anyway, Dave continued with his story, and man, was it one for the ages.

Dave proceeded to tell me that the reason he'd kept his potential Bigfoot Sasquatch story secret for so long was because he'd kept his true sexuality a secret up until just a few years ago. And by telling his story, he'd not only out himself, but another man, as well.

You see, Dave spent forty years as a happily married man, and he's the father of three children, all now grown and approximately my age.

"I went to Da Nang, Vietnam in 1968," he said, early on in his story. "I was in country before most people back here could even realize how messy that was gonna get. And man, where those different times, indeed. When I came back, why, it would have still been illegal for you to be married to your Asian wife and live with her here in the state of Virginia."

"What?" I said, feeling as if I were being lied to. I'd never heard of such a ridiculous thing.

"Google it!" Dave said. "There was a case of a white man married to a black lady here in Virginia that went all the way to the supreme court. Their case is what finally legalized biracial marriages in the U.S. And it wasn't until 1968, or 1969. Now, just think of how bad it was for us gay folk back then."

Later, after Dave had left, I *did* Google this and I found that he was right. Just before deciding to write this book, I read the book titled "Loving Vs. Virginia." What an amazing story. Some hick, racist sheriff in Virginia harassed this young couple and arrested them repeatedly for being married and for being of different races. The poor couple were found guilty and punished by not being allowed to live together in Virginia. If they snuck into the state to see family, they'd get arrested by this hick, racist sheriff and his deputies. And all this was going on less than half a dozen years before I was born. My mind was blown.

Anyway, Dave went on to tell me such a heartbreaking story of how he'd lived most of his life as a lie.

After returning from the war in Vietnam, and a year later getting out of the Marines, Dave was able to land a job with the Forest Service. He worked as a ranger in his home state, the name of which we'll omit, and he had a successful, long career doing so, retiring after nearly forty years.

"And I'm here to tell you," Dave said while talking of his work days. "I spent nearly half a century in the woods, and I will never lay claim to having seen anything that couldn't be explained by way of logic. I never saw any monsters, or aliens, or ghosts. None of that nonsense."

"I thought this was a Bigfoot Sasquatch story?" I said, after he'd said all this.

"It is, if you'll just listen."

Great, I thought. *I've met my match. Someone who can draw a story out longer than me.*

"There was this one secluded spot, where early in my career, we'd busted some marijuana farmers," Dave continued. "They had quite the little setup. They were probably farming two acres of plants in the absolute middle of nowhere.

"What they didn't know was that there was actually a service trail not too far away from them where my station's district met up with the next station district over. I mean, this place was really about as far away from any ranger station as you could get, but it happened to be in the geographical middle of two of them. These guys must have really done their homework. And that trail? Shoot, a deer could have missed it, so I can't fault them for missing that.

"As it turns out," Dave went further, "the ranger in charge of the next beat over was a guy about my age, who too, was gay. In the closet, just like me at the time and up until recently. We met and got to know each other while working together on the bust. He's actually the one who found it- the pot farm- and his office contacted mine to set up the sting, because they knew we were right across the border.

"So, long story short, we busted them, and this other guy, Mike, he and I said we'd get together and tear down this nice little shack they'd constructed to camp and work out of when they were up there farming."

"And did you?" I asked.

"No," Dave said. "For the next few years, we used that place as our love shack. We'd meet up there once, sometimes twice a week, and we'd do things that married people ought not do with each other if it ain't the other person they're married to."

"Oh," I said, picking up exactly what he was laying down.

"And here's the thing," Dave said. "Every time Mike and I were out there, having our little trist, I felt like someone was watching. Matter of fact, I take that back. I *knew* someone was watching." Dave looked down in contemplation before continuing. "There's only one other time I ever felt like that, and that was back in Nam, and any time I felt like that, a firefight was sure to break out. That's how I know, beyond any shadow of doubt, that they had their eyes on us," he paused, almost as if for effect, and looked up at me and made direct eye contact and said, "but they were not the eyes of a human."

I couldn't speak. There were questions I wanted to ask, but my mind was fuddled. Dave continued.

"It wasn't guilt. And I know it wasn't cameras, because again, this would have been early 1970's, and the technology just wasn't there. But I know we were being watched."

"What do you think it was?" I asked when I was finally able to speak again.

"Well, I had no idea until after we broke up," Dave said, pausing, pain still in his voice after all these years. Dave told me he's had two great heartbreaks in his life. Losing his wife to cancer just a couple years ago, and the ending of his relationship with Mike back before I was even born.

"Mike was living the same lie I was, you see," Dave said. "And he and his wife had recently had their first kid. He said he just couldn't do it anymore, because his greatest fear wasn't that people would find out that he was gay, but that his kid might find out, someday, that he'd been unfaithful to his mother. Didn't matter if it'd been with a woman or a man. Either way, it just wasn't right."

Dave told me that he'd stayed in touch with Mike, professionally at first, and then as acquaintances with a past, up until the time of his death, only recently. Just like Dave's wife, Mike had died of cancer. Another reason Dave wanted to finally come clean with his story was because Mike was no longer around.

"About a month after we'd broken up," Dave told me, I went back out to our love shack. I was still down and out about the breakup, and on top of that, my wife had informed me that we were with child, and I just felt like I needed someone to talk to. I guess for the past few years, that had been the place I'd gone when I felt this way.

"So I get out there," Dave continued, "and I was totally shocked to see that our love shack had been demolished. I mean, it had been torn apart, board by board, and frame pole by frame pole.

"But here's where it gets odd," he said. "After my initial shock, I started investigating the rubble. That's when I realized it hadn't been taken apart by any man. At least not by any tools made by man. There were no markings on the boards indicating that a crowbar or the claw of a hammer had been used.

"And then, I really got scared when I saw that the frame posts, four inches thick, oak mind you, had been snapped in half like twigs! No man could do that!"

"Do you think it was an animal?" I asked. "A bear maybe?"

"That was my next guess," he said. "But as I continued looking, I didn't find a single claw mark. Wasn't a bear, and no cougars were supposed to be in the area, though I'd always had my suspicions. But they would have left claw marks on the boards as well, and I'm telling you, there were none!'

"So what was your conclusion?" I asked.

"Well, and that's why I'm standing here telling you this story," he said. "I have every reason to believe, even though I cannot claim to have ever seen, heard or smelled one, that a Bigfoot Sasquatch was out there watching us every single time we got together, and out of frustration of us never returning, or having sensed our emotions when we broke up, just couldn't deal with the feelings, and took it out on our love shack by destroying the thing with its bare hands."

"Really?" I said.

Dave could sense the doubt in my voice, but he knew I wasn't doubting the Bigfoot Sasquatch part. "Really," he continued, as if reading my mind. "I believe these creatures are empaths. He, she or it could sense my pain, and Mike's, and not being perhaps as emotionally evolved as humans, he, she or it couldn't process that pain cognitively, so they went berserk on our shack, and ripped it to shreds."

It made sense the way Dave explained it, and as far as I'm concerned, there's less believable stories out there that make way less sense, so why not? In my own dealings with potential Bigfoot Sasquatch, I, too, have often felt as if he, she, it or they were empathic, and I believe it's largely why we may or may not have some in the forest behind our home. We seem to have a bond that's unspoken, because it's simply impossible to put into any kind of words. And it doesn't need to be put into words. It's a bond of emotion. And the ability to feel the emotions of the other.

Dave hung out for a little while longer before leaving. As he helped me finish mulching my trees he informed me that both he and Mike would go on to have three children each. Their wives never knew of their homosexuality. Dave said he finally came clean with his children after their mother's death.

"How'd they take it?" I asked.

"They laughed and said they already knew," he told me, laughing himself as he did.

"Really?" I said.

"Yeah," he said. "I guess being gay is kind of like being an alcoholic. You're actually the last one to know. Everyone around you already does."

We both laughed at that, and Dave got back in his car and started the long drive home. I turned to walk back to the house and for an instant, believed I'd caught something moving just inside the treeline of the forest as I did.

No need to go investigate, because I'd felt as if Dave and I had been watched from the spot the whole time he'd been there.

Who or what had been watching?

Potentially, him, her, it or they...

3

Tatata

I recently reconnected with someone from whom I should not have disconnected. I temporarily ended my rekindled friendship, about five years ago, due to the very issue that caused me to seek out friendship with the man, who we'll call Jim, in the first place.

Sadly, it's taken me nearly fifty years of living a life of drama, trauma, violence, war and grief, to come to the understanding that that which I desire most is peace. The problem has never been with other people, places, things, ideologies, etc. in my world. In most cases, most as in nearly all, the problem has been with me. It takes a mature man to admit this, and I finally realized that until I bucked up and did so, peace and a peaceful mindset would be, at most, temporary and fleeting for me.

Jim, who I met through other friends, struck me as the most Zen individual I'd ever met. I could tell the first time I got together with him and a couple other guys that he was more at peace with himself and the world around him than anyone with whom I've ever shared company. This impression, to this day, is so powerful in my mind, that I cannot even remember the reason that he and I and our other friends had gotten together in the first place.

I remember asking one of the guys the next time I saw him why Jim seemed to be so calm, cool and collected. He told me that Jim was huge into meditation. He actually called him a 'Zen Master.' Further, he told me that Jim loved to share his philosophy with anyone willing to listen, and that he was even willing to teach anyone willing to learn how to meditate how to do so.

I know that there's been many times in my past that I've come close to meditating unknowingly, mostly when I've been out in nature, by fixating on a tree, a beautiful mountain stream, or the way the tips of uncut hay sway in the wind, like waves on the ocean, during a hot, Autumn breeze, but I'd never done any *official* meditating, so to say, so I jumped at the opportunity to hook up with Jim and and see if he'd teach me his ways.

I called Jim and explained that our mutual friend had given me his phone number, and I let him know my interest. Jim was only too willing to meet with me, and he invited me over to his house the very next day.

Jim was about fifteen years older than me. When I got to his house, I quickly learned that he lived alone. He was not married. He had no children, he had no pets, and his simple twelve hundred square feet single level brick ranch house that looked like all those surrounding it, in one of those neighborhoods built in the late 1950's, was immaculately kept. A place for everything, and everything in its place.

"Why do you seek Zen?" Jim asked after a few minutes of meaningless pleasantries. Without the brashness of a businessman, he let me know he didn't like wasting time by getting straight to the point.

I explained how I sought what he seemed to have. The ability to wear the world around him like a loosely fitting garment. I told him quite a bit of my past. I was shocked at how much I shared with a man I'd just met, who was little more than a stranger. I went on, at length, about my divorce from years ago, about the war in Iraq, about losing my first family, about mistakes I'd made which drove those closest to me at the time away from me. I spoke about my ongoing, on again off again, battles with addiction. My attempts to numb the feelings of having made the huge mistake of being born, like it was somehow a bad thing, and it was somehow my fault.

"I could sense from the noise in your mind that you were deeply troubled," he said when I finished. "It was very difficult to focus on what the guys were talking about the other night due to the static coming from your mind. It's been a while since I've been around someone who's mind pushes out as much toxicity as yours."

Upon hearing this, I didn't know if I should feel offended, as if insulted, or as if I'd made a mistake and was sitting here speaking with a crazy person. However, I knew that was just a toxic *reflex*. My thinking brain told me that I should be in awe, due to this man's ability to see without seeing, and hear without hearing, because I knew everything he'd just said was right. I just didn't know how *he* knew.

"Don't worry," he said, a light laugh. "Not very many people can see and hear. You'd have to get really close to another empath."

"A what?" I asked.

"Another time," he said. "We've got work to do. You're in a bad way, and you need Zen, yesterday."

Jim gave me a quick class, so to say, on the art of meditation. He explained how Zen is basically the obtainment of an empty mind. "Mind without mind," as he said it. "It's not that you want to fill your mind with positive thoughts," he went on. "You want to clear your mind of any and all thoughts."

This was new to me. Like a lot of people, I thought that when you meditated, you conjured up positive images. A lamb lying with its mother. Cherry blossom petals being blown by a light, Spring breeze.

I was wrong.

"Your mind is like a dumpster," Jim explained. "It's filled with garbage; regrets, resentments, grudges. You want to clear it of everything in order to rid it of this garbage. All of this garbage is poison. And not to the people you resent or upon whom you hold grudges. You. It's killing you slowly, and robbing you of the highest quality of life you could have while you're still alive."

Jim taught me how to sit on my shins. He talked about the importance of keeping straight posture, and not slumping, so that I would not become so comfortable that I would end up sleeping. "Sleeping is not meditating," he would say. "It's sleeping."

I enjoyed getting together with Jim twice a week and learning all about meditation. I was a quick study, at least in the beginning, when it was easiest, but in time, I began to become frustrated when I wasn't seeing the rapid results I'd seen in the early stages of my new discovery.

"Don't get frustrated," Jim would say, when I found myself becoming frustrated, but before I said that I was, as if he were reading my mind. "It's like losing weight. The pounds always come off quickly at first, but after you start to level out, it's harder to lose weight. The tenth pound is always harder to lose than the first five."

"Yeah, but…" I would lament, and you could fill in the sentence with whatever 'woe is me' story you'd like after that. "The time this terrible thing happened in Iraq. The time I flew halfway around the globe to see my children and was denied visitation. The way I was blamed for these terrible things that happened in my life back home, while I wasn't even here, because I was half a world away fighting terrorists."

"That's the sick part of your mind speaking," Jim would say. "The part of your mind that does not want to be well, because it feels strength and power in sickness. It wants to cling to pain and negativity. This is the part we need to free. This is the mind we need to expel from your mind."

I'm very ashamed to admit this at this juncture, but things came to a head one day when I was at Jim's and during a difficult meditation session. I could not stop focussing on something from my past that is particularly painful. I could not push this particular piece of garbage from the dumpster that is my mind. When Jim started with his, 'that's the sick part of your mind,' thing again, I let him have it.

"So easy for you to say," I said. "You've never been to war. You're a single man who doesn't have a wife here to nag you or steal your kids and leave when you've had enough of the nagging. No kids to scream and drive you nuts, or to be taken away from you and rip your heart out in their absence, your only wish being they were still here to scream and drive you nuts! I guess if my life had always been about me and just me, I'd be pretty Zen, too," I said. "And I'd be able to sit here and stare at walls all day without a care in the world."

Jim said nothing, and he showed no physical signs of his mood changing in any way. This pissed me off even more, and I turned and walked out of his house. I did not see Jim for nearly five years. Not until I went to his house only recently, and knocked on his door to give a heartfelt and long overdue apology.

And to inquire further, about something he'd once said, Something that has kept me awake many nights wondering if it might just be…

Bigfoot Sasquatch!

***

Let me backtrack a bit...

At 'another time,' Jim finally *did* have that conversation with me about empaths. He explained to me, quite fully, what they were, and he let me know that not only was he an empath, but that I was one as well. For the first time in my life, I felt like I finally understood more about myself than I ever had. Why I had to spend so much time alone (recharging). Why I hate negative people like the plague (I sucked up their negativity like a sponge does water). And mostly, why narcissists always seemed to be drawn to me (I was their one stop shop for emotional output overload).

"When you become Zen," Jim told me that day, "as an empath, you can see and hear things that others cannot see and hear. It's as if you've been given a very special set of eyes and ears, but they're in your mind."

"Could you be a bit more clear?" I said. "This is all still so new to me. I've spent over forty years acting out of emotion, not reason or understanding, and certainly not any form of enlightenment."

"I can best explain it," he began, his face finally scrunching up a bit, as if his mind *finally* had to bend and flex a bit to make its point, "with the types of sounds my mind's ears hear around people, and the shades and colors my mind's eyes see with animals."

"Do tell," I said. I was totally intrigued. We were walking in the woods behind his house, which isn't far from my house, and the patch of woods we were in, if one were willing to walk the better part of a day, could be gotten to from my house without ever crossing any roads.

"Have a seat," Jim said, motioning to a downed red oak log. I did as he said. Jim sat a few feet away from me and began explaining a concept that blew my mind, not just then, but even more so now, as I've developed similar skills to Jim's, even if only to a slight degree. This is why I've gone back to see him after all these years. To talk more about this, and also, to make that long overdue apology, which I'll let you know now, he was more than happy to accept.

"When I'm around people," he began, "I can hear what sounds like a buzz, or static from a radio. Not overwhelmingly. I mean, it doesn't block my ability to listen during conversations, or to hear the background music in a restaurant. Usually," he said, looking at me as if having a sudden memory. And I'm sure he was. I got the feeling he was remembering the time he'd first met me. I can only imagine how interruptive my way out of whack, hyper-toxic mind frequencies were. "I can tell who's totally stressed out," he finally said, when he spoke again. "I can tell who'd rather be anywhere else than where they are at the time," he continued. "And once," he took a pause, as if not wanting to continue.

"Yes?" I said, curious.

"I'm hesitant to tell you this, because you'll think I'm trying to come off as a superhero."

"No," I assured him. "Go ahead."

"Once, I could tell a man was considering doing something very bad," he said. "I didn't know what, but it terrified me."

"What did you do?" I asked.

"I didn't know what to do, so I followed him home," Jim said, his eyes glancing downward and to the right, his mind recalling the memory.

"And?" I said. I was so excited to hear this part of his story that I couldn't wait for him to wrap up his dramatic pause, which I knew was entirely real and natural.

"He ended up driving his car, at extremely high speed, into a huge oak tree on the side of the road. It killed him. I'm sure instantly," he said.

"So you think the frequencies you were reading from him were thoughts of suicide?" I asked for clarification.

"No," he said. "I don't. I think he had something truly terrifying planned, and he ended up doing what he did so he wouldn't do the other."

"Any ideas?" I asked.

"No," Jim said. "But I remember reading an article about it in the paper a couple of days later. I was watching for it, because my curiosity was piqued. The article said that when the police arrived at the crash scene, they discovered three shotguns, two handguns, and over one thousand rounds of ammo in the trunk of his car."

"Holy shit!" I said.

"Yeah," Jim said, a tone of agreement. "Holy shit." It was the first and only time I'd ever heard him cuss.

"And then," he said, quickly transitioning.

I couldn't believe it. There was a 'and then?' A story that could top this one?

"No," he said. "I'm definitely not telling you this one. You won't think I'm a superhero. You'll think I'm a freaking nut case."

"Come on, man," I said, desperate. "You can't leave me hanging like this. Especially not after that last story."

"Okay," he said, looking down and to the right again, a sure sign of memory recall. "With animals, it's not a sound, I hear. It's not a vibration, or static. It's colors."

"Huh?" I said, not quite following.

"Colors," he said, now looking me straight in the eyes. I can sense hues and tones in my mind when I'm meditating in the forest, and when an animal is near."

Jim pointed off into the distance. A beautiful red cardinal was perched on an oak limb, calling, not for a mate, but simply to announce to the world that it was a happy camper. "Like that bird," he said. "If I were in deep meditation right now, I'd be seeing hues of bright green. Happiness."

"Oh," I said, beginning to follow.

"And if it were in distress," he said, "I'd see red."

"Really?" I said.

"Yeah," he said. "Actually, when I was a much younger man, and I was only first discovering all of this, I remember there was one place where I'd seen a bright red hue in my mind's eye one day. I went back the next day, and it was light red, almost pink. On the third day, it was gone. Nothing."

"What do you think it was?" I asked.

"Well," he began, his tone softening more. "On my way out of the woods that day, I found a dead coyote. It had been caught in a trap. It had probably only been dead a few hours. I believe that's what I'd been sensing."

"Okay," I said. "Well, that doesn't sound nuts."

"Because that's not the story," he said.

"Oh," I said, shutting up to listen more.

"I was out here meditating once," he said, continuing with his story, "and I heard what could only be described as a broken, or dead language."

"What?" I said, now totally confused.

"Yeah," Jim said. "I was as confused then as you are now." Then he smiled at me, as if to say, 'yes, I just read your mind.'

"I listened more closely," he said, and for some reason, while trying to figure out what type of language might be being spoken, I began thinking about painful parts of my past, and all of a sudden, I was no longer Zen. The dumpster that is my mind began filling up with garbage and clutter anew."

"And then?" I said, prodding him along, wanting him to rush through his peaceful pause of recall.

"And then I heard it speak, and I swear it wasn't mentally, it was verbally," he said, now staring me square in the face, with eyes that looked not filled with fear, but certainly with eyes that had more than just a hint of fear in them. "It said, tatata."

"What is tatata?" I asked.

"Tatata," Jim said, repeating the strange word. "Thusness. It's Buddhism. It means nothing matters but this moment."

***

This is the second reason I'd come back to Jim. Yes, to apologize for being such a selfish, self centered ass years ago, but also for clarification of this point.

"Remember that time," I said to Jim, now in the present, and then I reminded him of the time we spent together in the woods and he spoke of tatata.

"Yes," he said. "Very clearly."

"You never really said what you thought that was," I said. "At least that I can remember. I know it's been about five years ago now."

"Yes," he said, offering nothing else.

"Have you ever put any more thought into that event?" I asked.

"I haven't had to," Jim said.

"Why not?" I asked. It was as if Jim had dismissed the strange occurrence as if it had never happened.

"Because it's happened several times since," he said, flooring me, and once again, as if to prove he could read my mind. I knew he couldn't, but I also knew he could sense my aura well enough.

"When?" I asked. "How often?" My curiosity was leading to rapid fire questioning, diarrhea of the mouth.

"Whenever I need to be reminded," Jim said. "Reminded of tatata. Thusness. Of the power of now. Stay in this moment, for it's the only moment I have."

"I'm curious," I said. "You really are a Zen master. At least the closest to one I could imagine existing outside of a monk monastery in Tibet. I've got to know. What on earth could possibly pull you out of your place of peace? Something that would require this mysterious voice to speak to you? You seem like, more than anyone I've ever met, you have no problems in the world. Further, you seem like you never had. Like life's been even keel for you since birth."

"Have a seat," Jim said, motioning toward his couch. He'd invited me in after I'd arrived, but I'd gotten straight into my apology, and he'd not had the opportunity to ask me to sit. As I sat, Jim went into another room and shortly returned. When he did, he lay a photo album on my lap and said, "have a look."

I opened the album, and on the first page I saw a young couple posing for a wedding picture. I didn't recognize the beautiful woman in the image, but I knew right away that the groom was a forty year younger version of Jim.

"Is this you?" I said. Jim gave me confirmation with a light grunt, though I already knew.

I flipped through the book, and it was like following their lives. I saw the first baby come, and then the second. I saw them at the beach. At the carnival. I watched the kids grow, transitioning from diapers to big wheels to training wheels and then roller skates.

And then, when the kids were about nine and eight years old, the story ended. The book, about half full of pictures, was empty from that point on.

I looked up at Jim, a question on my face. A question he easily read and quickly answered before I could ask it verbally.

"They were hit and killed by a drunk driver in 1985," he said. "I never remarried. Never had other children."

I immediately remembered what I'd said to Jim the day I stormed out of his house five years before. Man, did I feel like an ever loving piece of crap.

"Jim, I am so sorry," I said, wanting to say more, but he quickly lifted a hand to cut me off.

"I know you are," he said. "And I know you had no idea when you said those things years ago. I'd never shared any of this with you. You had enough of your own pain. And I knew immediately that you were an empath, so the last thing I wanted to do was give you any more pain. You didn't need any of mine. You know the feeling of losing children, without having them die. I, my friend, could not imagine that pain. Longing due to loss, but knowing they're actually out there somewhere and not knowing the who, where or what of their lives.

Jim sat beside me. We fumbled through the pictures in the album together, neither of us saying a word at first. Jim finally started speaking, telling stories about what had gone on the day the pictures were taken, adding context to imagery. It was absolutely heartbreaking, and we both shed tears.

When it was over, Jim put the photo album back in the room where he kept it, and he came back and wished me well and bid me goodbye. He told me to come back again, which I have, several times since.

Before leaving, I turned to him and asked if he had any idea who or what might be reminding him of 'tatata' at times when he needs to be reminded.

"I have no clue," Jim said, not a moment of hesitation.

"This is going to sound nuts from my end," I said, looking him straight in the eyes. "But do you think it's, potentially, Bigfoot Sasquatch?"

Jim smiled, nearly ear to ear. But not in a 'man, this guy's bat shit crazy,' kind of way. But in a secretly knowing kind of way.

"I don't know," he said, light laughter in his voice. "And that's what makes it all the more mysterious, isn't it?"

I left Jim with a twinkle in his eyes, but with even *more* questions than I had before now floating around in my head.

One thing is for sure though. I'll never judge another man, or woman, for any reason, without having walked a mile in their shoes. It was already way past time in life for me to have learned this when I'd judged Jim, but thankfully, these lessons can never be learned too late.

And when I get bogged down in my own stinking thinking? Worrying about things I can't fix, because they're totally out of my control? Fearing the future or regretting the past? I'll do my best to remember something more powerful in order to stop the insanity.

Tatata…

4

The Tragic End To The Boy Who Cried Bigfoot Sasquatch

(Originally Titled 'The Unfortunate Demise Of Jittery Jay')

Once upon a time, in a land not too far away, there lived a man who knew it all.

And I mean EVERYTHING!

There wasn't ANYTHING this sumbitch didn't know!

If you were dealing with subject matter completely foreign to the man- a subject in which he had no experience or a subject of which he'd never even heard- he'd simply make up the 'facts.'

And no matter *your* expertise or experience with the subject matter, there was simply *no way* you could know anywhere *near* as much as this guy, this Mr. Know It All.

The man's name was Jittery Jay. Jay was short for his real name, which wasn't Jay, but which started with the letter J, and the jittery part preceded Jay, well, because it's what the man did.

Constantly and incessantly.

He jittered.

His beady little eyes would dart back and forth, left to right- looking off into space (which, by the way he could tell you *all* about), or up into the trees, which he never saw, because his mind was too cluttered with inner voices, mostly those of the talking heads of a particular left leaning mainstream media outlet, the voices of whom he relates to the gods, always telling him what to fear today. What he'll need to fear tomorrow.

The reason he jittered, this Jittery Jay, as most who knew him had come to call him, was not because he was always thinking, thinking, thinking, and only about how bad things were (the left leaning media outlet gurus told him so), or about how stupid everyone on earth except himself happened to be, and *certainly* not because he told incessant, ever-changing lies, which he did, as he was the very worst of compulsive liars among liars, but because he lacked the one thing his intelligence (not quite in abundance as he liked to think and claim, by the way) could never garner for him.

Confidence!

You see. Confidence is something that one earns in life, and Jittery Jay never quite grasped this concept. Confidence comes with doing. Itt comes with achievement. You cannot get a degree in confidence from that Ivy League college from which Jittery Jay had gotten a couple of degrees (history and fine arts- and it's *no wonder* he'd never been able to find gainful employment. That and the fact that you cannot obtain a degree in 'work ethic,' which is kind of a prerequisite to working, as well).

JIttery Jay, for all his Monday morning armchair quarterbacking throughout life- judging how everyone else who'd ever taken a risk in life, win or fail, had done it all wrong in his eyes- had never accomplished anything of note himself. So, as he stood in front of strangers and acquaintances alike, dressing down their accomplishments and achievements by way of explaining to them, in explicit detail, how he could have and would have done what they'd done so much better, simply because he was so much smarter than them, in all actually, Jittery Jay had never done diddly squat.

How does a man such as Jittery Jay survive in our world? How does he feed and clothe himself? How does he find a suitable roof to keep the elements off of his head?

Big government entitlement programs, we assume?

Maybe for some, but not Jittery Jay.

You see, Jittery Jay was a high class deadbeat. He was fortunate in that he'd married a woman who came from means.

Now, Jittery Jay's wife, mind you, who we'll call Crazy A (because she's batshit crazy and her first name starts with the letter A) has no more confidence that her husband. In fact, she has even less. It's why Jittery Jay was drawn to her in the first place. He saw in her, and in her extreme lack of confidence, relationship security.

You see, Crazy A was a middle aged two time divorcee with two children, one from both of her previous marriages. Both of Crazy A's first two husbands, like Jittery Jay, had been men who lacked confidence and work ethic, and who were not in any way physically or mentally challenged enough to be granted a check from big daddy Government, hence they'd tried to catch a ride on the gravy train of life by way of latching onto an Ugly Betty from a rich family. Her first husband had left her for a wealthier woman of slightly more physical attractiveness and less confidence (which, of course, meant even greater relationship stability), and her second husband, as gay as a roaring twenties speak easy, had left her for a very wealthy and somewhat attractive older man, who, too, despite his wealth and slightly better than average looks, lacked confidence.

Crazy A, who was not easy on the eyes by *any* stretch of the means, was more than a foot taller than the average sized American female, giving her a classic case of 'tall girl syndrome.' The abusive narcissist that was Jittery Jay saw in Crazy A a woman that he could not only look down on (not literally, or course, as she towered over him by a full eight inches), due to her complete lack of self-esteem, but an income stream by way of her wealthy parents, which would further enable his non-working ways in much more comfort than he'd known previously, which typically was handled by way of getting a job for a time, being an asshole to intentionally get fired, and then drawing unemployment benefits until they ran out, and then repeating the process. He'd tried for more than two decades to get some sort of permanent disability check, and had come darn close while working his last job before meeting Crazy A, having claimed to have permanently pulled a groin muscle by trying to lift a heavy tool box, conveniently, when no one else was around to witness the 'accident' which led to his supposed injury. He'd actually made his way to the third interview in the disability claims process without getting busted, but called the whole thing off when he quickly got Crazy A to agree to saying "I do" at the altar, which they did at the courthouse.

Jitter Jay, making sure to rule all the other birds in the roost, was always quick to point out to any new acquaintances that Crazy A's children were not his. He did not, as he put it with such chivalry, 'sire these dependents.'

By God's grace, these children, adults as of the time of this writing and long after the unfortunate demise (uh, hem) of Jittery Jay, are doing very well for themselves on their own, because fortunately they were constructed of true grit, which did not allow the shallow words and potentially harmful deeds of Jittery Jay to psychologically affect them as he'd hoped they would, and they've been living happily ever after, after having flown the coop.

Especially after having gotten word of this story!

And no, they did *not* attend the funeral!

Oh, how I digress.

Let me reverse.

As Jittery Jay's wife's family's circumstances allowed for Jittery Jay and Crazy A to live among the affluent, Jittery Jay had access to lots of well-to-do individuals upon whom to unleash his ego on a regular basis. But though all of the people living in close proximity to Crazy A and Jittery Jay had high finance in common, that's where their commonalities, for the most part, came to an end.

Within their immediate sphere, which was basically a small genteal farming community where only a few generational locals actually farmed as a livelihood, and where most residents simply had horses they paid others to actually care for, using all expenses, of course, as tax write offs, Jittery Jay and Crazy A were surrounded by businessmen and businesswomen who'd achieved great success. They lived alongside (well, as 'alongside' as one can get when everyone owns one hundred acre lots) 'first families,' whose ancestors had been granted land by King James himself shortly after the settlement of Jamestown. They were surrounded by trust babies, whose grandparents and great grandparents, and oftentimes great, *great* grandparents had founded fortune 400 companies more than a century before, this, by the way, being the way in which Crazy A's family had come into wealth.

Crazy A and clan could thank great, great grandaddy for inventing the pump that tops pretty much all personal pampering products today, such as body lotion, shampoo, conditioner, etc. Yes, something so simple turned out to be something so lucrative for generations to come by way of the patent ownership of the inventor.

Of course, one of the family's deep dark secrets had always been the fact that it was actually Crazy A's great, great *grandmother* who'd invented the pump, after she'd begun developing arthritis and needed a simpler means of dispensing her creams and lotions than the twist tops she could no longer open.

But who would have ever heard of a *woman* coming up with such a practical invention back in those times, and, well, no need to bring it all to light now, especially since the family had been sued for generations by another family who claimed the great, great grandfather had stolen the concept from their great, great grandfather. Alas, should word get out that he'd stolen it at all, even though he'd stolen it from his wife, the courts might decide to award the patent, and all those quarterly dividend checks, to the other family in question, and Crazy A's family would have to... wait for it...

Get jobs!

Oh, the terror associated with the thought!

There were a few of Crazy A and Jittery Jay's neighbors, albeit spread few and far between, and not accepted in any way by the rest of their well-to-do neighbors, self made men and women. These were individuals who'd not been born into wealth. They had not, as Warren Buffet puts it, "been lucky enough to enter the world by way of the right womb."

Actually, most of these folks had been born into below modest means. However, they'd been born with, not a 'special metal,' the kind out of which silver spoons placed so delicately into the mouths of trust babies are constructed, but, as was the case, fortunately, for Jittery Jay's step-children, true grit! A strength the weak like Jittery Jay would never know. And on top of that, they'd been raised in a way that instilled work ethic.

These were goal oriented, positive thinking individuals who didn't just think outside the box, but who threw the damn boxes away entirely! Men and women who came from nothing to spend their lives, by way of sheer hard work, and, at times, stubborn bullheadedness, marching their way to the top of the socio-economic food chain. Men and women who were not born into wealthy zip codes, but who'd spent their lifetimes earning their way into the ability to live in them.

These were the kind of men and women that Jittery Jay hated most, above all others, because they reminded him most of what he had not in the slightest degree, inside himself. That which he did not, nor would he ever possess.

True grit!

And despite all of his highfluteness, he knew, as did the rest of the trust babies in his area, true grit trumps birthright metal any day!

Imagine if you will, then, Jittery Jay's strong hatred toward his newest of neighbors, whose property bordered that of the hundred acre lot Crazy A's parents allowed him to reside on with their daughter, to the south. Crazy A's parents knew to *never* allow Crazy A to hold property in her name, as the risk of any of the ne'er do well men she had a taste for could easily and legally take it from her upon divorce. This, of course, led to further the lack of confidence in Crazy A, which, in turn led to further Jittery Jay's attraction toward her. And, despite Crazy A's parents' forward, defensive thinking, he was sure that with his supreme intelligence, he'd be able to figure out a way to snag their property from them at some point, anyway.

You see, Jittery Jay and Crazy A's new neighbors, the Drakes, were not only self made (oh, the indignity of people willing to get their hands dirty, Jittery Jay would lament in his mind, and often aloud, even if there was no one around to listen),but they had also come from very destitute backgrounds, Mr. Drake, having been born and raised in Appalachia (dumb hillbilly, Jittery Jay would always think of him as being, even before having met him and only having heard of where he was from by way of another nosy neighbor), and Mrs. Drake having been born and raised in a small third world country in Southeast Asia. Jittery Jay could never remember which one- Malaysia? Indonesia? Philippines?- but it mattered not, because in his mind's eye, Mrs. Drake, being nearly twenty years Mr. Drake's junior, must have been a hooker, or a stripper, and that's how she'd met her future American husband who she'd viewed as an immediate way out of third world poverty, is how Jittery Jay saw it. And they're all whores over there, anyway, he'd always say aloud, as if reminding himself not to forget this very important point. Jittery Jay, mind you, had never visited Asia, but like everything else, he didn't need to, because he already knew everything, anyway. And sometimes, he read.

On top of the non-pedigreed background of the new couple next door, it burned Jittery Jay up to no end, the way they'd accumulated their wealth. It made no sense to him, and it seemed an even more ridiculous family history than his wife's family's story of wealth accumulation- the whole lotion pump thing-a-muh-jig.

It appeared that Mr. Drake had accumulated his wealth by becoming somewhat of a world renowned cryptozoologist. When Jittery Jay had first heard this by way of the same nosy neighbor who'd informed him of where Drake had been raised, he'd said, "Ah, okay. Makes sense," in an attempt to sound blase about the information, the truth being he had no idea what the hell a cryptozoologist was, or what one did. He'd immediately rushed home and Googled the topic and found out that cryptozoology, a pseudoscience, was the study of mythical creatures, such as Bigfoot Sasquatch and the Loch Ness Monster. And one who pursued a course or career in cryptozoology was known as a cryptozoologist.

"You've gotta be fiddle fucking me!" Jittery Jay had said aloud upon reading this.

He'd done more Google searches and found that Mr. Drake was one of the premier cryptozoologists of the day.

Drake had hunted, with some success, according to the articles published by some very unscrupulous internet sites, who seemed to generate their revenues by way of massive amounts of clicks on articles with clickbait titles and sidebar ads leading to only the crudest of porn sites, the Filipino Kapre. It was there, one such article claimed, that he'd met his wife, Mrs. Drake, a beautiful young village girl who'd come from a long line of witches. She'd helped him navigate the haunted jungles of the Isle of Kapre, and the couple, aside from surviving a near all out war with many of the islands mythical creatures, such as the magical Filipino dwarves, known as duendes, and the murderous men with horses heads, known as tikbalang, had fallen in love.

Jittery Jay found a YouTube interview where Mr. Drake had explained what it was like swimming with Nesse in Scotland. "That water was cold," Drake had told his interviewer, "which isn't really surprising, with the lake being so high up in elevation. But 'ol Nesse would let me snuggle up with her for warmth when it got too bad."

"Fiddle Fuck!" Jitter Jay lamented. "How can anyone be stupid enough to believe this bullshit? How dumb *are* these people who read this shit?"

What really burned Jittery Jay up the most, however, was when he came across an article detailing the proud day that Drake had had an honorary doctorate bestowed upon him by an accredited University, making him an actual, bonafide doctor.

Sure, the degree was not in cryptozoology, as the study, as of yet, was still a pseudoscience. It had been awarded in the humanities, due to the fact that Drake did have a habit of donating a lot of the proceeds from his antics (it seems the pennies from all those millions of clicks from his social media accounts added up nicely), to various charities that contributed to the needs of the people in many of the third world locations where he did his cryptozoological studies. Alas, his new neighbor- the decent looking middle aged rich man with the beautiful, exotic, and much younger wife- was Doctor Drake!

"Hey neighbor," Jittery Jay said to Mr. Drake, (albeit Dr. Drake) one sunny, mid-summer morning. It was their first meeting. Jittery Jay had been stalking the Drakes for a month or so, after they'd moved in, the whole time continuing to compile as much information about them as he could by way of internet searches and by chitter chatting with anyone else in the community who seemed to know anything about the Drakes, and on this particular morning he was able to sneak up on Mr. Drake, after having worked his way through the treeline while Mr. Drake's back was turned. "The name's Jay. Nice to meet you."

Jittery Jay stood, eyes darting left and right, never making eye contact, of course, and after realizing that much longer than the appropriate amount of time for a response had passed without a response, he found himself doing something he rarely did, ever. Looking Mr. Drake in the eyes.

"I said my name is Jay," he said again.

"So," Mr. Drake said, matter of factly.

"We're neighbors," Jittery Jay said, a little less neighborly.

"So," Mr. Drake said.

"I just thought I'd come meet you."

"So."

Jittery Jay's eyes started darting back and forth again. Left, right. Left, right. He was at a loss. This is the time when everyone in America puts on a plastic exterior, and acts like they give a shit about people they don't know, and really don't care about, but are supposed to act like they do anyway. Especially when it's a neighbor.

"I guess you're busy," Jitty Jay said, taking a step back.

Mr. Drake did not respond.

"I'll catch you, perhaps another time," Jittery Jay said. "I see you're busy."

Once again, Mr. Drake said nothing, and Jittery Jay turned to leave, hating Mr. Drake (Jittery Jay refused to think of the man in terms of Dr. Drake) even more than he had before he'd met him.

***

He spent more time over the next few weeks, did Jittery Jay, asking around about his new neighbors- this Mr. Drake, (*Dr.* Drake, JIttery Jay would occasionally mumble in disbelief) and his exoticly beautiful wife- if he was able to buttonhole any of his *other* neighbors while they were out and about jogging or taking care of their lawns. To Jittery Jay's displeasure, any and all of his other neighbors he spoke with, and who had met them, seemed to really like the Drakes.

"They seem really nice," said Mr. Wesson, whose great great grandfather had partnered with a buddy to change the world of handguns forever a long, long time ago. "They seem to want to be left alone, and they seem to leave everyone else alone. Couldn't ask for better neighbors. Now if you'll excuse me," he added before returning to trimming the holly bushes that lined his driveway, letting Jittery Jay know with both his words and his body language, an abrupt one eighty spin after he finished speaking, that he'd like to be left alone, as well, this, something Mr. Wesson had quickly learned to do shortly after meeting Jittery Jay a few years back when that poor woman JIttery Jay had married (the one with no self-esteem but plenty of money) had moved him into the neighborhood.

Oh, how this rankled Jittery Jay! Not so much that Mr. Wesson, always such a sharp shooter, pun totally intended, had blown him off, yet again, but because Mr. Wesson liked the Drakes.

"Our kind of people," said Mr. Proctor, walking quickly, cooling down after a brisk jog when Jittery Jay approached him a few days after speaking with Mr. Wesson. Mr. Proctor's great, great patriarch had taken a gamble in the personal hygiene industry years ago that had paid off quite nicely. (And that pun was fully intended, as well, if you happened to catch it). "They don't bother us, and we don't bother them."

Mr. Proctor decided he hadn't jogged quite far enough, and he took off in fluid stride for an old man. At least until he rounded the next turn and was well out of sight of Jittery Jay, where he quickly stopped jogging and returned to a walk.

Jittery Jay was sulking later that day, just before sunset, when he could see, weaving between the trees, just on the other side of the property line, Mr. Drake and what appeared to be a small crowd of people. It appeared as if Mr. Drake was leading some sort of group expedition.

A house warming party? A family reunion? What could it be?

Being the ever so nosy neighbor that he was, Jittery Jay rose from his dignity, upon which he'd been sitting, and began making his way toward the property boundary he shared with the Drakes to find out!

***

As it was, Drake had been leading an actual, bonafide Bigfoot Sasquatch hunting expedition on his property. A month had passed now, and both Jittery Jay's curiosity and hatred for his newest neighbors were driving him completely insane. He had to get it out, and unfortunately for the woman who lived across the street from him, he happened to catch her out on trash night, and decided to use her as an outlet.

"Oh yes," Patricia Simmons, whose great great grandfather had been a pharmacist in Atlanta a century before- a pharmacist who liked to experiment with different drinks, sodas, and colas in five gallon buckets when there were no customers in the store, trying to find the perfect mix for a new drink he was concocting that he'd later call coca-cola, because of the perfect combination of cocaine and cola, (until, of course, the FDA took the first ingredient out, in time). "We know all about his Bigfoot Sasquatch hunts. Aren't they so interesting?"

"Really," Jittery Jay said. "A bit childish, don't you think?"

"Oh, not at all!" the lifelong Ms. Simmons said. Although seventy, and still gorgeous, she'd never been dumb enough to marry a man who she knew was probably attracted to her wealth as much as they might be her beauty. Oh, she'd had plenty of beaus, but she prided herself on not being dumb enough make anything legal, giving any of them the ability to tap into long standing family trust funds, potentially putting her into a position to have to… wait for it…

Get a job!

"You know," she continued, lining the corner of her trashcan up with the intersection of her driveway and the road, the ever obsessive compulsive sufferer that she was. "I'm really looking forward to squatchin' this weekend. We all are. Were you invited?"

"The what?" Jittery Jay said, incredulous, not just because, no, he and Crazy A had not been invited, but also because he'd just heard a word, squatchin', that he'd never heard before. Though he knew not what it meant, he was quite certain it was a stupid word used by stupid people, *because* he'd never heard of it.

"Oh," Ms. Simmons said, her left hand (the one she'd *not* been touching the trash can with, which would have required her to wash it nine times, like her other hand would be washed nine times, once back inside her house) covering her mouth, "I forgot. I wasn't supposed to mention it to you."

Ms. Simmons turned and began walking back up her lengthy driveway, intentionally not bidding Jittery Jay adu, looking down as she went, noting mentally upon how she'd have to have that lawn care company she used come out three times a week now instead of only twice to pull the weeds that grew along the drive. The dandelions had been popping up in even numbers lately, as she counted, and that was a bad omen. They had to come up in odd numbers if they were going to come up at all, so maybe having the guys come out three times a week instead of only twice, three, of course, being an odd number, would help.

"Fuck her," Jittery Jay mumbled aloud as he turned and headed back up his driveway. The type of long, elegant driveway Crazy A's great great someone had fantasized all of their descents enjoying due to their long ago efforts, but surely fearing the occasional ne'er do weller types like Jittery Jay may also enjoy from time to time, as every tree will have a few apples that aren't so much bad, but at least have bad taste fall from it. "She remembered damn well she wasn't supposed to mention it to me, that gas lighting whore!"

Jittery Jay was determined to throw a thorn under the saddle of whatever this group event thing he'd not been invited to was all about. But first, he had to 'God damn Google squatchin'!" as he put it, mumbling aloud up the driveway.

***

"So, these too good for me pricks are actually going out to look for a damn Bigfoot," Jittery Jay mumbled to himself. It was Saturday evening, just before dark. Three days had passed since he'd spoken briefly with Ms. OCD Queen, as he referred to his neighbor lady across the street, and he'd had plenty of time to *goddam Google squatchin'* and he'd found out all about it.

He snickered and sneered to himself from behind a tree as he watched his new, self made neighbors a hundred yards away on the other side of the property line. He could see that overly confident alpha male, Mr. Drake- Dr. Drake, technichly- chest out and shoulders back, all full of self esteem because he'd actually achieved so many things on his own in life.

Who couldn't, if they'd been born poor white trash in Appalachia, Jittery Jay thought to himself as he pondered Drake's achievements. *You'd have to to stop being poor. I could have done any number of things,* he thought further, *if I'd had to. But I come from a place of affluence with plenty of affluent people around me. Why go through the effort if you don't have to, unless you're an idiot.*

Jittery Jay had discovered, by way of his Google efforts, that people who believed in Bigfoot, or Sasquatch, or whatever the hell you called it, actually thought that you could identify their territories by strange marks these mythical creatures (at least mythical in Jittery Jay's mind) left in the forest. Trees bent over like arches were supposedly direction markers. If the trees were entirely broken off, they were territorial markers. If an "X" had been formed by placing the trunks of two trees together, it meant 'stay out.'

Jittery Jay had also discovered that these whacko's, as he saw them as being, these *idiots* who believed in such things as Bigfoot, or Sasquatch, or whatever the hell you called them, and who no doubt also believed in Santa Claus and the Easter Bunny- if not even the Great Pumpkin- thought that these fictitious creatures actually communicated with each other by way of knocking sticks on tree trunks and by clicking and banging rocks together.

"What idiots!" Jittery Jay said aloud, thinking of everything he'd learned and while watching the group of ten of his neighbors heading out into the forest at the edge of their field. Dr. Drake's half age, extremely beautiful, and extremely expensive in a whore bar at one point in time, Jittery Jay had convinced himself, though that was as far from the truth as all the other things Jittery Jay thought to be true, pulled up alongside the group as they exited the field. She'd come running from the house, as if hurrying not to be left behind, carrying what appeared to be a half coconut shell with smoke, perhaps from incense, drifting from the top.

"This outta be a riot," Jitty Jay said aloud, as he began to follow the group from what he felt was a safe distance. He'd spent the day before out in his neighbor's woods setting up 'props' as he thought of them. "X's" formed of downed limbs. He'd bent a few saplings over and pinned them down with large stones. He'd managed to break a few of them off. Not very big ones, but he'd assumed the group might attribute the tree breaks to a baby Bigfoot or Sasquatch or whatever the hell you called it.

What Jittery Jay had *not* known, while he'd been out galavanting in the forest, was that he'd been watched the whole time by way of security cameras. Had he ever spent a minute of his life thinking about anyone or anything else, other than himself and his own self importance, he might have figured out that the Drakes, who truly believed in the existence of cryptids (another word Jittery Jay had found during his goddam Googling efforts) had installed cameras around the entire perimeter of their property.

What he would *not* have known though, was that Mrs. Drake had been the one watching. Hence her lateness in joining the group and hence her bringing with her the smoking coconut.

***

"I heard that!" nearly half the group said together, in excitement, when they heard a tree knock about twenty minutes into their tour. It was not quite dark, but almost, and things were starting to get creepy. Or, in the new terminology the group was learning, squatchy.

Drake looked at his beautiful bride, who flashed him a devious grin. They'd heard the knock as well, and they knew it was made by no cryptid though it had been made by something creepy.

A creepy neighbor.

Mrs. Drake lightly inhaled some of the smoke coming up from the coconut. That which was smoldering inside the shell of the coconut was certainly not incense. It was a concoction she'd brought with her from her small, strange island in Southeast Asia, a concoction only to be used for special purposes, and this was one such purpose. Actually, it was the first time she'd used the concoction, composed of such ingredients as dried bat's blood, crushed pig eyes, and guava root, among many other gross oddities, since she'd come to the U.S.

Mrs. Drake held the smoke in her lungs for a few seconds. As she released the smoke through her nose, she mumbled, ever so softly, what a few of the neighbors were able to hear and would describe for years later as some sort of prayer. They would have no clue at the time or later what it really was.

What they'd never know was that it was a curse!

She whispered the words of unspeakable evil, native to the long line of ancestral witches from her small, scary island in the South Pacific.

As soon as all the smoke had left Mrs. Drake's nose, and her mumbling had ceased, the group heard another tree knock, this one coming from the opposite direction of the first. It came from the top of the hill above them. Mr. and Mrs. Drake exchanged excited looks, for they knew that the dip shit hanging out in the ravine below would have heard the knock as well, and he was no doubt doing one of two things as a result. Either trying to figure out which of their other neighbors might unknowingly be in on his game with him, or, pissing his pants, because he realized what had actually made the knock was no neighbor. It wasn't even human.

As the group moved forward, through the woods, Jittery Jay followed, flanking them from below. His thoughts were obviously the former of the previously mentioned two options, or he would have ran straight home like the cowardly beta male that he was. What he didn't know was that while the group moved- and he moved in the ravine below them- the entity that had made the responding knock only moments earlier did *not* move.

Not yet.

It waited. It waited for the group to move on, and then it went straight down the hill and drew a bead on Jittery Jay.

And then it stalked!

"Do you hear that?" someone from the group said, as they all came to a stop. It was Mr. Proctor. Drake was impressed with the sharp hearing of the old man. "It sounds like something's behind us. But like it's not following us, necessarily."

"I heard it," said Mr. Wesson. "It sounds like it's going down the hill."

"We have nothing to fear," Mrs. Drake said, beginning to move forward again, urging the group to follow her with a head nod. They did.

"They're harmless," Dr. Drake said, pulling up the rear of the group. "In all my research around the world, I've come to the conclusion that if you mean them no harm, they mean you no harm, either. But if you poke the bear, well."

Everyone laughed at that, especially since Drake had exaggerated his native, Appalachian accent, speaking in "dumb hillbilly" as Jittery Jay would have referred to it, had he been just close enough to hear, when he'd said it.

But as it turned out. Jittery Jay was *not* close enough to hear. He was just far enough away from the group now to where only a couple members of the group could faintly detect his first scream.

"What was that?" Ms. OCD Queen said, stopping and turning abruptly.

"Nothing at all," Dr. Drake said with a knowing smile, grabbing the older lady by the elbow and leading her on. He wanted to make sure that the group made enough noise, leaves and sticks crackling underfoot, to keep any of its other members from hearing what Drake knew would soon be a cacophony of screams. "Probably just an owl. Or a nighthawk."

***

The official report, several days later, would attribute the mauling to a bear.

"It happens," the closest stationed game warden would tell the curious neighbors who showed up to Crazy A's house when they saw the flashing lights out front. "I've never run into it, but I always figured with enough time on the job, I would in time. About time, too. I retire next spring."

Crazy A had actually *not* noticed that her husband, now deceased, had not come home from the Bigfoot Sasquatch hunt she'd never noticed he'd gone on. The two could not stand each other (but hey, it's better to be with someone you can't stand than to be alone, right? was always Crazy A's justification, and for Jittery Jay, well, as we well know, it was all about the finances), and through the years they had developed the almost instinctive practice of rarely being home at the same time. Despite the considerable commute into town, at least half an hour's drive, Crazy A was always able to come up with enough errands to run to have excuses to head into town at least three times a day. And she was always sure to text Jittery Jay when she was on the way home, allowing him ample time to get into his man room down in the basement and start surfing the ladyboy porn sites that he loved to visit so much.

So, it was of no notice to *anyone* that Jittery Jay was not around, until a drunken David Peters, retired arborist, and the man who'd inherited the estate bordering Crazy A's land on the backside of her property had stumbled upon the nearly half eaten corpse of the man formerly known as Jittery Jay earlier that morning. Peters had inherited a tract of land originally granted to his ancestors twenty generations before by King James when they came to the area to settle the land. Over the years, he'd allow nursery owners to pillage his land for desirable saplings to sell at their shops, like eastern redbud trees and dogwoods. And about every decade he'd sell off several dozen acres of timber to lumber companies. Since he made his spending money (albeing drinking money) off of trees, in one way or another, he referred to himself as an arborist, though he'd never taken a single class in the field, or, any class in any other field, having not continued his education beyond the high school equivalency level of the boarding school from which he'd graduated more than half a century before.

"Stunk to high heaven," Peters told the state police officer leading the investigation alongside the forest ranger. "I mean, smelled like pure shit put out in the sun to bake."

Crazy A had overheard Peters' less than colorful description of her former husband's remains, but it bothered her not. Her mind was elsewhere. Already, she was trying to decide who to move in next. That drunken bastard always hanging out at the bar, of all places, of the Harris Teeter Grocery store, or hell, why not Peters himself, if he'd have her. His third wife, young enough to be his granddaughter, had just left him and taken what she could from any money that wasn't safely guarded in his family's trust. Maybe it was time for a lateral marriage, money wise, instead of marrying down again, Crazy A thought.

Across the property line, and on the other side of the lawn, the Drakes sipped on mango nectar while they watched the scene.

"How in the hell did you conjure up the Kapre from here?" Dr. Drake asked his beautiful wife, referring to the Philippines version of Bigfoot Sasquatch.

"It was not Kapre," she said. "It was Bigfoot Sasquatch."

"So you can talk to them, too?" Drake said, turning to look at his beautiful bride. "I had no clue that island voodoo crap would work on these North American versions.

"My magic speaks many languages," she said. "Like me."

They continued to watch the proceedings on the neighboring property in silence, looking forward to their next squatchin' session, wondering if anyone else would be foolish enough to doubt their craft in the future.

Don't Feed The Trolls

I don't know if it's still the case for him, but I remember watching an interview with Stephen King, my favorite author, years back, in which he was asked about how much he used the internet, and he said that he used it very little, almost to the point of not at all. When further asked why this was, he said, in that ever eerie voice of his that has given many of us nightmares when translated to the written word or movie script to screen for decades, 'when you look out into the abyss, the abyss looks back at you.'

I've always kept that comment, and the profound concept behind it, in mind, but man, did it ever come to ring so true once my family and I got our YouTube channel, "Homesteading Off The Grid," really up and running.

The thing about being a successful social media content creator is that you never know what is really going to do well, and what isn't, as far as the content you create goes. Most of it is based on an algorithm that is a deep dark secret, even to the social media platform upon which you publish your content, and it's ever changing. So many factors go into that algorithm to determine what content is going to be pushed to the masses that week, that day, or even hour by hour or minute by minute. And the criteria can include everything from the title and cover image of your content, to the subject matter, and down to even the lighting of the video. Was it inside or outside? Overcast or cloudy?

Case in point. We'd been struggling just to get our channel monetized, making gardening and horticulture videos near daily for almost five months to no avail. The requirements for monetization approval at the time, which are the same as of this writing, were to reach one thousand subscribers and accumulate four thousand hours of watch time. YouTube had just reached a major settlement with the Government in regard to targeting children (as in, getting them to spend way too much time on YouTube- an unhealthy amount of time), and as part of their settlement, they were becoming far more strict in regard to who would be financially rewarded for creating content for their platform and who wouldn't. Basically, they were trying to garner more mature content creators with more meaningful content, and stop rewarding every assclown with a cellphone camera who was uploading thirty second long videos of pure rubbish which would entertain, however, nine year olds all day long.

We viewed this as a huge plus for us, seeing it as weeding out the weak, and we knew while we were plugging away to meet the requirements, that most people would not do the work we were doing, because it was hard and very time consuming. We knew tons of other people who had YouTube channels who simply stopped YouTubing as soon as these new requirements were put in place, because they viewed their efforts as hopeless.

We worked even harder!

So the surprise came when, one morning, I walked up to our campground with a camera that I'd bought at a Goodwill thrift store the day before for a whopping three dollars. I'd gotten some brand new batteries for it, and I was basically attempting to see if the camera even worked. My beautiful bride, Dearly, had tried to talk me out of even buying it the day before, being ever so thrifty as she always is, but I relented, and won out by telling her that if the camera didn't work I'd give her three dollars, so she acquiesced, hoping the camera wouldn't work and that she'd soon be three dollars richer.

I had no clue what I was going to video record, but just before I went up to the campground I'd read all three comments that had come in on our channel the night before and came up with an idea. One guy who'd watched a video we'd recently made about gnat repellent asked if we knew of a way to repel an annoying neighbor. With this in mind, I thought of an annoying neighbor we'd just dealt with for about a year, and of how I finally had gotten rid of him with the simple use of a crayon. We knew he was snooping around our place every time we went into town, and my idea to rid ourselves of him, which you can hear all about by watching our video titled, "How to get rid of an annoying neighbor with a crayon," actually worked. I remember clearly thinking to myself, what the hell. This camera probably doesn't even work. This is going to be the easiest three dollars Dearly ever made.

To my chagrin, the camera actually *did* work, and as of this writing, that eighteen and a half minute long video, which has garnered more than five million views, has generated the easiest twenty thousand dollars I've ever made in Google Adsense revenues.

Yes, that's kind of how our success with our channel all started. Testing out a three dollar camera from a thrift store, talking for nearly twenty minutes about some potentially inbred jerk that lives up the road, who may hold the world's record for being the world's oldest mamma's boy, who harassed us for a year, until I pulled out my crayon. The rest, as they say, is history.

But with success came a deluge of people from my past trying to catch up with me, some for better and some for worse. We brought about legions of trolls, mostly the competition, and this we knew from our previous work in social media, namely on Facebook. And then, there were the out and out psychopaths, one of which, completely blew my mind. Not just because of their actions, but because of who they actually were once I found out, quite some time later.

People from my past are easy. I ignore them. If we've been out of contact for twenty years, then they see me on YouTube and now want to be friends again? Hm, sounds like maybe they want something, like their ironically recently started YouTube channel plugged by me on my well established (from years of hard work in social media) YouTube channel.

Ban and ignore!

And then there are those with whom I'd had beef in the past who want to reopen old wounds now that they've located me in cyberspace. Sorry, brah, middle school (or high school, or college, or that first job or marriage, or whenever it was in the past) is over. Get therapy.

Ban and ignore!

However, the biggest batch of trolls anyone will face when working in social media is the competition. Yes, believe it or not, there are other content creators out there creating content in your same genre, who view the best way of getting ahead is to kill the competition. These are the typical, cynical, Negative Nelly types that we all see in everyday life. Instead of trying to figure out how to grow their channels, and perhaps partly by doing so by attempting to emulate what other successful people are doing, they spend their time making multiple fake profiles online and visiting their competitors and leaving nasty, degrading, very hateful and despicable remarks, all in an attempt to discourage the other content creator, their hope being, in eventually taking over their market share by getting them to become so discouraged they simply quit.

These life long losers will often seek each other out and form alliances and launch attacks on other content creators who either decline their request to join their alliance or ignore their request all together, which is what I always do. This is called gang stalking. It's very common, often successful in the short term, but relatively ineffective when these trolls are dealing with folks who've been around the block and know the game. Sickeningly, their other primary goal is to actually see the content creators they're cyberbullying commit suicide.

These folks must be banned and ignored repeatedly, as they'll simply create more fake userid's with different email addresses, etc., but eventually, they get approved for their social security disability they've been applying for for most of their adult lives (like our dear good buddy, Jittery Jay from our previous story tried so hard to do), and they give up their social media trollish ways and go away and live the good life on their thirty five hundred tax free for life dollars each month and leave the productive members of society alone. Hey, a small price for the taxpayers to pay to rid the otherwise peaceful pond of some nasty bottom dwelling scum.

And then there are the sheer, all out psychopaths. These people can range from the man who falls in love with your wife by way of your videos, and comes after you relentlessly for having what he wants, or the woman who develops a massive crush on you and goes after your wife (we've had both), to the super seriously mentally deranged who are only days away from walking into a crowd or a public school and start shooting away.

And then, there are the outliers. Trolls who you'd never suspect, never guess, and would have no way on God's green earth of figuring out who they were if they were never revealed to you. We had one such troll not too long ago, an outlier, and to this day, the story behind this troll blows my mind, and the only reason I tell this story now is because...

… he's dead…

***

About a year and a half ago, as of this writing, we began getting messages from a particular viewer, that at first, seemed pleasant and flattering. However, over time, these messages began to become bitter. I kept my eye on the user, assuming perhaps it was merely someone who was beginning to feel jaded because their replies never got a response from us.

When you're new to social media content creation, you get excited by comments, and you reply to many or most of them. However, as your viewer base grows, there simply is not enough time in a day to reply not just to many or most comments, but any of them. We're talking about, some days, thousands of comments that come in.

If you *do* attempt to reply to some of the comments, many other people who leave comments and never get replies have a tendency to get nasty. Seriously. It can be a nightmare. You actually end up creating some of your own trolls.

In the end, what most of us who end up getting a hundred thousand or more subscribers end up doing, is merely not reply to comments. It sounds ungrateful, but you reach the point where you have to pick your poison. Continue to create content in an enjoyable way, and patrol your comment section to ban abusers, and live your life, with your family, to the fullest, or to try to be all things to all people, and reply to everyone, and in pretty quick order, end up watching your channel shrink and become unsuccessful because you're spending too much time interacting with viewers and not enough time creating content. You'll also soon find that you're ignoring your family, making things bad on the homefront, and that's the last thing this guy is ever going to do.

With all this said, I continued following this particular commenter, and alas, they began making personal attacks against me, and warning my wife about how evil I was and how she must 'get out now.'

At first, I assumed it was merely some dude who'd fallen in love with my wife while watching our videos. But just as I was beginning to think this way, the troll started talking about events from my past that I'd never revealed on social media, or in any of my books- not even in fictional form. These were not 'deep dark secrets' from which I've tried to hide, simply parts of my past I've never shared publicly. I took it all as a message from this troll that they knew me very personally, and that they wanted me to know this.

At this point, I banned this troll, but only a day after banning him, we started getting comments from someone who appeared to be the same user. Knowing how easy it is to create a fake social media profile, I knew this person had merely opened another free email account somewhere and had come back to YouTube and created a new account, using the same profile name and profile image.

No matter how many times we banned this person, they would always be back the next day. And the insults and attacks got worse and worse, until the individual started commenting about some of the worst things I've ever gone through in life- things that would have killed most people, and nearly killed me- and of how I deserved it all, and they couldn't wait until it happened again. They wrote of how I'd "lost my first family," and was "getting ready to lose my new family." And of how they were having orgasms sitting back, watching it all unfold on the internet.

At this point, we felt as if we were in danger, and we took action. I will not tell you exactly what we did, as I may need to do this at some point again in the future, with some other psychopath, but what I'll tell you, is that if you are being cyberbullied in anyway, you can contact the authorities and they *will* act on your behalf. A lot of idiots are finding out the hard way that making fake profiles on the internet and harassing, bullying, or threatening people is not something that the authorities take lightly. It's not a joke to them, and there are a lot of people 'cooling their heels' in jail cells right now for cyberbullying.

It was shortly after we took this action, which was very effective (much more than the 'ol crayon trick), that we actually found out who our nightmarish troll was, and it absolutely blew my mind, because it was someone with whom I'd had no contact with for decades, someone who I'd forgotten, and someone, who once I *did* remember them, I would have least expected to be doing such a thing to anyone, let alone me. But I also found out they'd been doing it to dozens of people, others of whom had taken similar actions as us to protect themselves from this sick, twisted fuck as well.

So, is this person in jail?

No.

Like I said earlier, they're dead.

But they weren't killed by any of the dozens of people they were cyberstalking, nor did they go out in a blaze of glory during a Federal raid.

The story is much more unique than that, and sad at the root.

I've spent much of my adult life trying to unlearn most of what I'd learned as a child. I've sought enlightenment and spirituality, mostly due to being spoon fed hard, rigid religion from near infancy. I could never wrap my mind around the concept of a belief system that included a loving God, yet whose followers were filled with so much hate. There had to be a different way, and I was determined to find it.

One of the things I've learned along the way, is that in most scenarios in my life, good or bad, I've played a part. Now, I won't go as far as the mindset I had drilled into me as a child that I was a worthless piece of fly shit from birth and deserved nothing but bad things and my part in everything was that everything was my fault. However, I won't go to the opposite extreme, either, and say that everything that happens to be is because of someone else. I despise the victim mindset as much as I cringe away from the hell's fire and brimstone bullshit I was raised on.

However, I do realize my part in how I at least could become a target for the troll from hell, as I've come to refer to this individual.

I will not name this individual, and I doubt anyone else who was harassed and threatened by this individual will ever read this, but still, among the few things I may have learned on my spiritual journey in recent years, something I rank at the top as a must for spiritual growth, is forgiveness. This story is not being told out of vindictiveness, and it's certainly not being told to smear the name or image of someone unable to defend themselves, because they're not here to do so. They're dead.

This story is being told, because it's creepy as hell.

Period.

So here's the deal.

When I was a child in grade school, and this is going back almost forty years, mind you, there was another child approximately my age. This child had numerous, severe physical disabilities. And in order to actually protect the identity of this individual, I will not, in any way, describe any of his disabilities.

My part in it? This relentless online harassment which would eventually lead to the threatening of my family?

I was fake.

I was plastic.

I was very disingenuous.

I remember, distinctly, as a young child, staring at this other child, and if he noticed me staring, I would, of course, smile and say a kind word. I was friendly. At least it's what I thought. But what I was doing was covering my ass after being caught staring.

As we aged, and I became knowledgeable of how wrong it was to stare, or point out the differences in people, I remained fake, plastic and disingenuous toward this person. If our paths crossed, I would make sure to smile and say hello. Looking back now, I might not have realized that I never spoke to the dozens of other kids I happened to pass, but I'm sure the other kid, the one with severe disabilities, did. I was singling him out. I may have viewed it as friendly, but I'm sure he merely viewed it as being singled out, and I'm sure, because he was different.

We grew up, and where myself, as well as others like me, went on to college, and then careers, most of us leaving the state even, this child grew up to stay put, deal with constant medical procedures, and be pitied by those who passed him in public. Oh, but they always smiled, and they were always nice, so that made it all okay, right?

Wrong.

As time went on, our old friend, who wasn't really a friend to any of us, but who was someone who I or any of us easily could have and should have befriended, became bitter and jaded. He watched, while in physical pain, mind you, his peers go on to get married, have children, work for large corporations, own and operate their own businesses, get into journalism, become scientists and doctors, become war heroes, and some, successful social media content creators, working in an industry that would couldn't even have imagined existing back in our school days.

He watched all of this, through the years, mostly from beds in hospitals and wheelchairs in hospice centers.

And none of us who'd only offered those friendly, *oh, shit! You caught me staring!* smiles from years ago where there to watch any of this with him, nor did we ever go back to check on him and see how he was doing.

The time eventually came when, from the looks of it, he got word that death- his death- was not just imminent, but only months away.

I can't imagine getting such news. I don't know what I'd do or how I'd react. We all like to think we know what we'd do under such circumstances. We claim we'd wrap our arms around our loved ones and cherish every last living second we had with them, but the truth is, none of us know. The only way of finding out is by going through it.

It turns out, this individual decided to spend his final, living months stalking, by way of various social media sites and other online methods, people from his past, such as myself, and others. Those of us who always flashed the cold, fake, plastic veneer of a smile when he caught us staring. Those of us who showed such pity in our eyes, when we lay our eyes upon him, but who never had an ounce of empathy. Those of us who would consider him the last person we'd want to look up on this wicked new technology called social media, just to check in on him to see how he was doing. What he'd done in life. Who he'd become.

Because we didn't care.

And we never did.

I never did.

That's my part in it.

Did my family and I deserve to be stalked, harassed, intimidated and threatened in such a way?

No.

Can we sit here and justify the psychotic actions of an unstable man who'd spent his life dealing with difficulty and pain and who'd recently gotten word that his life, painful as it was, was about to come to an abrupt, sudden end?

No.

Can we, further, blame our actions as children, for how things all went down?

Again, a definitive no.

However, we can learn from this. We can teach our children, as I'm attempting to teach mine, that it is never okay to stare at someone because they are different. Also, if you're going to be nice to someone, if you're going to extend pleasantries, make sure it's real. Don't do it just because you think it's the right thing to do, or because others are watching. Either be nice to others because you truly want to be nice to them, or don't bother. I'm not saying be callous. I'm just saying, be real.

Because people can tell.

***

The following stories are from Bigfoot Sasquatch Files
Volume 2:

1

This Is How They Hid The Bodies

They'd known each other since kindergarten, and they'd loved each other for just as long. The only reason he bit her on the arm in first grade, and got sent to the principal's office for doing it, was because she'd asked him to. And she only asked because she wanted proof that he'd do whatever she said, no matter how ridiculous the request, and she got it that day, and his loyalty never swayed from that moment on, despite three slick licks he took across the backside.

The only reason he'd granted her strange request was because he wanted to show her, at the ripe young age of six, that he'd do anything she asked and grant her any wish her heart desired. Besides, he didn't bite her hard enough to hurt her, anyway- didn't even break the skin- and they both knew what that meant. Any request made, any request granted.

Oh, how she loved to torment him in middle school, by returning the flirtations from the high school boys while walking to and from the school house. But only when he was with her, and only for confirmation that he really cared, even though she never doubted that he did.

If she was alone, and the older boys flirted, she ignored them.

Because she, too, was loyal and always very faithful.

When he'd asked her to marry him after graduation (*before*, actually, though they couldn't tell their parents of such poppycock), she'd said yes, and they'd even set a date.

But the planes came over and bombed the harbor and Uncle Sam made different plans for them.

She used her time while awaiting his return (praying for it every night) wisely. She kept busy, in an ill attempt to keep her mind from wandering about what he might be going through by going to college and getting a degree. She got a degree in teaching from a normal school, as they were known back in those times, and it only took two years, back then, and just as she was finishing up, he was making his way back home.

Physically, he was fine, and whatever wars would forever fight on in his mind, he kept to himself, except for the times of nightmares. She cried for him at night when those came, but she always made sure never to tell him of them during the day. She figured those were his times of respite from the memories. When he was awake. That's when he had a say in keeping them away.

But she often wandered about it during the times he drifted off while wide awake, distant and away in his mind. Even then she gave him his space.

They'd gone through heartache when they'd discovered they couldn't conceive. And back in those days, the medical people couldn't tell who was 'at fault' as the folks of those days liked to say. Like there had to be someone to blame.

They both shed tears for what would never be, but then took it in stride and decided that the All Mighty simply wanted them to love on each other uninterruptedly, without having to share their love with little ones.

So they did just that!

For more than fifty years!

She retired from teaching, and he from selling insurance, and they'd saved way more money than most couples with such middle class incomes could have imagined. But hey, when you're not spending a quarter of a million dollars to raise a child to the age of eighteen per pop (converted to today's dollars, of course) such things are possible.

They decided to spend the inheritance for which they had no heirs to leave it, so they moved back to their native Virginia, and they bought the most beautiful six hundred acres parcel of land sitting right at the foot of the Blue Ridge Mountains that anyone could imagine laying eyes upon. They knew it to be true, because it was where they'd grown up, and despite him having been around the world (albeit, behind the sites of a fifty caliber machine gun), and both of them having been all around the U.S., they'd never seen any place as pretty.

And that's when it all started happening.

***

They'd discussed virtually everything throughout the years, but one topic they'd never breached was aging, and how it was possible that their minds might go once it began to happen; this dreaded thing called aging.

If anyone had asked either of them anything along these lines, they would not have been surprised to find that both held deep fear for *him*, and *none* for her. Sure, all those years as a public school teacher came with plenty of stressors, but she'd taught during a time when a teacher could still take a board across a youngster's ass if need be, and not get sued or be imprisoned ,though she'd never had to, because parents could freely do the same, and they did, back in those days, meaning that by the time their kids even *got* to school they knew how to mind their p's and q's.

So it came as quite a surprise when *she* began acting a bit odd- drifting off into the vast forest surrounding the relatively small cleared portion of their land- the part where they'd build their dream house- staying gone, sometimes for hours, the whole while never having even *mentioned* to the love of her life that she was heading out for a stroll.

The first few times it happened, he wouldn't have known, because he'd been out himself, running errands of some sort or another, or out hunting deer or turkeys (and always wondering just what in the hell those strange mounds he'd stumble over on certains parts of his land might be). So the first time he actually took note of it, his wife's odd behavior, it scared him out of his wits.

"Looks like that Clinton fellow from down Arkansas's gonna pull it off," he'd said, while reading the paper one morning. She'd been in the other room tidying up after breakfast. "They say he's leading among women, because he's the best looking candidate since Kennedy," he said, laughing lightly afterward. "What do you think?"

After waiting for a reply, and not getting one, he asked again. "Do you think this Slick Willy guy's cute, hon?"

Again, no reply, so he rose to his feet and ventured into the kitchen, only to find it empty, and to see the back door open.

He walked out back just in time to see her slipping into the woods on the far side of the field, nearly two hundred yards away. He yelled for her, but she didn't answer, so he closed the door behind himself and took off at a jog- at least as much of a jog as he could muster for his years.

"Wait up!" he yelled a couple of times as he crossed the field. It was to no avail. She was too deep inside the woods now to hear him.

He entered the forest, and though the morning's light was bright, it was nearly as dark as dusk underneath the heavy canopy. It was damp, humid, almost sticky. Typical summer morning in Virginia.

"Hon!" he called, louder, cupping his hands, and then repeating the effort in several directions. "Hon!"

She did not answer.

He looked for tracks but saw none. Not only was the ground firm here, the result of no rain in more than a week, but it was heavily covered with last fall's leaves. And she barely weighed a hundred pounds, anyway, so she'd be hard set to leave tracks under *any* conditions.

He continued moving through the forest, not knowing exactly where to go, and then he heard it.

A knock.

A tree knock.

For some reason, as his mind saw it at least, his wife had decided to pick up a stick and bang on the side of a tree rather than simply answering his calls by yelling in return. He followed the direction of the sound, and then he heard it again. This time, closer. He knew he was getting close to his wife, because she *had* to be the one doing the knocking, *right*?

"Hon," he said, when he'd made it to the top of a slight knoll and could see his wife standing not too far away, below. She was standing with her back turned to him, looking up the hill- the opposite direction from which he'd come- mesmerized. She paid no attention to him as he approached.

And then he heard the third knock!

He stopped, frozen in his tracks, suddenly realizing it had *not* been his beautiful bride of all these years who'd done the knocking.

His eyes followed her gaze to the top of the hill and for the rest of his days, he'd swear (never laying his hand on a Bible to do it, because he was too good a Christian for that, but he would swear to it with*out* one), that he saw someone, or some*thing*, large and dark, ducking its head behind a tree.

"Let's get you home, hon," he said, drawing up to her, quickly, after seeing what he'd thought he'd seen, and putting his arm around her. As he turned her toward the direction from which he'd come, it was as if she came to at the same time.

"Did you see him?" she asked.

"I saw *something*," he said, leading her out of the area, and back to what he *hoped* was the safety of their house.

"They're coming in closer," she said.

Neither of them spoke again until they'd gotten home...

...and went inside and locked the doors!

***

"I'm telling you," she said, glass of cold water in hand. "It's the forest people."

He'd looked into her eyes and he noticed that they weren't glossy. They didn't seem to have the far and away look of folks who were slipping in their minds. He could still remember that look distinctly from back when his grandparents had it, though it was nearly his entire lifetime ago. As far as he could tell, his wife's mental health was *not* off, and in a different way, this concerned him even more.

"Sometimes, I can feel them calling to me," she said, taking another sip of water and then handing him the glass. "It's hard to explain. It's like, I just know they're there. And they want me to come to them."

"Like with the kids," he said. "Little Missy, and the other ones."

"Yes," she said. "Very similar to that."

Despite the fact that she'd taught school during simpler times when children (and their parents, for that matter) seemed to be much more disciplined and respectful than many children and parents of today, and people seemed to have more character in general, there was the occasional bad apple. *Little Missy*, as her husband had referred to her, was a little girl she'd once taught back in the early sixties. She was a well disciplined little girl. She was clean and appeared to be well kept, and she was one of the brightest kids in the class. Never a problem. Yet every time she looked Little Missy's way, it was as if she could hear the girl's voice, in her mind, saying 'help me.'

She knew that if she were to tell anyone of this, what seemed to be the ability to read a little girl's mind, they'd write her off as mad, so she didn't. She kept it to herself. But she paid attention to it, this strange ability she seemed to possess, and she continued to listen to Missy's voice, and eventually, she acted.

One particular day when Little Missy's voice seemed to be particularly loud in her mind, she pulled Missy aside during recess, in such a way that none of the other children would notice, and she asked her if she was okay. Missy told her the most nightmarish stories of how her mother 'rented her out to her man friends,' as the little girl put it, on the weekends, and since it was Friday, she didn't want to go home.

She assured Missy that it would be okay to go home, and not to worry. Just go home and act as if everything was okay, and that she'd take care of it all for her. She would never have to fear weekends again.

Around 9:00 p.m. that evening, the local police, acting on what would forever be referred to only as an 'anonymous tip' when the story was told originally or retold hundreds of times over the years that followed, appeared at Missy's mother's house, and Missy's woes came to an abrupt end, though the girl, no doubt, was scarred for life.

And then there'd been Tommy, the boy always covered with bruises, because he was always running into things. An anonymous tip would save him from an abusive, drunken stepfather. And her abilities as an empath would later save Little Sarah from a much older stepbrother who couldn't seem to keep his hands, or other body parts, to himself.

"You never really believed those stories did you," her husband finally said, referring to the forest people she'd mentioned, not her strange abilities. He never doubted those. "I mean, those were just the stories our parents and grandparents told us when we were kids."

"I never believed *or* disbelieved," she said, remembering being told the stories quite well during her childhood, especially when it was bedtime and she didn't want to go to sleep. "I was always intrigued, and I always viewed it as if most anything's possible."

Both of their families had already lived down in the valley, but they remembered, when they'd been grade school children themselves, in the 1930's, the slew of families being driven from the mountain tops in order for the Government to build the Blue Ridge Parkway. A lot of the families held out as long as they could, some of them being forced out at the end of gun barrels before they'd leave.

There were stories of *some* families, way back in the sticks, who were supposedly protected by the people of the forest, or the forest people (the words were always interchangeable, but they had the same meaning), who would act on behalf of the locals (squatters, the *Guv'ment* men would call them). They would pull pranks on them, often disabling their vehicles, or throwing rocks at them during the day or night. Oh, and the sheer terror they would inflict upon them when darkness fell? With their ear shattering screams?

Stories for another time!

Supposedly, some of the locals who were way, deep, deep, *deep* back in the woods actually *were* able to remain on their land because of the efforts of the forest people. Every now and then, a hiker who gets too far off the beaten trails the Guv'ment men would later come through and cut out through what they'd call the Shenandoah National Park, will find the old homesteads. Sometimes they find the old houses, wells, frames from old vehicles, and every now and then old family cemeteries.

And sometimes, they even find bones.

"I know I'm getting old," she said, "and I know you have your worries. Trust me. I have mine for you. But I'm telling you. This is *not* dementia. My mind's as sharp as it's ever been."

"I'll take your word for it," he said, and he meant it. He remembered distinctly when she'd told him about the children way back when. He never doubted her then, as odd as those stories had sounded, so he wasn't about to doubt her now. Besides, he had fought in Japan, and he helped liberate the Philippine Islands before that, and he saw stuff over there that no one in Western culture would ever believe. And he *knew* they wouldn't believe it because he used to tell people about some of those things after he'd come home from the war, and he learned quickly to stop telling those stories when the people he told them to would hear him out then tell him he was crazy. So he had no doubt, back when she'd told him, that his wife probably *did* possess an ability that the majority of people simply didn't. And as they always say, the proof is in the pudding, and it all panned out when those 'anonymous tips' were followed up with by authorities.

As it turned out, that good looking smooth talker from Arkansas *did* push the man who reneged on his claim of 'no new taxes,' out of office, and the aged couple, lovers since childhood, would spend most of the eight years he'd spend in office together on their extremely large tract of land nestled at the foot of the beautiful Blue Ridge Mountains of Virginia, ever so close to their childhood homes.

They'd gone through the occasional spells of heading down into Charlottesville to be social, perhaps make new friends in their retirement, but no matter where they went or who they met, they always returned home, much earlier than they'd planned, and spent their time together watching the sunsets.

One beautiful Saturday morning, a crisp fall day, they decided to drive into town and support the local college during a football game. As the band played, well, but loudly, during a beautiful halftime show for the crowd of nearly forty thousand, they looked at each other, and with their eyes, agreed to leave. They went home and sat back on that beautiful front porch of theirs, the one with the even more beautiful view, and the one where they spent most of their time, weather permitting, and watched the leaves turn from green to gold, red, orange, and yellow. It was a better show than the band's field performance, entertaining and near excellent as it was.

As they spent their years together on their land, loving each other as much in their old age as they had in their youth, they noticed how many of the large properties around them were changing, and *not* for the better, at least in *their* opinions.

As the land values in the local real estate market skyrocketed, many families, whose land had been in the family for many generations, were being forced to sell their land, or at least the majority of it, as the patriarch and matriarch generation (proud members of the WWII generation, like themselves), were dying off, to appease the estate taxes.

Sure, on paper, these baby boomers inheriting the land were *loaded*. Anyone who owned even a hundred acres of land in the area, where raw land out in the sticks sold for thirty thousand dollars per acre, was worth three million dollars. But these were common folk. They were farmers. And if they worked away from home, they worked down at the public utilities for about forty grand a year, because a cousin of a cousin knew someone who had a cousin who worked there and who could get them a job. These were *not* rich people when it came to liquidity. As a result, when mom and pop died, and the Guv'ment men came around with their hands out, looking for fifty per cent of the value of their land to 'redistribute' to the masses who needed it so much more than the families who'd lived on it for generations, they didn't have it to give, and the family had to sell the land to satisfy these taxes.

The result of this- this 'redistribution of wealth'- was the tearing down of the most beautiful forests, the digging up of the most beautiful grazing fields, and the construction of the most God awful looking subdivision in the history of America.

Oh, but how so many of the young, middle class yuppies loved living in them so…

Around the time talk started up about the son of that one guy who'd reneged on the no new taxes running for office to avenge his father's loss (and who would win, and then go on to avenge his father in Iraq, for a time), she began spending a little more time than usual in the woods alone. They'd spent plenty of time walking the woods together through the years, but he knew that they'd only speak to her, or how ever it was they communicated with her (he never really understood) when she was alone.

"We've got to figure something out," she said one evening. They were sitting on the porch, sipping iced tea, watching the fireflies sporadically lighting up the field as the sun slipped behind the hills. "We can't let them come in here and tear this place down and throw up those over priced cookie cutter Mcmansions. It's *their* home!" And he knew *exactly* who she meant by 'their.'

They'd talk during their walks, and they'd talk while they sat on the porch, of all the ways they could protect the land. Try as they might, they couldn't seem to come up with a way to protect the property from the inevitable. They'd had their hopes up about the guy who was taking his daddy's old job in the White House, because he'd spoken of eliminating the estate tax, but as it was, once he'd gotten elected into the swamp, he did little more than swim with the alligators that were already in it, and he settled for simply waving the estate tax up to the first $1.3 million dollars worth of real property, cash and assets.

That would do them no good.

The couple wasn't so much worried about the continuation of the existence of the forest people, should their forest become a yuppified subdivision, because the forest people had proven for much longer than the U.S. had even been a country that they were adaptable. They were resourceful. They'd always been able to adjust to the changes forced upon them by mankind.

However, there *was* a particular part of the property that was sacred; a specific location that the couple felt needed to remain untouched.

The family cemetery.

The family cemetery of the forest people!

Yes, on the far back part of their property, a near two hour hike due to the sheer incline, all through extremely rough terrain (and it was the only way to get there), there was a dip in the land. The dip was not on the top of the ridge, but about fifty yards below it, and if one was standing on top of the ridge looking down, they'd never see it.

It was the perfect location. The ground itself here appeared as if a massive giant had taken a giant table spoon and taken a huge scoop right out of the earth. More than likely, millions of years ago, a meteor had hit the ground at the location, carving out the deep indentation.

Overhead of this hole, wild grapevines and Virginia Creeper grew so thick that if you were on top of the ridge, looking down into the dip, you'd never notice the change in topography. From above, the vines looked like the surface of the ground. One could not tell that they were the canopy of the dipped area beneath them. An area approximately half the size of a football field.

An area that held no less than forty graves of the forest people.

***

The only thing they couldn't figure out about the plan they came up with, ingenious if they didn't say so themselves, was which one of them would pass first.

It was more than just the, "I hope I die first, because I can't imagine spending a day without you," kind of things they jokingly said, but absolutely meant. And they always made sure to change the subject before they spent so much time on it that they actually started thinking about it too much, because they both knew the time was inevitable and drawing near.

There was also the morbid curiosity over whom the park would be named after. Him or her?

"It's not morbid," she'd say to him when they spoke of it, which was often. "How can we not be curious? It's only natural."

"I don't know," he'd say. "It just brings back so many memories. Bad ones. Like, talking to my battle buddies back in the war about who was going to mail whose letter home for them. You know. The death letters. To the families."

"Wow," she'd said, when he'd told her this. They'd actually been out in the forest behind their home that morning, hoping for a glimpse of the forest people. She almost always saw or heard them when she was alone, but they rarely did when he was with her. He never took it personal. He fully understood that she was an empath, and he knew full well that he was not.

"So who'd you write *your* letter to?" she'd asked him that day when it had come up. "Me or your mother?"

"Neither," he said, without a moment's hesitation. "I didn't write no damn death letter."

"Really?" she'd said, surprise in her voice.

"Dying was never something I considered an option," he'd told her. "I saw myself making it home, and I wasn't about to have a plan b, so I never wrote the damn letter, and let's change the subject."

And they did.

***

As fate would have it, the park would be named after her, though she didn't have to wait long for him to get there, wherever *there* was, to join her. He passed only six months after cancer came quick and took her away from him just as quickly. There was plenty of pain, despite how some might like to fantasize there *is* such a thing as a painless death by way of the Big C, but he'd been happy that it hadn't lasted long.

She went quick.

And he went in his sleep, the way he'd always boasted he wished to die if ever asked, and he went with a smile on his face.

And the county, to whom they'd donated the land, put up a trail park in her name since she'd been the one who'd gone first, and he stayed behind for all the paperwork and the official dedication.

Per the stipulation of the gift of the land- all of their land- the couple had made to the county, there was never to be allowed any hunting or straying from the main trails, which the country kept well cleared and clearly marked, and there was *never* to be any construction of any kind, and to this day, nearly twenty years after their passing, there hasn't been.

The yuppies come from far and wide to hike the rugged trails, which lead up the steep mountainside with its beautiful views at the peaks, especially the peak that has the steep drop down into what looks like nothing but tangles and brambles and briars and vines…

… at least from above.

And they take their group pictures, of family and friends, and those who go it alone take plenty of selfies, none of them realizing that down there in the backdrop of all those photos they're putting all over their social media sites and pages…

…are graves.

And that's *exactly* how they hid the bodies!

2

Where In The Hell Is Bigfoot Sasquatch When You Need Him Her It Or Them?

Thump!

I tried to ignore the first one and go back to sleep. My cat, Cleopatra- love her as I do- had decided to stay outside until 1:00 a.m., at which time she then decided to claw on the outside frame of the bedroom window to let me know she wanted to come in. This is her thing, and I could only *imagine* how we wouldn't have any screens left if we actually had screens.

That was two hours ago.

An hour ago, she decided to sit at my feet and meow incessantly to let me know she wanted back out.

Oh, just one of the many ways I know it's spring on the homestead. Sure, she's spayed, so she never has kittens, but she *does* love the attention she gets from the two tuxedo tom cats that come through the woods to see her this time each year. And it's warm enough for her to be comfortable while outside at night, so I don't mind. The spoiled thing hardly goes out in the winter. She's got her favorite spot on the love seat, only feet away from our woodstove and the warmth it provides, and she'll claw the eyes out of *anyone* who tries to take it from her.

Thump!

So there it is again. An hour after I let the cat out, and the thumps are back, and I can't ignore this second round. Not just because I know I'll never get back to sleep tonight- I've given up already- but because I know what it is. What's doing the thumping, that is.

"What is it?" my beautiful bride, Dearly, a.k.a. 'Giggly Girl' asks, sitting halfway up beside me in bed. She'd either heard it, too, or I'd awakened her by sitting up too forcefully upon recognition of what was making the sound.

"Nothing," I assure her. "Go back to sleep."

But you see. I know it's actually quite a bit *more* than nothing.

It's that everlovin' Dogman.

He's back!

***

So, I know these stories are supposed to be about Bigfoot Sasquatch, right? Well, they are, and so is this one. It's kind of about what happens during his, her, it or their absence from the homestead. This happens twice a year. First, in the spring, when the small clan of Bigfoot Sasquatch that may or may not be living on my property head to the top of the mountain and hang out for a time deep within their layer at a place I consider to be their breeding grounds. I think I've stumbled through it once or twice on my hikes.

And then, in the fall, they leave for a while, again. Never long. Maybe a week or two. I'm not quite sure if they're joining back up with their larger clan who are migrating south for the winter, and going part of the way with them before deciding they'd rather stay here and see what the hell Crazy Lake (that's me, by the way) is going to do next, or if it's intentional. Like, they travel with their clan for a way, and then come back, having known they were going to do just that before they left. Either way, that's how it's worked out for the past couple of years since they've been here. Or at least the past couple of years since I've noticed them here. Hell, for all I know, they've been here way longer than that. But as it seems to stand, they leave for a couple of weeks in the spring to get their sexy on, then they leave a couple of weeks each fall for their family reunion. But thus far, they've always returned.

But you see, in their absence, they leave a void. And we've had some really strange stuff fill that void. Potentially, we've had ghosts from little girls buried in an overgrown graveyard in a huge patch of briers and brambles behind our house. They actually come around, it seems, at times, when him, her, it or they are around, too. I'd be more than happy to clean the cemetery out- cut all those briers and brambles out of there and even leave flowers regularly, but it's just across the border of my property with a neighbor. But back when the girls actually died, as a result of the Spanish Flu Pandemic of 1918, they died in my house. It was all one property way back then, and this house, built for sharecroppers in 1903, was the house they lived in at the time. Come to think of it, they died, all three of them, in the very room in which I'm sitting while I write these words.

And yes, I just got the heebie jeebies.

And then there've been the civil war soldier ghosts marching through our fields and meadows. Sometimes you can hear the light tapping of snare drums. We've found some of the old cannon grapeshot and other relics while digging holes on our property to plant trees. There must have been a battle here. Or at least target practice.

There's that one thing that runs through the field, only on the darkest of nights- on nights when there is no moon- which puts off the sound of chains rattling, and it can be right beside you one instant, and then on the opposite end of the property, nearly a quarter of a mile away, the next. My gut is telling me that it might be the ghost of a formerly enslaved person. Perhaps more than one. But for some reason, these entities have chosen not to reveal too much about themselves to me, and I have reason to believe I know why. Virginia, where we live, is a very old state with a lot of history, and much of it, painful. And not all spirits realize they're trapped between worlds. These entities may be far more fearful of me than I ever could be them.

And then, there's this damn Dogman. A legend, I thought, at first. Until I met a funny turned old man on top of the mountain about a year or so ago who claims this damn thing followed him here from Michigan.

Hey, and they say I'm crazy?

Anyway, the first time this thing started coming around, I erroneously thought it was, potentially, Bigfoot Sasquatch. I explicitly remember a similar occurrence of what had happened tonight.

It was earlier in the year, just before spring, I believe. Still winter, but barely. The seasons just beginning to change. And I think him, her, it, or they had left to go up the mountain and get their groove on a bit early.

I was sitting in my office, the room I'm in now as I write (yes, the room where the little girls passed), and something thumped against the side of my house, just to the side of the window. It sounded like maybe a bird had flown into the side of the house, maybe attempting to avoid crashing through the window glass- veering off and missing the window at the last second- but then I realized it was still dark outside.

A bat, maybe?

Couldn't have been. It was close to freezing out and the bats were still in hibernation.

Just as I wrote it off to a wayward owl, it happened again. My first suspicion, after ruling out flying animals, was my former annoying neighbor. Anytime *anything* not to my pleasing happened around the homestead my first couple of years here, I would be quick to blame him, certain he was exacting some sort of revenge for having been told he could no longer take the hay off my land, as we'd bought our property for *our* use, not someone else's.

Reason would always win out in regard to this line of thinking, that it was the former annoying neighbor up to no good. There was no *way* it could be this man. I mean, if you were to look up the term "heart attack waiting to happen" in wikipedia, you'd probably see a picture of him in the article as an example of what a heart attack waiting to happen actually looks like. The man's about 5'9" and weighs closer to four hundred pounds than he does three hundred. We have a gate up at the end of the drive (a gate, I'll add, one hundred percent inspired by his existence), and he, honest to God, couldn't walk as far as from the gate to the house. It would *kill* him. It's a whopping fifty yards!

This has nothing to do with this story, but here's an odd thing about this man, the former annoying neighbor. As long as I've known him, I have *not* been able to accurately estimate his age. He's one of those guys who could be fifty three, or sixty eight. Does that make any sense? Hell, might even be just now nearing forty.

It's really strange.

Maybe he's actually a wendigo?

Oh, anyway!

So, as crazy as it sounds (have I mentioned they call me Crazy Lake?), I decided to go outside and investigate.

Yes, even though it was only 5:00 a.m. on a freezing cold, dark winter's morn' (almost spring, mind you) and I had no idea in hell what in the name of all things holy, or in this case, unholy, was outside waiting for me.

***

So, when I got outside, I had one of my handy dandy, very weak flashlights with me. I am notorious for not taking lights into the forest with me, and when I do, they're usually el-cheapo's.

Why is this?

I'm cheap.

Okay, I prefer the term, thrifty.

I will never understand the fixation so many middle class American men seem to have with gadgets and power tools. Is it an attempt to make up for some sort of lack in another area?

I mean, seriously. Look at all the guys who seem to spend hordes of money on all this crap and who never even use it. I mean, ever!

I know one guy out my way, for whom I used to do free lawn care, to a degree, for the simple fact that I felt sorry for him. He told me he didn't mow grass because he didn't want to spend money to have lawn care equipment maintained (lawn equipment he claimed he did not own), and he was lamenting over having to pay someone to weed along his driveway. It was ten minutes worth of work, and I was always out there, every ten days or so doing mine, so I told him not to waste his money paying someone else to do it, and that I'd do it for him for free. And I did for three years.

I cut up several downed trees for him, and I mean big ones- red oak- because he didn't have a chainsaw. I actually tried to give him one of my old ones, and he refused to take it, because it was nearing Christmas, and he said he was trying to talk his wife (whose family had lots of money and always gave her as much of it as she wanted) into buying him the best chainsaw on the market. After Christmas, I asked him if he'd gotten it, and he said no, and the reason why was because he didn't use all the other power tools she'd bought him in the past, so she wasn't wasting money on a chainsaw. This is when I finally found out that he actually owned a more than $300 Husquavarna weed eater that he'd never even taken out of the box! He let it slip by accident, this, the guy who three years earlier claimed to have no lawn equipment, because he didn't want to pay to maintain it, and boy, did his eyes get as big as saucers when he caught the slip.

I no longer weed his driveway or cut his trees.

I've always believed in helping the needy to the degree to which they cannot help themselves, as long as it does not jeopardize my *own* needs, but I have always taken issue with enabling the lazy, which was exactly what I'd been doing with this manipulative loser for three years.

Long story to get my point across about the flashlights, but if I can buy a great light that will work when the lights go out in the house, and last me years, and only costs me $20 down at Walmart, I'm not spending the hundred bucks or more I'm sure that guy got his wife to spend on the flashlight I'm sure he has that he never uses.

Besides. When did I ever say to myself. *Self? We're going to go buy a piece of property way out in the sticks that has Bigfoot Sasquatch, ghosts, Dogmen, and God only knows what else living on it, and we're gonna go out there and look for them all while it's still dark. We'd better get us the best flashlight money can buy.*

Um, never.

So I sneaked out the back door, making sure not to let it creak so as not to wake up my wife and kid (they had another hour before I had to get them up so that my wife and I could get our son ready for and off to school and then sit around and miss him all day), and then I slipped off into the field behind our house.

That's when the first walnut hit me upside the head! Just like a bottle of bub in that old Fifty Cent song!

You son of a whore, I whispered to myself. Again, I thought it was the former annoying neighbor, so I started creeping up to where it seemed the walnut had come from.

Whop!

Another one, but from a different direction. This one came from off to my three o'clock. And that would mean to my right, by the way. I'm always giving clock directions in my videos on our YouTube channel, "Homesteading Off The Grid," and so many newcomers ask, 'what does *get my six* mean?' You've got to view it as if you were looking at the face of a clock. If I'm looking straight ahead, watching for who knows what, and I say, 'get my six,' it means look behind me, because I'm facing the twelve. Whichever way you are facing right now, is your twelve. The three o'clock is to your right. And the nine o'clock is to your left. Your six o'clock is directly behind you.

Get it?

Okay, so the second walnut coming from a different direction allowed me to rule out Mr. Heart Attack Waiting To Happen, slash former annoying neighbor. Unless, of course, he had friends with him. But who the hell would be friends with that guy? Hell, he probably wore corduroy more than *I* did (inside joke- some internet trolls claim there is no way I could possibly have friends, because I wear corduroy pants in some of my videos). None of what was going on out in that field on that cold winter's (almost spring's) morning made any sense.

Then, all of a sudden, whop! One came from my left. And yes, that would be my nine o'clock.

I determined I was either surrounded by someone, or I was dealing with something that could move both quietly and quickly. I decided that when the next walnut came at me, I was going to bum rush in the direction from which it came.

As soon as I'd made my mind up to do this, another walnut came at me from straight ahead, just as the first had. I mustered up all the courage I could, got ready, set...

And froze in place, scared to move.

And then I quickly turned and ran back for the house, reaching it and making it safely inside quiet enough not to wake my family.

***

I'd always heard of Bigfoot Sasquatch while growing up. I mean, who hadn't? But this Dogman character?

Never!

The only thing remotely close to this cryptid I'd ever heard of was a werewolf, the difference between the two being, of course, that the werewolf spends most of its time in human form, taking the form of the wolf on the nights of the full moon, and the Dogman is *always* in the form of something partly humanoid, but mostly dog. Pure monster, all the time!

I did some further research into this thing as I continued to dig- and I can't even remember how I stumbled across the concept of the Dogman in the first place- and I seemed to have tracked it to its source.

Supposedly, as the story goes, the first Dogman sighting happened in Michigan in 1887. Allegedly (though I do prefer the word *potentially*), this cryptid is seen by someone every ten years, and only during years that end in the number seven.

However, in 1987, a radio D.J. in Michigan made up a song for April Fool's Day, and it was based on legends indiginous to North America. He included a bit about the Dogman, and this made the story go from being one rarely heard of by anyone, to now being a story quite popular and frequently retold by Michigan residents.

The D.J. would later state in interviews that he completely made up the bit about the Dogman in his song, and he was surprised to have actually stumbled upon an old legend, accidentally. Further, he said he doubted the actual existence of Dogman. Not to discredit his character, because I've never met him, but what does his opinion about something he stumbled upon by accident have to do with anything?

In more recent times, as in, this week, with what appears to be the revisiting, *potentially*, of a Dogman on our property as Bigfoot Sasquatch, *potentially* (did I mention I really like that word?), is off in the mating grounds getting their freak on, I've learned, by way of comments from our viewers from around the world, that this Dogman character has been spotted just about everywhere. Not just Michigan, and not just in the U.S. We have many, many wonderful viewers who constructively contribute to this conversation on our YouTube channel, and I've been finding out this thing has been spotted all over Europe, with many, many sightings in England.

One thing I've learned a lot about throughout life, and this really helped me when I was in the military and had to avoid them myself during combat, in order to stay alive, is patterns. Patterns tell their own story. Even if patterns don't reveal cold, hard facts, they do reveal cold, hard behaviors.

Not coincidences!

I have, indeed noticed, that during the two times of the year that I've previously mentioned, when I do believe our Bigfoot Sasquatches are gone, the Dogman, if not more than one of his, her, its, or their kind seems to move in and take their place.

For a while.

You see. I've learned, and I can't say how true this is or not, because who really knows- but we're determined to get to the bottom of it- that Bigfoot Sasquatch and Dogman are mortal enemies. They are both, allegedly, territorial, and being that they are two of the alleged flesh and blood type boogeymen roaming the woods, they are in the practice of running each other out of each other's domains. Not unlike the way a bear and a mountain lion will do the exact same thing.

***

So, here it is, the tail end of another sleepless night, and it appears that the Dogman is back, letting me know he rules the roost while our Bigfoot Sasquatches are gone. The cat's woken me up twice, and now he, the Dogman, has woken me up. I've convinced my wife to roll back over and go back to sleep.

What am I going to do?

Well, since in my research I discovered that Dogman is quite differently tempered than Bigfoot Sasquatch in that he probably will *not* simply duck behind a tree or a brush pile to remain hidden, and out of curiosity, observe my every move, but rather, come at me and rip me to shreds?

I think I'll just put the coffee on and curl up with a good book until it's time to wake my family.

On the couch.

Inside!

3

The Book Of Jane

She was four years old the first time she saw him. She was hiding behind the couch as the man she thought of as Daddy, but who wasn't, (even Mommy didn't know who her *real* Daddy was), was beating the ever loving shit out of Mommy.

Again.

And no, it wasn't her guardian angel, or any angel, and it wasn't the man called Jesus.

It was Bigfoot.

Sasquatch.

Potentially…

He (and it *was* a *he*, not a she, or an it, or a they, ((as he was alone))), was standing outside the window on the opposite side of the room as her, looking through the window, and waving a big furry hand, trying to get her attention. When he was certain that she'd finally noticed him, he started pointing at the door behind her. She turned to look, and she saw the face of another big, furry creature peeking through the small square of glass at the top of the aluminum door. This one, a *she*, opened the door, very quietly- though with the screaming of Mommy and the man she thought of as Daddy, it's not that silence was necessary- and motioned her to come outside, which she did.

The little girl followed the two juvenile Bigfoot Sasquatches into the woods, and oh what a marvelous time they had. They ran and jumped and swung from vines, and time flew by so fast that they couldn't believe dark was already falling when the sirens came screaming and the flashing lights came blaring through the distance, slicing the twilight like a knife. It seemed that some time after Mommy had been disciplined for whatever imagined offense she'd committed against the man who wasn't Daddy this time, Mommy had realized her daughter (her *afterthought*, more like it, Jane would always feel), was gone, and after not being able to find her, she'd called the police.

These were simpler times (unless you had that whole domestic violence thing going for you), and earlier days, and the authorities didn't require twenty four hours before they'd come looking for a missing person, and not just a child. So they came out blazing, loaded for bear, not realizing they'd need heavier loads than that, for something much bigger. As the would-be rescuers made their way into the coming darkness of the evening, the two juveniles walked Jane to the edge of the woods alongside the old country road up which the emergency, rescue and police vehicles were coming, motioned for her to stay put, safely on the side, where the authorities would find her less than a minute later, and then they disappeared into the underbrush and were gone. Or at least they *seemed* to be gone. But in fact, they would never stray far. They would always keep a close eye on Jane. She just wouldn't be able to see *them*.

At least for another eight years.

***

Back when Jane was four, and Mommy had taken one hell of a beating from the man Mommy had to explain to Jane wasn't her Daddy the next day, when the man never came home, Mommy promised she'd never get involved with a man who'd lay hands on her again.

And she didn't!

She got involved with a man who liked to lay hands on Jane.

And in the worst kind of ways.

Jane's daddy who wasn't really her daddy had been on his way home the night he'd beaten Jane's mommy. The kid had gone missing during the beating, and when his whore of a girlfriend, as he referred to her, said she was going to call the police to ask for help finding her child, he hit the road and headed for the farthest bar; one in the next town over. He wasn't about to be around when the po-po came by, with his old lady still bleeding and all. He knew they'd look the other way, again, as long as he wasn't there to question when they showed up.

But on his way home that night, he'd had an accident.

A strange accident.

He'd been driving out their old country road headed home, the last couple miles of which was dirt- zigzagging a bit, as he'd been drinking since just past noon- but managing to keep it on the road, when the damndest thing happened.

Now, exactly what that damndest thing *was*, no one was ever able to figure out. Not even the state police experts who investigated the crash scene the next day, at least momentarily, before getting another call about a pig roaming a local playground back in town and having to leave.

The man's car was found upside down, with him crushed and killed inside, about twenty yards away from the road. The damndest thing about it, this damndest thing that happened, was that he'd gone off the road where there were no curves and there was no hill. Further, there were no tire tracks heading to the spot where the car was found twenty yards away. It was as if someone, or some*thing*, had stopped his car in the middle of the road (they *did* find some half hearted skid marks there and what could have passed as some really strange tracks, had they not been so damn big), picked it up, carried it out into the middle of the woods, and flopped it down on its top, as if in all attempts to kill the man, using his car and its mass, as the murder weapon.

But what on earth could have done such a thing, all the investigating officers thought.

One county sheriff's deputy jokingly said it could have been aliens, and everybody had a laugh at that.

"Yeah, right," his frenemy beside him said. "Next thing, you're gonna claim it was Bigfoot."

Everyone laughed even harder.

But strangely- abruptly stopped- and all at the exact same time.

"Let's get lunch," one of them said, and the whole group disbanded.

It wasn't too long after the investigation was over, all ten minutes of it, that Jane's mommy moved in the frenemy of the officer who'd suggested it might be aliens. Jared was his name, and ironically, like the Subway Jared, he had a penchant for little girls.

His goosing and ass grabbing that seemed so playful at first, began getting out of line just around the time Jane started going through her middle school growth spurt, and unfortunately for Jared- who could commit to defending the public everyday that he suited up and badged up and gunned up and went out to patrol the streets of the town sitting at the foot of the mountain where he lived with Jane and her mother (and the town *did* have a population of *almost* a full one hundred), but who could not commit to saying "I do," to Jane's mother in the eight years they'd been together- made the grave mistake of attempting to play a little more than goosey goose grab ass with Jane while out in the woods one steamy, muggy morning in late June when he'd convinced her to go out with him to pick blackberries.

Jane made it home around noon, and the story she told was that they'd split up to find more berries, and she had no idea why he never made it back. His old frenemy from the department would later find one of his boots beside a creek not far from where he and Jane had been picking berries.

And that was it.

No further trace of Jared.

Everyone just assumed Jane's mom was back to giving him the ultimatum- either walk her down the aisle or walk his ass down the road and stay gone- and he finally chose the latter.

Later that year, during deer season, a hunter would find his other boot nearly eight miles away, and the boot was in perfect condition. No rips, no tears, no anything. The hunter who found it had no idea who it belonged to, and he hated to leave litter lying in the woods, but his hunting sack was already packed to capacity, and he had no way of carrying it out of the woods, comfortably, without compromising his ability to get a quick, clean shot off at the big one if it came through, sporting it horns in all its glory, so he just left it by the creek.

He never *did* see the big one, and Jared remained gone.

Forever.

***

By the time Jane entered high school, she was a real peach. And every boy in school couldn't help but notice her when she passed them by.

This really pissed off the cheerleader types- the always ever so popular girls- because Jane was neither. A cheerleader *or* popular. She was just some girl from up the hollow who had all of three different outfits to wear to school. And boy, did it burn the popular girls up even more when they'd point this petty little fact out to their beaus, when they caught them staring, and their beaus pointed out to them, and just as quickly, that they never noticed her clothes.

But, sad as it might be, behavior is learned and is often damn near next to impossible to unlearn. Though Jane could have had her pick from the pack- either the quarterback, who despite their little hick school only having forty students, would go on the start for the state's University- or the good looking (but like Jane) *shy* guy who would get a full ride to M.I.T., she had to have the hots for

Marty Flynn. Biggest piece of shit east of the Mississippi
River, second only, on a good day, to his dad, who was
rotting away in prison.

Marty liked to drink just like Jane's dear old Daddy who
wasn't really Daddy used to drink, back before that really
strange auto accident, and his mother knew to keep him
well stocked with booze if she knew what was good for her.
Before they'd hauled Marty's daddy off to prison for
shooting and killing a neighbor slash drinking buddy in a
gambling dispute, he'd trained Marty well, by way of
example, how to get Marty's momma to do what she was
told.

Marty was fascinated how the back of Momma's skull fit
perfectly in the palm of his hand, like a baseball in a glove.
And it even made the same sound a baseball makes when
caught in a glove, when he gave the back of her skull a
good hard whack.

He has his daddy's hands, his mother would think when
he'd hit her, but those times were few and far between,
because she made sure to keep him well stocked with
Stroh's.

"Huh," Marty said, patting Jane on the back of the head
one beautiful fall afternoon while he was walking her home
from school. He was familiar with the hollow she lived in,
as it was one of his favorite places to ride his four wheeler
while drinking. He could fill his cooler with a bunch of beer
and ice and spend all day up the hollow, with its main dirt
road and its many, many off shooting trails, mostly left over
from old logging operations- made by the skidders used to

haul the logs out of the woods and to the log trucks waiting near the road.

"What is it?" Jane asked, feeling him grope the back of her head. She didn't like the way it made her feel. It made her very uncomfortable. Unfortunately, everything dysfunctional about her, which was most of her, was completely comfortable with it.

"Oh, nothing," Marty said. "I was just thinking. You kinda remind me of my momma."

"Oh," she said. "That's good." After a long pause, she added, "I think."

It wouldn't be long before 'ol Marty started making that cracking leather baseball glove sound with his hand and the back of *Jane's* head. Marty, just like his dear old daddy had done with Momma, always made sure to do it when he thought no one was around, which meant out in the woods, on the way home up the holler, and after that year's Christmas break, when all the kids went back to school, Marty wasn't among them.

You see, just because Marty couldn't see him, her, it or they when he got the notion to tune up on the back of Jane's head, it didn't mean that he, she, it or they weren't watching Marty!

"Hm," Marty's homeroom teacher said, after his third straight absence in January. "He always said he was gonna drop out. I guess maybe he did?"

When the teacher mentioned the absences to the Principal that day when she bumped into him in the teacher's lounge, he said, "Hm. He always said he was gonna drop out. I guess maybe he did?"

The principal mentioned he'd keep his eye out for Marty's withdrawal paperwork to come through from the county school board office, but he forgot all about it before even leaving the lounge, and the paperwork never came through, anyway.

We all know that the best stories are the ones that have happy endings. The boy gets the girl, the girl gets the prince, and everyone gets their shit together and lives happily ever after.

Sadly, that's not the case here. As pretty as she was, and as much potential as she possessed, and how much she *never* asked to be born into the hell she endured, Jane was toxic and dysfunctional through and through. It's all she ever saw in life, sadly, and it's all she ever knew.

However, just as God will always look out for fools and drunks...

Bigfoot Sasquatch, et. al, will always look out for Jane...

And a hell of a lot of white trash shit bags go missing up her way.

She Got Too Close

(Originally Titled 'The Unfortunate Demise Of Whorry Torrie')

Whorry Torrie, pudding pie, kissed the boys and made them…

…lawyer up!

Well, she'd tried, anyway. With her first and only husband. But as it turned out, *she'd* been the one who had to lawyer up.

And *she* hadn't lawyered up to leave him and take all of his money. She'd lawyered up and left him because she found out she *couldn't* take all of his money.

Consusing, right?

Pay attention.

She should have *known* it was too good to be true, she remembered thinking even as she walked down the aisle to say "I do" on the day she'd married him. He never *once* asked her to sign a prenup, even though *he* knew that *she* knew he was worth millions.

What a sucker, she remembered thinking, the thought bringing a *true* smile to her face when the priest told him he could kiss her. She giggled, wondering if he could taste his best friend and best man's, well, nether regions, we'll call it, as she'd been kissing him and, well, them, less than an hour before the ceremony.

Torrie had always assumed that since she was from a filthy rich family- spoiled little rich girl her whole life- that *his* money was of no concern to *him*, at least as far as her potentially attempting to take it by way of divorce. She thought this was the reason he'd been dumb enough to marry her conceited, slutty ass in the first place. That and because he hadn't quite known about the whole slutty ass part. Sure, she was always screwing around on him, both before and after they were married, but she *was* discreet. She came from a well respected family. Someone in their family half a dozen generations ago had done something of note, allowing all the generations down to hers to benefit financially, though she had a hard time remembering what that notable accomplishment was. Something to do with a vaccine to prevent something or other that killed brown people in third world countries. Whatever it was, God had chosen her as one of his people to enter the world through the right womb.

In other words, she had the family name to protect, hence her discretion with her sluttiness. And that, only of course, because she couldn't risk Mommy and Daddy, as she still called them, even though she was in her forties, taking her name out of the family trust.

But the truth about *his* money hit her hard, right between the eyes, after Mommy and Daddy died (and God, had she been tired of waiting). "I'm leaving you," she'd said through crocodile tears whipped up for the event of her parents' death. "And I'm taking every goddamn dime you have!"

He walked over to her and sat on the couch beside her and put his arm around her as she cried. He might not have been a genius, especially when it came to his choice in women, but *his* mommy and daddy had taken all that into account, and this was when he broke the news to her.

"I'm sorry for your loss, Torrie," he said. And he meant it. How tragic their deaths had been. Torrie's mommy had faller off her horse, while out on a fox hunt, and had been dragged for more than a mile, her foot caught in the stirrup, and her father had died valiantly, and *instantly* when the horse kicked him a good one with it's right, back hoof when he'd made an attempt to unleash his wife at the start of the fiasco.

The investigators would claim that the horse must have seen a snake, but others in attendance attributed the horse being startled to something just inside the treeline along the side of the field in which they'd been hunting. Something tall, hairy, and fierce. A bear, they all claimed, when pressed to be more specific. Later, over Cognac back at the fox hunt club's lounge, they would all claim, but only in hushed tones, like when they talked about the people of color the club always hired as staff, that it hadn't been a bear. It had been something bigger. But what in the name of all things holey could live in the woods of central Virginia that was bigger than a bear?

"But all my money's tied up in trusts so tight they'd make an eighteen year old lesbian on her way to the nunnery seem loose."

"You fucking pig!" she'd shouted, rising quickly, slapping him across the face and turning to leave the room, not out of any form of real anger at his insensitivity or her emotional discomfort attached to the death of her parents (hell, it was hard for her to hide her happiness about that, because now she could get bumped up the line in *her* family trust and enjoy the big pay increase that came with it), but in a hurry to call her lawyer to see if the lying bastard was telling the truth, which, unfortunately for her, she'd soon find out he was.

Torrie quickly gained access to the three million dollars worth of cash (it had actually been assets, but she liquidated everything immediately) she had coming from Mommy and Daddy, and she got bumped up the line of succession in the trust, so her monthly pay went from the measly twenty grand a month she'd barely been able to live on to fifty grand a month. As long as she didn't increase the number of cruises and trips to Europe she usually took by any *great* degree, and if she could keep herself to trading in her beamers once a year, instead of every six months, like she'd fantasized about, had she been able to get her ex-husband's money, and if she just paid strict attention to a few other p's and q's, financially, she'd be okay. She'd be able to stretch that fifty thousand a month out and make it last! Hell, she might even figure out a way to save a few bucks every month and take a grand trip every other year or so.

The first thing Torrie did was go out and buy some land. She wanted as much space as she'd had growing up, but she couldn't have the exact space she'd had growing up, because, well, she'd liquidated mommy and daddy's house and land to get her hands on the cash. So, she bought some acreage about half an hour out from where she'd grown up. Raw land. And she'd had her house, a tiny little five thousand square foot cottage, as she referred to it, and her barns and stalls put up, and it was all conveniently located down the road from several of her favorite wineries, so if anyone ever *did* take her keys from her in order to keep her from driving drunk, as those asshole friends of hers often did- giving her rides home and arguing over who would have to go back and get her the next day and take her back to get whichever beemer she was driving at the time- she could just walk home, and tell them to go fuck themselves.

And she did just that.

About twice a week.

"This is cute," she said, turning into the drive of Bigfoot Brewery, one hot, summer afternoon. She'd been in her newly built house about six months, and she had pissed off more than just a few of the other regulars at the wineries scattered along the road she lived on. She never understood why so many of the uptight hussies that went to those places held grudges for so long after catching their men flirting with or fucking her. "You're just jealous, you bitch!" she'd drunkenly shouted at the last wife to catch her, just the week before. "You had to *marry* into money, and I have my own." That was the last thing she remembered before waking up in her "girl room" in the basement of her house the next day with a handwritten note that read, "Get your own fucking car tomorrow, you fucking bitch!"

And that's exactly what she'd done.

So, until people just calmed the hell down, Torrie was going to hit a couple of other spots while out and about, binge drinking locally between cruises and trips to Europe. She figured why not try a beer brewery?

Torrie parked her BMW beside a life size wooden cutout of what must have been a Bigfoot Sasquatch. "Cute," she said, flicking the bugger she'd been working out of her nose the whole way up the drive onto the cutout. "Bet he's hung like a beast!" She couldn't help but laugh out loud in spite of herself.

She walked into the tasting room of the brewery and was greeted by a cute, young college girl working her way through the summer. "Welcome to Bigfoot Brewery!" the girl said, chipper as hell. Torrie looked through her and walked right past her, heading toward the young man who was standing twenty feet away, also working his way through summer until returning to college in the fall.

"Well hello, good lookin'!" Torrie said, pinching the guy on the forearm. He did his best not to act disgusted. Sure, Torrie was okay looking for an older woman, and at least she wasn't fat, he thought. But still, she was older than his mom, and he knew it, and he'd never been into such things. But he'd been working at Bigfoot Brewery long enough to know that these whorry old rich bitches, and he and his male buddies who worked there called them, tipped really well.

"Hi there!" he said, just as chipper as the girl who Torrie ignored had been. "First time here?"

"Sure is," she said. "Break me in, but please be gentle." She tried to come across as innocent, but Travis, the young man she was ogling all over, knew she was anything but.

"Absolutely," he said. He walked her to a table, which sat by a large glass window, giving her a beautiful view of a large pond sitting at the foot of a hill, below, which joined the forest. It would have been a beautiful view in the opinion of anyone sitting there, but Torrie didn't notice it. She was eyeballing Travis' ass as he left to bring her a sampler.

"We call this one the Yeti," Travis said, pulling the first of four, six ounce samples out of the wooden slab he came back carrying. "It's my favorite," he continued. "Like the name implies, it's always best ice cold."

Torrie sampled just about every type of beer they made at the brewery, and though her favorite seemed to be a beer called the Yerin, named after the Chinese version of Bigfoot Sasquatch, what she really wanted to sample was Travis.

"So why do they call this place Bigfoot Brewery?" she asked, not quite three sheets to the wind, but at least two. "Trying to capitalize on the Bigfoot craze?"

"You mean you don't know about all the sightings over all the years?" Travis asked.

"Of Bigfoot?" she said. "Here? In Virginia?"

"Yeah," he said. "We actually have pictures on the wall." He pointed behind the bar.

Torrie turned and saw lots of old polaroids pinned up on the wall behind the bar. She walked over and looked at them, only briefly, and then came back and sat back down. "All I saw was trees," she said.

"You really have to know what you're looking for," Travis told her.

"You know what they say about guys with big feet, don't you?" Torrie said, sounding nice and slutty now that she was well into her cups.

"Yeah," Travis said. His guard had been slipping. He'd never pimped himself out to any of these rich bitches who came in and got drunk, but only because he'd never been propositioned. It would be nice if he could make enough jing off of one or a couple of them that he could afford to quit his summer job a few weeks earlier than he'd planned and squeeze in a nice summer trip somewhere before classes started again. "And just so you know," he followed up, these thoughts in mind, "I wear a size thirteen shoe."

"You naughty boy!" Torrie said, her eyes wide. "Mommy's gonna have to take you home and spank you!"

"I'm off in an hour," Travis said, trying not to throw up a little in his mouth. "Keep drinking and stick around, and I'll let you measure my toes."

"Bring me another Yerin and a side of wings, and you got it, big boy!" Torrie said.

An hour and a half later, Torrie was climbing behind the wheel of her orange BMW, drunk as shit as usual, and telling Travis exactly what she was going to do to him with *her* toes.

"Shouldn't I drive?" he asked. He wasn't really concerned, as she'd already told him that she lived only a couple miles away, and he figured she probably drove drunk more than she did sober, and so she was probably pretty good at it, but he knew the proper thing to do in American drinking culture was to at least verbally make an attempt.

"I got this, Trav," she said, and boy, had he always hated being called *Trav*.

***

Whorry Torrie was an avid tailgater, to the point you'd think it was as much of a passionate pastime for her as was drinking and fucking, but it wasn't. She was just always in a hurry to get to anywhere she wanted to go, whether she needed to be there by a specific time or not, because, well, just like every other aspect of her life, it was all about her.

It wasn't something new, this tailgating thing, since Mommy and Daddy had died, either. It had been the case since she'd started driving back in the eighties, when all the girls had big hair and wore lots of makeup, and a lot of the boys did, too. "Now, Torrie," her mother would admonish when she'd walk in the door on more than *many* occasions, "I got another call today from a neighbor up the road. Seems you almost ran them off the road on your way home from school yesterday."

"They drive like a damn grandpa," would be Torrie's response, always. Even if the complainant *had* been a grandpa.

"She was a forty year old woman," her mother might say. Or, "a thirty year old man." But all to no avail.

"Whatever," Torrie would say, turning up the volume on her Walkman as she jammed out to Def Leppord or Poison and headed upstairs to watch Family Ties on her remote controlled color t.v.

And that would be the end of it.

"Shouldn't you give them some space?" Travis said on this night, on the way back to Torrie's. Torrie was tailgating a couple who lived right across the road from her, though she wouldn't know it, because she never took notice of anyone she ever tailgated. What did they have to do with her? Other than the fact that they were in her way?

"They need to pick it up," she said. "If they won't, I'll make 'em."

Travis held onto the passenger door with his right hand and the console with his left, stiffening his entire body, as if bracing for impact at any moment. When the car in front of them reached the small community's post office beside the road, they whipped their car into the parking lot and gave incredulous looks, that couldn't be seen in the dark, to their neighbor Torrie's car as it passed them by, not even slowing down enough to allow them to ease off the road.

Torry simply threw the middle finger of her left hand into the air and kept driving, drunk, like a bat out of hello.

Just as Travis began to relax and tried to think of something to say- small talk, so to say- Torrie caught up with yet another car.

"What's up with all this goddamn traffic!" she said. "Jesus, we live out in the country. Shouldn't these mother fuckers be in bed, getting ready to get up and milk the cows in the morning?"

Just as she got the words out of her mouth, the car in front of her swerved, and it swerved hard, going off the road on the right side. It hadn't swerved out of fear of Torrie's aggressive driving. It was obvious, to Travis at least, who wasn't completely drunk, that the car had swerved to miss hitting something. And he'd seen what it had swerved to miss.

And there were two of them.

"Holy shit!" he said, looking back, not believing that he'd actually seen what he had just seen.

"What was it?" Torrie said, leaning forward and looking into her rearview mirror, paying absolutely no attention to the road in front of her. "A deer?"

Ka-thump!

When her car hit it, it hit it *hard*, raising the front right corner of the car off the road. The shock was enough to nearly sober Torrie up completely, at least for the few seconds it took for her to maneuver the car enough to keep it on the road.

"Holy shit!" she said. "Goddamn deer!"

"That wasn't a *deer!*" Travis said, turning and facing forward. "We have to go back!"

"I'm not going back for no goddamn deer," Torrie said, beginning to slow, only because her driveway was just around the next turn.

"It wasn't a deer," Travis said again. "It was way bigger than that."

"We're not going back for no goddamn bear," Torrie said, now driving up her driveway, thankful to have had the good sense to leave her porchlight on. After the adrenaline rush she'd gotten from hitting whatever she'd hit had passed, it made her drunkenness kick in even stronger, bordering a stupor. "Come on stud!" she said, exiting the car. Travis did as instructed, already counting up cash he hadn't yet received in his mind.

***

Travis lay beside her in bed as she snored loudly. He knew he wouldn't be able to get to sleep with all the ruckus, even if he'd wanted to, which he did not. He'd been waiting for this moment, the point when he was confident that Torrie was passed out to the point where he could leave without disturbing her and risking her trying to talk him into staying.

Fortunately for him, their intimacy hadn't lasted long. She came like a rocket as he entered her, and half a dozen times near as quickly as he worked his hips for all he was worth, eyes shut, thinking about the cute little coed that he worked with down at Bigfoot Brewery. The nice girl with the equally nice ass that Torrie had blown off when she'd walked into the joint. By the time he'd blown his load, Torrie was ready to call it quits, and Travis thanked God for small favors.

"Do I get rewarded for my efforts?" Travis had said when they were finished. "You tipped pretty well at the brewery. What about here?"

Torrie pulled herself up and staggered to the dresser. She reached in, pulled out a sock and threw it at him. "Take it all," she'd said, while he stared down at the near knee long Hanes, wondering what kind of shenanigan this was, until he squeezed it and heard the crinkle. He reached into the sock and pulled out ten, nice, new and crisp c-notes, obviously taken from an ATM machine from a bank where they'd just arrived from the Federal Reserve. A grand wouldn't allow for quite the trip he'd wished for, but if he pinched pennies, he could go down to the Outer Banks of North Carolina for a week. If he played his cards right, maybe he could convince that little cutie from the Brewery to join him.

After tossing him the money, Torrie had gone right the hell to bed, and passed right the fuck out, and now Travis was going to make his move and slip away. It was a long walk back to the brewery, but he was not about to be at this woman's home in the morning when the cops showed up after a dead body was reportedly found on the side of the road. A body whose shape matched the dent in Torrie's car and blood type which matched the blood all over her hood.

Travis didn't know exactly who or *what* she'd hit, but it wasn't a deer, and it wasn't a bear, because the damn thing hadn't been walking on all fours. It was running, upright, on two legs.

Travis made his way down the driveway, and when he reached the spot around the first turn where Torrie had hit whatever she'd hit, he stopped and glanced over the side of the road.

He saw nothing.

But he listened, and that's when he heard it.

Some*one* or some*thing* was dragging some*one* or some*thing* up through the woods, in the dark, and he would be willing to swear on a Bible the rest of his life that there was more than one some*one* or some*thing* doing the dragging, because he could hear at least two of them crying.

Travis figured it might be a good idea to take off at a jog to get back to the brewery and the hell out of here quicker. Besides, it would allow him to sweat off the rest of his buzz so he'd be better off to drive.

But instead of taking off at a jog, 'ol Trav, who'd always *hated* being called Trav, took off at an all out sprint!

***

Whorry Torrie slept the dreamless sleep of true drunks, completely unaware that Travis had left two hours before and even more unaware that there were two beings making their way up her drive.

Mommy and Daddy!

But these were not the ghosts of *her* mommy and daddy, back from the grave as apparitions, to futilely admonish her and her tailgating ways. Oh, no. This was a different kind of mommy and daddy. This mommy was seven feet tall and this daddy was eight feet tall, and they had a combined weight in the neighborhood of fourteen hundred pounds, and all fourteen hundred pounds of Mommy and Daddy were extremely pissed off and out for revenge!

Torrie never heard the crash of the large picture window in the living room, and she never heard the heavy footsteps coming up the stairs. She didn't even hear the growls they made before she'd make a scream or two, half asleep, half awake, and convinced, for just a second she was having some kind of nightmare, because just as she came to enough to start thinking it might not be a crazy drunk dream, it was all over.

Because no one can dream once their head's been ripped clean off their neck!

***

Travis would be questioned a few days later, and he started singing like a canary as soon as he saw the badges.

"I swear to God," he said, before being asked a single question. "I knew it wasn't a deer or a bear, and I begged her to go back, but she wouldn't."

"Son?" the older of the two state troopers who'd come to question him said. "What in the name of ever loving God are you talking about?"

"You're here about Torrie, right?" Travis said.

"Damn right, college boy!" the younger of the two troopers said. He'd never gone off to college, and he hated everyone from his generation who had. Look down at him, would they? His ass! He'd rough 'em up a bit and find something to charge them with.

"Calm down," the more experienced and obviously more self-confident trooper said, raising an arm and placing it over his sidekick's chest, as if in an attempt to hold him back. He looked back at Travis and said, "We know you're the last one to be seen with her. We want to ask you a few questions."

"What?" Travis said, doing the math. "She's dead?"

***

The cops didn't haul Travis down to the station. There wasn't any need. He sat with them at an empty table, out on the porch, and told them everything. Down to the last detail.

The younger of the two troopers wanted to charge Travis with prostitution, but the older trooper didn't give a rat's ass about that, and he decided that slight detail would be overlooked. As much as the story that Travis had told them simply didn't add up, minus the part about the dent and blood on Torrie's car, he knew that Travis was telling the truth.

But, you see, they'd never found a body by the road. There were no missing person reports filed. Everything else out in high net worth hicksville was a-okay, minus the rich trust baby bitch who'd been found by the UPS delivery guy lying on her bedroom floor, her body missing its head.

Travis was free to go, and he took off down to the Outer Banks as quickly as he could. He didn't even think to ask little miss cutie to go with him, but when she asked him where he was going on his way out of the brewery he told her, and she asked if she could go with him, so the angels were definitely with Travis on this day.

The veteran trooper pointed out to his young companion on the way back to town that he couldn't get over the irony that the woman who'd recently been found decapitated and dead was actually the daughter of the older couple who'd died in that freak horse riding accident just a few years back.

"What'd they say spooked that horse?" the Jr. officer asked. "A snake?"

"It's what they said," his partner said. "But others said it could have been a bear at the edge of the woods. Said they saw something huge over there, but it wasn't quite like a bear."

"What was it?" Jr. said.

"Huh?" his partner said, still contemplating so deeply he hadn't really heard the question.

"I said, if it wasn't a bear, what the hell was it?"

"I don't know," his partner said, the sound of doubt heavy in his voice.

"I just don't know."

5

Bigfoot Sasquatch Hunter Hunter Killed

Yes, you read that right. It's not a typo. It's exactly how the papers were titling the headlines, too.

The guy wasn't a Bigfoot hunter, or a Sasquatch hunter. Whichever the hell you call it.

He was a Bigfoot Sasquatch hunter, hunter!

See. When you add the comma, it makes more sense, but you're not supposed to use punctuation in headlines. Only the truly disgusting clickbait artists on the social media websites do such things.

It was a hard case to figure out, at first, and it was only because of some cop's kid that watched those stupid Bigfoot Sasquatch videos on YouTube that it was finally solved. Because at the time, when they found the body in the woods, the neck broke clean and a mile away from the vehicle, *none* of it made sense.

It was the vehicle that got the whole thing started. He'd parked at the mouth of what he'd *thought* was an old dirt road, but he'd actually parked at the mouth of the very long private driveway of one of those high falutin yuppie types of trust babies who didn't put up with trespassers. You know the type. Usually the first in line at all those immigration protests down at the college, their signs showing their full support for a world without borders, but by God, if you step *one foot* across the property line onto *their* land, across *their* border, a pox upon your eyes and a quick call to the county sheriff's office made!

It was Burt Reynolds who'd responded to the call, and yes, he'd heard all those jokes about how he was supposed to be the bandit, not the smokey, since joining the force twenty years before. And he caught hell about his name in school for many years before that, too, so go ahead and get it out now, because his namesake being the same as that other guy has nothing to do with the story.

He was used to getting calls from Crazy A about people parking at the end of her road. Batshit craziest neighbor up in that high falutin end of the county, now that her shitbag former husband (number three he was, if Burt could remember correctly), had gotten mauled by that bear the summer before. She'd shacked up with that drunken trust baby behind her who was always selling off a dozen or so acres of timber each year to support his drinking habit, ney, *raging addiction*, because the part of the funds from his trust he was allowed to touch (only the interest, never the principal, because his momma knew she'd raised a fool), never seemed to be enough. And it seemed that since doing so, she'd considered his property as much hers as his, and Burt had gotten three calls from her in the past six months alone. Man was that woman, whose name starts with the letter A, batshit crazy!

"Oh, just give 'em time," he'd told her when she'd called. Just like he'd told her all the other times. She'd told him she'd given it three days already and the car was still there. She mentioned something about someone in Florida probably missing them by now. Burt pressed her on that, and she told him the car, one of those little hybrid prius types that are smaller than most of the people who drive them, had Florida tags on it.

"I'm on my way," he'd said while rising and hanging up the phone at the same time.

Burt feared he might have another of those odd bear attacks on his hands.

***

Burt had a couple of the younger deputies meet him at the prius from Florida plates, and they got to work scouring the woods, and it didn't take them long to find the body. It was about a mile from the car, as stated earlier.

To cut to the chase, it was the body of a man formerly known as Peter Jackson. Jackson had been an adjunct biology professor at Eckerd College in St. Petersburg, Florida. What in the holy hell he'd been doing traipsing around the damn woods of central Virginia, armed with a Remington .243 deer rifle, with deer season being still three months away, was beyond Burt and the other deputies who'd found him.

"What do you make of it, boys?" Burt had said at the time, looking down at the body. When he'd gotten no response, he looked over and saw that the young deputies were standing at the edge of the woods, looking into the backyard of the property that met the woods where the body had been found.

Burt went over and saw a post middle aged man reading in a hammock. There was a beautiful, much younger Asian woman bent over, working in a flower bed just off to the side of the man, and Burt's wonderful assistants were fixated on her posterior.

"Guys," Burt said, hoping to bring their attention back to the matter at hand. "We've got a corpse over here, and ya'll are checking out the man's gardener?"

It was over dinner that evening, when Burt was telling his wife about his day, in a fashion suitable for their fifteen year old son who was eating with them, that he was put on the beginning of the trail. After he'd talked about Crazy A's call, and what him and the boys had found, and where they'd found it, his son piped up and said, "you probably found that serial killer."

"What?" Burt said, looking at his son, sadly, who he usually ignored when he gave any input into what Burt had going on with work or any other matter. But the words 'serial killer' will grab the attention of anyone, even an innocently often absentee father.

"That serial killer," his son said. "The one that's been killing those Bigfoot hunters."

"What?" Burt said, sounding just as incredulous as he had the first time he'd said it.

"Google it, Dad," his son said, and then he gulped down the rest of his milk and got up to run back upstairs and play the latest PS4 game he'd downloaded onto his console. "Not all conspiracy theories are conspiracies," he managed to get out, barely audible, on his way up the stairs. "Or theories."

"That kid spends too much time online," Burt's wife said as she rose and began collecting the dishes from the table. "I wish you didn't work as much and could spend more time with him. It's not like this is the crime capital of the mid Atlantic. Just all those damn protests down at the University every other week about something or other."

"I know," Burt said. "I've got some vacation time built up, and I'm going to take it soon."

"You've been saying that for years, Burt," his wife said, pulling his plate out from underneath his nose. "Better make soon, sooner."

Burt sat at the table, thinking, but not about his son and about how it seemed like yesterday that he was changing his diapers, and now the kid was as big as he was. He was thinking about the case. He rose from the table and he went to his den. He sat down at his laptop, and he began to Google.

And then he found them.

The articles.

All of them!

***

It wasn't too hard, as they were all published on one source. Some low budget blog site that seemed to have a penchant for UFO sightings, Bigfoot Sasquatch encounters, and various conspiracy theories. Back in the old days, before any nutcase could buy a site for only ninety nine cents per year, such information would have been much harder to find, as it wouldn't have been so centralized. It would have been scattered about in at least half a dozen different rags in the checkout lane at the grocery store. Tabloids they used to call them.

"Is this buzzkill187?" Burt said after calling the number on the blog and actually getting someone to answer the phone on the first ring.

"Depends," the voice on the other line said. "Whatchew got!"

"I'm actually interested in some of the stories you've been writing about the serial killer, as you see it, who's tracking down and killing Bigfoot Sasquatch hunters, as you see it."

"Whatchew got!" the voice said again, as if he hadn't heard what Burt had said. This guy, Burt thought, had a lot in common with his son.

"Look," Burt said. "I'm a sheriff's deputy out in Virginia, and I'm actually thinking there might be something to your train of thought."

And that was the last thing Burt got out before the call was dropped. He knew it hadn't been due to a poor connection. He should have *known* better than to tell a freaking conspiracy theorist that he was a cop. Especially one with an internet handle like Buzzkill187, the numerical portion of the nomenclature being police code for murder.

***

The story, based on several somewhat related stories, was pretty simple. It appeared as if there might be a serial killer out there trying to kill Bigfoot Sasquatch hunters. Absolutely zero of the investigations into the deaths of the three murdered men killed at the hands of the potential serial killer stated such, nor did any of the bonafide, what's considered *real* news sources make the connection, but Burt knew that official investigations rarely linked the activities of serial killers- hell, it was why serial killers were able to do what they did and get away with it for so long- and he also knew that pretty much all news these days was half fake, so why discredit the conspiracy blog site he'd found just because the lamestream news outlets may have missed the not so obvious?

Buzzkill187, no doubt a fine, upstanding member of his community, wherever that community was, who just happened, more than likely, to be living in and blogging out of mommy's basement, because the job market was so bad for high school dropouts where he lived (and who was probably earning six digits doing it, by the way) had pieced it together perfectly, as Burt would later find out when he followed up with the unsolved murders.

The first one to be taken out by way of a headshot via a Remington .243 deer rifle had been another blogger down in Texas. This guy, whose internet pen name was OICU812- just like the old Van Halen album title- had been stating loud and clear for at least two years that he was gonna "shoot me dead a Bigfoot Sasquatch and parade that mother fucker's head around on a slab so everyone will finally know once and for all that he's for real!"

It seems that OICU812 also had a YouTube channel and he often video recorded his expeditions and uploaded them to his channel, though most of his videos were filmed in his mother's basement, where he'd rant and rave, alcoholic beverage of his choice just off screen (showing it would violate YouTube's policies and community guideline standards) about "what he was going to do to that big, hairy sumbitch once he got him," which was pretty much, "shoot him in the mother fucking face."

In one of OICU812's videos, Burt actually thought he saw what might have been a mysterious, bipedal creature taking cover behind a rock outcropping in the Texas plains.

More than one thousand commenters thought they saw the same, and they must have been credible witnesses, with such screen names as MuhCoxHurts83 and TickleMyWhickle1@. Nonetheless, whatever it was, Burt could not, as the video's title even said, unsee it!

Less than a week after that particular video had been uploaded and published, OICU812 was found dead, close to the location where it had been recorded. His body lay in the Texas heat and swelled like a loaf of pre baked Texas toast with a double shot of yeast before it was found, only after OICU812's mother had reported him missing when she noticed he hadn't called out for pizza the night before, because it had been his turn. Though the investigators could name the weapon used, they could never find the weapon, nor could they find the man who had pulled the trigger, and there seemed to be no one with a motive, unless, of course, you counted that big hairy sumbitch OICU812 had relentlessly pursued for so long, but the local sheriff ruled that one out pretty quick.

***

The second of the three Bigfoot Sasquatch hunters who might have been- potentially, that is- killed by the Bigfoot Sasquatch hunter hunter (again, it's not a typo) would have been what would have murked the waters as far as any investigators making any sort of connection between the three killings would have gone. This guy did not broadcast to the world and everyone in it, by way of social media, that he was a Bigfoot Sasquatch hunter. In fact, his family tried to keep this fact, and many others about the man, hidden.

It truly was a sad story, Burt thought, as he read the online articles he could find about the man's death, after reading Buzzkill187's take on it.

It seemed that the man had a long history of mental illness, mainly paranoid schizophrenia. He'd been a star student and athlete not just in highschool, but also in college, but things in his life took a turn for the worse shortly thereafter.

The man, in his early forties at the time of his death- again, by way of a Remington .243 deer rifle, from a distance, and fired by a man who was never found- had majored in hotel and restaurant management in college and had gotten a general manager's position with Applebee's upon his graduation. He was on the fast track to being a regional manager before walking out into the dining area one night with a rolling pin in one hand, and a pyrex baking dish in the other and beating the living hell out of a man who he'd tell authorities was one of the greys, a particular breed of aliens, it appears, who were here (here being Earth, not Applebee's) to take over. It turned out the man was a beady eyed little preacher from one of the thirty seven local baptist churches, and he said he wouldn't press charges if the man who'd beaten him would attend his church. The man refused to attend a secret cult of grey aliens, and he spent thirty days on a psych ward for evaluation, instead, and it was there that he was prescribed merely the first half dozen of what would be hundreds of different medications he'd take for the next twenty years of his life before his untimely demise.

The serial killer who would eventually take him out of this world, this Bigfoot Sasquatch hunter hunter, must have gotten wind of him when the man had gone missing for more than a week, and the story of his search had made not just the local, but the national news. It seemed the man had gone missing on more than one occasion, but never for quite so long. However, the story he'd told once he'd been found is what had caused the sensation.

The man claimed that he'd found, in the woods behind his home, a clan of Bigfoot Sasquatch creatures. He said he'd moved in with them, and all was hunky dorey, until one of them had come home, drunk from drinking the shine he'd found in some hillbilly's hidden still, and he'd raped him. Strangely, the medical examination performed on the man would show evidence of forced penetration- of the sodomy type, of course- and he claimed he was going to 'get him a gun somewhere' and go 'shoot that hairy fucker dead before he rapes someone else!'

Less than a week later, he'd been taken out, sniper style, while walking (albeit, limping) rounds out on the grounds of the local lunatic asylum.

***

Burt Reynolds really had to give credit to Buzzkill187 for his handy detective work on the third victim of the Bigfoot Sasquatch hunter hunter…

…because the Bigfoot Sasquatch hunter hunter had travelled all the way to Australia for his next kill!

It seems there had been yet another social media standout in the world of all things Bigfoot Sasquatch who claimed to have found the beast of lore down under. Down there, in Australia, of course, the creature was known as the Yowie, not Bigfoot Sasquatch, but as the Australian vlogger always pointed out, especially when pressed and challenged by all those people who believe that they are the only people in the world who are allowed to have really seen Bigfoot Sasquatch, and everyone else is lying about it, in America- Bigfoot Sasquatch, Yowie- it was the same difference.

What Burt Reynolds couldn't figure out, however, was two things. Number one; how did the Bigfoot Sasquatch hunter hunter get his Remington .243 through customs, and number two; why would he have gone through the trouble, anyway, knowing beyond doubt that using the same murder weapon as the one he used in the states could end up being the common denominator of all the killings if anyone managed to look hard enough?

"Because he wanted to get caught!" Burt said, aloud, stating the simple truth about all serial killers who do eventually get caught. Their common thread, despite most of them being pre-middle aged white guys who usually vote Republican, was that they all suffered from extreme narcissism. They wanted the world to see how smart they were in their killings, and they wanted to make it clear that the only reason they were caught was because they intended to be.

But this guy- this adjunct professor from a small school in Florida even most people in Florida had never heard about- he hadn't gotten caught.

He'd gotten killed.

***

"I don't get it, though," Burt said over dinner the evening after putting it all together. "Why was he killing these people, and what was he doing in Virginia?"

"God, Dad!" his son said, slamming his fork down on his plate. "Do I have to solve the whole case for you?"

"Enlighten me," Burt said.

"He was killing these people, because they'd actually discovered a Bigfoot Sasquatch, and they were going to kill it. He was a tree hugger type. He was killing the Bigfoot Sasquatch hunters to protect the Bigfoot Sasquatches they were hunting."

The boy said it so nonchalantly, it was as if it was just commonly accepted these days that the world was round, taxation was theft, and Bigfoot Sasquatch was real.

"But why the hell was he in Virginia?"

"D'uh!" his son said, re-dropping the fork he'd just picked back up. "He was going to kill that YouTuber writer guy out there that has a Bigfoot Sasquatch in the woods behind his house."

"What YouTuber writer guy?"

"The one with the hot Malasian wife. Or Thai. Or whatever the hell she is. She's Asian."

Burt immediately remembered his peers ogling all over the young woman he'd thought had been the older man's gardener, or adopted Asian daughter. "You mean that guy out there killed this guy from Florida?" he said, when he spoke again. "You telling me this was an issue of self defense?"

"No," the boy said, but this time not loudly. He said the word lightly, defeated, realizing his father was the dumbest dad that anyone ever had in the world.

"Then why'd he do it?" Burt asked.

"He didn't," the boy said, not even able to open his eyes.

"Then who did?"

The boy simply got up and rose from the table and walked away. Just when he'd started to believe some of the 'restoring your faith in humanity' stories he saw on social media, he'd realized, by way of his father's stupidity, there was no help for humanity.

His faith was dead.

***

"You don't believe in any of that nonsense, now do you?" the man in the hammock said, not even looking up from his tabloid as Burt Reynolds immediately began questioning him after showing up in his backyard, unannounced, and introducing himself. "This, Bigfoot Sasquatch nonsense?"

"I've heard some tall tales," Burt said. "Like, there was this one woman down the road, with her head ripped clean off..." he trailed off, realizing someone was coming out the back door of the house. He looked over and saw the most amazingly beautiful young Asian woman he'd ever seen coming out the back door, carrying what appeared to be half a coconut shell, and there was smoke rising from the shell.

"It's okay, honey," the man Reynolds was questioning said. "Take that shit back in the house and douse it out."

"What's douse," the woman said, obviously hearing a *deep English word*, as she'd call it, with which she wasn't familiar.

"It means put water on it," her husband said, and she went back into the house, grumbling, "why you just don't say put water on it," and never returned while Burt was there.

"Look," burt said. "Let's just get right to it. Are you aware of the dead man found in your woods a few days back?"

"Very much," the man said.

"And you had nothing to do with it?"

"I'll answer no further questions in this regard without my attorney. Good day, Smokey, or the Bandit, or whichever one you are."

"Funny," Burt said. "Look, I'm not here to be an asshole. I know you didn't do it. I've got a hell of a case on my hands with this guy- the guy we found dead- that no one is aware of yet, and it's probably gonna allow for me to quit my job and write a book myself and live off of royalties. Hell, if my wife leaves me, maybe there'll be a smoking hot Asian girl in my future, too." Burt laughed after this last, but the man to which he'd said it, didn't, but *hey*, Burt thought, *if he's gonna pull that Smokey and the Bandit shit with me, everything's fair game.*

"I'm just trying to figure out," Burt continued, "who would have a motive. I mean, only me and one other guy, some online conspiracy theorist seems to have put this whole thing together."

"Buzzkill187," the man, whose last name was Drake, said.

"Yes!" Burt said, surprised.

"He gets it right every now and then," Drake said, now flipping pages, still not looking up at Burt. After a moment of silence, the man said, "don't ask yourself *who*, officer. Ask yourself *what*."

"I'm not following you," Burt said. The man with whom he was speaking closed his eyes, lowered his head, shaking it, and moaned, much like Burt's son had done the evening before at dinner.

"What did this man's other victims have in common?"

"They were all Bigfoot Sasquatch hunters," Burt said.

"You're partly correct," the man said, looking up, and for the first time making eye contact with Burt.

"What's the rest of it?" Burt asked.

"They had full intentions, and they'd made public these intentions, of killing the Bigfoot Sasquatch they'd discovered. In one man's case, the Yowie."

"Okay," Burt said, not following, bringing another look of disappointment from Drake.

"I have never made any claim, nor will I ever, that I will kill the Bigfoot Sasquatch that may or may not live in the woods behind my house, because I have no intentions of doing so, and I never will."

"And," Burt said, still not getting it.

"Look," Drake said, rising from his hammock. He stood right in front of Burt and stared him straight in the eyes. "You can take me in, you can print me, you can lock me up for 48 hours without charges, and you can even taser me and beat me up and shoot me. Whatever the hell you cops like to do to people these days. But here's the truth, and it's a truth you won't be able to handle."

Burt looked the man square in the eyes, feeling as if he'd been baited into abusing his power with the direct insult, certainly due a very small portion of law enforcement, but definitely not the majority. Being that Burt was part of that majority that did not abuse their power, he did nothing but wait for the man to finish the point he was obviously hell bent on making.

"I look out for him," the man said when he spoke again, seeing that Burt was not about to reach for his taser, "and he looks out for me."

Burt continued to stare, picking up what the man was laying down loud and clear. "So you're saying," he said, wanting verbal confirmation, "that this nutcase was on his way out here to make you his fourth victim, and that Bigfoot Sasquatch dispatched the mother fucker to keep you safe?"

The man smiled and said, "start paying closer attention to detail, and you just might figure out what's *really* going on around you," and he walked across the lawn and went inside the same door that his smoking hot, half his age Asian wife had come out of and reentered only moments before.

And he never looked back at Burt even once.

***

Burt never did write that book, though he did contact the authorities who'd been involved with the other Bigfoot Sasquatch hunters murders. As he'd suspected, they all bitched and moaned about having to dust off the files of the already closed cases, but they agreed with Burt that it would be the right thing to do, in order to bring some sort of closure for the families, odd as it might be. None of them ever bought the whole 'freak hunting accident' lines the police had given them for appeasement. Especially the family of the lunatic.

Burt would not come to believe in all things Bigfoot Sasquatch after this case, nor would he start searching the skies at night for UFO's or deep state Government spy drones. But he had to admit, he caught himself staring deeper out into the woods every time he patrolled a particular part of the county. Out where all those eccentric rich people lived, out past the Bigfoot Brewery and all the wineries. Out there close to where the fox hunting club was.

Something was going on out there, and perhaps, he thought, if he started paying closer attention to detail, like Drake had suggested, he just might figure out what.

6

Those Ain't My Tracks!

When you come from a rural place, far from the cities, especially from out in the country, or up in the mountains, there's a certain coming of age ritual that male children go through, and many females- more these days than in the past, it seems- and that is hunting.

Namely, deer hunting.

The cycle goes something like this; you cry on the first day of deer season, because you awaken, on your own, and rush into your father's room to find that he's already gone, and so is his deer rifle. This happens up until you're eight. Maybe up to ten, depending on how mature you are, and how much alone time your father wants.

Then, when you're ten (by the latest, and this was back when people knew that guns didn't kill people, people killed people, so it might have changed since the time I was ten) you get all excited as you listen to Mom and Dad 'discuss' we'll call it, whether or not you're really ready to go hunting, come deer season next week.

You see, going out with shotguns for squirrels and turkeys that you never seem to kill anyway is one thing, but deer season is different. If someone's blasting away in your direction with a shotgun, chances of you getting hit or hurt are much slimmer than if they were out there hunting with a high powered deer rifle, due to the scattering pattern of the projectiles- numerous little beads packed tightly into the shotgun shell's hull, all of which scatter in a wide pattern once ejected. But those high caliber deer rifles. Hell, you could get hit by an errant round from a quarter mile away and be dead on impact. Men use firearms of such caliber in war. It's a whole different ball game, and deer hunting is viewed as a much more dangerous activity than small game hunting, which it is, hence the reason many states require, by law, that people wear blaze orange while deer hunting. One hundred square inches at chest level or higher.

Google it!

So let's say you make it past the Mom checkpoint. Great! Comes now sleepless nights leading up to opening day. And the night before opening day is not too unlike Christmas Eve. You stay wide awake until an hour before you have to wake up, and then you fall into a coma. When you're awakened an hour later, you feel the way you'll find you feel so many Friday and Saturday nights, years later in college, (adrenaline being replaced, of course, by other substances) but you stagger out of bed anyway, because today's the day!

But don't get too excited.

It'll be another year or two before you're actually allowed to carry a gun. And even then, it's probably going to be a single shot shotgun with slugs.

Okay, let's fast forward a bit to get to the meat and potatoes of this story, because this is why we're here.

I was twelve years old when it happened. I'd been deer hunting for just a couple of years, and only this year had I graduated to the 'let's split up' stage of this right of passage. This was a big deal, as it was quite a leap from last year's 'you sit here and don't go anywhere until I come back to get you' stage. Sure, that had been great- the whole finally being alone in the woods hunting deer during deer season- but this, *this* was different.

Now I was alone and mobile!

The plan was pretty simple. And it wasn't the first time we'd done it. My father and I were splitting up about half way up the side of a considerable mountain peak.

Okay, it was in Appalachia, so it was technically a hill. Don't believe me? Go out west for a while, and you'll see the difference between the hills of the east coast and the actual mountains of the west coast. However, and in defense of those Appalachian and even the Blue Ridge and Smoky mountains of the east coast; go spend a day walking up and down them and see if you can get out of bed the next day if you're anything short of an endurance athlete.

So the plan, like last time, was for me to work my way up and around the side of the hill- oh hell, let's call it mountain, because it sounds better. Okay, so the plan was for me to make my way up and around the mountain by way of an old haul road- that's what the skidders would have used to haul logs out during the last timbering operation, which had probably been about twenty years before- and then work my way across the ridge and meet my father in the middle, up top. He would make his way up and around the other side of the mountain and cross the ridge from the other side, heading toward the middle, where he'd meet me, up top. The whole mountain was covered with deer, and we stood a good chance of getting one solo or by one of us driving a deer to the other. We were, or course, always conscious of the direction into which we shot, and the backdrop.

There was one variation this time. It was snowing. Not much, and this wasn't uncommon back in the hills of Appalachiastan. It could be a reasonably pleasant day down in the valleys, where the small communities we called towns were located, but once you got up in the hills (eh-hem, *mountains*), and the elevation rose by a thousand feet or more (again, they might not have been big enough to call mountains, technically, but they sure were steep) it could be blowing snow so hard you couldn't see.

So I was about half way up my side of the mountain when the snow picked up something fierce. Fortunately, I knew the trail well, and the haul road was actually easier to see in the snow, because the snow covered the individuality of all the shrubs and bushes and briars and brambles and rock outcroppings, and highlighted where the *trail* actually was.

The snow was falling so hard by the time I was nearly at the top, that I'd forgotten all about deer hunting, despite even seeing several sets of large deer tracks, and my primary focus had become simply getting to the top of the hill, crossing the ridge and meeting up with my father.

In a word, I was cold.

And I wanted to go home.

Just before I reached the peak, I heard a gunshot from my father's direction. My dad was a hell of a shot, and since I'd only heard one shot, I knew he'd gotten a deer. He did *not* miss.

When I was almost to the midway point of the ridge, I saw blood in the snow. It was obviously from the deer. And there was a huge set of tracks following the blood. I assumed it was my father tracking the deer he'd shot, so I abandoned my plans to meet up with him in the middle of the ridge, as his plans had obviously changed to tracking the animal. At least this had all been my train of thought at the time.

I began following the blood and what I thought were my father's tracks. I knew my dad had big feet, but man, the snow was really making them look a lot bigger. I guess maybe the way his heel would push the snow forward a few inches before his entire foot would rest on the ground's surface, beneath the snow, completing the step, and then from how the toe would drag snow as it came up out of the snow, forming the beginning of the next step, making it look like the track was nearly twice its actual size. At least this is what I was thinking at the time.

But then something happened.

I stopped to grab my old Army style canteen from my waist to get a drink of water, and I looked up and out as I did. About a hundred yards ahead of me, I saw what appeared to be something very large dragging a deer. I remember thinking distinctively that it couldn't be my father, because I did not see blaze orange, and it couldn't be a bear, because the only type of bears we had on the east coast were black bears, and whatever was dragging the deer was not black, but brown, just a subtle shade darker than the deer itself. And just as soon as I'd noticed this, it was gone. Out of sight over the next dip in the hill.

I sipped my water and holstered my canteen and began following the trail again. About fifty yards farther away I found the gut pile. For those reading this who don't hunt, this would be where the hunter who killed the deer would have cut open the deer and taken out its insides, making it much lighter and easier to drag out of the woods. Let me tell you, it's fun heading far out into the deep dark woods to get the big, elusive buck of your dreams, but once you do, the fun stops, as dragging an often two hundred pounds animal's carcass for miles through the woods is not much fun.

Anyway, I continued following the trail, which was now made up of those extremely large footprints and the bloody trail of an animal being dragged. I remember to this day wondering why my father would have killed this deer, gutted it, and then began dragging it back to the truck without waiting on me to let me know what was going on. I mean, why would he just start heading off the mountain like that, with his dear, while leaving his twelve year old son behind?

Because it wasn't my father!

I heard a sharp whistle come from behind me. I turned, and there, about fifty yards back was my father, brightly lit up by way of his blaze orange hunting coat and cap. I stood still and waited while he trudged through the snow to catch up with me. When he did, he asked me if I'd shot a deer, because he'd heard the shot and he'd been tracking the trail.

"No," I told him. "I thought you did."

I looked down at the trail in the snow and my father did that same. Our heads rose together and our eyes met, and I'll remember these words until the day I die. My father simply said, "those ain't my tracks."

"Who is it?" I asked, paying no attention to what seemed to be fear in my father's eyes. "Another hunter?"

"I have no idea," he said. "Whoever it is, they would have been in here before us, and I didn't see any cars down where we parked, did you?"

"No," I said, and where we'd parked was the closest place one could park to this location. If you were to come up this particular mountain from any other angle, it would be a day long hike, and who in their right mind would be camping out in November in these mountains where there was always the potential (I love that word) for snow squalls such as the one we were having?

"Let's follow it," my dad said, and I could tell that he was as curious as I was. "But let's not get too close."

We did as he suggested, continuing on and following the trail. It was a downhill trek, so it wasn't too taxing, but the snow continued to blow, and it even began picking up, making visibility even more poor.

We'd gone for about ten minutes when my father, a few steps in front of me, stopped immediately and raised a hand, motioning me to stop. I watched, as he raised his high powered rifle to his shoulder and peered through the scope. As stated earlier, I'd graduated to the 'splitting up' stage of this right of passage, but since I'd not yet graduated to the high powered rifle stage, and I still had a twenty gauge single shot shotgun with slugs, this meant I had no scope through which to peer at whatever my father was looking at.

Almost as quickly as my father had raised his rifle, he lowered it. He stood there, almost frozen in the snow, and then he raised his rifle again, peering once more through the scope. This time, as he lowered it, he turned, slowly and methodically toward me, and he raised his other hand to his face and gave me the universal 'stay quiet' sign of the index finger held to lips with the lips perched out in the 'sh' sound way. He slowly walked over to me and leaned into my ear and whispered, barely audible, which I didn't see as necessary since the wind was so loud, "follow me. Do not make a sound. And do not look back!"

This is weird, I remembered thinking at the time, but I was too cold and tired to question it, so I simply did as he said. I followed him, very quietly, which the snow made even easier, since there was no sounds of crumpling leaves under our feet, as the leaves were now under the snow, back to the top of the ridge we'd just descended, and we just as quietly and slowly began making our way down the other side.

When we were about halfway down the other side of the mountain, and not too far from the truck, my father stopped and took a drink of water from his canteen and told me to do the same. The snow had stopped, and by looking around, I could see that it hadn't snowed much at all over here. There was maybe an inch or two. The squall was trapped in the valley on the other side of the mountain, and by the time we'd later reach the truck, there was no snow on our side of the mountain at all.

"What did you see?" I asked my father as we sipped our water. You learn to walk the fine line of fluid intake while hunting. Enough to stay hydrated, but not enough to have to stop and piss every ten minutes.

"A bear," he said. "Come on. Let's get out of here." He turned and began walking again, this time a little faster and not so much concerned about how much noise he made.

"Who shot the deer?" I asked, now following my father. "Who else was out here?"

My father stopped abruptly and turned to face me. "I shot the deer," he said. "And a bear got it. Dragged it off to eat it before we could get to it. Now let's *get!*" And then he turned and began heading for the truck again.

And I knew my father had lied to me.

We reached the truck and began our long journey home in silence. I finally spoke, and when I did I said, "that wasn't a bear."

"What do you mean it wasn't a bear?" my father said, something in his voice letting me know that he knew I wasn't buying his story.

"I got a glimpse of it when I was tracking it," I said. "Before we met up. Whatever it was wasn't a bear, because it wasn't black. It was brown. Just a bit darker than the deer. And it was dragging it."

My father didn't say a word, and I remained silent. Years later, when I got into sales after college, I would learn the expression, "he who speaks first loses." This was a saying in regard to asking for the order. Once you ask the prospect to buy, you shut the hell up and wait, no matter how uncomfortable, and how long the silence. If you start babbling on and on about more reasons the prospect should buy what you're selling, you've lost, because you've shown weakness. If the prospect speaks first, usually showing hesitation due to some bullshit reason that isn't even relevant, you know you've won, and you've got your order, which translates, of course, into a commission.

They'd tell me years later that I was a natural in sales, and looking back on that day in the truck with my father on our way home from deer hunting I guess I could see their point, because I did not speak first. My father did.

And he lost.

"I'd like to say I have no idea what in holy hell that thing was that I saw through my scope, but unfortunately I'm afraid I do."

That's all he said, and I never pushed him for further explanation. I didn't want to put him in the uncomfortable position of speaking the actual words. Testifying orally that he'd seen something that is not supposed to exist outside of folklore and urban legend.

I'd hunt on that mountain for many years after that, sometimes with, and sometimes without my father, especially as I was older and had learned to appreciate my own alone time. Many years have passed since I've stepped foot on that mountain at all and I may never do so again. I have no particular reasons to go back to that spot, and hell, it's not the only place in the world where I've ever seen weird things. I wouldn't have the time left in life to go back to all those places, many of them in other countries, to see if I could get a repeat sighting.

But I'll always have the memories, especially the memory of that one day in deer season, the day it snowed, back when I was twelve years old. The day on which I'd graduated to the 'let's split up' part of a very special Appalachian American right of passage.

And I'll never forget the partial glimpse I got of what I'd seen, and what my father had seen through his rifle scope.

Because believe it or not, no matter how hokey some of those clickbait social media content titles might be, there are some things in this world that, once seen, cannot be unseen.

And that was one of them!

The End

***

The following stories are from Bigfoot Sasquatch Files Volume 3:

1

Footprints In The Sand...

Big Ones!

It was so much easier to be an atheist back in college, Jason thought, barrelling down the road, en route to another Bigfoot Sasquatch organization gathering. This weekend's trip was taking him to Corolla, a small, desolate village on the northern tip of the Outer Banks of North Carolina. At least he'd get some sun and sand, he thought, as he crossed the long bridge over the sound at Point Harbor. Take a nice little beach break after bursting some hillbilly belief bubbles, he thought, chuckling to himself as he made sure not to go more than five miles over the speed limit. He *did* have out-of-state plates, afterall.

What in the hell did Bigfoot Sasquatch have to do with being an atheist?

Simple.

The belief in Bigfoot Sasquatch, or other cryptids, was pretty much one of the few belief systems left that one could still publicly denounce, and who's believers one could still ridicule and shame for possessing a belief in things unseen- the very definition of faith- and *not* get locked up under the jail house for so doing. Or, in Jason's case, have their hand over fist money making social media accounts demonetized. All other belief systems based on faith were off limits.

Jason had missed the turbulent sixties, not having been born until the seventies, but he was happy to come of age during the nineties when there was a resurgence in bashing all things traditional, short lived as it was. And at first, as a caucasion male of European descent, he'd struggled with the concept of viewing himself as the root cause of all things bad in the world, but hey, he figured if he could hate so many people he didn't know personally, like all those Bible beating Christians, he could learn to hate himself to some degree, at least.

It took time, but he knew he'd achieved his goal of internalizing at least a small percentage of self hatred when he caught himself crying at the sight of his pasty pale skin in the mirror one morning. That was the morning when he had to have a heart to heart with himself about never having asked to be born white. But since he had been, and since he recognized that it was due to no choice of his, he could now relate even more to others who he felt were victims of circumstance, because now, he was one of them. He'd made the transition! He was practically a self made martyr! And man, did he feel guilty about it.

Jason had lost hope when that Texan took over the White House, the one whose father had stunk the place up during most of Jason's childhood, either as the man in charge, or as the man in charge's right hand man before that, when that no good actor from California was stinking the place up. Just as Jason was really beginning to enjoy his love hate relationship with himself, and participating in protests almost every week, he feared the geo-political winds were beginning to blow him in the direction of growing up and getting over himself, and his causes, for good.

Jason was all but ready to pack it in when the twin towers fell, because they'd fallen by the hands of followers of the wrong faith. How was he supposed to make Christians look like the most vile sect of believers in the history of God's green earth after this?

But then Jason discovered the train promoting the idea that not all Muslims were terrorists and not all terrorists were Muslims, which he and most level headed people knew to be true. But Jason, rarely level headed in regard to his hatred of all things traditional, quickly found the specific car on this train where all aboard went the extra mile of demonizing Christians and Christianity, by claiming all Christians were singling out all Muslims in the aftermath of the attacks. He jumped on board with his fellow radical leftists who saw the opportunity of a new way of going out and actively bashing the members of the Christian faith, and alas, he felt as if he'd refound his place in life.

And then the millennials came of age- those twerpy little snot nosed rugrats his sister used to babysit- and it wasn't okay to hate or bash *anyone*. Being nice was king, and since Jason was nearing fifty, he feared that being nice was here to stay, at least while he was still around, so he had to figure out another way.

And that's when he discovered Bigfoot Sasquatch!

Rather, those who believed in him, her, it or they.

"This is perfect!" Jason screamed, jumping up from his desk chair when the idea hit him several years before. "These people are idiots! And most of them are rural, backwood, family oriented Christians! I can bash these idiots all day long for believing in a bunch of ignorant horseshit no one's ever seen, just like God and Jesus, and I can get away with it and still make bank on social media doing it! This is *not* a protected group!"

Jason had spent most of his years after college as a newspaper writer, but like most of those guys lucky enough to still be relatively young when social media came out, he discovered that he could make way more money by blogging. He'd developed halfway decent writing skills through the years, and what he lacked in ability he made up for with passion. He poured his heart and soul into writing about what he loved.

Hate.

Namely, hating Christians and anything remotely conservative or traditional.

He'd developed quite the following through the years, and with each passing change in what would and would not be tolerated as far as hate in American society went, they were happy to jump ship with him when he had to leave one social media platform (that whole demonetization thing) and join another.

He'd been stuck at a pass when he got the idea to go about bashing Bigfoot Sasquatch believers. He'd been making bank blogging and posting his blogs on Facebook. That leftist leaning Mark Zuckerberg had no problem with him pointing out how ignorant Christians were, as long as they were American Christians. Jason laughed for years, when his competitors would post a meme to their Facebook pages referring to Islam as a religion of hate, and then end up having their accounts suspended or removed, knowing he could bash Christianity, labelling it as a religion of hate, or of incest and ignorance, or anything else bad he could think of, as much as he wanted on Facebook and get away with it, and he did.

But things changed after Zuckerberg started getting called out for his double standards by the rest of Silicon Valley and his advertisers. There had long stood an unspoken agreement between the billionaire entrepreneurs of the internet and the tax and regulate the hell out of everything Government men, and that unspoken agreement basically was that if the tech guys would mind their P's and Q's, then the Government men would take a laissez faire approach to the internet world (and of course there would be plenty of yacht parties with booze and drugs and 'she said she was legal' hookers for those Government men, courtesy of those Silicon Valley guys' lobbyists).

But Zuckerberg started bringing in the regulators with his shenanigans, like selling everyone's info to Chinese firms, so 'Ol Zuck started putting an end to the double standard bullcrap in a desperate attempt to make himself look good in the eyes of the people he'd conned, and thus, Jason found himself going from making tens of thousands of dollars a month bashing Christians and conservatives on Facebook to making zero dollars, and being banned, permanently, from the platform.

Enter YouTube, and Jason's ingenious idea of making a channel based on debunking these Bigfoot Sasquatch idiots. Oh, and how his somewhat massive following he'd collected through the years *loved* the idea as well, because they knew that most of the people who believed in such things were the very people they loved to hate as well.

Bigfoot!

Rubbish!

Just like God, and Jesus!

"Here we are," Jason said into his smartphone camera, "pulling up to the retreat." He was recording bits and pieces of his trip as he went along. He'd put it all together and upload and publish the video at the end of the weekend, and as most of his videos did, Jason was sure it would go viral.

***

Jason made sure to hang out in his car until a few minutes before the morning's first meeting started and then go into the rec center where the meetings for the weekend's festivities were being held. Actual Bigfoot Sasquatch hunts would take place later, on the beaches, and in the scrub brush, with several meetings, like the one Jason was about to enter, interspersed in between.

Jason had mastered his methods over the past couple of years, and today, he would do as he always did. He would sit during the meetings, act as if he was as interested, and like he believed in Bigfoot Sasquatch as much as everyone else in attendance, and then he would work his magic later by way of editing.

Jason entered the meeting and sat in the middle of the crowd, beside a couple in their late fifties. Jason knew that sitting in front might draw attention, and sitting in the back might make him look conspicuous, so sitting in the middle was the best way, as he saw it, to remain practically invisible.

"I'm so excited," Jason said, leaning over and speaking into the ear of the man beside him.

"Us, too," said the man's wife, leaning around her husband to do so, so that she could make eye contact with Jason as she spoke to him.

"First time?" Jason asked her.

"Oh, no," her husband said, answering for her. "We come to this one every year, and we usually make a couple of these a year. We were up at one in Virginia last month. The one where Dr. Drake spoke."

"Oh," Jason said, sounding excited. He knew of Drake and his work, as he was constantly attempting to debunk Drake's YouTube channel on his own. Unfortunately, he hadn't quite cracked the code for debunking Drake yet, because the man never actually claimed to see Bigfoot Sasquatch. He merely claimed to have potentially seen Bigfoot Sasquatch, and it's his channel's *viewers* who claim to see the alleged beast in the background of most of his videos. Boy, did Jason hate this Drake guy, and man, was he determined to get him someday, that bastard, Jason thought.

"That's awesome," Jason said. "I love Dr. Drake and his work."

"He's the best," the man's wife said.

"You know," Jason said, "I've been thinking about doing some stuff on social media myself, and I'd love to interview you guys a bit during this weekend's retreat, if it's okay with you."

"Why, sure," the couple said in unison. They had no idea they were dealing, not with the devil, but a man with devilish intent.

Jason had mastered his style of deception. He had learned to interview folks at Bigfoot Sasquatch retreats, just like this one, and then later think of different questions to edit into the video, so it appeared as if the people interviewed were actually answering questions they were never asked, but only Jason knew this. Jason was able to make them look completely ignorant and beyond ridiculous, and his hundreds of thousands of jaded viewers loved every minute of it, though they didn't realize they were being duped themselves by way of Jason's editing efforts. But they wouldn't have minded if they'd known, Jason knew, because, like him, they wouldn't care about the actual facts. Their minds were already made up.

***

With the first meeting of the day out of the way, the group of roughly thirty people in attendance for this weekend's Bigfoot Sasquatch retreat made their way out of the rec center and into the backs of pickup trucks that had football stadium bleachers built into them in order to seat as many people as possible. The trucks headed up the beach and into the brush, where very few people lived, where there were no paved roads, and where no one was allowed to feed the horses.

You see, in Corolla, there is a herd of wild Spanish ponies, and they're protected by the game and wildlife organizations of North Carolina, as well as a couple of various not for profit groups who make a *killing* on merchandise. The Bigfoot Sasquatch group guides talked about the importance of allowing the horses to remain wild, and ended by saying, "so if you see a Bigfoot Sasquatch, and you want to pet or feed him, her, it or they, that's fine. Do so at your own risk. But do not interfere, in any way, with the ponies!"

Bigfoot Sasquatch, ponies, whatever, Jason was thinking to himself, while eyeballing a cute girl in her mid twenties that he was *certainly* going to interview once the group got out of the trucks.

"Here we are," one of the guides said when the trucks stopped. "Again, break up into groups of three to five, spread out and see what you can see. Listen and see what you can hear. Remember to follow your nose, as well, as sometimes folks have reported to have smelled him, her, it or they. And let's all meet back in an hour for lunch. We'll eat, compare notes, then do another search before heading back and listening to one of our guest speakers lecture on the topic of which wild edibles are best to plant on your property in the hopes of attracting Bigfoot Sasquatch."

"Mind if I join you guys?" Jason said, jogging to catch up to the couple in their fifties he'd been talking to during the meeting. As luck would have it, the twenty something he'd been checking out in the truck was with them.

"Not at all," the girl said, turning at the sound of his voice, and smiling upon making eye contact. "My name is Becca."

"High, Becca," Jason said, extending his hand for a shake. "I'm Jason."

The groups all split up and went in separate directions. As some of the groups headed into the thick, bush scrub country that would pass for woods on the outer banks, Jason and his group remained on the beach, walking north, toward the Virginia state line.

"So how long have you been doing this?" Jason asked Becca, wondering if she'd smiled so nicely because she saw him more as the boy next door type he tried to portray, or if it was because she viewed him as one of her dad's friends types, which he'd always hated.

"First time," she said.

"Really," Jason said, surprised. "What inspired you to come?"

"My friend," she said. "Ricky."

"Who's Ricky?" Jason asked, hoping that he wasn't a boyfriend. "And what's his story?"

"Oh," he was just a friend from school," Becca said. "We'd been friends since we were kids."

Jason could tell that Becca was talking in past tense, and all of a sudden, he wasn't thinking about getting in her pants as much as he was interested in hearing about what happened to Ricky.

"What happened?" he asked.

"He died," Becca said. "About a year ago. A very rare cancer."

"Sorry to hear that," Jason said.

After walking further up the beach in silence for a full minute, Becca said, "he loved this Bigfoot Sasquatch stuff. We were actually going to come on this retreat together, but the angels swept him away before we could."

"Now, Becca," Jason caught himself saying before he could think before speaking, something he rarely did. "You don't really believe in that angel crap, do you?"

"Of course," Becca said. "Don't you?"

"Look!" It was the woman in her fifties. She and her husband were standing, frozen. "Something big and dark went behind that pile of brush over there!" She extended her right arm, her right index finger extended, pointing to the pile of brush.

"Come on," Jason said, taking Becca by the hand and beginning to run with her, toward the brush pile, seeing the opportunity to take his foot out of his mouth. "Let's check it out."

Jason and Becca and the married couple in their fifties grouped up behind a log about fifty yards behind the brush pile in question. "We'll go around on the left," the husband of the woman who'd potentially spotted the beast said. "You two go around the right!"

"Okay," Jason said. He took Becca by the hand and began to lead her in the direction in which they'd been assigned to go. She all too willingly followed, which led Jason to believe she'd forgiven him his trespasses, as these Christian types would say, and some actually had a tendency to do so, though those were not the ones Jason liked to focus on.

As the married couple made their way around the far side of the brush pile, and out of sight of Jason and Becca, Jason and Becca made their way around the other side, where they soon discovered the large, dark object that the woman had apparently seen.

"Jesus Christ!" Jason said, staring at the black Spanish pony. "A fucking horse!"

"Wow," Becca said. "Is that language really necessary? And, do you really need to take the Lord's name in vain?"

"The Lord," Jason said. "What Lord?" He walked over to Becca, until the distance between them couldn't have been more than a foot. "There is no Lord," Jason said. "There is no God. And there certainly is no such thing as Bigfoot Sasquatch!"

And that's when the Spanish pony, which Jason had gotten too close to while closing his distance with Becca, came up behind him and kicked him in the back of the head and knocked him the fuck out!

"Your parents were fucking deranged."

Jason heard the voice, but he hadn't seen who it belonged
to. His eyes were closed. His head was throbbing, and he
tasted blood. "What?" he said.

"I said your parents were fucking deranged."

Jason sat up, and sitting beside him, in the sand, was a
man about his age, wearing a tie dyed t-shirt with a peace
sign on the front. The man didn't have long hair, and he
didn't have a beard, but it looked like he could use a
haircut and a shave. Five o'clock shadow stuff. Too busy
this week to make it to the barber.

"But don't worry," the man said. "We've reserved a special
place in hell for them, and, well, they've taken up their
reservations."

"Who the hell are you?" Jason said, trying to rise to his feet
and falling back on his ass.

"Don't try to move," the man said. "You pissed that horse
off pretty bad. Didn't they tell you on the way up that the
horses don't like loud noises?"

Jason passed out, only momentarily, and when he woke
up, he found that the man who'd been speaking was now
carrying him down the beach.

"I'm sorry you endured all the abuse," the man carrying him said, when he saw that Jason's eyes were open. "Having to put up with all that bullshit. Always being told you were not good enough. Unworthy. And the beatings. No child deserves that."

"Then why the fuck did it happen?" Jason asked. It was the same question he'd asked countless therapists and thousands upon thousands of bottles of beer.

"That, my friend," the man said, "is a question that only my boss can answer. It's far above my paygrade."

And Jason passed out again.

"...you're going to get nothing but disappointment," the man said as Jason came to again.

"What?" Jason said.

"I said that if you hold everyone of a certain belief to such bullshit standards because your parents were fucked up, you're going to get nothing but disappointment. There are many wonderful Christians, Jews, Muslims and Budhists in this world. There are plenty of wonderful atheists whose seats are already reserved in Heaven."

Jason wanted to say *what?*, but he passed out again before he could.

When Jason awoke again, he was no longer being carried, but he was not alone, either. All roughly thirty members of the Bigfoot Sasquatch weekend retreat were there, in front of him, looking up the beach, in awe, as he came to.

Jason turned to look in the direction in which they were staring. For just an instant, he could have sworn that he saw a large, dark figure, a couple of hundred yards up the beach, duck into a stand of trees at the edge of the forest.

Jason's eyes worked their way back from the point where he believed he'd seen the dark figure, all the way back to where he sat, and what he saw was a single pair of footprints in the sand.

Big ones.

The End

2

Swimfan

(Originally Titled: "I Saw A Bigfoot Sasquatch And It Ruined My Life!)

"You're on the air. Go!"

"So, like. Am I on the air now? Live? Or is this being pre-recorded to be played later?"

"You're on the air, live. Now. Go."

Nick hated his job, and he didn't even need the money. But he had to work, per the judge's order. Nick was on probation for a year for his first D.U.I. conviction. He hoped it would be his last, but who knew. The whole twelve step program thing wasn't really working for him because, admittedly, he wasn't working it. That, too, had all been judge ordered.

"So like, I know Bigfoot Sasquatch is real, because he tried to rape my girlfriend back in college."

"Go on," Nick said to the caller, sounding interested, but totally rolling his eyeballs in the privacy of his a.m. radio station's small boothe. The radio station's office was in a spare room above a shity little regional bank. It was triangular shaped, due to the building's design, but it worked. Just enough space to serve the station's twenty thousand weekly listeners and growing (hopefully).

"I swear to God, it wasn't me! I'll tell ya that!" the caller said. "I didn't touch that bitch, and she was just trying to ruin my life, and that's exactly what she did. And it was that goddamn Bigfoot Sasquatch's fault for helping her!"

"Next caller," Nick said, hanging up on yet another psychopath, as he saw it. "And please, folks, let me remind you to watch your language when we're live. My grandmother's listening."

It wasn't true. Nick's grandmother had died when he was a very young child. But Nick was good at lying. All part of the job.

And it wasn't the belief in Bigfoot Sasquatch that he was lying about. He never claimed to believe or disbelieve. He figured anything was possible. The dishonest part came in pretending to give a shit about what the people who called into the show, his show, were calling about.

When Nick's very rich parents found out their very rich son was being ordered to work, they called Nick's very rich uncle who owned a radio station and hit him up for a favor. Nick's very rich uncle jumped at the opportunity to help his favorite nephew, little Nicky, because he agreed with Nick's parents, that Nick would absolutely *not* get some kind of labor job. Nick, despite being born into privilege, never took advantage of his circumstances and went to college or picked up any specific skill sets, because, he figured, what was the use? His grandmother who had died when he was a young child had invented waterproof cameras (she'd been an avid photographer and scuba diver), so it was highly unlikely anyone in the family would ever have to work for many, many, many generations.

Unless they were dumb enough to go out and get a D.U.I.

So here Nick was now, hosting the Bigfoot Sasquatch hour for his very rich uncle, in this little studio, putting up with total weirdos, as he saw it, but at least keeping his probation officer off his back in doing so.

"Am I on the air?" the caller said.

"You are," Nick said. "Go."

"Is this Nick?"

"The one and only," Nick said, rolling his eyes, but not as outrageously as he had toward the rapist.

"I know what you're doing," the caller said. "And I don't like it."

"Oh?" Nick said, hoping not everyone in the whole damn listening area knew about his D.U.I. Not that he cared, but still. "So what is it that I'm doing?"

"You're making fun of those of us who believe in Bigfoot Sasquatch."

"I've never done that," Nick said, surprised at hearing the defensiveness in his voice. "That's not who I am." And he was actually being honest about that. He never got his jollies off by making fun of anyone for any reason. He just liked to drink beer and watch sports.

"You're trying to pit believers and non-believers off against each other so you can sit back and laugh as we argue."

"Who is this?" Nick said.

"It's none of your goddamn business who this is," the caller said, just before Nick hung up on him due to his language.

"Okay," Nick said. "If you guys don't cut it with the language, I'm going to have to play some previously recorded phone calls. And that's no fun. So please watch your mouths. Remember. My grandmother."

Nick got lucky. No one else cussed for the rest of his shift, and he was able to kill the time in a much more relaxed way. An "uh huh" here and an "uh huh" there- here an "uh huh," there an "uh huh" and his shift was over.

"How in the name of God can you listen to those idiots without laughing your ass off?" Nick's best good beer drinking buddy, Quinn said, as Nick got into the passenger side of Quinn's car. Quinn was really good about taking Nick to work and picking him up and taking him back home afterward. Nick had also lost his license for a year due to the D.U.I. It helped that Nick was paying Quinn for it. A hundred dollars a day. Plus all the free beer the two of them could drink together, which was a lot. Nick knew he could possibly be given a piss test at any time, and if he popped hot, he would have to serve the rest of his time in jail. He had three months to go, and he figured he'd rather be in jail than stay sober. What was the difference, was how he saw it.

"My uncle would fire me," Nick said, reaching into the cooler between his feet, and then opening up the can of Devil's Backbone Vienna Lager he'd pulled out of it. None of that Bud Light shit for Nick. That was for rednecks and hillbillies. "Besides," he said after taking a long swig. "I've heard it all."

"That last guy," Quinn said, pointing to the radio, and then shutting it off. "A fucking Bigfoot Sasquatch kept him from being able to sell his house? Because everyone knew there was a Bigfoot Sasquatch in the area? So he got foreclosed on, and his finances have been shit ever since? He tried to make it sound like Bigfoot Sasquatch ruined his life."

"I get so much of that Bigfoot Sasquatch ruined my life shit," Nick said, and then he took another drink. "It's all the same. People claim to have seen Bigfoot Sasquatch, then they tell people about it, then they're written off as crazy, and they have no friends, and their wives leave them. They try to make it sound like seeing a Bigfoot Sasquatch is as shell shocking as going off and fighting in a goddamn war or something."

"Oh," Quinn said, reaching into his front pants pocket as he made the turn onto Willow Road, which would take them to Nick's house. Rather, Nick's parents' grand estate, on the back part of which had been built Nick's house ten years before when he'd hit the age of majority. He still spent quite a bit of time at mommy and daddy's though. Especially around meal time. "Some guy said to give you this."

"What's this?" Nick said, taking the folded piece of paper Quinn had handed him. He opened in up and read the handwritten note aloud. "I know what you're up to."

Nick only had to think for a millisecond before remembering the caller he'd spoken to earlier who had accused him of making fun of people who believed in Bigfoot Sasquatch.

"Who the hell gave you this?" Nick said, turning his head to face Quinn.

"Some dude," Quinn said. "About ten minutes before you came out."

"What did he look like?" Nick asked. "Did he tell you his name?"

"No name," Quinn said. "He looked about our age. White guy. I'm not gay, but I'd say he was good looking."

"And he didn't tell you his name?" Nick said.

"That's pretty much what no name means, Nick."

Nick's family's estate was around the next turn. The two men finished up the short remainder of the trip in silence. Once there, they went into Nick's house (he referred to it as a cottage, as his parents did, even though it was five thousand square feet), and got shitty drunk while watching some sports team score more points than their opponent in some game.

***

"You're on the air," Nick said, nursing a hangover by drinking a Bloody Mary. Sure, it was night already, but Nick and Quinn had stayed up until the sun had come up drinking, so time, for Nick and the lifestyle he led, and Quinn as well, since becoming Nick's best friend shortly after moving to the area a year ago, was irrelevant. "Go."

"There is a freaking Bigfoot Sasquatch right outside my house right now," the caller said. Nick could hear the fear in the man's voice, and he often wondered how these Bigfoot Sasquatch people could be so convincing. Were they having some sort of psychotic episode when they supposedly saw these eight feet tall, eight hundred pound creatures? Nick was convinced that had to be it. Either psychotic episodes, or they were on drugs. Nick sure did like his weed, but he couldn't remember ever seeing Bigfoot Sasquatch after smoking up a big fat bowl.

"What is the Bigfoot Sasquatch doing?" Nick asked, trying to keep the caller on the line. One hour was a long time to fill, and Nick had found that the key to burning it up the best was by keeping callers who were willing to talk, and who didn't use profanity when they did, on the line for as long as possible.

"It's ruining my life," the caller said. "Right now. As we speak."

"Can you please explain to our listeners how, specifically, the Bigfoot Sasquatch that's outside your house is ruining your life?" Nick said. He never got a straight answer on this one.

"Well," the caller said, sounding really nervous. "He cost me my job."

"How," Nick began, "did the Bigfoot Sasquatch outside your house cost you your job?"

"I haven't been able to go to work for a week, and my boss called me today and fired me for excessive absences. That's how."

"How is it that the Bigfoot Sasquatch kept you from going to work for a week?" Nick asked.

"Because he's right outside my house!" the caller screamed into the phone. "I can't go outside and get in my fucking car and go to fucking…"

"Next caller," Nick said, wishing he'd hung up just a little sooner. At least soon enough to have missed the second F bomb.

"I bet you thought that guy was a blast," an eerily familiar sounding voice said on the other line.

"Who is this?" Nick said.

"You know who I am," the caller said.

"Ah," Nick said, remembering where he'd heard the voice. "My mystery caller from last night. You're the guy who thinks I'm pranking everyone."

"That's right, buddy boy. And I know that you know that I know exactly where you are right now."

"You and our up to twenty thousand other listeners," Nick said, trying to sound brave, but feeling a little creeped out.

"You know what I think would be funny, Nick?" the caller said. "If you ran into one of these creatures one dark night, and he ripped your legs off and beat you over the head with them."

"That's not a very nice thing to say," Nick said.

"You have no idea what these people who've actually seen these things have gone through," the caller said. "Their lives have been absolutely destroyed, and then you sit up there in your little c budget radio station and make fun of us?"

"Wait a minute," NIck said. "I get it. You just said, *us*. So obviously, you've seen Bigfoot Sasquatch, too."

"Of course I have, you idiot!"

"Okay," Nick said. "How about instead of calling me and accusing me of doing something I'm not, like making fun of our loyal listeners, and insulting me, and wishing violence upon me, why don't you just tell us your story? Where and when did you see the Bigfoot Sasquatch? Under what circumstances? And most importantly, how in the name of God did it ruin your life?"

"Keep laughing," the caller said. "Bigfoot Sasquatch might not show up and give you the ass whooping you deserve, but by God, I will!"

And then the mysterious caller hung up.

"Just so you'll know, guys," Nick said, his voice riding over the sound of the dial tone from the disconnected call, "we have the ability to trace our calls. We can find you. It's not a good idea to call and make threats of violence with twenty thousand witnesses listening in. Keep that in mind as you're calling in. You don't want the boys in blue showing up at your house."

But that was all bullshit, and Nick was scared. He was texting away to Quinn as he was speaking the words over the radio.

"Don't worry," Quinn texted back, almost immediately. "I'm in the parking lot, and I heard the call. That crazy son of a whore will have a baseball bat waiting on him when he gets here if he's dumb enough to come."

Nick felt instantly relieved. He had no idea what forces in the cosmos were at work when Quinn had decided to uproot from his normal day job in Akron, Ohio (the type of job where they actually gave you five company polo shirts instead of three, so you wouldn't have to do laundry until the weekend if you didn't want to) a little more than a year ago, and move him into Nick's community. Further, he had no idea how the cosmos had arranged for Quinn to replace one of the guys on the lawn crew his family had used for years, shortly after Nick had gotten his D.U.I. and had started working at the radio station, but he was thankful it had happened.

And Nick was thankful for that first day that he'd met Quinn. The first day Nick had met Quinn, when he, Nick, had been binge drinking by the pool, and he'd asked Quinn if he wanted a beer, and Quinn said yes, and he did take a beer, and he did drink it, and he did not return to work with the rest of the crew, because he felt it was more important to drink a beer with the customers' adult son, and Nick knew he'd found a kindred soul. And when Quinn did get fired by the lawn crew boss for drinking with the customers' adult son instead of mowing grass, Nick did hire him to be his private driver.

Nick and Quinn had been inseparable, and rarely sober, since.

***

"So what in the hell do you think this guy's deal is?" Quinn asked Nick on the way home. Nick was already pounding down the brewskies.

"I have no fucking idea," Nick said.

The mysterious caller who'd alluded to hurting Nick had not shown up at the radio station, rather, the bank, with the radio station in the broom closet upstairs. Either that, or he had shown up, but when he'd seen Quinn's car, he decided not to stick around. This is what Quinn thought, at least, and he'd said as much to Nick.

"Why do you think that he thinks that you're making fun of people who claim to have seen Bigfoot Sasquatch?" Quinn asked.

"Gee, I don't know," Nick said. "Maybe becasue I fucking do?"

Quinn was silent for a moment. Confused. "Wait a minute," he said. "I thought you were, like, agnostic about the whole Bigfoot Sasquatch thing. That you didn't even care if he, she, it, or they exist or not?"

"I am," Nick said. "Shit, there might be some out there. I don't know, and I don't care." He popped the top of another beer, and then he said, "but how can you not make fun of the backwoods redneck fucks who claim to have actually seen one. They set themselves up. It's too fucking simple!"

Quinn continued to drive in silence. Nick paid no never mind, because he was too busy drinking beer and being thankful that Quinn had been on time, like he always was, and had saved him a potential ass beating.

When they got home, they went inside and watched some sports team score more points than their opponent, and got shitty drunk, and they did not go to bed until after the sun came up.

***

When Nick woke up late afternoon the next day, he found a note on the kitchen counter beside the coffee pot.

I made you breakfast. It's in a tupperware container in the ref. Just Nuke it. I'll be out running errands, and when I come home, I'll have more food. Don't worry. I'll be back in time to take you to work, boss.

Quinn

"A saint," Nick said to himself after reading Quinn's note. "The man is a fucking saint."

After a couple of cups of coffee, Nick nuked his breakfast and ate it, and then he made himself a Bloody Mary and went outside to sit under the shade of the giant magnolia tree his grandfather had planted a million years ago. God, he hated hangovers, but at least in three more months, when he got off probation, he'd be able to sleep them off entirely, like he always had in the past, because he wouldn't have to have his stupid job down at his uncle's stupid radio station anymore.

"How's that ex-con working out for you?"

The words rang in Nick's head like a gong. It was the voice of Chick, the head guy of the lawn crew.

"What?" Nick said, turning his head to his left to see Chick making his way over.

Chick pulled up a seat and stuffed the cold hard cash that Nick's parents had just given him for payment for last month's lawn care in his wallet. Chick wasn't an idiot. He knew these rich fuckers hated paying taxes as much as he, one of the truly hard working men of the world did, so he gave them two prices when they inquired about his services. There was the competitive, fair market value price which he'd offer to customers who paid with a check or credit card, and then there was the deeply discounted price he offered to anyone willing to pay him in cash. Chick made a lot of money and he didn't give much of it to the IRS because of his scheme, and his customers thought of him as a genius for doing it. They envied the way a man who actually had to work for his money could stick it to the IRS in such a slick way. It wasn't quite as easy for them to do it, with all their trust fund dividend and interest income being fully taxable, and all. They hated the IRS for taking so much of what they'd rightly been born into, so they loved the way Chick handled the bastards. He was their hero.

"That con you've got living with you," Chick said, sitting down and then adjusting his position in his chair, now that his wallet was so much fatter than it had been the last time he'd sat down anywhere. "Quinn."

"What do you mean, con?" Nick asked, and then he took a sip of his Bloody Mary.

"He didn't tell you?" Chick said. "As much time as you guys spend together?"

"Quinn's not a con," Nick said, surprised at the sound of his own voice. So defensive. It was as if someone had just told him his girlfriend was a slut. "He's a damned dependable dude. He always gets me to work on time, and he's never late in picking me up. And he runs all kinds of extra errands and stuff that he's not even paid to do."

"Whatever, chief," Chick said, rising to leave. "Just don't piss him off."

"Why?" Nick asked.

"He'll beat the living shit out of you like he did that poor bastard in Texas. Did three years for that one."

"Texas," Nick said, sounding incredulous. "He's never said shit about Texas. He's from Ohio."

Chick laughed so hard he nearly fell down. "That fucker's never been to Ohio," he said.

"Where did you hear all this?" Nick said.

"Dude," Chick said, walking back to get within feet of Nick before speaking again. "I hire my guys through the courts and probation officers. These are guys that can't get most jobs due to background checks. I knew this shit about Quinn before I even met him."

"You've got to be shitting me," Nick said, and all of a sudden, he found himself believing what he was being told.

"Look," Chick said, shrugging his shoulders. "People can change. Maybe he has. Just be careful."

And then Chick turned and walked away, heading off to collect his cash from the Browns down the road. He loved the Browns, because they, too, paid in cash, allowing him to stick it to the IRS, and the Browns loved Chick for doing it, because they couldn't, because the poor bastards had been born into extreme wealth and the IRS was all over them.

***

"Think you'll get any psycho calls tonight?" Quinn asked Nick several hours later on the way to work.

"I'm sure I'll get a few," Nick said. "It's the nature of the beast."

"Pun intended?" Quinn said, and they both laughed.

"As long as I don't get a call from one specific psycho," Nick said, and he slightly turned his head toward Quinn to see if he could note a reaction. "The night will go just fine."

"Oh," Quinn said after a moment's hesitation. "Don't worry about that guy. I'll wait outside in the parking lot your whole shift if it makes you feel safer."

"It's okay," Nlck said. "That's a long time to sit in a parking lot. Just be on time. If he calls back and makes more threats, I'll call the damn police."

Quinn dropped Nick off at the bank and then drove off. Nick hurried up to the office and replaced Jillian, a very lovely woman in her sixties who hosted *The B Sides*. And no, it wasn't a radio show showcasing big bands' lesser known songs. It was literally a show about bees. Honey bees. Jillian was a hippy, and Nick's very rich uncle had the hots for her, so he gave her her own radio show where she could talk about bees. It hadn't paid off for Nick's very rich uncle, as when he pressed Jillian for something in exchange, he found out she had a girlfriend. And only five hundred weekly listeners tuned in for the show. But Nick's very rich uncle kept Jillian and her show, anyway, because he liked Jillian.

And he hoped some day he would be able to turn her.

"We have something extra special for our listeners tonight," Nick said into the mic as he started his show. "Throwback Thursday! Even though it's Tuesday! That's right. We are going to start the show off by playing some of our best calls from the past. Let's get started with that guy from Pennsylvania who woke up one morning to find a couple of Bigfoot Sasquatches in his recently drained swimming pool!"

As Nick's listeners were hearing the story told from the guy who called a couple of months back, claiming that he had a suspicion Bigfoot Sasquatch was swimming in his pool at night, so he'd drained his pool, and ended up catching two of the creatures when they'd jumped into an empty pool on the deep end and ended up breaking their legs and therefore couldn't get out, Nick began Googling the ever loving hell out of his best good friend Quinn. He didn't dare risk doing so at home earlier, out of fear that Chick was most certainly telling the truth and that Nick had a real psychopath on his hands in his good buddy Quinn, and that that real psychopathic friend of his might catch him Googling him and take offense to it.

"Shit!" Nick said, aloud, before even finding any hits online. He'd glanced over to the side of the desk and saw the note that someone had supposedly given Quinn to pass on to him in the parking lot from the other night. He still had Quinn's note from earlier in the day, the note about breakfast, in his pocket. He pulled it out and compared the two notes and he saw that the handwriting was identical. "Shit!" Nick said again, after making the realization, and just because he liked to say the word shit.

As the man from Pennsylvania was telling the listeners in his previously recorded audio that of course he didn't call the Government men about the Bigfoot Sasquatches in his pool, because he knew they'd disappear him if he did, Nick hit paydirt with his internet search. It turned out that Quinn was from Texas, and that he had served three years in prison for attempted manslaughter.

Quinn read several articles about the case, and as it turned out, Quinn had actually been sentenced to twenty five years. However, the man who he'd been convicted of beating almost to death, and having put into a comma, came out of that comma after Quinn had been in prison for three years and told his side of the story, and as it turned out...

...it was the exact same story Quinn had told!

During Quinns trial, he'd claimed that while his best friend Randy and himself were out camping at South Llano River Park, just outside of Junction, Texas, they'd been attacked and badly beaten by a Bigfoot Sasquatch. Quinn claimed he'd barely been able to make it out alive, and he feared that Randy was dead.

There were no witnesses to the incident, and when authorities arrived at the scene, they found Randy, beaten so badly that he was in a coma. There were thirty eight empty beer cans found at the campsite, and Quinn's blood alcohol content (BAC) came back at more than three times the legal limit for driving after testing. Randy's BAC was about the same, but what had put him into the coma was blunt force trauma. Randy had been smacked in the head so hard that it knocked him out, and he stayed out, and on life support, for three years.

At the trial, Randy's family had gotten more than two dozen anti-character witnesses to claim that Quinn was pretty much the biggest piece of shit on earth. And the prosecutor claimed his whole story about Bigfoot Sasquatch was all being told in an attempt to claim insanity, because everyone knew there was no such thing as Bigfoot Sasquatch. In the end, the jury voted unanimously to convict him, and then the judge through the book at him.

However, when Randy finally woke from his coma, and was questioned by the authorities, he told the exact same story Quinn had told, and the Judge let Quinn out of prison early for good behavior. It was all done low key, so as not to draw media attention, but that one guy who has been kicked off of all the social media sites for blazing every conspiracy theory known to man, and who, ironically lives in Texas, got word of the release, and he went crazy with the story. That's how Nick had been able to find out all about it in the first place, here, tonight, while doing his Google searches.

"Oh, my God," Nick said aloud. "I get it. I get how having a Bigfoot Sasquatch encounter can ruin your life!"

Nick decided he would make things right, and he figured it might be a pretty good way of saving himself from an asswhooping that seemed to be coming his way pretty soon. When the guy from Pennsylvania, via replay, finished up about how all he could figure was that some other Bigfoot Sasquatches had come to the aid of the two he'd trapped in his pool the next night (because they were gone the next morning when he woke up, but by God, he swore, he was not lying), and the whole damn incident had ruined his life, Nick broke into the show to make a special announcement.

An apology.

"I have a very special statement I want to make tonight," Nick said, speaking into the mic. After a moment's pause, he said, "I'm sorry."

Nick let another moment pass before continuing, allowing his listeners' ears to prick up fully.

"I have never claimed to believe or disbelieve in the existence of Bigfoot Sasquatch," he said, being completely honest. "And I've always considered myself to be the kind of person who would never make fun of anyone else because of their beliefs. However, I've found myself doing that with many Bigfoot Sasquatch believers lately, and I humbly apologize. I would never make fun of someone for belonging to a specific religion, and I would certainly never make fun of someone due to their ethnicity or sexual preference. It's not okay to make fun of people who believe in Bigfoot Sasquatch, either."

Nick took a calculated pause before speaking again. He wanted to give what he'd just said time to sink in for his listeners, as well as see if he could get them to focus even more.

"I've only recently come to understand how having a run-in with one of these creatures could absolutely destroy one's life. And I want to go further and say that if your life has been negatively affected due to your personal encounter with Bigfoot Sasquatch, I wish you nothing but healing. It is to you that I apologize the most, and it is from you, that I ask forgiveness."

Nick was finished. He'd said everything he could think of to say.

And the phones started ringing off the hooks!

Believers and non-believers alike were condoning Nick for taking the high road and doing the right thing. No one said anything mean about anyone else who might think differently than them (at least on *this* night), and Nick's mysterious caller, his swimfan, did not call at all.

When Nick's shift was over, like clockwork, Quinn was waiting on him in the parking lot. "Nice show," Quinn said as Nick got into the car and took a beer out of the cooler sitting on the floor of the passenger side. "Thanks," Nick said, as he cracked the can open. "And our mystery caller never called."

"He came by," Quinn said, handing Nick a piece of paper as he put the car in drive and began making his way out of the bank's parking lot.

Nick felt hesitant, but he wanted to get it over with, so he wasted no time in opening the note.

"You're forgiven," was all it said.

"Is this good news?" Nick asked Quinn, knowing the proof was always in the pudding, and in this instance, the tone of Quinn's voice would be the pudding.

"It's good," Quinn said. "I don't think you'll have any problems with that guy again.

The two of them went home and got blitzkrieg drunk while watching some sports team score more points than another in some sporting event, and they drank beer until the sun came up. Quinn continued driving for Nick until he got his license back, at which time he "went back to Ohio" for a job opportunity.

Nick hated to see Quinn go, but he was also relieved to a degree. He now felt like he could sleep with both eyes shut.

Unless, of course, he ever decided to go camping at South Llano River Park just outside Junction, Texas, in which case he knew it would be best to not sleep at all.

 On second thought, Nick thought, there are just some places he decided he'd never go, and South Llano River Park outside of Junction, Texas just became one of those places.

The End

3

Gaslighting

(Originally Titled: The Unfortunate Demise Of 'Crazy A')

Stacy Pierce sat on her front porch. *Her* being the keyword here, because it was actually hers. No one else's. She wasn't paying some landlord *her* money to sit on *his* front porch. She was paying PennyMac to sit on *her* front porch.

Okay, so it was the bank's front porch, but the deed was in Stacy Pierce's name, and that was what mattered, because Stacy Pierce was a first time homebuyer, by God and Jesus and all the saints and sinners, too!

Stacy sat on that front porch of her's (we'll ignore the whole mortgaged for life thing for now), and she stared out into the woods that made up her front yard and that lined her driveway, and that went to the road, across which there were more woods. She tried to remember a more triumphant time in her life, and though there had been many triumphant times in her life- graduating at the top of her class Yale School of Law, etc.- none of them, at least that she could remember, felt so satisfying as this moment right now.

"Hi," Stacy heard the woman's voice call. Stacy looked down at the foot of the driveway, about one hundred yards down the hill, and she saw a woman, appearing to be in her mid-fifties, and very tall as far as American women in their mid fifties went, standing there, waving.

"Hi," Stacy said, waving and standing simultaneously. The woman simply stood there, at the end of the driveway, saying no more, but continuing to wave and smile, eerily, Stacy thought, like the Joker from the Batman series. "Would you like to come up?" Stacy said, not knowing if she was doing the right thing or not, but the tall woman seemed harmless enough.

"My name is Stacy," Stacy said, extending her hand for a shake after the tall woman made it up the drive and to the bottom step of the porch where Stacy had gone to greet her. "I'm new here. Just moved in."

"I know," the tall lady said. "I saw the moving trucks, but I've just stopped today, because it's overcast, and well, the sun *does* cause cancer." The tall lady then giggled, with one finger held to her lips, as if she were a silly little pre-teen girl. Stacy noted how her voice seemed to be a bit high pitched, and in a concerted effort kind of way. What most folks might refer to as fake. The woman actually seemed to be speaking in *Italics!*

"Do you live around here?" Stacy asked.

"Kind of," the tall lady said, and she said it in a whisper, while leaning forward, as if where she lived was some sort of secret that one needed to have clearance from certain Government agencies before being allowed to know such undisclosed location.

"What's your name?" Stacy asked, trying not to sound off. She wasn't nervous. Stacy didn't get nervous. Despite being only thirty years old, and pretty, and petite, and looking much younger than she actually was, even though thirty was young enough, Stacy was one of the most brazen courtroom attorneys anyone twice her age, size and of the opposite gender had ever been. She was simply trying not to show this tall woman in front of her that she could tell she was being disingenuous. Stacy, obviously, was trying to make a better effort than the other woman to make a good first impression on her new neighbor.

"Oh," the woman said. "You can just call me Crazy A."

"Crazy A?" Stacy asked.

"Yeah," Crazy A said. "That's what everyone else calls me."

"I'm curious," Stacy said. "Why does everyone call you Crazy A?"

"Oh," Crazy A said, in a voice she was using to try to sound like a twelve year old girl again, rather than a woman in her mid-fifties, "because I'm silly."

Crazy A knew *not* to confuse Stacy with facts. Confusing people with facts was not her reproitare. Besides, if Crazy A were to be honest, something she seemed almost naturally to be incapable of, she'd have to tell Stacy that the real reason everyone called her Crazy A was because she was completely and insanely batshit crazy, and her first name starts with the letter A.

"Well, Crazy A," Stacy said. "I'd ask you how long you've been here, and maybe some other insignificant facts about yourself, solely for the purposes of small talk with a new neighbor, but if you can't even tell me if you live around here or not, I'm not so sure you could answer any other questions."

"Shame about what happened to the woman living here before you," Crazy A said, ignoring Stacy's comment and painting her best joker smile yet on her face. She could see that Stacy was a strong woman, though she'd sized her up at first glance to be anything but, because she was young, petite and pretty. She was going to be a tough nut to crack, Crazy A thought, but she would crack her. Crazy A cracked everyone.

"Yeah," Stacy said. "I got bits and pieces. Something about a bear attack. Seems like there's been a few of them around here."

"Yes," Crazy A said, trying to sound sad, and trying to whip up a crocodile tear or two, but that had never been her strength. That whole sociopathic slash can't feel real emotions thing she had going on kind of got in the way of crying. "Believe it or not," she continued, putting her head down, "my previous husband- I'm remarried now- died the same way."

"Of a bear attack?" Stacy said.

"Yes," Crazy A said, pausing for effect. She'd learned years before that though she couldn't cry, because she was a sociopath, she could pause for effect. "But I've moved on. I'm remarried. To an arborist. And actually, I do live just down the road from you."

"Oh," Stacy said, thinking perhaps the woman just lacked social skills, or had been a nerd since birth. "Which way?"

"Just down there," Crazy A said, pointing to the right as if heading out of Stacy's driveway. "As a matter of fact, I'd better be on my way. The clouds might disperse, and I'd hate to get skin cancer."

"Thanks for stopping by," Stacy said. "You're actually the first neighbor I've met."

"Sure," Crazy A said. "Stop by sometime."

"I will," Stacy said, and then she turned and walked back up the steps of her porch, and she sat back down and stared into the forest surrounding her home, and she thought of how Crazy A just ranked at the top of the strangest people she'd ever met in her life list.

Oh, and she made a mental note to keep an eye out for rabid bears.

***

The first couple of weeks in her new house had flown by for Stacy. No moss, grass, or even anything that might grow faster than moss or grass grew under her feet. In the past two weeks, not only had she gotten all her things unpacked and properly arranged, but she had also won two big court cases, and she celebrated all of it by going out and getting herself that brand new Trek road bike she'd been wanting. Especially, since she now lived out in the country part of the county, and no longer in the city, where cycling was much harder, and not as safe to do.

Stacy had gotten a late start on her Saturday morning bike ride, so when she was almost home, the sun was already up, and it was a typical hot, Virginia summer day. Stacy, when less than a mile away from her new home that we're ignoring the fact about the bank actually owning, she just happened to glance to her right, and up a long driveway and in the front yard a large, beautiful home, she saw Crazy A.

"That couldn't have been her," Stacy said to herself. The woman she'd just seen up in the yard was sunbathing. She was even holding one of those silver, reflective cardboard looking things that reflexes the sunlight back into your face. "I thought she was scared of the sun?"

Stacy turned around and went back and risked being shot by the property owner by biking up the drive. It was an upscale place, but still, it was Virginia.

"Hi there," Stacy said. The woman laying in the sun dropped the reflective panel she held in her hands and stared at Stacy. "It's me. Stacy. The new girl from just down the road."

"I'm sorry," Crazy A said. "Who?"

"Stacy," Stacy said, feeling confused. Had the woman forgotten her already? Was she actually older than her mid-fifties and had just aged well? Was she entering senility? "I just bought the house down the road."

Crazy A lowered one side of her sunglasses and stared hard. "I'm sorry," she said. "I don't remember you."

Stacy said nothing, because she could think of nothing to say. Was this tall, unattractive woman who had gone out of her way to speak like a twelve year old high on drugs? Was she drunk? Was she schizophrenic?

"Nice meeting you though," Crazy A said, putting her shades back on fully and then reclining back and raising her reflective panel in order to soak up the sun. "Have a good day."

Stacy tried to figure out just what the hell was going on on her way back home, but she just figured some people were nuts, and she'd just met another fitting the criteria.

Until that evening.

Stacy was sitting on her new porch participating in her one unhealthy habit. She was binge eating ice cream. She sat in her favorite wicker chair with an entire quart and a half sized container of Eddy's double fudge brownie on her lap. She was eating away, enjoying her nasty pleasure, when a car came up her driveway.

It was Crazy A.

"I'm sorry," Crazy A said, sticking her head out the window. She was rocking the twelve year old girl voice again, speaking in Italics and all. "I thought you said your name was Tracy."

"What?" Stacy said, confused.

"When you came by earlier," Crazy A said, unnecessarily raising her voice, as if attempting to be heard over the car's engine. There was no need. It was a Prius hybrid. You couldn't hear the engine. "I thought when we met that you said your name was Tracy. I was just confused."

"I thought you were scared of the sun," Stacy said, laughing afterward, thinking it must have been an honest mistake- the whole Stacy Tracy thing. "I'm glad to see you were just joking."

"What ever would make you think I was scared of the sun?" Crazy A asked from her car, still speaking unnecessarily loudly, and in Italics, in the voice of a twelve year old girl.

"When you were out walking," Stacy said. "The day you stopped by. You said you only went out when it was overcast, because the sun causes cancer."

"That's *crazy*," Crazy A said.

"Well," Stacy said. "That's what I thought, but I didn't want to say anything.

"Who would say such a thing," Crazy A said. "Only walking because it was overcast? Scared of the sun? I'm sure I said something entirely different, and you're just confused."

And instantly, Stacy *did* feel confused. Had she misheard Crazy A?

"Anyway," Crazy A said, "I'm off. It appears you and I share the same guilty pleasure. And I'm out. I'm off to the store."

"How's that?" Stacy said, confused more.

"Icecream," Crazy A said, pointing at the Eddy's in Stacy's hands. "I am so addicted to ice cream that I actually went out and bought a separate deep freezer for my home, just to store ice cream in. When there's a sale, I'll, honest to God, buy dozens of containers of it, because I eat ice cream, literally, everyday. No idea how I allowed myself to run so low without restocking, but oh well," Crazy A raised her palms to the sky and rolled her eyes. "I told you I was silly. So it happened."

"What's your favorite kind?" Stacy asked.

"Eddy's double fudge brownie," Crazy A said.

"Mine, too," Stacy said, holding up her container.

"I saw that," Crazy A said. "See you next time Stacy, whose name isn't Tracy," and then she giggled like a little girl and put the car in reverse and began backing down the driveway.

"See you next time, Crazy A who isn't really crazy, just silly," Stacy said, waving, feeling much better about the misunderstandings and confusions being cleared up.

Until two weeks later.

When Stacy ran into Crazy A in the grocery store.

***

The last two weeks had flown by as quickly as the two weeks before them had for Stacy, and she found herself at the grocery store, restocking on ice cream herself now, among other things. She was probably going to have a six pack of Northern Lights IPA after the conversation she'd just had with her mother over the phone on the way to the store. When Stacy had mentioned how fast time was flying by, her mother had given her the old "yes, and before you know it, you won't be young and pretty anymore, and no decent looking man will have you, and I'll never have any grandbabies," speech again. Stacy had miraculously driven into a dead zone (at least that's what she said before hanging up on her mother) and felt the urge to drink now, which was rare for her.

"Crazy A," Stacy said, seeing her new neighbor in the beer aisle as she made her way around the corner. "How are you?"

Crazy A stared at Stacy like she'd never seen her before and said nothing. She wasn't pretending to not know her, like before, but it did seem as if she was putting off the vibe of not dignifying Stacy's greeting with a greeting in return.

"I've got mine," Stacy said, reaching into her shopping cart and pulling out her quart and a half container of Eddy's double fudge brownie. "Have you picked yours up yet?"

"Picked up my what?" Crazy A said, monotone.

"Your ice cream," Stacy said, still smiling. "You really are silly."

"We don't eat ice cream," Crazy A said. "I haven't eaten ice cream since I was a child."

"What?" Stacy said, feeling the exact same way she had when Crazy A had acted like she couldn't remember meeting her. And when she said she'd never claimed to be scared of the sun. Was this woman, this Crazy A character suffering from multiple personalities? Or was Stacy, herself, losing her mind. "You said this was your favorite," Stacy said, raising the ice cream higher. "You said you bought a freezer just for ice cream."

"Ice cream," Crazy A began, "and other dairy products, causes very painful kidney stones." She said it so matter of factly, Stacy was truly now doubting her own sanity. "My brother in law," Crazy A continued, "had a kidney stone several years ago, because he was eating too much ice cream, and he went through absolute agony passing it. It made me thank my lucky stars for not having eaten ice cream in forty years, and there's no way I'd start eating it now." And with that, Crazy A pushed her cart along, and went on her way, and left Stacy standing there in the beer aisle, her ice cream in hand and her shopping cart half filled.

Stacy put her ice cream back in her cart and decided on a twelve pack instead of a six pack. As she was hefting the box of beer out of the cooler and putting it into her cart, an older woman approached her and said hello.

"Hi," Stacy said, turning to make eye contact with the woman.

"I just saw all that," the woman said. She appeared to be in her seventies, yet still very attractive. She was wearing rubber gloves. The type dentists wear. When the woman noticed Stacy staring at her hands, she spoke again. "Look," she said. "I have OCD. I'm kind of a germaphobe. But I know it, and I get help. Not everyone who knows they're sick does, and I'm afraid you just dealt with one of the sickest people you could ever meet in your life."

"You mean Crazy A?" Stacy said.

"Yes," the older woman said. "Completely insane, batshit Crazy A."

Stacy was not a gossiper, but she didn't tell this woman as much, because she wanted to hear what she had to say.

"I don't like to talk about others behind their back," the older woman said when she spoke again, "but I feel it's my duty to tell you about Crazy A."

***

They say that in life, things happen in threes. Obviously, much is the same for marginally average written short stories, because two weeks later, (this being the third two weeks long period to pass in this story in a row between Stacy and Crazy A's meetings), here came Crazy A, running frantically up Stacy's driveway, screaming something incoherent, as Stacy sat on her porch, eating ice cream, because she loved it so much, and drinking beer, because she'd just gotten off of the phone with her mother. She figured she'd blow out all the excessive carbs and calories on tomorrow morning's bike ride.

And Stacy was ready for Crazy A and her bullshit this time!

The old woman that Stacy had met in the grocery store two weeks before, when Crazy A had denied ever eating ice cream, even though, just two weeks before that she'd claimed to have gone out and bought a deep freezer exclusively for ice cream, had been Crazy A's previous neighbor some time ago. The woman had lived across the road from Crazy A and her then husband, a man everyone referred to as Jittery J, back before Jittery J was mauled to death by a bear. Or at least that's how the *official* story went; that Jittery J had been mauled to death by a *bear*.

The old lady had invited Stacy to her home for a beer, and over more than just one, the old lady gave Stacy the skinny on Crazy A.

"It's called gaslighting," the old woman said, when she began explaining Crazy A's personality disorder.

To Stacy's understanding, from what the old lady told her, gaslighters are people who *do* have a personality disorder, known as gaslighting, and they *are* very much aware of it, but they choose to do nothing about it, because it's really an outward behavior induced by other disorders, mostly narcissism based on deep rooted insecurity and an antisocial personality disorder.

Gaslighters are knowingly manipulative. They will intentionally switch their stories around on you each time they see you, or, as Crazy A had done with Stacy, act as if they had no recollection of having said what they had said in the first place, which is basically the same thing. Many gaslighters will act like an event occurred that never did. They'll passive aggressively insult someone, and when called out for it, say it wasn't what was meant, and act hurt, because the person took it the wrong way, however, the other person took it exactly how they meant it.

Gaslighters are the kings and queens of lies of omission. They'll intentionally lead their listener down a certain path when telling a story of an event that occurred, get them thinking they see how things are going to go, or how things went, and then stop, knowing that the path veered, but they do not want their listener, albeit, their victim, to know the facts. And then, if ever called out on having misled their listener, when and if they find out the path veered, and what really happened, they always shrug, eyes wide and the palms of their hands up, and say, "I never told you that. That's what you chose to believe."

Some gaslighters will go as far as to claim to see things that aren't even there, all in order to get their victim, who obviously cannot see what they claim to be there, because it isn't there, to question their own sanity.

"It's all done to gain the power of control over someone," the old lady had told Stacy.

"Why would some random woman down the road," Stacy asked, "a neighbor at that, want to control me?"

"Because she has no control anywhere else in her life," the old woman had informed her. She explained how Crazy A was born into money, and instead of going out and doing anything meaningful with her life, she had done the bare minimum to keep Mommy and Daddy happy, so as not to get cut off. "She became part of the idle wealthy," as the woman put it. "And she simply has nothing better to do than go around gaslighting people. It's like a hobby. Or used to be, anyway. Sadly, it's become her way of life. She actually gets her rocks off from doing it."

The woman explained how so many of their other neighbors had had to learn the hard way, but most had gotten word from the others before they got too deep into thinking they were losing their minds at the hands of Crazy A's manipulation. Crazy A had actually moved just miles down the road, in the past, the old woman further informed Stacy, simply to have new neighbors she could gaslight, because her existing neighbors had figured her out and there was simply no more gaslighting excitement in her life.

"You're telling me this woman has moved, only miles away from her existing, perfectly good house, just to have new neighbors to gaslight?" Stacy said, knowing she'd heard some crazy shit in the courtroom before, but rarely, anything this crazy.

"Honey," the older woman said to Stacy. "Do you have any idea why everyone calls her Crazy A?"

"She told me it was because she was silly," Stacy said, "but I obviously know differently now."

"Yes," the old woman said. "It's because the truth is, the woman is completely and insanely batshit crazy, and her name starts with the letter A."

"Does anyone know what her real name is?" Stacy asked.

"Oh," the old woman said, in a voice sounding as if she was trying to remember something from long ago. "We used to. But we forgot."

The old woman went on to explain that there is only one way to deal with a gaslighter. You had to cut them off immediately by calling them out on their bullshit. The best way of doing it was to laugh, obnoxiously and loudly, at their next attempt of gaslighting and flat out tell them that you do not believe them. Burst their facade forcefully and immediately.

Further, the old woman explained, you must then insult them. Tell them you know they're full of shit, and that you've known they were full of shit the whole time and that you were simply trying to be friendly, but that you're not going to buy their shit anymore. Tell them that you know the truth. They're liars, they're losers who've never accomplished anything, hence the deep rooted insecurities that led to the gaslighting, and no matter what, under no circumstances- no matter how badly doing this to someone else makes you feel- you do *not* go back at a later date and apologize to the gaslighter. Gaslighters don't want help and they never stop gaslighting. It's the only way to a sense of power or authority that they have access to, and they will view any apology as a weakness, and they will use it as a door to get back into your life and your head and start gaslighting again.

"Wow," Stacy said after hearing the solution to her problem with Crazy A. "It sounds like gaslighters live lonely lives."

"They do," the old woman said. "But that's their preference. That's where that whole antisocial personality part comes in. Honestly, they hate most other people and have no use for them unless it's for personal gain. But they know this sort of attitude is not accepted in society, so they fake it. They act kind. They play nice. They come across as friendly. But underneath, they're planning their psychological attack on you. Gaslighters are some of the sickest mother fuckers you'll ever meet in your life, and I consider myself a lady, and I can't remember that last time I used that term, mother fucker."

"Wow!" Stacy said. Her mind had been blown.

But the talk had prepared Stacy, and she was ready, so as Crazy A came at her, running up the driveway, screaming something about something, Stacy stood to her feet, and...

...she started laughing.

Hysterically.

"Nice, try," Stacy said. "But I'm not buying it, you lying bitch."

"Help me," Crazy A said. "We have to get inside. We're going to be killed. We have to get inside."

Crazy A reached the foot of the steps leading up the porch, but Stacy had raced down them, and she confronted Crazy A face to face at the bottom of the steps. "You are not welcome in my house, or on my property, anymore, for that matter," Stacy said. "You are a lying, manipulative gaslighting bitch, and I'm calling you out." And then she laughed again for good measure.

"There's a fucking Bigfoot Sasquatch in the woods by the side of the road," Crazy A said, putting on the best act, as Stacy saw it, anyone could. Hell, if Crazy A had applied herself in life, Stacy thought, she could have been an actress. She really did seem terrified. Stacy, for just a second, thought there might be a Bigfoot Sasquatch in the woods. "We have to get in the fucking house, now!"

"Likely story," Stacy said, smiling, and still laughing. "Look, you lying sack of crap," she continued. "I know all about you. I talked with one of your old neighbors. I know who and what you are."

"We are going to be killed," Crazy A screamed. "Look!" she turned and pointed. "There's a fucking Bigfoot Sasquatch coming up your fucking driveway to kill us!"

"I'm not even going to dignify that bullshit story by turning my head to look anywhere in that direction," Stacy said, proud of herself to be acting on the advice Crazy A's old neighbor had given her. And she didn't even try to sneak a glance at the driveway. "Leave, and do *not* come back."

Stacy turned and began walking up her porch steps. Crazy A grabbed her by the back of the shoulder and tried to go with her.

Bam!

Stacy turned and punched Crazy A so hard on the chin, an upper-cut (it had to be, because Crazy A was so much taller than Stacy), and it knocked Crazy A flat on her back.

"You touched me first, bitch! I'm a lawyer, and I know the rules, so try to sue me," is all that Stacy said before continuing in the house and slamming and locking the door.

***

Just as Stacy was opening her door to go to work the next morning, she was met on the other side of the door by Burt Reynolds, a local lawman.

"Shit," Stacy said. She knew Burt, from work, and wasn't shy to be herself in front of him. "That bitch is actually going to try to sue me? She touched me first?"

"What bitch, Stacy?" Burt asked.

"Crazy A."

"Crazy A can't sue you," Burt said.

"I know, right?" Stacy said. "She touched me first."

"Stacy," Burt said. "Crazy A is dead."

"What?" Stacy said. "What happened?"

"Not sure yet," he said, trying not to let it show that he was afraid he may know a little too much. A little more than he could say without getting locked up in the nuthouse. "A jogger reported the body this morning just after daybreak. Saw her body strung out in the woods about twenty feet off the road. Just down here below your driveway. I was just coming up to ask you if you saw or heard anything strange yesterday evening, just before dark."

"She was here," Stacy said, now feeling like a real piece of shit for treating Crazy A the way she had. "She was frantic. She said something was chasing her."

"Why didn't you let her inside?" Burt asked.

"I didn't believe her," Stacy said. "I'd caught her up in a ton of lies, and I was actually breaking off our brief friendship." Stacy paused, looking down. "Burt, I had recently determined that the woman was completely and insanely batshit crazy, and having any sort of relationship with her was unhealthy, and I honest to God thought she was making up the whole being chased thing in order to weasel her way back into my life. Crazy people do that shit."

"Oh, I know," Burt said, agreeing. "I see some of the craziest stuff in law enforcement." Burt paused. And then he said, "Stacy? You got any idea what she said was chasing her?"

Stacy looked at Burt. Their eyes locked, and she felt as if he was reading her mind, but she also felt that if she told the truth, she'd be the one locked up in the nuthouse.

"A bear," she said, when she finally spoke. "I believe I remember her saying she'd seen a bear."

"A bear," Burt said, looking down, his hopes of Stacy being honest shattered. He might not have believed her had she been, but he could tell she was lying now. "Are you sure it wasn't something else?" He asked, looking up at her again.

"No," she said. "It was a bear."

"Thanks, Stacy," Burt said. "See you in court for that D.U.I. case you're defending this afternoon."

Burt walked down the porch steps and then down the driveway. His cruiser was still at the scene below, along with the other cruisers and an ambulance that should have been a hearse.

"Another fucking bear," Burt said to himself, feeling as if someday, he would eventually get to the truth.

But one thing was for sure.

Crazy A was no more.

She'd had a very unfortunate demise.

The End

4

Here's The Bigfoot Sasquatch Story You'll Never Hear Me Tell On YouTube

Some people get it, and some people don't. I'll never understand why so many people suffer from black and white thinking. It's got to be this, or it's got to be that, and there's absolutely *no* room for a gray area in the middle. At least that's what *they* think.

These black and white thinkers can be broken down into subcategories, too. There are too many to mention, but the ones that stand out on our YouTube channel are the ones who think that if you make one humorous video on your

YouTube channel, perhaps one with a giant spider (named, by the way, Ginormica Enormica, because it is both ginormous and enormous), then there is absolutely *no way* that any of your other videos were real, or that you were being serious in them, and there's even an old Roman expression, they'll tell you, which states that once you're caught in a falsehood once, you are to never be taken seriously or trusted again.

And then, there is the subcategory of black and white thinkers who believe that if you are unwilling to pick a side- either with those *do* definitely believe in Bigfoot Sasquatch, or with those who definitely do *not* believe in Bigfoot Sasquatch- then you are obviously making fun of one of the two sides, if not both. This whole idea of thinking that maybe, just maybe, some huge, two legged creature which no one has ever provided hardcore proof of existing might or might not exist, is ludicrous, these people think. How dare you not take sides, they scream. This is America (at least where I am, and thank you to our international readers and viewers for being here, we know there are many of you), and by God we pick sides here in America so we can agree with our sidemates and hate the people on the other side. That's what America is all about!

But then there's the truth.

Potentially.

Some of the behind the scenes stuff that you don't see on camera, because it is intentionally left out.

For protection.

And not just for the safety of me and my beautiful family, but potentially, for…

…him, her, it or they.

***

By the second half of 2019 we were getting close. I mean, really, really close. As close as what appeared to be about forty yards away in one of our videos.

Close to what? You ask?

Potentially, him, her, it or they, of course.

We'd captured several oddities in several of our videos recently that simply could not be explained. Months and months of refining my own, unique Bigfoot Sasquatch researching methods were appearing to pay off. All those construction paper cutouts. Strapping gopro cameras to my head. The fake hillbilly teeth and the miles upon endless miles of hiking and recording footage in the beautiful Blue Ridge Mountains of Virginia, sometimes in below freezing temperatures during winter, and sometimes with the heat index over one hundred in the summer. It was all culminating to the point of what may or may not be living in the woods behind my home allowing us to get closer.

Potentially.

Him, her, it or they were getting closer to us.

Potentially.

And then, in late October, just one week before Halloween, we may or may not have filmed, arguably, *the best* Bigfoot Sasquatch footage that currently exists on the internet!

Potentially.

And that's when it happened.

I do not JADE, though I have a very long history of doing so. JADE is when we 'justify, argue, defend, or explain' our points, our actions, our decisions to someone, either because we feel the need to do so, or because they *demand* we do so, and for some reason we cave to their demands and just start JADE'ing away.

Guilt and shame are two of the most useless emotions human beings can have. Sure, there's remorse- honestly being sorry for your words or actions- and remorse is good, especially when you combine some amends or even restitution with it if possible and if necessary. But after that, it's time to move onward and upward. It's called the healing process. To sit around and stew in guilt and shame is counterproductive. It is the opposite of healing, and it is futile.

And anyone who thinks that's where you should be? By continuously asking you to JADE?

Does not belong in your life.

No matter who they are!

Period.

No potentially about it.

What does this psychobabble have to do with Bigfoot Sasquatch? And this story?

A lot!

So, when you work in social media, especially around this topic, you often get two types of people or groups that JADE you, some of them even crossing lines most sane people would not cross. These groups or individuals want to either come out and confirm what you may or may not have found, or they want to come out and debunk you. The end goal of these groups or individuals, whichever their goal is, is basically rooted in the same reason.

They want to get the credit for your work if you were right.

Or they want to get famous for debunking your work if you were wrong.

Self centered egomaniacs who see you as opportunity, either way.

After publishing the video from October of 2019, where we may or may not have actually filmed him, her, it or they, I began getting even more emails and messages on our YouTube channel, Homesteading Off The Grid, by way of the comment section from these sorts of groups and individuals, and there was one group in particular, who will not be named, because I would never want to give them any free advertising, who thought their name and their popularity in the Bigfoot Sasquatch community would guarantee me returning their messages and actually meeting up with them, here, at my family's home, and that I would willingly take them on a personal tour and show them, exactly, where the potential lair of Bigfoot Sasquatch was.

Wrong!

Not to JADE, nay, *NEVER* to JADE, but I get completely dumbfounded by the number of people who don't stop to consider, for even a moment, that our homestead, this beautiful property that may appear to be a stage of our YouTube channel, is not a stage, but an actual, bonafide home.

Our home!

Who, in their right mind, watches someone on YouTube, a complete stranger who they never have, nor would probably never meet, and contact them and ask if they can come meet with them?

Nutcases!

That's who!

And we get it all the time. People who want to come camping on our property. People who want to go Bigfoot Sasquatch hunting with us. Oh, it would make your skin crawl if you saw all the messages we get in this regard. Most of them get held in the 'potentially inappropriate' filter on YouTube, so I'm able to ban the nutcases and their messages never appear on the channel publicly.

So, anyway, this particular group, who thought they were *somebody*, obviously didn't take a liking to me not returning their emails and replying to their comments.

So they actually freaking started coming by!

I shit you not!

These people had the audacity to contact me, after I'd never returned any of their messages, and told me that I might have the right to ignore them and keep them off of *my* property, but they by God had the right to contact people who lived around me and ask permission to go on *their* properties. They let me know that they knew all about the annoying neighbor I'd run off with a crayon, and that they were sure he wouldn't mind them actually setting up camp on his mommy and daddy's property so they could pull surveillance on mine.

Further, they let me know that they'd be watching, soon, and that when I took off to go back to the potential lair of Bigfoot Sasquatch, they'd be following, and whether I liked it or not, I would lead them right to him, her, it, or they, and they would forever be remembered as being the group who could provide undeniable proof of the existence of him, her, it, or they.

Or that they were going to destroy my career!

***

It's not hard to tell when someone's casing your house. Especially when you live out in the middle of nowhere, like we do, and especially after you've lived there long enough to be familiar with pretty much any vehicle that passes by your house on any sort of regular basis, like we have. Sure, we get plenty of touristy types passing through, especially in the fall, people who are driving around aimlessly, looking at the leaves, because it's simply so beautiful out here in the fall, but there's nothing much touristy about jacked up four wheel drive Jeeps and trucks with giant satellite dishes and dogs in the back of them.

So the first one I noticed was a Jeep with two guys, driving by my house one late morning, just before noon. The vehicle stuck out like a sore thumb, due to what appeared to be a giant satellite dish in the back. "Look at that Jeep," I said to my beautiful bride, Dearly, a.k.a. 'Giggly Girl,' as it passed by the first time. "I bet those are those Bigfoot Sasquatch people from that one group I'll never name and give free advertising to."

She just giggled and called me crazy.

But I didn't seem so crazy when I saw them going back the other way about ten minutes later. She wasn't giggling anymore, either. Because she wasn't there. She'd gone in the house. But had she been out there, she would have giggled, because that's what she does. She giggles, just like Jittery J used to jitter before having his unfortunate demise in volume 1 of this series.

Over the next few days, I would see several four wheel drive trucks, not muddy, quite clean on the contrary, and they seemed to be loaded down with camping gear and equipment. None of these people ever tried to approach me, and I'm sure it's because they knew they'd get a big fat no if they asked to come on my land or for me to guide them to the lair.

After about a week or so, I was convinced I was paranoid, and that it had to be ludicrous to think that any of these people driving around my place, back and forth, all day it seemed, had anything to do with the messages I'd received from the group I'll not name. Who the hell did I think *I* was? I'm not that important. Sure, we've got a pretty hefty loyal following of folks on our YouTube channel, but would this organization actually mobilize and deploy units to my central Virginia homestead? Besides, it *is* hunting season that time of year, and I was probably just seeing the vehicles of people who live outside of our area who'd come here to hunt.

Nine days after I'd originally captured the footage I may or may not have captured on the video I recorded at the end of October, I decided I'd head back up into the potential Bigfoot Sasquatch lair and see if I could have a repeat performance. I hadn't seen the guys in trucks for a few days, so I figured I'd waited them out and they'd gone back to wherever they'd come from. Or, they had been hunters, and they'd bagged their limit, and they were back in their cubicles at work lying to their coworkers about how big the deer they'd gotten the week before was. Hey, I used to hunt deer, and I'd turned many of little spikes into raging twelve pointers the size of moose back in my days of lying about deer hunting.

There are many ways to enter the area I refer to as the potential lair of Bigfoot Sasquatch, and I wasn't in the mood to walk forever that day, because I'd run a 5k road race that morning, my first road race in roughly fifteen years, and I was already tired, and I was in a foul mood after having been beaten in the race by so many women in their sixties and 20 year old college girls. I used to be a pretty good runner, and I was always racing, and I have no idea how all of a sudden, after having been away from the sport for so long, all these older ladies and young girls got so damn fast, but they have.

Anyway, I really stretched that video out. I think it was thirty minutes long. It wasn't intentional. I'd taken some pepperoni and fried chicken with me, and I was really just letting off steam in regard to my disappointment about the race, and I couldn't see any large, dark objects moving on the screen behind my back, where my six o'clock is, but I knew the video had gone on too long, so I wrapped it up and headed back out of the lair. I'd driven to one of the few places you could park at the foot of the mountain, and I'll be damned if when I got down there, I didn't see that funky looking Jeep and a couple of the four wheel drive trucks that had been passing by my house nearly two weeks before.

Some of the vehicles had people in them and some didn't. I assumed they had people out in the woods trying to see where I was, and others were watching from the vehicles to see which direction I'd exit the woods from, so they'd get a better sense of where the lair might be.

It took some time and some stealth, but I actually walked away from the parking area and went down the road, hidden in the woods, quite a way, and then I cross the road and came back up through the woods, so that when I exited the woods, I did so from the opposite side of the road I'd actually been on. It worked, as when I got in my vehicle, and I watched what these people were doing by the use of my mirrors, I could see that they weren't wasting any time in jumping out of their vehicles and gearing up and heading up into the woods I'd just exited.

Again, I might have just been paranoid, but I was convinced that I was being watched by a group of Bigfoot Sasquatch hunters, and the last thing I was going to do was lead them straight to where I may or may not have captured one of these creatures on video.

So I did not return to the potential lair of Bigfoot Sasquatch for months!

And I devised a plan.

Over the next few months, I nearly completely lost any credibility I may have built up in the Bigfoot Sasquatch community (and yes, I know that sounds like an oxymoron, and I love it, but it doesn't mean I'm making fun of anyone, damn it!) by making some of the most insane, asinine, and yes, fake videos that anyone could imagine making. Come on, if you're reading this, I know you probably watch my videos on Homesteading Off The Grid, on YouTube, so you know *exactly* which videos I'm talking about. You saw them. They were so obviously fake.

And I regret none of it.

Not only have I never set out to find Bigfoot Sasquatch for fame and glory, I never set out to find him, her, it, or they in the first place. If you've made it to volume three in this soon to be 100 volume series (well, maybe not so soon), then you know from the story I told in volume 1, we never asked for this nightmare. We were simply making videos about corn and green beans, and some really strange things were going on around our homestead, and sometimes, we'd unintentionally capture it on video.

With this said, there is one thing that I *am* definitely all about, and that is keeping these beautiful creatures, if they do indeed exist, and if they are what is actually coming around here and causing strange things to happen on our property, completely hidden. I don't need proof, and I know that at the hands of proof comes lots of destruction.

And dissection!

I can only imagine the damage that the Government and the scientific community would dish out on any population of any previously undiscovered species that resembles mankind to such a great degree. I'm sure it would all be done in the name of potentially finding a cure for cancer or Covid-19 or whatever, but these beautiful creatures would suffer, and I never liked the idea of lab test animals, and this is exactly what he, she, it or they would become.

Now, were the videos I made during this several months long period entertaining? Of course. Were they fun to make? Absolutely. And did I care about losing credibility? Not at all. I never knew I had any in the first place. Come on, this is cryptozoology, not biology. We're pseudoscientists, people.

But I do take great pride in knowing that I waited out those folks from that group that will not be named here. They all of a sudden, around the end of December, just before Christmas, stopped coming around. I never saw that Jeep with the satellite dish in the back and all those jacked up four wheel drive trucks again.

And I began, very erratically and over very dispersed time periods, going back into the potential lair of Bigfoot Sasquatch.

And most times, I never take my camera.

Oh, the things I see on those trips.

But who would believe me now? After destroying any credibility I might have once had?

So I'll just keep those moments where they belong.

Between me and him, her, it or they.

The End

The Tale Of The Bladeless Riding Lawn Mower Thieving Bladeless Riding Lawn Mower Riding Bigfoot Sasquatch!

I never thought that if I lived to be one hundred that I would come to believe there can be times when writer's block does not suck, but I am now a convinced man, because this story will detail, exactly, how if I had not been suffering from writer's block on one super hot summer day in Virginia, none of us would have ever gotten to hear the tale of the bladeless riding lawn mower thieving bladeless riding lawn mower riding bigfoot sasquatch!

Mark Twain put it best, the way he told the story in his book 'Roughing It.' You know the one. If you don't, you should read it. It was about his experiences when he went out west to try to get rich during the silver rush. In it, he details the time he got a job as an editor for a newspaper. At first, he loved it, because editor is a pretty important position. Editors are important people. They're much like college professors, in that they know all there is to know in their respective fields, in this case, the editor's field being writing, but for some reason, just like college professors and their respective fields, with all their knowledge on the subject, they're not any good at it.

But the point I'm trying to make here, a point that Twain made better than anyone else could, is in regard to content. Story. And the sheer amount of it.

Twain spoke of how you could be a really great writer, and write one really great book, and never have to work again and be remembered forever. J.D. Salinger, author of "Catcher in the Rye" comes to mind here. Salinger wrote one book in his life, and it just happened to be one of the best books ever written (be sure to read that one, too, if you haven't), and BAM! Just like that, he was done.

But an editor? Man, you have to come up with an editorial piece every single day. Twain, and he might have been exaggerating when he said this, and he might have just been trying to draw out the length of his story to make sure it was full length novel length (that's forty thousand words or more, by the way), because that 'ol rascal was known to do such things, but he said, that if you think about it, if a man or a woman were to be an editor of a paper for a full thirty year career span, they probably, over that period of thirty years, write enough words to fill a library.

And I believe him.

And he didn't last long as an editor. But fortunately for those of us who love a good story, well told, we remember that 'ol rascal.

So what does this have to do with writer's block? And the tale of the bladeless riding lawn mower thieving bladeless riding lawn mower riding bigfoot sasquatch? Well, I'm getting there, but I gotta tell it in order, and no, I'm not pulling a Mark Twain on you.

Potentially.

So, I'm no editor for any newspaper, though I used to work for several, but I am what you might call a modern day jack of all trades kind of guy when it comes to writing. I write books, like this one, a series of short story collections, and I write full length novels. Off and on, throughout the years, I've been a journalist, I've been a blogger, and I also have my YouTube channel which is really like writing in video form. I don't write any scripts for the channel, though many vertically challenged individuals who live under bridges often comment on the videos, stating that they appear to be scripted (I think they may be trying to compliment me, because the video came off so well it had to be planned out by professionals, but I'm not sure), but they're not.

So I was up in this super hot room where I write, on a super hot day in July, staring at the laptop, and not a single word would come to me. I'd been working on the next Bigfoot Sasquatch Files collection, the one you're reading now, as well as what I honestly believe will be remembered as my masterpiece, long after I'm gone. It's a collection of thirty one short stories, three thousand to six thousand words long each, like the stories in the Bigfoot Sasquatch Files series, and it's for the Halloween season, as all of the stories are paranormal, supernatural, and all around creepy in nature.

I'd been writing up to five thousand words a day (that's the equivalent of roughly twenty five pages in a book), and I was burned the hell out.

So I went fishing.

I've learned that when the words won't come, they just aren't going to come, and you just can't force them. You'll end up writing a bunch of crap that no one will like. This can be said with any form of work. If your heart's not in it, people can tell.

My beautiful bride Dearly, a.k.a. Giggly Girl and our son, Daniel, were off on a playdate with Daniel's best friend and his best friend's mother, so I didn't have my family here to go fishing with me, but I went anyway, something I rarely do. I just viewed it as if I'd be having a *me* day, something I do even more rarely.

It was ninety five degrees outside, with a heat index of one hundred, so I let the truck's air conditioner cool the cab down a bit before I actually jumped in and took off. I knew it was too hot to fish, and I didn't expect to catch anything, but a bad day fishing is always better than a good day at work, hell, even if the words *are* coming, so I went anyway, as soon as the truck's cab cooled down.

I got to one of my favorite spots on the Rivanna River in Charlottesville, but the air conditioning in the truck felt so good, and the outside temps were still so high, that I decided I didn't want to get out of the truck just yet so I just kept going. The next thing I know, I was in Scottsville, down in the southern part of Albemarle county, now riding along the banks of the James River, and it was still so damn hot, I didn't want to get out, so I just kept going, still.

I entered into Buckingham County, which is the geographic center of the state of Virginia, and I thought, well, I guess I am literally in the middle of nowhere now, and the temperature had dropped to ninety, so I decided I'd wet a line (that means go fishing for those of you reading this who are not from the south). I found a public boat loading area on the James and parked in the parking lot. I took my rod and tackle and my can of worms upstream, around the bend, so as not to interfere with or be disturbed by any boaters. I found a huge sycamore tree (those are the largest trees east of the Mississippi River, by the way), that provided plenty of shade, so I set up shop and started fishing.

"You done beat me to it," I heard a voice say, downstream from me, about ten minutes after I'd cast my line and sat down on one of the giant Sycamore roots protruding through the sandy bank and started sweating profusely. I looked downstream, and about twenty yards away was an older black gentleman coming my way with four rods and a chair and a can of worms in his hands. Once upon a time I would have referred to him as an old gentleman, because he was about sixty years old, but since I'm almost fifty, I've started using the term older instead of old, and I hope others will pay me the same respect.

"There's enough shade under this big ol' sycamore for both of us," I said.

"I reckon there is," he said. If you're not from the south, "reckon" means think."

He came under the tree with me and introduced himself as Michael. I told him my name, and then he went up about fifteen yards away from me and wet all four of his lines, then he sat back in that folding chair he'd brought with him and started sweating profusely. "Too danged hot to be a fishin' today," he said, and I agreed with him, and we both just kept on fishing.

Michael and I talked off and on for a bit. It was so damned hot it was even too hot to talk for too long. Every now and then, we'd see a catfish drifting by, riding the current, and they'd look over at our baited hooks, and we could tell they really wanted to go over there and eat those worms, but you see, fish are cold blooded animals, which means their body temperatures are whatever the temperature of their surroundings are, and as hungry as those catfish were, and as good as they thought our worms looked, it was just too damned hot for them to make the effort of swimming over there to eat the worms. And it's a damn shame, because some of them were among the biggest catfish I'd ever seen!

I guess those catfish just kept on riding that current, not putting forth any effort, and they probably made it down close to Richmond before the water temperatures cooled down enough to where they could swim without being miserable at night.

"You think those things spend all night swimming back up stream just to get home after drifting all the way down to Richmond during the day?" I asked Michael, since we'd gotten to talking about it and all. "And then just float all the way back down to Richmond the next day?"

"I reckon they do," Michael said. "In this heat. L'awd knows it's too damn hot to fish on a day like this." I agreed with him again and we both kept fishing.

As the hours passed, and man, do they pass slowly during the heat of these Virginia summers, the temperatures actually began to drop noticeably. The sun went back behind the horizon, we began sweating less profusely, and I could have sworn, some of those giant catfish started actually flapping their fins on one side, in hopes of making it over to our worms on hooks. We were able to start talking a little more, without getting worn out from the heat, and when Michael asked me what kind of work I did (he was a retired clerk from the post office, by the way), I told him. I explained just how much I write, and how I'd been writing up to five thousand words a day, and that I was suffering from writer's block so badly, I knew there was no way I could sit down and pump out a story that would be any good, nothing anyone would want to read, so even though it was hotter than hell's unairconditioned outhouse I decided to go fishing.

"What you trying to write about?" Michael asked.

"Bigfoot Sasquatch," I said, and man, did he start laughing so hard, he didn't *almost* fall out of his chair, he *did* fall out of his chair. I jumped up and went over to help him up, worried it might be heat related, or age related, because he wasn't old yet (wink, wink), but he *was* older. By the time I got to him, he'd gotten back up and got back in his chair, but he thanked me for my concern nonetheless and we both agreed we wished some of those giant catfish in the James River there, floating down to Richmond would make a similar effort for our worms.

"I wadn't laughin' at you," Michael said. "It's just that I've only heard one other person in my life refer to it as Bigfoot Sasquatch, rather than either or, and it's been years since I've heard it."

"Who else used to call it (or him, or her, or they) Bigfoot Sasquatch?" I asked, intrigued.

"Oh," Michael began, looking down at his feet, recalling a memory. "Just some crazy ol' white man."

"How is it that you know of this crazy 'ol white man?" I asked. "It wouldn't be by way of YouTube, would it?"

"What?" Michael said, looking over at me now.

"YouTube," I said. "Do you watch this crazy 'ol white man on YouTube?"

"Naw," he said, looking back down at his feet. "I don't do that internet stuff. D'rather be fishing. Even on days like this, when it's too hot to fish." I agreed with him and we both kept fishing, and then he said, "back when I was a boy. Here in Buckingham County. Used to be this crazy ol' white guy, probably the age I am now, he was known for going on and on about a Bigfoot Sasquatch stealing his bladeless riding lawn mower and running off with it."

"What?" I said. "You've got to be kidding me."

"I kid you not," he said. "And the strangest thing is?" He took a pause for effect, which I've been told I'm really good at doing on my YouTube channel by those vertically challenged individuals who live under bridges who say my videos appear to be scripted, and then he said, "I believe him, because me and a buddy was there the night it happened, and we saw it."

"You've got to be kidding me," I said.

"I done told ya I wasn't a kiddin' ya," he said. "And I don't know what exactly it was that I saw, but I know I saw something."

"You've got to give me details," I said.

"Well," he said. "If'n these here temperatures drop about two more degrees, I might be able to tell it without putting myself out too much. It's just too hot to talk for long today, and it's definitely too hot to fish." I agreed with him, and we kept fishing, and we picked a log that was out in the river, about twenty yards away from the bank we were sitting on and about ten feet further away than any of those ginormous catfish that were drifting by us, riding the currents downstream where they'd just have to start swimming back upstream to make it home in the middle of the night once the temperatures dropped. We agreed that once the first catfish made it over to that log, enroute to our worm baited hooks, which were about ten yards on the other side of that log, Michael would tell me the tale of the bladeless lawn mower thieving bladeless lawn mower riding bigfoot sasquatch.

Now here's where things take a turn for the weird. This was only supposed to be a story about a *story* about a bigfoot sasquatch, but as we were sitting there waiting for the temperatures to drop, Michael and I both kept getting glimpses of what appeared to be a large, bipedal creature on the other side of the James River, and if that was, indeed, what we were seeing, then this would no longer be a story about a story about Bigfoot Sasquatch, but that would actually make this a bonafide Bigfoot Sasquatch story itself.

Potentially.

"So when I was about thirteen," Michael bagan. I guess he'd seen one of those humongous catfish drifting down to Richmond reach the log, which, technically, meant that lucky fish might have ended up only floating down to Scottsville before he'd start swimming for home around midnight, when the water temperatures dropped enough for him to make an effort without putting himself out too much. "That's when it happened. And again, I ain't gonna put my hand on no Bible that it was a Bigfoot Sasquatch, but my buddy and me done seen something."

"There was this crazy ol' white guy," Michael said. "I think his name was Roy. I can't remember, exactly, but I believe it was Roy."

"Sounds about right," I said, and Michael asked me what *that* meant, because I wasn't there, and I told him when I was a kid I knew an older (not old) white guy whose name was Roy, and he was lunatic. Michael saw my point, and he continued his story.

"So this crazy 'ol white guy, whose name I think was Roy," Michael said, "everywhere he went, he went on a riding lawn mower that didn't have a blade on it."

"Why didn't it have a blade on it?" I asked.

"Cause it was his primary form of transportation," Michael said. "It was like his car. He didn't use it to actually mow grass."

"Why didn't he just have a car?" I asked.

"Story I got," Michael said, "was that he'd had about twenty drinking and driving convictions and had lost his license for life."

"How the hell was he not in jail?" I asked.

"This was back in the late sixties," Michael said. "Hell, most people had a pile of D.U.I.'s back then. You just paid a fine and went on. It wasn't until the eighties when all these congressmen and senators' kids started getting killed by drunk drivers that they really started laying the hammer down."

"Oh," I said, thankful for the brief history lesson on drunk driving laws."

"So anyways," Michael continued, "You'd just see crazy 'ol Roy. Can we agree on his name being Roy? Just for this story?"

"Sure," I said. "I've already told you I knew an older white guy named Roy, and he was a complete nutcase, so it's fitting."

"So you'd see crazy 'ol Roy," Michael continued, "just ridin' that bladeless riding lawn mower everywhere. It wasn't really a town. You know we have the town of Dillwyn down here in Buckingham County, and even that ain't much of a town, but way out in the county where I growed up, we didn't even have anything like Dillwyn. We were pretty much a wide spot in the road with a gas station on one end of the wide spot and a tasty freeze on the other."

"I get ya," I said, and I told him I was from Appalachiastan, so I knew. He asked me where the hell Appalachiastan was, and I told him my part of it was West "By God" Virginia, and he asked me why I called it Appalachiastan, because it made it sound like a third world country. I asked him if he'd ever been there, and he said no, and I told him that if he had, he'd understand. He said, "so you're saying it's like a third world country over there?" and I said, "In many ways, yes," and he said, "so it's fitting," and I said yes.

"So you'd see crazy 'ol Roy," he continued, "riding down to the gas station mostly to buy his beer every day. He only got gas once a month, cause that mower got real good fuel mileage, see. And you'd usually see him going to the gas station late morning, just after he woke up with a hangover. And you'd see him driving down to the Tasty Freeze just before sundown, no matter what time of year it was. If it was winter, he'd ride down there and get his dinner around four thirty, and if it was summer, he'd ride down there and get his dinner around eight thirty. Hell, I don't reckon the 'ol boy even had a watch or a clock in that mobile home of his he lived in back by the ballpark."

"Now wait a minute," I said to Michael, interrupting him. "You were saying earlier that this little wide spot in the road of yours only had a gas station and a Tasty Freeze. Now you're telling me it had a ballpark, too?"

"Oh, that's just what we called it," Michael said. "It really wasn't nothing but a wide spot off the side of the road of the wide spot along the road that made up our town. And it's where we kids would go play ball, or just sit around and hang out, so we just always called it the ballpark."

"I get it," I said, and I did, so it was most definitely fitting.

"So crazy 'ol Roy," Michael continued, "he had him a mobile home set up back behind the ballpark, just there at the edge of the woods."

"Uh, huh," I said, following.

"And most nights, and it didn't matter what time of year it was, he'd sit out there with his beer, I think he drank Stroh's. You ever heard of that?"

"Oh yea," I said. "Remember, I'm from Appalachiastan."

"That's right," Michael said. "So he'd sit out there with his Stroh's, and a flashlight, and a .22 caliber long rifle."

"What the hell would he do that for?" I asked.

"Well," Michael said. "He'd claim to be huntin' rabbits, up until around the time he got drunk. After that, he'd tell you he'd seen a Bigfoot Sasquatch up in the woods, back behind his mobile home, long time ago, like when he was a kid, and that he was gonna kill it and get rich and famous and leave our little wide spot alongside the road. Claimed he was gonna move to Charlottesville and buy him one of those fancy smancy houses close to the University and go to all the tennis matches."

"Was he a tennis fan?" I asked.

"Nah," Michael said. "He was just crazy. Thought maybe being seen at tennis matches might make him look more important."

"Oh," I said, and sat back to listen. Now, I was keeping my eye on our lines, because some of those big 'ol catfish were starting to swim their way past that long. The one where our baited hooks was only ten yards on the other side. I figured if the water temperatures dropped by another one or two degrees, those big 'ol fish might just be able to make it over there and take one of our baited hooks, without putting themselves out too much, due to the heat and all, and some of these fish had to weigh at least fifty pounds. You get down to the Richmond part of the James River, and you can catch catfish that way one hundred pounds all day long. I guess maybe they float down there from up here on these super hot summer days, and they're so danged big and heavy they just can't make it back up the river, so they end up just staying down there in Richmond.

"So me and this friend of mine," Michael was saying, "we were out here passing a football around one evening, and crazy 'ol Roy was over there with his .22, looking for rabbits or Bigfoot Sasquatch, or whatever. My friend, by the way, actually made it to Charlottesville, by way of a football scholarship to play for UVA. Made it to the NFL and won a superbowl. His name was Wendal Full. Ever heard of him?"

"Nope," I said.

"Anyways," Michael continued. "We just always figured he was just sitting outside drinking. And well, just about the time it was almost too dark to see, we heard that 'ol bladeless riding lawn mower's engine fire up and take off across the field. About ten second later we heard crazy 'ol Roy start a firing away with his .22."

"Was he trying to chase down a rabbit and shoot it while riding his bladeless riding lawn mower?" I asked.

"Well," Michael said. "That's what we thought. But we looked over, and crazy 'ol Roy was running behind the mower, about twenty yards back, shooting at the mower."

"What the hell?" I said. "Had he fallen off the mower, and he was shooting at his runaway mower?"

"That's what we thought," Michael said. "But when we took a good hard look at the mower, and mind you, it was right at the time of day when it was just almost too dark to see, but we squinted real hard, and by God, if we didn't see something big, and something dark, and something hairy riding away on that bladeless riding lawn mower."

"So you're telling me," I said, "that it appeared as if Bigfoot Sasquatch stole crazy 'ol Roy's bladeless riding lawn mower and then rode off on it?"

"That's exactly what I'm telling you," Michael said. "I ain't asking you to believe me, but that's how I remember it."

"Damn," I said. "I think you just cured my writer's block."

"How's that?" Michael asked.

"Well," I said. "This would make a great story for my next volume of the Bigfoot Sasquatch Files series I've been writing. Would you mind if I actually retold this story in a book?

"That'd be great," Michael said, and he smiled real big, lighting up like a Christmas tree. But after a hot minute, he said, "wait a minute."

"What's that?" I said.

"I'm not so sure that I want people knowing I told you this story."

"Why not?" I asked him.

"Well," he said. "If people heard me tell a story like this, they'd think I was as crazy as crazy 'ol Roy."

"Hm," I said, looking into the river in contemplation, and hoping those big 'ol fifty pound catfish would swim about another five yards over. "I've got it!" I said. "I'll change your name. I'll tell everyone your name was Michael."

"That'll work," he said. "For a start."

"What do you mean for a start?" I asked him.

"Well," he said. "I told you where I worked. What I retired from. If anyone down this way reads your story, they'll put two and two together, and they'll figure out who I am."

"Nah," I said. "I'll tell them you retired from the post office." I used to work for the post office, so it was the first thing to come to mind.

"That'll work," Michael said. Then we both sat in silence. He was looking for more holes we'd need to drill into the story, to protect his real identity, and I was hoping he wasn't going to back out of letting me use it, because it was a good one.

"What about my friend," Michael finally said. "I don't want to make it look like I'm one of those insecure name droppers by having named my buddy from childhood who went on to win a super bowl."

"I'll say his name is Wendell Full," I said. "No one will know who that is, because it's not a real person."

"Man," Michael said. "You *are* really good at this writing thing."

"Well," I said, feeling flattered. "I'm no Mark Twain, but I've put my time in. Been doing it for years."

Michael sat back for a minute, pondering a bit, and then he said, "you know, this place is so small, that I'm still afraid folks who read your story might figure out who told it to you, and they'd laugh me plum out of Buckingham County."

He had a point. People are pretty smart. They don't just believe what they read or see on the news. They question it. They think it might all be a bunch of highly spun half truths. And they know there might be more facts.

"I've got it!" I said. "In the story, I'll make you a black man!"

"Now you're talking," Micheal said. "And you know what? You should make crazy 'ol Roy white!"

"Done!" I said, "and I'll even say we were in Buckingham County, so even if anyone who might know you reads it, they'll never know it was you, because it didn't even happen in the place you lived your whole life!"

And just like that, we had ourselves an agreement on our story. Our little fishing tale, of sorts, and yes, that pun was intended.

Just about that time, one of those ginormous catfish *did* make its way over far enough on the other side of that log to take my baited hook. It hit so hard that it nearly pulled my rod into the river!

I jumped up and I started pulling and reeling. I didn't even need to set the hook, because that son of a gun had done it himself when he took the bait.

I reeled and reeled, but it was to to avail. This catfish was so big, he plum wore me out, and I had to actually hand the pole to Michael and let him reel for a while while I rested.

Once I got my wind and my strength back, I took the pole back from Michael, and it took me until well after dark to get that big 'ol catfish into the bank, but I by God did, and what a big one he was!

How big?

Well, he sure was a whopper!

I'd tell you.

But you wouldn't believe me.

The End!

***

The following stories are from Bigfoot Sasquatch Files Volume 4:

1

Poached

(Originally Titled: The Unfortunate Demise Of Old Man Singer)

My first runin with Old Man Singer came when I was about twelve years old. My childhood friends and I were sleigh riding on the steep road that ran up the hill leading to Old Man Singer's home. The road was steep, and when it snowed and the road iced over we could fly down it on our steel runners. It was the steepest hollow in our small community. Or, as we pronounced it in Appalachiastan, the steepest *holler*.

"You boys can stop this nonsense right now, or I can call the law on ya. Which is it gonna be?" It was Old Man Singer. He'd pulled over in the wide spot beside the road where we always burned an old car tire to stay warm when we went sleigh riding. (Yes, I hate to admit this all these years later, but we had no idea at the time that we were poisoning the world by doing it. It *was* Appalachiastan). He held a burning cigarette in his hand, and he must have smoked them one right after another, because when he'd rolled down his window to threaten us smoke came barrelling out of it.

"Fuck you, Singer!" my buddy Billy yelled. "You call the law on us, and I'll just tell 'em about that doe I saw you shoot last summer!"

"Them goddamn blades on them goddamn sleds make this road slicker than greased owl shit, you little shit! Now stop, or I'mma call the law!

"Call 'em, you old cocksucker," Billy yelled back. "We'll see who gets wrote up!"

With that, Old Man Singer stuck his cigarette in his mouth and cussed at us a little more while he cranked up the window on his old four wheel drive suburban, and then off he went, up the hollow to his home, and he didn't seem to have any problems getting up the hill despite the fact that we'd been sleigh riding on it for hours. He had chains on his tires, like most of the folks who lived up the hollow. There weren't many houses up there, but if the folks who *did* live up there wanted to get in and out during the winter, they knew to use chains.

"Who was that?" I asked Billy.

"Old Man Singer," he said, like I was supposed to know who Old Man Singer was. Then he spit into the fire. He'd lifted a box of his old man's Skoal again. Sure, I tried it. It made me puke. But not Billy. He loved the stuff.

"Who's Old Man Singer?" I asked, realizing Billy had no intentions of enlightening me further if I didn't.

"The biggest goddamn poacher in the county," Billy said, and yes, twelve year old kids in Appalachiastan really *do* speak that way. Hell, I'm sure twelve year old kids everywhere speak like that when grownups aren't around.

"How do you know?" I asked.

"I seen him kill a doe in his damn front yard last summer," Billy said. "Went home and told Dad, and he said he does it all the time. Everyone knows about it."

"Why don't he get in trouble?" I asked.

"No one gives a shit around here," Billy said, and his answer was sufficient. We lived in a small town in the middle of nowhere in the middle of Appalachiastan. Everyone knew everyone else, and most of the people who lived there were related to each other. The authorities didn't give a shit about a deer or six being killed out of season, especially when it was your third cousin twice removed, and a third time removed again by way of marriage doing the killing.

I'd later ask my father about Old Man Singer, when we were out hunting the following fall, and he filled in a lot of the gaps that Billy had left out.

"He likes to go spotlighting," my father said. Spotlighting is a highly illegal form of deer hunting in which one goes out at night and shines a bright, powerful spotlight out into the fields or into the woods, looking for the eyeshine of deer. Deer, just like when they see headlights from a car, will totally freeze up when they see the spotlight. The hunter, rather, the *poacher*, then shoots the deer while it's just standing there, staring into the light. Last I checked, it's a method that's illegal in all states.

"He'll bury the deer under the snow," my father said, "and then come back and get 'em the next day. Make it look like he killed 'em that morning. That way he doesn't run the risk of the game warden catching him at night.

"He's been known to set out traps, too, which isn't even legal around here," my father continued. "Basically, he hunts year round, and he follows no hunting laws."

"How come he doesn't get in trouble?" I asked.

"No one gives a shit around here," he said. He and Billy were on the same page in that regard.

Years would pass. I'd grow up and leave Appalachiastan. But I remember getting word by way of Billy, now living on the west coast and doing quite well for himself. I promised I wouldn't out him as far as what he's doing, because many of you reading this would know who he is, trust me, but what I will say is he's come a long way since being that cursing and tobacco spitting twelve year old hillbilly kid back in Appalachiastan. He quit chewing years ago, and he never took up smoking or drinking.

"Found him ripped to shreds," Billy told me over the phone when he'd called with the news.

"A bear?" I asked.

"Nope," Billy said.

"What was it?" I asked.

"No one knows," he said.

"Aren't they going to investigate further?" I asked.

"Nope," Billy said.

"Why not?" I asked.

"No one gives a shit around there," he said, and his answer was sufficient, but I went back the following summer and investigated myself. I talked to a few of his family members, and I spoke with the conservation officer who found his body. At least what was *left* of his body. Everyone seemed pretty convinced that a bitch named Karma paid Old Man Singer a visit out in those woods, but no one was convinced Karma had come in the form of a bear. When I pressed harder, and asked about a particular creature that's not supposed to exist, I got doors slammed in my face, but not before being given looks that said, *oh, my God! That's exactly what I thought!*

From the bits and pieces of information I gathered, and from hiking out into the woods where it all went down and searching around myself, this is how I believe Old Man Singer met his unfortunate demise.

***

Old Man Singer had been getting paranoid in his old age. Sure, he'd poached his whole life, just like his daddy before him, and his daddy's daddy before that- poaching was a long running family tradition in the Singer family- and he'd never been caught, but he didn't trust those conservation officers as much as he used to. Too many millennials of age now, filling such job positions, and every damn one of them out to be nice to everyone and everything. Including animals. Hell, Singer thought, if the good Lord hadn't wanted us all eating animals, he would have made them out of styrofoam instead of meat. But those damn millennials. Must all think the meat they eat grows in a garden, Singer thought.

Singer had gotten away from taking his rifles out into the middle of the woods and just blasting away at the wildlife in the middle of summer. He no longer wanted to take the risk of one of those young conservation officers hearing the shots, or have someone else report the shots, so he'd upped his trapping game.

Singer used the most horrific jaw type bear traps in existence, but he didn't use them to trap bears. He used them to trap deer. He'd take a solid number sixteen Duke trap, the springs of which were compressed with more than five hundred pounds of pressure each, and then bury the trap in half a bag of cracked corn. It never took long for a hungry deer to be caught in the trap while feeding on the corn, and once caught, it couldn't free itself. Singer would show up the next day and club the thing to death with a baseball bat he always carried into the woods with him for such purposes. If anyone were to ever ask, he'd claim the bat was for self defense- so many hippies out there smoking pot in the woods these days, he'd tell them, and God knows how violent people get when they're on the marijuanna- but no one ever asked, because no one gave a shit around there, but Singer always had his story ready.

Singer had gone out to check one of his traps on the day of his unfortunate demise. But once he got to the spot where he'd lain it out, it wasn't there. Nor was the corn he'd buried it in. There were a few kernels here and there, so he could tell something had eaten it, but there was absolutely no sign of his trap, whatsoever. Further, there was no sign that maybe a large animal, like a bear, had gotten caught in the trap and managed to walk off, dragging the trap along with it.

Singer got down on his knees and studied the ground where he'd staked the trap's chain. He had pounded the iron rod into the ground pretty deep, but it was gone as well. It looked like someone had simply pried it right up out of the ground and taken it- rod, chain, trap and all.

"Shit!" Singer said, aloud, having a sudden flash of insight. "Goddamn conservation officer got it!" The level of Singer's paranoia reached new heights. "Probably recording me right now on one of them goddamn hidden trail cams!"

Singer stood slowly and looked all around, turning a full circle as he did. First, he looked at ground level, and then he spun a full three sixty and looked at eye level. One more turn, while looking up, and he was convinced there were no cameras and he almost fell down from making himself dizzy.

He badly wanted to pull out a cigarette and light up, but he knew that if one of those millennial bastards were in the woods, waiting on him, he'd give away his position with the scent of the smoke. As hard as it was, he put off the urge to smoke and began slowly, cautiously and paranoidly as hell making his way out of the woods.

He'd only gone a few yards before noticing a pack of cigarettes lying on the forest floor. *Hm*, he thought. *There they are*. He'd had them with him the day before, when he'd come out to set the trap, but he didn't have them when he'd gotten back to his truck. "Must have fallen out of my pocket," he said to himself.

Singer bent over to pick up the box of Newports, and just as he touched the box, the mighty Duke number sixteen jaw trap closed on his forearm, breaking it instantly, the teeth of the trap deeply piercing his skin.

"Ahhhhhhh!" he screamed, and the echoes from his scream bounced back from all the different mountain tops from every different direction all around him.

He never saw what took his head off. He was too busy screaming and being in agonizing pain, but the pain didn't last long, because at least the one hunting him, poaching, rather, as such traps are illegal in the area for any reason, was more humane in regard to a quick kill than Singer had ever been.

But after that? Well, the thing just had fun ripping Singer's limbs off his body, years of rage finally being let loose.

They found the trap with Singer's arm in it two days later. His wife had reported him missing, but only because the Singers were a one vehicle family and she needed to run off the mountain and go to town, but she couldn't very well do that without the truck.

They found one of his legs a couple hundred yards away from his arm and the trap, but the boot had been taken off. The other leg was never found. His torso appeared to have had two giant hands shoved right into it, and his rib cage had been ripped clean open, the same way someone might open a package from Amazon.

The oddest thing of it all, and this is what piqued my curiosity enough to actually go back to Appalachiastan after being gone all these years and investigate this event, was that Old Man Singer's boots were found a few months later, during deer season, by an actual legal deer hunter. They were sitting together, beside a stream, as if someone had simply taken them off to wade in the water. The hunter claimed to have noticed them in the morning when he'd first entered the woods. He left them at the time, assuming their owner was nearby, but when he saw them at the same place on his way out of the woods that evening, he decided to take them with him. Upon doing so, he noticed they were covered in what appeared to be dried blood. He assumed the blood might be from an animal, perhaps killed by another hunter, but he decided to turn the boots into the authorities anyway. As it turned out, they had belonged to Old Man Singer, who had been mangled by someone, or something of great strength almost fifteen miles away the summer before.

Despite the finding of Old Man Singer's boots by the stream nearly fifteen miles away, and despite there being no animal native to the area which possessed the ability to rip a man's limbs off in such a fashion, except for a *really* large black bear, and despite a few pleas from Mrs. Singer to investigate the unfortunate demise of Old Man Singer further, no one ever did.

Because no one gives a shit around there.

The End

2

Sasquatchers Anonymous (SA)

(Originally Titled: The Unfortunate Demise Of Thomas G.)

"You have *got* to be kidding me," Thomas G. said to himself, aloud, reading over the search results he'd pulled up online. "Sasquatchers Anonymous?"

Thomas G. needed a new twelve step program. He was in a new town, in a new state, actually, and it was quite rural where he was, but he'd hoped to find a twelve step program or two where the members were addicted to some sort of substance, be it in chemical or drink form. Those were his niches. They'd *always* been his niches. The niches where he got his bitches, as he referred to the women he met in such programs.

Thomas G. was a shyster, and a shyster of the worst kind. Nay, Thomas G. was a predator, and a predator second only to those who prey on children.

Thomas G. was a registered, licensed, educated, professional and very effective psychologist and drug and alcohol counselor. The problem was, Thomas G. was also a sex addict, and he used his profession to feed his addiction; young beautiful women- and what better time to get them than when they were going through a great time of need in their lives. A time when they were trying to stay alive by overcoming their addiction to drugs or alcohol and sometimes both. And who better to help them through such times than a caring professional who actually had the answers they sought.

Thomas G. had been raised in privilege, being that his father had been very successful and had become very rich working in media after returning home from World War II a hero. It was simpler times, because people still trusted the media, and the media was simply much more trustworthy. After Thomas G.'s mother died while he was still in grade school, his father would marry a woman who went on to become an independently wealthy entrepreneur, having made millions off of her passion and hobby; candle making. She'd developed her own line of scented candles and gave it a quirky name, something that had to do with being a northerner, because Thomas G. and his father were from the south, and in a matter of only a few years, her line of candles went huge and to this day they are burned in many houses across America.

Thomas G.'s stepmother had loved him like her own child and she had spoiled him. With the passing of his mother at such a young age- a woman he loved- and the fine treatment from his stepmother- another woman he loved- he found himself growing up to be a man who truly loved women and who understood it was possible to love more than one- even if at the same time- and thus his course was set. Mommy issues led to sex addiction, and now here he was considering going to a Sasquatchers Anonymous meeting, well, because he wanted to get laid.

Thomas G. had never planned on preying on his patients. He'd never planned on opening an addiction center in order to have an ever ongoing flow of drunk and drugged up women coming in for treatment for him to prey on. He'd never intended to claim to be an alcoholic or addict himself in order to be accepted into all those meetings in order to have a constant pick of new women to prey on.

But he did.

All of it.

Thomas G. had the members of the twelve step groups he'd belonged two convinced that he'd been sober for nearly twenty years. But it all came crashing down on him, hard, when his third wife, half his age and bat shit crazier than the first two bat shit crazy women he'd married relapsed, again, and spilled the beans.

Drunk off her ass, bat shit crazy wife number three went to an open meeting with about fifty members and told of how Thomas G. had been going to meetings, nightly and for nearly twenty years, talking the talk and quoting the program's literature, word for word, and then going home afterward and drinking. No, he didn't always get drunk, but he usually did, and the next day he'd repeat the cycle.

Thomas G. had partnered with three other group members to open a rehab clinic, all three of whom were sober- *really* sober- and part of their pact had been that if any of them were to ever relapse, they had to forfeit their portion of ownership of the clinic to the other, sober members. After bat shit crazy wife number three spilled the beans, Thomas G. found himself without a business.

But hey, he thought. Fuck those t-totalers. He'd just go into private practice, but that only lasted a month before he lost his counselling license, because bat shit crazy wife number three had contacted the state psychiatry board and informed them that Thomas G. was fucking one of his patients; a twenty one year old college student who'd come to him for counselling because she knew that if she didn't get sober and stay sober she'd never graduate. Despite being old enough to be the girl's grandfather, Thomas G. had her pants off in his office on her first visit, and bat shit crazy wife number three, who'd actually been a patient of his when they'd met- very similar circumstances- walked in on her husband and the young coed in action, and the event is what led to bat shit crazy wife number three's relapse in the first place.

Thomas G. hadn't *really* been run out of town on a rail, but he'd been run out of town on a rail. Everyone hated him. They'd trusted him, accepted him, and they'd all loved him, believing that he suffered from the same deadly illness they did and they'd believed that he'd truly wanted to get it in check and keep it in check. The whole while, though, he'd only been using their programs to find needy women in needy times and using his psychological know how to tell them exactly what he knew they needed to hear, when they needed to hear it, making him appear to be savior like, while the whole time, he'd merely been another thirteenth stepper.

And now here he was, in some shit hole town nestled in the Appalachian Mountains, actually considering going to a Sasquatchers Anonymous meeting to find a needy young woman whom he could mind fuck and then fuck.

"Sasquatchers Anonymous," he said, aloud, again, as if hearing the words again would make it seem any less crazy.

Thomas G. found the group's website, and their program was pretty much mirrored after all the other twelve step programs. The members of Sasquatchers Anonymous all believed they'd seen Bigfoot Sasquatch at some point, and many of them claimed that the experience ruined their lives. They'd been dumb enough to speak of their sighting, publicly, and they'd been rediculed and laughed at ever since. Many of them lost their jobs, having been viewed as mentally unstable. And the worst of it, they'd gotten addicted to going back into the woods, or the desert, or along the beach where they'd seen what may or may not exist, and looking further, hoping for another sighting. Sasquatchers Anonymous had been set up in order to help these people overcome their addiction to going out and looking for the beast that may or may not exist. Return to a normal life. Be able to hold their heads up high in public and look other men and women in the eyes.

"Whatever," Thomas G. said, closing his laptop. He stood and pulled on a light jacket, because it was fall and the temperatures were much cooler at the higher elevations of Appalachiastan than what he was used to down south, and he exited his shitty little roadside no tell motel and he got in his car and headed to the meeting.

***

"My name is Jim R. and I'm powerless over Sasquatch."

The members of the small group, about ten of them, were starting the meeting by introducing themselves and proclaiming themselves to be bonafide members, the only requirement being a desire to stop seeking Bigfoot Sasquatch. Thomas G. could not believe he'd actually come to the meeting. Hell, he couldn't even believe such a group existed.

"And you, Sir?"

"Oh," Thomas G. said, realizing he was being addressed by the group's leader. "My name is Thomas G., and I'm powerless over Sasquatch."

"Thank you," the leader said, and then the introductions continued.

Not only had Thomas G. been preoccupied with disbelief of the existence of such a group, but he had also been preoccupied with checking out the twenty'ish year old blond sitting opposite from him in the circle. When it was her turn to introduce herself, she did so as Jane, and she proclaimed her complete and utter powerlessness over Sasquatch.

"Would you like to start tonight?" the group's leader, Ken R., said to Thomas G. "Since this is your first time here?"

"I think I'd rather just listen tonight," Thomas G. said. "Since it is my first time and all."

"Fair enough," Ken R. Said. "Jane," he then said, turning his attention to the beautiful young blond and only female in the group. "Any more disappearances up your way?"

"Not since my boyfriend. Back in high school. That's been three years now," Jane said.

Mumbles of 'good' and 'um-hum' circulated quietly around the room.

"So it's paid off not to go looking for the creature," Ken R. said.

Thomas G. was staring intently at Jane, and having spent more time in his field than Jane had yet spent on earth, he could clearly make out the signs of frustration on her face. Though she was obviously trying to keep the signs at bay,

Thomas took note of the tightening of her jaw, the crinkles around the corners of her mouth and eyes.

"I've never gone looking for them," Jane said, and though she was trying not to sound defensive, she clearly was.

"Now Jane," Ken R. said, trying to sound soothing but failing. "We've talked about this. It's called denial, and until you get brutally honest with yourself, you'll never recover. And we can't do it for you. We can only help you as far as you're willing to help yourself."

Thomas G. saw his opportunity. He'd easily be able to step into Jane's life and fill the void that the people in this program were not filling. Then, he was sure, he'd be able to step into her pants. But first, he needed to know at least a good portion of her story, so he baited her by way of good old fashion passive aggressive fishing.

"I'm Thomas G.," he said. "And I'm powerless of Sasquatch."

"Hi, Thomas G.," the group members said in unison.

"Sorry to chime in," he said, trying not to sound *too* cheesy by using the word 'chime,' the telltale sign of week writers, but marginally acceptable with spoken language. He was intentionally trying to come across as less intelligent as he was. People fear stupid people much less than geniuses. "But I think I can relate."

"How so?" Ken R. asked.

"Well," Thomas G. said. "I've never gone out, actively, seeking this creature, but he, she, it or they continually appear in my life, and I think this group might be able to help me if I could hear some instances of others being sought out, rather than being the seekers."

He'd looked at Jane while he'd spoken, laying the bait right at her feet, and boy, did she ever take it, setting the hook herself in so doing, and then run deep. Thomas G. sat back and listened as Jane basically spent half of the meeting sharing about how she'd first seen two of the creatures when she'd been about four years old. Her daddy, who wasn't actually her daddy, was tuning up on her mommy, and the creatures had helped her sneak out of the old trailer home the family lived in and they took her out into the woods and played with her all day to keep her entertained, away from the drama, and safe.

Jane further shared about times when men, and one high school kid, had tried to harm her in ways unimaginable, and from out of nowhere, Bigfoot Sasquatch would show up and save the day. "They're my guardian angels," she said when she wrapped it up, and Thomas G. knew exactly how to take things from here.

***

Thomas G. tread lightly. He first asked Jane to join him for coffee in a public place, so she would not feel threatened. "There's the gas station down on Main," she said. Thomas G. had forgotten. He was in Appalachiastan now, and there were no coffee shops. "How about the Mountaineer Mart?" he said, suggesting the only other alternative of the shit hole, meth infested town. "Okay," she'd said, and it was on.

Thomas G. attended every Sasquatchers Anonymous meeting held over the course of the next few weeks. Monday, Wednesday and Friday at five o'clock p.m., like clockwork, and he was never late. He respected the group. He was always at least ten minutes early, and on Fridays he went half an hour early to help set up the chairs and make the coffee. And after every meeting, he'd spend time with Jane, usually at the 'meeting after the meeting' in the parking lot, where there were other Bigfoot Sasquatch addicts, so that she would feel safe. But after nearly a month had passed, he decided the time had come to strike.

"You know," Thomas G. said to Jane while they were having coffee in the parking lot of the Mountaineer Mart one Friday after a meeting. "As you know, from our talks, and with all the time we've spent together, I am a licensed psychologist. I think I could help you overcome your Bigfoot Sasquatch addiction if we had a few private sessions. And I'd never dream of taking a dime from you for my services."

"But I've told you, Thomas G.," Jane said in her extremely sensual Appalachian American accent, "I don't go out a'lookin' for 'em. *They* find *me* when I need 'em."

"I know," Thomas G. said. "But maybe just spending some quality time alone for a few therapy sessions could help you in other ways. I know you come from a broken home. A lot of abuse. You just seem to have too much to offer the world not to get out of this shit hole and do something more with your life. Not to mention you're absolutely beautiful."

"Why, Thomas G.," Jane said, batting her eyelashes. "Are you trying to get me to take you home?" And then she smiled, daringly, flirtingly, and completely no way to say no to-ingly.

"Yes!" Thomas G. said. Sure, he was old enough to be this beautiful young woman's grandfather, and he knew it, but it had been so long since he'd lain with a twenty-ish year old girl, the gig was up. He could no longer take it. The time to strike had come!

"That's all well and good, Thomas G.," Jane said. "I ain't got no problem takin' ya back to my trailer, but you gott'a realize, these creatures are empaths. They can sense your true intentions. If you intend to do anything other than try to help me, they'll know, and it won't end well for you."

"It's okay," Thomas G. said, trying to mentally keep his manhood from rising, which it was, and no physical contact had even yet been made. "I can assure you my intentions are," he paused, looking for the right word. "Grandfatherly," he said when it finally came to him.

"Well," Jane said, looking down, a tempting smile on her face. "I never knew who my daddy was. And I sure as shit never knew who my grandaddies were, cause Mamma didn't know who her daddy was either."

Stay down, Thomas G. was mentally telling his manhood. *Stay down. Not yet.*

"Well," Jane finally said, matter of factly. "I reckon it's okay if you follow me out to my trailer. We can talk. I'll take me some of them counsellin' services you're offerin'."

"Lead the way," Thomas G. said, almost running to his car, the only Audi to be found in Appalachiastan.

***

Thomas G. followed Jane, who was driving a beaten, old Chevy S-10- the kind Thomas G. hadn't seen in years- and one that he couldn't believe even passed inspection. But with a smile and an ass like Jane's, Thomas G. figured she probably got just about everything she wanted or needed with little friction, like an inspection sticker for her truck that couldn't pass inspection. The girl had probably never opened a door for herself her entire life.

As they drove up Jane's hollow, pronounced 'holler' by the locals, the day's light grew dim. Evening was here. At least twilight.

The veil was thin.

Just before rounding the last turn and reaching Jane's mobile home, Thomas G. slammed on his brakes as two large, dark figures ran out in front of his car. They'd been fast, and he hadn't been able to make out what they were, but he could tell they were huge.

"Must have been bears," Thomas G. said to himself, massaging the bulge in the crotch of his pants with his left hand. "Bigfoot. Hah! What bullshit."

Thomas G. knew there was no such thing as Bigfoot Sasquatch. Only ignorant hicks, like Jane, believed in such poppycock. Sure, he knew, the girl was hot, but she was nothing more than hillbilly white trash like everyone else from Appalachiastan. They didn't have advanced degrees, from the University of Virginia, at that, like him. He'd decided from the time he first lay eyes on Jane that he'd play along with her silly belief system and her backwoods culture. Just long enough to get in her pants. And he'd continue to play along if he could stay in her pants for a while. But once he saw that he either wasn't going to get in her pants, or that she was going to kick him out of her pants once he'd worn out his welcome, he planned on giving her a good old highfalutin, sophisticated, smartest mother fucker in the room tongue lashing. One that would make her feel even more insecure than she probably already did because of her upbringing.

"Here we are," Jane said. She was standing at her truck when Thomas G. pulled into what passed as her drive, a wide spot beside the road. He'd never been in a mobile home before in his life, but he figured there was a first time for everything.

Thomas G. had played the role of the sophisticated older man for nearly a month now, but he'd massaged the bulging crotch of his jeans a little *too* much on the way up the hollow, and the jig was finally up as far as his acting skills went. He had one thought and one thought only, and that was to have Jane, this beautiful young hillbilly girl, right here, right now.

"Jane," he said, lunging toward her and kissing her. He wrapped his arms around her and nearly came in his pants when he pulled her tightly into him.

"Thomas G.," Jane said, pushing him off. "Now I done told you. You better be careful, or you're a cruisin' for a bruisin'."

"You know that's all bullshit!" Thomas G. said, and then he lunged in for another kiss. He knew she was just playing hard to get. Being a tease. He would call her bluff. He would have her.

Whack!

Something smacked Thomas G. across the back of the head, hard, sending him straight to the ground.

"Goddamn it!" he shouted. He rolled over, and standing over him was something that was not supposed to be real. It was only supposed to exist in urban legends and folklore. Only dumb hillbilly white trash believed in the existence of the kind of shit he was now staring at right in the hairy face.

"No!" Thomas G. screamed out, but it was too late. One powerful swipe from the creature's open hand, its long, sharp claws extended, took Thomas G.'s head clean off of his body.

Jane walked over to Thomas G.'s severed head and picked it up, turning its face toward hers. She'd read (yes, some dumb hillbilly's actually read, and believe it or not, some even write books) somewhere that some guy in France was doing studies on guillotine beheadings centuries ago to see how long a human head remained conscious after the beheading, and she remembered it was something like seventeen seconds.

Jane held the head in her hands and stared into its eyes. She got the distinct feeling that Thomas G. was still conscious. She smiled, and the head smiled back at her.

"Better watch that thirteenth step, Thomas G.," she said. "It's a doozy." And then she lightly kissed the head's mouth and as she did she could feel its lip muscles go limp. She knew that Thomas G.'s head had completely expired.

She lay the head softly on the ground. She stood and turned slowly, and there, before her eyes, was the guardian angel who'd severed Thomas G.'s head from his body and one of its buddies standing only a few feet behind him.

"Well come on, ya'll mother fuckers!" Jane said to them. "Drag this piece of shit's body off and get rid of it like ya'll did all the others!"

Jane walked into her trailer to grab a Miller Lite, and her guardian angels did as she'd instructed. They dragged Thomas G.'s body and carried his head out into the middle of the woods in the middle of Appalachiastan. No one would ever find either. But they made sure to take his shoes off and leave them, together, beside a stream in a very popular hunting location a considerable distance away, where *they* would be found.

Just to fuck with people.

The End

3

Final Vacation

(Originally Titled: The Unfortunate Demise of River Float
Karen)

It won't take too long to tell this one, because there's not
much to tell, really. Just a story about the very unfortunate
demise of a woman we'll call river float Karen. And we
won't be capitalizing the words river and float in front of the
name Karen, as they should be in order to remain
grammatically correct, and not because we're too lazy to
hit the shift key too many times, but because we will not
dignify her memory by doing so. Karen was *not* nearly as
important as she thought she was.

Why river float Karen? Well, because that's what she was
doing at the time of her unfortunate demise. She was
floating down the river.

And why Karen? Was that her real name? It's possible, but I doubt it. We're calling her Karen here, because she was a typical privileged white woman.

Oh, I'm getting ahead of myself again.

Let's start at the beginning.

So here's the deal. There's a particular spot on a particular river in my community, Charlottesville, Virginia, that is haunted as fuck. The land on both sides of the river used to be part of a massive plantation. Many enslaved people were worked to death, literally, along the banks of the river, and when they dropped dead, their bodies were simply buried in unmarked, shallow graves.

Many years before the land was part of a plantation, it was the living, hunting and warring grounds of many different Native American Indian tribes. Archeologists have found artifacts in the area dating back nearly fifteen thousand years. In a word, there have been a lot of tragic events take place in the area, hence its paranormal activity, and hence, in my opinion, the presence of- and I'm just saying 'potentially' here- Bigfoot Sasquatch.

There is one particular spot on the river, ironically just below its most popular swimming hole, that has always intrigued me the most. The reason why is because I have both fished and kayaked this portion of the river, and every single time that I have, I believe I have seen something, out of the corner of my eyes, watching me. At times from the bank, and one time, from within the water. It was like something large, but not aquatic, was in the water with me, hunkered down with only its eyes and nose above the surface.

Every now and then, my beautiful bride and our son will ask me to take them swimming in this river and at the swimming hole above the bend in the river that I've just described, and I always jump at the opportunity. Not just because I absolutely love doing anything and everything with my wife and our son, but because it gives me an opportunity to go squatching in a place I firmly believe may or may not harbor that which I'm constantly seeking; Bigfoot Sasquatch. One day this past summer we went to the river, and the swimming hole, which we'll call the Bigfoot Sasquatch hole, and this, dear reader, is where we met river float Karen.

I first noticed river float Karen from a distance. My family and I were swimming and playing in the water at the lower end of the Bigfoot Sasquatch hole. It had been my idea, because the position allowed me to peer around the bend where I'd felt like I was being watched so many times in the past. If a Bigfoot Sasquatch were to make its way out of the woods and slip over the bank and into the river, I would be able- potentially, now- to see it while safely keeping an eye on my family as well.

I heard what sounded like squawking. I could tell it wasn't coming from a duck or some other sort of water foul, because it was not a beautiful sound of nature. It was an annoying, bitching and complaining sound of a narcissistic post middle aged white woman. (Hey. We live in Charlottesville. You learn to recognize this sound quite well.) I glanced upstream, and there she was, in all of her two hundred pound plus glory, floating down the river on an innertube that looked like it wanted to commit suicide due to clinical depression induced by having to carry her wait. And not just the weight associated with her body, but the weight associated with her ego.

"Disgusting!" I heard her scream from about two hundred yards away, but I couldn't make out the rest of what she was saying. There were many families swimming in the river that day, as it is probably the most popular river swimming hole in town, and I could see that each time river float Karen got within speaking distance of anyone else in the river, she would speak to them, and every now and then she'd shout the word "disgusting" or "filthy" or "polluted" or "dirty" and then she would keep floating by.

I could tell by the body language and reaction of the people she spoke to that whatever she was saying must not have been very pleasant. Most of the people turned their backs to her and some of them even got out of the river until she passed. One family actually packed up their things and left.

"This should be interesting," I said to my wife, and she just giggled. That's what she does. She giggles. That's why we call her Giggly Girl, but that's another story. But I'll tell you the reason she was giggling at this time, and it's because she knows I don't put up with bullshit. I detest narcissists, and I don't cower to their passive aggressiveness. I call them out.

"Oh, this water looks filthy!" river float Karen said, aiming her bitchery in my direction once she was within speaking range of me. "How can you people be in it?" she asked, looking at me directly now.

Thinking that maybe I'd missed something, I looked around in the water, and just as I'd thought, and just as it has always been, the water was crystal clear. It's the Rivanna River, and it's a heavily protected part of the Chesapeake Bay Watershed, and the water has always been so clean, at least in the twenty years that I've been in the area, that you could drink it. I looked back up at river float Karen just in time for another derogatory statement about the water. "Isn't there sewage in here?" she asked.

"Yes," I said, totally lying. "There's a busted sewage pipe about a mile upstream. I'm actually standing in poop right now." My wife giggled as I said all of this and turned her back to river float Karen so she couldn't see.

"Are you serious?" river float Karen asked, and you could tell that she was serious. She was believing me.

"He's pulling your chain, and you're letting him," a thin man of about Karen's age said. He was floating in an innertube beside her. I'd noticed him, visually, but he'd not been bitching and moaning on his way down the river. As it turned out, the man was river float Karen's husband. We'll call him beta-male, because that's what he was. It was obvious that river float Karen had his balls in a jar somewhere, either hidden in her purse or locked away in a bank box, just in case he ever felt the urge to go searching for them.

"Hey, you," river float Karen said to me. "You better watch it buster, or someone's gonna be calling the cops to report that a teacher shot and killed an unarmed white man." Just the month before, police in Minneapolis had choked George Floyd to death, and just the week before, police in

Georgia, I believe, shot and killed an unarmed black man. The nation was being torn apart, at least in the major cities, all over the country by means of violent radical protests as a result. And river float Karen thought this was something worth joking about.

"How is that even remotely funny?" I asked her.

"Oh, come on, you!" she said. "Look at me. I'm a white woman. And I'm a teacher. I belong to a union."

"We're progressive liberals," beta-male chimed in. (And yes, the word "chimed" is a sign of weak writing, and I'm using it here because a weak word goes so well with such a weak man.) "From Montana."

"I think you might not be quite as progressive as you would like to think you are," I said.

"You must be from here," river float Karen said. She'd nailed me as the target she'd been looking for all day, and I was happy to oblige. "Only a southerner would consider this water clean."

"I've been in third world countries where the waterways were so polluted, you could walk across the rivers and be completely supported by the trash on top. You'd never get your feet wet. So to think of this water as filthy is asinine."

"We've vacationed in the Mediteranian," river float Karen said, "where the water is so clear you can see the bottom a hundred feet down."

"Then you should go back to the Mediteranian," I told her. "You should never come here again."

"Oh, we're *not*!" river float Karen said, annunciating the word 'not' so profoundly that she wanted to make it as crystal clear as the waters of the Mediteranian that our community would *never* have the privilege of being blessed with her presence again. "Ever!"

"We won't miss you," I told her. My wife was giggling so hard now Karen noticed.

"Who's that?" Karen asked. "Your daughter?"

"Yes," I said, putting my arm around my wife. "Doesn't she look just like me?"

Okay, so if you don't know me and my wife from our YouTube channel Homesteading Off the Grid, I'll spell it out for you. I'm a white man in my late forties, as of this writing, and my wife is a very beautiful, very petite Filipina lady in her early thirties. In a word, we look *nothing* alike.

"Why are you being so rude to us?" beta-male asked, and he almost made eye contact with me when he did. His voice cracked at the end, as if he were going through puberty, and it's possible he was, as he certainly didn't seem to possess the testicular fortitude that most men actually get after having gone through puberty.

"Because you fuckers want to come to *our* town, float down *our* river, and act like a couple of grasshoppers high on a leaf looking down on all us pissants, and let us know how much better than all of us you are," I said, and both river float Karen and beta-male were speechless. I'm used to this effect. There are a shit ton of privileged narcissists in Charlottesville and none of them are used to being called out on their shit by guys like me, because most people don't call them out on their shit.

I believe the reason there are so many privileged narcissists in Charlottesville is because of two things. Number one, the area is very affluent, and the people here who are *not* affluent want everyone to think they are, so they act like pricks, and number two, it's a college town, so it's filled with intellectual elitist wannabe's. A bunch of educated fools who aren't nearly as smart as they want everyone around them to believe they are. I can tell you, I know many people in Charlottesville who *are* affluent, and I've met many of the people who are extremely intelligent, and what I will tell you is that these people, the ones who are the real deal in both categories, are the salt of the earth. They put on *no* airs, they are humble, and it would blow your mind to know that you'd just talked to a multimillionaire or a scientist in charge of a major pharmaceutical company's research and development lab if you were to speak with them, because of this.

The narcissistic pricks? Like river float Karen and beta-male?

They're fakes!

"Why are you here anyway?" my wife asked. "You're not supposed to cross state lines."

We were at the peak of the coronavirus pandemic. In our state, you had to wear a mask in order to enter any businesses or public buildings. Many states were requiring that people self quarantine for up to two weeks if they were entering from other states. Yet, here was river float Karen and beta-male, self proclaimed progressive liberals from Montana, whatever the hell that means, twelve states away from home.

"Maybe your English isn't that good, sweetie," river float Karen said, and I guess there was nothing remotely racist about the comment because river float Karen *was* a progressive liberal, "but I said I am a teacher."

"What's that have to do with anything?" I asked river float Karen.

"I work *hard* for my three months of summer vacation, buster," she said, glaring at me while she said it. "I'm taking it!"

"We're never coming back to the south," beta-male said, but this time there was not even a sign of attempted bravado. He'd whispered it to river float Karen, but I'd heard it.

"Oh, five years from now, I'll be free, and I can go anywhere I want. We're leaving this whole damn country!" river float Karen said.

"Why don't you just leave now?" I said. "We'll help you pack. Are you on probation or something?"

"You listen," beta-male said, and he pointed at me, though he still made no eye contact.

"I'm listening?" I said, but beta-male had nothing further to say.

"I have five years to go until I get my pension," river float Karen said.

"Oh, yeah," I said. "The soul trap."

"The what?" river float Karen said.

"Pensions are part of the soul trap," I said. "Your sucked into a job you may or may not even like, but you refuse to leave once you've been there a few years, because you get free health insurance you never use and if you stick it out for thirty years, you will receive a pension, which pays you sixty percent of what you need to live on so that you only have to work part time for the rest of your life."

"We're done talking to you," river float Karen said, and she and beta-male began paddling backward with their arms to get further out into the river, where the current was much stronger, so they could float further down the river. To my surprise, I heard people clapping, and I turned and saw that we'd garnered an audience. My fellow dumb southerners along the river bank that day had been very pleased with the show I had given them.

I made my way to the lower portion of the Bigfoot Sasquatch hole and watched river float Karen and beta-male as they rounded the turn and made their way almost out of sight.

And that's when I saw it!

Finally!

Beta-male was drifting about twenty yards ahead of his wife. I guess that since he only weighed about half as much as his wife the current had carried him ahead, faster. Then Suddenly, something huge, which at first I thought was merely a boulder, shot quickly toward river float Karen. All of a sudden, what I'd thought was a boulder rose from the water. I knew the water in this part of the river was about five feet deep, yet the water came up only to this mighty creature's waist.

With one arm, it's right arm, the creature, which may or may not have been, potentially now, a Bigfoot Sasquatch reached out and grabbed river float Karen by the hair of her head. And even though river float Karen weighed every bit of two hundred pounds if she weighed an ounce, the creature lifted her off of her innertube (I think he, she, or it was merely showing off), and then slammed her into the water. It sunk back down into the water, giving the appearance of merely being a boulder again, and it held river float Karen under.

Forever!

She never came back up.

The End

(Postscript)

Whatever became of beta-male?

Who gives a fuck!

4

The Mysterious Case Of The Bigfoot Sasquatch Makeup Tutorial Girls

"I need your help, Dr. Drake," county sheriff's deputy Burt Reynolds said, approaching the area's local cryptozoologist, who was in his backyard reading a collection of short stories written by Ray Bradbury. "I sure hate to intrude on you unannounced like this, and I hope it's not a problem."

"As long as you don't mind coming up on another man in his drawers," Drake said. When the weather was nice, as it was on this mid-autumn afternoon, Drake preferred to read outside wearing only his boxers. There were no neighbors within sight of his yard, as he owned a sizable lot, and the lack of confinement by way of clothing had always allowed him to feel closer to nature and the universe as a whole.

"I had the damndest thing happen yesterday," Reynolds said, and he pulled a smartphone out of his pocket as he did. He looked down at it and said, "I listened to the whole story, and I know the girls aren't lying. It's their truth, as young women these days like to say. And I've gone over the evidence here on their phone, and it all checks out. But…" he trailed off, knowing not what to say next.

"And?" Drake said, dog-earing the page he was on and laying the book on the ground beside him. He was in his favorite vinyl camping/campfire/tailgating chair, and he had a can of Ovaltine beside him. Oh, how he loved to drink Ovaltine when he read outside in his boxers.

"Well," Reynolds said. "I really hate to put you out. And I'm sure your wife doesn't want company."

"My wife's in the Philippines," Drake said. "Off to see her parents."

"You didn't go?" Reynolds said, the statement more a question.

"I left that place for a reason," Drake said, "and we'll leave it at that."

"If you don't mind then," Reynold said, tapping the password one of the girls, Kim, had given him into the iphone. "I'd like to have you take a look at this video." He handed the phone to Drake. "I'll give you a little backstory first, though."

"I'm all ears," Drake said, picking up his Ovaltine and taking a sip.

***

Deputy Burt Reynonds had been driving his cruiser down state route 601 the day before, a day as clear and beautiful as the day he would visit Drake for his professional opinion. The day had been uneventful, like most days as far as any crime went, and Reynolds had no complaints. One of the advantages to working in a high net worth area was that most of the crime, if there ever *was* any, was white collar in nature. The IRS saw more action on Burt's beat than any actual police officer.

Then, all of a sudden, Burt saw something completely unusual in the road about one hundred yards in front of him after coming around a sharp turn. Two girls, who looked like Chinese Geishas to him, jumping up and down in the middle of the road, trying to flag him down.

"Help us!" both girls were shouting, to Burt's surprise, in perfect English and with a southern accent. "It's coming!"

Burt turned on his flashers and stopped right in the middle of the road. He got out of his cruiser and both girls, about twenty years old, came running to him and threw their arms around him. "We have to get out of here," they said. They'd been crying and sweating, and the very hideously applied makeup on their faces had run and now appeared even more hideous. Burt couldn't help but notice that under their Geisha type robes, both girls were earring bikinis. Bikinis with the design of the American flag on them.

"Get in the back," Burt said, opening the back door of his cruiser. The girls were more than happy to oblige him and they jumped in. Burt quickly drew his service revolver and turned and faced toward the forest, holding his weapon up at eye level. "How tall is he?" he asked. He'd left his driver's door open so the girls had no problem hearing him.

"About eight feet," one of the girls, Kim said.

"More like ten," the other girl, Sue said. And she pronounced *ten* with two syllables, like "tee-in." Though she looked Asian, Burt thought, this girl has got to be from the south.

Burt realized he was being duped. He lowered his revolver and holstered it. He turned to face the girls in the backseat of his car. They were beautiful, despite the make-up issues they were having, and they were sexy as could be. And though they appeared to be purely Asian, their accents were more southern American than his, and he'd been born and raised in central Virginia. "Do you girls mind telling me what's going on here?" he said.

"Get us out of here first," Kim said, and Burt knew that whether he was being put on or not, Kim was scared, and so was Sue. Just because something might not be as it seems, or even true, people who are convinced that something is as it seems, or that something false is true, aren't lying when making their statements. These girls were not lying, Burt could tell. He knew they were scared and they didn't feel safe, so he got in his cruiser and took them downtown to hear their story, and oh, what a story they had to tell.

***

"We're screwed!" Kim told Sue, storming into their shared apartment on Jefferson Park Avenue in Charlottesville,

Virginia. They'd been roommates the year before during their freshman year at UVA and they'd really hit it off well, so they decided to live together again, off campus, this year as sophomores.

"What's wrong?" Sue asked Kim, looking up from her smartphone. She had been watching the new Sam Hunt video on YouTube. Like Hunt, Sue, and ironically Kim as well, was from Georgia, and she absolutely loved country music, especially Sam Hunt's because she thought he was a hunk.

"We've been outed on Reddit," Kim said. "We've lost a thousand subscribers in the last hour.

"We're not *on* Reddit," Sue said.

"Our YouTube subscribers, you dumb hick!" Kim said.

"What!" Sue said, now sitting up quickly, dropping her i-phone to the floor, Sam Hunt immediately forgot.

"That little Japanese bitch, Himari, outed us on Reddit to steal our market share," Kim said, turning her phone around and showing Sue the post.

Their jig was up. Sue and Kim, both from Georgia, had built one hell of a following on YouTube by jointly hosting a channel called CuteKoreanGirlsMakeUpTutorials. Three times a week, for the past year, they would make videos where they dressed up like Geishas, wearing only bikinis under their robes which they always left untied and opened, and speaking in the cutest of Korean accents, and in broken English, of course, making them come across as more naive and innocent, and they would give tutorials on how to apply makeup Korean style.

The thing was, neither Kim nor Sue were Korean. They'd never even *been* to Korea. Both sets of their grandparents had migrated from Korea after the Korean war, escaping the North just before lockdown. Their grandparents, like many immigrants from other nations, clung strongly to the Korean community in Atlanta, where they'd set up shop after making the voyage to America. Kim and Sue's parents were products of that tightly knit second generation of Korean immigrants, and thus the girls' pure Korean ethnicities, but that's where it all stopped. Kim and Sue were raised in nice middle class suburban neighborhoods, and most of their friends were white, the second largest ethnicity represented among their childhood friends had been black, and they both only knew a handful of other Asians. The girls never knew each other before meeting at UVA, because they'd gone to different high schools in Atlanta, and the fact that they both came from Korean backgrounds was purely coincidental.

"Look at this shit," Sue said to Kim, pointing at one of the comments under Himari's post that outed them.

"If I wanted an American woman," the comment began," I'd get me one. I watch their YouTube show because I want an Asian woman! I've been duped. This is pure bait and switch!"

"I'm gonna kick Himari's ass when I see her," Kim said. "We helped her set up her channel and sent our subscribers to her so she could get monetized quicker, and now she's doing this? Stabbing us in the back just so she can take our audience?"

The girls continued reading the insults from their former fans, their base of which was diminishing by one thousand subscribers per hour now. The girls knew that their fans were not girls and women who wanted to know how to apply makeup in the traditional Korean way. They knew their fanbase was mostly a bunch of redneck white men, most of them older, who had a thing for young, petite, beautiful, sexy Asian women. They'd never had a problem with it, either. They were doing it purely for the Google Adsense revenues their videos generated, just like every other millennial who was making bank on social media. The girls often sat and talked with other social media content creators and they were all always wondering why they were even going to college in the first place. There was no way that the professions they'd pursue after graduation would provide as much income as many of them were already making on social media. Sue and Kim were both in education, and if they were to actually go into teaching after graduation they would take a massive pay cut.

"What are we gonna do?" Sue said.

"We're gonna kick Himari's ass," Kim said, again making her intentions for their little Japanese frenemy known.

"No we're not," Sue said.

"Why not?" Kim asked. "She wants the world to see who we really are? Let's get all redneck on her ass and give her a good, old fashioned southern beatdown!"

"That's exactly what she wants," Sue said, now feeling herself calming. "Then she could have one of those social media wars like those makeup dudes on YouTube. It would give her more power."

"So what do we do?" Kim asked.

"We switch gears," Sue said.

"How do you mean?" Kim said.

"Look," Sue said, now picking her i-phone up off the floor. "What a hunk he is," she said, seeing that Sam Hunt was still singing. She didn't listen to the rest of the song, though. She went to the homepage and scrolled down the recommended videos. "Look at all this shit," she said, holding the phone over for Kim to see.

"Bigfoot Sasquatch?" Kim said.

"Yeah," Sue said. "This shit is one of the most popular subjects on YouTube."

"What's that have to do with us?" Kim said.

"Who're our biggest fans?" Sue asked.

"Creepy old white guys," Kim said.

"Exactly!" Sue said. "And guess who makes up the biggest portion of the fanbase for Bigfoot Sasquatch?"

Kim's eyes widened, and a smile came to her face. "Creepy old white guys!" she said, excited.

"Exactly!" Sue said. "Get your boots, girl. We're going hiking."

***

"Can you believe that bullshit?" Kim said to Sue as she drove her Jeep Wrangler five over the speed limit through the city streets of Charlottesville, like most of the UVA students. The girls were heading to the outskirts of town. Ivy Creek Nature area. They'd done a Google search, and it was the closest place to their location that was off campus and had forested trails. They'd hiked through the trails on campus before and knew them to be too populated with people to be able to do what they needed to do. They needed to make it look like they were totally secluded and all alone. "There wasn't a damn thing in any of those videos, and all those people in the comments were putting time stamps where they saw shit, and there was nothing."

"I know," Sue said in agreement. "But you know, that one video. Where that guy was doing like a three sixty panoramic view of the leaves in the fall. That sure as shit looked like something huge on two legs walking down the hill. And it looked like it ducked behind a tree when he stopped panning the camera."

"You mean that one video from that dork that lives around here somewhere?" Kim said.

"Yeah."

"I'm sure he had his buddy in a monkey suit doing that," Kim said. "The timing was too perfect. There is *no way* he could capture something like that on film by tricking the creature into thinking he wasn't out there to actually capture it on film. I mean, who does that kind of shit? It had to be fake."

"Yeah," Sue said, thinking logically now. "You're right."

The girls may or may not have believed what they saw in the video of the guy discovering the lair of Bigfoot Sasquatch and being told he wasn't welcome, but they liked his strategy and they decided to adopt it. They were going to keep their YouTube channel named as it was, because they didn't want to go through the entire process of rebuilding a new one, but they were definitely going to make a pivot. Oh, they were still going to do the makeup tutorials, but they would now be doing them in the woods, claiming that they were trying to lure in the mysterious beast known as Bigfoot Sasquatch with their beauty and sexiness.

"Do you think this will actually work?" Sue asked Kim an hour later and after hiking for thirty minutes into the woods.

"Of course," Kim said. "What could creepy old white guys like more than smoking hot Asian chicks and Bigfoot Sasquatch?"

"Beer and Nascar?" Sue said.

"Oh ye of little faith," Kim said. She had been raised a southern baptist. "Let's do it here. Set the tripod up."

Sue did as she was told, and after a three, two, one, the camera was rolling, and Kim and Sue were confessing to their followers that they weren't really Korean. They were as American as baseball and apple pie. And they apologized to anyone who'd felt duped, but hey, they were still good to look at. They were still sweet and petite, and they would still do their makeup tutorials in their bikinis and Geisha robes, but there were going to be a few changes.

Another three, two, one and the girls lost their robes revealing a new style of bikinis. Old Glory! The red, white and blue!

"We're here to show you our true colors!" they said in unison. They'd practiced it on their hike out into the woods.

"Now," Kim said, peering into the camera at close range. "Here's something else we're going to be doing differently, too." Sue began looking all around them, really paranoid like, as if the two girls were being watched by some*one* or some*thing*. "We're going to attempt to use our beauty and our sexiness to lure in the mysterious creature known as Bigfoot Sasquatch," Kim said.

Kim drew away from the camera and Sue slowly, methodically, took her place. "We've heard it on good account that there have been several sightings in this area," Sue said as Kim was now looking around, all paranoid like, behind them. "Don't pay attention to what I'm doing," Sue said, pulling a tube of lipstick out of the pocket of her robe and beginning to apply it to her luscious lips. "Pay attention to what may or may not be behind me watching me put on my makeup." She was trying to do things just like that one weirdo who'd made the video about the lair.

The girls both applied their makeup in front of the camera, taking turns, of course, one doing makeup while the other acted all paranoid and crazy in the background. They made sure to take timed pauses and say, "did you hear that?" or "what was that?" every now and then to make it seem real, and they did their best to act scared a time or two.

"Do you really think this is going to work?" Kim asked Sue as she packed away the camera and tripod in her backpack when they were finished shooting the video.

"Where the fuck are we?" Sue said, as if she hadn't heard Kim's question.

"What do you mean?" Kim asked, looking around.

"When did we step off the trail?" Sue asked.

"Oh, fuck!" Kim said, realizing the trail was nowhere in sight. "Oh, fuck," she said again, as if saying it twice might help their situation.

"Follow me," Sue said. "We came from this direction."

"No we didn't," Kim said, refusing to move. "That's the way we were going. We came from the opposite direction."

"Shit!" Sue said, turning and following Kim. Though the girls were true southerners, they'd never spent much time in the woods. Much as in *any* away from the few times they'd hiked in the very well and populated trails on the campus of the University of Virginia. In a word, they were screwed, and they knew it.

"What was that?" Kim said a few minutes after they'd started their walk, not sure of where they were heading. She stopped upon having heard something and Sue had actually run into her back because she'd been following so closely.

"Come on," Sue said. "We're not recording anymore. Stop fucking around."

"I'm serious," said Kim. "It came from over there." She pointed her finger and Sue looked, and just as both girls thought they were staring at a giant stump from a fallen oak tree, what they'd thought was a stump stood, opened a large set of eyes, and let out a scream like nothing they'd ever heard before.

"Oh shit!" they both screamed, and then they turned and began running the opposite way. They ran and they ran, and they ran some more. They ran for a full ten minutes, grape vines and branches and briars whipping and scratching across their beautiful Korean looking but purely American faces.

"Oh, shit!" Sue yelled, stopping instantly in her tracks. "Another one!"

Kim looked twenty yards ahead and to the right, and sure enough, there, standing at least eight feet tall, if not taller, stood a creature that was only supposed to exist in urban legend and folklore. The girls took a quick turn to their left, about forty five degrees, and began running for their lives again.

"Are you getting this on camera?" Sue asked Kim.

"No," she yelled, and then she pulled out her i-phone and started recording. "But I will!"

Twice more during their time in the woods the girls were confronted by Bigfoot Sasquatch. Was it the same one? Were there multiple beasts among them? They did not know, but they dared not stop running, always changing their direction as dictated by the location of the beast or beasts, and with each new encounter, Kim captured at least fragments, blurry images at best, on her smartphone.

Finally, and at long last, the girls came to a road, old Virginia state route 601. And they came to the road just in time. A car was coming around the bend. They began jumping up and down, their Geisha gowns flowing in the light breeze created by their jumping. And as their good fortune would have it, the car that was pulling up to them, slowing as it came, turned out to be a police car. Its flashers were on, and it came to a stop and a not too unattractive man just old enough to be the girls' father stepped out of the car and came to their rescue.

***

"So what do you make of this?" Burt Reynolds asked local cryptozoologist Dr. Drake as Drake handed the deputy the girl's phone. He'd viewed the footage the girl was able to capture while running for what she thought was her life.

"Same thing you think but will never say in words," Drake said.

"So you're telling me," Reynolds said, "that this place is infested with Bigfoot Sasquatches."

"I don't know if I'd use the word *infested*," Drake said. "But there's a few."

"So what am I supposed to do?" Reynolds asked. "Ask the sheriff to ask the mayor to ask the Governor to call out the national guard? Track these things down and kill them?"

"Now why in the hell would you go and do a fool thing like that?" Drake asked in his Appalachian American accent. An accent that his former neighbor, Jittery Jay, used to mock, until, of course, Jittery Jay had had his unfortunate demise (see Bigfoot Sasquatch Files Volume 1).

"Well, it's clear these girls were running for their lives. These creatures, which may or may not be what they actually saw, were trying to kill them."

"Oh, my God," Drake said, rolling his eyes and putting a hand over his face. "Did you even watch the video?"

"Of course, I watched the video," Burt Reynolds said. "What am I missing."

"Obviously all of it," Drake said, removing his hand from his face and looking the sheriff's deputy square in the eyes.

"Enlighten me," Reynolds said.

"It was clear the girls were lost," Drake said. "The Bigfoot Sasquatch were helping them find their way out of the woods."

"What?" Reynolds said, incredulous.

"Watch it again if you need to," Drake said. "Every time the creatures showed up, it was to redirect the girls' direction of travel. The creatures could tell they were lost and needed to be shown the way out of the woods, so that's what they did. In a very nontraditional way, if you will."

"Hm," Reynolds said, and he pondered Drake's point. It made sense. It wasn't like these creatures, if that was indeed what they'd been, could just walk up to the girls and say, "hey, I can tell you're lost. Let me show you the way." The creatures know, for sure, that humans feared them, so the best they could do was scare the girls into heading in the right direction. "So what am I supposed to do about this, then?"

"What do you mean?" Drake asked, lost.

"You know," Reynolds said. "Just in the past couple of years we've had all these supposed bear attacks. That Jittery Jay guy and his wife. Crazy A (See Bigfoot Sasquatch Files Volume 3). And that Torrie woman. And her parents a few years before that (See Bigfoot Sasquatch Files Volume 2)."

"Weren't all those people assholes?" Drake asked.

"That's really no way to speak of the dead," Reynods said, "but yeah. Privilved snobs are what I'd call 'em."

"Then fuck 'em," Drake said. He took a sip of his Ovaltine and picked his book back up off the ground and began reading, dismissing the sheriff's deputy, in a word.

"So I should do nothing," Reynolds said. He didn't like being so nonchalantly dismissed.

"Maybe people shouldn't be assholes," Drake said. "Obviously those little Asian girls were okay. They made it out of their encounter without harm."

"So you're saying these things only kill assholes," Reynolds said.

"They are empaths," Drake said, and after that Reynolds simply turned and walked away. He went to see the girls at their apartment and convinced them that what they'd seen had not been what they'd thought they'd seen. "You were in a panic," he told them. "Your mind plays tricks on you when you're in a panic."

The girls bought it, hook line and sinker, and they said fuck social media and studied hard, and got their teaching degrees and went on to mold young minds and take a massive paycut…

And they never went into the woods again!

The End

Publish Or Perish

Professor Parish sat at the campfire with his six trusted students. These were the half dozen who'd made it through his trial by fire. Forty six students had begun the experiment, but only these six remained. He did his best to keep his eyes from favoring Marta, his favorite of these six elite, but it was difficult, because he was only human, and a very healthy *male* human, at that, and Marta *was* drop dead gorgeous. Twenty two, half black on her father's side, and half Thai on her mother's- Blasian, as the cool kids said- and she was one hundred percent gorgeous, Dr. Parish thought!

"So when does the first test begin?" Marta asked, as the group sat in a circle around the stoned blaze.

"Any time now," Dr. Parish said. "Though most likely, it will happen after dark."

"Why's that?" Ricky asked. Dr. Parish hated Ricky, because he had good reason to believe Marta was crushing on Ricky. Ricky *was* good looking, and he *was* pretty intelligent, but, well, Dr. Parish was hoping Marta might crush on him. Unfortunately, the girl showed no signs of daddy issues, so at nearly fifty years old, Dr. Parish would simply have to accept living with fantasies when it came to all things Marta. But he'd decided he'd still hate Ricky, anyway, just for the sake of things.

"I think you'll understand when the time comes," Dr. Parish said. Had Marta asked the question, he would have rambled on for half an hour or so, trying to impress her with big words and such, but Ricky, well, reference the last paragraph.

"I've never been camping before," Alice said. Alice was okay, for a freshman. Actually highly intelligent, and pretty mature, but she had a tendency to talk too much about stuff no one cared about. Dr. Parish didn't respond to her comment, but someone else did. Sarah, perhaps. Dr. Parish wasn't paying attention. He was reminiscing in his mind. Not just about the social experiment he was carrying out, or the fame that would certainly come his way once he published his results, or the tenure that the University would no doubt grant him because of it, or of getting into Marta's pants, but about what happened at this very campsite with Dr. Parish and his childhood best friend- a man who'd been killed in Afghanistan during the war about a decade before- and of how he knew he was going back on the promise he'd made with his now deceased friend.

And of how he did *not* care!

***

Once upon a time, Dr. Parish was simply known as Billy. And his best friend, before being known as Army Sergeant First Class Byron Jones, was simply known as Byron. And Billy and Byron spent every waking hour of their youth together, either on the river banks catching trout, or in the woods hunting deer and turkeys. Many of their adventures were had during overnight or weekend camping trips, here, at Byron's grandfather's place- a small homestead a couple miles outside the city limits of their small, Appalachian town. The property wasn't big enough to be considered a farm, and the old man never raised any livestock. He had a couple garden spots is all. But it was secluded- out in the middle of nowhere, and when the sun went down it was as dark as a coal miner's asshole, unless the moon was full, at which time you could almost see as if it were daytime, and it was peaceful and pleasant, and it held the best memories of their youth.

And it was haunted.

Or something.

But it definitely had a Bigfoot Sasquatch living on it, because that one fall, back in October of 1987, Billy and Byron saw it!

Or her.

Or him.

Or they (because it may or may not have been alone).

And neither of them had ever forgotten.

And that had only been the first time they'd seen it. The creature, or creatures, obviously felt safe in the boys' presence, and out of curiosity, when the boys would stay at Byron's grandfather's place, out in the middle of nowhere, they would often come right up to them while the boys were sitting around the campfire at night. Sure, they'd keep their distance, so everyone involved would feel safe, but the boys could always make out their eyeshine and the outlines of their bodies. The boys never felt threatened in their presence, and they knew they had something special, and they'd made a pact, somewhere around 1990- senior year- that no matter what, neither of them would ever disclose the fact that there was potentially a small clan of Bigfoot Sasquatch living on Byron's grandfather's land. And they'd cut their hands and became blood brothers on a handshake to seal the deal!

***

But Byron got obliterated by a roadside bomb just outside of Kandahar in 2009.

And Billy's wife left him for a woman in 2012.

And the University refused to grant him tenure because of his 'extracurricular activities' with beautiful young coeds (oh, if only he could get Marta to join that list!).

So Billy was reneging on his pact with Byron, and to hell with the safety of those Bigfoot Sasquatches. Whatever came to them after the disclosure of their existence and location was no concern to Billy. He needed the tenure, he needed the security, and he wanted Marta, and if he didn't publish something of substance, soon, he knew he would perish, professionally and then personally. Dr. Parish had to do something that had never been done before, and document it, or Dr. Parish would become Dr. Perished.

***

Dr. Parish had begun his social experiment at the beginning of the semester, the fall semester, and how fitting that here the finalists were, sitting around the campfire at Byron's grandad's place in October, the very month of the first encounter Billy and Byron had had with the creatures all those years ago.

The first test was simple. All forty six volunteers stood in a circle. Dr. Parish whispered in the first participant's ear, "my wife left me for a woman." The thing of it all was that that volunteer then had to whisper the exact same thing into the ear of the volunteer beside them. And so it went around the circle until they came to the end, and then the final volunteer loudly proclaimed the secret that had been passed around.

The first trial saw half the students eliminated. "Your brother slept with your mother?" The final student both asked and proclaimed at the end of it. Dr. Parish then *walked back the cat*, as they call it in the C.I.A. (you did *not* read that here), a process by which you go backward with your information seeking. The final student who stated the wrong information was not kicked out of the study, because the student just in front of them admitted that that was exactly what he'd told her. The difficulty lied in finding the broken links of the chain. Who flubbed it up? Several trials had to be done, and Dr. Parish's wife leaving him for a woman was retold as his father was really his brother, and his uncle was gay, and in one trial, that his mother knew why the sky was blue, all before the trial was over and successful.

Dr. Parish was convinced some of the students were flubbing things up on purpose, just because they were being assholes, but he did point out with each trial that this was a prime example of how rumors get started and spread, and why you should believe very little of what you hear when it comes to gossip. "Don't believe anything you hear," Dr. Parish told his student volunteers, "and only half of what you see."

But he'd finally narrowed the field down to a dozen. And then came the next set of trials. Witness account trials.

Dr. Parish would have all one dozen of his students observe an act, such as a dog walking through the park, unleashed, and then urinating on a tree or a trash can, and then trotting back to its human to be leashed. He would then have the students write exactly what had happened, in the fewest amount of words as possible, and once again, he was *not* amazed to find how many of these students, literally half, had difficulty in either remembering and noting things exactly as they'd happened, or at least being able to put the events that had occurred in properly worded fashion. One student had the dog urinating on a tree, when it had clearly urinated on a trashcan. One student said the dog was big and black, when it was clearly small and brown.

With the final six student volunteers expelled from the study, Dr. Parish finally had the six that he needed. These six were good at repeating stories exactly as they'd heard them, and they were good at writing stories about events exactly as they had occurred. In a word, they were credible.

***

"What was that?" Marta asked, turning to look behind her. Darkness had fallen now, and she couldn't see a thing that was any further than a foot behind her. She'd been staring into the light of the fire, hence, she was blinded for the darkness.

"I heard it, too," Ricky said. Dr. Parish didn't know if Ricky had actually heard anything or if he was just supporting Marta. *Goddamn you, Ricky*, Dr. Parish thought to himself. *Don't fuck this up over a peace of ass. I need this.*

Just as Marta turned around to face the fire again a sound came from the woods behind her that everyone in the group heard. They all turned to look, and there, about ten feet away, stood a being that had to be at least ten feet tall. Everyone present could see the shining of its eyes as the fire reflected off of them.

"Oh, my God," Alice said.

"Everyone's okay," Dr. Parish said. "There's no need to panic. If you'd feel more comfortable coming over here and sitting on this side of the fire, so your back isn't to it, feel free. Just move slowly so that you don't scare it away. I can assure you it is not going to hurt any of us."

"How can you be so sure?" Alice asked.

"Because I've been coming here and seeing these creatures for longer than you guys have been alive," Dr. Parish said.

The students sitting on the opposite side of the fire as Dr. Parish took him up on his recommendation and joined him and the others on their side of the fire. They sat in silence, staring at the hulking dark figure that was not supposed to be real. Five minutes later, another creature, this one about seven feet tall stepped out of the darkness and joined it.

"I've never seen two together," Dr. Parish said. "They must be really curious about you guys."

A minute later, another came out, this one about five feet tall.

"I think they're a family," Marta said.

"I'll be," Dr. Parish said. He was completely amazed.

The family of Bigfoot Sasquatch stared at the campers as the campers stared back for about ten more minutes, and then, just as mysteriously as they'd shown up, they slipped back into the cover of darkness and were gone.

***

Thirty days later, Dr. Parish was a worldwide celebrity. He'd published his piece on the existence of Bigfoot Sasquatch, and not only had he been given tenure by the University, but he'd already earned more money being paid for speaking engagements on the weekends than he would earn all year from his professorship. Sadly, he'd not gotten anywhere with Marta, but that was okay, because he knew in time that that might change. At least he hoped so.

And now, on a crisp, cool Saturday morning just before Thanksgiving, he was preparing to earn $100,000.00 from a speaking engagement which he'd hyped up by publicizing that he would now reveal the location of the Bigfoot Sasquatch family that he and his credible, trusted student aids had observed.

And Marta was pissed!

None of the other students cared much about the success that Dr. Parish was having as a result of his publication. They were happy for him, at most, but beyond that, they had other things to do, like go tailgating at the University's football games, and partying balls all night after the games, win or lose. And partying balls on the nights when there were no games to win or lose.

But Marta? Well, she was different.

Marta was an empath, and she could feel much more than even a Ph. D. in sociology, like Dr. Parish, could imagine, because, she knew, the higher one's education, the less likely one is to believe in things such as empaths.

Marta had known from the day she met him that Dr. Parish had dirty thoughts about her. She could tell he was a self-centered narcissist, not unlike many of the professors she'd known during her college years, and she could tell he was self-seeking. Still, she thought he was okay, and she'd jumped at the chance to be in his experiment, because binge drinking around campus was not her thing, and her gut instinct had told her during the entire experiment that the man was doing something for personal gain.

Marta made sure to be in attendance today with the thousands of others in attendance at the University's baseball stadium (there was a home football game today, or they would have used the football stadium in order to sell more tickets), as well as the millions and millions of people at home watching the livestream feeds.

"Today," Dr. Parish stated, after rambling about how important he was for about ten minutes, "I will disclose to the world, the very location of the small family of Bigfoot Sasquatches my trusted students and I observed, and the world of science and curiosity seekers alike can descend upon the location and the world can now see for themselves!"

The crowd cheered at that. So many people already had their car keys in hand, ready to go to this mysterious location so they could see a Bigfoot Sasquatch for themselves.

"The exact location of these creatures," Dr. Parish said, and then he took a dramatic pause in order to bask in the glory of such a large crowd's utter silence.

"He's lying!" a beautiful dark skinned girl with long black hair shouted from the middle of the crowd. "I was there. I was one of his aides. It was all a hoax for his fame and fortune, and it's gone on long enough!"

The crowd gasped, making it sound as if the air had just been released from the tiny tight nozzles of ten thousand car tires all at once.

Dr. Parish was floored. He knew not what to say. He stared out at Marta, now realizing that any fantasies he had that involved her would never be fulfilled.

"He never promised us money," Marta said, continuing after the crowd ceased gasping. "He didn't bribe us. We did it all on our own accord, because like him, we wanted to see how gullible the masses were." At this, the crowd began murmuring. They, the masses, were offended. "It was all a social experiment," Marta said. "This was all just one big social experiment, and you've all been duped. There is no such thing as Bigfoot Sasquatch." And with that, Marta simply walked away, first down the aisle where she'd been seated, and then, out the front gates of the stadium. As soon as she exited the stadium, everyone in attendance stood up and did the same.

"Wait!" Dr. Parish shouted. "She's lying!"

No one listened to him, because no one cared. They knew they'd been duped. They were all the butt of his big joke. They all knew that there is no such thing as Bigfoot Sasquatch.

Dr. Parish lost his tenure. He was not paid for the day's event. He was fired from the University, and he could not find new employment in academia, because his career was done.

In a word, Dr. Parish had become...

... Dr. Perished.

The End

6

Ask Me No Questions I'll Tell You No Lies

"So, I'm not trying to pry or anything," Jacob Mack said to his new hire, Jimmy Blake, as they trucked down the beautiful Virginia biway outside of Charlottesville. Jacob was driving the commercial sized dump truck, loaded to the gills with giant white oak and red oak logs that his tree removal service company had just cleared from the yard of a wealthy Virginia landowner. There were many wealthy Virginia landowners in this part of the state. Most of them were trust babies and Virginia first families, families whose ancestors had been awarded huge land grants by King James himself shortly after the settlement of Jamestown. Whereas most people in most other places would cut up any fallen timber themselves, and use said timber for firewood, most of the folks in this area were more than happy to pay Mack's Tree Removal Services up to five thousand dollars for each tree for cutting them up and hauling them away. The residents did not view their fallen trees as free firewood, rather, they viewed them as eyesores. Though most of their homes had multiple fireplaces, they burned gas in them so as to eliminate any labor, and most of them, sadly, simply covered their fireplaces up with large, flatscreen televisions. "But when you lost your CDL for drinking and driving, was that the first time you'd gone to work drinking like that?," Mack continued, prodding, "Or was it the first time you'd gotten caught?"

"Ask me no questions, I'll tell you no lies," Jimmy said. Jimmy was in his early thirties and had been only a handful of years away from actually retiring from a major delivery company. He'd started with the company at seventeen years old, driving forklifts in the warehouse, and he'd gotten his CDL at twenty and began hauling shipments by way of tractor trailers. Unfortunately, Jimmy had a drinking problem, and once he'd been switched to driving nights, he took his problem with him to work most nights, as well as a cooler with an iced down twelve pack of beer in it.

"But you're straight now," Mack said.

"Been sober just over a year," Jimmy said. "And I really do appreciate you giving me a second chance by hiring me. My old employer wouldn't even reply to my calls or emails, and a lot of former friends and family members have written me off as a deadbeat forever."

"Those who matter don't mind when we make mistakes, and we all do, and those that mind don't matter," Mack said.

"What?" Jimmy said, turning to face the older man. Mack was about sixty. Jimmy had been watching the scenery blow by. Though he was from Virginia, he wasn't from this part of Virginia, and he'd never been through this area. He found it to be absolutely beautiful, but he had to admit, his mouth had begun watering a bit a mile or so back when they'd passed Bigfoot Sasquatch Brewing Company, a microbrewery out here in the middle of nowhere, surrounded by nothing but natural scenic beauty and beautiful, vast estates.

"What it means is," Mack said, "that anyone who isn't your friend anymore because you got busted for doing something that most people have done at one point or another, they just never got caught, then they weren't your real friends in the first place."

"Yeah," Jimmy said, thinking about it for a minute. Mack had a point, he believed.

"And as far as family goes?" Mack said. "How many of those fuckers would you have had anything to do with, anyway, if you hadn't been kin?"

Jimmy again thought Mack had a pretty good point. He had a couple of sisters who he could never stand who always wanted to just through any mistake he'd ever made in his face. Last Thanksgiving, the last time he'd seen them, they were all about asking him how it felt to have been six years away from a pension at such a young age and then fucking it all up. "You're pretty wise," Jimmy said to Mack.

"I've been around the block, kid," Mack said. "And half the guys working for me fucked up at some point. You ain't the only one on my payroll with a D.U.I. on record. And them other guys- and I ain't gonna tell ya who they are, cause that's *their* business- well, they've turned out to be some of the best workers I've ever had."

Both men stared ahead. They were getting close to their destination; 'ol Leroy's, as Mack and his employees referred to the place. It was a huge farm, though no farming was done there. The man that owned the place was named Leroy Jenkins. A long time friend of Jacob Mack's.

"Looky, here," Mack said, pointing to a tractor trailer loaded down with split and stacked firewood coming out of the dirt road that was Leroy Jenkins' driveway. "'Ol Leroy sells more firewood, commercially, than anyone in central Virginia. That load there's probably going down to the Carolinas."

After the truck hauling the split and stacked firewood had cleared the turn, Jacob Mack turned his huge dump truck into Jenkins' drive. "I'll come out here with you the first couple times, for your training and all," Mack said. "Show you where to put the stuff. Introduce you to 'ol Leroy. But I'd say you'll be on your own by the end of the week."

Though Jimmy had lost his CDL license due to his D.U.I. the previous year, he could still drive a dump truck. The state of Virginia did not require a CDL for such purposes, just a driver's license, which Jimmy had just gotten back after having had it suspended for a year, and proper dump truck driver's training, which he was getting on the job now, at the hands of his new boss, Jacob Mack.

"There he sits, now," Mack said, slowing down as he pulled up to a somewhat dilapidated old farm house. There was a man of about seventy years old sitting on the front porch. He looked half asleep and half dead to Jimmy, but just as Jimmy started to think he really may be one or the other, the man stood, and with the use of a four legged walker, he made his way over to the big truck.

"Afternoon, 'ol buddy," Jenkins said to Mack when he got close enough to be heard over the truck's engine.

"Say there, partner," Mack said back. "Meet my new man, here. Name's Jimmy Blake. He'll be hauling this stuff out here by himself by next week, I'm sure."

Jenkins, very slowly, made his way around to the other side of the truck. Once there, he reached up toward the window and shook hands with Jimmy, who'd leaned out the window and reached down.

"You'll have to excuse me," Jenkins said. "I's out splittin' and stacking firewood this morning, and my back's a little sore. That's why I'mma usin' this here walker and gettin' around a little slower than usual."

"It's okay," Jimmy said. "It's a pleasure to meet you, Sir."

"They'll be none of that Sir nonsense around here," Jenkins said with a light laugh. "My dad was Sir, and he was the meanest son of a bitch I ever knew. You just call me 'ol Leroy, like everyone else."

"Will do," Jimmy said, and at that Mack pulled the dump truck forward.

The road that was Jenkins' driveway continued past the old house and headed into the woods. After about half a mile's drive of pure forest, things opened up again, revealing a large field about twenty acres in size and it was filled with firewood. Half split and stacked, and the other still in humongous log form. Another tractor trailer was just leaving the field having picked up a full load of split and stacked firewood. It was on it's way to Georgia.

"Damn," Jimmy said in awe. 'Ol Leroy's firewood operation was larger than most lumber mills Jimmy had ever seen.

"We ain't the only one that brings him wood," Mack said. "See, if we hauled this here load we have now to a landfill, they'd charge us seventy five dollars to dump it. 'Ol Leroy lets us bring it here for free, and, well, you can see what he does with it. He turns it into one hundred percent profit. I don't care that he makes a small fortune off of what we give him for free, because he saves us three hundred dollars a day. Do the math on that. Comes out to over seventy thousand dollars a year. That's profit of mine I get to keep in my bank and use to pay my men. I'm happy to give him all this wood for free."

"How long's he been doing this?" Jimmy asked, looking around, still amazed.

"About twenty years," Mack said.

"Where's all his workers?" Jimmy asked, realizing now that since the other trucker had left, he and Jacob Mack were the only two people to be seen. Mack didn't answer. He actually acted like he hadn't heard the question. "Where's his equipment?" Jimmy then asked, realizing there were no woodmizers or firewood belt operated cutting machines. An operation of this size, Jimmy assumed, would require the most state of the art commercial grade firewood cutting equipment money could buy. Again, Mack didn't answer.

"This is our area," Mack said when he finally did speak again. "Jump out and guide me back, and lets dump this load up as tight against the last load we brought as we can, so we can fit as much in here as we can in the future. That's the key. Pack it in tight in case it takes him a while to get around to it."

Jimmy hopped down from the truck and guided Jacob Mack back. Jacob Mack dumped their load and Jimmy jumped back in the truck and the two men began heading back to the home where they'd been working, expecting their crew to have another large oak that had fallen in a recent storm ready for loading.

Jimmy looked all around as they drove out of the massive log yard, and what he did see in the way of firewood splitting equipment was axes. Dozens of them. All scattered around, stuck into variously placed splitting blocks. It looked as if a couple dozen people had been out in the log yard splitting these massive logs with splitting axes.

"What's going on here?" Jimmy said, looking over as Mack as they entered the wooded portion of the drive before reaching Jenkins' house.

"Word is," Mack said, "'Ol Leroy splits and stacks all this wood himself.'"

"What?" Jimmy said. "At his age? With that back? And enough to supply the eastern seaboard with firewood?"

Mack did not reply.

"What's really going on here?" Jimmy asked.

"Ask me no questions, I'll tell you no lies," Mack said, and he looked over at Jimmy and gave him a wink that said *if you aren't willing to talk to me about certain truths, I'm not willing to talk to you about certain truths.*

As they drove past 'ol Leroy's house, Jimmy looked over and noticed that 'ol Leroy was enjoying his afternoon nap in a hammock he had set up in his yard over on the side of his house opposite the driveway. He was so fast asleep, Jimmy could hear him snoring over the loud engine of the dump truck he was in. Well, Jimmy thought, at least he isn't dead.

***

Jimmy finished up his first week, his training week, and just as Mack had told him, he was now driving on his own. During his first week solo, he'd gone to 'ol Leroy's three times, but all three times, 'ol Leroy had been nowhere to be seen. Jimmy put the large logs where he'd been instructed to put them during his training week, and each of the three times he'd taken loads out, he saw that the load previously taken before each had already been sawed down, split and stacked. There was no way, Jimmy thought, that a seventy year old man who could barely hobble around in his yard, with the use of a walker at that, could cut, split and stack so much wood in such a short period of time. Especially without industrial equipment. Something was going on here, Jimmy knew, and he was determined to figure out what it was.

"Maybe he's breaking child labor laws," Jimmy said to himself the following week while driving his first load of logs out to 'ol Leroys' place. These logs were maple. Still an excellent wood for burning. "Or prisoners," Jimmy said. "I bet he's buddies with the warden over at the county jail, and he buses some of the prisoners in here at night and makes 'em chop all that wood with axes. Hard labor."

Jimmy reached 'ol Leroy's drive and waited patiently as not one, nor two, but three tractor trailers filled with split and stacked firewood pulled out of the drive. Once the coast was clear, he turned into the drive, and he was happy to see 'ol Leroy standing in the front yard, propping himself up on his walker.

"Afternoon, 'ol Leroy," Jimmy said, sticking his head out the window.

"How's things going, 'ol buddy?" Leroy said, hobbling over toward the truck.

"Good," Jimmy said. "Real good. Hey," Jimmy said, excitedly, thinking quick on his feet, "it's about my lunch break. I packed a lunch, but how about after I dump this load I come back around here and sit with you for a spell while I eat, so we can get to know each other a little better."

"Sounds good to me, 'ol buddy," Leroy said. "I'll be a sittin' there on the porch. If I doze off, why, just wake me up. Not too sudden though," he said. "I was in Nam, and I might come to and knock ya a good one upside the head."

"All right," Jimmy said, laughing lightly. "We wouldn't want that." And with that, he began moving forward again. He made his way through the forested part of Leroy's property and then was in the twenty acre field that was the largest commercial firewood operation he'd ever seen. Again, he took note of how he saw no employees today, just like he'd never seen any employees ever. Still, no commercial equipment. Just dozens of splitting axes stuck into dozens of chopping blocks sporadically placed around the field.

***

"Glad you're awake," Jimmy said, carrying his small cooler onto Leroy's porch. It was actually the cooler he used to use to keep his beer cold while driving for his former employer, but these days it only held food. "I was hoping I wouldn't have to wake you. I sure do enjoy my naps when I can get 'em."

"I'll just take mine after you leave," Leroy said. "So how's the new job workin' out for ya?"

"Going good," Jimmy said. "Real good." He sat down and pulled a roast beef and provolone cheese sandwich with mustard on a hamburger bun out of his cooler. He took the sandwich out of the ziplock back it was in and ate almost half of it with the first bite.

"You're hungry," 'ol Leroy said.

"I don't eat breakfast," Jimmy said.

"Gotta eat," Leroy said. "If you're gonna work, you need the calories."

"I bet you eat like a buffalo," Jimmy said, just before putting almost the entirety of the remainder of his sandwich in his mouth. Alas, it would take him three bits to devour this one.

"Ha, ha, ha," Leroy laughed, but he spoke no real words.

"I mean, with all the wood splittin' you do," Jimmy said, talking with his mouth full. "How on earth do you do all that by yourself?"

"Well," 'ol Leroy said. "I get a little help."

"From who?" Jimmy said. "Must be more than a little. You couldn't split and stack as much firewood as you do as quickly as you do if you had the best machinery you could get. And you don't have *any* machinery." Jimmy swallowed the food in his mouth then stuck the small bit of sandwich that remained into his mouth. "And what's up with all the axes? There is *no way* all that wood's gettin' split up by some of your buddies using axes."

"Why don't you come on out tonight and help me and my buddies," 'ol Leroy said. "If you really want to know."

"Tonight?" Jimmy said, looking up. He'd been digging through his cooler for his next sandwich. "Your helpers come out and do all this work at night?"

"Yeah," Leroy said.

"But I didn't even see any lights out there," Jimmy said.

"They don't need 'em," Leroy said.

"Why not?" Jimmy said, now taking the sandwich he'd dug out of the cooler out of its ziplock bag.

"Because they can see in the dark," Leroy said.

Jimmy had just bitten into his sandwich, and with Leroy's last comment, he'd stopped moving entirely. He looked like the frozen statue of The Thinker, but with a sandwich in his mouth.

Leroy stood and turned toward the door of his house. "I think I'll be takin' me that nap now," he said. "Stay and eat all your lunch. And if you wanna see how the most amazing firewood operation the world over operates, show up about ten o'clock." And with that, he went inside to have his nap.

Jimmy ate the bite of sandwich that was in his mouth, but he put the rest of his sandwich in his cooler and stood and began making his way back to Jacob Mack's dump truck. Curiosity had just killed his appetite.

***

Jimmy pulled his personally owned vehicle, an old Jeep Wrangler, into 'ol Leroy's driveway as darkness fell, about seven p.m., as it was now mid-October in Virginia. He got out and began walking up the porch steps before looking up and noticing that 'ol Leroy was sitting on the porch in the same chair he always seemed to be sitting in.

"You're early," 'ol Leroy said. He was drinking a cup of coffee. He offered Jimmy a cup, but Jimmy declined, claiming he'd never sleep if he drank coffee this late.

"I live an hour south of Charlottesville," Jimmy said. "I don't think I could wait until ten to come out and then make it home by a decent time and then get up for work tomorrow. I hope you don't mind me coming out early."

"Not at all," Leroy said. "But the action ain't gonna start for a few more hours."

"Look," Jimmy said, sitting on the top porch step. "I don't have to see it. You seem like a pretty straight shooter. I'd like to just hear what's going on out here, from your mouth, to settle my curiosity, I guess. I'll take you at your word, and then I'll get home before it's too late so I can get some sleep."

"Well," 'ol Leroy said. "I can tell you exactly how it all happened, but I'm tellin' ya now, you ain't gonna believe a word of it, and you'll be convinced I'm crazier than a shithouse rat."

"Try me," Jimmy said.

"All right," Leroy said. He took a sip of coffee, and then he began telling his story, and it went like this.

***

Thirty years before, Leroy Jenkins had been a mail carrier. He'd lost his job because everyday, after getting his route done early, he'd stop by one of the local pubs to have a few beers and milk out the clock for the rest of the day. He would joke about it when he got back to the post office, half lit or more than half lit, about how he was getting paid to drink beer.

Until the day he drove his mail truck into the ass end of a school bus.

The bus was stopped, and the last child had just gotten off. No one was injured. Not a single scratch. But the police came, of course, to file a report, and they noticed that Jenkins had been drinking. He failed their field sobriety test, was given a D.U.I. and summarily lost his job as a mailman.

Jenkins knew a guy who knew a guy who knew a guy who had just started up a tree removal service company and who was looking for help. Jenkins met up with the guy, Jacob Mack, and was not only given a second chance at employment, but would find a good, true friend in Mack, in time. Mack, too, benefited professionally, because as it turned out, Jenkins had been left his family's farm just a few years before when his mother had died. Mack was making money hand over fist removing fallen trees for all the rich people in the area, but a considerable portion of his profits were being handed out by having to pay landfills and private landowners to dump the removed trees on their properties. When Jenkins first heard of this, he told Mack that that was poppycock, and that he had a twenty acre field out in the middle of the woods about a half mile behind his old farmhouse, and that Mack could put as many trees as he wanted back there for free.

"I'm gonna tell ya now, though," Jenkins had said. "I'm probably gonna cut and split it up and sell it as firewood. So I'll be making something off of it."

"So what," Mack had told him in reply. "You'll be saving me a small fortune. I don't care what you do with it."

And with that, their deal had been struck.

***

Jenkins' family's farm had been in the family since the mid 1800's, and during that entire period, the family had never allowed anyone to hunt on the land. Sure, they took the occasional deer and a bunch of squirrels and rabbits at times, especially when times were tough, which they occasionally were, but no one else had ever been granted that permission. The story as to why this was, a story passed down from generation to generation, was that it was because there were certain forest creatures living on the property that the family felt needed to be protected. The family had learned that in protecting these creatures, these creatures would protect them in return.

How?

Well, there were several occasions back in the late 1920's and early 1930's, during the depression, when times had been really tough. Even wild game was hard to come by, because so many people were out there hunting, killing everything that moved, because if they didn't, they would have no meat to eat. The American wild turkey nearly became extinct during this period, and all because so many people were so hungry.

The Jenkins family fared well during that period, because, once a week, and for a number of years, they would open their front door of an early morning, and there, hanging in an old hickory nut tree in the front yard, by wild grapevine, would be a whitetail deer, only recently killed. The family would have meat for the entire week. And the following week? Like clockwork, they'd have fresh vinision hanging in their old hickory nut tree again.

And then there was that time in the 1950's ('ol Leroy had been a boy and could remember this time well), when the house caught on fire in the middle of the night. It had been during the last harvest of the year. It was the first night of the year that the family was actually burning wood in their woodstove, and there had been a bird's nest built in the top of the flu earlier in the year that had caught fire. The cinders scattered across the roof and set the top portion of the eastward facing side of the house on fire. Everyone inside was exhausted from having worked the harvest all day and they did not wake up.

Until the banging on the outside of the house started! Just outside the downstairs bedroom windows.

The family rose and escaped the blaze. They fell back, fifty yards from the house to watch it burn, as they huddled together in blankets they'd brought with them from their beds, doing their best to stay warm in the chill night's air.

Their saviors' favors had not stopped with waking them. The family watched as tall, dark figures moving frantically in the night carried bucket after bucket of water from the pond in the backyard to the blaze and extinguished the flames, allowing them to have caused only minor damage.

But the most amazing part, at least as far as what Jimmy was here for tonight, was when they'd come to 'ol Leroy's aid when his back started going out and he was no longer able to do the backbreaking work that he'd been doing for about ten years for his new, best good buddy Jacob Mack.

True to his word, 'ol Leroy began cutting, splitting and stacking quite a bit of the wood that his buddy Jacob Mack was delivering to his giant field at the back of his farm. But 'ol Leroy was no spring chicken. He was beginning to get up there in years, and there had been a time or two when he'd lifted with his back instead of his legs. When he'd twisted this way when he should have twisted that way. And he didn't even like to *think* about what his body had been put through back in the war. The amount of work he was able to do was becoming greatly limited, and he knew that Jacob Mack could tell, and he had the feeling that the only reason his buddy was keeping him on at the job was because he didn't want to fire him because he was a friend. And he also knew that as his injuries progressed, he would be hard pressed to feed himself in his old age.

So he came up with a plan.

Jacob went through his out buildings and collected all the axes and splitting mauls and wedges and sledgehammers that he had. He put them in the back of his old Ford F250 and hauled them out to the field where Jacob had given him so much free firewood. He set up splitting stations throughout, and he went around, throughout the day, splitting and stacking wood at the various stations. The entire time he could feel eyes upon him, and knew that the entire time there were eyes upon him.

At the end of the day, he walked to the treeline, where field met forest. "I have a favor to ask," he yelled into the forest. "I can't do this very much anymore. It hurts."

He listened, yet he heard nothing. Even the crickets had stopped chirping, but he knew that was a good thing, because that meant the ones for whom his message was meant were near.

"Now, we've helped each other out for a right good while now," Jenkins shouted into the forest. "I could have exploited you. Charged people five dollars to come see you. Sold t-shirts and coffee mugs on this new thing they call the internet, but I haven't done that." He took a pause, choosing his next words carefully. "I'm gettin' awful down in the back now," he said when he spoke again. "And I could use a little help. It's all I'm askin'."

And with that, he said no more. He limped over to his old F250 pickup, after having worked hard all day splitting and stacking firewood at the various stations he'd set up, and he drove home and fell asleep almost instantly once getting into bed.

And the next day he returned to the field to find that every single log that had been lying in the field- literally hundreds of them- had been cleanly split and properly stacked!

***

"So you're telling me," Jimmy said after 'ol Leroy had finished his story. "That you expect me to believe that you've got a couple dozen Bigfoot Sasquatches out there in your back twenty splittin' and stackin' firewood every night?"

Just as Jimmy finished speaking, the two men on the front porch of 'ol Leroy's house heard the first smack. It was the smacking sound of an ax, in a field half a mile behind the house, crashing through the first piece of unsplit, yet soon to be cleanly split, firewood. Jimmy's eyes grew big after having heard the sound, but they grew even bigger when he heard the next one only seconds later. And then the next, and then the next.

"Looks like they're startin' a little early tonight," 'ol Leroy said, glancing down at his wrist watch. It was still just a bit before nine o'clock. He'd stretched his story out a while as he'd told it, because that's what any truly good storyteller does. They stretch their stories out. "But that's okay, I guess."

"I'd best be leavin'," Jimmy said, standing and turning toward his Jeep. "I have a long day tomorrow. I'm sure I'll be bringing you out a load."

"You sure you don't wanna go out to the back twenty and have a look?" 'ol Leroy said with a smile on his face, because he knew that Jimmy was convinced. He didn't need to see.

"That's okay," Jimmy said, and he got in his Jeep without even saying goodbye, and he made his way out of 'ol Leroy's driveway and onto the main Virginia biway that would take him to Charlottesville and then home from there. He promised himself, especially after having heard such a story, that no matter how tempting it was to take a drink or twelve, he would *not* stop at the Bigfoot Sasquatch micro-brewery just down the road from 'ol Leroys.

He kept his promise.

The End

***

The following stories are from Bigfoot Sasquatch Files Volume 5:

1

Letter From Hollywood

I've never believed in luck. Unless, of course, we put it into view as Yogi Berra saw it. As he said, "the harder I work, the luckier I get."

I've always viewed people who say anything about anyone else being lucky to have achieved anything as a statement coming from a place of sour grapes. For some reason, they just don't want to give credit where credit is due. But then, of course, much of it *could* be that the person who's always referring to everyone else as lucky is really just lazy.

And then there are those who always talk about their ship coming in. Ever notice how they never even go down to the docks to look for it? And what I mean by that is, instead of getting up off their asses and going after whatever it is that they want, be it a promotion at work, more success with their small business, etc., they simply talk about their ship coming in. This, too, strikes me as lazy.

But for the past ten years I've caught myself doing both! Relying on luck and waiting for my ship to come in. *Time to take control and get up off my ass*, I thought, a couple months back, when I'd come to this realization, and I did, and here's how it all went.

Okay, what am I talking about? In what area of my life did I want to get lucky? What ship was I waiting to come into my personal port of existence?

A letter from Hollywood!

Yes, you read that right. A letter from Hollywood.

So here's the deal. My family and I used to be poor. Very poor. No, that's not very accurate. We were even poorer than that.

We were *third world* poor!

And let me tell you, poverty does *not* exist *anywhere* in America like it does in third world countries. There *are* no benefits offices to run to. There *are* no EBT cards for free food. And you do *not* get free medical treatment if you get sick or injured and go to the hospital. If you don't have the money to pay for your treatment, they will *not* treat you. They will let you *die* in the waiting room and then charge your survivors a fee for having to remove your body. And *none* of this is an exaggeration.

My wife is Filipina, and I lived in the Philippines with her for nearly six years, and it's where our son was born, so he was there, too, of course, and man, were we desperate. There were so many nights, and by 'so many' I mean *most* nights, that my wife and I would go to bed raging hungry, but happy in knowing that we'd somehow managed to see that our son ate again that day.

While lying in bed, hungry, my wife and I would often talk of just about anything in order to keep the other from hearing our stomachs growling. One of our favorite fantasies to talk about was getting a letter from Hollywood. Some big production studio claiming that they'd read one of my novels or short story collections and that they thought it was so damn good that it just *had* to be turned into a movie for the big screen, and since I was still relatively young and marginally attractive, I just *had* to star in it. We'd laugh so hard while having this conversation we couldn't hear our bellies growling, and sometimes, we'd wake up our son.

"Damn it!" I said a couple months back when I came to my 'ah ha moment' about waiting around on luck and boats, and realizing I was only being lazy.

"What?" my wife asked.

"The letter from Hollywood."

"Oh, yeah," she said, and laughed, thinking of the memories. "What about it?"

"Why am I waiting around on it?" I said. "I'm going to go to them!"

"You're going to go to Hollywood?" my wife said. "I want to go."

"No," I told her. "I'm not going to go to Hollywood. I'm going to contact some of these online companies that make all these made for internet originals. Like Amazon and Netflix. Even Hulu.

"Why?" she asked.

"Bigfoot Sasquatch Files," I told her, wondering why she hadn't seen it before me and pointed it out.

"What?" she asked.

"Bigfoot Sasquatch Files," I said again. "All those short stories in that series are really starting to pile up. And they're great. People love them. I get tons of five star reviews on Amazon, and a bunch of one stars from trolls I've banned from our YouTube channel (yes, we know you happily spend a few bucks to buy the e-versions of my books so you can leave a one out of five stars review. Please, please, PRETTY please keep doing it, because we need your money).

"That's a good idea," she said.

I immediately ran upstairs to my office, which is in one of our spare bedrooms, to send out inquiry emails to all the online movie studios. However, the bed in my office looked inviting, so I took a nap. But I sent those emails out after I woke up, by God!

No more waiting on Hollywood! I was going to them!

***

Weeks passed, and I heard nothing from any of the online studios, and I'd pretty much started thinking the whole thing had just been another one of my pie in the sky ideas. I've had plenty throughout my lifetime, but hey, sometimes they've worked out.

And then.

I received an email from one of the online studios.

"They're coming!" I yelled while running down the stairs to tell my wife.

"Who comes?" she said.

"Hollywood!" I said, still screaming even though I was now downstairs and in the kitchen where she was. She was cooking something that involved chicken feet and tons of soy sauce. We'd no doubt be eating whatever this strange concoction was over mountains of plain white rice.

"Really?" she said, not sounding too enthusiastic, but I knew her mind was elsewhere. On the chicken feet. It's her favorite food.

"Yeah," I said. "And they're gonna let me be in the show. I get to play the role of Crazy Lake."

"Who they get to play Bigfoot Sasquatch?" my wife asked.

"Well, that's just it," I said. "I've convinced them not to get an actor to play the role of Bigfoot Sasquatch. I told them I'd draw the real ones onto the sets by doing the weird shit I do to draw them into my YouTube videos. I'll run around like a madman with my clothes inside out while brushing my teeth and wielding a sledgehammer. Low crawl with a chainsaw in one hand and a machete in the other. You know how I roll."

"When they come here?" my wife asked.

"Day after tomorrow," I said, and we were so happy about our letter from Hollywood, even though I'd actually been the one to send it, and it was an e-version, by way of email, and this online movie studio was out of Newark, New Jersey, but hey, it's all the same thing, just more modernized, right?

Our letter from Hollywood had become a reality!

***

I'd like to say that things went great, and that we shot our entire first season of Bigfoot Sasquatch Files, the e-show, but that's not how things went.

"Okay. I've just got one question," the director said after going over the screenplay for the first episode. It's the first time I'd ever written a screenplay. You'd think it would have been easy, since I simply converted one of my old YouTube videos to screenplay form, but there is way more to it than that. You have to write in, like, the instructions for the cameraman and all kinds of stuff. Here's an example:

Camera zooms in on Crazy Lake
Crazy Lake: "Get my six!"
Camera zooms out and focuses on forested area behind Crazy Lake.
Camera pans, slowly, left. Pauses for a three count.
Camera does slow pan right.
Camera zooms in on Crazy Lake.
Crazy Lake (while brushing his teeth with one hand and holding up a sledgehammer in the other): "The comptroller of the ultimate contraption shall neither hate the poor nor envy the rich!"
Crazy Lake spits toothpaste toward the camera.

"What in the name of Fuckola is this shit?" the director asked.

"It's art," I said. "And I'll draw him, her, it or they out into the open and then you can get them on camera."

"You're telling me," he said, "that you run around here acting like a crazy bastard the entire first episode of season one, and not only will it draw Bigfoot Sasquatch out of hiding, but you expect people to come back for episode two?"

"Potentially," I said.

"Potentially what?" he said. He sounded very frustrated, and we'd only been working together for half an hour, but I kept my chin up. I'd always seen these director types portrayed as primadonnas in the movies, so I figured that's all it was.

"Potentially both," I said. "We'll draw the creature out, get him, her, it or them, if there's more than one of them, on camera. Just for a glimpse. And then people will come back to watch episode two to see if I've completely lost my marbles. It's like a trainwreck. People just can't look away from that shit."

"Let's try the first scene," the director said, sinking his head- his shaking head- into the palm of his right hand as he held his right arm up at the elbow with his left hand, which was crossed over his chest. Man, one thing was for sure. This guy was striking me as a pretty good director. He looked completely disgusted by my screenplay and ideas. I really felt like we were going to do great with this.

But we didn't.

We shot the first scene, which showcased me shaving only half my face. I left the other half for another time.

"Cut!" the director yelled. "Why in fuckall did you only shave half your face before you started running up the hill with that goddamn sledgehammer?"

"It's in the script," I said. "Didn't you even read it?"

He sunk his head- his shaking head- back into the palm of his hand, and he directed me to shave off the other half of my face, because he just thought it looked stupid. I tried to explain that that was how my entire research method worked. You had to get the potential Bigfoot Sasquatch that may or may not live in the woods behind my house curious enough to come out and see what in the name of fuckall Crazy Lake is doing today. If you're just out there doing normal shit like a normal person, he, she, it or they are not going to come out. Normal is boring.

We tried shooting a few more scenes, but the director had had enough. He just kept holding his shaking head, and he just kept complaining, and he finally said, "where in the hell is this supposed Bigfoot Sasquatch thing, anyway? You said he'd show up if we did this."

"First of all, it's not a supposed Bigfoot Sasquatch. It's a *potential* Bigfoot Sasquatch," I said, correcting him. "And I don't know if it's a he, a she, an it, or a they."

"What's that even mean?" he asked.

"It means I don't know enough about these creatures that may or may not exist to assign them a pronoun."

"Pack it up," he screamed to his assistants. All two of them. "We've wasted enough time with this horseshit already, and we're not wasting any more. Let's head back up to Newark."

"Why did you even come down here?" I asked the director as I followed him and his crew of two off the hill behind my house and down to their rented minivan in the driveway.

"I saw that you had a large YouTube following," he said. "I assumed it meant there was actually hope for this project. But I think all it says is there's a fuckton of really stupid people on YouTube who like watching stupid fucking videos."

"Wow," I said. "I'll pray for you." And I did. I asked God to please bring him and his crew and their families the same health, wealth and prosperity that he (or she, or it, or they) have so blessed me and my family with, and then I told him not to forget to shut the gate on his way out, and not to let it hit him where the good Lord split him, and not to waste his time in coming back, because he wasn't welcome.

And they left.

But our hopes of achieving our show did not, as only three days later, the next crew from the next online e-version of Hollywood, a group fresh out of Atlanta, Georgia, came to our homestead to give us a shot!

Here's how that went.

***

"Listen," I told the director of the next outfit when they arrived. "You have got to give me full creative license, or this isn't going to work out any better than it did with the last jacklegs."

"Someone else has already been here?" the guy said, and right off the bat I knew I'd be able to work with him. He was a younger millennial. One of the typical beta-males of his generation. You know, the ones who were raised to believe that masculinity is offensive, because it represents an unfair advantage over women? So masculinity should thereby be avoided at all costs? It was the reason Hooters restaurants have been shutting down all over the country in recent years. These young males actually find breasts to be offensive. Well, the admiration of breasts for any purpose other than nursing an infant.

"Yeah," I said, "and I've got three more outfits lined up to come out after you if this doesn't work." I was lying, not something I like to do, or that I do very much, but I've been working in social media for more than a decade, and let me tell you, it's an industry filled with dishonest scumbags. Most of the folks who work in social media don't even use their real names. Mostly so they can make fake news, claim to have reliable sources, etc., and then avoid any repercussions when and if the truth comes out. This guy was going by the name PeaceB4All, and I seriously doubt his mother named him that. But hell, who knows. Anyone who would raise a male to view masculinity as offensive and the admiration of breasts for any purpose other than feeding an infant as offensive would probably mind fuck her young male child in just about anyway, to include giving him a fucked up name like PeaceB4All.

"We'll do it your way, then," PeaceB4All said, barely audible, because he spoke mostly in whispers. I guess he didn't want to give any indication that he'd gone through puberty a few years back and the influx of testosterone had made his voice deeper. It might offend someone.

At any rate, we got set up, they got the cameras rolling (well, their i-phone 11-s's), and we were off. I started out with the typical "get my six" and started going around my place acting batshit crazy. I figured I'd throw in a new trick or two. Something that the potential Bigfoot Sasquatch that may or may not live in the woods behind my house may or may not have seen yet (because it's always possible while sleepwalking or while having a PTSD induced flashback, I might have unknowingly been outside doing this shit before).

I got one of my wife's sports bras and strapped it to my forehead, like those guys in the old movie from the 1980's, Weird Science. You know, when the guys were trying to create a woman. It had no effect on the director, because I don't think he knew what it was. But he was not my primary concern. Bigfoot Sasquatch was, and I always felt as if the males of the species probably had pretty high labidos. Men were still men where Bigfoot Sasquatch came from, as I saw it.

Next, I put a burlap sack over myself. I'd cut a whole in the bottom of the center, so when I turned it upside down and slipped it over my head, my head poked through. I didn't create any holes for my arms. Instead, I folded my arms up in front of me and used my elbows to push the bag out, giving the appearance of having two really big infant feeders, to put it in the words of our director, PeaceB4All. I knew I was taking a risk of any alpha-male Bigfoot Sasquatches that may or may not have been hiding in the woodline coming at me to have his way with me, but I'd been running and cycling a lot, and despite looking like an old man with a big twinkie tummy, I knew I could run fast enough to escape him, because I was not getting any closer than fifty yards from the woodline. This would give me just enough of a head start to make it into the house. As far as PeaceB4All went, well, may the God of his choosing be him.

So I did a couple of passes in front of the woodline behind our family's campsite at the top of the hill behind our house, and on my third pass, I turned to face the camera (well, the i-Phone 11s) that was at my twelve o'clock, making sure not to look directly into the camera (that's how the viewers can tell the video is fake), and what I saw was that the entire film crew, all three of them, were looking up in a tree, about twenty feet above my head, and their mouths were so agap that they were nearly touching the ground. Well, not really, but this is literature, and I'm trying to be descriptive. Okay, their mouths were agap enough to where they might have been able to stick a McDonald's Big Mac in them and barely scrape the bun with their teeth.

The next thing I know, all three of the crew members scream bloody murder. Well, I could hear two of them screaming bloody murder. I couldn't really hear PeaceB4All screaming, because it was a whispered scream, but his face gave all indication that had he been born a generation before, when men were still men, he would be screaming. All three of them, making sure to powerfully secure their i-Phones took off running down the hill. They jumped in their little Prius (God bless them for being part of that group who's trying to save the world one half electric car at a time), and headed back down to Atlanta. They never said a word before leaving, and I never heard from them after that.

After they'd driven off, I slowly turned and looked up in the tree where they had been gazing. I may or may not have seen what it was that scared them off, and it may or may not have been salivating at the mouth, eyeballing me not as if I were the feeder of infants, but as if I was skankily making my way across the dining room floor, a platter holding a greasy ass cheeseburger and soggy, undercooked fries in one hand and a mug of stale beer in the other. Needless to say, I ran like hell for the house, and there was no potentially about it.

Unfortunately, our letter from Hollywood, which had actually been a letter from me to Newark, New Jersey and Atlanta, Georgia, didn't pan out.

Yet!

We've not given up hope, but I guess for the meantime, I'm kind of taking the loser's way out in that I'll just wait a little longer for my ship to come in, and hopefully, in time, I'll get lucky.

The End

The One That Got Away

(For A Friend)

"Momma thinks we should go camping together to get to know each other better before the semester starts."

It was J.R. My roommate for the upcoming fall semester at college. Rather, as I viewed it at the time, my lackey, and I his liege.

J.R. was the kid brother of a girl I'd gone to high school with. She was a year behind me, and despite the fact that she was absolutely gorgeous, we'd never been anything more than friends. But not 'just friends,' as people might say in defense when accused of there being more to it than that, but 'good friends.' You see, we both ran track, and we were both awesome at it, and we were both obsessed with the sport. Sure, when people saw us together at the meets, or sitting together on the bus on the way to or from the meets, or hanging out together at lunch in school, they'd make their accusations, but even they knew the truth.

When J.R.'s sister was a junior, and I a senior, J.R. was still in middle school. My only memories of him before our camping trip and the school year that would follow was of a near snot nosed little kid who always sat between his mother and father at track meets and who never said a word. I'd tried talking to him, just to be polite and respectful, when I'd see him at meets, but he never had anything to say. Literally. I mean he wouldn't even speak back.

"Is your brother dim?" I'd asked his sister once at a track meet.

"No," she'd said. "He just hasn't come out of his shell yet."

***

"Sure," I said, into the phone. This was back when there was nothing but landlines. "Let's go camping. It'll be fun."

Oh, God, is what I really thought. *This is going to be boring as shit!*

The semester started at the end of August, only three weeks from the time I received J.R.'s call. It was early August and hot as hell in Appalachiastan. We decided we'd go camping at one of the few places public camping was allowed in our region. Like most third world provinces, the Government owned most of the land in our area, in this case, the United States Department of the Interior was our Lord, as our entire province, outside of a few small municipalities was designated National Forest.

Our campground of choice was made up of a dozen or so tent sites. Each site provided a large, wooden picnic table, a metal fire ring for a campfire, and a grill which was cemented into the ground so none of the local rabal could steal it and take it back to their mobile homes. There was a wooden box with envelopes at the gate of the campground, which was never locked, and you simply stuck three one dollar bills in the envelope, wrote your campsite number on the envelope, and dropped it in the box. The park ranger would come by each evening at dark to get the money. If you forgot, or if you were trying to squat for a night, he'd usually just let you. No one gives a shit in Appalachiastan. Like any third world country, it's why the region is nearly third world poor.

Apathy!

I was twenty two years old at the time and going into my sixth and what would finally turn out be my last year in college. Sure, it was taking me a little longer than most to graduate because I worked almost full time almost every year I was in college, but I also have to admit, that like any good college student, I had a tendency to party balls at night and miss those early morning classes the next day. It didn't really matter much, because I'd make sure to show up for a class or two before any tests, and I'd ace the tests, but what I would find out is that the intellectual elitist types who were known as professors considered it an insult that some hillbilly kid from Appalachiastan could party balls, entertain all the pretty college girls they all had their sick fantasies about, never go to class, and then show up on test days and get A's. They would eventually start kicking me out of their classes for "excessive absences" thereby giving me a grade of "F" for the course, shattering my GPA, but despite this, I would still go on to graduate, barely, and continue to succeed in the real world which they claimed to know so much about, yet spent no real time in...

...and I continued to entertain the ladies of which they could only fantasize.

Na na na, boo boo, bitches!

Remembering J.R. as a knot on a log, I made sure to get a case of beer for our camping trip. Sure, it was only going to be a one-nighter, but one night can be a very long time when you're stuck with someone who carries on a conversation with only a few words, those words being, "uh-huh," "yup," and "oh." I figured a few cold ones, or a dozen, would get me through it. I was sure J.R. didn't even drink, so I was confident I wouldn't run out.

I was spending the summer at my apartment where J.R. and I would live during the upcoming school year, so I drove into our craphole Appalachian American town and picked him and his supplies up and headed up to our campground. As fate would have it, his big sister, my old friend, was visiting their parents, so I got to see her for the first time in several years. I'll say two things here. As a young man who was no longer obsessed with track and field, I certainly saw her through different eyes. She was absolutely drop dead gorgeous, as she'd always been, and I began mentally kicking myself in the ass for never having pushed the envelope a little more in regard to my relationship with her all those years ago. The insult to go with this injury was that she had her fiance with her. He was a recent accounting grad who'd landed a gig with a large investment firm, and he looked like a Ken doll. I took the high road, and I wished them the best, but that old Billy Ray Cirus song, "It Could Have Been Me," which was new at the time, was blaring inside my head.

Oh, well.

J.R. and I drove to our campsite in half silence. I call it half silence, because I talked, but he didn't, except for the occasional, "uh-huh," "yup," or "oh." The hour long drive felt like a day, but alas, we finally reached our destination. We put our three dollars in the little envelope at the front gate, took the campsite furthest back, which would end up being the closest to the approximately five acre lake only a one hundred yard hike through the woods, and we set up our tent. After doing so, I cracked open a can of Stroh's (hey, it was Appalachiastan), and offered one to J.R. "No thanks," he said, and I considered it a small victory to have gotten two new words out of him.

After I had a couple brewskies, we decided we'd grab our fishing poles and walk to the lake and go fishing. I knew our efforts would be futile because of the heat. Here it was, early August, and it had to be every bit of ninety eight degrees. The humidity was so high that our clothes were sticking to us. We'd taken off our shirts, only to find that the local mosquitos found us quite tasty, so we'd put them back on just as quickly as we'd shedded them for at least a slight layer of protection. There were no other campers at the campground, because despite the local populace being referred to as 'dumb hillbillies' by those who lived outside of the semi-autonomous, culturally and economiclly wise, region of Appalachianstan, they'd had enough sense to stay inside where there was air conditioning or fans. There was simply no way any cold blooded animal, like fish, was going to move on a day like this. You'd have to get lucky enough to cast your bait into it's open mouth while it was breathing.

Sure enough, as I'd suspected, the fish weren't biting. J.R. and I stood on the lonely dock of the lake, heat waves glistening in every direction, throwing cast after cast to no avail. The more we cast, the more we sweat, and what little bit of a noticeable effect I'd gotten off my two cans of Stroh's was now gone.

Just as I was about to recommend we head back to the campsite and wait until evening, when the temperatures would be cooler and we might have a better chance of actually catching something, which was really my well thought out excuse of heading back to drink more beer, we heard what sounded like a broken airplane coming up the mountain. Not by way of air, but on the road.

"What the hell is that?" I said, turning to look behind us.

"Huh?" J.R. said, the only word in his vocabulary which would be fitting.

"Do you hear that?" I said.

"Uh, huh," he said, turning to face the same direction I was.

A few minutes later, we saw it. The golden calf, pulling into the driveway behind us and heading straight for us.

The stock truck!

For those reading this who don't know what the stock truck is, it's the truck owned and operated by the local fish hatcheries that carries large tanks of highly oxygenated water on the back, and those highly oxygenated tanks of water are filled with fish! In this case, trout!

Now, here's something that even most people who understand all this might not understand. At this time of year, the tail end of the dog days of summer, those stock trucks carry what's called 'breeders.' These are the absolutely oldest fish from the hatcheries that they'd used for egg laying and fertilizing for many years, and which are probably only months away from dying due to old age. The hatcheries tend to do the humane thing by releasing them into the wild so they can spend their final months living like real fish.

Translation?

These fish are freaking HUGE!

Ginormous!

As in, Ginormica Enormica!

J.R. and I reeled our lines in and watched in awe as the two men operating the truck pulled right up to the water's edge, got out, took two big nets on long poles off the side of the truck, climbed onto the top of the truck, opened the water tanks and began scooping up the largest trout either of us had ever seen in our lives and tossing them into the lake. It was as if every other fish they threw into the water was a full three feet long, and every other one was pretty damn close to it.

"Jesus Christ," J.R. said, barely audible, but he'd said it. I didn't know which amazed me more at the time. The size of the trout being stocked into the lake, right before our eyes, or that there were other words in J.R.'s vocabulary.

After throwing in what seemed like an endless amount of netted fish, the two men closed the lids to the tanks and then climbed down off of the top of the truck. They hooked their nets back to the side of the stock truck. The man riding shotgun jumped in the truck and buckled up, and the driver, just before getting in, looked at us, smiled big, and said, "have fun, boys."

And boy, did we!

We watched the stock truck drive off out of sight, and we were blinking, over and over, as if to make sure the sight was really real, not some sort of Appalachiastanian mirage. And as soon as the truck was gone, and after we could no longer hear the rumbling of its engine heading down the mountain, we turned around and cast our baits into the lake.

"Son of a bitch!" J.R. screamed, having hooked into a trout the second his bait hit the water. We were using salmon eggs, little red balls that may or may not have actually been salmon eggs, but they smelled like fish, and they usually worked, and boy, did they work on this hot August afternoon. "Gaaaawwwwwdamn!" he screamed as he worked his reel, which was screeching insanely as the giant fish on the other end of the line pulled out more line, despite J.R.'s best efforts. You could tell the kid was a pretty regular fisherman, because he reached down and tightened his drag, just enough to where the giant trout he had on the line could fight without snapping the line. The mistake many anglers make is that they set the drag too tight and the big fish merely snap the line. J.R. did not make this mistake.

It took nearly ten minutes, and I halfway thought J.R. was prolonging the fight to be melodramatic, but when he finally landed that fish, I was able to see that the whole thing had been legit. He pulled in a ginormous brown trout, the likes of which I'd never seen. We measured it, and the thing, from tip of its snout to the end of its tail, was thirty eight inches in length! It had to have weighed fifteen pounds! I had never seen a trout that big in my life and neither had J.R., nor have I since.

"Dad's gonna shit his pants when he sees this," J.R. said. I couldn't believe what I'd heard. This young man actually *did* understand and speak the English language! His vocabulary was made up of more than three simple words and/or grunts. I was witnessing magic happening.

I cast my line into the water, and sure enough, as soon as my bait hit, a mouth the likes of which I'd never seen on a trout came up and took my bait and the fish attached to the mouth began heading out into the middle of the lake. I set the hook and tried to reel, and alas, my drag had been set too tightly, and SNAP! My line broke and the big one, at least *my* big one, got away.

J.R. and I fished only another fifteen minutes longer, because that's all the time it took for us to both catch our limit of six trout each. We had, between us, a dozen trout, and the smallest of our catch was eighteen inches long. The largest, of course, was J.R.'s monster of a brown trout.

"Let's go fry these sumbitches up and drink some beer!" J.R. said, and I felt like I was hanging out with a different guy than I'd come up to camp with.

J.R. and I made our way through the trail back to the campsite, and we did just as he'd recommended. Before we even lit a fire in the grill, we opened up a can of Stroh's each, we toasted our miraculous trout fishing success, and then we began to drink. And we drank like thirsty men lost in the desert for days with no water, but our water had hops and yeast and barley, and these ingredients had been allowed to ferment and the results had been cold filtered, and we did drink of the results of this fine refining process and we did become drunk upon the alcohol because it was in excess.

And at some point, we actually cooked some fish and ate them, too.

J.R. and I partied into the night. I found out so much about J.R. He actually had a girlfriend. They'd actually known each other in the Biblical sense, though I had to swear not to tell his sister, because she might tell their mom. I confided in J.R. that I regretted not taking my relationship with his smoking hot sister to another level, and he confided in me that he thought that was gross and that if I had, he might have had to whoop me. I kept it to myself that I didn't think he could, because we were drunk upon the alcohol that had been in excess, afterall, and when you get two hillbillies in Appalachianstan drunk on alcohol wherein excess, best good buddies and future roommates and all, or not, you're more likely to get a fistfight than you're not.

And then we passed the fuck out, just before the sun came up.

"Do you hear that?"

It was J.R. He started by pushing me in the head to wake me up. I was still drunk. I looked at my watch and saw that it was just a little after 7:00 a.m. We'd slept maybe two hours at best.

"Hear what?" I mumbled, but J.R. didn't need to answer, for just as I'd said it, I *did* hear it. It sounded as if someone or some*thing* was opening our cooler outside.

"My fish!" J.R. said, jumping up to his knees, and then falling over, because he was obviously still drunk, too, and then he jumped back up to his knees and made his way to the tent's door and unzipped it. He stuck his head out and yelled, "Get-ah-outtah-heh!" Appalachian American for "get on out of here."

I rose to my knees, slowly, and joined him at the tent's door. I looked out and saw what had to have been the biggest black bear I'd ever seen in my life. The thing had to weigh nearly four hundred pounds. If it were to stand on its hind legs, it would have had to have been nearly seven feet tall. The bear had just knocked the lid off of our cooler.

"Get-ah-outtah-heh!" J.R. yelled again.

"Are you fucking crazy?" I said to J.R., and in not much more than a whisper.

"My fish," he said.

The day and night before, when we'd fried up our trout and eaten it, we did not fry up J.R.'s giant brown. We didn't even cut its head off or gut it. We'd put it on ice for two reasons. Number one, he wanted to show his father, because he wanted him to be proud of him (this is something Appalachian American males spend their lifetimes doing, trying to make their father's proud of them, though few if any ever achieve this, because their fathers' fathers had never shown any pride in them, so it had not been a learned trait), and secondly, he wanted to have it officially weighed and measured for we both thought it might have been a new state record.

We watched out the tent door as J.R.'s worst fears came true. The giant bear took the giant brown trout up in its mouth and simply sauntered out into the woods, no doubt taking it off somewhere more private to devour it.

"Come on!" J.R. said, and he jumped out of the tent and scooped up a handful of rocks. He began following the bear, pelting it with rocks, and cursing its mother's maiden name.

"Are you fucking crazy?" I said, crawling out of the tent and picking up a handful of rocks myself. Since I was still drunk and not thinking too clearly, I began pelting the big black bear with rocks as well. I figured since J.R. was cursing its mother's maiden name, I said a few derogatory things about its father.

We followed the bear about a hundred yards down a different trail than the one that led to the lake. This one led in the opposite direction, deeper into the woods on the other side of our campsite. At this point, the bear looked back at us, as if just now noticing us. We saw the giant brown trout in its mouth. So far it had not been damaged. There may have been hope after all. The bear turned back to face the direction in which it had been heading and then it moved further down the trail, deeper into the forest.

We scooped up more rocks and continued to follow the bear. We had reverted to cursing it's siblings and offspring since cursing its parents had no effect. Four hundred yards into the woods now, and we were about to give up all hope, but that's when it happened. An event that I will remember until my dying day.

At first, we thought the bear had had enough. It turned and looked at us, and we saw its eyes grow even larger than they were. The bear stood up on its hind legs, and just as I'd suspected, it was every bit of seven feet tall. It opened its mouth, we thought to let out a mighty roar, but it made not a sound. We watched, as the giant brown trout dropped from its mouth, still undamaged, and fell to the forest floor.

And then we heard the roar.

But it came *not* from the bear!

The mighty roar came from behind and above us. We turned and looked upward, expecting to see a mountain lion in a tree. Allegedly, the last mountain lion seen in our part of Appalachiastan, officially, had been back during the Civil War, when our state had split from the much more prosperous state of Virginia. It had been shot and killed by a guard at a nearby Union prison camp which held Confederate P.O.W.'s. But rumors were always circulating about these giant cats being around, though in very small numbers.

However, what we saw sitting on the sizable limb of a giant oak was not a mountain lion. It was something even more rare. It was something that was not supposed to exist at all. It was…

Bigfoot Sasquatch!!!

We could hear the bear behind us taking off at full speed on all fours. It obviously wasn't even trying to miss running into the small saplings and seedlings and even some trees of considerable size that stood in its way. It merely ran *through* them, leaving a trail of destruction that looked very much like a small tornado had ripped through the area.

J.R. and I watched in both fear and disbelief as the Bigfoot Sasquatch, with only one leep, jumped to a limb every bit of twenty feet away, and then dropped to the ground, its back toward us, and then reach down and pick up the giant brown trout. It turned slowly to face us. We thought the bear had been amazingly tall, but this creature was taller by at least a foot. We thought the bear's shoulders had been broad, and they had been, but the shoulders of this creature were broader.

As we continued to look in disbelief, the giant Bigfoot Sasquatch raised the giant brown trout to its mouth, making it look like a sardine in comparison to itself, and then in one bite, a small bite, as if to see it it was even worth eating, the Bigfoot Sasquatch bit the entire head off of the giant trout. It chewed, once, twice, three times and then swallowed. For an instant, I would have sworn I'd seen a smile of approval, and then in only two giant, hungry bites, it ate the rest of the fish. Then, as if we weren't even there, it turned and merely walked slowly down the trail the bear had been travelling. We watched, as within a matter of mere seconds, it rounded the turn and disappeared into the forests' thick underbrush of mostly mountain laurel and scrag oak.

***

J.R. and I returned to our tent and attempted to sleep off our drunk. But after what we'd just seen, sleep eluded us. We waited until late afternoon that day, so that our drunks would at least have time to wear off, and then we packed our shit and headed off of the mountain.

I took J.R. back to his parents' house before heading back to what would soon be our shared apartment just off campus of our little hick college. Unfortunately, his sister had already left, so I didn't get to ogle at her, I mean, say goodbye to her again.

We told J.R.'s parents about the great fishing success we had, and we told them of J.R.'s giant brown trout. We told of how we ate all the fish except that one, and of how a giant black bear took it from our cooler that morning and carried it off into the woods. We ended our story there, daring not to run the risk of being committed to the local lunatic asylum for telling of the events that took place after that.

After we told our fishing story, J.R.'s parents looked at us intently for a full ten seconds, and then in unison, they began laughing their asses off.

"Yeah, right!" his mother said. "Did you guys practice that story the whole way home?"

"Yeah," his father said. "If you're gonna tell a whopper like that, why not go for broke?" J.R. and I looked at each other in disbelief. How could they *not* believe this story? It was certainly more believable than the truth. "Why not say," his father continued, "that a damn Bigfoot Sasquatch took your fish?"

With that, J.R.'s parents laughed even more hysterically.

Until they saw the look that J.R. and I exchanged.

And then they stopped laughing.

***

J.R. and I would go on to live for an entire school year together. We had our ups and downs as roommates will have, but there were far more ups than downs. We partied balls in our apartment, we partied balls at the college football games, and we partied balls at the bars. We played musical beds with many a fair lady, and we commiserated, enduring many a hangover together. But through it all, we were friends.

Sadly, like so many of my friends from my youth, J.R. and I ended up losing touch with each other. You see, we only spent one year together as roommates, because that would *indeed* be my last year of school. I graduated and left Appalachiastan, because I wanted something more out of life than digging coal or stacking lumber. Not that there's anything wrong with either profession- they are admirable, and they are necessary- but neither are for me.

I went back to the motherland of Virginia, and I would move on to other places from time to time- the west coast, the Middle East, Asia, and then eventually back to the motherland- but I never *did* reconnect with J.R.

And then sadly, and just recently, I got news that he'd passed on way too early.

J.R. never escaped Appalachiastan. He didn't manage to graduate from college and he ended up in the mines, like his father before him, and like his father's fathers for countless generations before that. J.R. had married a beautiful young woman and they'd enjoyed several children together, and then J.R. was killed in a motorcycle accident one night while on his way home from the mines. He was forty one years old.

We've all heard stories of the one that got away. *Who* or *what* was the one that got away in this story? Was it J.R.'s smoking hot sister? Was it the giant trout that snapped my line in the lake that day? A trout that I'm still convinced was larger than the one that J.R. caught? Was it the giant Bigfoot Sasquatch that we saw eat J.R.'s giant brown trout? And the opportunity to snap a picture of him, her, or it and have the undeniable evidence that researchers have been looking for for decades?

It was none of these.

It was J.R.

When we find a true friend in life. One who accepts us despite our faults, our flaws, our shortcomings, our human errors, our personal character defects- someone who loves us and approves of us in spite of ourselves- we should cherish them, nurture the friendship, and by all means, never let them go. Stay in touch. Because friends like that? Well, they are rare. They are more rare than the beauty of certain women. They are more rare than the giant fish raised in hatcheries and released into the wild in their final months of living. And, they are more rare than the elusive cryptids that I'm convinced roam the world around us, rarely seen as they may be.

J.R. was one of those friends.

And he was my friend.

I miss you, J.R., and I love you.

The End

3

Peekaboo!

(Originally Titled: The Unfortunate Demise Of The Campus Peeping Tom)

"Peekaboo!"

"Oh, my Christ!" Christie screamed as she jumped back three feet. She'd been walking up the bricked walkway of the campus, just in front of the Rotunda, when the large, smelly, in desperate need of a shave, shower and haircut sixty year old man jumped out from behind the large magnolia tree. He appeared to be about sixty years old, and though only five feet and nine inches tall, he had to have weighed three hundred pounds if he weighed an ounce. "What the fuck, dude!"

"Need me to carry your books for ya, there, sweetie?" the man said. He was wearing a long sleeved t-shirt that read 'grounds crew' so Christie assumed he worked for the university.

"No way, creeper!" Christie said, and she walked a huge circle around the guy, intentionally giving him a wide berth, and she increased the pace of her steps once around him and she headed for her dorm room.

Christie was the first girl with whom P.T., as he was known on campus by students and his co-workers alike (it stood for Peeping Tom) had played his little game of peekaboo today, but she would not be his last. For you see, his shift had just started.

***

"So, what was it like?" Ginger asked Jane. "Growing up poor. In Appalachiastan and all."

It was the end of the first month of the fall semester at the university. Ginger and Jane had had a bit of a rough start as roommates, because they'd come from two entirely different worlds, even though they grew up only a four hour's drive away from each other; Jane in the mountains of Appalachiastan, and Ginger in the rolling Blue Ridge Mountains of Albemarle County, Virginia.

Jane had known a toxic home where her single mother always entertained various men, many of which had tried to entertain Jane a time or two (before these men ended up having unfortunate demises and were never seen or heard from again), and Ginger had grown up with loving parents who'd met while attending their ivy league university, and they had raised Ginger in privilege- a four thousand square foot house on two hundred acres, and barns filled with horses and a dozen immigrants who may or may not have been in the country legally who tended to the horses.

"What was it like growing up rich and privileged?" Jane asked Ginger, turning the question around on her.

"I don't know," Ginger said. "Like, it's just how it always was. I thought it was normal. I've never met a poor person from Appalachiastan before. I thought that like, if you were white, there was no way you could be poor."

"You're shitting me, right?" Jane said.

"No," Ginger said. "I mean, like, we have privilege."

"Jesus," Jane said, barely audible. "I think you've got a lot more to learn than the bullshit they've filled our textbooks with."

When the girls had first met, Jane had to try really, really hard not to punch Ginger in the throat. Ginger came across as a pretentious snob, but Jane had learned to read people pretty well, and she knew that there was no maliciousness in anything that Ginger said. Jane could tell the girl had just been raised in a bubble and had no clue how the other ninety five percent of the population lived.

"How about I take you home with me some weekend?" Jane said. "I mean, I don't have any family or anything to visit, just a few aunts and uncles and cousins, but I still have my mobile home on my small tract of land up the hollow, and you could at least go back with me and take a look around. You could see first hand what it's like to be poor and white in America and have no one give a fuck about you. Maybe explain to some of my fellow hillbillies this privilege thing we're supposed to have to keep us from being poor."

"I didn't mean to make you mad," Ginger said.

"I know," Jane said. "But you bring this up all the time, and it's getting old. Maybe I should just take you to Appalachiastan so you can see for yourself. Satisfy your curiosities."

"I've got volleyball practice," Ginger said.

Ginger got up, grabbed her gym bag and headed for the gymnasium where she and the other members of the university's women's volleyball team would spend the next three hours busting their asses so they would be prepared to kick Wake Forest's asses at the end of the week in the first volleyball match of the year. Jane stuck her nose back in her history of world cultures textbook, reading about the wonderful attributes of the cultures of places like Thailand, Indonesia, Beleruz and Bolivia. "Nice how these elitist types glorify the impoverished cultures of third world countries," Jane said to herself, "yet no one minds bashing the third world subcultures of this one."

***

Ginger, who, by the way, was *not* a redhead, but a six feet two inches tall buxom blond who was built like a runway model and who looked like one, too, had to stay after practice with two other girls, because they'd not been aggressive enough in regard to their digs. They'd let too many balls hit the floor right in front of them. "Too pretty to dive for it?" Coach Carter had screamed at all three of them, and the truth of it was that they were, so she'd made them stay late and practice their digs. No one was allowed to leave until all three of the girls, one of which had actually been Miss Teen Tennessee the year before, got ten saves each.

"What a bitch!" Ginger said to the former teen queen in the shower after their extended practice.

"I know," the third girl, who, by the way, *would* go on to drop out of college the following year in order to take a huge, six digit figured modelling contract, said. "And you know she just singled us out because we're the prettiest girls on the team. The old butch just wanted to check us out longer."

"I know, right?" Ginger said.

Little did the girls know, Coach Carter wasn't the only one who wanted to check them out. Lingering just inside the locker room, hiding around the side of the far lockers was P.T., the very much heterosexual grounds keeper who loved checking out the numerous, beautiful young ladies on the campus of the university. Oh, how he was enjoying checking out three of the most gorgeous young women not just on campus, but in the U.S., right now in the shower, and oh, how he did pleasure himself as he watched.

***

"How was practice?" Jane asked Ginger when she got back to their dorm room.

"Hard," Ginger said. "Coach made a few of us stay after and work on our digs. At least that's what she said. We're pretty convinced she just wanted to check us out more."

"You mean," Jane said, "your coach is a lesbian?"

"Of course," Ginger said, bordering incredulity. "All college volleyball coaches are lesbians. Jesus, you really were raised out in the sticks, weren't you?"

"Yeah," Jane said. "And my offer of going home with me some weekend so you can enlighten my fellow hillbillies on how the world really turns will remain open."

"Not anytime soon," Ginger said.

The girls didn't speak for a moment or two, and when Jane looked over at Ginger, she could tell that she was in deep thought. "Something wrong?" Jane asked.

"Well," Ginger said, trailing off at the end of the word, though it was only one syllable.

"What is it?" Jane pressed.

"I think I was followed home from practice."

"By who?" Jane asked.

"One of the groundskeepers," Ginger said. "Some fat, really old guy. He's like a hundred or something."

"Okay," Jane said. "I know you well enough now to know that that probably means fifty or so. Would you say he was fifty or so?"

"Maybe a little older," Ginger said. "And he was fat. And he looked dirty. But not, like, from working. He looked like he never bathes."

"Hm," Jane said, looking down. "You know, there's a guy that fits that bill that I've seen in the hall a time or two when I've come in and you've been here alone. Once, it was almost like I'd startled him when the elevator doors opened. It looked like he was jumping back from our door, but I told myself there was no way. I mean, who does that?"

"Did he have one of those scruffy beards that looks like he needs to shave, but never does, but like, his beard won't actually grow into a full beard? One of those guys that seem like they were born to just naturally look filthy and unkempt?"

"I've never heard it put like that before," Jane said. "But that's pretty accurate." After another moment of silence, Jane added, "Let's just remain vigilant. Talk to your teammates about it, and see if they've had any similar experiences, and if we need to, we'll do something about it."

***

"Peekaboo!" the fat, dirty bastard yelled as he jumped out from behind the large ash tree beside the brick walkway. It was the next day, and Ginger was on her way back to the dorms following practice. Once again, she and her fellow beauty queens were held after to work on their digs and so that Coach Carter could indeed check them out longer.

"Jesus Christ!" Ginger screamed. She had nearly had a heart attack when the fat, dirty bastard that was P.T. jumped out from the tree

"Want me to carry your bag for ya, sweetie?" P.T. asked.

"No! God No!," she almost screamed. She made a wide circle around him, almost reaching up to hold her nose as she did, and once around him, she began running for the dorms. P.T. attempted to keep pace with her in order to tell her that he was just kidding around, but in his condition, he could only jog three steps before having to stop and catch his breath. Once he did, he went on his merry way in the opposite direction Ginger had gone, in hopes of finding another young, beautiful coed to creep on.

***

"We want to file a complaint against one of the groundskeepers."

It was Jane. She'd accompanied Ginger, nay, she had nearly *dragged* Ginger around to complain about the dirty fat bastard who appeared to be stalking her, if not others, due to Ginger's insecurities in regard to *rocking the boat* in any fashion. First, Jane had taken Ginger to talk to the volleyball coach. Though the coach was very excited to meet Jane, who, though not an athlete and a few years older than the traditional freshman, was still quite fit and very beautiful. The coach had particularly found her Appalachian American accent quite sexy. However, the coach said there was nothing she could do, and she recommended they go straight to the dean. She also recommended Jane stop by some evening for dinner and wine, and Jane had told her she would consider it, but Jane had knowingly lied. Jane wasn't judging, but Jane liked boys.

The girls had had to set an appointment to meet with the dean, Dean Franco, but they finally got in to see him. "Oh, no," Dean Franco said, instantly dropping his head into the palm of one hand and shaking both his head and hand lightly. "Let me guess," he said, now looking up, but at the ceiling, not at the girls. "Dirty fat bastard. About sixty years old. Smelly. Filthy."

"Yes!" Ginger said, nearly coming out of her chair. It was the first time she's spoken during the entire round of complaints. "How did you know?"

"It's not the first time," Dean Franco said. "Actually, it's probably not the one hundreth time."

"What?" Jane said. "How can you people know about this and allow him to stay here?"

"By 'you people' do you mean we Episcipalians?" Dean Franco asked, defensiveness in his tone.

"What?" Jane asked, confused.

"What exactly do you mean by 'you people'?," he asked. "I know where you're from."

"Get over it!" Ginger said, sounding more assertive than Jane had ever heard her be, and truth be known, Ginger was being more assertive than she had ever been. "How can you have a pervert like that working on a college campus and do nothing?"

"The staff here at the university have a union," Dean Franco said, dropping the front, having pretended to have been offended for some unknown reason like the good progressive liberal college dean that he was. "And it's a strong union."

"That's good, right?" Ginger said. "But what's that have to do with it?"

"Welcome to the real world people like this guy will never tell you about," Jane said. "A strong union means that you can't fire anyone. Even shitbags like this dirty old pervert bastard."

Dean Franco glared at Jane, trying to find offense in something she'd said, but sadly, he knew she was right. But how dare she introduce the innocent, pampered and thus far brainwashed mind of Ginger to such cold, hard truths about life at such a young innocent age, he thought. This was university. Minds were supposed to focus on how life *should* be, not on how life really *is*.

"Sadly," Dean Franco said when he finally spoke, "there's truth to what she said. I'd perhaps word it differently."

"What?" Ginger said.

"Look," Dean Franco said, and then he leaned forward, resting both elbows on his desk and clasping his hands. He gave the girls the rundown on the fat, dirty bastard that was stalking Ginger, and indeed, others, and it went like this:

The fat, dirty bastard- this creepy pervert- this peeping tom, was known as P.T., because of the very fact that he was a peeping tom. Everyone simply called him P.T. Ironically, those were actually his real initials, and since the man wasn't the sharpest tool in the shed, he'd never made the connection that people were actually insulting him by calling him P.T.

P.T. was a local hick from out in the county. Like a number of local hicks from out in the county, P.T. was land rich and cash flow poor. He'd inherited hundreds of acres of land that had been in the family for many generations. Once upon a time, his ancestors actually worked, and they'd worked hard. Proof of such was their past ability to acquire and keep such large tracts of land. However, with each successive new generation, the level of work ethic within the family faded. Now, by P.T.'s generation, after several generations before him simply having had a few acres of land carved off and given to them, and mommy and daddy springing for a mobile home to put on it for Junior or Sally to live in, there was *no* work ethic left. Junior and Sally had to drive into town each day and work at whatever job they could get with their tenth grade education (because having finished high school would have required too much work), in order to get health insurance which they would soon desperately need, as obesity, tobacco and alcohol abuse, and a diet of frozen and fast foods takes a hefty toll after about sixty years, and what little income they could earn in order to pay the personal property taxes on all that land they'd inherited.

"We've fired him once," Dean Franco said, after having explained P.T.'s persona. "He waited a year. Until the girls who'd filed the complaint had graduated and moved far from here and on with their lives. Then he sued us. And he won. We had to pay him a year's worth of back pay and give him his job back. We've not been able to get rid of him since. Any time we've tried, the union's interfered."

"What am I supposed to do?" Ginger asked, now feeling entirely helpless.

"Keep your doors locked," Dean Franco said. "And I'll call Coach Carter and have her post a guard in the locker room so you don't have to worry about him hiding in there while you're in the showers again."

"We never said anything about that," Jane said. "Why would you…"

"Because we know him better than we'd care to," Dean Franco said. "Honey," he said, now facing Ginger. She was not offended by being called honey, because she could tell that like her and Jane, Dean Franco preferred boys, too. "I know you don't know this, and you don't want to hear this, but I'm sure he's watched you girls in the shower."

"Gross!" Ginger said, and she shivered as if ten thousand cockroaches had crawled across her skin.

And with that, the girls got up and left.

***

"I've got a plan," Jane said as the girls walked back to the dorms. And that's *all* that was said until the girls got back to their dorm room and were safe behind their locked door.

***

"You know," Ginger said, staring out the window of the passenger's side of Jane's truck in both disbelief and disgust. She'd never seen poor white America before, and until now, she'd thought there was no actual way it could possibly exist. *White people should just know better*, she and her privileged friends had always lamented if the conversation of poor whites in America were to come up, which it rarely did. Only around election time, when she and her friends, as children, would sit around and listen to their parents blame poor, non-college educated white men for all the problems of the world. "You never did tell me why you finally decided to go to college. Especially so late in life. I mean, how old are you? Twenty two?"

"Yeah," Jane said, taking Ginger's comment with a grain of salt, as she'd learned to take all of Ginger's comments since meeting her. "I'm almost ready to start drawing social security."

"You know what I mean," Ginger said.

"Yeah," Jane said. Ginger said nothing. She looked at Jane, hoping she'd expand on the subject, because she felt that if she were to continue to look out the window and see more mobile home trailers or cars up on blocks she would puck in her mouth.

"So there was this guy," Jane began.

"Ooh," Ginger said. "I was starting to wonder about you. I saw the way you looked at Coach Carter."

"That's not even remotely accurate, and by *a guy*, I don't mean in *that* way," Jane said.

"Oh," Ginger said.

"He was older," Jane said. "Quite a bit older. He was old enough to be my grandfather, actually."

"Ooh, gross!" Ginger said and she actually *did* throw up in her mouth just a little at the thought of it. Anyone over twenty five was ancient in Ginger's book.

"Yeah," Jane said. "Actually, he had some pretty nefarious intentions I came to find out. His name was Thomas G. I actually thought he saw something in me other than a piece of ass and high sitting tits. But I guess he wasn't much different than P.T., actually. Just more refined. More sophisticated."

"So what happened?" Ginger asked.

"He had an unfortunate demise," Jane said.

"Um," Ginger said. "What does that even mean?"

"I think you're going to find out when our friend gets up here," Jane said. "Anyway, before he had his unfortunate demise, and before he tried to force himself on me, he said a few things that really got me thinking."

"Like what?" Ginger asked.

"Well," Jane began. "I know now that it was mostly a bunch of flattering bullshit. All trying to get into my pants. But some of it really stuck. Like, he told me I had too much to offer the world to just stay up here in Appalachiastan. The way I started viewing it, though, was that maybe the world had more to offer *me*. So why not go out there and get an education. Maybe get a job doing something I like. Get the fuck out of Appalachiastan."

"I don't blame you," Ginger said, looking back out the window now. It seemed like every house they passed belonged to a hoarder of some type. This household hoarded broken appliances. This one broken cars. That one firewood. Filth everywhere. Even the road signs were filthy and hard to read, covered in coal dust and soot from the exhaust of the trucks that hauled the coal and timber.

"Anyway," Jane said. "I'm really enjoying learning all that stuff that's pressed into those twenty pound textbooks, but I think I learned a thing or two about real life and about dealing with people back here in the mountains that is going to help me get a little further ahead than many of our peers who have been pampered. No offense."

"I haven't been as pampered as you'd think," Ginger said, trying to sound defensive but failing. "I had to muck out my own horse stalls."

"Okay," Jane said, not even acting as if she had any empathy. "By the way," she said, "here it is." She pulled off into the wide spot at the side of the road that was the driveway for her old mobile home. It was sitting there, at the side of the rarely travelled dirt road, or holler, as Jane and her fellow Appalacian Americans called it, and the padlock she'd put on the outside of the door when she'd left a month before was still there.

"What now?" Ginger asked.

"We go inside and wait," Jane said, and then she opened the door and got out of the car.

"Oh, my God," Ginger said to herself. "I can't believe I am actually going to step foot inside a trailer."

***

Jane had actually devised the plan while Dean Franco was going on and on about the good side of unions, trying to make it appear as if their fine job of securing employment for life for the likes of non-productive shitbags like P.T. should merely be overlooked. She'd told Ginger about it once back in their dorm room, and despite Ginger's slight hesitation, she went for it.

"Your uncles," Ginger said, after Jane had explained that she had a couple of very protective uncles back in Appalachiastan who had helped her deal with the likes of P.T. types in the past. Thomas G. for instance. "They're not going to kill him, are they?"

"I can assure you," Jane had said. "No one is going to find P.T.'s dead body, anywhere." Sure, it had been a lie of omission, but it wasn't a full blown lie. Jane knew they'd never find the body. His shoes, however, might be found by a hunter at some point in the future, more than likely sitting beside a stream, as if their owner had merely decided to go for a barefoot wade in the water and forgot to come back and retrieve his shoes.

"And they're not going to rough him up really bad, are they?" Ginger asked next.

"I can assure you," Jane said. "You are not going to see P.T. walking around campus with his arm in a sling. No black eyes. You won't see him with a single mark or bruise." Another lie of omission. She left out the part about how Ginger, nor anyone, would see P.T. again at all.

"Well," Ginger said. "If it's worked in the past, and if it gets this creepo to leave me alone. Sure. I'm in. Besides, I said I wanted to see Appalachiastan."

"Let's kill two birds with one stone, then," Jane said, and she giggled a little at her little inside joke.

Setting P.T. up took a full two weeks, and only because Jane was having such a good time doing it. She'd gone out looking for P.T. on campus while she was in between classes, and when she finally found him, on her second day of looking, she decided to turn the tables on him.

"Peekaboo!" Jane shouted, jumping out from behind a large sycamore tree in front of the Rotunda, one of the most famous works of architecture in the world, designed by the man who'd built the university more than two hundred years before. "I see you!"

P.T. had been startled. He'd not expected a fellow gamer. He staggered back a few feet (he was too obese to actually *jump* back a few feet), and grabbed his chest as his heart began fluttering. He then reached down and grabbed his crotch, realizing he had blood flowing to his man member. *Oh, my God!* He thought. *I'm in love!*

"Well, now," he said, his heart rate slowing. "Who are you?"

"I'm Jane," Jane said, walking up to him, sauntering her hips. She knew the way men had looked at her for many years, and she knew exactly how to move to make them look even harder. "Who are you?"

"Folks call me P.T., ma'am," he said.

"Ooh, ma'am," Jane said. "I love a southern gentleman. Too many of these boys on campus are from up north and they have no manners. Why, they make me open my own doors."

"You'd never have to open a door in my presence, ma'am," P.T. said, now reaching up and taking his cap off.

"Prove it," Jane said. "Walk me to my dorm and open my door. And stop calling me ma'am. Call me Jane."

"I'd be honored, Jane," P.T. said, and he did.

***

It had been Jane's goal to meet up with P.T. every other day or so, to lead him on- walk him right into her trap- but the man was so instantly infatuated with her that he made sure to meet up with her *everyday.* He would walk her to class, and like a faithful little puppy dog (well, a puppy dog that pushed the scales to three hundred pounds), he would wait outside and then walk her back to her dorm. The two spent so much time together, that if it had been a generation before, people would have started asking questions. However, since it was 2020, and Generation Z was of age and populating the university's campus, everyone was glued to their smartphones so not a soul noticed the two of them spending so much time together, nor much else of anything going on around them, as their eyes were constantly guled to the screens of their gadgets.

"By the way," Jane said at the end of the two week 'rope a dope' period. "You doing anything tonight?" It was roughly

9:00 a.m. P.T. had walked Jane to her only class for Friday.

"I don't reckon I am, Miss Jane," he said.

"Here," she said, handing him a slip of paper that had the address of her mobile home back in Appalachiastan on it. "It's about a three hour drive, but I think if you come it'll be worth it."

"How so, Miss Jane?" P.T. asked, and he could feel, again, the swelling in his pants.

"I'm taking my roommate back with me this weekend," she said. "She and I are going to have a panty party."

"A what?" P.T. asked, and he lowered Jane's books he'd been carrying for her to the front of his pants so she would not see the tent he was pitching.

"Oh," she said. "Silly me. I shouldn't have said it that way." She giggled and looked down for a second and then looked back up and said, "I've been working on my mobile home. It needs painted, and there are no curtains or blinds, so basically, my roommate and I are going to be painting in our panties inside, and, well, it would be quite a show for anyone on the outside looking in."

P.T. didn't even question how Jane could have known that he was a voyeur, and that his biggest turn on was watching people who had no idea they were being watched. P.T. was not healthy. He'd never been involved in any sort of functional relationship with a woman. Actually, he'd never been involved in any relationship with a woman. And if he were to be honest about it, he had never wanted to be. He just wanted to watch them. And pleasure himself while doing so. He really got off knowing he was having pleasure at someone else's expense without them even knowing about it.

"It'd be great if you'd come help us paint," Jane said, taking her books from P.T., and intentionally pressing down on his pitched tent with the back of her left hand as she did. "Or, you could just sit outside and watch. It would be dark by the time you got there, if you finished up work today and all. You could just hang out outside and watch through the windows. We'd never know you were there."

P.T.'s eyes were wide. His tent was fully pitched. Saliva began running down his jaw, tricking out of the left side of his mouth.

"You could even take care of this," Jane said, flipping the peek of P.T.'s pitched tent with her middle finger. She then turned and walked into class, making sure to saunter her hips in her special way, and P.T. made a handsfree mess in his pants.

***

"So, like, how is this going to work if you actually have blinds and curtains up?" Ginger asked. The girls were in the trailer watching "Bigfoot Sasquatch The Movie" on YouTube. Jane thought it would be comical in its irony that Ginger would never know about. "And I can't believe you have an internet connection up here."

"Yeah," Jane said. "We dumb hillbillies have internet, and electricity, and running water, and…"

"You know what I mean," Ginger said.

"I know," Jane said. "And it doesn't matter that we have blinds and curtains on the windows. He'll come. Literally, probably." And Jane laughed in spite of herself.

"And you're sure your uncles are going to take care of this?"

"Absolutely," Jane said. "They live at the foot of the hill we came up, and if they see any car that's not mine come by? Well, they come up to investigate."

As the girls got to the part of the movie (arguably both the best Bigfoot Sasquatch movie ever made, as well as the best full length movie ever recorded exclusively on an Apple i-phone 11-s) where the main character, some nutter called "Crazy Lake" was boarding a plane in Charlottesville, Virginia (ironically, where the girls were attending university) to fly to Nepal in order to track down the Yeti, P.T. pulled into the drive. He'd killed his headlights a hundred yards or so before reaching the trailer home, because he'd seen the lights from within (the girls had at least left the blind covering the living room window open). His fetish worked best when his victims had no idea they were being victimized. True voyeurism only worked when the person being watched had no clue they were being watched.

P.T. had been rubbing his crotch the whole way from Charlottesville to Appalachiastan, but he'd teased himself, not allowing himself to make another mess in his pants, which he'd never changed. Being dirty and filthy in all sorts of ways was part of who P.T. was. He slowly got out of his Subaru Forester, quietly shut the door and then made his way toward the trailer home. He made sure to stand back a full twenty feet, knowing that he could see in, but since it was dark outside and the lights were on inside, the girls could not see out.

"Hey now," P.T. said, very quietly, aloud, after peering through the window. "Them girls is fully dressed!" He felt the blood leave his netherregions, his pitched tent taken down to be packed away for later use.

Just then, P.T. heard a stick snap behind him. He turned, sensing that someone, or some*thing*, was creeping up on him. He looked, first, into what he thought was darkness. Then, he realized he was staring into the body of some large creature that stood only six feet away from him. Slowly, he worked his head and eyes upward. As his eyes adjusted to the dark, he realized the creature standing before him was manlike in build, yet covered in hair, and when his head and eyes finally stopped their upward ascent, he noticed that this thing before him stood every bit of eight feet high.

"What in the name of Goddamn!" P.T. said, still not in a loud voice, but definitely louder than a whisper.

The moon was near full on this night, and there was not a cloud in the sky, so by the time P.T.'s eyes had fully adjusted he could see almost as well as he could during the day. He noticed that the creature was salivating a bit out of the left side of its mouth. Spittle was trickling down its hairy chin. P.T.'s eyes followed the flow of the spittle, back down the creature's chest, and since his head was going downward, he allowed it to continue, and he took note once his eyes fell below the waistline of the creature, which was pretty much even with his own face, that the creature was pleasuring itself, and man, P.T. thought, if the thing had been wearing pants it would be pitching a tent large enough to house an entire circus!

"Oh... my... God..." P.T. said, merely a mumble, and as soon as the words left his mouth, another creature, one which P.T. had *not* noticed slipping up behind him from a different angle, grabbed P.T. around the waste with one giant arm while using its free hand to cover his mouth so he could not scream, though P.T. did attempt to scream.

"Did you hear something?" Ginger said to Jane inside the trailer.

"Just a coyote," Jane said, but she knew better. She didn't even try to hide her smile.

The movie was nearly over, and the nutter in it, this "Crazy Lake" was going on some sort of tirade about following your heart and pursuing your passions. Doing in life what makes you happy, despite what anyone else says, because no matter what you do, people are always going to judge you, anyway, so fuck 'em.

It was so boring, the girls fell asleep.

***

"Do you think it worked?" Ginger said. It was 10:00 a.m. the following morning. The girls were outside drinking coffee.

"Yeah," Jane said, staring down at a set of car tires that didn't belong to her truck. "You can see that he parked here," she said.

Ginger came over and stared down at the tire tracks. "I guess he got his talking to and went the hell back to the motherland," she said.

"Yeah," Jane said. "Something like that." She knew the 'something like that' had been something else entirely, and that the car had been pushed over the revine only a hundred yards away which fell straight into an old coal mining drainage pond that was more than fifty feet deep and probably held as many vehicles deposited in it throughout the years. Not just at the hand of Bigfoot Sasquatch, but at the hands of so much hillbilly crime and deeds that take place in Appalachiastan that the folks on the outside world, the more prosperous parts of America, would never know about and wouldn't care about anyway, because, well, they'd just say 'those people should just know better.' Or they'd write the victim of some of the crimes and deeds off as just 'one less non-college educated white man' to go around destroying the world.' "I don't think you'll have any more problems with P.T."

The girls went back to the motherland of Virginia that afternoon. Ginger feared that if she spent another night in a mobile home in Appalachiastan she might catch something she couldn't wash off. Jane took her concerns with a grain of salt, and then she took her back to the dorm room a few hours away.

No one ever saw P.T. on the university's campus again after that. And it wasn't like they'd noticed he wasn't around. They'd just never noticed him playing his little game of peekaboo again. It was a welcomed change that again, no one really noticed.

The head of the grounds crew didn't notice P.T.'s absence for quite some time, because P.T. had never been a productive grounds crew member. The grounds crew, without P.T., actually increased their productivity in his absence due to the lack of dead weight. In a word, life around the university, and any sphere in which P.T. had had influence or any sort of presence, went on without him, and no one ever asked a thing about him.

The following spring, while out fishing in the heavily trout laden streams of Appalachiastan, an old man, recently retired, was casting his line, hoping to hook into a sizeable native brook trout (which is actually *not* a trout, but a type of arctic char) when he nearly tripped over a pair of size nine, non-name brand work boots. "Damn litterbugs," the man said, bending over and picking up the boots. He looked at them closely and saw that there was some sort of dried fluid on them. It was not blood, as it was not red in color. It was more… cream.

The old man took his backpack off and placed the boots inside. He would carry them out of the woods with him, and once reaching the closest town where he could get a decent meal, which was actually across the state line in

Maryland, he threw the boots in the dumpster behind the restaurant.

The End

4

Confession

(Originally Titled: The Unfortunate Demise Of My First Wife)

(Then, after realizing she's probably still alive: Secondarily Titled: Toxic Love Will Kill You)

(But then, realizing, for a second time, that she is probably still alive, we went with 'Confession')

I have a confession. And I want to get it off my chest now, not just before I die, or at least not when I *think* I'm about to die (boy, do I have a story about someone who did *that* and was wrong, because they lived longer and wished they'd never made their confession), but because I want to stop secretly obsessing over it. I've carried this weight for more than twenty years, and it's become far too heavy to bear. You know the saying, let go or be dragged? Well, this has dragged me down for years, so the time has come to let go. Please don't judge me too harshly.

First and foremost, let me state right off the bat that no, I didn't kill anyone. I donated them. Kinda, sorta. And no, not to science, but I guess you could say to science fiction. However, this really happened, so it's not fiction, but I know no one will believe me, so I'll claim it's in that genre.

What's that? The story about the person I knew who made a confession because they thought they were dying but then they didn't? Okay, I won't leave you hanging. I'll go ahead and tell you that one now. The short version.

I promise.

So off and on, I attend various twelve step program meetings. We're not supposed to write about it, or talk about it in the press, media or film, so I won't say what group it is, but I'm sure you'll be able to figure it out. Anyway, many years ago, probably ten now, just before I went to Iraq for a year's deployment, I had befriended this old man from one of these groups. He was a retired full bird Colonel from the U.S. Army, and he'd been in the Korean War, Vietnam and Desert Storm. And, on top of having lived through all that, he'd managed to go for forty years without drinking and drugging after having spent many years struggling with both.

At least that's what the story was.

Just before I deployed to Iraq, I got a call from this guy. He wanted to see me in private. He had cancer and he felt as if he were going to die while I was deployed, so when I went to his house where he was being cared for by hospice workers, it was more than likely, we thought at the time, the last time we'd ever see each other. Technically, it was the last time we ever saw each other, but not because he died. He didn't. He lived for another eight years. We never saw each other again because of the confession he made to me. After coming clean (pun intended), he couldn't face me, and he spent the next eight years hoping I wouldn't tell his dirty little secret, which I never did while he was still alive. But I am now.

It's pretty simple. The guy really had not been clean and sober for forty years. He'd never been clean and sober for an entire year. He lived a lie, and he admitted to me during our meeting that it was because of his ego. He'd gotten used to being *big man on campus* in the Army, and by claiming to have been sober for nearly half a century, he got to be *big man on campus* in our twelve step program. The truth was, however, that he'd married a woman he'd gotten together with in Vietnam, and the couple spent the winter months in her homeland, and they came back to the U.S. for the spring, summer and fall. He told me that for the three months he's in Vietnam each year, he never sees a single sober day. Then, when he returns, he jumps right into our twelve step program again, and writes the obvious months long hangover off to jetlag, and after thirty days dry, he's all bright eyed and bushy tailed again, and blowing smoke up everyone's ass like he's some kind of spiritual guru.

He told me this, because he *did* feel guilty about it, but also, he said, because he liked me and he could tell I was naive. He wanted me to stop trusting so much in other people and start trusting a little more, or a lot more, in myself. It was great advice, and he said it would help me survive the war- listening to my gut- and he was right about that, too. Oh, and something else he was right about? He said that he was just one of many, many, many smoke blowers in our twelve step program, and he cautioned me about putting too much faith in pretty much anyone.

All of his points were well taken by me.

Okay, none of that has anything to do with *my* confession, but I guess I had to elaborate since I'd mentioned it. My confession has to do with my wife. No, not the sweat, dear lady I'm married to now. The woman I've been married to for the past ten years, and with whom I share a son.

My first wife.

To whom I was miserably married for a little more than a year.

So here's the deal. You can put me in a crowded room with hundreds of other people, and if you insert simply one dysfunctional individual into that crowded room, either I will find them or they will find me within minutes. It's how it goes.

Why?

Because dysfunctionalism is such a way of life for those of us who suffer from it that it's almost like a subculture. You have urban black people, rural whites, wealthy tech engineers in Silicon Valley, and then you have us dysfunctional fucks. We're our own demographic.

Dysfunctionalism is a learned behavior, passed down from generation to generation, and it is a very hard cycle to break. I came up in a very dysfunctional way, and though I feel I've broken the cycle to a pretty great degree, now, it took me a long time to do so, and I left a long line or wreckage in my past. And yes, I've burned bridges, but I had to to get to where I am, because sometimes you have to burn the bridges behind you so the crazy, dysfunctional fucks from your past can't catch up to you. Let me tell you, when you come from a place of dysfunctionalism, those around you do *not* want to see you make it out, because misery *does* love company, and man, are dysfunctional fuckers miserable!

So, on with the story.

I first lay eyes on my ex wife in a college science class. I believe it was biology. It was my last semester in school. I only needed six hours to graduate. I was taking twelve, in order to qualify for the student loans I needed to pay my way, and this particular science class wasn't necessary for me to graduate. I was taking it because I knew the professor. I liked him and he liked me and I knew he'd give me a gentleman's C as long as I just showed up.

We were ten minutes into the lecture on the second day of class when she walked through the door- fashionably late (like, really fashionably late- she'd missed the first day) like so many dysfunctional people are. You see, people who are constantly late, I've found, are quite self-centered. They don't respect other people enough to be on time. The whole world can wait on them.

She was sweet and petite, about five feet tall and a hundred and ten pounds. She had strawberry blonde hair and emerald green eyes. Her skin was fair, but not sickly looking, and she wore a beautiful little sundress, and it was tight around the waist, and I felt as if I could probably wrap my hands around her waist and touch my fingers of both hands together, yet she didn't look anorexic. She was just built small.

Her name was Mandy, and Mandy made her way over to the far side of the class, where I was sitting, and she sat in the only open seat available, the one beside me, and as she crossed the room, she made eye contact with me, and she maintained it all the way to her seat, and I could tell that beneath that beautiful, sexy exterior she had to be batshit crazy. I could see it in her sparkling, emerald green eyes. And as she sat in her seat, she continued to look my way, and she said hello, and I knew I was in love.

***

"I can give you my notes from yesterday," I said to her as soon as class was over. "Since you missed class and all."

"Okay," she said, and I could tell by her smile that her intentions of getting my notes were just as low on her priority list as they were mine in giving them to her. I believe that she could tell I was dysfunctional as hell, and she had fallen instantly in love, too.

"I have an apartment just off campus," I told her. "Wanna come over? For the notes?"

"Yeah," she said. "I have a car outside. I'll drive us down."

"Okay," I said. I'd walked to class, because it wasn't far.

Her car was a total piece of shit. A little 1988 Toyota Camry, rusted and filthy on the outside, and completely littered with what looked like a week's worth of living necessities on the inside. As I opened the passenger door to get in, the smell of fermented fast food wafted out and hit me in the face like a bully in gym class. "I've been meaning to clean my car," she said, and I knew she was lying, and it made me fall for her even more. You see, that's another thing about dysfunctional people. Their cars are like pigsties. Every aspect of dysfunctional people's lives are a total wreck. Their cars, the inside of their houses (especially their kitchens and bedrooms), and even their yards and lawns. Shit strewn everywhere. And if you clean this mess up for them? They get freaked out and have anxiety attacks and they will actually intentionally make everything a mess again, because this is their sense of normal. Yes, this all sounds fucked up if you're not dysfunctional, but let me tell you, as someone who spent the first half of his life in this lifestyle, it makes perfect sense to those who live this way.

We said little as we drove to my apartment. The trip only took a few minutes, and when we arrived, Mandy didn't even take her backpack and her notebooks inside with her. There was no need. We both knew exactly why we'd gone to my apartment.

As soon as we stepped inside, I locked the door, and the instant I turned around, she was on me. We made our way through the living room, completely entangled with each other, ripping each others' clothes off, and into the bedroom where we did what you know comes next. I'll save you the details. But what I'll tell you is that when we were finished was actually the time that I learned her name.

"What's your name, anyway?" she asked me, as she lay on her back, catching her breath. I told her and asked her hers. This is when I found out her name was Mandy. However, I already knew that I was in love and that this was the girl I wanted to spend the rest of my life with.

Mandy and I had the science class together on Monday, Wednesday and Friday. Everyday, after class, we would head down to my apartment and repeat our activities of that first day that we'd met. On Tuesday and Thursday, though Mandy didn't have classes at all those days, she would come over and we'd fornicate on those days as well.

This went on for nearly a month, and I'd not learned anything about Mandy. Where she was from, what her family structure was. What she was majoring in, etc. I didn't care. All I knew was that the sex was great and that everytime she came over, she'd make my already filthy apartment even filthier, usually by springing for some sort of fast food after our sexipades, and leaving all the wrappers and leftovers all over the place. During that month, she'd brought in quite a bit of her personal belongings, mostly clothes, and she'd scattered that around the place, too. Not as if she were moving in, because she wasn't, but just so she'd feel more comfortable having some of her own mess around the place where she was spending so much time as of late.

"Do you want to go with me this weekend to visit my son?" Mandy asked, out of the blue, one day after we'd had sex and eaten Big Macs and fries.

"You have a son?" I asked.

"Yeah," she said, taking up another fry and making sure to dip it in the ketchup she'd just opened and squeezed out onto the coffee table that day, not the little collections of ketchup that we'd squeezed out and onto the table over the course of the last week. When one is a dysfunctional slob, one must always be vigilant in order to avoid food poisoning.

"I didn't know you had a kid," I said.

"There's a lot you don't know about me," she said.

"Sure," I said, feeling myself becoming aroused again at the idea of just how dysfunctional this strawberry blonde actually was. "I'll go with you."

***

The following weekend, Mandy picked me up and we drove a couple of hours away to see her son. He was three years old, even though Mandy was only twenty, and he was being raised by Mandy's wealthy grandmother, just as Mandy had been.

"Are your parents dead?" I asked her when she told me this.

"No," she said. "They're just dysfunctional fucks. It's why I'm so fucked up. But hey, we do what we can, right?" She said it nonchalantly. It sounded beautiful. My favorite type of dysfunctional fucks back in the day were the ones who admitted it. The ones who are in denial? The ones who try to pass their fucked up ways of living off as normal? Those are the true lunatics we must all watch out for. Those are the crazy fuckers who walk into movie theaters and schools and shoot the places up. It's like drunks. The ones who claim they don't have a problem are the ones who wrap their cars around telephone poles or other people in their attempts to prove they can handle it. Going out for a drink, and then driving home after having had fifteen. The *good* drunks- the *safe* ones- know they're pickled for life and they make sure to stay home and drink behind the safety of their own closed doors.

Mandy went on to explain about how her father and mother were both homosexuals. They'd met at some protest during the Vietnam war and they felt as if they were soulmates. Though they were both openly gay, even back then, they decided to procreate and make a love child. This is how Mandy came into being. Her parents actually got married when she was two years old, and they tried to conform, because the war was over and America was in the beginning of its longest post world war two period of peace, so they found themselves at a loss of what to do. They figured raising a child and living in a subdivision, the newest craze in housing among baby boomer yuppies at the time, would fill their empty voids. However, when the cocaine craze of the eighties hit its peak, Mandy's parents were right there in the thick of it, and her father ended up leaving her mother for a man, and her mother was fine with it, because she'd been secretly seeing a woman from work for nearly a year.

Neither Mandy's mother nor her father wanted the responsibility of raising a little girl, so they pawned her off on her maternal grandmother. The grandmother was happy about it, because she never approved of her daughter's dysfunctional lifestyle, though she knew she was largely to blame for it as she had been just as dysfunctional in her youth (remember, that whole *vicious cycle* thing?). It was actually how she'd come into wealth. She'd had a very dysfunctional relationship with her father, as in he'd left the family while she had still been in diapers, so she never knew him, so after growing up with severe daddy issues, at nineteen years old she'd married a seventy seven year old coal baron who she'd actually been sleeping with for three years. She was his fifth and final wife, as the old man would die, on top of her in their wedding bed, just not on their wedding night- he'd lasted about six months- from a massive cardiac arrest. Though his other nine children had sued for their share of the estate, the woman was still left with millions, and hence, Mandy's grandmother was now wealthy. The old woman would never marry again, though she did cat around quite a bit until she was in her forties. It's how Mandy's mother came into being. And no one knew who Mandy's mother's father was.

"Wow," I said after Mandy gave me her family's history. "Quite a story."

"What about you?" she asked. "I knew you were as fucked up as me the moment I laid eyes on you. Are your parents divorced, too?"

"No," I said. "They should have been, but they never did it."
And it was true. I was raised in a house where my mother
and father pretty much hated each other. They had
opposite views and opinions on everything, and I know
now, looking back on it, that it was all simply to spite each
other. My mother was a Catholic, so my dad was a bible
beating protestant. My father was a conservative
Republican, so my mother chose to be a liberal Democrat.
In all my years around them, I never heard either of them
tell the other that they loved them. To date, neither have
told me the same. And that day will never come, as part of
my getting over being batshit crazy dysfunctional involved
becoming estranged from them both nearly a decade ago,
as of this writing, and my true take on that is that I wish I
had done it ten, if not twenty years earlier. I learned the
hard way that just because someone shares your DNA, or
even if they are responsible for having brought you into this
world, it does *not* give them the right to talk to you and treat
you like you are the lowest form of whale shit on the
bottom of the ocean floor. If a friend, neighbor or a mere
acquaintance had ever treated me the way my family did, I
would have never given them another opportunity to do it
again, as I'd merely push them out of my life and keep
them out. Sadly, I felt as if I had to let those with whom I
share DNA back in to do it over and over and over.

Never again!

But at the time I met Mandy, I had not come to this
revelation, so abuse was something I accepted as freely as
living and breathing.

***

"What's this one's name?" Mandy's grandmother said once we'd arrived and walked into her house.

Mandy told her grandmother my name. I hadn't realized I was who she was referring to as "this one" until then. I offered my to the old woman for a shake, and she just waved her hand at me and said, "don't bother. I don't care anything about you."

Mandy had made her way into the living room where a very cute little boy was playing with Lincoln logs. "Come to mommy," she said, after having squatted down on her knees. The boy looked up, and recognizing Mandy, he ran straight into the foyer and wrapped his arms tightly around his great grandmother's legs.

"Don't worry, Jackson," the old woman said to the child. "She won't be here long. She never is."

After comforting the child, who appeared scared, for a minute or two, the old woman put him down and he returned to his Lincoln logs. Mandy made no further attempts to communicate with him- hell, she didn't even acknowledge him anymore- so it appeared as if all were right with his world again.

"How much do you need?" Mandy's grandmother asked, pulling her checkbook out of her purse which was hanging in the foyer.

"How ever much you'll give me," Mandy said, staring out the door, a longing look in her eyes. I could tell she wanted to leave already.

"You," the old woman said. I realized she was addressing me, so I said, "Yeah?"

"You'd do good to run as far away from this sweet piece of ass as you can as quickly as you can."

I needed no further confirmation that I was in love with Mandy, but this certainly did provide it. Mandy's grandmother knew her better than anyone else in the world, and she was warning me against staying with her. I'd managed to meet the most beautiful, and most dysfunctional young woman of my generation, I was sure, and I felt as if I'd won the lottery.

"She will destroy your soul," the old woman said, and then she turned around and gave Mandy a check for two grand. "That should keep you away for a while," she then said to Mandy. Mandy simply walked out the door, and I guess I was supposed to follow her, so I did. We got in the car and headed back to my apartment.

Mandy never even said goodbye to Jackson.

***

"I'm pregnant," Mandy said one afternoon after we'd had sex. We skipped science class altogether that day.

"Shit," I said.

"I'm not saying it's *yours*," she said.

"What?" I said, and this was the first time I actually felt concerned in regard to my fucked up dysfunctional relationship with Mandy. I thought she was *my* psycho. I didn't realize I'd been sharing my psycho with another. "When would you have had time to be with someone else?"

"There's twenty four hours in a day, dipshit," she said, getting up and slipping her blue jeans on. I guess she was right. Though we got together and screwed each others' brains out almost everyday, we actually only spent a couple of hours a day together. I had no idea what she was doing with her time after that. Hell, I'd never even been to her place. I remember fantasizing how messy it must be. How drafty the windows might be. Pure white trash dysfunctionalism (well, in Mandy's case, white trash with money, due to her grandmother and all).

"But you're going to be the one to marry me," she said, now buttoning her blouse.

"What?" I said, incredulous.

"You're graduating in a couple months," she said. "You're going to be able to get a good job and make decent money. The other guys I've been screwing are losers. They're just good lays."

"The *fuck* I'm marrying you!" I said, enraged at the idea of my strawberry blonde little psychopath being with other guys. Losers at that who were just good lays.

"Then you are going to go to jail," she said.

"What the fuck are you talking about?" I said.

"I'll say you raped me," she said, and her voice was smooth, cool. There was no sign of emotion in it. I would later in life, while trying to leave my dysfunctional ways behind me by way of a fuckton of therapy, learn that the exact type of crazy that Mandy was was termed sociopath. "I'll say you raped me repeatedly, and I'll say that you touched my son when we went to see him."

"What?" I said, not believing what I was hearing.

"Do you want to contact the courthouse to set the wedding date? Or do you want me to contact the courthouse and file my charges?" She said this as she slipped her shoes on her feet.

Two weeks later we were married in front of the local magistrate.

***

So here's the deal. I know all this now, because Mandy's rich grandmother told me later, but I didn't know it at the time. As it turns out, when Mandy found out she was pregnant, she actually talked to her grandmother about it first. The old woman told her that if she had another child out of wedlock that she was going to completely cut her off financially. Her grandmother had two agendas with this threat. First, she really *did* want Mandy to abandon her dysfunctional ways of living, and secondly, she wanted *me* to marry Mandy so that she, the grandmother, would not be the sole economic provider for Mandy and her soon to be *two* bastard children. And I do say bastard, because when Mandy's second child was born, it turned out that it was half Mexican. I am a white man, and I've described Mandy already, so as you'll remember, she is not Mexican. The child obviously was not fathered by me, and Mandy never told me or her rich grandmother who the child's father was. I have every reason to believe that Mandy might not have known, because I would soon begin to believe that not only was Mandy a sociopath, but that she was also psychophrenic.

Mandy's rich grandmother did me a solid in taking the young half Mexican child in to raise, along with Jackson. She said she was doing it so Mandy and I could "get on our feet, financially," but I knew she was really trying to save me some face. She didn't want to make it obvious to the world that I was a cuckold.

But Mandy didn't mind doing so.

We moved to a town about halfway between where I had attended college and where Mandy's grandmother lived. After I graduated, Mandy simply never went back to college. She would admit to me later that the only reason she'd gone in the first place was to 'rope a dope,' as Muhammid Ali might have called it. She actually worded it as 'find a husband,' but it was the same thing. And I was that dope.

Shortly after I'd gotten a job with an insurance agency, where I'd be taught the true art of instilling the fear of God into parents that they were going to die and their children would be raised by child molesting foster parents unless they bought a variable life insurance plan from me, Mandy started fucking around on me.

With two guys I worked with.

She said she wanted to make it obvious that I was a cuckold. I would be the one to earn the money to support her, and in part, the two children she'd had with other men. It was her full intentions to make me miserable, and by the end of our first full year of marriage, she had. During that year, we'd had sex twice, at most, and I'd slept on the couch, waiting on her to come home from screwing one of my fellow insurance agent shmucks, who, by the way, would spend the entire next day telling me how great of a fuck my wife was. I guess the story that she'd given them was that I okayed her infidelity, because I couldn't get it up, and that my turn on was listening to her go into the details of what her and my coworkers had done after she'd gotten home. I played the part of the fool in the eyes of Mandy and in the eyes of my co-workers.

But only because I had a plan.

***

I'd grown up a considerable distance away from the small town where I was now selling life insurance. It was a place far away from the small town where I'd attended college, and where I'd met this beautiful, strawberry blonde of a wife of mine who was making me miserable. It was in the southern part of the state, a very secluded, rural area. A place where things that are not supposed to exist, do. Things like…

…Bigfoot Sasquatch!

There was one hollow, in particular, where no one dared go. Sure, there was a family or two that lived up the hollow, and for some reason, these people exclusively were safe up the hollow, as if the beasts were protecting them, but if anyone else went up the hollow, the likelihood of them returning could not be guaranteed. Especially, for some reason, beautiful women.

The local stories were always that Bigfoot Sasquatch had a very high labido, and if a male Bigfoot Sasquatch saw something he liked, in the way of a woman, that is, he was likely to kidnap her and take her to his underground domains and sexually and domestically enslave her for the rest of her days.

"I want to introduce you to someone," I said to Mandy one morning over coffee. I'd just woken up, and she'd just come in from the night before. She'd actually just recently started screwing my office manager. She said one of the other guys had gotten her pregnant, but she was going to pin it on our office manager and extort him. She figured he was the highest paid guy in our branch, which he was, so it simply made sense in her mind to do it this way. But, she had no intentions of letting me out of my miserable marriage. I would remain her cuckold for life, as she put it. But she simply wasn't going to pass up another income stream by way of my office manager.

"Who?" she asked.

"He's a big man back where I'm from," I told her, and I wasn't lying.

"In what way?" she asked. "Importance or manmeat?"

"Both," I said. "I think you'll enjoy what he can offer you."

"You're not trying to weasel out of this marriage, are you?" she asked. She could have replaced me financially with little trouble if she'd wanted to. And she'd already replaced me sexually. But I think she really enjoyed keeping me around, under her thumb, because I accepted the abuse as if it were natural, because for me, with my upbringing, it was. If people truly care about you, I'd been raised to believe, they'll treat you like shit. This had to be how things worked, because the people who were supposed to care about me most treated me like shit, right?

Oh, how wrong I would find this to be at midlife. The fact is, if someone treats you like shit, they do not care about you a bit. No matter their relation to you.

Anyway, Mandy's curiosity was piqued and she agreed to join me on a three hour road trip south. I told her the big guy had a private, mountain top resort, and we could only drive so far. We would have to hike the last mile in. I told her he had a private helicopter, and that that was how he reached his place, and she actually believed me.

The three hour drive passed quickly. I got to listen to all the different ways in which my coworkers made love to my wife. I got to hear about how they all did so much more for her than I ever had. I listened to how the whole time we'd been fuck buddies in college, she'd never really liked me, and she'd never really enjoyed the sex, but she knew I was only months away from being able to make her an honest woman, at least in the eyes of her rich grandmother.

After reaching our destination in southern Appalachiastan we parked our car at the side of the road. There was a single mobile home here, and I actually knew the woman who lived there. We'd gone to high school together, at least until she'd gotten pregnant and dropped out. She actually happened to be there that day, outside with her daughter, a little girl named Jane.

"She's beautiful," I told my old acquaintance while staring down at Jane. She was about six years old at the time. Sadly, her stepfather had gotten killed in some freak car accident a couple of years before. Somehow, his car had been turned upside down, with him in it, and he'd been crushed. Jane's mother was now dating a local cop, a man who'd actually been involved in the investigation of the strange car accident that had claimed the life of Jane's daddy who really wasn't her daddy. Like I said, I come from a place riddled with dysfunctionalism.

"Who's this little tart?" Jane's mother asked me, looking, spitefully, at Mandy.

"This is my wife," I said. "Mandy. We're going up to see if we can meet up with the big guy."

"Oh," Jane's mother said, a knowing smile on her face. You see, people where I'm from know quite a few things about life and the real world that people of privilege, like Mandy, do not. "Y'all take care." And then she took Jane by the hand and they went back into their mobile home. I could tell Jane was going to grow up and be a heartbreaker someday.

Mandy and I hit the woods and were close to the top of the mountain in no time. She bitched and complained about the mosquitoes and the briars and the heat (even though it wasn't hot) the entire time, but her hopes of meeting a well endowed rich man at the top of the mountain kept her going. "Who knows," she said at one point. "If he's insecure enough, I might actually give you your freedom."

When we reached the top of the mountain, we stopped to catch our breath, and I heard a light growl coming from behind a rock outcropping only fifty yards away.

"What was that?" Mandy asked, and I could see the fear in her eyes.

"Just a deer," I said.

"Deer sound like that?" she asked.

"Yeah," I said. "In the woods. But not the deer you see in yards and stuff. They're different. That's why you've never heard it."

"Oh," she said, buying the lie I'd made up on the spot.

"Yeah," I said, spotting opportunity. "And they only have one horn, not two. And it grows out of the center of their skulls. Like a unicorn."

"You're fucking with me now," she said, but I could hear the doubt in her voice.

"Seriously," I said. "Walk over there, real slow, and check it out."

Mandy took the bait. She began making her way to the rock outcropping. I could hear another grunt or two from the other side, and I could tell that they were grunts of excitement. Grunts of lust. The Bigfoot Sasquatch hiding behind the rocks had either gotten a glimpse of Mandy- the sexy little strawberry blonde whore that she was- or they could smell her pheromones, or both.

Just as Mandy got to the rock outcropping and placed her left hand against a large boulder and began to peer around the other side of it, a large, as in eight feet tall and eight hundred pound bipedal creature- truly the stuff of nightmares- stepped out from the other side. Mandy first looked up in fear, and then down, and seeing that this creature was indeed aroused, curious.

The beast gave Mandy no time to make her mind up about what this new experience might be like. He grabbed her by the waist and picked her up off of her feet like a miniature King Kong would a mini-Ann Darrow, and he turned and vanished behind the rock outcropping and I heard nothing more. I waited a couple of minutes and then I went behind the rock outcropping and I saw the hidden entrance to what appeared to be a large cave. This, I knew, would be Mandy's new home.

I made my way off the mountain and back to the little town where I sold insurance. I waited a couple of days and then I went to Mandy's grandmother's house and told her that Mandy had apparently ran off with another man. She acted like she believed me, but I could tell that she didn't, but all she said was, "well, you and these two boys here will be a lot better off." I left after that and I never went back. I never saw or heard from Mandy's rich grandmother again. I have no clue what came of those two little boys.

I quit my job the following week. I packed my shit and I left Appalachiastan. I moved a state away and I put myself into therapy. I spent many years unravelling my dysfunctional ways. I have a new wife now. I had to file for an uncontested no fault divorce years ago, and since no one showed up to contest it, it was granted. My new wife and I have a healthy relationship. We have a cat, a dog, and two point three children.

Just kidding.

We have only one child; a son.

But we do have the picket fence.

Okay, that's a lie, too. We have a huge ass homestead, and it's beautiful.

My wife and I are faithful to each other. And when we have a disagreement, we have a discussion. We do not argue. We do not treat each other like shit. Nor do we treat our son like shit. And we tell him that we love him.

Everyday!

So he will always know.

And we show him through our actions, and we display for him what a healthy relationship between a husband and a wife looks like. It is my hope in doing all these things that I have broken the vicious cycle of dysfunctionalism. It is my hopes that my son grows up and only gets involved with people who truly love him, or at least care about him enough to respect him and not treat him like shit.

Because NO one deserves to be treated like shit.

By anyone else.

And I stay the everloving hell out of Appalachiastan!

The End

(Potentially)

***

The following stories are from Bigfoot Sasquatch Files
Volume 6:

1

Winds Of November

The scariest night we ever spent in our house (so far) was the first. It's been four years ago now, and I'll never forget it. We'd finally gotten everything we'd been wanting for the longest time and we had no idea just how frightening that would be.

Silence.

Total.

We'd only recently moved to the U.S., central Virginia to be exact, from the Philippine Islands, where we'd spent our last six months in the capital city of Manila, close to the U.S. embassy, so that the second my now wife's fiance visa was granted we could jump on the next plane to the U.S., which we did. While there, we lived in a nice condo on the thirty third floor of a seventy story high skyscraper right in the middle of the city. And despite the height, all we heard, all day and all night, was the honking of horns, the screeching of brakes and tires, and the shouts and screams of people. All we saw were lights, lights, and more lights at night, and smog, smog and more smog by day. It made us long for a place out in the middle of nowhere, where there were no people, and where there was no smog, and where there were no noises other than the noises of nature. After having made it to the U.S., and spending a few months in an apartment complex nearly as rambunctious as Manila, we finally found our little homestead out in the middle of nowhere, we bought it, and the dream had been achieved.

And that first night, again, was absolutely terrifying!

I grew up in the mountains of Appalachiastan, and all I'd ever known for the first quarter century of my life was silence at night, and mostly by day, once you got off the well beaten path, that is. But that was years ago. I left Appalachiastan and I spent time in places like Seattle, and then on to Iraq (yes, a war zone), and then the Philippines. Somehow, and though it drove me crazy at first, I'd gotten used to the noises of the city, the combat zone, and both the rural and urban jungles of Southeast Asia. I'd forgotten the peace and tranquility of those beautiful country nights, though after years away from them, I longed for them, and yet when I got them back? Well, we've discussed this. No need to be redundant. I know, too late.

I remember that first night, lying in bed. It was a brand new king size that we'd had custom made for our new home. Well, new to us. It's nearly one hundred and twenty years old, one of the last sharecropper houses built in the U.S., just before the industrial revolution would come along and change the landscape of the world economy, and with it, the world's way of living. My wife was on the opposite side of the bed that night, and our son, only five years old at the time, was sleeping in between us.

Neither my wife nor my son had any problem falling asleep that first night. Not only had we spent the entire weekend moving our belongings from our apartment twenty miles away in the city (it took a few trips and two days of work), but our son had started kindergarten just a couple of weeks before. It was September. And we'd just gone through the jumping through hoops bullshit with his school in order for them to allow him to attend.

You see, when we had our apartment in the city, we were in one of the overcrowded, understaffed city school districts. But where our house is located, we are in the most privileged school district in the county. Many of the kids who attend this school come from the families of trust babies and celebrities, and the school, though public, is better than most expensive private schools in the U.S. It's a huge part of the reason we bought our house where we did.

We finally stood on one leg long enough, while rubbing our bellies with one hand and patting our heads with the other, after having given the principal a notarized copy of our real estate contract, showing we were closing on our house, in his school district, only two weeks after the beginning of the school year, and permission for our son to attend the school was finally granted. It was an emotionally exhaustive process to go through while also going through the emotional process of buying a house, all while going through the physically draining process of moving from our apartment to our house only three months after having moved nine thousand miles away from the Philippines to Virginia.

Ugh!

But despite this, and being plenty exhausted myself, I could not sleep.

It was too quiet.

Far too quiet.

And my mind began playing tricks on me.

In Mosul, Iraq, where I was stationed, our team ran night missions, and we tried to sleep during the day. *Tried* being the key word here. It was difficult, as our base, Diamondback it was called, was right in the center of the city, and our enemies who lived in the city would lob mortars at us all day, trying to kill us while we tried to sleep in their attempts to keep us from coming out at night. Just like the diamondback rattlesnakes that we were. Eventually, by about halfway through the deployment, we were all on trazadone, which I equate to a horse tranquilizer, because trust me, once you take it, you are knocked the fuck out for the next eight hours. It allowed us to sleep through the barrage of mortars that never stopped the entire time we were there.

And you might think that sleep in the middle of the jungle in the most remote locations of the Philippines, after that, would be easier, but it was actually harder. You see, Filipinos love to sing, especially when they're drunk, and there are these little karaoke bars all over the islands. And by bars, I mean just these little bamboo shacks where the proprietor is one of the few in the village fortunate enough to be able to afford electricity, allowing them to purchase or lease a karaoke machine that the locals pay one pesos (about two cents in U.S. money) to sing a karaoke song. And they do this until 3:00 a.m., with the volume on high, and the entire village gets to hear it all. And then, at 5:00 a.m., the morning vendors start roaming through the villages, screaming at the top of their lungs, what it is they're selling.

"Isda! Isda!" the fish vendors yell.

"Gulai! Gulai!" the vegetable vendors yell.

And sleep, at least for westerners not accustomed to such behavior, becomes as elusive as, well, for the lack of a better comparison…

…Bigfoot Sasquatch.

But as I lay in that brand new, overpriced custom made king size bed that first night in our new house on our Virginia homestead, my mind got the better of me and it kept me from sleep. At least in Iraq, when I heard the mortars, I knew who or what was out there. A bunch of people trying to kill me. When I was in the Philippines, as loud as it was out in the jungles at night, I knew what was out there. Drunken Filipinos crucifying Bon Jovi and Journey. Little old men with slimy eats from the sea and their little old wives selling the products of their labor in their gardens. And even in Manilla I'd learned to differentiate the sound of a taxi cab's horn and that of a jeepney. But here? In central Virginia? Where there wasn't a streetlight for twenty miles? There could be *anything* out there just on the other side of the walls of our house, and it could be creeping up on our house, and it could even be peering into the windows of our house and we would have *no way* of knowing because it was so freaking dark!

I'd forgotten how dark it gets at night when there are no artificial lights. I'd forgotten how quiet it is where there are no bombs, car horns, or drunken Filipinos or vendors. Sure, I could hear the frogs in the pond in the front yard, and it was a welcome sound, and I could hear the crickets chirping, and their presence was welcome as well, but when both would go silent, and then a floorboard would creek as the house settled, or the tin roof would pop as it cooled in the night after having baked in the sun all day, I was out of bed, on my feet, and walking around to investigate with an aluminum baseball bat in my hands.

Eventually, and just a few nights later, I would finally accept the fact that I was where I was, and this is how the nights were where I was, and it's what I'd wanted, and not to fear it but to embrace it. In a word, I began sleeping like a baby by the end of the first week in our new (to us) house.

Until November.

When the winds of November came.

And brought something ominous and fearsome with them.

***

We settled into our new routine in our new home on our new land, relatively quickly. A lot of it simply had to do with the fact that we were worn out from our topsy turvy life of the past year. I'd spent six months, alone, in the U.S., getting Dearly's visa, we'd moved my family back in the Philippines three times during that time after getting word of kidnapping plots on my son in hopes of hefty ransoms, and then I'd gone back, stayed with my family in Manila for six months before coming to the U.S., together, and then renting for three months, appeasing the powers that be in the public school system, and then finally settling down on our homestead after moving in. It was literally our eighth move in a year, this is counting another time we moved while living in Manila, simply because my wife had picked a real shithole of a place to live there, right across from the mall of Asia, before I'd flown back to live with her and our son. It was a small room, about the size of a closet- the typical type of living arrangements made by many of the service workers in the area who work twelve hour days and merely need a small space to sleep when not working. This was not good for us, by my standards, so I'd moved us to Makati City, the most high end part of Manila, and we quite enjoyed our stay there for the five months we were there after having spent a month in the broom closet.

Though settled, we were still quite busy. Our son's school was nearly half an hour's drive away from our property and we were taking him there in the mornings and going and picking him up in the afternoons. Yes, there is a bus, and yes, he does ride it these days, but it took us that first year to get over the idea of someone constantly trying to kidnap him for ransom, so we were not about to let him out of our sight.

When we'd get home from picking him up from school in the afternoons, we'd often lay on air mattress out on the lawn, underneath one of our many walnut trees, for shade, because it was still September, and then October, and in our part of central Virginia, it is still quite hot that time of year. We would lay together, the three of us, and stare into our fields (which are now meadows, and quickly on their way to becoming a forest), and watch the deer and the rabbits. We've seen the occasional bear and turkey. So many hawks fly above our place, regularly, you'd think it was a bird of prey preserve. And there are far too many gray squirrels to count. Often, on these first afternoons at our new home, (and it was, *finally*, our home, after all those years of moving around due to poverty and safety) we would fall asleep in the field, on our air mattress, and wake up just in time to go inside, have dinner, and then fall asleep for the night in our bed.

Then, as if the winds had a calendar, just as it turned November 1, a few minutes after midnight, the winds whipped up something fierce, as they'd say here in the south, and my feeling of peace left and I was right back to where I'd been that first week in our home.

You see, as our land lay, and as the land around it lies, it makes for the perfect scenario for heavy winds. There is a small river down the road and over the hill from our property. It's about two hundred yards away. And all the land beside the road, once passing our property, is wooded. Our land is the first open land in the immediate area (it was formerly hay fields) so when the temperatures begin dropping drastically in November, and the water's temperature is actually higher than the air temperature around it, it creates a draft. And since the land around the river, except for the road, is all wooded, the easiest way for the draft to escape, and rise, as warm air does, is to come up the road. Then, once these warm drafts reach our property, they go batshit crazy, because they can, because they have the space. The winds (fyi, wind is defined as the result of the uneven heating and cooling of the earth's surface, in case you didn't know) then whip around like crazy on our six acres. It's as if they run around, playing tag with each other, until they spin themselves out.

Our old house has beautiful old eaves that hang over each window. They're angled perfectly for keeping the sun's direct shine out of the windows during the summer, but they allow for it to shine in during winter. . These were necessary when the house was built, because air conditioning, at the time, was a fantasy at most, as was heating systems outside of woodstoves and fireplaces. Neither had been invented yet. These days, the eaves are not necessary, but we leave them, because it helps our old house look more rustic. We feel like we're living in an antique, which I guess we are. The house is listed on the historical registry here in Virginia.

Anyway, the point to all of this is that as those winds on that first night of November reached our property, and then our house, they lifted these eaves above the windows, at least the ones upstairs, and then as the winds passed on, the eaves would drop back into their natural place and it sounded as if someone was jumping around in the upstairs bedrooms of our house.

When this first happened, I awoke with a start, immediately believing I was back in Mosul, Iraq, and that another s-vbied (suicide vehicle bourne improvised explosive devise) had rammed into the gate, killing all the guards and making a hole for an insurgent attack. I sat up, and I reached to the side of my bed to grab my M-4, but alas, it was not there. I jumped up, ready to find it, and that's when I saw my wife and our son sleeping in our custom made king sized bed, and I remembered where I was.

And then it happened again!

Another slam from upstairs convinced me someone was in the house. I may not have had an M-4 ready by my bed, but I did have an aluminum baseball bat that I keep there to this day for such events. For some reason, I've had a couple people out this way ask me if I have firearms. I had no idea why I was asked this at first, but I've since come to believe that they asked this because they are anti-gun types (yes, I'm out in the country, but it is right outside of a university town, and there are tons of those types out here), and they wanted to judge me as as 'gun nutter' had I said yes. I did not answer their question, and I will not answer it here, but what I told them was exactly where my bedroom window was located, and I challenged them to come climbing through it at 2 a.m. some night and find out.

They both (two different beta-males on two separate occasions), simply turned and walked away and never came back!

Anyway, I took my bat and I headed upstairs. I heard the slams a couple more times on my way up. They were coming from our son's room. He hadn't actually moved into his room yet, because allowing him to sleep with us that first year here, even though he was already in kindergarten, was part of our cooling down process as well. Let me tell you, when you have to spend the first five years of your kid's life worrying about them being kidnapped for ransom, because their father is a white foreigner living in a non-white third world country riddled with terrorists and common criminals, old habits are hard to break. However, we since have, and it's a really nice feeling being able to let our guards down just a bit.

The door to my son's room was open, and though the light was off, I could still see into the room quite well. We had not hung the blinds yet, and the moon happened to be almost full that night, and there wasn't a cloud in the sky, so the light from the moon was coming through the windows lighting the place up almost as if it were day.

As I was looking out the window, a gust picked up and slammed the eave again, and this time, I saw the actual movement of the eave, and I heard and felt the resulting slam, and I was immediately set to ease. I laughed at myself as I lowered the baseball bat from my shoulder.

But then I immediately raised it again!

As I was peering outside the window, I saw something large scurry around the side of our detached garage which sits outside and below the window. And what I'd seen was no animal on all fours. What I'd seen, for just a moment, was walking upright on two legs, and it was big.

Very big!

I didn't go to the window, knowing that I was far enough away from the window so that I could see out of it, but if anyone or anything was outside looking in they could not see me. If I were to get close to the window, whoever or whatever was out there would be able to see me.

I stood, motionless, for a minute, and realizing a drawn bat would be of no use to someone or something outside the window, I lowered it again, but I remained vigilant. A couple more minutes passed, during which time the eave outside the window banged and slammed a couple of more times, and then I saw it again.

Actually, two of them!

I could not believe what I was seeing at first, and I actually *did* move to the window this time to get a better view. What

I saw completely blew my mind, and it would take me nearly a year to come to accept what it is that I saw, though I have to admit, that at the time, I believe I already knew.

At first, there was only one. One large, and I mean *really* large, creature, walking on two legs, away from the back of the detached garage and up the hill of what was then our upper field. It had recently been cut for hay, as we'd allowed the man who'd taken the hay from the land for years (the land had belonged to his mother's cousin before we bought it) take one last cut before using the land exclusively for our own purposes. The man was, and still is, a total dickbag, and my immediate instincts told me at the time that it was this very man, the annoying neighbor that I would eventually have to run off with a crayon, that I was seeing outside that night. I believed he was stalking us (because he actually did for a while), and that he was outside being a peeping tom (which he'd been fired from the University of Virginia for being, I would later find out), and I was about to run out the back door and give him a good, old fashioned Appalachiastanian hillbilly ass whoopin'!

But then, the first creature was joined by a second. This one was just a bit smaller, but it was still massive in size!

It occurred to me that these creatures were not men. They were not human, though they appeared to take human form. That is, as long as you consider professional NFL tight ends and WWE wrestlers. They had to be nearly eight feet tall, and if I were a betting man, which I'm not, because I've always been too good at math to gamble or play the lottery, I would wager they weighed close to eight hundred pounds.

I watched in awe as these two entities, slowly and methodically, while looking back on occasion, made their way to the top of the hill, about four hundred yards away, before slipping into the woods behind my house. I rubbed my eyes a few times as they made their way up the hill, and I even pinched myself once, and sure enough, I was fully awake, as I would remain the rest of the night, despite the winds of November finally dying down and the ceasing of the banging of the eaves.

As I lay in bed the rest of the night, I questioned my sanity. I mean, I knew I was messed up a bit from the war. I knew I was messed up due to my time in the Philippines, and the events that took place there. I knew I had issues due to personal losses resulting from both.

But I knew I wasn't crazy!

Well, that much.

But I knew what I'd seen!

It would take more experiences like this one, and it would later take confirmation from some really supportive and credible people on a YouTube channel we now have that did not exist at the time- that first fall that we were in our new home on our new property- but today I have every reason to believe I know exactly what I saw, and only for the first time, on that November night when I'd been awakened by the winds of November.

Potentially…

…two…

Bigfoot Sasquatch!

Bigfoot Sasquatch Saves The World

Okay, so I'm pretty open with my life on our YouTube channel "Homesteading Off The Grid." I'm open with my daily affairs, many of which are 'same 'ol, same 'ol,' and honestly, becoming boring. Splitting wood, mowing grass, growing weed gardens (no, not *that* kind of weed, and they're meant to be vegetable gardens, but if you miss a few days straight of weeding, the weeds get the better of you, and we have a tendency to miss a few *weeks* straight every year, so come harvest time, we're wading chest high in weeds looking for vegetables. It's much like an Easter egg hunt.). Oh, and going around the woods and meadows behind my house looking for him, her, it or they.

And I've been pretty open with much of my past. Mostly, by way of writing about it in my novels under the guise of fiction. Especially all those 'down and out years' in the Philippines.

"How did you go from being a batshit crazy, drunk, down and out disabled vet in the Philippines to an upper middle class Virginia landowner just outside of Charlottesville?" people often ask.

"Why," I begin in response, "by never giving up. I focussed on my writing, and in time, I got good at it. Eventually, I got on the map and the money started coming in, and we were able to leave the jungle and get back to the city, and a couple of years after that we were able to come to the U.S., and well, things were going so well that we were able to buy a house on six acres out in the country, just outside of Charlottesville, and well," I say, just like I started with, "everything just worked out."

"There seems to be some holes in your story," the most astute of naysayers will say.

"How so?" I'll ask.

"How did you survive?" they'll say. "During those *down and out years* as you call them. I mean, you had to be making money somehow. At least enough to sustain yourself and your *beautiful bride*, as you call her, and your son. How did you do it?"

At this point, I don't plead the fifth. But I come close. I refer my examiner to my novel, "Isle of Kapre," and I say to them, "good luck figuring out which part of the story is fact, and which part is fiction."

At this point, I'll get a look of confusion. However, I get no further questioning, because the people who tend to make it this far along in their inquisition do have a half a brain cell or two more than the average bear, and some of them actually do read the book. And of those who get back to me after reading the book? They all say the same thing.

"You really *are* batshit crazy!"

What's my point to all this? Well, it's simple, really. In my previous life, I made many contacts. Contacts in high places who relay messages through common friends in low places. If this sounds like I'm speaking (well, typing) in riddles, it's because I am, and it's for a reason.

"Why?" you ask.

Again, if you haven't read it, go read "Isle of Kapre," and you'll totally get it.

And you, too, will be convinced I'm batshit crazy if you're not already.

Anyway, here's what all this has to do with this story.

Be prepared for a validated, actual, bonafide, effective vaccine for Covid-19, no later than the end of February, 2021, if, indeed, it's not out by the time you read this book!

"What in the name of all things holy are you talking (well, typing) about now, Crazy Lake?" you might be asking yourself?

This!

***

Ring!

It was my cell phone. It was early on a Sunday morning in October of 2020. I'd planned to sleep in, because I'd been up late the night before doing a night hunt for Bigfoot Sasquatch in the woods behind my house, and making a video of it for my YouTube channel, as well as approving final edits for my most recent novella length collection of short stories, "Bigfoot Sasquatch Files Volume 5." It was a busy night, a night on which I was up well past midnight, and I was, as our friends in the U.K. would say, cream crackered! That means worn out in American.

I grabbed the phone and looked at the number calling. I sat straight up in bed, instantly wide awake, and I answered before it had a chance to ring a second time. The number calling was from an individual I'd never given my number to, but I guess guys like him have the ability to find you. Or anyone. Anywhere. The events that took place on the Isle of Kapre is proof enough of that.

"Yes, sir?" I said.

"You're not gonna believe this," the voice on the other side of the line said. It was the voice from a fifty year old man who was supposed to be dead.

"I'm kinda having a hard time believing you're still alive," I said.

"Remember," he said. "Believe nothing you hear and only half of what you see."

"Fuck you," I said.

"Why?" he said.

"I cried for a minute when I thought you were dead."

"Wow," he said. "A whole minute?"

"You think you're worth more time than that?"

"I love you, too, but we'll catch up later. I have a job for you."

"Um, do you know where I am?" I asked.

"Yes," he said. "You're sitting up in your bed in the downstairs master bedroom of your old sharecropper house out in the country, just outside of Charlottesville. You're staring at the far wall telling yourself you need to get around to painting it, and the rest of the inside of your house, again, because four winters worth of smoke from your woodstove has taken its toll on the last paint job."

"Did you mother fuckers put cameras up in my house?" I asked, the feeling of panic like I'd not felt in years instantly returning.

"No," he said, laughing. "I'm just fucking with you." He was laughing so hard it took him a hot second to be able to speak again. "Lucky guess, but look."

"Fuck you," I said, now feeling my heart rate coming back down.

"Okay, we're done with the fuck yous. You need to listen. I have a job for you. But yes, we know exactly where you live and how you live."

"How?" I asked, now looking around for pinhole sized camera lenses in the corners of the room.

"You broadcast your life on YouTube," he said.

"Oh," I said, feeling myself disarming again.

"Look," he said. "We need you to go back to the lair."

"What lair?" I asked.

"The lair of Bigfoot Sasquatch, you dumb fucker," he said.

"Are you serious?" I asked.

"It's either there or the Isle of Kapre," he said. "Take your pick."

"What do you," I began, but then I thought better of it and reworded my question. "What do *they* need from me now?"

"DNA," he said, short and sweet with no further explanation, and I'd worked with him enough in the past to know that he would give no further explanation so there was no need for me to press. And I didn't blame him. Guys who work in his capacity have a tendency to be disappeared for giving too much information, and frankly, guys like me who've performed certain 'odd jobs' in the past, like the odd jobs I was performing leading up to and even during my time spent on the Isle of Kapre had a tendency to be disappeared for knowing too much, too.

"Why me?" I asked. "I thought I was done. I thought that was part of the deal. I work for your guys once, and I get to come home and live happily ever after and all that bullshit. We got their man in office. We set up their puppet Government. We eliminated the threat from those networks these fucking know it all, pampered, smartest assholes in the room Americans over here have never even heard about, because we never allowed them and their actions to reach the scale of making mainsteam news, where all the smartest assholes in the room garner all their information."

"A little bitter, or just a lot?" he asked. "Let me know when you're done. If you'd like to persist, I can have my assistant run out and pick up some cheese to go along with your whine."

"Fuck you," I said.

"We're done with that," he said. "Remember?"

"What's in it for me?" I asked.

"You get to keep living your happily ever after," he said.

"And if I don't do it?" I asked, already knowing the answer.

"They're going to take it all away," he said. "Remember, what the large print giveth, the fine print taketh away."

And I knew there was no need to argue my case. Trust me, the people he contracted for had a way of not just disappearing people, but destroying people in such a way that makes them *wish* they'd disappeared, and it was the promises that they *didn't* renege on that always amazed me.

"Tell me what I need to do," I said, swinging my feet over the side of the bed, rising, and then heading into the kitchen to start the coffee while my informant gave me the mission.

***

When I've got shit to do, I have a tendency to get it done- like, now, not later- hence, only an hour after having my coffee and breakfast, I was off to go hiking through the woods behind my house, the potential lair of the potential Bigfoot Sasquatch being my final intended destination. I'd told my beautiful bride, Dearly, also known as 'Giggly Girl' on our YouTube channel, that I was burned out on running and cycling, and so my morning exercise was going to be hiking.

"You are going to da lair to make to da YouTube video?" she asked in her ever-cute and ever-broken English.

"Something like that," I said.

"Oh," she said. "Was that..." she trailed off.

"Yeah," I said.

"I thought he was dead?" she said.

"Guess not," I said, lacing up my hiking boots.

"I wish he dead," she said.

"That's not nice," I said.

"He not nice," she said.

"It's not his job to be nice," I said. "It's his job to get shit done so the world keeps spinning and the protected can remain protected, and bitch and complain about it the whole time because they have no fucking clue how protected they are."

"You go," she said. "Just don't bring any of that shit back with you."

By 'that shit," she meant anything of paranormal, supernatural, or cryptozoological nature, but little did she know, *shit* is exactly what I planned on bringing back with me. I had to. It was the mission. Shit contained DNA, and yes, I could have gone after saliva or hair, or even blood (which could have ended badly for me), but I'd made it my little personal prank on humanity to go after shit.

You see, I've been a manbrat/smartass bastard since the days of the old testament, my friends!

***

Two hours and a roughly five mile hike later, I'd reached my destination. I was, potentially, in the middle of the lair that may or may not have belonged to Bigfoot Sasquatch.

"Jesus," I said to myself, half a complaint rooted in a complete loss of knowing what to do now, and half in the form of an actual prayer. "What do I do now?"

No answer came to me, but I figured I'd just get to doing what I'd come to do. I slipped off my backpack, which is my old Army assault pack from Iraq, and I took out the pair of purple latex gloves I'd brought with me and slipped them on. I took out the half a dozen plastic grocery store bags I'd brought with me (which, by the way, are of the devil. They are pure evil. They are responsible for so much pollution and death of wildlife around the world. And I *do* mean around the world. I have seen plastic bags from Food Lion ((a major grocery store chain in the southern U.S.)) blowing around in the wind all over the world. I have seen these plastic bags blowing through the Arabian Desert in Iraq. I have seen them blowing along the beaches and through the jungles of Southeast Asia. Yes, actual plastic bags from Food Lion in the southern U.S.! I guess they caught some really intense upward heat drafts), and I began searching the forest floor all around me for shit.

Bigfoot Sasquatch shit!

"This is deer shit," I said aloud, finding my first pile of droppings. At first, I had no intentions of bagging up this deer shit and turning it into my superior (God, I hate referring to that asshole as my superior), but I figured that if I went back empty handed I'd be accused of not having tried hard enough, so, bag it up I did.

I continued walking around, slowly, and in pretty short order, I managed to bag up more deer shit, some racoon shit, some groundhog shit, and finally, after searching for nearly an hour, I found a big steaming pile of bear shit. Now, it was pretty easy for an experienced woodsman like me (yes, I'm an experienced woodsman, even though so many vertically challenged individuals who live under bridges accuse me of being a 'city boy' on our YouTube channel) to be able to tell that this was only bear shit, but I'd be able to use the excuse that it was so fresh that I couldn't tell, and that would get me a pass. At least long enough to get a second chance to come back.

Next, after having been awakened early by the phone call after a late night, and hiking for hours, and searching for shit, literally, for hours, I sat down, my back against a large red oak tree, and I fell asleep.

***

I don't know how long I slept, but when I woke up, I was ravishingly hungry. I immediately thought of the twinkies I'd brought in my assault pack. Realizing I was probably a good quarter mile away from my pack, I immediately got up and began walking back to my pack, making sure to take my bags of shit with me. I hurried the pace, because I was really, really hungry (yes, I know that's redundant, and it's intentional, because I want to really make the point about how hungry I was), and I really, really love twinkies.

Alas, as I got to within sight of my assault pack, only fifty yards away through the forest, I saw a scene that was heartbreaking. A large, dark figure was opening my assault pack, and I knew it was going to take my twinkies.

"You fucking bear!" I yelled, assuming that the thief was the black bear that had recently deposited the huge, steaming pile of shit I now held in the bag in my left hand. "Leave my twinkies alone, you fucking fuck!"

I began running at the thief, knowing that black bears are relatively docile creatures, and that they, like all wild animals (except wild hogs, which, fortunately, are only found considerably further south of where I live) fear humans more than anything.

Once I'd cut the distance between myself and my assault pack and the large, hairy thief in half, I stopped in my tracks. I nearly deposited my own steaming pile of that which I was carrying in my plastic Food Lion grocery bags, because what stood before me, on two legs, not four, was no black bear.

It was...

...potentially...

...Bigfoot Sasquatch!

"Oh, shit," I said.

The creature let out a mighty roar. Then, while holding my now open assault pack with one hand, it jammed its other hand inside it and pulled out, not my twinkies, but...

...wait for it...

...a spicy Italian sub on flatbread from Subway that I'd bought and forgotten to eat more than a month before. It had been in one of the different pouches on my assault pack that I'd not checked before leaving for my hike because I'd been in such a hurry. I mean, I was doing the job as a subcontractor for a guy who was doing his job as a subcontractor for a group of people who are not known for their patience, so I simply hadn't taken the time to check all the pouches, even though I could smell quite a stench. A stench like that made by rotten meat.

"Argh!" the creature yelled again, like a big hairy pirate, and if I were to translate what the 'argh' meant, I mean, with my morning phone conversation still fresh in my mind, I would have reason to believe that the 'argh' meant, "fuck you!" The beast crammed the entire sub of rotten meat and wilted vegetables into his, her or its mouth, wrapper and all, and gave me a hard stare, that I would equally translate into a 'fuck you,' and then it dropped my assault pack and then turned and ran over the mountainside with such speed it was gone instantly.

I hurried to my assault pack, and fortunately, my twinkies, all of them, were still in it. I took the twinkies out of my assault pack and I ate of them. And I became full of the twinkies that were in my assault pack. And I was pleased by the feeling of being filled of the twinkies that had been in my assault pack all was good with the world.

***

"Shit," I said, walking back down the mountain after having finished my twinkies. "Now what?" Again, it was part complaint and part prayer.

But this time, the answer came to me in the way of a moan. A moan emanating from the middle of a laurel thicket about one hundred yards to my right. I stopped, I listened, and I was pleased!

Bigfoot Sasquatch had eaten a rotten Italian sub from Subway! Bigfoot Sasquatch had a terrible tummy ache as a result of a mild case of food poisoning!

Bigfoot Sasquatch had the shits!

My job had just become simple. All I had to do was wait, and wait was all I did. I hunkered down beside a large poplar tree, and I was conveniently hidden behind my own thicket of laurel, and it was all I could do to not laugh my ass off while listening to the large, bipedal beast shitting his, her or its guts out only a hundred yards away. I mean, I wasn't trying to be mean, taking pleasure in his, her, or its pain, but Karma is real. You steal a man's food, you get a case of the shits, right? And besides, the creature could have been lucky enough to have opened the other pocket on my assault pack and stolen my twinkies. Then where would I be? Would I have eaten the spoiled sub? Would I be the one with the shits now? I mean, I *am* batshit crazy, so maybe.

Anyway, after a quarter of an hour or so, the beast seemed to be finished, and I knew that out here in the wild, there was no paperwork to do, so once it (or him, or her) crept further down the hill after making its deposit, I waited another fifteen minutes or so to make sure it was gone, and then I went to the laurel thicket where it (or him, or her) had made its extremely large deposit.

I'd hit the mother load!

Knowing this was exactly what I'd come for, I dumped out all the other shit I'd already collected- deer shit, raccoon shit, bear shit- and I'd even found what I thought was bat shit, and I almost kept that as a suveigner, you know, because I'm told it's the type of crazy I am? But no! I needed all the room in my plastic bags I could get, so I dumped out the bat shit, too. Once my bags were all shit free, I reloaded them, this time with nothing but shit from him, her, it, or... well, there was only one, so there was no they. And then I headed off the mountain, considering this yet another successful mission. I felt elated, because I'd not actually performed any type of missions for these guys since leaving Mindanao more than five years ago. Even though I hated the bastards, familiar territory felt good.

***

Here's what I can tell you about the outcome of my mission. I left the 'package' where I was instructed to leave it, and where I'm sure it was picked up the second I was out of sight.

Like all my missions, I'm never told the exact specifics, or, like I discussed earlier, any specifics, but I always have my hypothesis, and here's my hypothesis in regard to this mission:

I know this mission was carried out during the peak days of the Covid-19 virus. Further, I know that the amount of DNA similarities that we share with him, her, it or they are so close it would terrify most people, especially all those know it all smartest assholes in the room who believe these creatures don't exist, anyway, because, well, mainstream media has never confirmed their existence, and that's where they garner all their information.

Further, I have reason to believe that there are no such things as 'new viruses.' I believe that everything is cyclical. I believe that this Covid-19 virus has visited us before, however, it did so during the days before we were nearly as advanced as we are today, and I don't mean only in regard to science and medicine. I mean in regard to record keeping, as well. I believe this virus, and many others, visited us thousands of years ago, and I do believe that it wiped out large populations.

However, I also believe that large populations developed herd immunity to the virus, and I believe that the Bigfoot Sasquatch population happens to be one of those populations.

And I believe the people who subcontracted me for this mission, through a subcontractor, knew this, hence this mission.

So, like I said, look for the 'miracle vaccine' within ninety days of the publishing of this story, unless, like I also said, it's here already, before this story even has time to be published.

Oh, and I got word a couple days after completing this mission that my contact died in a single car vehicular accident.

I'm sure I'll hear from him again. As soon as *they* want something from me again.

Oh, and know, that when you receive the vaccine for Covid-19, should you choose to, or, should we all be forced to…

…wait for it…

…you're (potentially) being shot up with a big 'ol steaming dose of Bigfoot Sasquatch shit!

The End

3

The Things We Leave Behind

"Ya'll ain't never gonna see it, what, with the piss poor attitudes ya'll have about it."

It was Herb. He wasn't *really* a cop, but they let him wear the uniform and walk the streets- not drive the cruiser, mind you, but walk. And they let him have a billy club, but not a handgun.

"Shoot, what with the piss poor attitudes ya'll boys have about everything."

"Ah, come on, Herb," my childhood best friend, Ricky said. "Just tell us exactly where it is so we can go see it. We just want a glimpse." We were thirteen years old and had nothing better to do than to harass the man we viewed as the town's fool.

"Now, I ain't tellin' ya'll boys where it is. I know ya'll better than you *think* I do. Why, you're liable to go up there and try to shoot it," Herb said. And he was right. If he told us where it was, that's *exactly* what we were going to do. We were going to go into the woods, up on the hill behind Herb's house, which overlooked our entire small town, and we were going to kill us a Bigfoot Sasquatch, and we were going to become rich and famous for doing so.

But really? We didn't believe any of Herb's stories, so more than anything, we were going to debunk him.

"Now, that time I went and told ya'll boys about where the spaceships were landin', ya'll went up there with your flashlights, and your tent, and you built your bonfire, and they ain't been back!"

Herbs thing, for years, when Ricky and I had been younger, had been aliens and U.F.O.'s. He'd claimed he knew where their landing strip was. At least the one in our area, where they would park their ship while visiting and taking samples of the lifeforms that lived in our area.

"They don't hurt nothin' that breathes," Herb used to go on and on, back in those days. "They only want to study our plantlife. Why, they know how harmful them meats are to a body, so they don't touch it." Herb had claimed to become a vegetarian after having not just observed the aliens he claimed to see from afar, but after having, or at least he claimed, conversed with them telepathically. "Why, they don't even waste time and energy with speakin'," he'd told us back then. "They do it all mentally. Inside their heads."

We'd actually gotten Herb to tell us the specific location of this alleged (or, potential) U.F.O. landing area, and we had gone camping up there, and though we never saw any U.F.O.'s or strange lights in the night sky, we *did* find an area that looked as if it had been burned up in a forest fire. It was only the size of a basketball court. Nothing big at all. And there were several very strange indentations in the soil in the area, as if something large and heavy had sat in the area. We wrote it all off to Herb trying to set us up. Make us believe his idiotic story about the U.F.O.'s. I mean,we knew he was our village idiot. At least that's what we'd thought at the time.

"I can only imagine how bad things would have been back then," Herb said, reflecting on the night that Ricky and I had gone camping at his alleged (or, potential) U.F.O. landing pad, "if ya'll'd been totin' around firearms like ya'll are nowadays."

I'll tell you this, here and now, and just by way of being honest when looking back on it. Herb was right. Had any unidentified flying objects come around Ricky and me back in the day (circa 1987), we would have shot them out of the sky.

But that was a long time ago.

A very long time ago.

In time, Ricky and I would outgrow our infatuation with passivily aggressively harassing the man we viewed as the town's idiot by listening to his tall tales about aliens and Bigfoot Sasquatch. We would discover a new infatuation.

Girls!

We started chasing them shortly after giving up on getting Herb to let us in on the specific location of this alleged (or, potential) Bigfoot Sasquatch that he claimed lived in the woods behind his house. Herb soon became an afterthought. He would become that weirdo we'd see walking up and down the sidewalk in front of the theater (this being back when our little town in Appalachiastan had not yet become the meth and pill riddled shithole that it is today, like so many small towns in Appalachiastan that once thrived before the days of the internet), one hand on his holstered billy club, the other on his pants waist, opposite side the billy club, in order to hold them up, because they were a size too large. The department was not going to put in an order for a new uniform for a guy who was merely an 'honorary policeman' as they called him.

"There's the guy that claims to see aliens and Bigfoot Sasquatch," Ricky and I would whisper to our dates as we prepared to pass Herb on our way to see the latest Friday the 13'th installment, or the newest Rocky or Indiana Jones. Ricky or I, or both of us, would make some sort of snide comment to Herb about the claims he'd made to us when we were younger. He'd put his head down and act like he hadn't heard us, and our dates would tell us we were mean and they would never go out with us again. It took us a while to learn that girls, the good ones, at least- the ones worth keeping- didn't view being mean to other people, especially those who came across as weaker-than, as a turn on.

Ricky and I grew up, and this is the point in which most stories would read that we went our separate ways and conquered the world, but it's not how this story goes. I left that little Appalachian town and I went on to college, and after graduating, I left Appalachiastan entirely.

Ricky didn't.

He never got out.

And neither of us conquered the world. The world would eventually conquer Ricky, and me? Well, let's just say I'm still fighting.

Ricky wasn't the brightest tool in the shed. At least that's how we'd referred to him as kids. As it turns out, he suffered from dyslexia and a very mild case of Aspergers. We just thought he struggled with reading and was funny as shit- the guy willing to say the things the rest of us weren't- but I guess we were wrong.

Ricky stayed behind, and as the middle class fled Appalachiastan, beginning in the mid-nineties, as a result of the then, newly internet driven economy- an economy that allowed for people to work from home, hence, allowing them to work from anywhere- Ricky's economic options began to shrink. He'd barely graduated high school, and the only jobs he could get were labor jobs. He'd started out doing okay in the coal mines, but with the restrictive regulations President Clinton would put on mining, causing many of the mines back in Appalachiastan to close, Ricky would soon find himself unemployed and unemployable at the ripe old age of twenty six.

However, a new industry was taking over much of Appalachiastan.

Methamphetamine!

As the infomercials we all grew up watching in the 80's would put it, Ricky would not just become the president of his own little meth lab and distribution business, he would also become a client. And he would soon begin his vicious cycle of jail, court ordered rehab, the street. Jail, court ordered rehab, the street.

Like so many addicts in Appalachiastan, or hell, anywhere else in the world for that matter, everyone who knew Ricky would soon distance themselves from him. His family, friends, and sadly, even me, wrote him off as dead, though, for a while, he was still very much alive. It was a mix of not wanting to be associated with him and loving him too much to watch him continue to kill himself slowly, as addiction is basically a form of suicide on installment.

But not Herb.

Herb always saw Ricky as that smartass little ten year old who wanted to know where the U.F.O.'s landed. Then, as that smartass thirteen year old who wanted to go and shoot himself a Bigfoot Sasquatch and become famous for doing so. And later, as that older teen who was feeling his oates so rowdy that he'd say the occasional mean thing he didn't really mean, in the hopes of impressing a beautiful member of the opposite sex.

Herb never had the validated capacity to arrest Ricky, and he never did. But there had been many a night when Herb had spent the night with Ricky in the drunk tank. There were so many times that Herb would catch a ride to the regional jail with whatever officer was taking someone up for their next stay, and he would visit with Ricky while there, the other officer- the *real* officer- processing the new intake while he did.

Herb would visit with Ricky in his cheap, no-tell hotel room that he could rent for twenty dollars a night (and sometimes the heating system in the room actually worked in the winters) on those rare occasions that Ricky was not locked up in either jail or rehab. On more than one occasion Herb allowed Ricky to stay with him when he didn't have a twenty to rent his room and no one else would. This is how it went all the way up until about ten years ago. Until Herb died at the ripe old age of eighty three.

Then Ricky had absolutely no one.

No one knew the specifics, but Ricky got himself stabbed to death about a month ago. He was forty five years old. The surprising part of the whole thing is that everyone was shocked he'd actually lived *that* long. It was a given assumption that Ricky probably died due to a drug deal. Either he'd bought and not paid, or he was selling to someone who had no intentions of paying. Either way, most folks thought, it was for the better. And not just for the community, but for Ricky. Everyone viewed it as if he was merely a suffering animal being put out of its misery.

But not me.

I cried when I got the news.

I hadn't spoken with or communicated online with Ricky for more than a decade. It broke my heart to do it, but what I'll say is, to this day, I feel it had to be that way. You see, I may have left Appalachiastan, but none of us, anywhere, are free from the threat of addiction to the things that make us feel good. Especially, if for some reason, we have an addictive personality, the addiction gene, or, if we merely mess around with the wrong things for too long.

I've struggled myself, off and on, and I have reason to believe I always will, though each day I pray the struggle is over, and that true freedom from addiction has arrived, but experience has shown me that it's a back and forth battle I may never win, but I swear, God as my witness, I will *never* give up fighting. The point here is that not only did I have to distance myself from Ricky because I didn't want to be associated with him and because I loved him too much to continue watching him kill himself, but I had to distance myself from him in order to have a better chance of staying clean and sober myself.

I once had almost a year sober, and Ricky came up to see me. It was my last year in college, and I'll admit that I hadn't really dried out in order to stay dry, but to finish my senior year and graduate. Ricky and I went out and celebrated getting together for the first time in a long while. We got blackout drunk for a week, and I missed class for a week, and I ended up having to spend another semester in school because I'd failed a class, and I didn't see another sober day for several years.

Later in life, Ricky was the one actually trying to get straight. He had six months clean and sober, and who do you think went back to our little shit hole town in Appalachiastan to do some fly fishing? Why, me, of course, and I had to go see my old friend Ricky, and I just happened to have a case of beer with me, because when you go fishing, if you don't end up catching any fish, the least you can do is end up catching a buzz, and Ricky and I got shitfaced all week, and I never even *went* fishing, and a month after I left that shithole little town in Appalachiastan, Ricky would get his first of *many* D.U.I.'s.

And this is how it went for many years. When Ricky was straight, I'd take him back through the narrows. When I was dry, he'd wet me up.

We were no longer good for each other.

So, painfully, we parted ways, and I was the one who'd made that painful decision for both of us.

I didn't attend Ricky's funeral, and I doubt many people did. But the weight of the pain of our relationship weighed on me heavily, and finally, about two weeks ago, I took a day and drove back into that shithole town in Appalachiastan. Well, not really "into" as much as "on the outskirts of." You see, this is where the cemetery is.

I found Ricky's grave and I smirked and laughed lightly at the irony that it was so close to Herb's. They weren't next to each other. There were a few other graves in between them, but they were close enough to where you could see one while sitting beside the other. And that's what I did. I would sit by Ricky's, having telepathic conversations, in my head, with him *and* Herb (remembering Herb's aliens and laughing about it), and then I would move over to Herb's and do the same from there.

I caught myself reading the inscription on Herb's tombstone. I don't know why I didn't at first. I guess my mind was elsewhere. And I guess I just always viewed him as the village idiot, and I assumed the inscription on his tombstone would simply read that he was the village idiot.

Boy, was I wrong!

The inscription on Herb's tombstone was quite lengthy, and I read it all, and to sum it up in fewer words than were written, Herb was a hero!

Herb had served in the United States Army during World War Two. He'd been an airborne infantryman, and he was part of the group that stormed the beach at Normandy on D-Day. Then, he spent months fighting his way all across Europe, finally reaching Hitler's 'Crow's Nest,' and he was part of the group that delivered the final death blow to the Nazi regime.

"Wow!" I said aloud after having read the inscription. I looked up, skyward, to say a prayer for both of my fallen friends, and as I did, and as my eyes connected with the skyline, where the top of the hill met the sky, I saw something large, something dark, dart behind a large tree.

It was early November, and the leaves had already fallen from the trees. Whatever it was that I saw was a couple of miles away from me, but it could easily be seen because of the lack of leaves, and also because its sheer size.

I'd grown up in these mountains, and I'd seen plenty of black bears in my day. Large ones. But there is no such thing as a black bear as large as what I'd seen dart behind that tree. I watched, and I waited, but I did not see it again. Eventually, my curiosity got the better of me and I left the cemetery, and I went hiking.

Ironically, the closest place to the location where I'd seen something large and dark dart behind a tree on top of the mountain overlooking the cemetery, and the entire town, for that matter, was by way of Herb's back yard.

***

I didn't go to my car and drive to the other side of town to hike up the hill to see if I could get a better look at what I thought I'd seen. And I didn't even run. I walked. Slowly.

The town was small, and it had eroded since I'd left a quarter of a century ago. I ambled through what was once downtown, now a ghost town, and through the neighborhood on the opposite side of the town as the cemetery, receiving suspicious glares from the few people I saw as I did, until I reached Herb's old house. He'd been dead and gone a while now, and his house looked just as abandoned and dilapidated as so many of those surrounding it and just like so many of those that I'd passed on my way through the small hamlet.

This was the kind of place where when one died, and their beneficiaries inherited their property, their beneficiaries did *not* rejoice. There was no value to a crap house that could not sell, because there was nothing in the area to draw people in. And to use as a rental? Good luck! A revolving door of druggies and drunks who never pay rent and which require court orders that take nearly a year to obtain to evict. To inherit anything in this near third world shithole community is a burden, not a blessing, and it was no surprise to me that Herb's house had been allowed to merely fall apart at the hands of time, erosion, and a one hundred percent lack of care and upkeep.

I made my way through Herb's front yard, and then the back, and finally, into the woods. It took only twenty five minutes to hike to the top of the hill which overlooked the small community. Once on top, I found a large boulder that I'd known well in my childhood, and I sat on it, and I peered out over the once middle class community that now was just one little spot of existence in the great meth and opioid belt of Appalachia that has replaced what was once referred to as the rust belt. No, the industrial, labor type jobs never came back after the advent of computer technology, and for some reason the folks in the area never got on board with the new economy, and when there was no prosperity rushing in, the pills and the powders filled the void.

As I sat, attempting to shed tears for Ricky and Herb, tears that would not come, I fondled the pint of Jim Beam I had on the inside pocket of my coat. When I'd left home, it had not been cold, but I knew temperatures would be much lower here in the hills of Appalachiastan, and I'd been right, and I was thankful for the decision to have brought the coat, but I was wrestling with the decision I'd made about the bottle. I'd told myself I was going to have one last drink with Ricky, right there at his gravesite. I would take a swig, and then dump a shot on Ricky's grave. I'd take another swig and then give another to the earth that covered my old friend from whom I'd been estranged for the last decade of his life.

I was lying to myself again and I knew it. Rather, my disease, the only disease that spends its entire existence trying to convince those that have it that they do *not* have a disease, addiction, was whispering in my ear. The disease was doing the lying, and I was believing it. The diseases' lie went; *come on. It's a special occasion. You're drinking to the loss and memory of two old friends. It's just this once. Besides, you're giving half the bottle to the grave, so it's not like you're going to drink the whole pint.*

I pulled the bottle from my coat pocket, and as I held it in my left hand, I began to unscrew the lid with the fingers on my right.

"To Ricky," I said aloud.

And to Herb.

I turned quickly, assuming someone was standing right behind me, but no one was there. And with the realization that no one was there also came the realization that I'd not actually heard the words spoken. At least not aloud. I'd heard them in my mind.

Telepathically!

I stopped twisting the lid. I'd broken the seal, but I'd not taken the lid off. I lay it on the boulder I'd been sitting on and I began creeping around the woods, only in close proximity to where I already was. Though the leaves were off the trees, the mountain laurel for which Appalachiastan is famous was still out in its full evergreen bloom, so there could have been someone or something within only a few yards of me and it, or they, would be able to remain well hidden.

After getting about twenty yards away from the boulder where I'd been sitting, I began to hear weeping, and I did not hear it telepathically. I heard it here, in the physical realm. Someone, or some*thing*, was crying in the forest, but just as quickly as I'd caught the sounds of weeping, they disappeared. They hadn't lasted long enough for me to draw a bead on their exact location.

"I'm being emotional," I said to myself, and then I made my way back to the boulder where I'd been sitting. I took up the bottle and I sat down, and once again, I stared out across what I was now convinced was the precipice of my insanity.

"Ricky," I said, only a whisper.

"Herb," I heard, and the spoken word- spoken, by the way, in a very rough, guttural, almost growl sort of way- came from no more than ten yards to my right. I chose to ignore it, convinced I was losing my mind. It was my disease talking to me. I knew it's language well. I've heard it speak to me for many, many years. Since the time of my first drink many, many years ago. I knew that "Herb" actually translated to "hurry the fuck up and open that bottle and fucking feed me, you pussified mother fucker!"

I twisted the cap and took it off. I didn't even need to hold the bottle to my nose to smell the fumes of the sweet poison the bottle contained. My mouth began watering, instantly, and I felt my hands begin shaking. I instantly thought of those mornings after, when my hands would shake so wildly I couldn't put sugar in my coffee without spilling half of it from the spoon and onto the counter.

But that won't come until tomorrow, the disease whispered to me. *And like 'ol Bob Seagar said*, it continued. *We've got tonight!*

"You first, Ricky," I said, and I held the bottle up and out in front of me, using it like a site on a rifle, drawing a bead on which grave I thought might be Ricky's approximately a mile and a half away and at about three hundred feet lower in elevation. "For you, old friend."

I dumped half the contents of the bottle on the ground. Back in the day, during my active drinking days, I would call such an act alcohol abuse. But I was dumping out half, immediately, for Ricky, because I was going to pull on the rest of the bottle, hard, and drink the entire other half of the bottle in one fell swoop. I'd been clean and sober a number of years at this time, and I figured if I was going to go back to my old ways, I was going to do it right. I'd slam this half a pint into my blood system almost immediately, stagger out of the woods and to my car, and then get a case of beer at the local shithole convenient store and lock myself into a shithole no-tell motel room, hell, maybe even the one Ricky used to stay in, and I'd leave Appalachiastan at some point later.

Maybe…

And maybe in handcuffs or in a pine box.

But this mattered not to my disease, for it merely wanted fed.

And it mattered not to me at the time. I'd lost two friends I'd been out of contact with for years. This was my justification.

I hung my head and cried. It wasn't a light weeping, it was a full blown crybaby bawl. I held the bottle out and away from me, and I kept it steady, so I would not spill its precious contents, and that's when someone, or something, took it from my hand.

It took me a hot second to realize what had happened, and the instant I *did* realize what had happened, I heard the snapping of a stick only two feet away from me. This was *not* my crazy mind. This was *not* my disease. And this was *not* a sound that had been delivered telepathically.

This was real.

I raised my head, and I opened my eyes, but all that was before me was blurry. It was the first time I'd had a good cry in many years, and I guess my tears had been building up for some time, and when I'd finally had my cry, it was as if tiny dams had burst at the inner corners of my eyes, and for the *life* of me, all that I could see before me were blurry images. Shades, really.

The shade that stood out most was a large, dark shade smack dab in front of me and only two feet away. This shade was every bit of eight feet tall, and this shade was shaped like a WWE superstar. The shape extended what appeared to be an arm out to its side and it tipped over the bottle that it had taken from me.

"To Herb," the shape said as it dumped out the remainder of the bottle's contents.

I rubbed my eyes fiercely. My coat was still unzipped from where I'd opened it to pull the bottle out of my inside pocket. I reached in and grabbed my shirt and quickly brought it to my eyes to wipe away the tears. I rubbed hard, and when I took my shirt away from my face, my tears were gone, but now all was blurry from the pressure with which I'd rubbed my eyes.

But I could see clearly enough to see it!

There, about twenty yards away from me and heading into the laurel thickets was the dark shape I'd seen. The dark shape that had taken the bottle from me and dumped its contents to the ground in memory and honor of our old, mutual friend Herb. As the dark shape slipped away into the obscurity of the laurel thicket, my vision cleared just enough to where I could get one, crisp, clear view of what this shape truly was, and it was…

…potentially…

Bigfoot Sasquatch!

***

This story I've just told happened several weeks ago as of this writing. I'm happy to report that after what may or may not have been an actual (well, at least a *potential*) Bigfoot

Sasquatch slipped out of my life, the thoughts of having that drink, for now at least, have done the same.

I managed to make my way off the mountain and out of the woods without incident. I weaved my way back through Herb's old neighborhood and through the streets of that old shithole, drug infested Appalachiastanian town, and I got into my car and made my way back home.

I've gotten back in touch with several of my *new* friends where I live now. Friends that have healthy, clean lifestyles. Friends with whom it's good and healthy for me to spend my time. But I *do* pray, daily, for those with whom I had to part ways simply out of the sheer necessity to stay alive, some of them living, but some of them gone far too soon.

And I continue to fight.

Daily.

The demons...

The End

In The Beginning

God created the heavens and the earth…

Wrong book.

This is the book of Bigfoot Sasquatch!

The sixth in this series, actually.

But before there was Bigfoot Sasquatch, there was…

Kapre…

And it's not about which came first, the chicken or the egg. The Bigfoot Sasquatch or the Kapre.

Let me explain.

I tell this story, one I've told more than once on our YouTube channel, "Homesteading Off The Grid," because I want it preserved in writing. When I began this venture, this 'Bigfoot Sasquatch Files," venture, I had no idea it would become a venture. Honestly, I thought I'd merely be wasting more time, spilling out more of my talents onto the page, only to have it fall on deaf ears, rather, no ears.

I've got too many carts before the horse here, so let me move them out of our way, one by one.

Firstly, I've worked in social media for more than a decade, and what I can tell you about the folks who spend a lot of time on social media, and who comment on posts often, are often fake. They are bored, they have nothing better to do with their time, and they piss endless hours of their days away scrolling, scrolling, scrolling. A good number of them use fake profiles so they can troll, or, and this is the true minority, simply remain anonymous (and if they're not trolling maliciously, I see no harm in this. It's actually a good idea for many reasons). My point here, in regard to the fakeness, at least, is that many of the comments they leave are left merely so they can 'look good.' They're not sincere.

At least this is what I thought.

Before my beautiful bride Dearly, who we know as Giggly Girl on YouTube, (because that's what she does. She giggles. Incessantly. And it's quite contagious), and I was successful on YouTube, we had success for a number of years on Fakebook. Most of you will know this social media platform as Facebook, but we've come to call it Fakebook, because it's as fake as it gets. From the users, which I described above, to the founder and owner, Mark Zuckerburg, who's all about promoting privacy and ethics, until someone like China waves some money in front of his face, at which time he waves the ethics he never had in the first place and sells China all of his Fakebook user's private information.

So, for many years, while we worked on Fakebook, and after I'd publish a book, the subscribers on our pages would shout, "If you make this book available in print, I'll buy a copy." I bought this hook, line and sinker, as hundreds of people said this, and after making my books available in print, I might sell four or five copies. The way the math actually worked, was that I would sell nearly one hundred e-copies of my books for every single print copy. But I would buy the lies, the fakeness, hook line and sinker, and go through the extra efforts, and back then, the extra costs associated with making my books available in print, only to be duped time after time after time.

So I eventually stopped.

But not so with our YouTube audience.

I'd not made any of my new books available in print for years by the time we became successful on YouTube after having left Fakebook. Once again, however, the commenters began clamoring, "If you'd write a book about Bigfoot Sasquatch, and make it available in print, we'd buy it." I ignored this for more than a year and a half, but after hearing it so much for so long, I finally decided to test the waters again, for the first time in years, and man, am I glad I did.

This is a big kudos, I guess, to our YouTube followers. These folks are not fake, like those Fakebook bastards. I was completely floored when, as a test, I put together a novella length collection of short stories for 'Bigfoot Sasquatch Files Volume 1' and made it available in print, and saw that our YouTube followers were actually putting their money where their mouths are. I mean, to put it bluntly, this whole 'Bigfoot Sasquatch Files' venture as I'm not referring to it, has given my family and me a second income stream that competes with our YouTube revenues. That was never the objective. We'd never even considered it as a goal. But we're flabbergasted that it's happened, and you'd better believe I plan on hanging on to this tiger's tail for quite some time to come. And not out of greed. We know enough about social media platforms to know that they may view you as one of their darlings one day, but should the winds of what's politically correct or socially cooth, or not, change, they have no problem killing their darlings, so having an active, profitable plan B in place is a nice thing, and it's brought us quite a bit of peace of mind.

Besides, and as I've said on our channel over and over and over. When you do what you love, you'll never work a day in your life. And I absolutely, profoundly, and as much as I love anything else in life (except my wife and our son), I love writing. It's my mistress. I can tell her anything, and she loves to listen, and she doesn't judge. She appreciates my honesty, and she doesn't care about the occassional fucking bad words. She doesn't tell me Jesus is coming to judge me first, and some of that other stupid shit the verically challenged individuals who live under bridges of the world constantly tell me on social media. She simply listens. And she accepts.

Okay, that went a little overboard, but my point is, our YouTube users are real, so as much for myself and my love of my mistress, writing, these Bigfoot Sasquatch Files collections will continue!

Now, the next cart in front of the horse.

The Kapre.

Now that I know these stories are being preserved in print (ah, the reason for my recently completed rant), I want to get my story of my night with the Kapre on paper. For you see, it was the experience which I'll now describe, for the first time, in print, that would lead to the creation of my novel "Isle of Kapre" and I do believe, open the door, if not a portal, or a slip in the veil, on our property in Virginia, years later, that would allow for the entire Bigfoot Sasquatch stuff we have going on (potentially), anyway.

Trust me.

It'll all make sense by the end.

***

To say that my beginning with the Potential Bigfoot Sasquatch only dates back to the events I'm about to describe- events that took place on a white, sandy beach in Southeast Asia, rather than the rugged, hemlock and giant western cedar studded Cascade Mountains of the Pacific Northwest, would be a lie. My beginning would actually start with a fascination with all things cryptic, paranormal, horrific and out of this world in childhood that I directly correlate to my mother's decision to allow me to watch the movie 'The Exorcist' when I was four years old. Since that dreaded night of terror, I became a firm believer in all things that could not be seen with the nake eye, be it demonic possession or large, hairy manlike beasts roaming the forests of the world.

But I'll take you to that white sandy beach of Mindanao, the southernmost island in the Philippines- an island riddled with mysteries and terrorist organizations (I'm telling you, if you haven't read 'Isle of Kapre' you don't' know what supercalifragilisticexpialidocious fiction based on *fact* is all about) in order to relate this particular tale of all things Bigfoot Sasquatch, well, at least all things closely related to Bigfoot Sasquatch (as in first cousins, perhaps, and you'll understand this, soon, too), because this is the tale of my first, up close and personal experience with, potentially, one of these amazing creatures that may or may not exist.

So, to give you the quick backstory in a paragraph or less, the year was 2011, and I'd recently returned to the Philippines after unsuccessfully securing proper employment in the U.S. I would spend the next four years straight there, after having gone back and forth, for several months at a time in each place, for the previous two years. I had a nine month old son there, Daniel, and a beautiful soul mate, Dearly, and it would be a long, hard four years of work, work, work, in the realm of literature and social media, creating something out of nothing, in order to get home (the U.S.) and be able to afford to live here.

During my first month back in the Philippines full time, Dearly and I got her aunt Marissa to keep our son for a night so we could take a fisherman's boat to a small island a couple miles off the coast of Mindanao in order to spend the night at a private resort. And don't think that's anything fancy. As I described in the previous paragraph, we were broke. But for two U.S. dollars, you could sleep in a bamboo shack without amenities pretty much anywhere on the beaches of the Philippines, and as long as it was a place away from where you usually stayed, it felt like a vacay.

We'd gotten to the other island late, as in an hour before dark, and the place where we wanted to stay had no vacancies, so we had to keep going up the beach. We found quickly that all the huts at all the small, privately owned properties had sold out for the night. We would soon be facing a very uncomfortable dilemma as the last boat to head back to Mindanao had already left for the evening. We were facing being stuck on this small island with no place to go.

Fortunately, just before nightfall (which comes at 5:30 p.m. in the Philippines, 365 days a year, as they're only seven degrees above the equator), we reached what seemed to be the end of the rocky, upward sloping road we'd been travelling by way of a rickety old tricycle (motorcar attached to the side of a moped), and there was a little old woman closing and locking a gate to a property on the side of the road, getting ready to go home for the evening. It would literally be dark in about ten minutes.

Dearly jumped off the tricycle and ran to the old woman and asked her if we could rent a hut for the night. The woman explained that their huts were only available for day rental and that no one ever spent the night at this resort, which lay at beach level about two hundred yards down a rocky trail. Dearly explained that we had nowhere else to stay, and the woman then explained to Dearly that the place was haunted. "Many Aswang," I heard her say. I didn't speak the Visayan language fluently yet, though I would in time, but I knew what 'Aswang' meant. It meant 'paranormal.'

"Cool!" I said, jumping off of the tricycle myself now and running over to the old woman. The old woman begged and begged us not to stay at the haunted resort, but I insisted. When I offered her two hundred pesos, roughly four U.S. dollars, her eyes grew big and she unlocked the gate and told us to take any hut that we wanted. However, she said she would be locking us in for the night, and that a guard would be showing up soon (he should have been there by then, but finding anyone in the Philippines who's ever on time is like finding a needle in a haystack), and that he would be the only one around for a mile. This, I know now, but I did not know at the time, should have let me know how scared the locals were of this location. I mean, if you see ten square meters of free space in the Philippines, you'd better store the spot to memory, because within minutes, they'll have a dozen plywood shacks built on it with fifty people living there. And this is said with no disrespect. The place is severely overpopulated. Roughly one hundred and ten million people are living on a total land space only half the size of the state of Texas in the Philippines.

At any rate, Dearly and I entered the 'resort' (again, a term being used very loosely here), were locked in by the old woman, and we made our way down to the beach, each of us carrying a backpack. We'd brought only the bare essentials. Food enough for both of us, and booze enough for me, which would have been the equivalent of booze enough for three people, as I was still drinking quite heavily at the time.

We settled into the farthest hut from the main hut on the beach which was obviously used as an office. Though it was now dark, the moon was full, the sky was cloudless and we could see as clearly as if it was day. We enjoyed a late dinner of rice and chicken (it wasn't cold, because it was ninety degrees, but it wasn't nice and hot, either), and then we spent time walking up and down the beach, me carrying a serving tray in one hand with a Filipino candle on it, and my glass of tanduay rum and coke in the other. We had no ice, but the booze had a high alcohol content, so it didn't matter. I was more concerned with effectiveness than pleasantness.

Now, for those of you who don't know what a Filipino candle is, let me explain. You simply take a small jar, or a glass, and you fill it about halfway with sand. Then, you simply pour enough cooking oil into the glass to meet the top of the sand. It will look like mush. Then, you take a toothpick, and you wrap it with a cotton ball by stabbing the toothpick into the ball and then carefully pulling the cotton down over the toothpick, covering it entirely. Next, stick the cotton covered toothpick into the mushy oil soaked sand in the jar, or glass. Wait only a couple of minutes and the oil will entirely soak up and coat all the cotton. You then light the top of the cotton covered toothpick. This is your wick. And it will burn slowly until all the oil from the sand is soaked up through the cotton. This type of candle will actually allow for hours of light.

"I have to pee," I said, after we'd made our way down the beach a way. Our bellies were full, a feeling we'd soon come to forget for a very extended period of time- a time I refer to as my 'down and out years in the Philippines'- and we were going back and forth between wading in the water and walking just where the surf ended against the sand.

"Don't pee there," Dearly warned as I got ready to spray against an old coconut tree stump a few years up from the water's breaking point.

"Why not?" I asked.

"It is the home of the Duende," she said, and I could tell she was serious.

Okay, so the Duende is the magical Filipino dwarf. They are said to live in the jungles, housing in caves they burrow underneath old, coconut tree stumps. This particular stump, where I was about to pee, *did* have a hole in it, but my western, logical mind attributed it to erosion. I laughed and peed on the stump, anyway.

"The Duende," Dearly warned. "He plays many tricks."

I laughed at her, finding her broken English as adorable then as I still do today, after having been with her for eleven years as of this writing, and then I packed my member back into my shorts and turned to walk back to Dearly and return to strolling along the beach, but all of a sudden the Filipino candle that had been resting securely on my serving tray jumped up, flipped in the air, and went crashing to the ground and shattered into pieces. It looked like it happened in slow motion, but in real time I'd been in mid stride and I was unable to stop. When my right foot came down, I sliced the corner of the joint of my big toe, where it meets my foot, clean open on the largest piece of the glass from the candle, and blood began spurting out of my foot like water from a hose.

"Oh, my God!" I shouted. Not only was the injury painful from the slicing from the glass, but the glass was hot from the flame, and it added to the pain. "I'm going to die!"

"Pesti, mata baka!" Dearly said, which is Visayan for 'fuck your eyes.' "I told you the Duende plays tricks. You pee to his house, he cuts to your foot!"

"Fuck my life!" I yelled, a phrase that was pretty common in American pop-culture when I'd left the states. I'd been wanting the opportunity to use it before it died out, like all pop-culture bullshit always does, and thank God for small favors, and this seemed like the perfect opportunity. So perfect, in fact, that I decided to shout it again. "Fuck my life!"

Dearly and I made it back to our hut, me wobbling and her propping me up. Once there, I sat in the bathroom, which was nothing more than a tiled section of the small hut with a hole to defecate and urinate into and a smaller hole under a water spigot which stood as a bathing area. I held a washcloth on my cut and applied pressure, and Dearly left to see if the guard was at the gate. It turned out he was, and both of them returned in just a matter of minutes.

Now, if you have read 'Isle of Kapre' (good on ya, mate, as our English and Australian friends would say), then you'll recognize this scene. When Dearly and the guard came into the hut, they were both carrying the small leaves of the Mulungi tree. I'd eaten these leaves many times in soups and nearly every other Filipino dish I'd ever eaten, but on this night, Dearly and the guard were crushing the leaves up and allowing the juice to drain onto my cut. The instant the juice from the leaves hit my cut, it stopped bleeding, it stopped hurting, and I could almost see it begin to heel. And I would never have the hint of infection as it did hear. It was absolutely amazing. I said these things, and Dearly and the guard both laughed.

"You are Americano?" the guard asked.

"Oh-oh," I said, which means 'yes,' in Visayan.

"In your country," he began, "you take pill for everything. In Philippines, we still use nature. What God gives us."

He had a point.

"In your country," he continued. "You cut foot. You go hospital. You get stitches. You get medicine. You get big bill." He and Dearly both laughed at that. "Here," he said, "you get Mulungi. You go on your way. You keep your money if you have it," he said, and they laughed again.

The guard was at our shack for no more than five minutes. Just long enough to apply ample Mulungi juice to my wound and insult my culture repeatedly. You see, that's one thing about life as a white foreigner in the Philippines. The overwhelming majority of the women love you. They fantasize about you. It's their dream to marry a western man and leave third world poverty behind forever. And anyone who wants to judge them? I would challenge the judge to go without eating for days at a time, and when the judge does eat again, make their meal a chicken neck and a cup of rice, and then go a few more days without eating before repeating the process.

It's not about being whores.

It's about being hungry.

And the men?

Well, many of them, at least, are insanely jealous for aforementioned reasons. Could you imagine being a guy and hearing every female in your life, from your sisters to your mother to the girl you've got a crush on constantly talking about their fantasy of marrying a white foreigner? An entire book could be written on all of this from this point, but… oh yeah.

It was.

It's called 'Isle of Kapre.' Have I mentioned it yet?

Anyway, after the guard left, and I was back on my feet- well, at least one of them- Dearly and I went out and sat on the small front porch of the hut, she eating left over chicken, and me drinking rot-gut Tanduay Rum, now straight, only chasing it with water. Sure, the Mulungi had killed the pain, but I wanted to make sure the Tanduay would perform well as my second stringer in case the Mulungi wore off.

And that's when we smelled it. The smell of sweet cigar smoke. It smelled like the smoke of a cherry flavored Swisher Sweet, something I never saw in the Philippines all the years I was there. .

"It is Kapre," Dearly said, jumping up faster than I've ever seen her move, to this day- well, except the time she stepped on an eight feet long cobra when we were hiking in the jungle, once- and she ran inside and shut the door, leaving me on the porch. "Come inside," I heard her yell from the other side of the door.

"The what?" I said.

Through the door, Dearly reminded me of the Kapre. Sure, I'd heard about it, as well as much of the folklore of the

Philippines, but at the time I'd originally heard about it I hadn't taken any of it seriously enough to store it to memory.

And then I heard a twig snap only yards away from the hut, followed by a low growl!

I quickly joined Dearly in the hut, now taking this shit seriously.

Again, and as is fully described in 'Isle of Kapre,' the Kapre is the Filipino version of the North American Bigfoot Sasquatch. However, there are a few stark differences.

Okay, whereas the North American Bigfoot Sasquatch is a forest dweller, the Kapre, who is said to incessantly smoke sweet smelling cigars, lives in the tops of giant trees. Also, he's interdimensional. You see, the Filipino people believe that there is a portal to another dimension in the tops of the trees where this mystical and mythical creature lives, and he uses this portal to go back and forth between our worlds.

Why does he come here? (By the way, Kapres are all males). Well, he comes into our world to kidnap beautiful, young Filipina ladies. He then takes them through the portal and enslaves them as part of his harem on the other side of the portal where he lives in a giant, stately castle.

Think 'Beauty and the Beast.'

Now, in the Kapre's defense, once he gets these young maidens to the other side of the veil, they aren't enslaved by a huge, hairy, hideous beast anymore. You see, the

Filipinos believe that once back in his own dimension, the Kapre sheds his hide and alas, he is one hell of a good looking dude.

Anyway, no beautiful, young Filipina lady wants to be taken from her family and her friends on this side of the veil, so it is all so horrifying, and inside our little hut that night, Dearly and I didn't sleep a wink. Oh, we tried, but whatever was on the outside of that hut would not allow it.

"Come on," I said, once in the hut. I'd crawled into bed and got underneath the sheet. In the six years I spent in the Philippines, I never saw a blanket. Hell, they weren't necessary. The temperatures may have dropped to eighty five degrees fahrenheit at night during the two rainy seasons. And you were lucky if you could even find a sheet, but on this night, we were in luck.

"No," she said from somewhere in the hut. She was huddled in a dark corner, as far away from both the door and the one window the hut had as she could get. I looked over at the window, and I saw that Dearly had managed to latch shut the wooden shutters from the inside just before I'd come into the hut, and just as I made the outline of the shutters out in the darkness, they began shaking.

Someone, or some*thing*, was on the outside of the hut, shaking the shudders!

Instantly, I'd forgotten all the jokes I'd made about the Kapre and the Duende and all the other mythical creatures of Philippines folklore. I found myself pulling the sheet up and over my head like a kid watching a scary movie, just like back when I'd watched 'The Exorcist' at four years old, yet this was no movie.

This was real!

Potentially!

Throughout the night Dearly and I would be disturbed, intermittently, by either the shaking of the shutters or the smell of sweet cigar smoke. Every time I'd fall asleep, one or the other, or both, would wake me up, and poor Dearly never even fell asleep at all.

You can only imagine our relief when the sun came up the next morning. You see, just like a vampire, the Kapre will never be seen when the sun is up. It's not that the sun could kill him, he just doesn't want to be seen, so he only comes out, through his portal, under the cover of darkness at night.

When day did come, Dearly and I packed our few belongings. Before leaving his shift, the guard actually came down and helped us carry our stuff up to the gate since he knew my foot was injured. That's one thing I'll give the men of the Philippines. They may be insanely jealous of white foreigners for reasons described earlier, but many of them are still kind, do the right thing and follow the golden rule.

As we made our way past the small hut that was used as an office, Dearly told the old woman of our night. The old woman merely shook her head. She said she didn't sleep all night, knowing something bad was going to happen, and she was just happy that we were still alive. She begged us not to tell of our experience, to anyone, because she was afraid that though the events took place at night, the story might hurt her day business. We promised her we wouldn't tell a soul, but I kept my fingers crossed behind my back, because I knew this story was too good *not* to be told, and now I've told it in two separate books and I've talked about it in several YouTube videos.

But I wish anyone interested in finding this island the best of luck.

It's not even charted on any maps.

My attitude about the Kapre and the Duende and the rest of Philippines folklore changed after that night, and a couple of years and a few 'odd jobs' later, during my 'down and out in the Philippines years,' I would have enough material, by way of actual experience, to pen 'Isle of Kapre,' and to date, it is the most haunting book I've ever written, for you see, though poised as fiction, and though much of it is, I know which parts are not.

I know which parts are real.

And these things, to this day, cost me sleep at night.

Especially since…

…there may be other portals and other large, humanoid cryptids among us…

And there may or may not be one in the woods behind my house on our small homestead here in Virginia.

One that is an entry and exit way for…

…potentially…

Bigfoot Sasquatch!

The End

5

Lt. Bee Must Die!

(Originally Titled: "The Unfortunate Demise Of Lieutenant Bee)

If you haven't noticed, our stories in this issue of 'Bigfoot Sasquatch Files' are following a particular theme.

Reflection.

It's just occurred to me, over coffee, a blank page, and the sight of two does and one buck eating the few remaining leaves of a peach tree in my fruit orchard just on the other side of the window and down at ground level, as my office is in a second story bedroom, that many of these 'Bigfoot Sasquatch Files' volume focus on themes.

Perhaps it's because I'm in a particular mood when I write them? Perhaps there are issues over which I'm stewing as I type the words?

Well, this is obviously the case, and I'm not too surprised that this issue, Volume 6, written in and released in the month of November, seems to be themed upon the past, for you see, November is the month of my birth, and often, during the month of November, I reflect on my past. It's probably worth noting that November comes toward the end of the calendar year which I'm sure sparks the reflection process in many of us.

So if our last tale was a reflection on the events which inspired my novel 'Isle of Kapre,' I'll take this last tale in our sixth volume to focus on just one of the many stories which inspired much of my novel 'Off Switch;' this work being fresh on my mind as I've recently just made it available in print edition again on Amazon.

There is a particular bad guy in my novel 'Off Switch,' a really shitty lieutenant by the name of Lt. Bee. At least that's what he's called in the book. The book version is a fictional character, but as with most of my works, his character is very tightly based on a real person. It's one of my tricks to the trade, you see. People often ask for advice on writing, and one of my tricks, at least in regard to character development, is that if you tightly base a character on a real person, the work is really already done for you. Is it cheating? Maybe. Is it lazy writing? Maybe. But what I've found is that it's very effective.

Anyway, if you've read the novel "Off Switch" then you know Lt. Bee was a prick. He took great pleasure in abusing and mistreating his troops. Just as it says in the novel, I believe the underlying reason to this day was that he suffered from a severe Napoleonic complex. You see, Lt. Bee was only 5'6" tall. He spent hours in the gym everyday, trying to get buff, which he did, but at most, he put one in the mind of Mighty Mouse, still a somewhat comical sight.

Lt. Bee naturally hated anyone who had what he did not, or at least what he viewed as if he did not have. Things like natural intelligence (he wasn't stupid), or alpha-male strength, speed and/or natural leadership qualities. He worked hard to obtain these things, and that's commendable, but I honestly believe he always viewed himself as lesserthan because he hadn't been born with or naturally gifted with these attributes. And I'm sure it didn't help him in our unit that our first sergeant was pure alpha-male stud! An airborne infantryman who stood six feet six inches tall, weighed a solid two hundred and twenty pounds, and who had women melting whenever he passed because of his movie star and manly rugged, good looks.

And then here came Lt. Bee, nearly jogging, having to take almost three strides to keep up with the first sergeant's one.

Here is a fact about our deployment that Lt. Bee was completely unaware of while we were in Mosul, Iraq fighting for our lives, the freedom of the Iraqi people, and, despite what so many of my neighbors in my very 'enlightened' community of Charlottesville, Virginia (a

University town), tell me- the sheer survival of Western Civilization, as the factions we faced in Iraq were desperately trying to reunite with other factions in the region to deliver a death blow to Western Civilization. Here is a fact I thought I'd take to my grave. Yes, this fact that Lt. Bee never knew of while he was abusing many of his troops, treating us as if *we* were his enemy, because we'd been gifted with what he lacked.

People were trying to kill him.

Not the terrorists.

His troops.

Here is a cold hard fact of war that most folks who've never been to war do not know. Even those who served in the military but who never deployed do not know this.

There's nothing friendly about friendly fire.

It's intentional.

So much so, that in the recent wars in the Middle East the Defense Department actually changed the term 'friendly fire' to 'fratricide,' meaning 'to kill my brother.'

Why?

Because even those at the Defense Department knew that what had been called friendly fire for centuries was not friendly, but intentional.

So, here's the deal. I had no idea, until after we'd left Iraq and were de-mobing in Ft. McCoy, Wisconsin, just how many of my fellow troops had it out for Lt. Bee. You see, despite being surrounded by your fellow soldiers, enemies, explosions and gunfire while in a combat zone, your brain turns so much of what is around you off. It has to in order to maintain any semblance of a brain. In order to avoid going completely and unrecognizably insane. Nothing about war makes sense, and nothing that takes place in a combat zone is logical. But one does what one must do in order to survive, and after the insanities pile up so deep, the brain simply shuts down.

So, here is a list of things that were going on around me in regard to the close demise of Lt. Bee while in Iraq, things of which I had no idea, because I was walking around with combat induced tunnel vision (if anyone or anything steps within my life of sight, I either kill it or I don't kill it. It's that simple).

1- Sgt. T- whom Lt. Bee hated with a passion, because Sgt. T's father was a command sergeant major with another unit (by the way, that's the highest rank one can achieve in the enlisted ranks), cut the brake cables one night, toward the end of our deployment, of the uparmored humvee that Lt. Bee would be riding in that night. Sgt. T would be driving, and his plan was to simply go out in a blaze of glory, over a cliff with a two hundred feet drop in a particularly mountainous region of northern Iraq that we crossed through every night while out on convoy, taking, of course, Lt. Bee out with him.

What stopped Sgt. T's plan? At the last minute, they switched out his machine gunner. Sgt. T didn't particularly care for his regular gunner. He didn't hate him, but he had no problem with considering him collateral damage in Lt. Bee's demise, but he was rather fond of the gunner with which he had been switched. His new gunner was a young private whose mother Sgt. T had personally promised he would make sure came home. So, while in the motor pool, preparing to go on mission that night, Sgt. T declared the guntruck inoperable due to a problem with the brakes, and the truck was switched out for another.

Lt. Bee would live to abuse his troops another day.

2- Specialist C was the gunner on the truck that roamed our convoy for side security. Specialist C's truck was positioned in the middle of the convoy, and if any of our gun trucks had issues and needed to stop for any reason, it was Specialist C's truck's duty to hurry up and pull side security, while another truck hurried into place on the other side of the stopped truck, and yet another rushed to pull rear security (this, by the way, was my truck). This way, any stopped truck in our convoy always had full, three hundred and sixty degree security, and each gunner only had to secure a forty five degree piece of the line of fire pie.

One of of SOP's (standard operating procedures) was that we were *never* to dismount (that means get out of) our gun trucks, because the most effective weapon our enemies were using against us was IED's (improvised explosive devices). They knew they could not fight us, and win, toe to toe. They knew their weaponry was far inferior to ours (we could shoot them dead from ranges their weapons could not even reach us from), so they would bury bombs along the roadsides and try to lure us into their detonation zones and blow us up. It was much safer to be inside those uparmored vehicles in case an IED exploded than it was to be outside them.

Lt. Bee fancied himself a cowboy. Anytime we stopped for any reason, he would jump out of his truck and strut around with his M-4 assault rifle drawn, like he was going to kill every damn terrorist in the Middle East all by himself. And what he didn't know was that by eighty percent of the way through the deployment, every time he got out of the gun truck to strut around with his assault rifle, Specialist C, from high atop his turret in the gun truck parked alongside Lt. Bee's, had the sights of his fifty caliber machine gun trained on the back of Lt. Bee's head.

His plan?

Should a firefight go down?

Specialist C was going to take Lt. Bee's top knot (that would be his head, for you civilians reading this), off with his fifty caliber machine gun and write it all up to 'friendly fire.' He knew he'd be taking a risk now that the term used was 'fratricide,' but it was a risk he was willing to take.

Now, at this point, you may find yourself feeling sorry for Lt. Bee. You might be asking yourself what it was that he was doing that would lead so many among our unit to think of ways to kill him?

I won't prolong this point, because many of the things he was doing were clearly pointed out in 'Off Switch,' but what I'll tell you, is that at the time of his abuses, many of us feared his abuses would have very long lasting effects on those of us he was abusing, and now, more than ten years after the abuses were dealt out by way of Lt. Bee, I can tell you that we were right.

To this day, I have three adult children who were innocent little kids while their Daddy was in Iraq fighting monsters, and being abused by a monster who wore the same uniform as Daddy, who I have not seen or heard from in nearly a decade, and the beginning rift in this sad relationship split was a direct result of Lt. Bee's abusive actions toward me in Iraq (that whole taking me off the payroll and not allowing me to go to the payroll department and get put back on- hence- having no ability to send money home to my family while deployed, setting it up perfectly for my ex-wife to take my kids and go anywhere she pleased with them ((she picked England, of all places)), and not giving me a say, because I was a 'deadbeat dad' anyway, and yes, there are soldiers who fight in combat zones without pay, while their families suffer back home, you just never hear about it... because those stories don't work as tear jerker space fillers in mainstream media like the ones they use where Daddy comes home from deployment and surprises his daughter who is out cheering at the local high school football game).

I must stop at this point, because the previous sentence (which looks more like a paragraph) that I just wrote is completely incoherent. I've intentionally not edited it, because some things cannot be edited. They must not be, for it takes away the true feeling and meaning. Let's consider that last sentence (that looks like a paragraph) a practice in what's called point of conscious writing.

The point is.

I still suffer from the effects of Lt. Bee's abuses more than a decade after the fact.

And I didn't even mention his disallowing of me to seek medical treatment when I was injured for the entire remaining three months of our deployment, which would lead to a six month Army hospital stay with surgery and rehab and the onset of painkiller addiction, ending what had previously been eight years of being clean and sober before that, and...

Here we go again.

The point is (seriously, this time).

Lt. Bee had to die.

But he didn't.

Yet...

***

As I mentioned, I learned of all these plots against the life of Lt. Bee only after returning to the U.S. from Iraq. I've mentioned only two, but there were many, many more (and I'd be lying not to admit that I had a few of my own). The most haunting, however, was the plot that was described in the least detail.

Danny's plot.

Danny and I had been CHU (company housing unit) mates in Iraq with a couple of other guys. That means roommates. The four of us shared a plywood box twenty feet by twenty feet for nearly a year. It was like a sweatbox. There was enough room for all our gear, and then we'd somehow manage to find a place to lay within our gear and sleep for four hours or so when we were on base.

Oh, and the whole sweatbox reference? It's because our air conditioner was always going out, and Lt. Bee wouldn't allow us to go to the maintenance guys who fixed such things and report it. One of us would always sneak, and then the officer in charge of repairs would ride up one side of Lt. Bee's ass and down the other for abusing his troops, and then Lt. Bee would ride up one side of our asses and down the other, like taking us off the payroll, etc. for having gotten our air conditioner fixed and him in trouble while doing so.

Danny didn't talk much, but when he did, what he said was profound. He was a computer whizz, knew more about world history than any professor I ever had in college, read more books than anyone I ever knew (including me, and at times I read ten books a month), and in a word, was just an all around genius.

And he'd never finished high school.

Danny didn't look it, but physically, he was formidable. He looked kind of 'doughy,' which as you know, is a state that precedes fat. Yet he could run mile after endless mile and nearly keep up with me, and I have an extensive track and field background. He wasn't buff, and he didn't look strong, but he could lift far more weight than me. And though he moved slowly and methodically, and had a babyface, on the combatives mat (that means MMA mat for any civilians reading this), he would choke out our most skilled fighters.

Oh, and he was obsessed with Bigfoot Sasquatch.

It didn't come to any surprise for me, at the time, because we were in Washington State, and many of the guys in our unit were obsessed with Bigfoot Sasquatch. Well, we were in Ft. McCoy, Wisconsin, but my unit was with the Washington Army National Guard, so you get my drift.

What the hell was I doing in Washington State?

I'd moved to Washtington from Virginia, because my ex wife had moved to Seattle, in order to try to get my kids away from me (as far as possible, obviously), and max out child support payments, due to that whole number of nights at each parent's house thing. Too bad for her, when she moved, leaving the kids with me for six month so she could get set up in Seattle, all unannounced to us, she lost custody and I was awarded full custody, and she was supposed to pay child support (which she never did, but of which I never cared, because I just wanted my kids). I'd sent the kids to stay with her while I did my military training then took the high road and moved out to Washington once I was finished so that our kids could have their mother *and* their father in their lives. It was never about money. It was about the kids.

And three months later I was in Iraq with the Washington Army National Guard.

And I've already told you the rest.

"He's going to die," Danny said. Again, we were at Ft. McCoy when this conversation took place. We'd just finished our little pow-wow. The one where all the guys who'd been planning on killing Lt. Bee in Iraq but who never did had left. Only Danny and I remained in the room. "He's going to die in six or eight years. No one from our unit will be suspected."

"What are you talking about?" I asked Danny, knowing him well enough to know that the words he spoke were not empty. There was meaning to them. I knew that Danny had a plan.

"I know where he lives," Danny said. "I know where he hunts."

Lt. Bee was one of those psychos who'd joined the Army to kill people, not to defend his county. And for anyone wondering, there *is* a difference. Lt. Bee hunted to kill animals, not for food, though he did eat what he killed, but again, he hunted for the sheer joy of killing.

In his free time Lt Bee watched a DVD series called "Prison Fights," an illegal blackmarket film series where prison guards would set up fights in prisons and sell the DVDs for profit. One of the rules in "Prison Fights" which drew Lt. Bee's sick mind to the series was that once you knocked out or choked out your opponent, you did *not* have to stop fighting. Fighters could and often would continue to beat the man they'd knocked out, often to death. These were the fights that Lt. Bee watched over and over while we were in Iraq.

"I've seen shit in those woods," Danny continued, "and that shit is empathic, and he's going to get a little too close to what I've seen, and they're going to know exactly what he's thinking and why he's out there, and…"

"This isn't more of your Bigfoot Sasquatch bullshit, is it, Danny?" I said.

"Lake," he said, sounding irritated, but he really wasn't. Not by now. He had been at first, but we knew each other well now. "It's either Bigfoot, or it's Sasquatch. It's not both."

"It's all make believe," I said, so it can be whatever I want it to be."

"Let's go to chow," Danny said, and we did.

***

So, I guess you were hoping for a more detailed, lengthy conversation between Danny and me, about what sort of unfortunate demise Lt. Bee would end up having? I wish I could give you one, but that's all there was to it. Like Mark Twain said, fiction is harder to write than non-fiction, because fiction has to at least make sense. Well, here's his case in point. This short, simple, almost nothing burger conversation between Danny and me about Lt. Bee's future death, at the hands of a Bigfoot Sasquatch nonetheless, seems hardly worth writing about, right?

Wrong!

While reminiscing a few days ago, because it is November and all, November, of course, being the month of my birth and the tail end of the calendar year, I decided to look up my old friend Danny. Unfortunately, and as with all the guys I deployed with, I'd lost touch. I'd spend six months in the Army hospital after our deployment, and then I lived in the Philippines for the better part of six years, and I was fighting for my life as much over there in many different (yet a couple similar) ways as I had been in Iraq, and staying in touch with best good buddies just wasn't on the top of my priority list at the time, and now I'm settled in Virginia, and, well, people just lose touch is what I'm getting at in this near incoherent paragraph of a sentence.

I Googled him, and I found out that Danny was dead.

Danny had died by way of a single vehicular accident on an old state route just outside of the small timber town in Washington State in which he'd been born and raised. The only times he'd left that small town was to go to a rock concert (Linkin Park) in Seattle, basic training in Ft. Sill, Oklahoma, and to defend his country and all western civilization in a little shithole of a city known as Mosul, Iraq.

He was thirty years old at the time of his death.

I shed a tear for my old friend, though I wasted no energy on the emotion of guilt for having been out of touch. Shame and guilt are the two most worthless emotions we can spend energy on, and it took me nearly forty years to learn this, and I refuse to unlearn it. It is what it is.

Though it is unfortunate.

And Lt. Bee?

Well, of course I had to Google that son-of-a-whore after shedding a tear for Danny.

He's dead, too.

I wish I could say that he'd died at the hands of Bigfoot Sasquatch, but he did not.

Since our unit was a national guard unit, the guys in the unit *did* have day jobs when not deployed and not training one weekend a month and two weeks a year during summer annual training.

Lt. Bee was a computer programer, and, as it turned out, after getting home from Iraq he landed a job working with computers for none other than the Washington State Department of Corrections.

He was programming computers in prisons!

About a year after Danny's deadly car accident, Lt. Bee, by then *Major* Bee, as his illustrious actions in Iraq had earned him a promotion, was found dead in a library in one of Washington's many state prisons. He'd been beaten to death, it's assumed by an inmate, though it's never been determined who the inmate who'd allegedly beaten him to death was. No one's talking, because as even those of us who've never been to prison know, in prison, snitches get stitches, bitches!

No motive of the deadly beating was ever revealed. And investigators, to this day, have never been able to figure out why Lt. Bee's body (again, Major Bee at the time of death) was found, lying on the floor of the library, with a camcorder lying on one side of his body and a crisp, one hundred dollar bill on the other.

Personally, I have reason to believe I know what Lt. Bee had been up to just before his unfortunate demise. I have reason to believe that he propositioned the wrong inmate to star in one of his warped videos he'd planned on selling on the black market, and he got his just deserts.

But what do I know?

I'm just some batshit crazy war vet now obsessed with Bigfoot Sasquatch himself.

Like my old friend, Danny.

God rest his soul.

The End

***

The following stories are from Bigfoot Sasquatch Files Volume 7:

(FYI, Volume 7 was released in December of 2020, and was billed as a 'special Christmas edition,' hence the stories pertaining to Christmas.)

1

Customer Service Is Dead

(Originally Titled: The Unfortunate Demise Of Karen The Clerk)

Her name wasn't really Karen, but we'll call her that, because she sure as hell acted like a Karen. We must point out, however, that though she was white, she hadn't come from privilege. Just the opposite, actually. Opposite as in you might refer to her as poor white trash and be pretty spot on.

She wasn't bad looking for a woman nearing fifty. However, she wasn't nearing fifty. She was only thirty five. You see, just like everyone whose hearts have been hardened early in life by bitternous, jealousy, rage, and hatred (mostly self-hatred) Karen's outer shell had aged prematurely, letting anyone with a keen eye see just how toxic and venomous she truly was on the inside.

But if you couldn't see these things about Karen with your eyes, and you wanted to find out about them the hard way, all you had to do was go to the post office.

Karen's post office.

Karen had started out as a mail carrier shortly after dropping out of high school. Oh, how she'd hated having to go back and get her G.E.D. in order to get the job, but after Mommy and her Mommy's boyfriend, who had also been Karen's boyfriend (but Mommy never knew, and Karen had been eighteen the first time she and Jim Bob had gotten together, so it *was* legal eagle) died of an overdose together on Christmas Eve of all days, Karen had no choice. If only she'd been a minor when Mommy had passed on, she thought, she could have gotten social security checks for a while- until she could have lassoed some older schmuck of a guy who got them full time because he'd already suckered the SSI Disability people into believing he had a cause worthy of a tax free check for life- but no. Mommy had to go and kill herself with the pills when Karen was already the ripe old age of nineteen, forcing Karen to make an honest effort to enter the workforce and support herself.

No worries, Karen thought, at first. She'd just get herself a somewhat decent paying job and then fake an injury while on said job, then get her one of those SSI disability checks for life, just like the generations of poor white trash that came before her, and hell, it would all work out better in the end, because then she wouldn't need one of those schmucks of a man who was already getting a check, because she'd have her own. As Karen saw it, it was the perfect plan!

Wrong!

These had been the days of the great recession, and Karen found that jobs were few and far between. There was but one hope, as Karen saw it.

Government!

And why not the post office?

Karen sure as shit wasn't going to join the military. Sure, the Army and all the other branches of brave, honorable men and women who fought for the protection of the free world (and the occasional deposit of oil) was always hiring, but Karen was neither brave *nor* honorable. She was lazy, entitled (hey, at least she possessed *that* real Karen traight), and the farthest thing from honorable. Karen cared only about herself, her own basic needs being met, and fuck everyone else, in Karen's mind. The military would not do, but the post office was the perfect fit for her. It was right up her alley. So many people who possessed her shitty attitude and complete lack of concern for quality of work found lifelong careers at the post office. Sure, there were those who worked at the post office who were some of the hardest workers in society, *many* actually- and many with very *positive* attitudes- but at the post office, these folks were the minority. These people made up the ten percent of the post office's work force that carried the other ninety percent for thirty years and to their pensions.

But again, Karen had no desire to spend thirty years at the post office, or at *any* job. She only wanted to work long enough to fake an injury and get herself one of those SSI disability checks for life. Hell, she thought, if she was lucky, she could make it look *really* good and she might even end up getting herself a lifelong prescription for something like

Vicodin or Oxycodone and then she wouldn't have to spend any of her hard earned monthly SSI disability check money on pills. Boy, Karen thought, if Mommy were still alive, she'd be so proud!

Long story short (I know, too late) Karen jumped through the necessary hoops to get her G.E.D., she took and passed (with flying colors) the postal exam, and in pretty quick order she found herself shucking mail into the boxes of the shitty little houses in her shitty little Appalachiastanian community for almost twenty dollars an hour, and the pay, she was surprised, was so good, for a minute (well, maybe for half a minute), she actually considered doing the right thing- keeping the job long term, not faking an injury to get her Government money- but alas, she came to her senses, and on a cold, snowy day in February, during the middle of the fourth week of her job as a letter carrier, Karen threw herself down a flight of steps (okay, there were only three steps leading up to a porch, but technically, it counts as a flight), and she landed flat on her back and she began moaning and screaming in agony. Her fall really had hurt, but she wasn't in as much pain as she was letting on to be in, but it was all part of her great plot. In her heart of hearts, with each agonizing scream, that wasn't really that agonizing, Karen knew her lifelong SSI disability check was as good as in the mail!

Wrong!

What Karen had been completely unaware of at the time of her 'fall' was the fact that one of her supervisors had been trailing her, secretly, observing her work. The supervisor, a lifer as they're known in all Government job circles- someone who possesses *no* work ethic, a *shitty* attitude, yet cannot be gotten rid of due to a strong union, and who *always* gets bumped up into management at Government jobs- had actually felt intimidated by Karen up until this point. Despite Karen's shitty attitude, the supervisor knew she was getting her work done in the projected time to do it, and he'd thrown her on some of the longer routes to test her. Actually, to set her up for failure. Little did he know that Karen's shitty attitude was worse than his, and anger and frustration fueled Karen. Though she hated the longer routes, it was the energy derived from that hatred that allowed her to finish them under time.

Ah, the supervisor thought now, watching Karen make snow angels on the walkway of the property where she'd fallen, waiting on the homeowner (or renter, or squatter) to come to her aid, be her witness, and to later be forced by the SSI disability people to write a sworn statement on her behalf so she could get her check. However, the homeowner never came. Unbeknownst to Karen, they'd gone on a Schlitz Malt Liquor run just before she'd reached their house, and the only face that Karen soon saw standing over her, bearing witness to the events that had just taken place, was the face of her supervisor.

"What the fuck, Karen?" he said. "What in the actual fuck?"

"Shit," Karen said from her position on her back on the ground. She knew the jig was up, so she said it again. "Shit!'

***

Karen was summarily fired from the post office for what they perceived as being an attempt to intentionally get injured on the job for the sake of getting an SSI disability check for life. Hey, it was the post office. They were used to it. However, her union, the National Association of Letter Carriers, quickly went to bat for Karen, as they did all the shitbags at the post office (and it is important to note this, for the union rarely represents hard, honest workers who are actually getting screwed by management), and sure enough, Karen got her job back, as well as back pay for the six weeks she'd been out due to having been fired. However, Karen was no longer a mail carrier. Karen was now a clerk.

There were no available clerk spaces where Karen lived, and it had been the post office's hopes that upon having to transfer in order to regain employment with the postal system, that Karen would merely quit and the postal service could wash their hands of her. But no. Not *this* Karen. This Karen was determined to get her SSI disability check for life at all costs, and if she had to actually work for a year or two to let bygones be bygones, then so be it. And just as soon as all those bys were gone, she'd figure out a way to fake an injury in the mailroom, and by God, that SSI check for life would be hers!

Wrong!

They'd not just transferred Karen out of her small town in Appalachiastan, they'd transferred Karen out of Appalachiastan entirely! They'd moved her over the mountain, into Virginia! And not just *any* part of Virginia. They'd moved her to the outskirts of Charlottesville, a town affluent with blue blood trust babies and Virginia first families, both groups of which came from generational wealth, generational ivy league educations, and generational pretentiousness. Karen was now, truly, a fish out of water, surrounded by real Karens and the beta-males they marry.

The postal service was wise enough, at least, not to throw Karen directly into the center of C'ville, as the town was known by locals (as well as Hoo'ville, and not because of Doctor Seuss and that *other* Christmas book- that story of Seuss living in C'ville during the time he wrote *that* book about some grinchy old green bastard and basing it off of the town and town's people and yada yada is all a lie), fearing she'd be so lost in the weeds due to the extremely high volume of mail and packages it received (more in a day than her shithole little town back in Appalachian received in a month) so they put her in one of the tiny little branch offices on the outskirts of town. One of those tiny little post offices that actually closed and locked their doors for an hour for lunch, because there was only one clerk in the branch.

When the postmaster at Karen's previous post had told her that she would be transferring a state away as a condition of keeping her job, and Karen had agreed to the transfer, the post office intentionally chose a spot to put her where she would feel so out of place that she would quit (since the idea of a transfer in and of itself hadn't been enough to do the trick), and the tiny little branch they stuck her in was the perfect spot. You see, volume would not be an issue. The clientele, many of the clientele, at least, would be the ingredient needed to make for the perfect mix of getting almost *anyone* to want to quit the job. To describe them? In a word? Or a few, at least?

Stuck up, pretentious, narcissistic snobs who looked down on anyone who was just not *as* wealthy as them, but who'd not been *born* into wealth like them, meaning, they actually looked down their noses at self made millionaires and even self made billionaires. You see, the affluent of Charlottesville viewed themselves as God's chosen people. Why else, they figured, had they been *born* into affluence, while the other ninety seven percent of the human race had not been? Oh, there was *no way* Karen would feel comfortable in their presence, and she would quit her job in short order, for sure! This, at least, is what the post office's H.R. people had thought.

Wrong!

The post office did not know Karen as well as they thought they did!

***

"Maybe if you'd pull that silver spoon out of your ass, you'd be able to make it down here in time before I close up for lunch," Karen screamed at a middle aged trust baby at 11:59 a.m. on the first day of her second week on the job at her new location. She'd spent her first week with a trainer, but she knew the ropes of the small branch now (there were only two hundred and fifty customers who rented boxes, less than her post office back in Appalachiastan), and Karen had no problem running the show on her own. Oh, and how she *loved* the concept of closing for an hour for lunch.

Nap time!

"It's a birthday card for my mother," the middle aged trust baby said to Karen. "I'm already late in getting it out. I fear if it gets there *too* late, she won't send me my next dividend check. "You know," the woman said, tilting her chin in and her nose up, raising the index finger of her right hand to her pursed lips, "my great grandfather invented velcro. Our family still owns the patent."

"Yeah?" Karen said, coming across as if she gave a shit. The middle aged trust baby, the *real* Karen, bought it for a second, but then not real Karen said, "my great grandfather invented the ass whoopin', and my family still hands them out! Now you go on and get the fuck on outt'a here and come back in an hour, or I'mma whoop your highflutin' ass!"

"Why, I never!" the woman said and then turned to walk out.

"I bet you never, you bitch!" not real Karen the clerk yelled after her. "Can't get them tight ass legs holding that silver spoon up your ass apart long enough to do it!"

Real Karen left and she mailed her mother's birthday card from the main office in C'ville. It got there just before her mother was about to rip up her daughter's dividend check. Real Karen never went back to see fake Karen again.

***

"How much to send this to Philippines?"

Karen heard the voice, but she hadn't seen who it belonged to. She was putting mail in boxes. She looked over at the counter and all she saw was the top of a head. Long, jet black hair.

"What?" Karen said, moving over to the counter. It was only two weeks from Christmas, and ordinarily, every post office in America would be packed with customers, but Karen had been at her post for nine months now. She'd summarily ran off all the regular customers. Those she could not piss off or offend enough into never coming back, she banned. When they'd called the main branch's postmaster to complain, and the postmaster had tried to unban them, Karen's new union, The American Postal Workers Union, jumped in on her behalf, stating that if the area's postmaster were to allow barred customers to return, that they would be putting Karen in an unsafe work environment. As was always the case, the postmaster did not listen to the union, and each time one of Karen's barred customers entered her branch, Karen was awarded five thousand dollars in grievance pay. And though Karen's grievance pay, combined with her salary, was closing in on making it possible for her to actually buy a house in the new highfalutin area she lived and worked in (she was currently renting 'urban' living space in the middle of city limits), she still fully intended on only working another six months or so before faking her injury, this time, she was certain, without witnesses, and finally obtaining that SSI disability check for life.

"How much to send this to Philippines?" the stunningly beautiful, petite Asian woman on the other side of the counter asked. Ironically, this woman, a Filipina beauty who was married to local Cryptozoologist, Dr. (honorary) Drake and Karen were the exact same age. But whereas Karen appeared to be nearing fifty, due to her hardened heart, shitty attitude, and all the other negative attributes of which we're all now fully aware, Mrs. Drake looked like a teenager. She didn't appear to be a day over twenty. Sure, her petite stature and beautiful, Asian complexion helped add to her youthful appearance, but it was the true, beautiful and kind nature of her heart that helped her stay young.

Karen looked down at her watch. It was eleven thirty. Damn it, she thought. She couldn't blow this little oriental bitch off with the closing for lunch excuse. She really wanted to get all the mail put away before lunch so she wouldn't have to deal with it later, and there was something about this little Asian woman she didn't like. There was always something about people who were happy and not toxic that Karen didn't like. Mostly the facts that they were happy and not toxic.

"Cut off for international is at eleven thirty," Karen said, thinking quickly on her feet. "Come back when I reopen at one o'clock."

"No time," Mrs. Drake said. "Many errand."

"Many errand," Karen said, mocking her. "Many errand."

"Why you make me fun?" Mrs Drake asked, feeling a bit of anger beginning to boil up inside her. Sure, Mrs. Drake was a cute little beauty- a true pearl of the orient- but as Mr. Drake could and *would* tell anyone, if you pissed her off, hide the mother fucking machette!

Karen reached up with both hands and grabbed at the outer edges of both of her eyes with her fingers. She pulled her skin tight, making her eyes slant. "Why you make me fun?" she said. "Why you make me fun?"

"Pesti mata, ka!" Mrs. Drake said.

Though Karen did not speak VIsayan, Mrs. Drake's native tongue, and therefore did not know that what Mrs. Drake had said in Visayan translated to 'fuck your eyes' in English, she pretty much knew she'd just been insulted by Mrs. Drake's tone.

"Get your little fuckin' foreign ass outt'a here and don't come back!" Karen yelled. "You're banned!" And already, Karen was adding another five K to next month's paycheck, because she was hoping the woman in front of her didn't understand English enough to know what it meant to be banned, and that she would return again before Christmas.

"Pesti mata, ka!" Mrs. Drake said, again, as she turned to go. She knew exactly what Karen had meant, and she knew exactly what she was going to do about it.

Mrs. Drake left the post office and got into her car, but she did not leave. She waited, and she watched, and at noon, after Karen had locked the post office up for lunch and gone to her own car, Mrs. Drake followed her.

Karen drove up the road, heading away from C'ville, and she stopped at a roadside shithole, one of the few in the area, and she went in to have a beer and a burger and another beer for desert. She had not locked her car, allowing Mrs. Drake to slip something under the driver's seat. Just a little trinket, one would think, if they were to find it. Part of a coconut husk. A coconut husk that had been treated with a special potion and then allowed to burn.

Unknown to anyone who might view it as a trinket…

… a fully cocked and loaded weapon!

But not a bomb.

Unless, of course…

…you considered it to be…

A Bigfoot Sasquatch bomb!

***

Karen made it back to the post office after having one for the road after desert, three beers total, and she finished out her day relatively uneventful. A beautiful young lady, one of the local college girls, Karen assumed, came into the post office to mail something out with less than a minute before close, and Karen was about to go up one side of her and down the other, but she didn't. She hesitated. This beautiful young lady looked familiar.

"Do I know you?" Karen asked.

"I don't think so," the girl said, but her facial expression said differently. She squinted her eyes a bit and turned her head sideways, trying to recall where *she* might have seen *Karen* before.

Karen looked at the return address on the envelope the girl had handed her. The girl's name was Jane. She then looked at the receivers address and noted that it was going to a location familiar to her back in Appalachiastan.

Karen realized she *did* recognize the girl. She was that crazy bitch from the next town over from Karen's hometown back in Appalachiastan who was rumored to have killed off several men. Only rumors, however, as Jane had never even been *questioned* in any of the disappearances. Also, Karen remembered, Jane's town was infatuated with tales of Bigfoot Sasquatch and all kinds of other weird beliefs.

"Fifty cents," Karen said, deciding not to get any friendlier with this beautiful young lady than she did anyone else. Jane handed Karen two quarters then turned to leave.

"Fucking hillbilly," Jane said as she exited the post office, having recognized Karen. She knew where she'd seen her before. She'd gone back to Appalachiastan to show one of her privileged white friends from college, her roommate and a real Karen, how the other half lived some time back, and she'd seen fake Karen out delivering mail when she'd almost reached home. She was from the next town over from hers, Jane remembered.

"Fucking hillbilly," fake Karen said, watching Jane drive off as she, Karen, locked the door to the post office behind her. She was done for the day and it was time to go home and get shitfaced. Karen, though only having been with the post office just over a year now, had already succumbed to the typical lifestyle of far too many postal workers. Go to the job you hate that makes you miserable by day, then go home and get shitfaced drunk and pass out by night. Wake up the next day and repeat the process. Except for on Sundays and Federal holidays. On Sundays and Federal holidays you just get shitfaced all day. No work.

But hey, at least after thirty years you get a pension! And that pension meets sixty percent of your financial needs! So you only have to work part time in order to survive!

More time to get shitfaced!

One of the things that sucks most in life, Karen thought, as did any true alcoholic, was catching that three beer buzz at lunchtime and then feeling it wear off over the course of the next hour. This feeling sucked. Karen, having had experienced this today, decided she'd take a shortcut to her urban housing development in Charlottesville. There was a back road that weaved its way through one of the rich people areas that she could take and it would save her seven minutes. Why, Karen thought, she could chug a beer in that amount of time. So, instead of staying on the main road on her way into town, she took the shortcut just past the train tracks and began weaving her way down the dark, winding road. With the winter solstice only days away, it got dark early this time of year, and it was already dark now.

"Huh," Karen said, peering through her windshield about a mile down the old backroad. Snowflakes were beginning to fall. Though everyone was up to their assholes in snow back in Appalachiastan the climate was much more mild where she lived now and this was actually the first time she'd seen it snow for the year.

As Karen was admiring the snow hitting the windshield, as well as all the beautifully decorated mansions and estates she was passing- Christmas lights and lit wreaths and artificial deer covered in lights in many of the lawns- she noticed a peculiar smell inside her car. "What the fuck is that?" she said aloud, taking a deep whiff through her nose.

Karen looked down for just a minute, as she surmised that the smell was coming from the driver's well. For an instant, she thought maybe she'd stepped in dog shit, even though the odor wasn't quite that rank. As she looked back up, she saw more than just snow on the other side of the windshield. There, standing in the middle of the road, just as Karen was about to enter a very sharp turn, stood, what she at first thought to be a man, but was not. It *was* something man*like*, but it was much larger than an actual man. Much, much larger.

Karen screamed and cut the wheel hard to the right, sending her car off the road and straight into the front field of one of the local estates. She'd been wearing her seatbelt, so though her car had come to an abrupt halt once it had gone about twenty yards off the road and into the field, where it became engulfed in a mushy soft portion of the property owner's lawn- a low part where standing water stood for long periods of time after any amount of rainfall- she had not been hurt.

"What the fuck was that?" she asked herself as she turned the car off and took off her seatbelt to get out. She hadn't even tried to back out of the lawn, because though she might be dumb, she was not stupid. She wasn't getting out of this predicament without a tow. She knew the best she could hope for would be to flag someone down, and the later it got, the less likely that would be possible, with less traffic on the road and all, so she decided to get out quickly and get back to the road. She was not concerned about the large, upright standing creature she'd seen in the road before her accident, because she was already convinced it was merely a shadow or sorts. Or a spot in the road that had recently been patched, hence a darker shade of pavement at that particular spot than the rest of the road surrounding it. That was so common back in Appalachiastan, where most of the old country roads were pure shit, because there was not enough of a tax base to pay for them to be kept up, unlike the roads here in Albemarle County, Virginia, where there was a huge tax base due to all the wealth. Hell, the Virginia Department of Transportation paved these roads every three years just so the locals who paid more money in taxes each year than the average American earned in a year could see where some of those tax dollars were going.

"Help!" Karen yelled as she reached the road. A car was coming, and as she waved her arms while yelling, she was happy to see that it was slowing down. "I've gone off the road," Karen said as the car that had been coming pulled up beside her and came to a stop. The driver had already rolled down the window.

"Wait a minute," the driver of the car, a middle aged white woman said. "Don't you work at the post office down the road?"

"I do," Karen said, smiling.

"Go fuck yourself, cunt!" the driver said, and then she put the petal of her Saab to the metal and left Karen in her dust.

"Fuck!" Karen said. However, she didn't revel in her misfortune for long, as the sound of breaking twigs, as if someone or some*thing* was walking in the forest behind her caught her attention. She turned suddenly and stared into the darkness. "Hello?" she said. "Anyone there?"

She heard the sound of footsteps in the dark again, and they sounded closer, but they came to an abrupt halt as the headlights from another vehicle came up the road from the same direction as the last car. Karen began waving her arms, and once again, this car pulled up beside her, it's window down.

"I ran off the road…" Karen began.

"Go fuck yourself, bitch!" the older gentleman in the car said, having recognized Karen from the post office before she'd even finished speaking, and as quickly as he'd stopped, he sped away in his Mercedes Benz, leaving Karen to her predicament.

"Fuck!" Karen said as the Benz' tail lights made their way around the bend.

Snap!

It was another twig snapping, and the sound had come from right behind her.

Karen turned, very slowly, as she could sense the presence of someone or some*thing* standing behind her, and once she'd turned around, she looked straight into the chest of something huge and hairy. Karen began moving her head and her eyes upward, and once reaching a height of about eight feet, she looked into the eyes of…

Bigfoot Sasquatch!

The Bigfoot Sasquatch that stood only a foot away from Karen let out a mighty roar of anger as it raised both fisted hands high into the sky and then brought them both down with the force of a sledgehammer, bashing Karen on top of the head. The blow had not *killed* Karen, but it had knocked her the fuck out. After she fell, the beast picked her up, flung her over its (or his, or her) back, and vanished into the woods just as mysteriously as it had crept out of them.

Karen was never seen or heard from again.

***

Local Sheriff's deputy Burt Reynolds would end up being the lead investigator into the disappearance of a local postal clerk, but his investigation would turn up nothing. Karen's car was impounded, and it remained impounded, indefinitely, as none of Karen's next of kin wanted to come all the way from Appalachiastan to claim it. When they'd been contacted and informed of Karen's disappearance, their response had been "Hm." When asked if they'd seen her, all of her relatives stated, "no. But if *you* do, tell her she still ain't welcome around here." Reynolds had no idea what that meant, but he'd known a few folks from

Appalachiastan and he'd always noted how so many of them seemed to completely hate their entire families.

Reynold chalked Karen's mysterious disappearance up to the same unexplained phenomena he'd been chalking so many recent disappearances and deaths in the area up to.

The unexplained.

But in his heart, he knew the truth.

Sure, he thought to himself. He could go out and question Dr. (honorable) Drake some more, about that whole Bigfoot Sasquatch thing, but he was sure he'd pretty much get the same response from the man that he'd gotten last time- the time he found those two smoking hot Asian girls who weren't really Asian standing in the middle of the road, in the same part of the county as Karen's recent disappearance, wearing U.S. flag embroidered bikinis and geisha gowns with make-up running down their beautiful faces.

"Was she a bitch?" Drake would ask. "That's what most people thought," Reynolds would say. "Then you know what happened," Drake would respond, and then he'd take back up whatever book he'd been reading when Reynolds had shown up, unannounced, dismissing Reynolds without formally dismissing him.

"Maybe I'll go see him after the new year," Reynolds said to himself while leaving the sheriff's office for the day and heading home to enjoy a couple of days off. He was looking forward to putting up the Christmas tree with his family. He smiled at the thought, thinking of how he and his teenage son were finally spending more time together. Then, thinking of actually taking some of that time away from his son, and his wife, for that matter, to investigate the disappearance of a miserable, disgruntled degenerate that no one in the area seemed to like, anyway, knowing what the end result would be, anyway, he had another thought.

Maybe not!

The End

2

Snow Angels

Carolyn was forty now, and she couldn't figure out why she was so unhappy. Especially on this day. The day after Thanksgiving. The day that she and her husband Tom, and their two beautiful daughters, Ella and Jenna, were putting up and decorating the Christmas tree.

Tom was taking the easy way out, as he'd begun to do in recent years. At forty two years old, Tom was feeling tired these days, and he was taking full advantage of his sales skills by sitting on the couch and watching his girls, as he referred to his wife and daughters, do all the work.

"I *am* working," he'd told them when they'd adamately admonished him for his lazy ways. "I'm supervising." And to prove it, every now and then, between sips of ale, he'd tell one of his daughters, or Carolyn, that the left side of the tree had far more ornaments than the right side, and to make sure to place their next few ornaments on the right side of the tree to even it out.

After hanging every third ornament or so, Carolyn would stand back and take it all in. Her girls- Ella ten years old now and Jenna eight- were so adorable, she thought. They'd both gotten the best genes that she and Tom had to give. They were already dominating all the other kids, including the boys, in any and all sports they played. Carolyn wasn't surprised, and it was due to those aforementioned genes. She and Tom had met while competing together on the track team back in college.

And Tom, Carolyn thought. So handsome, despite his middle aged spread. Sure, he still jogged and ate mostly healthy, but the occasional six pack (or twelve) of beer and four slices of pizza at a time a couple times a month (or week) contributed to the stereotypical *dad bod* so many men his age sported.

But through it all, his ever growing belly and all, Tom had always been faithful. He'd always been supportive. He had always been loving to both Carolyn and his daughters.

Carolyn, herself, had done everything the way she was supposed to do it. She never got in trouble in school, avoiding any negative marks on her proverbial *permanent record* that people never figure out doesn't *really* exist until they hit forty. Her grades and athletic achievements had gotten her into college, where she'd graduated cum laude, just like both of her parents before her. Yet, and like so many middle class yuppie types with whom she fully identified, she felt as if having done everything the right way was one big recipe that led up to nothing more than a feeling of emptiness. It's like, it had all been one big lie. At times she actually felt regret for never having been more daring- taken a risk- gotten arrested, even- just to see if having strayed down the proverbial *wrong road* for a while may have added more spice to what she felt was her extremely boring perfect life.

Carolyn thought more of her past as she watched Ella and Jenna struggle over the star for the top of the tree. Tom, just like last year, would have to get up off his rump and help them with this part of the project, putting an end to his supervisorial ways.

What was coming to Carolyn's mind now was the ten years she'd spent teaching before getting pregnant with Ella and making the decision to stop working and stay at home to be the best full time mommy she could be. Tom was pulling down six digits pretty easily at his brokerage firm by then, and they'd never lived above their means, unlike many of their middle class yuppie type peers who were so far in debt they'd never get out, so they believed they'd be able to make it off of one income, and for the last ten years they had.

Carolyn knew she had lived the poster image of a life the way it was supposed to be lived. She had everything in life that any non-materialistic/consumeristic yuppie (rare as they are) could want. A beautiful and healthy family. A wonderful home in which to live. Her bills were paid and there was more than plenty of money left over afterward. The only debt she and Tom had was the mortgage, and it was less than half the amount it had started out to be, and Tom's financial prowess had allowed them to accumulate a sizable nest egg.

So why did she feel so empty?

Her mother, God rest her soul, now gone these past three years, had labelled it psychosis immediately after *the event*, as that night when Carolyn had been ten years old, her daughter Ella's age, would always be referred to in hushed tones by Carolyn's parents and doctors. A night and an event of which to this day even her husband Tom was unaware. She would certainly never tell her daughters. This was one of those 'take it to the grave' type things.

A couple of years after *the event*, Carolyn's father, an actual psychiatrist- not the armchair kind, like her mother- would label Carolyn's condition depression. And in order to keep all things ethical, he would send her to see his best good buddy in the business, and his best good buddy, per the orders of Carolyn's father, of course, would put her on a steady stream of meds.

Carolynd never liked the meds. She couldn't stand the side effects. She'd go on and off of them, back and forth, over and over, but her father always figured it out, and he would make sure to witness her taking the pills and he would ground her indefinitely until she could be trusted to self administer. This went on for a number of years, until one day, Carolyn discovered running.

It came first out of anger. Having been caught not taking her pills again and, being fifteen and hormonal and refusing to take them despite her mother and father's demands, she'd ran out of the house, and, well, she'd just kept running.

Carolyn's parents, having decided Carolyn might *not* be coming home after having given her what they'd felt was ample time to cool down, had jumped in the car and gone looking for her and they discovered her four miles down the road from their house. She was standing at the side of the road, hands on her hips, though not bent over. She was standing tall, having already caught her breath, and she wore only a slight glisten of sweat on her face.

"How did you get here so fast?" her father asked, after rolling down the window.

"I ran," she said.

"Want a ride home?" her father asked, the sound of amazement in his voice. Carolyn took his tone as a complement of her achievement and she got in the car and went home with her parents.

As it was, it just so happened to be a month into the new school year. Carolyn's father made a deal with Carolyn that day on the way home in the car. He'd read study after study which proved that long distance running was as effective in treating certain mental illnesses as was many medications. He told Carolyn that if she joined the cross country team at her high school, and if the running seemed to work in her case, then she could quit the meds. Carolyn agreed, and after her father successfully convinced the cross country coach to allow Carolyn to join the team even though they'd started the season two weeks before, the deal was struck. Carolyn got off the meds and she would end up being an all state runner that year as a sophomore, having had no running experience other than the time she'd set out in an angry rage and ran four miles nonstop, mind you, in blue jeans and shoes that, though casual and sporty in nature, were not running shoes.

Caroly's senior year in high school, she was state cross country champion, and she would win the two mile state championship as well in track and field and finish second in the mile. A'la college scholarship, a'la meeting her husband Tom on the college track team, and a'la everything else ever since.

Until a year ago.

When she'd broken her ankle.

Carolyn had been running a 5K fun run, with her daughters, pacing them, when she'd come down off the side of a sidewalk the wrong way, shattering her ankle instantly, and then falling to the ground and writhing in pain.

Her running days, at least for the foreseeable future, were over.

About three months after her injury, Carolyn began slipping into what her father (and God rest his soul, too, as he'd died a year before her mother) had referred to as depression way back when. Carolyn knew it. She knew the signs well. However, she could remember the side effects of the meds, and she refused to go see a doctor, who she felt would insist she begin taking them again, despite Tom's pleas to get her to make an appointment with someone.

"I'm sure they've come a long way with those things," Tom had told her when he and Carolyn had talked about her blues. He could tell she was down, and he knew most of it had to do with the fact that she'd lost a very important part of her lifestyle- part of who she was, with the loss of her running- and it was only then that Carolyn had confided in him that, as a child, she'd been diagnosed with depression and that she'd been on meds. It was the first time in their more than twenty years together that Tom, a former All-American steeplechaser back in college, truly knew the reason Carolyn had become a runner in the first place. However, she certainly did *not* tell him about the night of *the event*. Oh, no! That one- *the event*- was going with her to the grave.

Even the girls were now noticing Carolyn's long naps and though they never voiced their concern, they did *have* concern over Mommy's drinking. They'd never seen Mommy touch a beer, but a few months after her injury, Mommy started having a beer with Daddy. Now, on more than one occasion, they were finding themselves peeking around the corner of their room and down the hall on nights when Daddy had to carry Mommy to bed because she'd gotten drunk and passed out on the couch again.

"Who's going to plug in the lights?" Carolyn asked as she helped herself to one of Tom's beers, the thought of a beer having popped into her mind. Everyone acted as if they hadn't noticed, and as if they were not concerned, but they had, and they were.

"Me!" the girls yelled in unison, and just like every year in the past, they held the plug and stuck it into the outlet together. The tree lit up brightly, and just like every year in the past, it was absolutely beautiful! Carolyn and her family would no doubt have yet another wonderful Christmas.

Their lives were perfect.

Absolute bliss!

And Carolyn was miserable…

***

Nothing could have made for a more perfect day for putting up the tree than what had happened during the last hour of the day.

Snow!

It was the first snow of the year, and it was coming down now, an hour after dark, hard and heavy. It hadn't come as a surprise, as the weather forecast had been calling for it, but Carolyn and Tom had both warned the girls not to get their hopes up too much, because the forecast was so often wrong. However, the forecast had been right on the money this time.

The couch in the living room was positioned so that when sitting on it, one could either turn their head slightly to the right and see the fireplace, or, turn their head slightly to the left and look out the large picture window. There was no television in the living room of this house. Never had been; never would be. And the family of four had sat on the couch in that last hour of daylight, alternating glances between the fire in the fireplace and the snow coming down outside, and of course, their beautiful tree, which stood in the middle.

The girls had cuddled up between Tom and Carolyn, going on and on about what they wanted for Christmas, now only weeks away. Their parents had teased them about having doubts that they could behave for the final weeks leading into Christmas, this, as every child knew, a requirement to get what they wanted.

It had been a long, emotional and adrenaline filled day, and it was no surprise to Carolyn that both the girls and Tom dozed off shortly after dark. Carolyn had made her way well past the three beer buzz well *before* dark and she was now well on her way to oblivion. Sure, it would have been the perfect lead in for passing out drunk on the couch, but with the snow, still visible as it came down outside by moonlight, sleep was the furthest thing from Carolyn's mind.

What filled Carolyn's mind at this time, while the most important people in her life slept beside her, was memories, vivid memories of *the event* from all those years ago.

***

Carolyn had been eight years old at the time, the same age of her younger daughter, Jenna, now. It was the same time of year, potentially to the day. Mommy and Daddy were finishing up getting ready for a Holiday party (not a Christmas party, mind you, because Mommy and Daddy's friends were politically correct long before being politically correct was cool- or even a thing, for that matter), and Carolyn had been staring out the window, witnessing the year's first snowfall.

"It's snowing!" she yelled with the excitement only a child could muster for such weather. "It's snowing!"

"Uh, huh," her father had said, tying a tie around his neck. Her mother had chosen to ignore her entirely, as her mother would do most of her life.

Carolyn paid no never mind. She continued staring out the window, and as she did so, she saw the headlights of a car pull into her drive. She stared down from her second story bedroom window, through the windshield of the car in the driveway, and she saw her babysitter, Laurie, leaning over from the passenger seat and kissing her boyfriend, Michael, who had brought her. Carolyn knew that about fifteen minutes after her parents had left, Michael would drive back around and stop, and he would come in, and after Laurie and Michael thought Carolyn was asleep, they would make all those weird sounds they always made down in the living room on the couch. The very sounds that kept her from being able to fall asleep for the longest of times when Laurie came over to babysit. It was as if, Carolyn thought, while lying in bed so many nights listening, after children go to sleep, or at least the adults thought, adults reverted back to the language of primitive grunts and groans for communication, rather than sticking with the actual words used in modern language. Except for the words "oh God," and "I'm coming." That one had *really* thrown Carolyn the first time she'd heard it. To her knowledge, Laurie and Michael had never left.

Mommy and Daddy had given Carolyn kisses and hugs, and Daddy's had been half-heartfelt. Mommys had felt as cold as the snow blowing outside, but that hadn't been new. And then, Mommy and Daddy were off, and within minutes, Michael was pulling back into the driveway. An hour after that, Carolyn was in bed, listening to the 'ooh's' and the 'awe's' and the occasional 'oh Gods,' and after Laurie and Michael had both come back, even though Carolyn had never heard them leave, things got pretty quiet downstairs, but still, Carolyn could not sleep. She was too excited about the snow and the upcoming Christmas that it always brought with it.

Deciding not to even *try* to fight sleep, Carolyn had gotten out of bed and she'd made her way back to the window to watch the snow. However, something was different this time. As she peered out the window, down to the snow covered lawn below, she saw a figure.

At first, she thought there was a man standing at the edge of her yard, just on the lawn side of the treeline that represented the beginning of the forest that stretched for miles beyond her family's property. But as she squinted her eyes and looked closer, she realized this was no man. Men don't get that big, except for those guys that Daddy liked to watch put on those pads and helmets and throw footballs around to each other on Sundays. But even those guys looked small in comparison to the figure she now saw on her lawn.

Carolyn watched, in awe, as the figure moved further away from the treeline and closer to her house. It was standing in the middle of the lawn when all of a sudden it flopped down on its back and it began, of all things, making snow angels.

Carolyn laughed, and she put her hand over her mouth, realizing how loud she'd been. She had the feeling that Laurie and Michael were asleep downstairs, both now having come back from never having left, and she didn't want to wake them. She laughed again, more quietly, but somehow, the figure on her lawn seemed to have heard her. It stopped it's flapping motion and lifted its head. It peered up, as if looking right into Carolyn's eyes, like it could somehow see in the dark, and then, it waved.

Carolyn, with the innocence of a child, waved back, convinced she was looking at a bear or some silly circus animal that had been highly trained and then had escaped, having been a bit *too* highly trained. Whatever the case, and whatever it was, she did not fear it. She watched it play in the snow, and she giggled at its antics, and she acted scared when it formed a snowball in its giant hands, or paws, as Carolyn saw it, and threw it in her direction, but even then she wasn't *really* scared. And when it waved for her to come down and join it? She had no reservations, and she did.

Carolyn had sneaked downstairs, and she had sneaked right by Laurie and Michael. They were both sleeping on the couch, without their clothes, and Carolyn could never understand why they seemed to get so hot every time they came over, but she did her best to cover her eyes as she made her way past them and to the backdoor, which was actually on the *side* of the house. She then made her way out onto the lawn to join the silly circus animal that had obviously escaped and had ventured out to play in the snow. She'd slipped her coat and snow boots on just before going out. She'd had them both by the door in the hopes it would, indeed, snow.

When Carolyn reached the creature standing in her yard, she stared straight up and into its face. She'd never seen anything so tall. Anything that stood on two legs, of course. The creature was covered with hair and it looked like no circus animal Carolyn had ever seen, but just before she might have gotten scared, for real, considering what the creature before her might be, the creature smiled and it giggled and Carolyn did the same, and in unison, as if reading each other's' minds, they fell to their backs and they began making snow angels.

Carolyn and her new, strange friend played for hours. Sure, it was cold, but when Carolyn would shiver, her new, strange friend would pick her up in its warm, harry arms, and it would warm her. It would give her hugs that were *not* half-hearted, and certainly not cold. For the first time in her life, Carolyn felt loved.

How could this be? Carolyn could remember thinking, even years later, and even as an adult. *How could I feel so loved and accepted by something not even human that didn't know me any better than I even knew what the hell it even was?*

Carolyn, at one point during a college psychology 101 class would hear the term 'empath' and she would instantly think back on the night of *the event,* but just as the professor said the idea of 'empathy' could not be scientifically proven and therefor was nothing more than a myth- a psychological superstition- she'd written the idea off just as quickly as it had entered her mind. After having felt found for half a second, she once again felt lost.

But not on the night of *the event*. Oh, on that special, snowy night Carolyn had felt loved and accepted for the first time in her life, and she had had so much fun playing with her new friend, and it mattered not to her what sort of animal it might be. It was her new companion, and with her new companion she made snow angels. She built a snowman. She and her new companion threw snowballs at each other and a few at Michael's car. They were doing all the things that Mommy and Daddy had never made the time to do with her, and after having done these wonderful, wonderful things for some time, and Carolyn having caught cold again, her new companion picked her up in its arms and hugged her, for real, and warmed her...

...and then they were hit right in the face with blaring headlights!

Mommy and Daddy had just pulled into the drive, and they'd seen Carolyn and her friend.

"Let my daughter go!"

It was Daddy's voice. Without even turning the car off, he'd jumped out and had begun running into the yard, through the snow, toward Carolyn and her new friend.

Carolyn's new friend put her down, kissed her lightly on the head, and as if it had never been there at all, it disappeared into the treeline...

...never to be seen again.

***

Daddy had thought of calling the police on the night of *the event*, but after having gone back to the car to get a flashlight in order to see which way the perpetrator had fled, based upon his (or hers or its) tracks, and having seen the tracks left behind, Daddy did *not* call the police. Further, Daddy had instructed Carolyn and Mommy that no one was to *ever* speak of the event. *EVER!* And *the event* was certainly never to be spoken of in the presence of others, because there was *no way* the good psychiatrist would be labelled crazy. Why, it would cost him his business and his family their livelihood.

Daddy, or course, would spend the rest of Carolyn's childhood trying to convince her that *she* was crazy. She had not, he would tell her when she broached the subject, played in the snow, for well more than two hours, with something that does *not* exist. She, he would tell her, was so fortunate not to have been kidnapped by some psychotic lunatic child molestor who had obviously been out on that dark, snowy night, seeking his next victim. Carolyn, her father would go on to put the proverbial icing on the cake, had been one lucky little girl.

But Carolyn had always known the truth.

And never having spoken of it, aloud, to anyone, her entire life, had driven her into a very painful, lifelong depression.

As now forty year old Carolyn reminisced about the night of *the event* when, then *eight* year old Carolyn had had the time of her life, playing in the snow with something that was not supposed to exist, and of how innocent and wonderful it had been- the complete opposite of having to bury the lie of *the event* and the creature's existence for the next thirty two years of her life- she was brought back to the present time and present events by way of noticing a large, dark figure standing just outside the treeline, in her yard, where the lawn bordered the forest.

Could it be?

"I'm seeing things," Carolyn said to herself, softly, as she rose, ever so carefully, making sure not to wake her family. She then made her way to the large picture window and stared out into the snowy darkness for a better look.

"Oh, my God," she said. Either her eyes were deceiving her, or she was shitfaced drunk, she thought, because she was still seeing what appeared to be standing by the edge of the forest.

Carolyn, as quietly and stealthily as she'd gotten off the couch and made her way to the picture window slipped out the front door of her family's home and into the dark, snowy night. She hadn't put on her coat, and she wore only houseshoes on her feet. She was wearing flannel pajama pants and an old Nike hoodie that was ragged and worn and because of both factors, more comfortable than anything else she usually wore around the house. It was cold, but she was well into her cups, so she wasn't feeling the effects of the weather, and besides, her focus was not on the temperature, but on the figure she believed she'd seen at the edge of the woods.

Just as Carolyn made her way out of the realm of light being cast onto the snow from within her house out of the picture window, and into the shadows, the figure she believed she'd seen appeared to have ducked into the woods. Carolyn decided to follow.

Carolyn made her way fifty yards or so into the woods before the effects of the weather and the temperature really hit her, and in a word, sobered her up. She realized she was cold, she realized she was out in the snow, and in the woods at that, and in what she referred to her outfit as her 'skivvies' and wearing only house slippers. She realized that the creature that she thought she'd seen could not have been real. Sure, it might have been real all those years before, when she'd seen it as a little girl, but what she was experiencing now was merely what her parents might have referred to as an episode of psychosis. Mostly alcohol and memory induced.

Carolyn was convinced she'd finally lost all her marbles, and that she was now completely, indefinitely, totally and undeniably, batshit crazy.

Carolyn stood, figuratively staring over the precipice of her insanity, at a spot in the forest where there was a wide opening in the canopy above her. The moon was full and its light shone down brightly through the opening in the canopy above her. She looked up, through the tree tops and to the moon, and she said, "fuck it. What the fuck is it all for, anyway?"

With that, she fell flat on her back, she made several snow angels, and then, and for the last time, she hoped, she fell asleep.

***

"Daddy!"

It was Ella. She'd woken up to find that Mommy was gone, and she was scared.

"What is it?" Tom said, waking and sitting upright, rubbing tired eyes.

"Mommy's gone!"

"There she is," Jenna said. She'd woken up when her sister had woken their father. She hadn't even noticed her mother was gone. She'd simply run to the picture window to see if it was still snowing.

Tom and Ella rose from the couch and they made their way to the window. They joined Jenna in staring out of the window and what they saw shocked them all. Jenna had been right. There was Mommy.

Outside.

Being carried!

Someone, or some*thing*, was carrying Mommy, limp in its arms, from out of the forest. Just as it reached where the light cast through the window met the darkness, it knelt, and it ever so gingerly lay Mommy in the snow. Then, it stood, it turned, and it slowly made its way back into the forest.

"What in the name of God?" Tom said, just a whisper.

"Go get her, Daddy," Ella said. "Before that bear comes back."

Tom knew that what had carried his wife out of the forest and lain her on the snow covered lawn was certainly no bear, but he did agree that it would be best for him to retrieve his wife and bring her into the house before it, whatever in God's name it (or he, or she) was, returned, and he did.

When Tom brought Carolyn into the house he carried her straight to their bedroom and put her in bed. She slept the rest of the night, the alcohol running through her veins a big help. When she woke up the next morning, fortunately with no hangover, she believed she'd had a very vivid dream, brought on, no doubt, by a combination of the time of year, the snow, the booze, but mostly, memories of *the event* from all those years ago.

However, Tom and the girls, after allowing Carolyn plenty of time to wake up over coffee, informed her that the events of the night before had not been a dream. They had been real.

Very real.

Carolyn's family decided they'd keep the events between themselves. However, unlike her parents when she'd been a child, they decided that they could and would speak of the events, amongst themselves, as freely and as often as they liked.

Carolyn found immediate comfort in being able to talk about things no one else would ever believe with the people who mattered to her the most. She found comfort in knowing she was not crazy, and she found comfort in no longer having to live the lie.

Carolyn gave up drinking as a New Year's resolution a little more than a month later. By the following spring, her injury had healed to the point that she could begin running, lightly, again, and by fall she was running local 5K's and 10K's again.

And every Christmas, while families all over the world stare out their windows, waiting on a fat man in a red suit who is said to ride around the entire world, giving gifts to all the children of the world, Carolyn and her family stare out their big picture window waiting to catch a glimpse of something else. Something as reclusive, if not more so than the man they call Saint Nick. They wait, sometimes patiently, sometimes not, to see if they can capture just a glimpse of...

...potentially...

...Bigfoot Sasquatch!

The End

Look What The Cat Dragged In

"So far, so good," Robert said to Nick, leaning up against the small table that worked as a counter. Nick had just rung up another satisfied customer, the new, proud owner of a six feet tall spruce tree they'd paid Nick and Robert sixty hard earned dollars for, but for which Nick and Robert only paid only ten, having bought an entire tractor trailer load's worth from a Christmas tree farm in Pennsylvania. Sure, Robert and Nick had nearly a thousand trees planted on their property, a beautifully lain out five acres homestead in Greene County, Virginia, which sat in a small valley just below the Blue Ridge Parkway- the two of them could almost see their place while driving across the Parkway during the winter months once the leaves had fallen from the trees- but it was the trees they bought in bulk, at deep discount, and had trucked down to their Christmas tree farm in Virginia where they made the majority of their profit.

"We're killing it," Nick said. "As long as we don't have any problems."

"We never have before," Robert said, a hushed tone.

"Yeah," Nick said. "But there's never been as many sightings as there has been this year."

"These things are afraid of humans," Robert said. "I'm sure there's not one within miles of us, what with all these people we've been having come out."

"One can hope," Nick said, and then quickly put on his big, plastic smile as he saw another smiling family coming toward the register, the patriarch of which carried another six feet tall spruce. When Nick thought of the fifty dollars profit the tree was about to bring, his fake smile became real.

Robert and Nick had moved to Virginia from New York twenty years before. They hadn't been old when they'd made the move, only early forties at the time, but they knew old age was coming and both of them had been getting less tolerable of the cold, New York winters, which had seemed to be getting colder and more tolerable as they aged.

"Let's move to Virginia," Robert had suggested after having driven down to spend a weekend with an old college pal in Charlottesville.

"Are you serious?" Nick said. "They'll lynch us!"

"Not if we stay close to Charlottesville," Robert had told him. "It's a really progressive area."

"In Virginia?" Nick said, not believing what he was hearing. "A progressive area in the South?"

"It's technically not the South," Robert had told him. "It's the Mid-Atlantic, but you're not supposed to tell the locals."

The two of them laughed, and then after a week spent together in Charlottesville, with Robert's old college pal being their guide, their plans were made and ninety days later, Robert and Nick closed on a five acre tract of land that had a beautiful, antebellum home on it which had been built in 1840, just outside of Charlottesville, and they became two progressive liberals from the northeast who were unknowingly playing a small part in an unforeseen big role or turning the historic red state of Virginia blue. The two of them had fixed the old house on their new land up nicely with the profits from the sale of their apartment in New York, and with the rest, they'd invested in their Christmas tree farm.

"The trees we actually plant and grow are not where we'll make our money," Robert had explained to Nick, understanding the business a bit because he'd had an uncle back in Maine, where he'd grown up before moving away to New York for college and then having stayed for fifteen years after graduating, who had owned and operated a Christmas tree farm. "The trees we'll be planting will be merely for ambience. And we'll have plenty of people who will come just for the experience of harvesting their own tree. But the real money is in wholesale retail. We can get nearly a ten times markup by buying in bulk."

Nick had taken Robert at his word. It had been Robert who'd come up with every business idea the two of them had pursued since having met at a rave and then having had the most passionate night of what had been meant to be one night stand sex either had ever had, and then shaking up together within weeks, having decided the chemistry they had between them was too strong to be used up in only one night. And every business idea Robert had suggested and which they'd pursued had always been profitable. As it would turn out, the Christmas tree farm idea would be yet another of Robert's wonderful and successful ideas. And now, nearly thirty years after having met at the now long defunk rave (cocaine and the advent of a mysterious virus… and not covid... that would wreak havoc on their community closed down most of the raves), here the two of them were, living happily ever after on their five acres Christmas tree farm in the middle of a state which had been red when they'd come, but which they'd helped turn blue, but neither of which mattered to them now, because all of their tree sales converted to green, pun intended. Oh, and they only had to work six weeks out of the year. From the day after Thanksgiving until Christmas Eve. And even then, only Friday through Sunday, from 10:00 a.m. until 5:00 p.m.

"Excuse me," a severely hungover thirty-ish year old man asked, walking, almost painfully, toward Robert. Robert had made his way back into the field where he and Nick grew their white pines. Most were between four and six feet tall now, but there were many that were only a couple of feet tall, having only been planted either this spring or last, and there were the occasional ten to fifteen footers that were the result of the trees not even having been close to perfect looking saplings in their youth that had never been sold. Robert, always keen to spot economic opportunity, always donated these tall, ugly, gangly giants to churches and municipalities and was more than happy to take the tax write-offs from doing so. "Do you have any saws?"

"Sure," Robert said. He had two limb saws in his left hand, and he had one in his right. He handed the man the one in his right. "Here alone?" Robert asked, his hopes high.

"No," the man said. "My wife and kids are here." And just as he'd finished speaking, his beautiful, not hungover wife appeared, carrying a one year old in her arms, and with a three year old and a five year old following behind her. The children were all boys.

"Have fun," Robert said, turning away from the family, immediately, to dismiss them. It wasn't, however, just because he'd just found out that the younger man was straight and married. It was in order to do yet another safety check of the treeline which bordered his and Nick's property. Their five acres consisted entirely of fields, and their neighbors' properties to the south and the east were fielded properties as well. However, to the north and west? All forested. This was the direction of the Blue Ridge Mountains and the Blue Ridge Parkway. The direction from which all the sightings had occurred, and the direction in which if one were to get lost, they might not be seen again. And not because the area between Robert and Nick's homestead and the distant Blue Ridge Parkway was so vast. It wasn't. It was merely a six mile hike up to the Parkway. It was, however, due to what lived and hunted within that six mile patch of forest that could lead to one's disappearance.

**

"You guys are actually going to stay open until Christmas Eve, huh?" Emerson Eckles said, sipping his complimentary cup of hot cocoa. He was leaning up against the table that Nick used as a counter. Robert had made his way back to the register area after having walked a loop around the planted trees and having seen nothing alarming. Eckles, the local Game Warden, had stopped by as he'd been doing twice a day since the happy, aged couple had opened shop for the season.

"We've made it this long," Robert said. "We've only got ten days to go. I think we'll be fine."

"I hope so," Emerson said, taking another sip of his cocoa. "You know, 'ol Pete Singer over on Pea Ridge saw one of them damn things last week. Said it would'a made off with one of his sheep if he hadn't had his rifle with him and he hadn't shot at it. He'd been out deer huntin'. Perfect timing and situation to see one of them sonsabitches, I guess, if you're gonna see one."

"I don't think we'll have any problems," Nick said, scanning the treelines on the north and west edge of his property with his eyes as he spoke. "Too many people around here. The odor should keep them away."

"Help us! Help us!"

The woman came running and screaming from the field where Robert and Nick grew their white pines. Robert recognized her as the woman that had been with the hungover younger man he'd found attractive, but, unfortunately, also straight and married.

"It got my baby! It got my baby!"

Robert, at first, took the woman literally, seeing that her arms were now empty, but when he saw her good looking and hungover, but unfortunately straight and married husband come running through the trees behind her, he saw that *he* was now holding the baby in one arm, while holding, tightly, onto the hand of the couple's oldest child with his other hand. But subconsciously, he knew the math didn't add up. Someone was missing.

"It got my baby," the woman said, again, pulling up to a stop at Nick, Robert and Emerson. She saw all three men staring at the actual baby her husband was carrying, and she said, "our middle child! Ryan! He's autistic!"

"What?" Emerson said, dropping his half full cup of cocoa to the ground.

"Ryan," the woman's husband said, now coming to a stop alongside the group. "He's autistic. He just wanders off. All the time. And he did it today."

"I went looking for him," the mother said, "and that's when I saw it. It had Ryan by the nape of the neck, holding him by his coat. And it just trotted off into the woods with him as if he were a doll." She fell to her knees and broke further into hysterics.

"I told you guys not to open up this year," Emerson said to Robert and Nick, beginning to unholster his sidearm while walking away from the group and in the direction from which the distraught family had come. "I'll call backup."

"You fuckers shouldn't have reintroduced the mother fuckers?" Nick said, entirely having lost his cool. "Or you should have at least let the public know about it."

***

Once upon a time, long before white settlers ever stepped foot on the eastern shores of what is now the United States of America, great predators roamed the eastern forests; large wolves, giant cats, and, potentially (and not to mention according to more than one now non-existent, formerly local indigenous tribes) Bigfoot Sasquatch. These creatures lived in harmony with each other in the wild, fulfilling their duty as an intricate part of the food chain and biosystem. Like most non-herbivorous wild animals, if something was smaller than them, they killed it and ate it, and if something was larger than them, they hid from it or ran from it.

And then the settlers came.

Oh, how these settlers loved particular animals they'd never seen in the old world, like white tailed deer and wild turkeys. Especially when they ate them. But the wolves? The giant cats that weighed more than the white tailed deer? And especially that large, hairy man of the forest? Oh, how these creatures instilled the fear of the almighty God into these settlers, so they did what their kind had done for thousands of years.

They killed them all!

The men of any and all local populations in the new world would ban together, often, and perform what was known as 'circle hunts.' The men would determine how much land they could surround, this being based upon the number of men who'd shown up for the hunt, and then they would form a large, outer perimeter and then hunt their way into the center, killing anything and everything that wasn't human, occasionally, however, killing or severely wounding one of their own, as well, by way of poor and usafe shooting.

As flourishing as many of these large, fierce, wild predators were when the fair skinned settlers first came to this land, by the end of the fair skinned settlers' first century, many of these creatures no longer existed east of the Appalachian Mountains. And, as the fair skinned settlers would work their way west, these creatures would cease to exist east of the Mississippi. Only because these fair skinned settlers, all these centuries later, had no desire to live in large numbers in some of the most uninhabitable conditions (for humans) at the top of the Rocky Mountains or the Cascades in the far and extreme west, do these animals still exist in the continental United States. In just about any and all other terrains with climates suitable for the human condition, these beautiful creatures have been entirely extirpated.

It is said that the last official sightings of the eastern mountain lions took place around the time of the end of the American Civil War. Sure, there have been many folks claim to have seen them, or heard them at night- sounding like women being murdered, screaming from somewhere deep in the forests- since, but those who have made such claims have been summarily written off as crackpots. Many of them, still yet, had heard the cries of foxes or the screeching of screech owls, and had merely never spent enough time in the wild to be familiar with the often terrifying sounds such animals can make.

However, in more recent times, as in, the past two decades, many of the sightings and the reports of hearing strange sounds may have carried more validity. For you see? There has been quite a change in the mindset of those fair skinned settlers' descendants that has caused yet another rift in the biosystem, namely, in the food chain.

Once upon a time, it was highly understood that people's food came from farms. Vegetables were grown, meat came from animals that were raised and slaughtered and then butchered. Everything was packaged up and sold by way of the market, and then later, the grocery store.

So much time has passed, however, since the masses of fair skinned settlers and their descendants lived in any such way that would place them in a situation where they might witness part of this process with their own eyes. With the industrial revolution of the early part of the twentieth century, Americans made a great exodus from the country and the farms, and they flocked to the cities to work in jobs that hadn't existed in times before. As time does, time marched on, and as economies and societies do, both evolved, and for more than a century, the overwhelming population of Americans would live in urban or suburban areas. Farms were something they had sung about in kindergarten, along with all those e-i's and o's. And all the farm animals wore smiles on their faces and loved being scratched behind the ears. And even the grocery stores were now sporting meat neatly packed in packages that bore stickers on the front that said, to the effect, "the animal which provided this meat for your consumption lived in better conditions than eighty percent of the world's human population (and that part was true), and when it was slaughtered and butchered for your consumption, it was only after it had led a nice, long life, and it was in full consent of the process, and the process was only carried out after the animal had naturally expired, and before having expired, of course, the animal had given its full consent to be butchered and consumed by humans, much like organ donors give consent at the D.M.V. (this part was not true- but the masses were convinced).

In a word, the killing of animals (and by the way, the only *safe* word to use in this regard on social media and *not* have your account suspended is "dispatch") for the sole purpose of human consumption had become kin to evil incarnate. Sure, these yuppie types who believed and pushed this tripe still ate meat, but again, meat from animals who'd been petted and loved and blah, blah, blah…

So, here's the point.

Certain wild animal populations, such as the white tailed deer, which had always been properly held in check largely by way of hunting, became overpopulated by the end of the twentieth century. By the end of the first decade of the twenty-first century, there were literally more deer being killed by drivers and cars than by hunters and guns than a generation before. And the damage these out of control deer herds were inflicting on crops? People's gardens, flowerbeds, shrubs, trees, bushes and lawns?

Monumental!

Oh, but how dare the Division of Natural Resources carry out culls to control the herds! This was tried, and all those Karens and whatever you call the beta-males Karens marry came running out of their houses, banging on pots and pans to scare away the cute little sixty eight pound malnourished deer that were in their yard when the Government people came by with their crossbows to *dispatch* them.

It didn't work.

So, what did they do next?

Well, and here's the part you won't hear about…

…they secretly reintroduced the natural predators of such overpopulated, now nuisance animals like the white tailed deer. The very predators their ancestors had extirpated generations before.

They started in remote areas with coyotes; these being the least dangerous wild predator to human populations. Though there is the occasional story of a coyote carrying away a three year old child at least annually, the endings of those stories are relatively positive. The coyote only carries the child a few yards before realizing they're too heavy and then it drops them and then heads for the hills. Coyotes hunt in packs, and they specialize in going after wounded animals, and at first, it was a perfect fit, what with all those wounded white tailed deer limping around after having been hit by Karen in her K-car. However, Karen would in time begin driving priuses. Tiny little half electric cars that would get demolished if they hit a squirrel, let alone a full grown sixty eight pound malnourished deer. And sometimes the deer were healthy and actually weighed a hundred pounds or more. How on earth could a Prius stand up to that?

It couldn't.

Obviously, there was no way to minimize the Karen population, so a way to combat the Karen populations' mindset and lifestyle of privilege and comfort and the utter destruction on the very environment these Karens were claiming to save with their Priuses and reusable shopping bags had to be come up with, so, "they" began introducing even more fierce predators to the scene. Predators like gray wolves and cougars.

But "they" had to be careful here. These animals, if given an opportunity, would attack humans, and they didn't need their pack of buddies, like coyotes (though the wolves preferred it). Especially those cats. The world's most lethal hunters. The only animals that weighed nearly two hundred pounds and measured nearly eight feet in length that could sneak up on the most vigilant human standing in the middle of an empty field without being detected.

But "they" did it.

And the result?

The deer herds began diminishing, which led to less crop damage and less deer induced auto-accidents. People could plant ornamental trees and shrubs in their yards again without having to cage them in with chicken wire to protect them from the deer. And the best part? It all happened out of the range of the eyes and the ears (except for the occasional late night scream from the forest that was overheard by clueless campers, but the DNR could always convince them it had been a fox) of Karen, her beta-male husband, and the children of Karen and whoever she'd cheated on her beta-male husband with to produce said children.

Oh, and…

…well…

Welcome to the Christmas tree farm!

***

"What do you mean, 'reintroduced the mother fuckers?'" the hungover father asked Nick as everyone except Emerson stood by, clueless as to what to do.

"Long story," Nick said, not wanting to tell of everything this writer just wrote. "Things will be okay."

"Okay?" the distraught mother said. "Okay? I just saw my baby get carried off by a mountain lion, and you're telling me everything's going to be okay?"

God, Nick thought. *I'm so glad I'm gay.*

"I'll get the car," Robert said. "Everyone jump in when I pull up, and we'll do what we can."

Robert drove a Toyota Sequoia with a third row of seats, so he, Nick and the distraught family all fit with plenty of room to spare, and once all where in, Robert locked the four wheel drive mechanism and off they went, out into the wild blue yonder, Robert knowing his actions were making the family feel better, but also having the full understanding that there wasn't a goddamn thing anyone was going to be able to do.

In his mind, Nick was weighing the ferocity of the upcoming lawsuit.

***

Three miles away and straight up the steepest part of the mountain, and while Robert was just reaching the edge of his and Nick's Christmas tree farm, with their hysteric and distraught passengers aboard, the mighty, fierce mountain lion eyed a moss covered boulder. This particular boulder was as large as a single story house, and it appeared to butt up against the exposed mountain here as it continued, equally steeply, to the top, another half mile above.

But it did not!

If one were to walk around to the eastward facing side of this large boulder, not only covered in moss but also surrounded with mountain laurel, if they had been fool enough to hike nearly three miles straight up the side of the mountain in the first place, they would notice a crevice where the boulder was disconnected, ever so slightly, from the mountain proper. This crevice measured four feet wide and four feet tall. It was almost perfectly square.

If, persey, one *did* walk three miles straight up the steepest side of the steepest mountain in this part of the Blue Ride, and one *were* to notice the giant boulder covered with moss and surrounded by mountain laurel, and, *further*, should one make their way around to the crevice on the eastward facing side and, out of curiosity, *squat* down and shimmy into the crevice, one would find that just two feet into the crevice, the opening grew wide, and the opening then took a sharp turn northward, heading, by way of tunnel, several hundred feet into the mountain proper. And, at the end of this several hundreds of feet long tunnel, one would find a vast opening, a room for the lack of a better description. And this room, measuring a whopping one hundred feet by one hundred feet served as a home.

And this home, served as a home for...

...Bigfoot Sasquatch!

***

Bigfoot Sasquatch sat, cross legged, at his (or hers or its, but not their, as there was but one) fire, warming large hands attached by thick wrists on the end of long, strong arms. The hidden cave, which had served as the home for the Bigfoot Sasquatch for some time (in southern terms, that could be from a few seconds to a few millennium, so use your imagination here, and forget that the story is actually taking place in the Mid-Atlantic) never got too cold in the winter, nor did it get too hot in the summer, due to its location hundreds of feet beneath the earth's surface. It was perfectly insulated.

The cave was equipped with running water, as it had an underground stream which flowed through it, conveniently pooling in a perfectly formed hole, created by millenniums of erosion, the size of a bathtub, where enough fresh mountain water to meet long term needs continuously flowed, always providing a great amount, yet due to the continuous flow, always being refreshed.

The smoke from the creature's fire easily and efficiently made its way out of the vast cave by way of literally thousands of tiny openings on the cave's ceiling which channeled through the ground stone, above, like comb of a bee's hive, working like the perfect filter, so that the small amount of smoke given off by the Bigfoot Sasquatch's fires was always absorbed by the soil and stone before even reaching the earth's surface. A hiker could be sitting right on top of the cave, hundreds of feet up through stone and soil and tree roots, and never even smell a hint of smoke coming from the Bigfoot Sasquatch's fire. The cave was the perfect place for creatures that are not supposed to exist to exist.

"Oh, no," Bigfoot Sasquatch thought as the giant cat that had no name came traipsing into the cave, something smaller than itself, yet quite sizable compared to the cat's other previous catches, and fortunately still alive, dangling from its mouth.

"What have you done?" Bigfoot Sasquatch spoke, telepathically, to the cat that had no name. Bigfoot Sasquatch and the cat came from a world that did not use proper names, and as a result, pronouns. Man knew their world as nature, yet though beyond giving it a name, like every goddamn thing else man came across, he respected it little. However, and as they'd honestly admit, due to reasons of self preservation, Bigfoot Sasquatch and his, her, it or their kind respected the world of mankind. They'd (he'd, she'd, It'd) found, throughout time, that it was the best way, nay, the *only* way, to remain undetected, and not become extirpated themselves, if not entirely extinct.

"Tastes good," the large cat with no name said, telepathically, of course.

The language of animals was another area in which man felt he had come so far, yet was so cluelessly unaware. Sure, animals made noises. And many of those noises meant specific things. For instance, in the bird families, this tweet meant, 'hey guys, I found food,' and that chirp meant, 'hey baby, wanna make an eggy?' but the true, meaningful conversations between the animals, even across species, took place telepathically. Even the cavemen had known that, but modern man? Well, to modern man, things had to make sense. Things had to be proven. Without proof, things were not real. So, as advanced as modern man liked to think they were, they were not, and in many ways, this was all the better for the creatures of the fields and the forests.

"We cannot eat their kind," Bigfoot Sasquatch said, telepathically, to the large cat with no name.

"Ah," the large cat with no name replied, telepathically. "Just once?"

(Author's note- henceforth, when writing of the communication between Bigfoot Sasquatch and the large cat with no name, the word *telepathically* will be omitted, as one of Stephen King's (this writer's favorite author) suggestions on writing is to eliminate unnecessary words. This will allow this writer to eliminate up to forty seven unnecessary words. However, always keep in mind throughout this reading, that when these creatures communicate, they are doing so telepathically.)

"No," Bigfoot Sasquatch said.

"Can I keep it as a play toy?" the large cat with no name said.

"No," Bigfoot Sasquatch said. "Take it back."

"Ah," the large cat with no name said. "Do I have to?"

"Yes," Bigfoot Sasquatch said. "Come on," he (or she, or it) said, and together, the two creatures, one of which was not supposed to exist in Virginia, and the other, which was not supposed to exist at all, made their way out of the cave, down the long tunnel, and then they slipped out of the crevice between their hidden passage and the large boulder which camouflaged it, and then they began making their way down the mountain and toward the Christmas tree farm.

***

"What was that!" It was Nick. He was sitting in the second row of the Sequoia's seats. He'd allowed the father of the missing child to ride in front, with Robert (though he'd kept his eyes on Robert, because Robert hadn't always been faithful, and Nick knew Robert had a thing for younger men with drinking problems, often stooping as low as going to AA meetings and picking up men during their first ninety days of sobriety, their greatest time of need, and when they were most vulnerable and easily gotten, even, many of them, if they were straight).

"I saw it!" the father of the missing child said. His hangover had worn off now. It was just after dark. He was really jonesing for a drink, especially with the added emotional strain of the current situation. "Was that a fucking mountain lion?"

"Where's fucking Emerson when you need him," Robert said. "If he was here he could shoot that fucking thing."

"I could have shot the fucking thing twice already if you weren't so anti-gun," Nick said from the second row of seats. Robert chose not to dignify the comment with a response. As much as Robert loved Nick, he would be the first to admit that Nick was a bit of a redneck. But it had always been his alpha, manly ways that had turned him on. And at least he still voted Democrat.

"What the fuck is that?"

This comment stopped all conversation, as it came from five year old Billy who was sitting in the third row of seats.

After everyone turned to look back at the small child who had just dropped a massive F bomb, their mouths agape, they slowly turned their heads, their mouths becoming even more agape, as if it were even possible, as they then stared at, standing dead center in the Sequoia's bright headlights and only twenty feet in front of the vehicle…

…Bigfoot Sasquatch!

And in the arms of Bigfoot Sasquatch, reaching up and tugging at the hair on Bigfoot Sasquatch's chinny chin chin…

…was Ryan. Safe and sound and uninjured.

The group inside the S.U.V. was silent. They could not believe what they were seeing. They remained silent as the Bigfoot Sasquatch in front of them lowered the small child to the ground, let him go, and then slowly walked out of the road and into the woods. A giant cat, one that had no name, because names and certainly not pronouns were used in its world, leaped back across the road, heading now in the direction the Bigfoot Sasquatch had gone, and neither creature was ever seen again.

***

As it turned out, the family who'd been put through the ordeal of having their autistic three year old child taken by a large predator that was not supposed to exist in Virginia chose *not* to sue Robert and Nick. They were grateful to get their child back, unharmed, and they were grateful that Robert had stayed in touch with the patriarch of the family and had actually convinced him to take positive steps (twelve of them, actually) toward combating his drinking problem.

And no, they never got it on, because though Robert strayed from Nick from time to time, the man was faithful to his wife.

And not gay.

The story of what happened at the Christmas tree farm that day never made its way into the media. Had it, Emerson would have done what he'd done a time or two in the past when stories of strange sightings and missing or mutilated livestock *had* made their way into the media.

Deny, deny, deny.

Emerson had been prepared to use the excuse that "distraught mothers' emotions run high and make them see things that aren't there" had the mother of the child gone to the papers (or the shady blogs on the internet) and told her story, but he was grateful it hadn't come to that.

And the story the group had told Emerson about the Bigfoot Sasquatch? Well, he knew there were cougars in the area, thirteen of them for sure, for they were being tracked after having been reintroduced to the wild, secretly, by his department. It was hoped that they were breeding, but his department had still not garnered any evidence that this was the case, yet.

But Bigfoot Sasquatch?

Poppycock!

Those aren't real, and everyone knows it, Emerson thought. Why, modern man has come so far that we know goddam everything! He'd tell you you could even go ask an old acquaintance of his, Jittery J, but Jittery J was dead. "Goddamn, if that 'ol boy didn't know goddamn everything," Emerson said aloud, the thought of Jittery J entering his mind.

And as far as Bigfoot Sasquatch and the large cat that has no name? Well, Bigfoot Sasquatch had a good talking to with that large cat, and that large cat never went anywhere close to where humans resided again, and as a result, was never spotted again.

But that talking to had taken place the day *after* the day of the events that took place on the Christmas tree farm. For you see, on their way home, Bigfoot Sasquatch had received a message. A message transmitted by way of a spell carried out through a burnt coconut husk. A spell cast by a beautiful young Pacific Island woman now as much out of place in Central Virginia as Bigfoot Sasquatch and the large cat with no name themselves.

"You go home," Bigfoot Sasquatch told the large cat with no name (and you remember how they communicate, right? I'm choosing not to use that word for the sake of eliminating unnecessary words, remember). "I'll be home late. I have work."

The large cat with no name headed one way, toward the secret cave, and Bigfoot Sasquatch headed the other. There was a real bitch of a postal clerk about to head home by way of a short cut just a short distance from where Bigfoot Sasquatch now was, but for some reason, a spell had been cast, calling upon Bigfoot Sasquatch's to make sure the woman would not make it home.

Per the final events in the closing paragraphs of story one of this collection…

…she did not.

The End

4

Sisters Of The Secret

I had a best good buddy back in the Philippines. His name
was Ray. He was a seventy-ish year old Englishman who
thought and lived like he was still in his twenties, and man,
did me and that guy have some good times together.

"Why the long face, friend?" were the first words Ray ever
spoke to me. But I had no idea what he was saying,
because he was speaking in Tagalog, the national
language of the Philippines, and it would be quite some
time before I'd actually learn to understand and speak the
language. I had been sitting at the bar in a hotel restaurant
in Manila, the country's capital, having a lukewarm beer
(ice seemed to be a precious commodity all over the
country, except for at the highly priced five star joints I
could not afford to visit) when Ray came in to do the same.
It was two o'clock in the afternoon, and aside from the two
waitresses who were sleeping behind the counter (they'd
given us the go ahead to help ourselves to as much
lukewarm beer as we wanted, as long as we left payment

on the bar when we left, and asked that we just not wake them) we had the place to ourselves.

I let Ray know I had no clue what he was saying, and since he was pronouncing the Tagalog words with a thick English accent, it sounded like Czechoslovakian to me, anyway, and I doubt I would have understood what he was saying even if I'd spoken Tagalog at the time.

Ray switched over to speaking English, and after I told him my tale- the short version being that I'd gone to the Philippines to meet a girl I'd met online, had been taken major advantages of, had spent twenty 'k' U.S. in three weeks bankrolling her village, and was on my way back to the U.S., my tail between my legs, to nothing waiting on me there- and I explained how I'd recently returned from Iraq to no home, no family, little money. Nothing but problems and people who viewed me as a hero a year before, but a dead-beat embarrassment now.

So much for the short version, huh?

"You got the wrong introduction of the Philippines," Ray informed me. "Have you already bought your plane ticket home?"

"No," I said. "I'm getting it directly from the counter at the airport tomorrow. I don't care how much it costs. This place sucks."

"Give it another two weeks," Ray said. "Come with me to Davao City. Let me show you around. Teach you about the culture, which begins with trusting no one. You can have a lot of fun here. You can meet a lot of beautiful young ladies. And I even know a few who are wonderful. They're not whores and scammers. They're hard working, honest, trustworthy, and did I mention gorgeous?"

"No," I said.

"Well, they are gorgeous," he said. And after more beers than I care to remember, I decided to give it a shot. I did not return to the U.S. at that time. I would go to Davao City, in Mindanao, with my new best good buddy, an ageless man with the wisdom of an old testament prophet, and I would, in time, meet such a girl Ray had described. Actually, Ray is the man who introduced me to her. Her name is Dearly, and she is now my wife, and she was *nothing* like the girl I'd gone to the Philippines to meet (she refused to go out with me for more than a month at first- claiming I talked too much- and she would *never* take *any* of the money I offered her to help her navigate her way through her third world impoverished lifestyle with more ease, no matter how hard I tried to make her take it). When we met, she was in her third year of college and she had a full time job in order to pay her tuition and rent and other living expenses.

Dearly was nothing like any woman I'd ever met in the U.S., either. She was a one of a kind, and after meeting her, I instantly forgot that I was surrounded by thousands upon thousands of the world's most beautiful women who, and I'm just saying it like it is, would jump (and many who *did* jump) at the opportunity to hook up with me, simply because of my skin color and nationality. They viewed me as an instant escape from poverty, and I knew it. They viewed me as a ticket to the U.S. and I knew it. Though they were wonderful people in so many ways, I just couldn't come to terms with the idea of being used for an agenda. But Dearly? Well, like I said, she couldn't stand me and she wanted nothing to do with me nor anything from me, and I was in love with her at first sight, and her lack of an agenda (she said she never wanted to leave the Philippines, let alone travel half a world away to the U.S.) made me want her even more!

So what does this walk down memory lane- a 'how I met my wife' saga- have anything to do with Bigfoot Sasquatch? And Christmas?

Correlations!

My mind works in very mysterious ways, and it draws connections to past events, facts, and theories at times, and this story begins with one of those times.

So, before I met Dearly and began the long process of getting my shit straight (it helped that she actually learned to like me and then love me, and we had a son and came to the U.S. and got married, and have been living happily ever after, etc. etc.) I was a bit of a man whore. This is nothing I'm proud of, but I'm not ashamed, either, as I know I can look back and recognize the fact that I was completely and insanely batshit crazy at that time in my life. And I somehow ended up in a place where all there is to do, even for the locals, is get drunk and screw. And I spent a hell of a lot of time, as if all the time I was awake, doing both.

"Let me show you how to find some of the most interesting places," Ray said one day while we were walking down the street in Davao City. I'd gone to his apartment bright and early at noon. He'd just finished up his breakfast. Having anticipated my visit, he'd made sure to get up bright and early at 11:00 a.m. and have a slice of toast with coffee before showering and going out with me. This was the beginning of what had been our daily routine for months and would be until I would meet Dearly. Ray had no idea that by introducing me to my future wife he'd end up losing his running buddy.

Ray and I began strolling down what appeared to be a deserted alleyway. (Well, I mean, there were people in the alley, but come on, man, this was the Philippines. There were people everywhere. But for the Philippines it seemed deserted.) The alley made a turn or two, and then it opened up to another barangay (neighborhood) which was located on the beach, and man, what a time we had that day. We visited the barangay's various drinking holes, and got to know quite a few of the local beauties, and ended up discovering what would become one of our favorite places to hang out from time to time, until, of course, I would meet Dearly and change my bad boy ways.

"I've been around the world many times," Ray said as we sat on that white sandy beach, drinking beer that was actually cold, for once, staring out across the Pacific, wondering if we were directly across the ocean from North America or South America. "And what I've found," he continued, "is that most of the greatest treasures truly are off the well beaten path. There are mines with gems, like this place, and like these gems (he nodded his head toward our two companions for the day- two beautiful young ladies in their early twenties who could have and probably would have been pinup models or neurosurgeons had they been lucky enough to enter the world through wombs in the West) all over the place. Most people simply never find them, because they dare not venture off the well worn paths of their lives."

Ray took a big swig of his San Miguel Light, the beer we were drinking and began staring again, across the Pacific. "God, I wish I would have discovered this place when I was your age." He'd spoken the words, and the words before these words like a sex and alcohol addicted Robert Frost, and I was hanging on every one of them.

And then there was Dearly… and then monogamy, and eventually, sobriety, and… well, our homestead in Central Virginia, an S.U.V. driving down an old dirt road our first fall here, enjoying the beauty of the changing of the leaves on the deciduous trees, and a spoiled little boy of five years old sleeping in the back of the vehicle. That was our daily routine back in those days. Our son, Daniel, was in kindergarten. We'd pick him up after school and we'd take one of the various backroads home to look at the leaves and find out more about what was around the area in which we now lived, and, then, on that day, there was…

… a monastery?

Yes, an actual monastery.

""I've been around the world many times," Ray's words from that white sandy beach and all those years ago came to my mind instantly upon seeing something in the middle of the Blue Ridge Mountains of Virginia that seemed so out of place in the middle of this nowhere. "And what I've found," he'd continued that day as we drank cold beer and spent time with young women as beautiful as supermodels, "is that most of the greatest treasures truly are off the well beaten path."

And here was an example of his case in point.

"That's really odd," I commented to my wife. "Who would have thought there would be a monastery out here in the middle of nowhere?"

And then I forgot all about it.

For about two months.

***

Until the morning of election day, 2016.

After I'd voted (I'd gotten there early and was third in line), and I was leaving, I hesitated while opening my car door in the parking lot outside the church that served as our polling station. It was still dark, but I noticed the headlights of half a dozen vans pulling up. They parked by the side of the road, and hordes of nuns stepped out of the vans and went into the church to cast their votes.

"Huh," I said, aloud. "I guess nuns vote."

And then I forgot all about the nuns and their hidden monastery again.

For another three years.

***

Until one overcast afternoon in the late fall of 2019!

I'd been tracking an elusive creature that may or may not
have been, potentially, a Bigfoot Sasquatch. The creature,
potentially, had been haunting our homestead since long
before we'd purchased the land. I mean, I really don't think
he, she, it or they showed up just because we moved in.
However, this is still a possibility that we've not ruled out,
what with our experiences with the Kapre in the
Philippines, and whatnot. I sometimes think that cryptids
and spirits and all things paranormal and unexplainable
attach themselves to those who can see them, and
especially, those who can see them and acknowledge
them. It's as if, though they don't want to be harmed in any
way, nor harm anyone or anything else, they absolutely
love the attention of being noticed. And who or what
doesn't, right?

Anyway, I'd been pretty heavy into the whole Squatchin'
thing for more than a year by this point. And I was taking
my camera out into the woods with me on a pretty regular
basis and everything, because I'd managed to garner a
sizable audience on our YouTube channel, "Homesteading
Off The Grid" (ever heard of it?), who were also curious in
finding out more about this potential, mythical creature that
may or may not exist and which may or may not be living in
the woods behind my house. Not to mention, watch to see
what sort of ass clown shenanigans I might get up to each
episode in my attempts to harness the creature's curiosity
bone and pull it far enough out of the woodline to catch a
glimpse.

On this particular November day I'd been canvassing a
region just outside of an area we've come to call the lair of

Bigfoot Sasquatch. It's a location a considerable distance from my home, as far as hiking or driving would be concerned, but not so much as far as the crow flies, or, in this case, the way that Bigfoot Sasquatch travels over hill and dale and mountains and valleys.

All of the leaves from the trees, except for the leaves of the oak trees, had fallen, which gave me greater visibility than usual (the oak leaves fall after Christmas). However, I also knew that this allowed for anyone or anything out there in the forest with me to see me from a greater distance, as well. So, though I could see farther, I was moving much slower than usual, having greater spaces of land in front of me to scope out with my eyes before taking the next steps forward with my feet.

I'd been following what I thought was a large, dark figure that seemed to cloak in and out of our dimension. You see, that's one of the things I've noticed during my cryptozoological explorations. There are times when, and this is not just when viewing things through the screen of my iphone and its, what is often referred to, shitty, archaic 360 uploaded videos, but with my naked eyes, I often see areas in the forest, areas sometimes the size of a man, sometimes a small as a squirrel, where there just seems to be pixelation. I grew up in the mountains of Appalachiastan, and I spent a good portion of my youth in the woods, and I never saw anything like this until I moved to this homestead. Well, except for in the Philippines, on a particular, very creepy island, and, well, I've already hit on this point.

So, on that day, I followed the pixelation. Again, at one point it would be pixelation, and at another it would be a large, dark, blurry object. I'd been following for hours, and I knew I was going to run out of daylight soon, but my curiosity had gotten the better of me hours before, so I continued following. Besides, I'd heard a car or two way down in the valley below me, so I knew there was a road down there, and if I were to get stuck in these woods after dark, my plan was to merely go down to the road and flag a ride. I had been following this pixelated/large, dark, blurry image for too long to give up now.

When I crested the next ridge and stared down over the precipice, low and behold, there was that damned monastery, out in the middle of nowhere. Further, the apparition, if you will, I'd been following, just drifting down the hill, toward the monastery, and once it reached the treeline, where the forest gave way to a large, open field (a field with several nuns tending the past year's garden, I'll add), it formed fully. I stared, in awe and wonder, as what had been pixels one minute, and then a large, dark, blurry image the next, became, in the flesh and fur...

...Bigfoot Sasquatch!

I watched, from a distance of nearly a quarter of a mile, three nuns approach this large, manlike creature. I could not hear what they were saying, but I could tell by their body language that they were speaking. I knew my eyes were seeing what I believed they were seeing, because I was not viewing this scene through naked eyes. I'd taken with me, as part of my potential Bigfoot Sasquatch field research kit (available for purchase, by the way, in our Etsy store, "Homesteading Haven") not only an empty toilet paper roll to use as optics, but one of the long, empty Christmas gift wrapping rolls we'd recently emptied wrapping our son's Christmas presents. It had a much longer range than the toilet paper roll, and I could clearly see the nuns' lips moving as they spoke.

The creature seemed to grunt or growl, or hell, maybe even speak itself. Though I could see clearly through my gift wrapping roll, I was still too far away to hear. And after the exchange, which seemed to last only thirty seconds or so, the creature walked off, but not back into the forest, rather, into a garden that appeared to be walled off with about an eight feet high brick wall. It looked much like the beautiful bricked wall gardens on the campus of the University of Virginia down the road in Charlottesville.

Knowing that which I had been tracking for hours was no longer in the forest with me, I picked up my pace in heading down to the monastery. When I reached the field, the three nuns who'd spoken with the potential Bigfoot Sasquatch approached me, gardening hoes raised over their shoulders as if they were ready to smite me. "You're on private property, pervert!" one of them yelled at me. "You'd best get, or we will eviscerate you!"

"What?" I said.

"That means we'll cut off your balls, you disgusting male creature!" one of the other two nuns said.

"Sisters!"

I turned and saw another nun coming our way. Upon the sound of this nun's voice, the others had lowered their gardening hoes, and I felt my testicles relaxing and dropping back into my scrotum. Instantly, upon having one of the nuns explain to me what 'eviscerate' meant, they'd crawled back up the tubes they'd hidden in until that fateful day puberty would come along and give me body hair in places I'd never had it (and the body odors that came with that), zits, emotional insecurities, and a full sack instead of an empty bag, like many of the local beta-males in my college town who's alpha wives have obviously eviscerated *them* and who have been hiding their jewels in a jar, somewhere, ever since the day they'd been idiots enough to say "I do."

I saw, approaching us, another nun- the nun who had spoken- but she looked nothing like the nuns prepared to turn me into a eunuch. These old biddies had been in their seventies. The nun approaching us, hips swaggering like a goddamn bluejeans model- and yes, this was noticeable despite the black robe she was wearing- was young, much younger. She appeared to be younger than me, even. I was in my mid-forties at the time, and I doubt this woman had hit forty yet. She was in her late thirties at most.

"Put that shit down and get inside," the nun said.

"Sister," one of the old biddies said, under her breath but still loud enough for me to hear, as she passed the much younger, and need I say further, extremely more attractive nun who was still coming toward me. "Your language."

"Shit," the hot nun said. "I forgot." I smiled when this happened, and the hot nun caught my smile and she returned it.

"Lost?" she said when she'd reached me.

"No," I said.

"Then why are you here?" she asked. And by the way, her name was April. I'd find this out, as well as quite a bit more about this hot nun in pretty quick order, but at first, things were a little testy.

"I followed it. Here. All the way from my place."

"Followed what?" April asked.

"You know," I said.

April stared at me hard for a hot second, but then she rolled her head, said, "shit," again, and I could tell, by the way her body, which had been entirely rigid (except for those hips that had sauntered so sexily across the field) until now relaxed, that she wasn't going to play any games.

"Are you alone?" she asked.

"Yeah," I said.

"Do you have a camera? Are you recording?"

"I do have a camera," I said, "and I have been recording. But I'm not now." I pulled my cell phone out of my pocket and showed her that it was off.

"What's that?" she asked, pointing to the empty gift wrapping tube I was holding in my other hand.

"My optics," I said, handing her the tube. She took it from me and held it up to her right eye and she closed her left.

"This doesn't work," she said. "Are you crazy?"

"Maybe," I said.

She looked at me, a very serious look on her face, and then she broke into hysterics and nearly fell to the ground laughing.

"You're a trip," she said. "I would have loved to have done a line with you." She laughed more at that thought.

"A line?" I said. "You mean, like..."

"Yeah," she said. Coke! And not the kind that comes in a bottle."

"Well," I said, warming up to this beautiful, sexy, younger me and not very nunnish nun. "That's never been my thing, but you mention bottle, and well, once upon a time, that was. And, well, I would have loved to have killed a bottle of the top shelf shit with you."

"Oh," she said, regaining her composure. "I can see how *that* would have gone." She stood straight now, pressing the wrinkles that weren't there out of her robe with the palms of her hands. "I would have ended up with *four* illegitimate babies instead of three had that happened."

"Are you serious?" I said.

"You're not gay, are you?" she asked, matter of factly.

"Not that," I said. "I mean, you have three kids?" Then I realized I'd left out an important fact. The answer to her question. So I added it. "And no. I'm not gay."

"Buddy," she said. "Not all of us end up in here because of our love of Baby Jesus." She looked at me in a knowing way. A way that let me know that she knew my mind was blown, quite a feat in internet language, even though we were having this discussion in person. "Not at first," she continued to explain. "But it does come to that. With what people on the outside might call indoctrination. I've come to call it faith. And it's faith based on knowledge."

"How is that possible?" I asked her. "Faith is defined as a belief in things unseen. How can you have actual knowledge of things that have not been seen?"

"The definition does not say unseen by all," she said. "It just says unseen. Some see, some do not see."

She had me. I could relate entirely. It was the reason I'd ended up here in her presence in the first place.

"Speaking of which," I said.

"Ask me no questions, I'll tell you no lies," April said.

"Well, what's up with that?" I asked, wanting the truth, not lies. "I mean, why here?"

"Safe haven," she said. "Sanctuary. They can live in peace and not be hunted."

"They?" I said. "You mean there is more than one?"

"More than one what?" she asked, playing dumb, though smiling coyly, and looking like a naughty-nurse fetish model from an adult website in so doing.

"You've got to give me more than that," I said. "I've been seeing these things on my homestead for the four years I've lived there. I've been tracking them through the forest between here and there for two years now. We finally got one on video, I believe, just last month (this would be the 25 October 2019 video titled "He Discovers The Lair Of Bigfoot Sasquatch And Is Told Loud And Clear He Is NOT Welcome" on our YouTube channel 'Homesteading Off The Grid').

"Where is your homestead?" she asked. I told her, and she said, "give me your cell phone. Let me hold onto it while we're together. I'll drive you home, since it's gonna be dark in, like, five minutes. On the way there, I'll tell you a tale or two, but you are not allowed to repeat what I tell you. And then I'll give you your phone back."

I agreed to her terms, mostly because I didn't want to have to walk home in the dark. It was a long way. I'd been hiking and following what I'd been following all day.

At one point, the thought of my wife getting pissed off and running to the garage to find the machete I keep hidden from her upon seeing me being brought home by a hottie crossed my mind, but I found safety in the fact that the hottie was a nun. Like the majority of people in the Philippines, my wife was a catholic, so she'd recognize the outfit.

On the way home, April told me many things that blew my mind. Not just about that which I'd tracked from my homestead, to the lair, and then to the secret monastery hidden in the middle of nowhere in the beautiful Blue Ridge Mountains of Virginia, but of her own life and her past. As she talked, I did get a flashback to my best good buddy in the Philippines, Ray, and that day he led me down the alleyway to a secret neighborhood by the beach, and it's secret beauty and secret beauties. How ironic this secret monastery and this beautiful nun turned out to be.

See, I always tie my segways together!

In many ways, April's story was a sad one. She'd been a promising young lady, having graduated high school at the top of her class and then going on to college at a prestigious university (though not U.V.A.). However, she'd never graduated from that prestigious university, because during her second year there, after having gotten a 4.0 GPA for both semesters of her freshman year, April was introduced to cocaine. She quickly became addicted to the garbage, and with the addiction came the sad, destructive lifestyle that so many addicts deal with. Promiscuous sex, abusive relationships, loss off job (in April's case, failing out of school), and often, and as was the case for April, homelessness.

"My parents still hate my guts," she told me while sharing her story with me. "And let me tell you, there's no love lost from my end. But I give them props, because they're raising my kids, and they're doing a good job of it."

"And you have no idea who their dads are?" I said.

"Dude," she said. "I don't even remember having sex with anyone. When I'd binge, it was like, blackout every time."

April did tell me many stories of, potentially, Bigfoot Sasquatch, and she shared with me her disbelief when she'd been transferred to the monastery and told of the secret. She'd started out her studies at a monastery in New York City, where she was from, but after leaving the grounds to party on three separate occasions, she'd been transferred to the monastery in the middle of the woods in Virginia.

"How can I confirm any of this?" I asked as I was getting out of the van she'd driven to take me home. It was my assumption that it was one of the very vans I'd seen on election day two years prior.

"Well," she said. "You can't, really. I mean, I'm not allowed to show you one and all, but…" she trailed off, and I felt hope rise in my chest. "I can tell you where one is buried," she said. "And you can try to find the grave. As long as you promise not to dig it up."

"I promise!" I said, sounding like a kid whose parents just gave them permission to do something special- maybe open one of the gifts under the tree on Christmas Eve. April gave me directions to where, potentially, a Bigfoot Sasquatch was buried. She warned me that it was heavily guarded by centuries, for it was the grave of the 'aged one.' One of the tribe's elders.

"And you can record it, if you want, because no one will believe you," she said. "Let me tell you," she continued. "The sisters and I are excellent at guarding our secrets."

"You've been pretty open with me," I said.

"Just wait," April said, smiling her coy, inviting smile, and after giving me directions to the grave of the aged one, she drove off, bound for the monastery hidden deep in the Blue Ridge Mountains of Virginia.

It didn't take me long to go looking for the grave of the aged one. And though it would take me until the following spring, this past spring, as a matter of fact, as of this writing, I actually found it! I'll save you the details by telling you to simply go watch the video I made of the hunt. It's on our YouTube channel, 'Homesteading Off The Grid,' and it's titled "Flanked On All Sides And Followed Throughout He Keeps Going And Finds The Grave Of Bigfoot Sasquatch." Many of the people who watched that video asked 'who' I was talking about when I kept referring to 'her' and 'she' when speaking of the woman who'd told me of the grave. Well, if you were one of those people, now you know.

It was April.

And why do I bring all this up now? Why do I include this story in a 'Christmas edition' of Bigfoot Sasquatch stories?

Because recently, as in last week, I stopped by the monastery to see April. I'd bought a Christmas card for her, and I wanted to see if she was well. I wanted to thank her for leading me, by way of her somewhat shitty directions that took six months to figure out, to the grave of Bigfoot Sasquatch. And admittedly, I wanted to question her further on these creatures and why it was that she and her sisters were given the charge of guarding the secret of their existence in our area.

But April was not there.

According to the old biddy who answered the main office's door when I knocked, April had never been there. It was as if the woman didn't even exist.

"You were there when I met her," I said, recognizing the old bitty. "You threatened to castrate me with a gardening hoe!"

"Oh, dear," the old lady said. "I would never do such a thing. Especially to such a sweet young man like you."

I couldn't believe it. This very woman had been a man hating bitch two years before. But now she was acting like a sweet little grandmother. I was being had. And I *knew* it.

"Where is she!" I demanded. "April!"

"There's no April here," a voice came from behind the old biddy. I looked up, and there she was.

April!

"*You're* April!" I said. "It's me. Kevin. Remember?"

"My name is May," she said, and she smiled, coyly, knowing I'd catch the play on words. You know, that whole months of the year thing? "And I've never laid eyes on you in my life."

"Seriously?" I said, my voice letting her know I wasn't buying it, but she continued playing her game.

"Oh, I'd remember you," she said, giving me a onceover from head to toe.

"Now, May," the old biddy who I'd nearly forgotten was there said. "You go back to your room and say three Hail Marys and four Our Fathers." The old biddy then turned and looked at me, embarrassment on her face, and said, "she's not been through the change yet. She still gets honry," and then she shut the door in my face.

I left, taking the Christmas card I'd taken for April with me. I scratched out April's name when I got home and wrote the name of my mail carrier on it and left it in the mailbox for *her*, along with a fifty dollar bill. The card had cost me six dollars and fifty cents so someone was getting it.

I have no plans on going back to the monastery. I can figure out what happened. The night April gave me a ride home, she'd merely had loose lips. She was excited to talk to me. She hadn't seen a man in God only knew how long, well, God and his nuns, and she was just excited to talk to anyone other than the old hags with whom she lived and who saw day in and day out. She'd done a good job at protecting most of the secrets, but I knew that she knew she should have never told me of the grave.

I don't begrudge April for what she did last week (as of this writing), acting like she didn't know me and all. I know she's had her own struggles, and she still does. And despite not getting any more answers to the questions so many of us have about these creatures that are not supposed to exist, like, why some of us can see them and others can't, etc. etc. I still do wish her the best.

And like it said in the card that she never got. The card I'm sure the mail lady didn't even read after taking the fifty dollar bill out of its center. I do wish her a very Merry Christmas.

As I do each and every one of you reading this.

And as I do him, her, it or they, wherever he, she, it or they may be hiding this holiday season.

Merry Christmas!!!

The End

***

The following stories are from Bigfoot Sasquatch Files Volume 8:

***Author's note: The letters in this volume were submitted to us by many of our YouTube channel 'Homesteading Off The Grid' viewers. Full, written permission to use these stories, here, and on our YouTube channel has been extended by the original authors of all letters used in this volume and with any letter that was read on our YouTube channel. The only changes made to any of these stories were in regard to the editing of typos, spelling and grammar, except in the cases where the author's local vernacular simply made for a better telling of the story than 'proper English' would have, thus, those parts were left alone.

Besides, only the Queen speaks proper English. But don't just take my word for it.

Ask her.

Enjoy!

1

Why Now?

Two reasons.

Number one; I have enough of my own stories, and I always have had enough of my own stories, that I've never needed to tell the stories of others.

Number two; massive trust issues.

Look, I've worked in social media for more than a decade, and what I can tell you, is people are fake. Okay, that's true enough in real life, but when you allow people to hide behind a screen, up to thousands of miles away from your location, and you arm them with a keyboard?

Man, you just upped the fake factor to infinity!

You have no idea who it is you're talking to on the other side of your computer screen. And I'm not talking about all the stuff they make reality television shows about- 'To Catch A Predator,' etc. I'm talking about on a much lower scale than that, even. But a scale where, if you derive the majority of your income from social media as a content creator, like I do, your time, which is your most valuable asset (though most humans don't realize this) is completely sucked out of you like the blood of a young damsel's neck in a b budget vampire flick.

Sadly, many of the folks who use social media, regularly, are merely bored. They're looking for unproductive ways to fill the great void of time that is their life, and what better way to do it than by scrolling, scrolling and then scrolling some more through stupid posts about cats on Fakebook (fingers crossed that *that* doomsday machine will be split up by the Government, and this author is a full supporter of capitalism- but Zuckerberg is an evil, pasty skinned little boy that needs to be stopped), or watching marginally creepy video after marginally creepy video on YouTube.

I'll tell you what better way.

By finding a content creator who posts those stupid memes about cats or who spends the majority of their working hours creating those marginally creepy videos who will engage them in communication. Yes, I'm talking about messaging or emailing back and forth.

Okay, this sounds cruel. And I know that there are people reading this right now who are my loyal, faithful subscribers on YouTube who watch every video I make and who've read every book I've ever written, etc. I'm not talking about you. I know, you're saying, 'how can you not be talking about me? I even leave comments regularly in the comment section of your videos.'

Look, that's what you call support. And I can tell by your comments that the overwhelming majority of you are healthy. You have a life. You come to my channel and you read my books for the very reason you should.

ENTERTAINMENT!

Now, with this said, does that mean that some of that sketchy stuff you've seen in some of our videos is fake?

Absolutely not!

What it means is that healthy people know where to draw the line between understanding that content creators who share part of their lives with the masses (of strangers, at that) on social media are merely working in an industry that is still relatively new. They've (we've) harnessed the ability of technologies to basically support themselves (ourselves) by sharing part of themselves (ourselves), in a limited and harmless way.

But then there are the unhealthy people, and these people scare the hell out of me, and this is why we have never even considered accepting stories from other people, until now, and only by way of hand written or typed and printed and then mailed letters to our P.O. box, the address of which can be found in the description boxes of most of our videos on our YouTube channel.

You see, I've met some of the unhealthy people out there, and it's enough to make you look for another job!

I'll tell of this tale here, but never on YouTube. This is the tale of the first perhaps not so healthy individual we ever had experience with, in person, as YouTubers.

It was the summer of 2018. I'd recently gone viral with that whole 'neighbor with a crayon' video, and our channel was getting about ten thousand new subscribers a day! I had no idea what kind of videos to make at the time, because no one seemed to give a shit about our gardening videos or my wife's cooking videos (the trolls love to claim they do, telling us they liked our channel better when we made those types of videos, but numbers don't lie. Hm, let's see. My wife makes a cooking video and I make a gardening video, and both videos might get eight hundred views. We make a Bigfoot Sasquatch video and it gets eight thousand views. Where is our time better spent? And who's telling big fat bold face lies?- I might be 'crazy' but I'm not stupid).

Anyway, for some reason, it seemed people just liked hearing me talk, so I'd make videos where I would basically just tell stories of my life's experiences. The series was called "the morning ramble." It worked for a while, until I got sick and tired of the harassment from certain 'vertically challenged individuals who lived under bridges.' Many of them were actually dysfunctional blood relations and former friends and acquaintances from whom I've been estranged for many years who'd found me on YouTube by way of YouTube recommending they watch my videos. I guess they were like, "Hey, there's Kevin. Let's make fake profiles and go to his comment section and remind him of the absolute lowest points in his life, when he was really down and out, and of how much of a piece of shit he was back then, and let's let him know we've not forgotten, and that no matter how much he's cleaned his life up and turned things around and found happiness (and who knows, maybe even God?), that he's still just a worthless piece of shit, and he's not fooling anyone, no matter what this here YouTube's telling him!"

And that's exactly what they did.

Anyway, that's not even the scary part. That's the part to be expected by anyone who decides to bravely work in social media and put themselves out there. I mean, I've had people I knew and have not seen since college (a quarter of a century ago) try to reach out to me because of this gig.

Anyway, as you know, if you watch my videos, I have a tendency to digress and get off topic. So let me get back on at this time.

So, one day, while wrapping up my morning ramble, I mentioned that I needed to go, because my family and I were taking a trip. I actually said where we were going and when we'd be there. And when we got there?

Someone was waiting on us!

Seriously!

I won't say where this event took place, and if you've noticed that I don't disclose my locations on YouTube, it's not just because I'm trying to protect the location of any potential Bigfoot Sasquatches. I'm trying to protect myself and my family, and I learned to do so by way of this creeper, who we'll call Tom. That's not his real name, so that's the one we'll use.

So my family and I were at this place we'd gone to (it was a public event with hundreds of people in attendance), and we'd split up. After about ten minutes, I heard my wife say, "honey," and I looked over, and here comes my beautiful bride, Dearly, and our son, Daniel, and some old guy, about sixty, who looked like he was drugged up on all kinds of happy pills was walking with them. "We have a fan here," my wife said.

"Cool," I said, and what I was thinking was that someone who also happened to be attending the event for the day just happened to notice my family from our channel. This happens. Especially when we go into town in Charlottesville. We've had people come out of shops on the downtown mall and say hello, and tell us they watch our channel. We've run into people hiking in local trails who've told us the same. We run into people at the UVA football games who tell us they're our viewers. None of these people, not a single one of them, have ever creeped me out. They've always been kind, pleasant, and respectful of our space and our time. They basically say hello, tell us they watch, and then wish us a great day and continue on with theirs.

But not the *happy pill creeper* at the event I'm writing about here.

He'd gone to the event looking for us!

I know I have a tendency to make a short story long, as I've already done here, so I know it's too late to say long story short, but long story short, this guy happened to live not too far away from where the event we'd gone to was taking place. He told us he'd watched my morning ramble that morning and that when I'd said I was going to this event he decided he'd just hang out at the event all day until he ran into us.

Okay, that's not so creepy, right?

But then, he wouldn't leave us!

He followed us around the event like he was our best good buddy. He didn't just say hi and by and then leave. He literally never left, and he made us so uncomfortable, we decided to leave after we couldn't ditch the guy. We'd planned on staying all afternoon, but we split after about an hour of trying to ditch this guy.

But even then, he wouldn't stop!

He told us where he lived, and he told us that he wanted us to go home with him and meet his entire family. He explained that he had grandchildren our son's age, and that they should become best friends. At this point, he actually picked my son up, like he was his.

We were standing by the parking lot, and our car was in sight, and in my head, I knew that if this guy refused to put my son down, I was going to end up in jail, and I would be indicted for manslaughter.

I walked over and took my son from this creeper, and he actually relented, like he didn't want to let go. As if he was going to use Daniel as leverage to get us to go to his house and meet his family. I wrestled Daniel from his arms, and as we were making our way to our vehicle, this guy kept taking pictures of himself with us.

On the way home, Dearly and I decided there were certain precautions we needed to take if we were going to continue to be YouTubers. We decided we would NEVER say where we were going again. We decided that if we ever made videos while out and about in other cities, or while on vacation, that we wouldn't publish those videos until after we got home, not just so creepers wouldn't come looking for us, but also so no one would know we weren't home and try to rob our house in our absence.

If you knew how many people have contacted us and told us they know where we live, and they want to come meet us, or, more recently, even told us they know where they live and they love driving by and they get excited when they see us outside, but don't worry, they'll never stop, because, and this is their words, they're not crazy, it would absolutely blow your mind.

I've said recently that if I could support my family without having any social media presence, I wouldn't have any social media presence.

Anyway, I totally digress, but I hope this gives you more insight into why I rarely, if ever, engage viewers on our channel. I'd love to engage with the majority of you who are healthy, but the minority who are nut jobs scares the living shit out of me.

But, alas, and to my point!

I figured if anyone out there was willing to actually handwrite, or type, and then pay postage to send their story to a P.O. box, so that their story would actually get to me- in a very safe, non-stalkerish way- then, number one- they're not just bored, but sincere in wanting their story told, and, number two- there is probably some validity to it. Any vertically challenged individual who lives under a bridge can copy and paste some bullshit story about Bigfoot Sasquatch for shits and giggles, but it takes effort and time to go through the process of getting a story to me the way I've set it up for stories to get to me.

The good old fashioned way.

By way of an old fashioned letter.

By way of the old fashioned and outdated postal system (which I still hate, by the way, but I like many of the employees).

So, with no further do, as my beautiful bride Dearly, a.k.a. Giggly Girl would say, let's get to the stories!

The Doctor's (retired) Story

*From a letter dated 12-02-2020.

Kevin,

It is my hope that I do not come across as if I'm talking down to you in this letter, either from the standpoint of a father figure, for I am old enough to be your father, or from the standpoint of my former profession before retirement. I worked for more than thirty years as a certified counsellor.

Further, I know you do not respond well to criticism. I am also tempering myself not to make this letter about diagnosing you. All I'll say in this regard is that I'd wager that you have a long, vast history of abusive, critical relationships that have left indelible scars on your psyche. Good news, my young friend. You are not alone. Many of us had fathers who were pricks. Bad news. Unless you get help with that some day, not only with the scars never leave, but the underlying wounds will never fully heal.

Well, so much for that effort.

However, before leaving this point, I do want to point out that some of the most creative individuals throughout history have been people who spend their childhoods being criticized by emotionally abusive parents, and by way of trying to prove to the world that they were worthy, and that they were okay at the endeavors they pursued, many of them changed the world. As a wise man once put it, "everyone can hear the music, but it is those who live outside of the box who create it." By the way, your book 'The Box' was my favorite book of yours. I'm surprised it's the one in your collection of many wonderful books you've written (and yes, I've read them all) that seems to have received the least amount of fanfare. However, I get it. Most folks who come to your literary works seem to do so by way of your YouTube endeavors, and I do know that that work centers almost entirely around the mythical creature which may or may not exist and which may or may not live in the woods behind your home.

Speaking of both your literary works and the 'creepy crawlies' on your land (and yes, that was an amazing video. It was the first of your videos I ever watched, and it was offered to me by way of YouTube recommendations), there was a story you wrote in one of your recent Bigfoot Sasquatch Files volumes that brought back memories from nearly three quarters of a century ago. The story I'm referencing was, I believe titled, "The Things We Leave Behind," or "Those We Leave Behind." Something to that effect. It was the story where you wrote of having to leave your best friend from childhood behind because you were both toxic for each other in regard to your addictions.

Firstly, if that story is true (and I have reason to believe the majority of what is put into most of your stories, even your novels, *is* true) I would like to point out as a former counsellor, and though I said in the opening of this communica that I would attempt to refrain from such things, you made the right decision. It was always so frustrating to me, when working with patients, when we would come so far in therapy, to the point where my patients were about to be 'healed' for the lack of a better term, because in this field there is no healing, rather, constant treatment, and then, the progress would stop, and usually emotional relapse would occur, because my patients simply refused to sever their ties with the most toxic people in their lives. Often, and most of the time, it was a toxic family member who was holding back my patient, and as difficult as it is to sever ties with spouses, parents and children (and I know you have first hand experiences with all of the above), it is of absolute necessity if one wants to truly get better, though as heartbreaking as it was to watch, the vast majority of the people I worked with throughout the years could not do this. I worked with people who I knew in my soul could have contributed to society in such a way that they would be remembered throughout the annals of history, yet they've spent their lives working in low wage, meaningless jobs, earning just enough to survive, because they've bought the lies that an abusive parent, spouse, or other family member sold them; they were worthless, their ideas were stupid, they were immature and irresponsible for wanting to pursue their passions, etc. And still others, who may not have gone on to achieve greatness, yet who could have known happiness, are, to this day, if they are still alive, miserable. And I don't even want to attempt counting up the number of funerals I have attended due to death at the hands of overdoses, accute alcoholism and suicide. I can only imagine that had you not cut ties with many of the people in your past, your funeral, had I known you personally, would have been another I would have attended.

However, I want to point out that it was not the character portrayed as the best friend of the main character in your story that brought memories rushing back from many years ago, rather, it was the quirky character of the honorary town cop in the story that brought back the memories. For you see, when I was a child, I knew a man just like that man, and the story of that man and things he claimed to see and know of are so strikingly similar to the real man that I knew, and his stories, that it's as if you were given a view into my very memories.

There is something else I must tell you about myself at this juncture, and the return address on the envelope in which this letter is enclosed may have given this away. I am Algonquin, and for centuries, my family has lived in the great lakes region, between the U.S. and Canada (and yes, I hate winters up here).

The man I knew, we simply called 'the old lunatic,' because that's what he was, and my family focussed on speaking English. Though I regret having lost some of our old ways, I do appreciate my parent's concern in my survival in modern times, and I was not able to simply survive, but I honestly feel as if I thrived throughout most of my life, yet this has nothing to do with the old lunatic, so I'll get back on track. It appears as if I may have been watching too many 'Crazy Lake' videos as of late with such a segway (just kidding… maybe).

So, for as early as I can remember, this was this man, the old lunatic, who was always digging holes in his yard. And I don't mean with a shovel. This guy had a backhoe. He would dig a hole about ten feet by ten feet by ten feet, and then he would bury it. At least this is what he appeared to be doing. When I once asked my father what the old lunatic was doing, he told me that the man was 'digging for dinosaur eggs.'

You might imagine that as a young child, I found this intriguing. Dinosaur eggs? What healthy, red blooded young boy wouldn't want a piece of that action? Around the time I turned twelve, my curiosity of the old lunatic and his endeavors had reached a boiling point, and one day, along with my childhood best friend, Steve, I approached the old lunatic and I engaged him in conversation.

What I discovered when talking to the old lunatic was that he was not a lunatic at all. He's what someone who lived life off of a reservation might refer to as a wealthy eccentric. He'd made a fortune off of a series of convenient stores back before convenient stores were even a regular thing, and though he did spend most of his time digging those giant holes in his yard and then covering them up, he was *not* digging for dinosaur eggs, it turned out, and he was *not* simply filling in those giant holes after he'd finished digging them for the sake of staying busy.

He was building traps.

And he was capturing and burying cryptids…

…alive!

Namely…

…wendigos!

The old man, whose name, by the way, was Robert, and who was no more a lunatic than you, Crazy Lake, are crazy, explained to us of how there were things in this world that most people will never believe in, mostly because they will never have any sort of experience with them. Robert went further and explained that there are so many people in the world who simply refuse to believe anything that they don't already believe, bigots he called them, and until then I thought that was a term referencing racists, but I learned that day, that a bigot is merely anyone who refuses to consider ways of thinking that are not already a part of the way they think- people who are unbending when it comes to different thoughts and the consideration of new or different ideas than their own. But Robert, that day, convinced Steve and me that he was a believer, and after hearing the story he told us, we were believers, too.

To make a long story short, unlike you in your videos (sorry, I had to put that in there), Robert's parents had been eaten by a wendigo. He told us these were creatures from our tribe's ancient legends. Basically, there is a form of bad energy that will consume a man, or a woman, who is already consumed with greed. It turns them into a monster; a flesh eating, cannibal, who must haunt the forests and eat human beings, and despite how much they eat, they are never satiated. Just like people who suffer from the deadly sin of greed are never satisfied with having enough, no matter how much stuff they acquire, the wendigo is never full, no matter how much they eat.

That day, Steve and I picked up shovels and began helping Robert dig and set his traps. In time, he would teach us to operate his backhoe.

But then something happened.

Steve and I got older. We stopped believing. And when we did, we realized that Robert was not an old sage. Robert, we would now agree with the rest of our community, was an old lunatic.

We were not rude to Robert, like the two boys were in the story you wrote about the kids who had a similar relationship with the honorary town cop who everyone thought was crazy. And just as it turned out that your town cop wasn't crazy, but right in what he saw and experienced (sorry for the spoiler alert for anyone who hasn't read Bigfoot Sasquatch Files Volume 6 yet), Robert had been correct and honest about what he'd seen and experienced as well.

I remember receiving a call from Steve, years later, when I was in graduate school at the University of Wisconsin, working on my masters degree in psychology. He called to tell me not just that Robert, the old lunatic, had died, because as it turned out, Robert had died more than two years before that- I simply had never heard of his passing- but of what they found in Robert's back yard.

It turns out that they were clearing the land to build a subdivision type of neighborhood. And just like Robert's convenient store chain, this was back in a time when subdivisions were not even a thing yet. And when they began digging to lay the foundations and build the basements of the new houses that were going to be built in the area, according to Steve, they found skeletons...

...everywhere!

So if you've read my letter this far, I know what you might be thinking. Robert was a serial killer, and Steve and I had been accomplices, albeit unknowingly, in hiding some of his victims' bodies. This was not the case. For you see? As Steve explained to me, they could not identify the skeletons. Sure, they were human-like, but they were not human. And many of them had- and make sure you are sitting down for this part- deer like antlers attached to their skulls. However, they'd not been artificially attached, as if some sort of sadistic ritual had taken place before their murders.

They were bonafide parts of the skulls!

They'd grown there!

You can Google my story all you want, Kevin, and you will not find evidence of it on the internet. This all happened long before you were born, and since it happened in one of our sovereign communities, this story would have never leaked to the press. You see, that's one thing about my people that hasn't changed. We do not air our dirty laundry.

Kevin, I know your channel focuses on Bigfoot Sasquatch. I know that you think you may or may not have a Bigfoot Sasquatch or a clan of Bigfoot Sasquatches living in the woods behind your house. And to be honest with you, I don't even know if you honestly believe this or not, or if you're putting us all on. And I'm not trying to be one of those "vertically challenged individuals who live under bridges" as you refer to the degenerates who troll your channel. I'm just being honest, and I hope you can appreciate that.

However, I do know that there have been times in your videos when I could tell that you were genuinely, and flat out, as you southerners like to say, scared. And I know it was genuine. Remember, I was a counsellor. And what I'll say, going out on a limb here, is that though one can fake monsters in the woods, and though one can genuinely act scared, one cannot really be scared unless they are truly scared, and I have seen that in you in many of your videos.

Also, I have seen things in your videos. And I have heard the screams of the 'mysterious creatures in the woods,' as you refer to them, and these things I've seen and heard in your videos bring back memories from my childhood. Things I'd hear late at night in the great lakes region- the home of my youth- and things I'd catch a mere glimpse of out of the corner of my eyes in the same place.

Kevin, please be careful. Again, I do not think you are crazy in any way. Frankly, I consider your work a sign of genius. However, I do believe it is crazy to continue to go into those woods alone, all for the sake of making your videos that I feel not enough people truly appreciate, not knowing exactly what it may or may not be, as you would say, that you are dealing with. For you see, I do believe I know what you are dealing with, and it is not, in my humble opinion, a Bigfoot Sasquatch. It is, rather...

...the wendigo.

Sincerely yours,

Peter S. (last name omitted)

The End

3

Homesick

*From a letter dated: December 2, 2020

Dear Kevin,

I can't remember when or why I started watching your channel. I know I've been a regular viewer for about three years now. So I must have started watching before all of this "Bigfoot Sasquatch" stuff, as you call it, started.

I remember why I kept watching, though. Your videos made me homesick!

I have lived my whole life in Morgantown, West Virginia. I know our states border each other, but it's quite a drive from where I live down to your neck of the woods. I know this well, because my parents were both from the south western part of Virginia. A town named Christiansburg, which is not too far from Blacksburg. Home of those dreaded Virginia Tech Hokies. As you might imagine, being a West Virginia Mountaineer, I hate the Hokies as much if not more than you probably do, since you live in Charlottesville, or thereabouts. However, don't think for a minute that I'm any fan of the UVA Cavaliers, because I'm not.

Okay, sports talk aside (and honestly, I don't really care about any of it, but I know you like your UVA hats), watching your videos, especially the ones that have you and your wife and your son in them, on your homestead, brings back so many memories from the summers I would spend with my grandparents down in Christiansburg. The videos you guys have made of fishing on the local rivers in your area reminds me of all the times my grandfather would drive us over to the New River, on the southern border of West Virginia to go fishing. Those years, some fifty years past now, were a magical time in my life.

I'll admit that once you started this "Bigfoot Sasquatch" stuff, originally, I unsubscribed from your channel. I'm sorry to say, but I also left a comment on the last video I watched telling you that I was unsubscribing. I know that you banned me, because when I returned to your channel only a few months later (it was winter, and I was up to my ass in snow, and I couldn't stay away from the views of those much milder winters in Virginia that I could see daily on your channel) I tried to comment and I could not. I don't blame you for banning me. I was negative. I could have unsubscribed and moved on, but I felt that I had to get a dig in at you. It was immature, and I'm sorry. I can't imagine how many 'vertically challenged individuals who live under bridges' you have to deal with, and it wasn't right for me to have been one of them. If you ever feel like unbanning me (my YouTube userid is FatJack55) I promise, I won't do it again.

Now, with sports talk and past grievances aside, it's time for me to get to my point. Like you, I've always had an issue with that, but alas, we're two salty old souls adrift in this great vast universe who were meant to be connected. Potentially. (hehehe)

I had completely forgotten about all the stories that my grandfather used to tell my sister and me when we'd go camping at night, either on our grandparent's farm or on the banks of the New River. It was only during this past Thanksgiving, when I was talking to my sister on the phone (goddamn Covid) that I was reminded, because she reminded me.

Sadly, once I'd reached my teens, I no longer wanted to go to my grandparents' place down in Christiansburg for the summers. I had friends. I had a girlfriend (who, by the way, is now my wife), and I was playing sports. The last thing I wanted to do was hang out with an old couple who had funny accents (listen to me, a 'dumb hillbilly' as I know you know we're known outside of West Virginia calling the kettle black), who sat on their porch talking about how danged hot it was most of the summer and listening to what I thought was a half crazy old man telling stories about things that do not exist most evenings.

The summer of my senior year of high school, my sister, two years younger than me, went and spent the summer, alone, with my grandparents. Our parents had recently gotten divorced (a rare occurrence in my youth, but an event my generation, the baby boomers, would make quite popular) and I guilt shamed my mother into allowing me to stay in Morgantown. She worked almost all the time, so I got to spend all my time with my girlfriend. We ended up "getting in trouble" if you know what I mean, and it sped up the "I do's" at the altar, but I don't regret any of it. And I'm proud to say that she and I are still together, having never participated in the divorce game, and we have three kids, all of which are about your age.

My little sister came back with quite the tale at the end of that summer. Allegedly, she and our grandfather, while out camping early in the summer, were visited by someone or something that would walk circles around their tent at night. At first, they thought it was a deer or a bear passing through. However, the first night it happened, it happened for the entire night. Whatever was walking around the tent did not leave until just before dawn.

Our grandfather had fallen asleep, convinced that what they were hearing was merely an animal, but my sister, she told me, was too scared to sleep. I know Morgantown is not a big city as far as big cities go, but we did live in the middle of town, and we didn't have deer walking around in our yard at night.

A week later, my sister and grandfather went camping again. They were camping on our grandparent's property, so the likelihood of what they'd heard being a trespasser was small. You know, living in Virginia yourself, that people there do not trespass, because they know they are more likely to get shot for so doing than not, and that was even more true back in those days.

Anyway, my sister and grandfather tried an experiment. They left a half dozen apples out, about twenty yards from their tent, as well as a candy bar. Yes, a candy bar.

My little sister thought the idea of leaving a candy bar out was as crazy as you probably do reading this, but my grandfather's point was that any animal could eat the apples without leaving any sort of trace of what, specifically, at the apples, but if anything ate the candy bar, you would clearly be able to tell it was an animal by the way it would have to maul the wrapper to get to the food inside. Most animals, my grandfather said, wouldn't even touch a candy bar.

The next morning, my sister and grandfather found no apples and only the wrapper from the candy bar. And it had not been mauled and gnawed on, as if from an animal, like a bear or a racoon. It had been opened, neatly, by someone or something which obviously had opposable thumbs!

When my sister and grandfather told me of this tale when I went down to Christiansburg with my mother to pick my sister up at the end of that summer, I thought it was all just a bunch of bull they'd made up in order to make me feel guilty for not having gone down and spent the summer on my grandparent's farm. I did not believe it for a minute, and I let them know about it. They didn't seem to care that I didn't believe. They said it would always be something special between the two of them. When they made not a single effort to try to convince me to believe, I thought there might actually be some truth to it.

I would go on to college after high school (Go Mountaineers!), and my grandfather passed away during my senior year. My grandmother passed away only six months later. We believe she died of a broken heart, as she and my grandfather had been together since childhood.

I attended my grandfather's funeral. It was actually held at his farm. He'd wanted to be buried at the top of a hill overlooking the old farmhouse. Ironically, it was one of the locations where we'd often camp when I spent the summers there, and it was the same location where he and my little sister had claimed to have had their experience with what I'd jokingly call the 'candy bar eating Bigfoot,' which I'm sure you'd call the 'candy bar eating Bigfoot Sasquatch.'

There were not a whole lot of people in attendance for my grandfather's funeral. He was a shy, private man. He didn't have many friends, but the ones he had were close. Ironically, I think that's another reason I found myself drawn to your YouTube channel. You kind of remind me of him.

After the funeral, a few people walked over and put flowers beside the headstone of my grandfather's grave. My little sister placed a candy bar on top of it. Though the jury of my mind was still out on the validity of their story from years before, I found her gesture sweet and sincere, and it brought tears to my eyes.

That evening, my little sister and I sat on the old porch swing on the front porch of the old farmhouse. We talked well into the night, mostly reminiscing about all the summer's we'd spent on the farm. We went to bed just before midnight.

Some time in the middle of the night, I was awakened by what sounded like a loud stomp on the front porch. The room my sister and I were sleeping in was the master bedroom of the house, which was on the first floor. The window looked out over the porch.

After hearing the stomp, I raised my head to look out the window, but it was pitch black dark outside. There was no moon. I could see nothing. I lay my head back on my pillow and went back to sleep as quickly as I had awakened.

The next morning, I rose early. I wanted to take advantage of seeing the sunrise over my grandparent's farm, so I made my way out to the front porch and I sat in the old porch swing. When I rested my hands beside me on the swing, I felt something with the fingertips of my left hand. I instinctively wrapped my fingers around what was there, and I raised it to my face.

It was a candy bar wrapper!

To this day, I have no idea how the candy bar wrapper got on the swing. I never asked my sister about it, for you see, part of me believed the story she and our grandfather had told me. I erred to the side of caution, and I viewed the wrapper as having been left as a message for my sister, so I left it on the swing.

I watched, shortly after my sister woke that morning, as she, too, made her way to the porch swing. I peered through the bedroom window, making sure to do so from the opposite side of the room as the window so that my sister would not see me, and I saw that she took up the wrapper, and when she did, she cried.

At long last, I had my answer, as far as whether or not their story had been true.

I also believe that I've had confirmation about their story being true. Did I see the Bigfoot Sasquatch myself?

No!

Then what's the confirmation?

My sister never mentioned the wrapper that she found on the porch swing to me, and to this day, I've never asked her about it. As they say, some things are better left unsaid, and in this case, I believe that what is being left unsaid is the truth.

Kevin, thank you so much for the time you put into making your videos. The memories some of them have brought back to me are worth a priceless fortune. I would imagine there are better things you could be doing with your time, but I, for one, appreciate every minute that you put into your videos.

Though you've banned me, I'll be a viewer for life!

Kindest Regards

J.S.

Morgantown, WV

4

Faces In The Fields And Forest

*Author's explanation: I have always felt that there are things, if not beings, for a better word, around us, that cannot necessarily be seen, heard, or even understood. This is a touchy subject, because so many people who believe in just about anything think that their way is the only way, and the minute you mention anything about other realms, dimensions, planets with life, the spirit world, or cryptids, you are written off, not just as crazy, but as demonic, a satanist, an occultist, a true lunatic whose soul (if these exist) is hellbound (if that place exists).

I'm going to go out on a limb here, but could it be possible, just, well, I'll say potentially, because I love that word so much, that all that Bible stuff is true, as is all the other stuff that cannot be explained? I'm not trying to offend anyone who believes in Jesus and all that stuff, as I do myself, but just because one states a belief in one idea or concept, it does not believe that one does not believe in another. In a word, it's okay to believe in multiple explanations, especially when it comes to things that cannot necessarily be explained (I know that sounds like an oxymoron, but I know what I'm doing here), without having to state your abandonment in other beliefs. Remember, the more we learn, the more we realize we don't know, and I know most people's absolute, bullheaded, stubborn refusal to believe in concepts they don't already know, understand or believe in (the word is bigotry) is based in the fear of realizing just how much is out there that they don't know about or understand.

"If it ain't mentioned in the Bible, then it ain't real." That's a quote. Who said it? Damn near every adult in my circle of influence while growing up in Appalachiastan. Not trying to knock them, but geez, there's a reason I left, and the last time I read my Bible (yes, I actually have), I saw no mention of the internet, social media, electricity or cancer.

Just sayin'.

For a long time I've simply felt that some have the eyes to see and the ears to hear, while so many do not. And I'm talking in the literal sense here, not just the anti-bigot sense. Some people can literally see things that are there, that remain hidden to others, and hear some of these things as well.

One such phenomena that fits into this description would be faces in the fields and forests surrounding my homestead. And I'm sure there are plenty of these faces everywhere else around the world. I know I've seen them in the Middle East and Southeast Asia.

One thing I've gotten in the habit of doing is making sure not to look any of these faces in the eye. Well, the ones that have eyes, because some of them don't, and those are the ones that can be a bit terrifying.

Now, am I alone in seeing these faces?

Absolutely not!

For years, we have been having viewers of our YouTube channel, Homesteading Off The Grid, comment in the comment section that they, too, have seen faces in our fields and forests. And these comments were coming in long before we ever got on the Bigfoot Sasquatch kick. I'm talking about back when we made all those exciting videos about corn and green beans! (uh-hem).

Recently, one of our viewers, a lady by the name of Brittany, contacted us and sent us pictures of some of the actual faces in our field and forest that she was able to isolate on film, somehow, from our videos. If you would like to see these faces, if you've not already, simply go to our YouTube channel and watch a video called "Disturbing Images Submitted By Obserant Viewer Is Proof That Things Are Worse Than Imagined." Not to mention, if you watch that video, you'll hear about one hell of a crazy dream I remember having had at the age of four, forty three years ago, as of this writing.

Here, printed with permission, is some of the communication I received from Brittany:

"Hi Kevin,

My name is Brittany. It's a pleasure to meet you. I've enjoyed your channel since the very beginning with the bunnies and Roger. I was working with behaviorally challenged bunnies, cats, dogs, lizards, chinchillas, rats, etc. I am furloughed from my job due to Covid.

Some people consider me to be empathic or clairvoyant. I just think I'm Brittany. I can pick up on weird things quickly, like you, and from the start saw things like you did. I spent too many years hiding the true "me" and ignored my gut instincts because I didn't want to be seen as a weirdo. My boss from my Animal Shelter dog—who is a Shaman/Holistic Healer and a real paranormal investigator encouraged me to use my "gifts" which I didn't know I had. Now that I've seen how the world really works and operates I sometimes miss the days of being blissfully ignorant. c'est la vie!

How do you stay sober with all the creepy going on around you? Some of those faces are terrifying, like the yellow eyed wendigo /werewolf thingy.

Speaking of faces. You have one dude that follows you constantly. I think he's the one playing the pranks and throwing walnuts. I also believe he is the ringleader of the bunch. Wherever he goes, the Yeti army goes. I think the dude is alien. Ya know your video that shows a strange creature standing next to the life size Halloween figures in your yard.....well... that's him.

I will enclose some alien races he could be a part of. I call him Kermit, because he looks like Kermit the frog. Wherever he goes, the army of Squatch is sure to follow...

I have just been filtering screenshots.

I see the moving blurs, faint faces, and lots of eyeballs. I was genuinely frightened by some things I uncovered. Your scariest video is the one where Kermit jumped into the tree and left that freaky carving of himself (he looks like that too!) I could see frustration and fear in your face. I deal with a similar but different situation. Nothing is more stressful than someone or something insinuating itself into your life, and the life of your loved ones. What's worse is when that unseen force is causing a multitude of problems, and the people around don't believe you because you don't have clear cut photographic evidence. Your wife seems like a doll...and your son is adorable. It's hard to see you guys dealing with that (and then trolls running their mouths). I just want you to know, it's not you. That stuff is there and it's scary. Plus you're a dad and a husband, and your first priority is keeping them safe and sound.

Like you said in your uploads, the craziness becomes a part of your life. It starts to blend into the background like white noise. I love that you use humour as a way to offset the absurdity of the situation. Dearly is a great support. It's great to see that.

I don't know if my images will be of help. I'm not a crazy fan girl type. I hate the spotlight and I've had my share of stalkers.

(This portion of Brittany's message is being withheld, as she mentions some of the specifics about the stalkers I shared with her we've dealt with in the past, and two of them are involved in pending legal actions, so we cannot disclose details here).

I'll send you a couple pics. If I attach them to the letter—I'll somehow erase all the texts.

Thank you, and I hope you and your family have a wonderful morning.

Brittany

***

*Author's note (again): Brittany, by far, is NOT the only viewer who has spotted faces in our fields and forest. Below is a list of other comments that have been left on our channel in this regard. These comments have been left over the years on many, many different videos.

~ I have been watching your channel, with interest, for about four months now. I have never seen the Bigfoot Sasquatch you claim may or may not live in the woods behind your home, so I'm leaning toward the 'may not' part of that statement. However, I cannot help but notice that you have many, many faces in the forest behind your home. They are even in the trees. I believe they are demonic in nature, so please be careful.

~ I am a believer in all things Bigfoot Sasquatch, but I don't believe this guy. I think he's nuttier than a squirrel turd. But I see lots of faces in his field. Freaky. I thought he was doing some kind of editing at first, but there's no way these things can be edited into the video like this. Some of them are scary. I know I see them. But fuck this guy. He's crazy.

~ I know Bigfoot is real. Down here in Louisiana where I live we have something similar. It's called the skunk ape. I've never seen the skunk ape, but I know it's real, because he raped my cousin. I don't believe a word this crazy legs says in these videos, and I think he's making fun of those of us who believe, but I see a lot of weird things in the background behind him. Like faces.

~ I hope that one of these days this ass clown comes face to face with a real bigfoot and it tears him limb to limb. But can anyone else see all those faces? Why doesn't he talk about those? Bigfoot is real, but there's not one in this guy's yard, but there sure are a lot of faces.

~ Kevin I love your videos. I watch every one of them. I don't care if they are about gardening or Bigfoot or fishing. I love them all. I have to admit, I'm not buying into the Bigfoot stuff, but I'll also admit that I have seen a few things in your videos that are kind of creepy. Also, there have been times when I could tell you were seriously scared. In one of your videos, you kept looking behind you saying you were being followed. I didn't see Bigfoot, because Bigfoot isn't real, and I have reason to believe you know that, but it looked like there was this really creepy mist following you. When you would stop, the mist would disappear. And then when you started walking again, it would reappear, and then form into a face, and then form back into mist and follow you again. I don't know if that's something you're doing with editing or what, but it's kind of creepy. Be careful.

~ Your wife's laugh is infectious. I can understand why she doesn't like to go into the woods and do a lot of videos with you anymore. I see the faces in the trees. Please don't point them out to her. I'm afraid she would get so scared if she saw them she would go running back to Puerto Rico.

*Author's note- my wife is from the Philippines.

~ This guy is a fake and a fraud and he is going to lose everything once he's properly exposed. But what the fuck is up with all those faces in his woods?

~ Kevin, I wish you would stop doing those night hunts. Every time you point out that the temperature drops, and a mist moves in, I can see faces in the mist. I don't believe in Bigfoot, and I don't think that you really do either. I know that it gets you views on YouTube and that translates to money and you need that to take care of your family. However, I don't think it's worth the continued risks you take, especially at night, to make these videos. The faces that surround you in the mist at night appear to be dominic in nature, and I fear they are set upon dring you even crazier than you already claim to be, which, I don't believe you are either.

~ First and foremost, this guy is fake and so is his videos. How stupid does he think we are? Bigfoot? Seriously? The next thing you know, he is going to be making videos claiming that the Loch Ness Monster lives in that little pud puddle of a pond in front of his house. But what the fuck is up with all the faces I see hovering just above the ground all over his fields?

~Don't you people get it? Bigfoot is real, but it's assholes like this guy that make it so hard to believe those of us who have actually encountered the real thing. This asshat is nothing more than some douchebag crying wolf. The best thing we could do to stop him is band together and stop watching his videos. He gets paid for this. By watching his videos, we are encouraging bad behavior. I for one will never, ever, EVER watch another one of this asshole's videos again. But what the fuck is up with all the faces in his fields and forest?

*Author's note (again, times two): The list could go on indefinitely, but I'll stop because I'm sure you now get the point. I'm suck. I'm fucking crazy, because at times, I think I may see what may or may not be Bigfoot in the forest and fields behind my home. And that, obviously, makes me certifiable. But, by God, there are goddamn faces everywhere!

The End

The Crazy Bird Lady

*From a letter dated January 4, 2021

Hi Kevin,

Give my regards to your giggly wife and your adorable son. It's easy to see why a man as blessed as you are, having those two special people in your life, is always so happy, despite the level of crap you have to put up with from assholes who are miserable and who obviously hate their lives, on YouTube.

As I sit and write you this letter (thank you for finally getting a P.O. Box, because I'm a little older, and I still like letters, and I don't trust that there internet) I am sitting in my screened in and heated front porch, watching birds and squirrels at the various bird feeders in my front yard. Like you, I have assholes for neighbors, so I had a fence put up years ago so I didn't have to see the bastards. I found that just the sight of them made me angry. So I blocked the sight of the sonsabitches. But the fence looked very impersonal, so I planted a few bushes in front of it and then hung bird feeders, and little did I know, over the course of the last ten years or so since I did all this, I would become an avid bird watcher. The only problem? Those asshole neighbors had an asshole cat that used to come around the fence and eat my birds.

One of my granddaughters happened to be over one weekend about a year or so ago, completely ignoring me while she stayed glued to her smartphone. I asked her what she was watching that was so important it would draw her into ignoring her dear old grandmother, and she said YouTube. I asked her what was on that, and she said everything. I asked her if there was a way to keep asshole neighbors' asshole cats from eating your birds at your feeder and she typed a few buttons and then gave me her phone. She had pulled up a video of you showing how you piled sticks around your feeders to keep your asshole cat from eating your birds.

And if you haven't been able to tell, though people write me off as the crazy cat lady of my neighborhood, because I don't go out much, and I get a lot of mail, I'm anything but. I absolutely hate cats. Their assholes!

My granddaughter said she needed some fresh air, so she went out in the backyard. I know that what she really meant was that she needed to go smoke some of that Mary Jane. So when she didn't come back quickly, and your video went off, your next video came up. I think it was how to keep your windows from fogging up in cold weather, or something. But I kept watching, because my granddaughter was still out back toking up, as I've heard her call it. And then when the next video came on, and it was yours, it was something about Bigfoot Sasquatch.

I remember at first asking myself how someone could be so smart and yet so stupid at the same time. I mean, Bigfoot Sasquatch? Are you for real?

When my granddaughter came back in, high as a kite, I gave the phone back to her and I told her what I thought of you. Both smart but dumb, and she asked me if I wanted her to troll you. I asked her what that meant, and she said she would call you a cocksucker in the comment section, but I told her there was no need to be rude. You seemed like an okay guy, just a bit off your rocker. But aren't we all sometimes?

Well, just a month later was Christmas, and that spoiled ass daughter of mine bought that spoiled ass daughter of hers, the chain toker, a new smartphone even though there was nothing wrong with her old one, so the little chain toker, and her name's Serena, by the way, gave me her old phone. I told her to teach me how to use that YouTube thing so I could see if you'd either been committed or solved the problem of world poverty yet, and I'll be a son of a saint if I didn't find that I quite enjoyed your videos more than I could have ever imagined. A lot of it might be that I didn't know how to use the phone or the YouTube too good and I was afraid to touch anything, and your videos just kept playing, one after the other. I'll go on and admit it. I'm as hooked to your videos as my granddaughter is the Mary Jane.

Now, back to my birdfeeders.

At first, I thought it was just my imagination playing tricks on me. Maybe my mind was being influenced by all your silly videos. Or maybe I had inhaled some of Serena's second hand smoke. But I swear to the Arc Angel Michael that just before dark, about a week ago, I looked up and I saw something large, dark and seemingly ominous out there at my bird feeders. My sighting only lasted a second. It looked like I caught the him, her or it (it wasn't a they, because there was just one of them) holding up one of my danged bird feeders, shaking the seeds out of it and into their mouth, just like you or I might do with a potato chip bag once we'd eaten all the chips and want to suck down the crumbs.

Then, just like that, it was gone!

Now, reason kicked in pretty quick, and I told myself there's no such thing as a Bigfoot, or a Sasquatch, and there definitely ain't no such thing as a Bigfoot Sasquatch, like you're always a'callin' it. So I knew it had to be my asshole neighbor. Much like you've described one of your asshole neighbors, I refer to this man as the smartest guy in the room. He knows everything about everything, even though he's done nothing and does nothing. I reckon he has a lot of dignity, and he prefers to sit around on it all day long. He's got him one of them women that likes wearing the pants in the family taking care of him. I guess it's win win. He gets to do nothing, and she gets to brag about how she's superior and all that. Hell, my husband, before he passed, never minded digging a ditch if that's what he needed to do to take care of his family, and I was damn proud of him for doing it.

I figured I'd confront that asshole. I should have years ago. Could have saved me money on that fence, though I do enjoy watching the birds.

Anyway, I go over there, and I'll be damned if not just the neighbors aren't there anymore, but the house isn't there anymore, either!

While I was standing there, wondering how a whole damn house could vanish without me noticing, though as I've already told you, I don't go out much and I get a lot of mail, I noticed that another neighbor further down, a woman, was looking at me, so I waved to her. She came over and asked if I was okay. I guess maybe she thought I wasn't because I was standing out in the cold with my bathrobe on over my nightgown and I was in my favorite pair of pink bunny house slippers. Leaning on my walker and all. Looking all crazy myself, I guess, 'cause my hair was a mess.

I told that lady that came over to check on me that I was just fine and not to touch me, but I asked what happened to the house that used to be there, too, and she said it burned down. Now, how in the hell can the house right beside me burn down and me not know about it, is what I asked her. She looked embarrassed for me (I know the look), and she said that sometimes people just miss things.

"Well did you miss the Bigfoot Sasquatch that just came a runnin' around the side of my fence?" I asked her. She looked at me, her jaw lookin' like it might fall off entirely, the way she was a holdin' her mouth open, and I said, "Well, did ya?"

"I saw something," she said, and then she just kept looking at me like I was senile, which, hell, I guess I might be, but at least she shut her damn mouth. She was starting to look like someone who'd been touched. I don't know if you can say that these days, but back in my time, that's exactly what we would have called her. Touched.

Well, the woman's husband came over just as I was turning around to go back around my side of the fence. He was yelling something about seeing something. I just turned around and looked at him and told him if he had something to say then just say it, and that's when he told me that him and a couple of the other neighbors had been seeing whatever I thought I'd seen.

"It comes around in the winter," the man said. "It seems to like bird seed."

"You're kidding me," I said.

"I know, right?" the man said. Now just what in the hell does that even mean? I know right?

By the way, I asked him how the house on the other side of my fence had burned. He told me the smartest guy in the room had set it on fire. He tried to make it look like an accident so he could collect insurance money, because I guess that miss 'bring home the bacon and fry it up in a pan bitch' he'd married had given him an ultimatum. Either contribute to the household, financially, or find some other woman who would take him in based upon his all knowing intellect. I guess he's doing time somewhere. And, according to my other neighbors, his wife done went and shacked up with some woman she works with. Oh well. As the world turns.

Anyway. I just wanted to let you know that I love your YouTube channel, and not just because it's the only one I know how to watch. You're okay to look at. Pretty easy on the eyes. Not that I'd expect you to know what that even means, but you can always go ask an old lady.

Take Care,

J.P.

Barboursville, West "By God" Virginia (or as you'd say, Appalachiastan)

The End

6

John's Story

*From a letter dated January 5, 2021

Dear Kevin,

I hope this letter reaches you. As you can tell, I do not want you to know my location, or any true specifics about me. I'll refer to myself as John, because that is not my real name.

I absolutely have to tell you my story. You have no idea how happy I am that you set up a post office box so I could mail you this letter. Though I've been watching your YouTube channel for three years now, I have never commented and I have never subscribed. I will never do either on your channel or anyone else's. I do not leave tracks on the internet, because they know everything about everybody when you do that. I don't even have a sign in for YouTube. I simply search out your channel and videos from the search box.

Okay, so here's the deal.

The Bigfoots and aliens and faces on your property and all the other weird things you see are holograms. I know how they look, because they are showing them to me, too.

I know that you were in the military, and I know that you were in other parts of the world doing some really badass shit, and I thank you for your service, but I know that you have also seen things that you are probably not supposed to talk about. And the thing is, they are afraid you are going to talk about them, so they want to discredit you. They want to make you look crazy so that if you talk about some of the stuff you saw or that you may have done overseas, everyone will think you're lying, because you believe you have a Bigfoot Sasquatch, among other things, in your backyard.

I know this, because they're doing it to me, too!

Now, I'll admit, I never served in the armed forces, though I very much wanted to. My father was a Naval officer, and I was in ROTC in high school and college, but I never actually served after that. You see? I was too smart, and I don't follow orders well, and they knew it, based on various aptitude tests I was given while I was in ROTC in college.

Basically, and to keep it simple, they viewed me as a dangerous threat. My IQ is higher than anyone else you've ever met. And aside from simply being highly intelligent, I also know how to think for myself, and I do so on a regular basis.

This would make for a very poor fit with the military. If they told me what to do, and I knew it was not the right thing to do, then I wouldn't do it. It's just that simple. And then the military industrial complex would not be able to achieve their total goal of world domination. I would be the burr under their saddle. The chink in their armor. And they knew all this, so they did the exact same thing to me that they've been doing to you.

I never leave my house, unless I run out of beer, because every time I go out I see images of their destruction. With you, they show you Bigfoot and aliens. With me? They show holograms of my yard being ocean front property, and I live at least a thousand miles in from the coast. I believe they do this, because they track me on the internet, using my IP address, and they know that global warming is of great concern to me. They fear that if I sound the alarm about how serious this problem really is, the masses might listen to me, because they would be able to tell how smart I am just from listening to me talk, so they project these holograms from outer space, with a satellite they keep hovering over my house, so they can discredit me if I were to sound the alarm.

Let me tell you, Kevin, these people are dangerous. I can only imagine some of the things you may have done or seen while you were in the military. Things they absolutely do not want the general public to know. I'm convinced that if they were to view you as enough of a threat, they would kill you. Please don't let it come to that.

I know you probably think I'm crazy, but I'm not. This is a deep state military operation called MK-Ultra, and my friend, you have been part of it for a long time, you are probably just now finding out about it.

Google it. You'll see.

Take care, and please keep making your videos. Though I know Bigfoot is not real, and you're only seeing holograms, I do find your videos entertaining. They help me pass the time while I stay secluded in my humble home, mostly in the basement.

John.

The End

7

I Know He's Real But You Don't Got One

*From a letter dated January 5, 2021

Kevin,

You have summarily banned six of my various fake profiles, but I know you'll read this letter. You cannot get rid of me as easily as the stroke of a mouse click.

I know Bigfoot is real. And that's what it's called. Bigfoot. Not Bigfoot Sasquatch, you buffoon!

And I know he's real, because I've seen him!

I was a logger back in Maine when I saw him. I had been on the job for a year. I was out in the woods, by myself, because my team had gone into town for lunch. We were logging a stand of timber not too far away from a small community that had a Subway, so they wanted to get sandwiches.

I remember laying my back up against my backpack. I don't remember falling to sleep. But I do remember waking up, and seeing that eight feet tall, probably eight hundred pound monstrosity standing over me, looking down at me as if he was wondering what I was doing trespassing.

The only thing that saved me was that my buddies were coming back at that very instant and when the thing standing over me heard the truck, it took off running into the forest.

Now, here's the part about you that really pisses me off, and it's why you'll never stop hearing from me. I was a good worker. The best. And I had big plans. I wanted to become a foreman and then a manager after that. I aspired to gain all the knowledge about timbering that I could and then eventually start my own logging company. But no. None of that was to be. For you see? When I told my friends about what I had seen, lumbering over me, pun intended as your dumbass might say, I became the laughing stock not just of our small timbering operation, but of our small town back home, about two hours south of where we were working that day.

My sighting occurred more than a decade ago, and to this day, because of it, I am still merely a worker bee. My income has barely increased since the time I started on the job, and any likelihood of me achieving this mythical upward mobility is little to none.

I don't blame you, Kevin, for the way I was treated originally, but I do blame you for the way I continue to be treated. People watch fake-ass hoaxers like you on the internet, someone who obviously has a screw or two loose, and they assume that anyone who claims to have seen a Bigfoot, like myself, is batshit crazy. Just because you're batshit crazy doesn't mean I'm batshit crazy, but I cannot convince others of this.

It's safe to say that my experience with Bigfoot has ruined my life, and I certainly wish that you would stop your shenanigans, because you make the case for people like me a lot worse.

I hate you,

Rex in Maine

P.S.- This won't be the last you hear of me.

The End

8

Riding That Dame High On Cocaine

*From a letter dated January 5, 2021

Dear Kevin,

First of all, I want to commend you for the work you do in a field few others would touch due to the sure fired guarantee that they will be ridiculed, mocked and discredited. You are a shining beacon in a world gone dark of real heroes. I commend you.

I thank God for you, because I now have a safe place I can come to with my story. For years, the raw emotions inside me, raw emotions brought about by an experience I had years ago that have never lessened in rawness, because until now, I've never been able to tell my tale.

You see, Kevin, I am an educated professional. I have a master's degree in business, and I am very successful. I earn more than a quarter of a million dollars a year as a private financial advisor. I work exclusively with high net worth individuals, and as such, I only have to have a couple of dozen clients to make the money that I do. I do not work with anyone who is not willing to bring me at least two millions dollars.

I state all this not to brag, or to sound like the arrogant prick that many people in my line of work are, but to make it clear to you why I have never come forward with my story until now. I would no doubt be written off as insane, and who, especially among high net worth individuals is going to invest their life savings with a man who is insane? I know I wouldn't.

So here's the story.

I haven't always been an upstanding member of my small community. Small community here, being the key phrase, as you know how people talk so much in small towns. And once branded bad, you stay bad.

Sure, I was always good at covering my tracks, and one of the ways I did so was by being bad, as it were, *outside* of my community, and this is where my profession came into play so well.

You see, I wasn't always a private financial planner. I used to work for a major brokerage firm, and I won't name which one, but I've followed your videos long enough to know that you used to do the same thing, and though you've never mentioned the large firm you used to work for, I have reason to believe it was the same one I worked for. The cultures sound too similar for the firms to be different.

Anyway, once per quarter, our firm would hold a regional meeting. These were basically 'rah rah' sessions where our region's top producers would sit on a podium and tell all of us underlings how great they were and why they were so great. You used to work in the business, so I know that you know how it all went. They would make it sound like they were Billy Badass, and like they basically told their clients to invest all their money with them, the way they told them to invest it, or else. And the clients would tremble in fear and not just open their checkbooks but run out to the banks and finance companies after leaving the office to borrow more money to invest with these Billy Badass brokers.

Of course, Billy Badass always left a hole in their stories. A big one. The part about how their mothers were the sweet little old ladies who everyone loved in the H.R. department down at the factory that employed ninety five percent of the town's working populations. And how that dear, little old lady (mom) handed each new retiree her son's business card and said, "Okay, now that you're retiring, you need to go see Jasper here, and make sure to do a 401k rollover. And you can't wait on this. Here, as a matter of fact, I'm gonna call and schedule your appointment."

They leave out the part of how the retirees just couldn't believe that the little old lady in the H.R. department that they loved so much already was actually calling Jasper for them and setting up their appointment, and why, how good it felt and how easy it was just to walk into Jasper's office on their way home that day, their last day of their thirty five years long career at the plant and sign papers to allow Jasper (such a fine, outstanding young man any mother would be proud of, though they'd never learn that the little old lady back at H.R. actually was Jasper's mother- that whole conflict of interest thing), to transfer all six hundred and fifty thousand of their 401k dollars into an IRA at Jasper's firm.

Anyway, after a while, and after I'd garnered enough of a book of business on my own (like you, I'm a self made man- I had no contacts in the real world), I said fuck 'em all and went independant.

However, it was during the last regional meeting I attended while still with the big brokerage firm that I had my experience with a creature that is not supposed to exist. An experience that would reshape the rest of my life, as I have not, and I repeat, I have NOT ventured into the woods since.

And this was back in 1986!

Okay, so I've aged myself, but that's okay, because you've got to understand the time when this happened, because a lot of what was going on had everything to do with the time. And I know you're probably too young to remember some of the most unflattering parts of the era.

So back in the mid 1980's, while you were probably watching a shitty movie remake of Flash Gordon (the old t.v. show I watched as a youth was way better) and Footloose, and listening to Culture Club and Cindy Lauper, those of us who were of age, and who worked in professional circles, were doing mountains of cocaine and throwing our car keys into salad bowls or hats at parties and then pulling out someone else's keys and then going home and having sex with whomever owned the keys we pulled from the hat or salad bowl.

Yes, I hate to admit that this is how I spent much of my late twenties and early thirties, but alas, it is. The past is the past, and I cannot change it. And besides, I don't think I'd want to, anyway. Some of my associates had some pretty hot wives.

Okay, so we were at a place you might actually know. Smith Mountain Lake, in the southern portion of Virginia (yes, I live in Virginia, too). We were partying balls that night after having our awards dinner, where we saw the Jaspers of the firm given huge accolades for having done more than a million dollars in gross production (though they should have given the award to their mothers, whom they never even mentioned). After our first round of cocaine, someone started passing the salad bowl. I dropped my keys in, and realizing I was the last in line, I went ahead and pulled out a pair as well.

I'll admit, I cheated. Our regional leader's wife was smoking hot. She was the typical trophy wife these guys would marry. And while she'd been walking around during dinner just hours earlier, she'd left her keychain conveniently hanging out of the side of her purse. To this day I remember it. It looked like Prince's white guitar that he made famous in the movie Purple Rain. Oh, how I miss the eighties.

Anyway, having had the hots for this woman since I'd first seen her, about two years earlier, I pulled her keys from the hat, and in pretty short order, she and I were walking through the woods surrounding the lake, hand in hand, looking for a secluded area.

Most of the other folks at the party were simply going to each other's cabins, but for some reason, this woman, Judy was her name, wanted to do it outside. Looking back on it, I think it is because she loved not letting her husband know who she'd had sex with during those escapades. Of all the couples who were honest with each other during those times, I never remember any of them breaking up when we all grew up, which was quickened by the advent of the AIDS virus. But among those who were secretive, I would say they all got divorced by the 1990's. I think Judy wanted to be able to hold secrets over her husband's head in order to make him both paranoid and jealous.

Anyway, I'm happy to report two things. Judy and I got it on hot and heavy, and secondly, I didn't catch anything that I couldn't wash off. Again, when I look back on how I lived all those years ago, it amazes me that I'm still here. Thank God for good luck and three different rehabs, the third of which took. Twenty three years clean and sober now, by the grace of God and a secret society I'm not allowed to mention in the press, radio or film (wink, wink).

Anyway, I'll be discreet in saving you the details of mine and Judy's quick escapade, but what I won't spare you is any detail in regard to the hideous creature we encountered on our way back to the party cabin.

Kevin, I know that you like to think of these creatures as being kind and benevolent. I can tell you they are not. Not that the beast that Judy and I encountered harmed a single hair on our head, because it didn't, but because of the look of death it wore on its face and the howl from hell that it emitted.

Imagine, there you are, walking down a moonlit path in the forest, having had just made love to the most beautiful woman you've ever known personally, actually fantasizing about ways to break her and her husband up (I actually was not married at the time), so that you could spend happily ever after with her (and of course, removing the idea from your head that she would want to be shared with others at social get togethers), when a beast standing nearly eight feet tall and weighing nearly eight hundred pounds just jumps out onto the trail in front of you. Well, that's exactly what happened to us.

"Oh, shit!" Judy yelled. "I knew we were snorting some bad blow!" Somehow, at the regional meeting before this one, we'd gotten ahold of some bad shit. It had been laced with something, and a couple of the brokers and their wives ended up the E.R. It turned out to be a good thing, actually, because while there, they all tested positive for Hepatitis C, and one was found to be carrying the AIDS virus. So had we never gotten that bad blow, those who were sick, but who did not know it, might not have found out until it was too late. And by the way, the cheap ass broker who brought the bad blow was asked to leave the firm the following week and he went into private practice, which he'd planned on doing, anyway. It didn't help him that his wife was a heifer and no one ever wanted to end up with her keys at a party.

Anway, I assured Judy that we were not on a bad trip (even though we weren't doing acid, but you know what I mean). I assured her the thing in front of us was real, very real, and that we were probably going to die.

The thing started walking toward us, slowly, sniffing as it did, trying to figure out what we were, though I have every reason to believe that it already knew. Sure, it may have never been seen by humans before, but I'm sure it had seen plenty of humans in its past.

The damn thing got only feet away from us, looking at us like a midnight snack, working its sniffer like there was no tomorrow. To this day, I have no idea how I came up with the idea, I guess it just came to me, but I did it, and it worked.

What am I talking about?

Cocaine!

I had a vile of cocaine in my pocket. I reached into my pocket with my left hand to pull it out and took up Judy's left hand with my right. Thank the God of your choosing, as you would say, that she had long, luxurious nails.

"What are you doing?" she asked. She was terrified of what was in front of us and of what I was doing, and she was also frozen stiff due to her terror, and I told her not to worry about it and to keep her mouth shut. Fortunately for both of us, she did.

I spread a line of coke out on Judy's pinky nail and I held her hand up toward the face of the monstrous beast that was now no less than an arm's length away from us. As I'd hoped would be the case, the creature sniffed the blow off of Judy's finger. It took a couple of steps back, sniffing violently as it did, and then came to a sudden stop.

I could tell from experience that the buzz had just kicked in full bore. I'm sure the creature had a pretty healthy, drug and alcohol free diet, which meant it had no tolerance to man made drugs. This thing was all jacked up on cocaine, and it started shaking, I mean its whole body, and it summarily let out a scream more terrifying than the scream it had emitted only a minute before.

I literally pissed my pants when the beast let out that second scream and Judy actually collapsed. And it was just then, when I thought the creature was going to rip us both limb from limb, that the creature began itching like crazy. I know that if you take too many prescription pills you'll itch like that (did I mention three rehabs? I think I did), so I just assumed the creature was having some sort of allergic reaction to the blow. Whatever the case was, it took off into the forest, disappearing as quickly and mysteriously as it had appeared. I heard it running for all it was worth, until I couldn't hear it running anymore, and then I heard a super loud splash. I guess it jumped into the lake, hoping the water would cure it of its itch. Sadly, it had no idea that the only true remedy for a bad trip and a hangover is time.

I bent over Judy and coaxed her to consciousness by slapping her, lightly and painlessly, on the cheek. When she came to, she had absolutely no recollection of what had just happened. Actually, she had no recollection of us having had sex, and she told me that I was gross and how in God had she pulled my keys, and for me to take her back to the party shack.

Fantasy over.

But the good news is, Judy never remembered our encounter with Bigfoot Sasquatch. At least not that she ever spoke of, and I honestly believe that she does not remember. This is good, because she was never able to pull me into having to talk about what had happened, which would surely have discredited me and I'm sure it would have ruined my life.

Jesus Christ, Kevin, it has been so many years that I've held this story inside of me, and I have wanted so badly to share it with someone, and finally, Thank God for you, because you are that someone.

I know that assholes who have no life and who live in their mother's basements give you ever loving hell in the comment section of your YouTube channel due to the videos you make. But listen, they are going to do that no matter what type of videos you make. Those people are just miserable and hate their lives. You could go back to making those boring ass videos about green beans and corn and you'll still have them. So please, please, pretty please, whatever you do, do NOT stop making your Bigfoot Sasquatch videos. I don't know if this goes as far as some sort of Government coverup, but I do know that these creatures are out here, and the masses need to be informed. So please, keep being that shining beckon in the dark for those of us who you are so bravely leading to your light.

Sincerely yours,

P.T.

Somewhere in Southwestern Virginia

The End

9

Oh Well, Anyway

*From a letter dated January 12, 2021

Kevin,

First of all, I want to let you know that I love your YouTube
channel "Homesteading Off The Grid." I hated it when your
giggly wife, Dearly, stopped making videos with you, but I can
understand the fear and concern she had with all things Bigfoot
Sasquatch. I'm glad she started her own channel, "Life With
Dearly," and as with your channel, I never miss a single one of
her videos. She is such a sweet little lady. I'm a retired RN from

a nursing home and I used to work with a Filipina lady who looked almost identical to Dearly. We're still friends. She's a lot younger than me and she still works. I showed her one of Dearly's videos and told her I thought they two of them looked alike and she just laughed, and when she did, she kind of sounded like Dearly, too.

Oh, well.

Anyway, I wanted to let you know that I love your approach to Bigfoot Sasquatch. The way you don't claim that him, her, it or they are definitely real or that him, her, it or they definitely are not real. You keep an open minded approach that I believe would make the world a better place if more people could do the same about more topics. Like you, I absolutely hate politics, and I'm glad that you never discuss them on your channel. I have seen that issue divide the best of friends and the closest of family members, but I guess that's the underlying purpose of the two party system, anyway.

Oh, well.

No room for gray. It's got to be either black or white, and you're either for 'em or you're again' 'em, or you're not welcome in their home, by God. At least that seems to be the belief system of so many single minded assholes who are absorbed with the issues. Look at me. Just discussing the idea of politics gets me worked up.

Oh, well.

Anyway, here's why I'm writing, and thank you for setting up a P.O. box. I hope you got my Christmas card. You never said. But I saw the fistfuls of cards you were getting in a couple of your videos you made around the holidays and I understand.

Oh, well.

Anyway, I have never seen Bigfoot Sasquatch. However, my grandfather, back when he was alive- and this was a long time ago, as he died when I was still in grade school, and I was born in 1950, so do the math- used to always tell us a story about having seen something in the forests of Pennsylvania back when he was a kid that very much sounded like a Bigfoot Sasquatch to me.

Now, my grandfather claims to have had his experience when he was about thirteen years old, so that would have had to have been just before the turn of the last century. Probably in the 1890's. Wow! It blows my mind to even think of a time back that far.

Oh, well.

Anyway, my grandfather used to love to fish for these tiny little native brook trout. Small fish that were not stocked by the hatcheries. They existed in just about every little creek or stream that flowed through most mountains in Appalachiastan. We grew up in the rust belt portion of Pennsylvania, just south of Pittsburgh and not far from the West Virginia border.

My grandfather had always been a loner. I guess going back to birth. So it comes as no surprise that on the day of his experience, he was alone.

It's a pretty simple story, really. Grandaddy said he was catching so many fish on this particular day that he was leaving them all strung in groups on lengths of fishing line, scattered on the bank of the stream he was fishing that day. His plan was to collect each string filled with small trout on his way back downstream. Grandaddy always said that one of his few regrets in life is having kept every single fish he ever caught and taking it home to eat. He said that times were tough back then, and they needed the food, and not a single critter he ever killed went uneaten, but it broke his heart that by the time he was an old man, many of the streams that used to be filled with "tubs of fish" as he always put it, when he'd been younger, "didn't have a blame fish in 'em," as he also put it.

Oh, well.

Anyway, he had caught nearly a hundred fish on that particular day, and as he was heading back down stream, collecting them all, he came around a sharp bend in the river, and just as he popped around the bend, something huge, as in eight feet tall and eight hundred pounds, stood up downstream. It had been crouched down. Grandaddy said when it stood up that it was holding one of his strings filled with small trout.

Grandaddy said the strangest part of it all was that he was never scared. He never felt threatened or as if he was in harm's way. He said he actually felt a sense of peace.

Grandaddy said that big 'ol thing that took his fish merely walked across the stream, heading away from Grandaddy, and disappeared into the woods.

No one, for Grandaddy's entire life, ever doubted Grandaddy's story. Sure, there were folks who would say that it was probably a bear, but no one ever called Grandaddy a liar. Grandaddy would go on to work in the steel mills until he retired, and his story would never change.

Anyway, I've been reading your "Bigfoot Sasquatch Files" books and when I read the story of you and your old college roomate going fishing and having that big 'ol brown trout stolen from you by a bear, who in turn had it stolen from him by a Bigfoot Sasquatch, I just felt like I had to share my Grandaddy's story with you. I hope you liked it, and you can share it with other people if you want. Just don't tell them my name, because I see how rude people are to you on your YouTube channel, just for making silly videos. I don't want any part of that.

Oh, well.

Anyway, have a great day and give my best to your beautiful family!

Yours Truly,

R.G.

Somerset, Pennsylvania

The End

10

There's Only Room In This World For One Bigfoot Sasquatch

*Author's explanation: One of the biggest time consuming tasks for social media content creators, which is also one of the least liked activities for social content creators, is 'policing your page or site or channel, etc.' This basically involves going through the comment section a couple times a day and banning people who post inappropriate comments. Many people claim this is a violation of 'free speech' but it is anything but. You see, most viewers of YouTube channels, in time, actually come to care for the content creator, albeit, from afar (unless they have issues with boundaries and end up becoming stalkers, which was discussed at the beginning of this book). And when they see their favorite YouTuber constant getting bashed and berated in the comment section, they will actually stop coming around, because they do not like it. And, people commenting in our YouTube channel's comment section, asking me such questions as "how much did it cost to mail your mail order bride to the U.S.?" and "was your wife even eighteen when you started fucking her?" which, believe it or not, are comments we receive daily, all these years into our social media careers, are hardly representations of free speech. It is one thing to have the right to state your comments, opinions or beliefs in regard to any situation or topic, but referring the woman that I love as a mail order bride, or a whore (we get that one a lot), or to me as a pedophile, is not free speech. That's being an asshole, and those assholes are summarily banned.

I do an excellent job of policing my channel's comment section, which is great for our supportive viewers, but what I can tell you is that starting your day, each and every day, before the sun comes up, blocking all the assholes who hit your hard during the night while you slept is not an enjoyable experience. In time, I do believe it will lead me out of being a YouTuber. Imagine if you will, every morning for the past five years, waking up, having coffee, and then reading dozens of comments telling you how much you suck, how you are a liar, a scammer, etc. (and don't forget, a pedophile), and that the woman you love more than life is an opportunistic whore.

Anyway, there is one particular type of troll that has stood out over the course of the past two years that we've been doing the Bigfoot Sasquatch stuff on our YouTube channel 'Homesteading Off The Grid." And it's not the "you're a chime-o and your wife's a whore," type of troll. And it's not even the smartest guy in the room type troll who comes on and claims there is no such thing as Bigfoot sasquatch and then states that all our viewers are a bunch of ignorant, inbred hillbillies (yes, this is one of our most common forms of trolls). It's the trolls who absolutely believe in Bigfoot Sasquatch, claim to have had an experiences with him, her, it or they, yet for some reason, think that no one else can have a Bigfoot Sasquatch living in the woods behind their home, because, by God, they're the only ones allowed to have a Bigfoot Sasquatch living in the woods behind their home. Ironically, and not by much of a surprise, many of these vertically challenged individuals who live under bridges have small, dickless YouTube channels and they (surprise, surprise) make videos about Bigfoot Sasquatch, and they usually have all of fifteen or twenty subscribers and in truth, they're trying to drive my viewers to their channels. It amazes me how some people simply never learn two things. 1- the golden rule, and 2- you draw more flies with honey than vinegar.

At any rate, here are a few recent examples of people who I've recently prayed for (God, please bring this vertically challenged individual who lives under a bridge the same health, wealth and prosperity you have so blessed my family and me with), and then summarily banned!

~ This guy is a liar. I can't believe he has so many subscribers. I know Bigfoot is real, because I've seen him, but this guy hasn't. He's doing this for money, because he gets money from YouTube, and all you idiots are falling for it. I'm out. Come watch my channel. Where shit is real.

~ I live in Washington State, and I have had first hand encounters with Sasquatch. Everyone knows he lives in the Pacific Northwest. Where is this guy even at? Somewhere in the south? He talks like a hick. I know he's lying. There are no Sasquatches in the south. It's too fucking hot for them.

~ I know this guy is a liar and a fake, but I know Bigfoot is real. We have one in our woods. But we live in Oregon, where Bigfoot does, too. Who has ever heard of Bigfoot living in the south? I hope this guy loses his YouTube channel. His videos are a complete waste of bandwidth.

~ Anything for attention. I know Bigfoot is real. I saw him while hiking in the Rocky's many years ago. I have always kept it to myself, because I don't want the attention. But you can tell this guy is lying. There are too many tells. He just wants attention. All you people who are buying this need to stop giving it to him. It's the only way he'll ever go away. By the way, I never go back to Colorado, because I never want to see Bigfoot again.

~ You can tell these videos are staged. Sure, bigfoot is real, but this guy is fake. If you really want to see a channel that has real bigfoots in it, come to my channel. Please subscribe to it and tell all of your friends to do the same. This guy is a flim flam man.

~ When I was a small child, hiking through the woods with my daddy, I saw a bigfoot. My daddy told me never to tell anyone, because he said it lived in the woods behind our house. I never saw it again, but I know it's back there, all these years later. That's how I know this guy is fake. Yes, bigfoot is real, but he lives in the woods behind my house, and I live in Arkansas. This man claims to be in Virginia, and that's probably a lie, too, but let's give him the benefit of the doubt and say he's up there in Virginia, well then, like I said, he's a liar, because Bigfoot's down here in Arkansas.

~ My husband and I used to be the most outdoorsy couple you'd ever meet. Our love story is one that goes back to childhood. We actually met at 4-H camp, which shows how long we've both been together and outdoorsy. We're in our late forties now, though we don't look like it, because though we're not outdoorsy anymore, for reasons you'll soon understand, we still work out all the time, but in the safe confines of a gym.

Anyway, while on a hiking trip in Idaho, just outside of Coeur D'alene, back at the turn of the current century, we saw something on the trail ahead of us, coming right at us, that was, without a doubt, a Bigfoot Sasquatch. At first, we thought that once it saw us, it would simply turn and run the other way, but that's not what happened.

As we stood there, too afraid to move, we saw that the thing had clearly spotted us. Then, it threw its nose up in the air and started sniffing around. Then, it came running toward us!

"Oh, shit!" I screamed. "I'm on my period!" And I was, and my husband knew I was, because he wanted to start that day with a romp in the sack, but we didn't because of it.

Anyway, I knew that if Bigfoot caught us, he was going to kill my husband and rape me. We have never run as fast as we did that day before or since that day, and we both do 5K charity runs on a regular basis, so that tells you something. We're good runners, and we love giving.

Anyway, we made it safely to our car, a hybrid I'd like to point out, back before hybrids were cool, and though we hated to do it, we decided to become gerbils on treadmills rather than free range spirits in the wild. Though we still run our 5k's, we only run them in the cities, because we love running and we're so giving, and because everyone knows Bigfoot isn't in the cities.

Which brings me to my main point!

Everyone knows there's no bigfoot in the woods behind this guy's house. Virginia? Seriously? Fat rednecks and hillbilly transplants from nearby Appalachia? Sure! Bigfoot? No way. This guy is a liar, and everyone knows it. Does he even run?

The End

(I wish it were, but there'll be more like this tomorrow morning
when I wake up.)

11

Bigfoot Sasquatch Beat Him Into Serenity

*From a letter dated 01-13-2021

Dear Kevin,

I have been an avid follower of your YouTube channel
"Homesteading Off The Grid" since before you went big. I
remember I was one of your first one hundred subscribers. I was
happy for you and your family when you went viral with the
crayon video, which allowed you to quit your 'job you hated that
made you miserable' down at the post office.

Now, with that said, I was a little hesitant about all your Bigfoot
Sasquatch videos once they started, but not because I didn't
believe- trust me, I'm a believer- or because I thought you were
making fun of those of us who do believe, because I knew you
were not. You have a very dry, witty sense of humor that can
come across as something it's not to both the less intelligent
who simply don't get it, as well as the intellectual elitists who

take themselves too seriously to know humor when it presents itself- the smartest guys in the room, as you call them on your YouTube channel. However, I pride myself in being a middler, as Ben Franklin called us, and I get the humor quick and fast, and I am very appreciative of it, especially in this overly serious, overly politicized and overly polarized world.

Why did your Bigfoot Sasquatch videos bother me so much then, you might ask?

Because they simply hit too close to home.

Yes, Kevin, and anyone you care to share this story with (I do give you permission to do so, but please edit my writing first so I don't look uneducated ((*Author's/editor's/Crazy Lake's note- DONE!))), I do have quite the Bigfoot Sasquatch story to tell.

I'm well into retirement now, and I have a wife of more than thirty years, and we raised two kids who I hope turn out okay. So far so good, but they are in their twenties, and they don't seem to know how to hold a conversation that isn't digital. However, I am very proud of the fact that neither of them are violent. They are very peaceful.

And this brings me to my story.

When I was a kid, growing up in Appalachia, like you did, (but a different part of Appalachiastan, not West "By God" Virginia), I was as much a product of hillbilly culture as I'm sure you were and still are, though I'm sure, like me, you fight it. I was quick to anger, I was defensive, and I was insecure as all get out, as we'd say back there back then (I got out, too, and as you can tell by my return address, I now live in Ohio), and would rather punch it out than talk it out, whatever the it was.

I wasn't a big guy, but I was mean as a rattlesnake. For a guy to be named Stacey, like me, you can imagine the bullying one would procure. In traditional hillbilly fashion, anytime anyone picked on me because of my name, calling me a girl and all, I'd light into them like a bolt of lighting. Being as my persecutors were hillbillies as well, they never learned their lesson, nor quit just because of a good old fashioned hillbilly ass whoopin', and they'd come at me again the next day.

However, there was another reason I was always fighting. I had an older brother, who died many years ago now due to health complications associated with a lifetime of illnesses and physical deformities, who all the other kids liked to pick on as well. We all know the saying, "kids can be so cruel." As you know, Kevin, make those kids hillbilly kids in Appalachia and it gets even worse.

My parents, from the time I could remember, put me in charge of my brother's wellbeing when we were out of their sight. While we were out playing, or in the woods, and especially at school. I didn't mind, at first, as it made me feel important- responsible- but in time, this duty became too much for a young child to bear. Not only did I have to defend myself from my own bullies, those mean hillbilly kids who saw fit to make fun of my name, but I also had to defend my brother from all the little assholes who chose to pick on him for having been born differently than they were. And to add insult to injury, if I didn't do it, or if I simply hadn't been with my brother during a time when he'd been bullied, my parents would light my ass up with the buckle end of a belt when I got home.

Anyway, fast forward to our teen years. You can imagine throwing the hormones of puberty into this mix, and I was a hot mess. I was even more angry than usual, fighting and getting into trouble more often, and I remember feeling like I wanted to either run away or die. The only good part of the story during those days is that the beatings at home stopped, because when I was fifteen, I took the belt away from my step father (mom's third husband), and beat holy hell out of him with it. No one in that household ever touched me again.

Though I might be proud of having dealt out an asswhoopin' as a fifteen year old kid to an abusive adult who deserved it, a year after that, I dealt out an asswhoopin' to someone who didn't deserve it.

My brother.

A bunch of us had gone camping up at this old abandoned cabin that used to be occupied by moonshiners back in the day. As always, I had to take my brother with me. My friends were used to this by now, but you see, we had something with us, rather, we'd found something under the old floor boards of that old cabin, that we weren't used to.

Moonshine!

Sure, we'd sneaked the occasional Stroh's beer (and I know you know what that is, since you're a hillbilly, too), from our step-fathers, but we'd never had liquor, especially white lightning. Suffice to say, we got pretty well lit up pretty quick.

For some reason, my brother started talking about Bigfoot. He claimed that during many of the times he slipped away, without anyone knowing exactly where he was, he was up in those very woods where we were camping, hanging out with Bigfoot.

Well, our two other friends who were with us started making fun of my brother for this, and before they even knew what day of the week it was I'd lit into them and whooped 'em both and told 'em to head on off the hill before I put 'em in a grave. They didn't need to be told twice.

I watched those two boys leave, and then I turned around and looked at my brother. I told him I was sick and tired of fighting his fights for him and that if he wasn't able to fight for himself, he needed to stop being such a dipshit. I remember to this day what happened next. He pointed behind me, smiled, and said "Bigfoot."

"You retarded mother fucker!" I said, and for the first and only time in our lives, I punched my brother square in the chin. The place I'd learn while in basic training in the Army (I was drafted during the Vietnam War), they called 'the button.' It's the place boxers aim for, because if you hit it square on, like I did with my brother, you knock your opponent out, and it doesn't even really take a whole lot of pressure.

Well, my brother hit the ground, and just a split second after he did, I heard a growl from behind me. I turned around, and there, only feet away, was…

…you guessed it…

…Bigfoot Sasquatch!

And let me tell ya, it wasn't one of those experiences you hear so much about, where the creature and I made eye contact, and I wet my pants, and the creature turned and ran away, and then I told people about it and it ruined my life, etc. etc. I mean, all that happened, except for the creature turning away part. Oh, it didn't turn away. No, sir!

It gave me one rightly deserved asswhoopin'!

But it was the strangest asswhoopin' I could have imagined.

It didn't really hurt!

You see, the creature didn't rip my head off with his brute strength. He (or she, or it, as you'd say on your YouTube channel) didn't slice and dice me (as we said about the bayonet in the infantry) with its super sharp claws. It simply picked me up and held me above its at least eight feet tall head, and then it threw me down to the ground. And then it did it again.

And again.

And again.

And again!

It was as if the creature was trying to punish me for what I'd done to my brother. But unlike my hillbilly parents and step-parents, it wasn't punishing me, while angry, trying to hurt me for what I'd done- a style of punishment I'd fortunately learn in my own adult years is never acceptable- but it was trying to discipline me out of caring- out of the desire to let me know I'd done wrong and my behavior was not acceptable.

After the beast threw me down for what would be the last time, and then turned and walked away, I felt an odd feeling come over me. It wasn't fear and it wasn't anger. For the first time in my life, I had a sense of serenity. The beast had actually beaten me into a sense of serenity! Other than watching my children enter the world, it is the closest thing to a spiritual experience I've ever had.

When I sat up, my brother was jumping up and down, clapping his hands, saying "Bigfoot! Bigfoot!" over and over.

I stood, dusted my britches off, and I walked up to my brother and I told him I was sorry. He just smiled and laughed and kept saying Bigfoot over and over, like I'd never hit him in the first place. I gave him a big hug and I never hurt him again.

And amazingly, I never hurt anyone else after that, either.

After that experience with this amazing creature that is not supposed to exist, I never had a temper problem. My fuse, which had always been so short, became so lengthy no one could ever burn it down to the detonator.

The following year was my senior year in high school. My teachers noticed the change in me, and upon the urging of our guidance counselor, I actually went to college (a small in state school, but hey, college was like a foreign nation to my family and all the other hillbillies around us), and I graduated, and I was able to leave Appalachiastan and lead what many would call an average, middle class American life, but a life, which as you know, is anything but average when you come from an Appalachian background.

Sadly, my brother passed away before I finished college. He'd outlived the life expectancy they'd given him at birth by many years, so we knew we were blessed to have him when we did and for much longer than we should have, but to this day, his passing is the second biggest heartache I've experienced, the first, of course, being the heartache associated with the time I whooped up on him up there in the woods.

Kevin, I commend you for doing the work that you're doing with your YouTube channel. You are bringing awareness to many people that there are things in this world that are not supposed to exist, but do. And I can't even tell you how much I related to so many of the stories in your completely awesome short story collection, "October Nights." I bought a print copy of the book on Amazon as soon as it came out, and admittedly, read the entire thing before the month of October even rolled around. But I didn't regret it, because having done so allowed me to sit and watch and listen as you read each story from the book each night of October on your YouTube channel. That was a great experience that I hope you do again next fall. I saw some reviews of your book on Amazon that were not flattering due to this fact. People actually giving you shitty reviews because you read the stories on YouTube. I guess they felt like they'd wasted their money buying the book, because they could have just listened to the stories on your YouTube channel, but I guess those people have no idea what it's like to grow up poor in Appalachia, and not have the resources to buy a book (something that is simple for me now, thank God), and have no one care, because you don't belong to the right demographic that garners special interest votes come election day.

Sorry for that digression, as I know you despise politics, as do I, and I'm sure for much of the same reason. Our hillbilly roots.

Anway, I just wanted to send you this letter and share my Bigfoot Sasquatch experience with you and anyone else who would be interested in either hearing about it on your YouTube channel or reading about it in one of your upcoming "Bigfoot Sasquatch Files" volumes, frankly, which is where I'd like to see it, because I've read every one of them and anxiously anticipate the publication of each new volume. (*Author's/editor's/Crazy Lake's note- DONE!)

It's my hope and wish that God continues to bless you and your beautiful little family there on your beautiful little homestead in Virginia. It looks like the perfect place. The beauty of nearby Appalachiastan, without all the dysfunction of, not all, but so damn many of its people.

Your forever fan and YouTube viewer,

Stacey P.

Akron, Ohio

The End

***

The following stories are from Bigfoot Sasquatch Files Volume 9:

1

Uncle Burton's Diary

Uncle Burt, as we called him, though I'm sure his mother would have called him Burton, as a child, at times when he was in trouble, was not a rich man. He was a 'just enough to get by and by God grateful for it' kind of guy.

Uncle Burt, like our entire clan, came from hard working stock, where a man's hard work was rewarded by enough to survive, and even better, the affordance of a great night's sleep. Our people never fancied the finer things in life so materialism was never part of our way. I guess it's why I was surprised when I got a call, last spring, telling me that I'd "inherited" something from my recently deceased uncle Burt.

When I found out that my inheritance was merely a diary, a diary I had no clue the man had kept, my mind was set at ease, rather, my mind was set back to reality, as for a fleeting moment I fancied Uncle Burt having had jars of cold hard cash buried around his property, which his attorney had collected and pooled together, and that I had been deemed the lone recipient of all that cold hard cash.

I asked Mr. Esquire, while I had him on the phone, if he could mail the diary. It was then that I was made aware of the very odd condition that came with my inheritance, that being, that I would only accept the diary while in the presence of Mr. Esquire and only in his offices. I would be locked in the drawing room of Mr. Esquire's offices (as his offices were found to be in an old house built in the late 1880's) where I would read the diary, in its entirety, alone, and then burn the diary in the fireplace, which would be burning hot upon my arrival.

As you can imagine, I found this condition quite odd. Why would I, or anyone, drive nearly four hours, in one direction, to read the diary of a recently deceased man who'd, and with all respect given as I say this, never accomplished *anything* that *anyone* would consider meaningful outside of our little village in Appalachiastan?

As I stated earlier, Uncle Burt was one hell of a hard worker. He was an honest man, and boy, could he really spin a yarn. I'd listened to plenty of his yarns in my youth. But the fact of the matter is, the man never made it past the eighth grade, he spent forty years working as a lumberjack, either logging or driving log trucks, and though he'd been all over the mountains of his native Appalachiastan, he'd never left them, save for the time or two when he ventured back to the motherland of Virginia to visit the beach, both times of which he stated upon returning home, he could have "saved time and money heading over to the lake for a dip." He also pointed out that there, "wouldn't have been so damned many other people around, either."

However, just as I was about to decline my inheritance, I remembered something that Uncle Burt had said to me after telling me one whopper of his yarns. He'd told me the story more than forty years ago, and I remember asking him, when he was finished with the telling, if it were true, and he'd told me that as sure as he and I were breathing air, that it was true. When I'd asked him to prove it to me, which he could have easily done at the time, he told me that he feared doing so, because, in his own words, "the thing was so goddamn close to human (and he *never* took the Lord's name in vain), that I'm a'skeered they'll put me away for manslaughter. And I trust you, boy," he'd continued," but not with my life. Look, let me tell you what I've learned about secrets. The only way to keep a secret between three people is if two of them are dead." But even more chilling than this, what he said next led me to believe that the story was true, and I feel as if I've known this for these past forty years. What he said was, "when I'm dead and safe, I'll prove it to you. Beyond the shadow of any doubt, I'll prove it to you."

"Can I come and do the reading this evening?" I asked Mr. Esquire over the phone after having this memory.

"My offices are open until 5:00 p.m., but I can stay a little later if needed," he said.

"If I leave now," I said, "I can be there by five. I'll call ahead if I'm running behind."

"That will do," he said, and we ended the call. Fifteen minutes later, I was on the road, heading back to the hills of Appalachiastan. The whole while driving, I heard uncle Burt's voice in my head. The voice was retelling the stories from all those years ago. But the story that the voice told the most- over and over as if none of the other stories had even mattered- was the story I will relate to you now.

***

Uncle Burt and I had gone native brook trout fishing. For those readers unfamiliar with the activity, I will point out that it's actually a combination of many activities in one. Firstly, it's part hiking. One cannot successfully fish for native brook trout without walking, at least, five or six miles on an average day of doing so. And it's more than the most simple form of hiking, as there's no trail. There is a slippery, rocky creek bank that often winds, with the creek, under laurel bushes, or through rocky ravines hardly surpassable by a billy goat. There are often steep climbs and equally steep descents, often laden with moss covered rocks and logs. There are briar and bramble patches to crawl through, around, or over, and among all these already treacherous obstacles, there lies the occasional rattlesnake or copperhead, both deadly venomous.

Native brook trout fishing requires quite the stalking ability, so it's one part sniper, for lack of a better description. You see, the very small fish, which, technically are not even a form of trout, but rather an arctic char which were left in certain northeastern streams during the last ice age, when the glaciers had actually pushed their way as far south as central West "By God" Virginia, before retreating and melting, are very skittish. Even if a stiff wind blows a tree branch which is hanging above the small pool of water which they inhabit, the small fish will dart under a rock or the edge of the bank and stay hidden, at times, for the rest of the day, upon sight of said tree branch. So, while one is traversing the rugged terrain where the streams are located that house these small fish (catching one of eight inches or more in length is to catch a real monster), one must do so quietly and cautiously. More than once this writer had spent ten minutes or more sneaking up on a beautiful hole of water, maybe three feet wide by the same length, and about a foot deep, only to stumble over a fallen limb or slip on a rock at the last second and sadly see that beautiful six inch long native brook trout dart up underneath the bank on either side, and not come out again for the day.

One must be a naturalist and a keen observer to successfully fish for native brook trout, for you see, there are constantly different types of insects hatching at different times of the year, and in order to have the most success with catches, one must match one's bait to the hatch. If black gnats are hatching like mad the first of June, using what worked only a week before, a may fly pattern dry fly, won't work at all.

And certainly not lastly, one must be quite proficient at casting. It's not just about hitting one's mark on the water, it's about not hitting the many obstacles before the bait even gets there, like numerous tree branches, boulders, logs, bushes, etc.

"Almost there," Uncle Burt said. We had hiked about four miles upstream. We'd set out at first light and it was nearing noon. Four miles of native brook trout fishing on a stream about a foot and a half wide and eight inches deep, on average, with the occasional pools of six feet by six feet that might have been eighteen inches deep, meant that we were making pretty good time. To this day, I hate to admit this, and it certainly isn't the way I would do things if I could go back and do them differently, Uncle Burt and I both had two dozen brook trout each in our plastic bread bags we used to carry our catches in. We put one hell of a hurting on the native brook trout populations in those mountains. And we had a pretty shitty attitude about it, too. You see, we knew that everyone else kept all the fish they caught. "Catch and release" was a practice we viewed as being for the yuppies who came into our areas from the cities to fly fish once or twice a year so they could go back to their doctors and lawyers offices, where they proudly hung their far too expensive Orvis fly rods over their fake, gas burning fireplaces, and prattle on to their patients and clients about how they are prodigious fly fisherman, and of how they brave the natives and travel into the heart of Appalachiastan twice a year, once in the spring and once in the fall, to catch the most elusive fish to be caught in North America. We locals? "Dumb hillbillies," as those yuppies called us in hushed tones?

We, on the other hand, kept and ate every goddamn fish we caught!

"Right up here's the head of it," Uncle Burt said as we made our final push to where this stream actually started. You see, many of these native brook trout streams we fished were so small that they didn't even show up on any of the topographical maps produced by the Forest Service. Many of them simply shot up out of a spring hole at either the top of a mountain or part of the way down one. The streams may run for only a few miles before flowing into a larger stream (these, of course, are called tributaries), but a good many of them simply gave out. One minute, water is flowing, the next, it just stops. Admittedly, very few of the streams that just stopped had any trout in them, but most of the ones that were tributaries did. The one we'd been fishing on that day was a small tributary that flowed into yet another tributary that was actually recorded on a map, but this stream was too small to have been recorded.

Just above us, the whole time we'd been making our way up the stream, there was a road- the type of road called a haul road. It derived its name from the purpose it had been cut through the forest anyway to serve; the hauling logs from mountain to mill.

Uncle Burt had cut the haul road above us the spring before. We were out on a beautiful fall day, and we'd actually pondered weather to go native brook trout fishing on this particular day or turkey hunting. We had chosen fishing over hunting, knowing that winter would soon come to our part of Appalachiastan, freezing the waters of these small streams and burying the land in feet of snow. We could at least hunt in such weather, so we'd chosen to fish while the weather still permitted, though, there was one such time when this writer went fishing on this same stream later in life, at the age of 17, just to prove that fish could be caught in sub freezing temperatures. I caught three on a day when it was 20 degrees fahrenheit. I had to suck on the last eyelet on my fishing rod after reeling in every cast, because the tiny water beads would turn to ice and lock the line so that I could not cast unless unfreezing the whole mess with my mouth first. By catching those three brook trout that day I'd won a bet with a naysayer. Though the naysayer never paid up, I'd proven my point. Despite weather conditions, all animals must eat.

"Let's head up here to the road and have our lunch," Uncle Burt said.

We walked up the hill just below the point where the stream we'd been fishing actually began. Sure enough, it shot up, as a spring, from underneath a huge limestone boulder. I'd noticed while crawling up the bank to get to the haul road, which was already beginning to grow over with new vegetation, that it appeared as if there was a "sister spring" or "twin spring" as they were both frequently called, coming from underneath an entire collection of rocks that looked almost as if they'd been bulldozed over the hill, as if to cover up the stream.

"Looks like another spring," I said to Uncle Burt as I maneuvered over the rocks and reached the road.

"Yeah," he said. But that was all he said. He made his way to what would have been the log landing, the wide point at the end of this haul road, where he would have loaded, with a huge piece of machinery called a log loader, the actual logs he'd cut down and dragged to this collection point onto the back of whatever timber truck he would have driven up this tight, steep, barely surprassible road. FYI, if you have never watched a logging operation, it is worth searching up and watching on YouTube. It is absolutely amazing, some of the places these loggers take vehicles into the woods, and the work they do there. These men, and a few women who work in the industry, manage to take these behemoth pieces of machinery up what are practically trails that would be challenging for a four wheeler, load them up with an entire truck's worth of logs, and then haul them back off of the mountain and to the mills.

"I was up here alone the last day of this job," Uncle Burt said, biting into a Spam sandwich, a hillbilly delicacy. "I'd already hauled all the logs to the landing, here," he said between chews, "and I was just loading them onto the truck. It was a Saturday. I remember that. It's why Billy and Cephus were off. I came out and got the job wrapped up by myself so that on Monday we could start a new job over in the next county."

Uncle Burt described how he was loading the logs onto the truck by way of the log loader, which actually sits on top of the back of the timber truck. Though separate parts, a timber truck is often one large 'do it all' piece of machinery. It's got to be in order to get all the different parts up into the working area conveniently.

"I'd noticed that big pool of water down there," he said, continuing his story. "I'd been glancing over there the whole time I'd swing around to the left there to grab another log to bring over to the right and load up on the truck. I just knew there were trout in there, and if I could just see one, why, I was gonna bring you up here fishing with me."

"I guess you saw one," I said, lifting my bread bag overfilled with fish.

"I reckon you can say that," Uncle Burt said. "Not just one, but two. And they were both about the biggest native brook trout I'd ever seen in my life. Had to be at least a foot long, each."

"My God," I said. At that time, I'd never caught a native brook trout that big. Years later I would catch one that was thirteen inches long, and to this day, nearly forty years later, I've never caught one that big, since.

"*My God* is right," he said. "But what happened next brought me back to my senses real quick."

"What happened?" I asked. I remember being hungry, but I also remember being so into Uncle Burt's story that I couldn't take another bite of my pb & j until he continued.

"Now, you probably ain't gonna believe this next part," he said, and I became even more excited to hear the next part. How could I not? If he'd already told me it was unbelievable.

"Well," he said, continuing, looking down at the ground as if in deep thought, remembering the events of that day, and completely forgetting that he held a delicious, half eaten Spam sandwich in his hand. "While I was still staring down at those two fish, I was swinging the log I'd just picked up in the pinchers around to the right, over toward the truck. And all of a sudden, I hit something. The boom stopped as the log bounced off of whatever I'd hit."

"What'd'ya hit?" I asked.

"Well," he said. "That's just it. I knew the coast was clear. I'd done swung half a dozen other logs through there. There weren't no other people around. We're miles outta town up here. And it couldn't have been an obstruction. Why, I looked down from the cab, and I couldn't see anything. I figured there might have been a kink in the boom gears or something, so I just loaded that log up and kept on going. I loaded eight or ten more logs and filled the whole truck. It was only after that, when I climbed down from the cab that I realized what I'd done."

Uncle Burt hanged his head, not in shame, but in a way that looked remorseful. "What was it?" I asked.

"This here's the part you probably ain't gonna believe," he said. I said nothing, even as a child knowing it was best to give the man the time needed to collect his next spoken words properly.

"I saw," he said, when he finally spoke, "laying right there in the mud, something that looked like the biggest goddamn man I'd ever seen in my life, except it was naked, and covered with hair, and had the face of…"

"Of what?" I asked after he'd trailed off and didn't seem like he was coming back.

"Well," he said. "That's part of the story. See, I guess when I'd swung that big red oak log around, while I was gawkin' over the hill at those fish, this thing, or this guy, just snuck right up on me, and I never saw him, or it, and I smashed him right in the face with that big 'ol log that had to weigh a ton if it weighed an ounce, and I just caved his whole face right in. Looked like the front of his head had been smashed in by a cannonball the size of a large watermelon."

I sat in silence, knowing not what to say. Burt sat in silence, as well, fearing he might say too much. When he finally spoke again, he said, "I'll be goddamned if I didn't go and kill one of them there Bigfoot Sasquatches!"

"No way!" I said.

"Yes way!" he said, and as if he'd never been touched, emotionally, by the retelling of the story, he once again took up eating his delicious Spam sandwich.

"Is this story true?" I asked him. I knew he could tell some whoppers, but the way he'd acted during the telling of this particular story led me to believe that this story was not a whopper, but a confession.

"As sure as you and I are breathing air right now, this story is true," he said.

"Prove it," I said. He told me that he could and that he'd love to, but that the thing he'd killed with the log had so closely resembled a human being that he was afraid that he'd get locked up for manslaughter. He told me he trusted me as much as he trusted anyone, but that one of the cold hard facts that he'd learned about life was that the only way to keep a secret between three people was if two of them were dead. He told me not to worry, though, because he said that when he died, and could no longer be carted off to prison, he'd prove it.

***

For the life of me, I will never cease to be amazed how steep the mountains of Appalachiastan are. No matter how many times I go back, though I'll admit it is not often, and it's intentional, I'm always aghast at the sheer, steep climbs. I spent a couple of years living on the west coast, and folks out there liked to tell me that we didn't even *have* mountains back east. We only had *hills* they claimed. Their Rockies and their Cascades were real mountains, they would tell me. I had to give it to them, because in so many ways they were right. But I'd always challenge these one uppers to come back east with me and hike a day through the Appalachians and see if they could walk the next day. I never got any takers.

I rolled into the offices of Mr. Esquire just as darkness fell. It wasn't quite night yet, it was evening, but being that it was the month of March, and the shifting of the clocks forward had not yet occurred, it was still getting darker a bit earlier than I preferred.

"Are you prepared to follow the instructions as I gave them to you?" Mr. Esquire asked.

"I am," I said. He then handed me the diary, which had a lock on the front of it as well as a sealed envelope. "What's this?" I asked, nodding toward the envelope I held in my left hand, while holding the diary in my right.

"Instructions to find the key," he said.

He grabbed me by the elbow, ever so lightly, and guided me into an adjacent room where a single, straight backed leather chair sat before a raging fire. There was a couch off to the side of the room with an end table beside it. "I'll lock you in from the outside," he said. "When you are finished and want out, simply knock."

"Okay," I said, feeling as if I'd somehow been swept into an early 1900's English novel.

Mr. Esquire left the room. I could hear the lock latch as he turned the key from the outside. I sat in the straight backed chair before the fire and stared into the flames. I found myself thinking that I could not believe I'd just driven four hours to perform such a task. What on earth could be in this diary? And how more could it answer my question from all those years before than by simply stating the story was true? Weren't there better things I could be doing with my time?

Without further thinking or further hesitation I opened the envelope. There was a piece of paper inside, upon which was written a single, simple sentence.

"Look under your cushion."

I stood and pulled up the cushion on the chair upon which I'd been sitting, and sure enough, there was a small, silver key there. I took it up, replaced the cushion, then sat back down before the fire. I put the key in the latch of the diary, opened it, and found that the entire book was empty, save for one page. A page close to the middle had been marked by way of the ribbon marker protruding from the spine of the diary. There was a note here- nay, a letter- and it read...

"K,

If you're reading this, before a blazing fire in Mr. Esquires offices, then I trust you never quite got over your curiosity of the story I told you years ago.

Before I "prove" to you, the truth of my tale, I must first point out my fascination about the single biggest question you never asked me either at the time I told you my tale, or later, when you had nearly forty years to ask it, that question being, 'what did I do with the body?'

I'm glad, K, that you never asked this question, because as an honest man, I was never good at lying, and I feared this question would come from you, and there would be no way I could get out of letting you know the answer. If your lack of questioning in this regard was intentional, I thank you, from my grave, for saving me the awful situation of having to either lie or answer it out right.

With this said, I will now give you the answer to that question you never asked.

I buried it!

Where?

I must first point out that on the day that I told you the story, I did tell one lie. I hesitated, forgetting I held a delicious Spam sandwich in my hand at the time, doing my best to keep a poker face so you would not discover my dishonesty. I suppose it worked.

It wasn't untrue that my mind had been distracted by my viewing of two large native brook trout in the hole of water off to my left. That is very true. The part that is not true is that it was the wrong hole of water.

If you'll remember, as we climbed that creek bank, all those years ago, you pointed out that it appeared as if another stream was coming from another spring which was under rocks- rocks, if you'll remember, that appeared to have been pushed over the hillside by a bulldozer.

K, it appeared as if there was another stream here, coming from another spring, because there was. Before those rocks were there, rocks that I did, indeed, push into the hollow with the blade on the front end of my log skidder, there was a sister hole which appeared nearly identical to the other hole of water that you did see. It was in this hole that two large native brook trout tread water, and into this hole that I did peer, as I carelessly swung a log around to my right, without looking first, and smashing it into the face of a creature that was nearly as human as you and I.

As I mentioned to you the day I told you this story, what I'd killed was so human that I honestly felt as if I might go to prison for killing it. I had not harmed the creature intentionally, and I meant no malice in what I did next, but I was out to save my own hide.

I pushed the creature, which had to have been eight feet tall and weigh nearly eight hundred pounds, over the hill and into that beautiful pull of water where I'd been staring at those beautiful trout, though understandably, trout were the furthest things from my mind by this time. Then, I pushed every large rock and small boulder I could find into the ravine, burying the body with mostly limestone and sandstone, and then I was sure to flatten it out, as best as I could, so as to make it all appear natural. I'll admit that part of taking you fishing there so that you could see the area was to make sure someone who didn't know what had happened wouldn't be able to tell that the land had been manipulated. I guess my workmanship passed the test, at least yours.

Does this prove to you, K, that my story is true? In my mind, it does. In your mind, it might not. If you want further proof from this point, well, that is up to you. You're a clever man. I know you can figure out what to do next if there is a next step for you. As far as I'm concerned, I know I can rest in eternity, having taken this secret to my grave, but also having made my confession posthumous.

Now, burn this diary, you dumb hillbilly!

Love,

Uncle Burt"

***

I sat, staring into the fire, pondering the validity of the "confession" as it were, that I'd just read. Could this be true? Was this a prank from Uncle Burt from beyond the grave? An excellent storyteller he'd always been, but a prankster? It had never been his way.

I stood slowly, tossed the diary into the fire, which was now beginning to burn down a bit, and I sat back down and watched the book burn. After it had burned beyond recognition, I rose, turned and walked to the door. I rapped on it lightly with the knuckle of the middle finger on my right hand. I could hear the more than a century old floor boards on the other side of the room creaking as Mr. Esquire came to free me from my chamber.

As Mr. Esquire opened the door, he held a pillow and a folded blanket. "I know it's quite a drive back to the motherland of

Virginia," he said. "And it's getting late. FYI, the couch in the same room in which you are leaving is more comfortable than any motel bed in the county (there *are* no hotels in this part of Appalachiastan- only really shitty run down motels), and if you'd like to spend the night, you're welcome to do so. There is food a'plenty in the kitchen, and you can let yourself out in the morning.

I thought for a minute, and it was obvious that Mr. Esquire could read my thoughts as he grinned at my ponderance. It was not the long drive back to the motherland of Virginia that made me consider staying. It was the certain head of a certain hollow between two certain hills where a stream not located on any topographical maps lay that was piquing my curiosity and tempting me to stay.

"That's kind of you, Mr. Esquire," I said. "I believe I'll take you up on your offer."

He smiled as he handed me the pillow and the blanket. He turned to leave, and as he grabbed the doorknob of the front door, he turned, and simply said, "there are a few things in a sack you might be needing. Just inside the closet, there." With this, he nodded toward a door in the room in which I would sleep before the fire, and then he walked out the front door, shut it and locked it.

With that I was alone.

Out of curiosity, I made my way to the door which he'd nodded toward, opened it, and within found a large, green military style luggage sack. I opened it and found that it contained a pickaxe and a shovel and three pairs of gloves.

I went to the couch, lay out my bedding, got under the blanket and shut my eyes.

But I didn't sleep a wink all night!

***

Around 4:00 a.m. I gave up. What was the use? It was well into the next day, though the sun still lacked a couple hours from rising. I would not wait for it. I would leave. However, my destination was not my comfortable, vast estate back in the motherland of Virginia. It was up one of the deepest, darkest hollows in Appalachiastan. So far up, as our native son and hero Chuck Yaeger would have said, that they "had to pump sunshine into it."

After an hour and a half's drive up several old roads that got only smaller and smaller, more narrow with each passing mile, I came to the point where vehicle would no longer take me, even though said vehicle is a totally awesome Dodge Ram 1500 four wheel drive pick 'em up truck that would make any Prius owner's you know what go limp upon sight. Came now the rest of the journey that could only be made on foot.

I was a mile up the trail when the sun came up bright enough for me to see. I'd had no problem making my way in the pre-dawn light, more like a glow for those late risers who aren't familiar with the light of early dawn, as the old haul road Uncle Burt had cut himself all those years ago still remained, though there were now trees littered throughout it, some nearly two feet in diameter. Time marches on, saplings and seedlings become mighty trees, and men and women grow old.

An hour after the sun had risen, I reached my destination. The old log landing on top of the mountain. Though I remain, to this day, in great shape, participating in the occasional 5k road race for charity, it had been so long since I'd hiked up one of those "hills" in Appalachiastan, and I was reminded of the challenge I used to give my mates back on the west coast- the challenge that none of them ever accepted- and it damned near got the best of me.

Without wasting any time I began removing rocks that made flat land of where I knew originally there was a ravine. Though temperatures had been in the eighties the day before when I'd left my beautiful home in Virginia, the temperatures, at this high elevation in Appalachiastan, hovered around forty. There was still snow and ice, and it made for a slower go of it, but rock by rock, stone by stone, I made my way through the earth. After an hour's time of work, I reached running water. The original spring.

But I found nothing.

No skeleton, no skull, no nothing.

"I'd been had!" I said to myself, sitting beside the bank well into mid morning. I opened the old military luggage sack again and took out two sandwiches I'd made just before leaving the offices of Mr. Esquire. Havarti cheese and uncured salami on wheat bread with fat free mayonnaise. Mr. Esquire and I, it appeared, had similar tastes in cheese and meats. I could not imagine how far Mr. Esquire had driven, though, to find the havarti, for they certainly did not sell havarti cheese in the part of Appalachiastan where his offices were located.

"That's it!" I said, thinking of Mr. Esquire. "They are in on it together!"

And they had to be. How could they not be? The way Mr. Esquire had simply told me of the tools in the sack in the closet. Tools he knew would come in handy for some sort of digging. How could he not have been aware of that for which I'd be digging?

Further, he'd intentionally lured me into staying the night at his offices. He seemed far too ready with that pillow and blanket when he'd unlocked the door and opened it. It was as if he wanted to make sure I did not flee.

"Those sons-a-bitches!" I said, peeling the crust off my sandwich and throwing it to the other side of the water hole that I'd uncovered. It was then, and only then, that my thoughts stopped in their tracks.

The bit of bread I'd tossed to the other side of the water hold had been caught, just above ground level, by what appeared to be a stick. But this stick was not quite the color of any stick I'd seen before. At most, it resembled the color of a sycamore tree, but there were no sycamores in the area. Further, the end of it appeared to have been whittled, by a knife, and the odds of such a thing seemed completely remote to me.

I stood, and already wet from the knees down, walked through the water and to the other side of the small pool. I bent over to inspect the bread and the "stick" upon which it had been caught. This is when a sudden terror came over me, as I realized this was no stick.

It was a bone.

A finger bone!

But unlike any finger bone I'd ever seen (not that I'd seen many finger bones, if any), it was huge!

I removed the bread crust from the bone and then began removing some of the other stones and soil around the finger. What I found was that this finger was attached to an entire hand!

I've attended only one NBA basketball game in my life. It was the Washington Wizards vs. the Miami Heat, and the game had been held in Washington, D.C. This was during the second, and what would be the final year of Michael Jordan playing for the

Wizards, as well as in the NBA, despite having already retired twice before this. I knew that seeing Jordan play (Shaquile O'neal was playing that night, as well, for the Heat), live, would be a piece of history that I would regret missing if I didn't go to at least one game that year, and to this day, I'm glad I did.

My point here is that during that game, I remember being so impressed by how small the basketball looked in the hands of those NBA players. They palmed the basketball like I would palm a baseball. Their hands were that big! And I explain this to the reader, now, because what I can tell you of the skeletal remains of the hand I unearthed that day in the spring which had formerly been hidden for the past forty years would have made those NBA players' hands appear as small as their hands made my hand appear to be.

"Oh, my God!" I said, as I stared at the hand, now coming up from the soil and the rocks. And it was so much more than just a hand. It was a hand that was attached to a wrist, which I would assume was attached to an arm, which was attached to a torso, etc. etc. "Oh, my mother fucking God!"

Immediately, without taking the time to think, I climbed out of the ravine, bringing my luggage sack and tools with me. Tired as I was, I made sure to bury the hand and the pool itself with a couple feet's worth of stone and rock. I hadn't covered it nearly as well as Uncle Burt had forty years before, but I'd covered it enough to allow that which had been hidden for an equal period of time to remain hidden going forward.

Fortunately, the long walk back to my totally awesome, like new Dodge Ram 1500 4x4 pick 'em up truck that would make the you know what of any Prius owner go limp upon sight was all downhill. Once back to my truck, I threw my supplies in the back seat and began the long drive back to my beautiful, comfortable, vast estate in the motherland of Virginia. I did not return Mr.

Esquire's sack and the tools within, but I will be sending them back UPS (because the post office sucks!).

And I am certain that Uncle Burton's secret, the secret that he took to the grave, will become a secret once again, once either Mr. Esquire or myself pass on to the other side.

The End

2

Are They Hunters? Or Haint They?

"This one would be easy to solve," comment number 87 said. "Just go talk to the neighbors and see if they're letting people hunt on their land."

Of course every other word of the sentence you just read was misspelled before I fixed it.

"I'm done!" read comment number 103. "This asshat could easily go up there and talk to the people on the next property and find out if they hunt or if they let other people hunt on their land. This guy is so fake. He is a scam artist. If you really want to see Bigfoot, come over to my channel (name of channel omitted), where I will show you real proof."

Ah, the joys of working in social media, where everyone's an expert, a critic, and just an all around asshole in general.

Okay, not those of you reading this book. Especially if you read all of the preceding volumes before it. Honestly, you guys are part of the select few that keep me going. I know that not everyone who watches the videos on my YouTube channel "Homesteading off the Grid" is a vertically challenged individual who lives under a bridge.

There's just so damn many of them!

Okay, what is this tirade about?

It's about a series of just a few videos that I uploaded between Christmas of 2020 and just after the New Year of 2021. In the videos, we could very clearly see at least one, at times two, and potentially three upright walking, bipedal creatures. In all of the videos, it was just before dark, and they were spotted toward the top of the hill behind my property, close to where the property line is with one of my neighbors. In one of the videos, the culprits were clearly caught walking toward the setting sun in the west, and in another, they were captured walking away from the setting sun, heading east. In one of the videos, it appeared as if what may have been the third of these "entities" (I'll refrain from calling them 'creatures' at this time, as the jury is still out), actually shimmied up a tree and then simply vanished.

There's a bit of backstory to these videos, and I believe it's worth noting here, though I did note most of it in the videos themselves, but it bears repeating.

There are three things I love most in this life. My wife, our son, and my afternoon naps. I have a real love hate relationship with my afternoon naps in the winter because of the short daylight hours. It's actually easier for me to grab my naps in the winter, because the weather outside is often such that I can easily choose not to do any work outside on bad days without feeling guilty, and I can choose, instead, to nap in front of the woodstove- if aforementioned wife and son are not home- or I can nap upstairs in the bed that's in my office- the very room in which I sit now as I write these words. It helps that there is no gardening or lawn work going on in the winter. Winter is the time of year in which I get most of my reading, writing, well, and napping done.

Oh, and another part of these naps? I wear earplugs. My wife and our son have not learned the fine art of verbally communicating with each other by actually walking into the same room where the other is before addressing them. So, if I want to actually get to sleep and stay to sleep if my family is home, I have to use earplugs. They help, unless my son lets our psychotic cat, Cleopatra, in or out of the house, as my son, who is now ten as of this writing, has not mastered the fine art of shutting a door without slamming it.

I digress.

But that's what I do.

And supposedly (ooh, the word 'potentially' was almost appropriate here, but not quite), you folks who have made it to volume nine of this epic endeavor that has no planned end in sight like that.

So, anyway, I remember the first time I saw the figures on the hill above my house. I'd been taking one of my beautiful, beautiful naps, and when I awakened, I glanced out my bedroom window that faces the back of our property. I stared up into the beautiful, beautiful woods, as I so often do, trying to gauge how much daylight I might have left to go outside and split and stack some firewood, not just a necessary chore due to our lifestyle, but one of my most enjoyable hobbies. I honestly believe I would cut, split and stack firewood even if I didn't have a woodstove or a fireplace, I love doing it so much.

There have been times I've laid in bed, watching out the window, that I've seen deer walking through the woods or in my field or meadow. I've seen hawks, turkeys and even bears. But on this particular late afternoon in December of 2020, I saw something out my window that had me bolting straight up and my heart racing.

Two of them!

I'd seen what appeared to be, at first, two men walking through the woods. Actually, 'walking' isn't the best description here. A better term might be 'stalking.' For you see, it was as if each of the two figures had been hiding behind a tree- separate trees- and almost like synchronized swimmers, they moved from behind the trees hiding them, and simply positioned themselves behind trees that were only a few feet behind the original trees, again, both choosing to hide behind separate trees.

Now, I'll point out that my mind had already decided that I would not be going out and splitting and stacking any firewood, because there couldn't have been twenty minutes of daylight left. This was late December, when the days are shortest, when it gets dark at 5:00 p.m. It was a quarter till five, so the best I could do, as I saw it at the time, was to remain in bed, still as a church mouse, and keep my eyes on the trees where the two figures seemed to be hiding. I watched, until it was too dark to see outside, and I did not see the figures come back out from behind those trees.

I hadn't had my smartphone with me that first day that I saw the figures in the woods from my window, but I made sure to take it upstairs with me when I napped every day after that. Sure enough, three days later, my mysterious figures returned. It was as if they'd been watching me nap the whole while, from a distance of nearly a quarter of a mile away, and then began heading up the hill once they'd noticed I'd woken up.

This time, having my smartphone, I was ready for them. I actually opened my window and walked out onto the snow and ice covered roof to record them. Probably not the smartest idea I'd ever had, but I wanted to get the scene on camera. I did, though I could not detect the perpetrators in the video, so I took things a step farther and uploaded and published the video to my YouTube channel, hoping maybe some of our viewers could spot the beings. No one did, to my knowledge, and I'm sure the whole thing made me look like a paranoid, delusional schizophrenic. But hey, when the word "crazy" is part of your nickname, you don't allow such trifles to bother you and you live the way you want to live, despite what others who see you doing so care or say. We've all heard the saying, "dance like nobody's watching." I've tweaked that a bit to my liking, which is "I dance like I don't give a fuck who's watching," and there is a difference, and I'm willing to bet that if you're reading this book, meaning you've made it this far with me on this journey called life, you totally get the difference. Peas in a pod we are, you salty old soul!

Anyway, as much as I really hated to do it, I put off my naps for the next several days. I wanted to make sure that I was awake, and outside, and armed and loaded with my smartphone when and if these sons-a-gunses came back.

And they did come back!

On two separate occasions!

Long story short (I know, too late), I captured the figures on camera and published the capture in two separate videos. You can go to my YouTube channel "Homesteading Off The Grid" and watch the videos and clearly see these figures for yourself. The titles of the videos are, "VINDICATED!!! He Clearly Captures TWO Of Them Walking Through The Woods On Camera! TWICE!!!" and "Two Stand Guard At The Top Of The

Hill While A Third Swings THROUGH THE TREETOPS To Take The Candy!" The titles are long and so are the videos, but hey, that's me, and you can see 'em.

Though I could not tell, from the distance, exactly what the figures were- neighbors, hunters, trespassers, or... wait for it...

Bigfoot Sasquatch!

...I was tickled pink to get it on video and upload and publish it to the channel. For years now, since I've been pursuing what in the hell ever it is that may or may not live in the woods behind my home, I have been called crazy, paranoid, a drug addict, and many, many other things. Like the title of the first of the two videos suggests, I was happy to finally be vindicated.

Or so I thought.

Though I've worked in social media for more than ten years now, and though I understand it to be the gutter of the internet better than anyone, my best- actually capturing these unexplainable entities on camera- still wasn't good enough, as evidence by the way this story started, as well as the hundreds of other similarly flavored comments left on those videos.

So, you might be asking, what's the big deal about going up and asking your neighbors if they hunt or if they allow others to hunt on their property?

Okay, here's the big deal.

It's none of my goddamn business what my neighbors are doing or allowing others to do on their properties!

Nor is it any of my neighbor's goddamn business what I do, or what I allow others to do on my property.

It's as simple as that.

Well, you might ask, why not explain the situation to your neighbor, and yada yada yada...

Because it doesn't matter!

Many people who watch our videos have no idea what it's like to live out in the country and in the south. Sure, there's that stereotypical southern charm shit we're known for, and a lot of it's real, but when it comes to a man's (or woman's) home here in the south, which includes their laid, that is his or her castle, and one really needs to view that property line as a mental moat, because if crossed, uninvited, one faces meeting real life crocodiles in the form of the land or homeowner meeting you with a firearm, and the fact that your property borders there's doesn't make a lick of a shit's difference. If you go uninvited and unwanted (and trust me, if you've not been invited, it's because you're not wanted), you stand to face a good ass-whooping, to have no-trespass papers served against you, or getting shot!

And yes, I'm serious!

"My neighbors in my subdivision aren't like that, thank God," people have commented on videos where I've pointed this out.

I've held back responding to these people thus: "Dear yuppie. That's why you live in a subdivision, and we country folk don't. Please do us all a favor and stay in your subdivision (we actually had a couple yuppies from a subdivision buy a property close by and what asshole nightmares *they* were for a couple years- always wanting to come over and 'pull on your ear' if they saw you out- faking an interest in *how* you're doing to find out *what* you're doing- fucking assholes). Oh, and keep driving your Priuses, because we need all the gasoline for our big four wheel drive pickups and SUVs."

Sorry, I regress.

But that's what I do.

Most call it a segway in storytelling.

And FYI, I've had dealings with these bastards that live around me. Most notably, the annoying neighbor I drove off with the crayon. But that's not the property in question here. This guy, and I've had one dealing with him as well, and it was pleasant and cordial, would eat that guy for lunch. Once, our first year here, when a large tree limb from a large oak had fallen right on our property line, I made my way back to his multi-million dollar spread and asked permission to cut it up. I told him I wasn't sure exactly where the line was, so I wanted to ask permission first. He thanked me for asking, told me to take it, as well as any other free fallen timber or branches or sticks that are close to the line and to never, under any circumstances step foot on his property again. He didn't care about me, my family, what we did, where we've been. He assured us that he felt we were pretty good people, just by the way we asked before taking that limb, but he wanted us to understand fully that he didn't give a goddamn about us or anyone else, thank you, have a good day.

My take on it?

He is the perfect neighbor in my book, because I feel the very same way about him and the rest of the people who live around me. I have always viewed friends, neighbors, and business associates as three separate entities that should never mix, and for the life of me, I can't understand why so many other people cannot grasp that simple concept.

Oh well, for them there are subdivisions.

So, I'm no expert on getting on well with neighbors, but I know a guy...

Okay, that was my lame impression of that Pawn Stars guy that inspired all those memes years ago. But I actually do know a guy who lives on the foot of the mountain behind my house, at the other side of the guy's property I just described. It's not so much a mountain as it is a hill in a series of mountains; the Blue Ridge Mountains to be specific.

We're going to call this guy Carl, because that's not his real name. If one were to walk up the hill behind my house, to the point where we captured the two, if not three figures on film, you would hit the top of the hill which consists of about one thousand acres, which is now split up and owned by half a dozen different families. It was once all part of one piece of property, but the guy who bought it last in its entirety has sold it off piecemeal over the years. The original house he'd built up there was worth about a million, but I guess the woman who bought it from him considered it substandard living, so she immediately put another million dollars worth of upgrades in it.

Once you cross down the other side of the hill, you hit Carl's land. Carl probably has half a dozen acres or so, like myself. Carl is about seventy years old and retired (I'll not say from what), and he strikes me as a gentleman homesteader, much like myself. However, he actually has some horses and cows and chickens, whereas I just have some chickens and rabbits, and potentially, a few head of Bigfoot Sasquatch.

Now, to be honest about it, I rode my mountain bike up the road that goes up that hill behind my house once. I was scared half to death the whole time I was doing it, because of reasons I've mentioned earlier. Some folks wouldn't hesitate a bit to blow a mountain biker off of his mountain bike with a shotgun. The road itself is a state road, which legally means one can travel on the road, but let me tell you, there is court house laws, and then there are country laws, and some folks wouldn't hesitate to drag your mountain bike just inside their property line once they blasted you off of it with their twelve gauge.

I can hear you as you're reading this. "I don't think these people, especially if they're so rich, would behave this way, Crazy Lake."

What I would say to you is, "you don't know too many rich Rednecks."

As it happened, I was out jogging past Carl's homestead around mid-January, about a week after I'd captured whatever I'd captured on video, and I saw that Carl was out. Now, I'd waved at Carl a time or two, and he always waved back, but he never smiled. In "out in the country" body language that means, "I'll be friendly to you and wave at you in passing, but for the love of Christ don't waste my time trying to come over here and talk to me."

I took a big chance that day, because I'd actually intended to jog up the mountain. Since I'd been up there once on my bike and hadn't been shot, I was willing to take the chance. I knew the mountain was steep, but I wanted to see if I could get a glimpse of anything strange from a closer vantage point.

"Excuse me, Sir," I said, slowing down as I got closer to Carl. He was petting one of his horses which was on their side of the fence, just off from the side of the road. "Is it okay if I jog up that road? Or do you think I'll get shot?"

"Well," he said, taking the hand he'd been scratching his horse behind the ear with and beginning to scratch behind his own ear. "I don't want to say you'd get shot, but there's some assholes live up there that would probably come out and tell you what for if they saw you."

"Oh," I said, deflated.

"It's a state road," he continued. "But you know how assholes are."

"I do," I said. "I found out real quick shortly after I moved in." I went on to tell him, the brief version- not the eighteen minutes and thirty six seconds long version- of my experience with the annoying neighbor I had to run off with a crayon.

"If he ever comes back," he said, referencing the annoying neighbor. "Just pick up the biggest stick you can find and go upside his head with it."

"Really?" I said.

"Yeah," he said. "Oh, (name omitted, but he was talking about the annoying neighbor) ain't nothing but an old pervert. He got fired from the university for being a peeping Tom."

"Really," I said.

"Yeah," he said again. "Really."

I got some more dirt on the old pervert hay collector, dirt that so far has turned out at least four more totally awesome short stories (remember a few volumes back? When our heroine Jane took 'ol PT back to Appalachiastan and had him disappeared? Well, that's where that story came from- but how did I write it before Carl told me about it? Well, some of this is being told out of order- I mean, I *am* a storyteller- but you get the point), and then I got to the point.

"I'm curious," I said to Carl. "And it's none of my business, but I'm just curious. But do you know if any of them assholes up there have been hunting or allowing others to hunt on their property above mine lately?" I didn't have to tell Carl where I lived, because that's another thing about country life. I'd been here four years by this time, so I guarantee you everyone with five miles of me knows where I live. And, since I jog and mountainbike all over the place, I can pretty much tell you who lives where within a four or five mile radius of my house.

"Been hearing gunshots?" Carl asked, and I could tell by the way he cocked one eye when he looked at me, and by the tone of his voice when he asked, that he knew I'd not been hearing any gunshots.

"No," I said.

"Then why would you think that there may be someone hunting up there?"

"Well," I began, and then I gave him the short version of the story I've written of here, in regard to the two videos I recorded and published on YouTube. After I finished my story, Carl just stared at me, saying nothing.

"Well," I said. "Are they hunters or ain't they?"

"What you should say," he said, "is, are they hunters or haint they?"

"That's what I said," I said.

"No," Carl said. "You said ain't. I said haint."

"Haint," I said. "You mean like ghosts?"

"Well, you're a southern boy, afterall, aren't ya," Carl said, and he lightened up and laughed for the first time.

"Not really," I said. "I grew up across the state line in Appalachiastan, but I've spent the majority of my adult life over here."

"I thought you talked funny," he said, and then he laughed again. "Hey, did you know the toothbrush was invented in Appalachiastan?" He asked.

"Yeah, I know," I said, rolling my eyes, "because if it had been invented in any other state it would have been called the teethbrush."

"I bet you've heard 'em all, haven't you," Carl said, his laughter finally dying down.

"Yeah," I said.

"Okay," Carl said, serious now. "All I'll tell you, is that there's been times, all around these parts, when folks have thought they've seen people out hunting or trespassing in general on their land. They've run out, sometimes guns a blazin', to run 'em off, only to get almost right up on 'em and have 'em disappear, as if into thin air."

"Really," I said.

"Boy, you love that word, don't you," Carl said, and then he kept on talking like I'd never spoken at all.

"And there's been some folks," he continued, "who have sworn the folks they'd run up on were wearing civil war uniforms. Some blue. Some gray."

He paused and looked at the ground, as if in deep thought. I remained silent, not wanting to interrupt his train of thought, but after he went past the standard eleven seconds of silence no American can comfortably take any longer while in conversation I spoke again.

"Do you believe them?"

"Believe, 'em," he said, and he laughed again. "I not just believe. I agree with 'em, because I've experienced it myself."

"Really?" I said.

"Back to that word again," he said, chuckling. "Oh, every few years or so, I see 'em. I call 'em the sentries. Like you, I've noticed 'em up on the top of the hill, up on that asshole's land there. So I never went up and approached 'em. But I used to be friends with that old asshole up there, back when he owned the whole mountain, before he drank away most of his money he'd inherited and became paranoid about everyone and everything. What I'll tell you is he don't hunt and he don't allow no one else to hunt up there, either. And you aint' seein' no trespassers."

"So you're telling me I'm seeing ghosts," I said.

"You say last week was the first time you've seen 'em?" he said.

"Yeah."

"And you've been out here for four years now?"

"Yeah."

"Sounds about right," he said.

"What do you mean?" I asked.

"That's about how long it's been since I've seen 'em," Carl said. "And they stay pretty regular. Every few years, no more than five years apart at most, they come around. Doin' their rounds."

I couldn't believe what I was hearing, but I fully did believe what I was hearing.

"I'm gettin' up there in years," Carl said. "And my vision isn't quite what it used to be. Nor is my memory. I used to remember to look up there and see if I could see 'em, but I guess I'd forgot almost plum about 'em until you just brought it all back up."

"Wow," I said. "That is freaking amazing."

"Guess they don't believe in that stuff where you come from," he said, as if he felt I was doubting his story.

"Oh, no," I said. "Quite the opposite. Especially with me, personally." I hesitated a minute, but figured I'd strike while the iron was hot. "Have you ever seen or heard tell of any cryptids out here?"

"Any what?" Carl said, obviously having never heard the word before.

"Cryptids," I said. "You know, like Bigfoot Sasquatch."

Carl looked me straight in the eyes, with a look on his face that was as serious as a heart attack, and said, "why you wise ass little punk."

"What?" I said.

"So I tell you I've seen some civil war ghosts, and you're gonna go and call me crazy like that?"

"Crazy!" I said. "I wasn't trying to call you crazy. I was trying to find out if there's been any Bigfoot Sasquatch sightings around here, because frankly, when I saw those figures, I thought that might be what it was."

"Bigfoot," he said, disapprovingly. "Sasquatch."

"Yeah," I said, and I stood, speechless, as did he. We were having a stare down and a saying nothing down. He who spoke first would surely lose.

"Bigfoot Sasquatch," he said.

"Yeah," I said. Again we stood at a stalemate.

Suddenly, Carl threw his head back with the most maniacal laughter I'd heard in years. "Bigfoot Sasquatch! Hole-e-hell-shit boy! Ah hahahaha. Bigfoot Sasquatch!" And he continued to laugh.

"That's okay, Carl," I said and I turned to leave. "You don't have to call me crazy, either."

I began jogging back toward my house, on the other side of the asshole's mountain above us, and I heard Carl shout out, "hey" after I'd gotten about twenty yards away from him.

I stopped, and I turned to look at Carl. He was standing by his horse, giving me a look as serious as he'd given me any other time that day. "Around here," he said, "we just call him

Sasquatch," and then he turned and began walking up the hill toward his house.

I ran back to where we'd been standing while we'd been talking and shouted at Carl as he walked away. "So you've seen him, too?" I asked. "Have others?"

Carl simply threw his hand up in the air, to both wave at me and to wave me off. He never spoke again, and he never turned back around to face me. Discouraged, I turned and was back on my way to finish my run.

I've seen Carl a couple of times since that day, and each time I've started to either jog toward him or bike toward him to follow up with the questions he wouldn't answer that day, and both times, he saw me coming, and he conveniently darted back to his house.

I guess, in a way, that's Carl's way of giving me the answer I was looking for, anyway.

The End

The Unfortunate Demise Of Dirty Dick

(Originally Titled: The Unfortunate Demise Of The Dirty Dick)

"We have a problem," sheriff's deputy Burt Reynolds said to Dr. (honorary) Drake as he took off his patrol cap and held it in front of his crotch, as if trying to hide a woody. Drake, who'd been at the side of his house splitting firewood, the old fashioned way, with a ten pound sledge hammer and a diamond maul, had seen him pull up the long drive and walked over at the end of the drive to meet him.

"What's the problem, Bandit?" Drake asked, holding in a laugh.

"Yeah," Reynolds said, emotionless, "like I said when we first met, that one never gets old." He glanced over Drake's shoulder at the work he'd been doing. He mentally noted that Drake appeared to have literal dump truck loads of logs on his property, most of which, it appeared, had already been split into firewood and stacked neatly to season. "You cutting and splitting all this by hand?" he said.

"Yeah," Drake said.

"You need a gas powered log splitter."

"People who can't, or who don't, being critical of people who can, or who do, never gets old," Drake said.

"Touche," Reynolds said. "Look," he spoke again, quickly. "We got something we've got to deal with."

"What asshole who I'm sure deserved it went missing this time?" Drake asked, resting his ten pound sledge hammer at his right side and resting most of his body weight on that.

"No one," Reynolds said. "Well," he hesitated. "There was a postal worker just before Christmas past, but…"

"But?" Drake said.

"I was in there to mail something out once. Just as she was going on her lunch break. Trust me, that bitch deserved it, so I never came to see you."

Drake said nothing. He continued to look at Reynolds, waiting for the reasoning of his business that constituted his visit. Most people, at surface value, would think that one of Drake's greatest combined blessings and curses was his astute ability to locate, communicate with and live in peace and harmony with the various cryptids around the world. An ability that had garnered him both internet fame and a huge following of vertically challenged individuals who lived under bridges who absolutely hated his guts. But if one were to ask Drake himself what he felt his biggest combination blessings with a curse was, he would tell them that it was his amazing people skills that made him come across as so approachable and folksy. He had an aura that made people feel as if he'd never met a stranger. So many people felt like they could just sit and have coffee with him and solve the world's problem from his front porch. The problematic curse of this, which Drake would point out? He didn't hate people, but he had no use for them in general, and he viewed spending any time with them, outside of his family and the less than a handful of very carefully chosen confidants, and extreme waste of his time, which he guarded closely and greedily, and he preferred the masses would simply leave him the ever loving fuck alone.

"Why are you here," Drake finally said, the point of the previous paragraph made.

"There's a girl sitting down at the station right now. A college girl from down at the university. She's getting grilled by this asshole out of D.C.- Manassas, really- for something I know she didn't do. And he's trying to link her to a whole shit ton of shit she didn't do."

"Like what?" Drake asked.

"All these assholes around here who deserved to disappear did that," Reynolds said.

"Oh," Drake said. "You mean like Jittery Jay, Whorrie Torrie, Crazy A and the like?"

"Yeah," Reynolds said. "There was one in particular that put her on this guy's radar. Some old sick fucker that used to work on the grounds crew over at the university. Went by the name "P.T.," both because those were his initials and also because he was a peeping tom. I guess he'd actually been fired for it once, but the union got him his job back. Someone claimed this girl, Jane, her name is, was seen hanging out with the old fuck just before he, well, had an unfortunate demise of sorts and was never seen or heard from again. So this dick from Manassas- who, by the way, is a detective and who is named Dick- is trying to connect this poor girl to all the other unexplained deaths."

"I thought you attributed all those to bear attacks," Drake said. "How could he even draw a link between those passive aggressive, gaslighting lunatics Jittery Jay and Crazy A and someone like that old whore Torrie who'd obviously been mauled to death by a wild beast and some college girl?"

"I know it doesn't make any sense," Reynolds said, "but I sure could use your help on this one. This old bastard's got his hooks in this young girl, and I need to get him off of her."

"I bet she's really torn up," Drake said, looking down, pondering in his mind how he might be able to help. How could he convince some FBI dick, named Dick, that whoever this young girl he was grilling was wasn't some sort of fair gendered serial killer, but that the true culprit, or culprits behind the missing assholes who deserved to go missing was one or more Bigfoot Sasquatch. Especially since his one fourth witch of a wife from the South Pacific had a bad habit of using her spells to control some of the weaker minded of this lot of creatures that are not supposed to even exist?

"Actually," Reynolds said, "she's not upset. That's what's getting me about the whole thing, and it's why I've come to you. It's as if this girl knows something."

"What else do you know about her?" Drake asked, his curiosity piqued. Could it be, he thought, that he might have a young, cryptozoologist in the making on his hands, here?

"Just that she came over here from Appalachiastan. First generation college student. No family to speak off. Her mother died when she was a teen."

"And you said her name was Jane?" Drake asked.

"Yeah," Reynolds said. "Jane (last name omitted from this text due to legal purposes)."

"You don't know what part of Appalachiastan she's from, do you?" Drake asked.

"I can't remember," Reynolds said. "She said it was somewhere down toward the southern part. Just above the coal fields. Timber country."

Drake looked off to one side, as if in deep thought. "Could it be?" he said, barely audible.

"Could it be what?" Reynolds asked.

"Give me a few minutes to shower up and I'll meet you at the station. I need to see this girl."

"What's going on here?" Reynolds asked.

"Maybe nothing," Drake said. He paused for a moment, and then he said, "maybe a lot."

                                    ****

Dick's actual name was Richard, but everyone called him Dick. He always knew that was because Dick was short for Richard, but he also knew that most people that knew him, most, as in all, thought he was a dick. And he was a dick, and it was intentional, so he never took offense to any of it.

Dick, now in his late forties, had always been one of those guys that always did the right thing, as long as there was no harm toward himself to come from it. And he'd always been one of those guys that made sure to point out the wrong in others. He'd formed the habit, in childhood, of being a snitch- a tattle tale. He'd learned something about himself early in life- something most people would find alarming if they weren't sociopathic themselves- and that was that he took great pleasure in watching others suffer or endure hardship. It got him off much like watching girl on girl porn did others.

Mind you, Dick was not violent. He did not physically abuse others, or even small animals, but he'd found, as a very young boy, that he gained a morbid sense of both stimulation and gratification out of watching others suffer.

He'd come across this discovery in a very odd way. When he was ten years old, his mother's brother, Dick's Uncle Rick, had come to stay with them. The man was sick, and he would eventually die in the family's guest room. Looking back on it, Dick might tell you he never concerned himself with what ailed Uncle Rick, and he hadn't, but he fully understood now, as an adult, that his Uncle Rick had been one of the first wave of Americans who was not gay, a drug addict, or a poor black man to die from AIDS. Uncle Rick had been an unsafe manwhore. Professionally, he'd been a cop, and he was always screwing around on his wife, and it wasn't a secret at all. When he'd contracted the virus, and needed homecare, as he lay dying, slowly, his wife, fortunate not to have been infected by her adultrous manwhore husband, threw him out on his ass. Rick went to his little sister's house (Dick's mother), and there, in the words of William Faulkner, he lay dying, until he died. And until he did, his service revolver and badge lay on the nightstand beside him.

While Uncle Rick lay dying, Dick spent much time with him, listening to story after story from copland. Dick was enthralled by just how stupid some of the criminals Uncle Rick had busted had been. And as Uncle Rick's mind began to go more and more, he'd even shared the occasional story of some of his more adultish exploits.

These adult stories didn't do much for Dick, but once, when his younger brother was told to clean up Uncle Rick's bed mess (Uncle Rick was always making a mess, and the boys were to take turns, along with their mother, cleaning them up), and had got caught up in lying, claiming he'd already had his turn, when his mother knew he clearly had not, and he had gotten punished, corporally, for the first time ever (Dick's mother has reached her wit's end), and right in front of Dick, Dick felt his nether regions swell with blood. It was the first time in his young life this had ever happened, except for on times when he'd awakened with a full bladder, and though he could not explain the experience, he discovered that he very much liked it.

Shortly after this experience, while at school, he witnessed one of his classmates cheating on a test. The student, another boy, continually leaned over to view the answers on a girl's answer sheet at the desk beside him. Simply the thought of this other student being punished for his dirty deed was enough for Dick to experience the rapid blood flow to a certain appendage of his body. Without realizing he was walking across the classroom with what he and his friends would be referring to as a "pitched tent" just a few years later, Dick strode to the teacher's desk and ratted out the cheating student. Being that these were the days before "no such thing as a wrong answer" in the public schools, and the days when bad behavior was not given a diagnosis and a prescription, the offending student was summarily pulled into the hallway and given three swift smacks across the ass with a two inch thick board, known the the old days, as a paddle. With the sound of the third smack, Dick felt something that was not urine oozing into his underwear.

And thus, a quesa sadist was born.

Later, after school, the boy who'd gotten the paddling due to Dick having narked him out caught up to Dick on the way home and taught Dick, first hand, the saying, "snitches get stitches, bitches!" Dick found himself experiencing pleasure from this experience as well.

And thus, a masochist was born!

Sadist plus masochist equals sado-masochist.

So thus, a sado-masochist was born!

Dick, however, was a shy boy, and he found himself very much enjoying voyeurism as well. Not in any traditional sense, such as peeping on the girl or the boy next door as they undressed to shower or change. More like a "Needful Things" kind of way. Yes, a nod to the Stephen King work, here, where the old man would pit people off against each other and take pleasure in their infighting.

Dick learned early how to spot people who didn't like each other. He learned how to pit them off against each other. He learned how to hide in the bushes, behind the edge of a building, or between vehicles, and take pleasure in pleasuring himself as the two enemies squared off. He learned that the suffering didn't have to be physical. He learned to have his fellow students sent to detention, where he'd often climb a tree outside of the school and peer into the windows of the detention room and pleasure himself while the slew of students, many of whom were there because of his tattle tale ways, spent two agonizing hours after school, sitting at their empty desks, doing nothing.

After high school, Dick didn't waste any time heading off to college. He knew exactly what he wanted to do. He wanted to be a police officer just like dear dead Uncle Rick. He went to the academy and started out as a local sheriff's deputy after graduation. During his short stint as a sheriff's deputy, he went after old grudges. The guys who maybe got the attention from the girls he'd always crushed on but didn't have the balls to talk to himself. One of his favorites was following around the people who he knew were stoners and busting them for smoking a joint. He would often go as far as to throw them in the back seat of his cruiser, under the cover of darkness of night, and sit in the front and masturbate, unbeknownst to them, as they pleaded with him not to file charges for their simple, recreational use of God's magical green leaves. Their exclamations of suffering from glaucoma always brought him to climax. Usually, though he hated the bastards, he'd let them off, only so he could follow them around and bust them again later.

Dick's career skyrocketed when the opioid crisis hit the rust belt. An Ohio native and resident, his small town was hit extremely hard. It didn't help that the region bordered Appalachiastan, which was totally devastated during the crisis.

Dick took part in a large sweep that ended up netting sixty eight potheads and pill poppers one morning, and as he watched dozens upon dozens of druggies thrown into the police vans, all pleading for leniency, Dick found himself having to actually leave the scene due to his levels of hyper excitement. The part of it all that made it so exciting was not so much the sheer numbers of people suffering, but the fact that he'd helped set the sting up. He'd actually given a large portion of the drugs being confiscated to the dealers, in order for them to sell them to the users, making sure the bust would be like shooting fish out of a barrel.

"That's it!" he said to himself while changing underwear, though he knew his efforts were more than likely futile, as he'd no doubt be needing to change again in only a short while. "I have foiled my own plot! I am ready to join the F.B.I.!

And he did!

It took him a while to climb the ranks, but Dick eventually made his way into a lead detective role with the F.B.I., and this was where he'd spent the ten years prior to coming to county sheriff deputy Burt Reynolds' jurisdiction setting up and busting minor marijuana infracters for major crimes. Nothing made a dime bag dealer squeal like making sure to set him up with pounds and pounds of weed one day, and then coming by the next day and starting the ball rolling to have them sent up for the next twenty years. The climax after climax that came with each foiled plot was indescribable.

But then the states started legalizing the shit, and it had almost driven Dick to sheer impetence.

But then there were all the unsolved serial killer cases. Oh, how Dick did love a knowingly innocent person squirming in the back of his unmarked suburban after having been picked up for questioning in regard to a cold case involving someone the accused, momentarily by him, at least, had never even heard of. And since the windows on his unmarked suburban were blacked out, dark as night, he could pleasure himself up front, in the middle of broad daylight, while the accused cried like a baby and begged in the backseat after having been told that they would never see the sun or the moon again for the rest of their lives.

In a word, Dick was one twisted, demented fuck of a human being. He would have been an excellent counter sick fuck for an entire season of the old serial killer show 'Dexter.' But since he was part of the long arm of the law? It was society who would pay for his twisted ways, not him.

And now, Jane sat across the table from him in the questioning room in sheriff deputy Burt Reynolds' offices, as Reynolds, along with Dr. (honorary) Drake watched from the other side of the two way mirror.

***

"Is he jerking off?" Drake asked.

"He's trying," Reynolds said. The two men watched as Dick was clearly rubbing his dick, though his pants, underneath the table that separated him from the young college girl.

"She's really pretty," Drake said, "and I'm not judging, but Jesus, couldn't he wait until he got home?"

"I could tell you stories I've heard about this guy," Reynolds said, "that would make your skin crawl."

"So how do we handle this?" Drake said.

"I was hoping you'd have some ideas," Reynolds said. "I don't know what he expects to get out of this girl. But this is a dead end group of cases. You and I both know where it leads, and if we come out with the real culprit to all these unfortunate demises, they'll lock us up in the looney bin. How in holy hell are we supposed to save this girl from this creepy mother fucker without making ourselves look like a couple of lunatics?"

"I've got an idea," Dr. (honorary) Drake said, and he turned and headed toward the door to enter the questioning room. "Just go with it," he said, and then he turned the knob. Reynolds followed him into the questioning room.

***

"I helped her," Dr. (honorary) Drake blurted out as he and Reynolds burst into the questioning room. Jane looked up, her face still expressionless, and Dick quickly removed his hand from his dick.

"And just who the holy hell are you?" Dick asked.

"He's with me," Reynolds said. "I've had this guy in mind for this for a long time, and he's finally come clean." Drake thought Reynolds was doing an excellent job of following his lead so far, but, he also thought, with a name like Burt Reynolds, how could he not be a great actor?

"I'll take you to the remaining bodies you've not yet found out about," Drake said, "but you've got to promise leniency for the girl. I've been the mastermind the whole time, and I completely took advantage of her youth and inexperience."

"Are you willing to beg for her leniency?" Dick asked. Drake dropped to one knee and put his hands together, intertwining his fingers and resting them double clenched under his jaw. "Please," he said. "I am begging you now."

Dick almost creamed his khakis.

***

Dick pulled his unmarked suburban to the wide spot in the road where Dr. (honorable) Drake had instructed. They were in the middle of nowhere now, with Reynolds riding shotgun and Drake and Jane in the back.

Dick had allowed Drake his one phone call, by way of his cellphone, while driving to their destination. Drake had called his beautiful Pacific island princess of a wife, and said something about, "remember that time at the rocky overlook on our favorite trail? Out where the wild blueberry bushes cover the mountainside? It would be great for one last trip there, if only to smell the wonderful burning of a very powerful coconut husk." Dick had thought maybe it was some sort of code when he'd overheard it, but how on earth could such a ridiculous statement be code?

"Why are you doing this?" Jane had asked Drake after he'd hung up the phone. "This is the craziest bullshit I've ever been put through, and I'm going to make this dick internet famous the minute this is over. I know a couple of Asian chicks," she'd caught herself and she had amended her statement, "well, they're not really Asian," she'd said. "They're from

Georgia. But I think they're Korean, ethnically, but my point is, they have a really successful YouTube channel, or Instagram or TikTok, or something, and I'm going to ruin this guy's career the minute this bullshit is done with."

"You're not gonna have that opportunity, sweet cheeks," Dick had said from the front seat. "Everybody out. You fucking soon to be folons lead the way. No funny shit."

The group started walking through the woods, Dr. (honorary) Drake leading the way. Jane was a couple of paces behind him, then Reynolds, and Dick was pulling up the rear, his right hand holding his service revolver, and his left resting just over his crotch.

"I think you'll find," Drake said to Jane, giving her a solemn look back over his shoulder as he did, "that it would be best to say nothing about any of this when it's all over." Jane gave him a look that let him know understanding was beginning to enter her mind and then he faced forward again, making sure to watch where he was going so he would not trip. "By the way," Drake said. "You remind me of someone I used to know. A long, long time ago."

"I bet you say that to all the girls young enough to be your daughter," Jane said.

"Seriously," Drake said. "Reynolds mentioned you were from Appalachiastan. What part?"

"It's all one part," she said, stepping over a fallen branch.

"Yup," Drake said. "True hillbilly."

"Fuck you, yuppie!" Jane said.

"I might look like a yuppie," Drake said, laughing lightly as he did. "But I can guaran-Goddamn-tee you I'm more hillbilly than you are."

"Yeah, right."

"Girl, I was spot lighting deer and skinning them and butchering them up before the sun came up in the middle of summer time years before you were born. I've dug ramps in two feet of snow, caught trout in subfreezing temperatures, and suffered heartache after heartache every time the Mountaineers had a winning season only to get slaughtered in whatever bowl game they went to."

"Really," Jane said, her voice softer.

"Really," Drake said. "I am a tried and true Cavalier fan for life now. I've adopted this place as my home town, but it ain't where my roots sprouted."

"That's enough," Dick said from the back. The group had walked nearly half a mile into the woods. "Where the hell are we going, anyway?" he asked.

"Right over there," Drake said, pointing to an outcropping of rocks where a steep incline began.

"Oh, my God," Jane said, not seeing what waited, hidden, behind the rocks, but feeling its presence with every bit of her empathic abilities. She looked at Drake and said, "You mean you can..." and she trailed off.

"You're not the only one," he told her. "There aren't many of us, but there's a few of us."

"How long have you been able to…"

"Shut, the fuck up!"

It was Dick. He was clueless as to the significance of the conversation he was interrupting, but he wouldn't have believed the idea of the subject matter anyway.

"This has gone on long enough. Everybody stop, and nobody move!" Dick walked up to Drake and got right in his face. "Show me!" he demanded.

"See that log sticking out over the last big boulder on the right?" he asked.

"Yeah," Dick said, looking over where Drake was suggesting.

"Just go to that log. Look around the other side of that boulder and you'll see the bodies. At least what's left."

Dick was so excited. He didn't even attempt to hide the erection which was rising in his pants. He would be able to threaten to have the girl executed, causing this Drake guy, who seemed so stoic, to beg for her life so much the memories of it alone would later allow Dick to fill the spank tank in his mind. He would probably be able to retire.

"What's your folks' names?" Drake asked Jane as Dick made his way over to the rock outcropping. Jane confessed that she had no clue who her real daddy was. She told him her mother had never been sure. She told him her mother's name, and Drake said, "oh, shit."

"What?" Jane said, looking over at him quickly.

"I mean," he said, and then clasped his hands before his mouth and shouted, "a little more to your left," to Dick.

Jane didn't turn her glare away from Drake. Suddenly, she felt as if he were familiar to her as well. "Did you know my momma?" she asked. She had visions in her mind of a man, a man that looked like Drake, but younger, visiting her and her mother when she had been a little girl. They hadn't stayed long. Just long enough to say hi. The man had said something about taking the woman that was with him to meet someone. The only other thing Jane could remember about the events was that when the man came back out of the woods, a couple of hours later, the woman was not with him.

"Holy fuck!" Dick screamed from just to the side of the large boulder. Jane and Drake looked over at him. He was staring upward. Reynolds began making his way to Jane and Drake to see what they were witnessing, but he wasn't quick enough. What he was not in time to see, but what Jane and Drake clearly did see, was a huge, hair covered hand reaching quickly from behind the boulder. The hair covered hand grabbed Dick around the neck and both squeezed and lifted at the same time.

Reynolds reached Jane and Drake just in time to hear both a crunching sound and a light groan. All he saw were Dick's feet being sucked, it seemed, behind the boulder at a height of about four feet above the ground. "What the…" he said, and

Drake said, "You don't want to know, though I know you already do."

"What now?" Reynolds asked.

"Well," Drake said. "We've got about a half mile's hike to figure it out."

***

By the time the group of three got back to the road, they had their story straight. Reynolds would radio one of his young deputies to come pick them up. They would tell the naive lawman that Dick wanted to investigate the area alone, and that he sent them all back and told them to arrange their own ride. Everyone already knew that Dick was a dick, so that part of the story would never be questioned.

Later, when someone would eventually find what was left of Dick's body? Well, that would all simply be written off to yet another bear attack. The group wasn't worried.

Jane pressed Drake on his knowledge not just of the Bigfoot Sasquatch that had been so readily available when and where they needed it, him or her to be (no *they*, as it had been alone), as well as what he might have known about her mother or her part of Appalachian. She couldn't shake the feeling she had that he somehow seemed familiar to her, and she kept thinking back to the memory from when she'd been so young.

"There's a lot I need to explain to you," is all he said the whole way back to the station. Once they got to the station, Reynolds got his squad car and offered the two rides home. They accepted.

When the squad car pulled up to Drake's house, he looked into the backseat at Jane. He'd been riding shotgun. "If you'd like to come in for a bit, I can explain a lot." Jane stared at him, a questioning look on her face, but she said nothing. "My wife is home," he said. "I have no inappropriate intentions. And I will be more than happy to drive you back to your dorm later. I bet you could use something to eat, anyway. Especially something other than cafeteria food. Have you ever had adobo?"

There was one thing Jane knew, and that was the intentions of men. She could tell that Drake was sincere, and she in no way deemed him to be any sort of threat.

"I can stay for a bit," she said.

Drake got out of the car and then walked around to the back of the driver's side of the car and opened the door for Jane. They both thanked Reynolds for the ride, and he told them not to worry about anything going forward, at least as far as Dick went, because he'd make sure to clear everything up.

"So he knows?" Jane asked as they watched Reynolds pull away in his cruiser. "I mean, about…"

"Yeah," Drake said. "He knows." He began walking toward the front porch of his house. Jane walked beside him. "He thought it was me, at first," he said. "But someone actually tried to kill me a while back, and he came around to the truth of it all."

"Who tried to kill you?" Jane asked.

"Some fucking inbred redneck who was obsessed with Bigfoot Sasquatch and thought I was making fun of dumbfucks like him who believe in it."

"But you don't do that," Jane said as they began climbing the stairs to the porch. "I mean," she said, trailing off. "You actually know the truth about these things. Like me. Why would someone think you were making fun of them for believing in them?"

"Because, my new young companion," Drake said, "people are fucking nutcases. And they are going to believe what they want to believe, and you cannot confuse them with facts once their minds are already made up."

Jane needed no further explanation. She was attending university in town, and she knew all too well what Drake was saying. She'd never run into so many educated fools in her life as there were on campus. Sure, many of them truly were intelligent, but as far as actual real world smarts went? Well, she was thankful for all she'd learned during her hard way of life coming up in Appalachiastan.

Drake opened the door and held it for Jane. "After you," he said. She walked in and he followed, closing the door behind himself. The two of them were greeted by a beautiful young Asian woman who didn't appear to be much older than Jane. Jane felt that the woman looked familiar somehow. Like she'd seen her around town. The post office, maybe?

"Who this?" the beautiful young Asian woman said.

"Jane," Drake said. "Meet my wife. The beautiful Mrs. Drake."

"Hello," Jane said.

"Honey?" Drake said. "Meet Jane...

...My daughter."

The End

(For now)

4

Through The Eyes Of Bigfoot Sasquatch

Dark.

Lighter.

Gray. Mist.

Chirp, chirp, chirp.

Peep, peep.

Stretching. Yawning.

Sitting.

Standing.

Moving forward.

Inside new place. Wooden walls. Piles of hay.

Flashback:

"I swear to Jesus Christ as my witness, if that's that goddamn fox that got 'ol Perty, I'mma fill its face with lead!"

The other one said, "do you kiss your momma with that mouth?"

"Yes. And I go to church twice every Sunday and never miss a Wednesday evening worship. That's how goddamn tired I am of this son of a bitch gettin' my chickens!"

The other one said, "you can't kill foxes in this county. All them rich folks up at the hunt club made sure of it with the commissioner. Or the board. Or whoever the hell makes the laws at the county level. You better not shoot no fox, or your ass is goin' to jail."

Ducking into new place. Large wooden building. Hay. Hide in hay. Don't move!

"Ain't nobody goin' to jail for killin' no chicken killin' fox!"

The other one said, "you know how it is around here. Fuckin' animals have more rights than humans. I blame the goddamn university crowd."

"Awe, it looks like that son of a bitch got away again!"

The other one said, "come on now. Let's get back on in the house. It's freezing out here, and our beer's gettin' cold!"

"Fuck you! You chicken thieving son of a whore!" (Loud. So loud ears hurt.)

Watching them leave through crack in side of wooden walls. See them enter house. Light outside goes off.

Rip open feathery dead thing.

Eat warm insides.

Sleep...

Morning-

Walking past house. Looking in window. Two men sleeping. One on couch. One on floor.

Walking away from house. Into woods.

Trees. Bushes.

Hills.

Creek.

Drink.

Water cold.

Walking more.

Hungry.

Find food place.

Walking more.

Close. Closer. Closest.

Here.

Vroom, vrooms. Vroom, vrooms.

Locked.

Locked.

Open.

Bag. Large M.

Food!

Take.

Eat.

"Look at that, mommy!"

Little girl.

Big girl says, "look at what, honey?"

Drop to ground. Roll over embankment in front of vroom vrooms. Lay still. Don't move. Hide in tall grasses.

"It was a bear, mommy."

"A bear," says big girl. "You have a very vivid imagination, young lady. There's no bear out here. But there could be. You never know what you might see hiking on these trails."

"The bear went over the hill, mommy."

"Oh," said the big girl. "I get it. Did you guys sing that song in pre-school yesterday? The bear went over the mountain, the bear went over the mountain, the bear went over the mountain, to see what he could see!"

"No mommy. That's a stupid song."

"Now Sigma, why would you say that? That's not a nice word. Remember, sticks and stones may break our bones, but words will completely ruin our lives."

"I'm sorry mommy. But the bear really did roll over the mountain."

"Where?" the big girl said.

"Over there," the little girl said.

Tall one walks to edge of hill. Looks over.

Take deep breath and hold. Holding breath. Hold, hold, holding. Holding means cloaking. Can hold and cloak for long time. Giant lungs. Healthy lungs. Can hold breath and cloak for long, long time.

"There's nothing there, honey."

"Why are the weeds smooshed down right there?"

"Maybe a deer slept there last night."

"It would have been a big deer."

Hold breath longer. No problem. Can hold breath long, long time. Hold breath. Can't see me. Hold breath. Can't see me.

"Come on, honey. Let's go. Daddy's coming home for lunch today."

"Why is my car door open, Mommy?"

"Son of a bitch!" the big girl says. "Goddamn degenerates!"

"Words, Mommy," the little girl says. "Your words. You're going to destroy someone's life with your words."

Doors shut.

Vroom vroom starts. Leaves. Can hear it rolling away.

Breathe again. Can be seen again.

Sit.

Eat contents of bag with M on it.

Gross.

Greasy.

Hurts heart.

Spit rest out.

Rise.

Walk.

***

Later that afternoon...

***

Napping in bushes beside old country store.

Sun high. Energy low.

Must sleep.

Can't sleep.

Voices. Coming from bench in front of store. Too loud.

"Did you hear the one about the 'ol boy was sitting out here last week? Looked over and saw 'ol Clem's dog just a lickin' his nuts?"

"No," the other one said.

"'Ol boy said he wished he could do that, too. Why, I told him he could go on over there and try it, but that old dog would probably bite his face off."

"That one's older than you are," the other one said.

"Well let's hear you tell one, goddamn it!"

"I ain't gotta tell a 'ol worn out joke," the other one said. "I can just tell you what happened to my nephew Mark last week."

"That queer nephew of you'rn considers hisself a actor?"

"That's the one," the other one said. "But he ain't a queer, and he ain't a actor. He got him a girl prettier than you ever seen, and he's a entertainer. Magician."

"If he got a girl, he's a pretty good magician. Magic enough to make people think he ain't a queer."

"Well," the other one said. "Could be. You never really know with people. Especially family."

"So what happened to that queer nephew of your'n that's so worth telling?"

"Well," the other one said. "He was on his way over to Harrisonburg to do a show at JMU."

"That's where I'm tryin'a get my grandkids to go," the first one said. "Ain't as goddamn liberal as the university down in Charlottesville."

"Do you wanna hear it, or don't ya?" the other one said.

"Oh, go on and tell it, then."

"So he was headin' over there on thirty three west, and he got pulled over by the poe lease."

"What the poe lease pull him over for?"

"If'n you'll just shut the hell up, I'll tell ya."

"Oh, go on then," the first one said.

"Well, my nephew Mark said the poe lease pulled him over for speedin'. Asked him why he was goin' so fast, and well, Mark told him he was a magician of sorts, and that he had 'im a show over there at JMU.

"Well, that poe lease man told him that if he could juggle somethin' for him, he wouldn't write him a ticket. Mark told 'im he'd sent all of his equipment ahead with his lovely assistant. Now, that would be that pretty girl I was tellin' you about. And he said he did't have anything to juggle.

"So the poe lease tells him he's got some flares in the back of his squad car. Mark tells him, alright, he'll juggle those.

"So the poe lease man lights five flares up and hands them to Mark. He's a jugglin' 'em all, real nice, right there beside the road. All of a sudden, some yuppie, probably from over here in Charlottesville, seein' how there's so many yuppies here and all, pulls over to the side of the road in his BMW. He gets out and goes over and lets himself into the backseat of that poe lease man's car.

"So the poe lease man walks over and asks the yuppie what he's'a doin' and the yuppie tells him to go on ahead and haul 'im in, because there ain't no way in holy hell he's gonna be able to pass that field sobriety test."

"Ah, ha, ha, ha! you old son of a bitch!" the first one said. "You done went and got me good! Hey, you know the difference between a BMW and a porcupine, don't you?"

"What's that," the other one asked.

"With a porcupine, the pricks are on the outside!"

Ah-ha-ha! Loud laughing from both.

Porcupine!

Ouch!

Sit half up! Fast. Turning. Looking for porcupine!

"What was that!" first one says. "Did you hear that?"

"Hear what?" the other one said.

"In the bushes. Behind us."

"Where in the bushes?"

"At our six, you dumbass! Where else would they be if I said behind us?"

Hold breath. Cloak. Hold breath. Can't be seen.

"Ah, it was probably just one of them old dumpster cats," the other one said. "Come on. It's well past noon. Let's get us a case of somethin' cheap and take it out to my place and get ta drinkin'. Faye's done gone over't'er sister's again. Prolly won't come back 'til tomorah."

***

Several hours later.

***

Walking along fence line. Sun heading lower.

BANG!

"Aurgh!" ears hurt.

Bang!

Bang!

"Aurgh!" ears hurt.

Changing direction. Walking over hill. Look down into open meadow through woods.

See man.

Crazy man. Slamming hammer down on steel anvil, driving anvil into wood.

Hat on inside out. White tag waving in breeze.

Man holding up red circle. Man talking into small thing in hand.

Walking closer.

Hiding behind trees.

Creeping.

Holding breath. Clocking. Can't be seen while holding breath. Creep to just inside tree line of field.

"What was that?" crazy man says, staring at small thing holding in hand. "Did you hear that?" Crazy man looks around. Eyes wide. Hat still on inside out. Why is hat on inside out? Man is crazy.

Crazy man holds up red circle again. "Right there," crazy man says. "It's like, I heard footsteps from something walking, but there's no one or nothing there. But I clearly heard footsteps. Rewind and listen."

Crazy man moving small thing in hand around. Pointing small thing in hand everywhere. "Get my six," crazy man with inside out hat says.

Have to breathe. Must breathe.

Deep breath. Ducking behind tree.

"Did you see that?" Crazy man says. "That tree back there. At my eight o'clock. I saw movement. Rewind and watch again."

Crazy man walks back toward middle of field. Crazy man talking to small thing in hand. Crazy man talking fast, then slow. Fast then slow.

Follow crazy man. Crazy man entertaining. Where crazy man flares? Crazy man juggle? Follow crazy man to find out.

"What's that!" crazy man says. Stops in field. "Okay, get my six. And as I was saying. Do I believe in Bigfoot Sasquatch? What about all the people who claim to have had sightings?

"Here's what I think about all those who've claimed to have seen Bigfoot Sasquatch," crazy man says. "I think half of them are lying, and I think the other half are not telling the truth."

This man crazy. Must follow crazy man.

Hold breath. Cloak. Walk. Stop.

"Did you hear that?" crazy man says. "It's like, there's something walking in this meadow with me. Something that can be heard, and felt with my spidey senses, but not seen. Rewind and see if you can see the sawgrass moving."

Crazy man very aware. Better hold breath long time. Crazy man not crazy.

"So here's what I mean by that. Okay, it is so obvious a great percentage of these assholes who claimed to have seen Bigfoot Sasquatch are simply lying. I don't know why. Maybe they want attention. Maybe they committed a crime and they want to blame it on their imaginary accomplice, Bigfoot

Sasquatch. Maybe they are gaslighters who want to make others question their sanity. I don't know.

"But the other half? They are not telling the truth. However, I do not think they're lying. There's a difference. I do believe there are people out there who have seen things or had experiences that cannot be explained, and they attribute it to Bigfoot Sasquatch. Maybe, in their mind's eye, that's what they believed they saw when they got the glimpse of a bear, or a moose. Or they saw an actual human being from a far distance walking in the woods."

Gotta breathe.

Exhale.

Inhale.

Hold.

"Did you see that?" crazy man says. "It's like, there was something there, and then there wasn't. Rewind and watch. And with that said, I'm going to lay this drumstick here on the gifting stump and head in for the night. Thanks for joining me for another episode of the PBS...

"...S...

"The potential, Bigfoot... Sasquatch...

"...show."

Crazy man stop talking to small device in hand. Crazy guy push buttons on small device. Crazy guy walking toward house. Crazy guy going in house.

Breathe.

Dark now.

Tired.

Hungry.

Pick up drumstick crazy man left on stump.

Eat.

Put bone back so crazy man won't know.

Go inside crazy man's outbuilding.

Lay down on pile of hay.

Sleep.

The End

(At least for another day in the life of Bigfoot Sasquatch)

***

The following stories are from Bigfoot Sasquatch Files Volume 10:

Recidivates

(Originally Titled: The Unfortunate Demise Of The Regional Three)

"Son of a whore," Martin said, aloud, as he read the headline from the *Richmond Harold* online.

"Virginia *Becomes First Southern State To Legalize Recreational Use Of Marijuana*"

"I knew I should have stayed with Dad," Martin mumbled, thinking all the way back to his parents' divorce thirty years before. His father had gone back to his native Virginia to take a job he'd been refusing to take, due to his mother's desire to stay in Appalachiastan because, and *only* because, she had family in Appalachiastan. She'd lacked any education beyond high school, she had *no* social clout outside of her family and small community (which didn't amount to a hill of pigeon shit's worth of social clout, anyway), and instead of following the man of her dreams (for the season) who she'd met at the Appalachiastan State Fair one summer while he'd been in Appalachiastan visiting his grandparents, Martin's mother had stayed in Appalachiastan, clinging to her fear of the outside world, and thus, catapulting Martin and her two other children (fathered by two other men- *not* Martin's father- but who's counting?) into the same cycle of generational poverty and lack of opportunity that she and all her people before her had always known. *But hey, she'd thought to herself at the time, despite Martin's knowledge of her thoughts, there's safety in the same old same old. Change is scary as hell, and the devil you know, albeit ignorance and poverty, is safer than the devil you don't.*

Though he'd done no time of any sort, only months after his father had gone back to Virginia, Martin's reputation, at least locally (and locally was all he had), had been ruined when he'd gotten caught smoking a joint with a couple of buddies after school one day back in middle school. They'd all told their parents they were on the wrestling team, and they *had* been for the first week of wrestling season, but man, that shit was hard, they'd discovered, and one of them, Thomas, now dead for more than a decade, had discovered more than just that he wasn't any good at the sport. He'd also discovered that rolling around on the mat with the other boys made certain of his body parts become stimulated in such ways he didn't think were supposed to become stimulated, and, being that he resided deep in the heart of Appalachiastan, he figured it might be best to quit the team before any of the other boys found out about this and summarily beat him to a bloody pulp. Especially any of the others who might have discovered themselves being in the same situation. Better to deflect by way of a good old fashioned hillbilly beat down than to draw attention to one's self for the same offense. This was the Appalachia- By God- Stanian way!

Martin hadn't gotten in much trouble at home as he'd feared he would- he'd been grounded from television for two weeks (he didn't really miss the radical right views of Michael J. Fox's character on 'Family Ties,' though he *did* miss seeing his celebrity crush, Alyssa Milano, on 'Who's The Boss'), and that had been that, but he certainly remembered the first time he realized he now carried a scarlet letter of sorts.

He'd been hanging out with one of the girls from school, Stacy- a girl he'd been friends with since kindergarten, and who he'd never thought anything more of than simply one of his buddies- but who, in the past year or so at the time had become in all ways different. It was during that magic time of life when boys noticed that girls were different in a very special way, and visa versa, and that they liked these differences, unless, of course they were like Thomas, and preferred the sameness of their own gender, which was okay by Martin (he'd just never admit it publicly, i.e. fear of aforementioned hillbilly beat down).

Martin had been intentionally walking up and down Stacy's street, much like in the scene where Jimmy Stewart's character did the same with Donna Reed's character in the classic film, "It's A Wonderful Life," (it's where he'd gotten the idea), and Stacy had finally noticed him, asked him if he was going to 'come in or aren't you,' as if she'd seen the movie, too (though she never got around to saying that Martin's mother had called, because she hadn't), and Martin had been only too eager to go inside, and he didn't act like he wasn't, like Stewart's character in the Christmas classic.

Martin and Stacy, after all awkwardness of recent pubescent crushness was lain to rest, were on the couch, in the living room, watching Kirk Cameron's character give his television sister a good 'ol tongue lashing for something, back, of course, when Kirk Cameron gave people tongue lashings about things other than the blood and the life of his Lord and Savior Jesus Christ, when Stacy's mother came home.

"Stacy, hon, come here a minute," she'd called from her bedroom after walking straight through the house and not even acknowledging Martin. "You get that Goddamn pothead out of my house! You stay away from that piece of white trash shit!" Stacy's mother had said, intentionally a little *too* loud, Martin felt, once Stacy had entered her mother's bedroom. And just like that, Martin's hopes of becoming a statistic in the rampant outbreak of teen pregnancy that was sweeping its way through his part of Appalachiastan back in those days (his county took pride in having the highest teen pregnancy rate in all of Appalachiastan the entire time Martin was in middle school and high school), were crushed like a wave on a rocky shore.

At some point, though Martin couldn't remember quite when, he gave up the ghost. He quit trying to fight the reputation, which seemed as if it would be lifelong, that he'd earned from smoking a joint and having been caught. Though he'd only done it a couple of times before getting caught, and though he never touched the stuff for several years after having gotten caught, he'd become a regular toker by senior year, because the title of good for nothing white trash pothead would not leave him, and it was one of those 'if you're going to do the time, why not do the time' kinda things, and besides, there was this super smoking hot pothead named Paula, and, in time, and many, many dime bags smoked between them, later, she would introduce Martin to the world of Appalachiastanian teen pregnancy!

Just to be a dick, Martin insisted they name the baby, a girl, Stacy.

And they did.

***

And then there was Robbie!

Robbie was the petty thief that Martin got to meet and spend up close and personal time with at the Regional jail his first stint in.

As fate would have it, Martin would get popped buying a bag of the sticky stuff from a nark wearing a wire for the po po just a month after having turned eighteen. The judge had given him a thirty day sentence to ensure that he'd be out of jail in time to celebrate his daughter Stacy's first birthday, which was only a couple of months away at the time. "I don't want you to miss an important event like that," the judge had told him, "but I want to make sure you learn your lesson so I don't see you in here again." Little did the judge know (though he'd suspected it at the time) Martin was to become one of his regular customers, albeit at the hands of the local po po's game of wiring up everyone they busted and getting them to nark on all their buddies, keeping the same girls and guys on a vicious cycle of in and out of regional jail due to smoking joints and bowls and selling dime bags, etc. etc., but hey, it was good for business.

Martin would find during his first few days shacked up with Robbie that Robbie's troubles had started out much the same way as his, though they'd started at a much younger age, and, admittedly, more innocently.

Though most of the folks in Appalachiastan were dirt poor, Robbie's family were worse off than most. Though Robbie had the rare blessing of having the same adult male play the father figure role throughout his childhood (though, technically, the man wasn't his biological father, but again, who's counting?), the man that played that role had a tendency to sell the family's food stamps (these, dear Generation Z'ers reading this, were what welfare recipients used to purchase food back before EBT cards), for cash, fifty cents on the dollar, in order to buy booze and marijuanna (and this, dear Generation Z'ers reading this, is why Uncle Sugar switched from food stamps to EBT cards). This 'side business' of the father figure resulted in a houseful of hungry kids, and Robbie had earned the title of petty thief all the way back in kindergarten, where he'd gotten caught, repeatedly, digging into the other kids' lunchboxes during class and lifting their food and eating it.

The people who worked in the school system, bless their hearts, did their best to understand, and they made sure that Robbie and a handful of other kids like him were fed before class with the state's free breakfast program, but Robbie knew there would be no food at home afterschool, and he was only thinking of all his half-siblings as well, and, well, he become quite prolific in his thievery. And soon enough, he figured, why just take food when there were all those nice coats and rainboots and neat toys on show and tell days, etc.

By middle school, few people would associate with Robbie, out of fear of him taking the shirts off of their backs while they spoke with him. By high school, he was not allowed in the changing room during gym class, unsupervised, because of his thieving ways. And by the day after graduation, the po po were trailing him, knowing he was eighteen, and figuring they could throw him into their mix of wired up pothead and petty thief narks- at least as far as the in and out of regional went- and hey man, that would be even greater job security for them!

Martin was in for a bag of the sticky stuff, and Robbie was in for joy riding on a four wheeler that didn't belong to him. Well, that's what had resulted in the chase with the po po. It actually led to the po po finding the Ford Bronco and the Chevy Blazer, neither belonging to him, either, that he had hidden out back where he parked the four wheeler, as well.

***

But their buddy Jason, who Martin and Robbie had met their first time in regional, and who they'd come to know quite well by way of all their future stints together in regional- stints that would lead to them being known as the regional three, since they always seemed to pull their stints at the same time- was certainly, at least in Martin and Robbie's minds, the odd man out in their threesome. The one who didn't quite fit in.

Jason, the other two thought, should have never ended up in regional, and he should have been able to escape from Appalachiastan with ease- going off somewhere and living the proverbial "boring middle class lifestyle," which, as any hillbilly could tell you, when you're from Appalachiastan, is in no way boring at all. Food? Clothing? Shelter? No po po coming around all the time due to their 'war on drugs' bullshit? Giving them the perfect excuse to bother you? No petty theft required because there's money in the bank? How could Jason *not* have fled the hills of Appalachiastan for a piece of *that* action, Martin and Robbie thought?

Jason had truly been raised in privilege. He was the son of a doctor who was making fifty thousand dollars a month back in the early 1990's. When the term 'white privilege' would become prevalent many years after this, and when it would finally make its way to Appalachiastan, everyone would joke about how they couldn't find their white privilege and the reason had to be because Jason had gotten it all.

Way back when the regional three had pulled their first stint together, a stint during which Martin and Robbie were both terrified of getting beaten up and ass raped (neither of which happened), Martin and Robbie marveled at the treatment Jason received. They witnessed it, for days, before finally asking Jason about it one day during lunch chow.

"How did you get your own cell?" Martin asked after setting his prison tray down across from Jason at the table.

"Yeah," Robbie said, sitting down beside Martin. "And how come you get to shower alone?"

"My uncle is the judge," Jason said.

"Really?" Martin and Robbie said in unison.

"Yeah," Jason said. "Besides," he said, shoveling something that was supposed to be meat into his mouth. "I've never even been arrested."

"What the fuck are you doing in here if you've never been arrested?" Martin asked.

"My dad's a dick," Jason said. "He found a fucking bong in my room, so he's convinced I'm a dealer or some shit. Afraid of how that might make the good doctor look. He's a doctor," Jason added when he caught the looks of 'what the fuck are you talking about' from the guys across the table. "Anyway," he said, continuing, "he's going with that tough love bulllshit. He's never around, because he loves his work more than his family. So he thinks that by having uncle Rick lock me up in here for ten days I'll be scared straight and start clicking my fucking heels together saying, 'there's no place like med school. There's no place like med school.'"

Martin and Robbie gave each other a look that loosely translated to "what the fuck?"

"Yeah," Jason said, reading the look. He knew it well. "It's all good though. I've got a pretty good hook up with some of my dad's nurses. I'm fucking one of them. I've made some connections in here, and I think I can put something together that's gonna allow for me to pull in some pretty good jing when I get out of here."

"What do you mean?" Martin asked.

"Fucking drugs, man," Jason said, dropping the cool kid m.o. "I can get my hands on practically anything. Fuck marijuana, man. I can get narcotics. I'm meeting guys in here who are already offering to become customers. I'm gonna make fucking bank with these jailhouse connections I'm making in here. My old man will never know the favor he did me with this bullshit."

"Seriously?" Martin said.

"Yeah, man!" Jason said. "Where are you guys from?"

Martin and Robbie told Jason from which parts of Appalachiastan they hailed, to which Jason responded, "Mother fucker! We could corner the market on the fucking state! We're all in different counties. Man, you guys need to become part of my supply chain!"

And they did.

***

Though the trio would prefer to be referred to as *the three amigos*, or *the trilogy three we be* (Robbie's stupid idea) they would never be able to shed the moniker the regional three.

It took only a month after the three's release from that first group sting at regional, way, way back in the 90's before Martin and Robbie were busted hauling a Ziplock freezer bag of little white oxycodone across county lines. They'd proven their metal to Jason by not outing him as their supplier, and he rewarded them by dipping into some of his trust funds to post their bail. At sentencing they were given a year's worth of supervised probation, but they kept working- Jason just made the deliveries to them during that period- and since they had to piss in cups quite frequently, they never consumed any of the profits by way of gestation.

Jason would eventually get caught taking large quantities of narcotics from the hospital in which his father worked, and it had nearly cost his father his job, but everyone agreed that if Jason went to a thirty day rehab center the slate would be wiped clean. Since Jason never used narcotics in the first place (it was always all about the money with Jason, and he simply enjoyed toking up on a bowl of the sticky and kicking back and relaxing with a cold beer, anyway) he did the time in rehab standing on his head. Since his homelife was pretty Richy Rich, down to the part of his absentee father ignoring the holy hell out of him, he was able to pin his addictions on his daddy issues enough to please his head shrinks, and after pissing clean on day 30, he graduated rehab with flying colors and was summarily released.

And he'd garnered a couple dozen new clients while on the inside of *that* institution, as well!

Over the years, the regional three would spend their time together at regional jail, Robbie and Martin always being allowed to be cellmates (they were on a first name basis with all the guards and knew the names of most of their children), and Jason was always given his private suite, due to his uncle's position as judge.

However, and as fate would have it, Jason's uncle would eventually lose re-election for his seat as judge, a shocking turn of events, as most folks thought he'd retain the seat for life- but during the Trumpublican rising of 2016, anyone who had a (D) in front of their name on the voting ballots in Appalachiastan were summarily handed defeat at the polls, regardless of how many generations they'd been in office. Jason's uncle was a lifelong blue dog Democrat (these are closet republicans who despise minorities and gays, but who vote democrat, because among the few of them who work, they work labor jobs, and they need union protection from their evil capitalist masters, and among those who do *not* work- well- they need welfare- and all of them are still waiting on John F. Kennedy to come back from the grave and save them, just like he said he would do when he rolled through Appalachiastan a million years ago- but these people were were definitely *not* democrats), so, circa 2018, when Robbie and Martin would get busted, again, just after Jason had made a product drop and had been caught on surveillance camera having made said product drop, the three would spend time in regional, again, and this time, Jason got to shack up with his buddies. "No more special treatment for you by way of your Hussein Obama supporting uncle," the guards had told him while locking him up with Martin and Robbie. He tried to explain that whole blue dog democrat closet republic thing to them, and of how it meant his uncle would never vote for a black muslim, but it went over their heads.

***

"This is bullshit!" Jason said that first night in their cell.

"Welcome to how the other half live," Martin said.

"Yeah," Robbie said. "Wait till you try the burlap blanket."

***

Over the next ninety days, while they pulled their time, the regional three commiserated on how they should have left Appalachiastan after the first time they'd gotten in trouble all those years before. "Once you're on their radar," Martin had said during that conversation, "you never get off of it."

"That's right," Robbie said. "Once they get your number. I had an uncle who told me that, back in the day. He told me to leave Appalachiastan and never come back, but where the hell was I supposed to go? I didn't know anyone anywhere?"

Martin and Robbie had gone on and on about how they could not understand why Jason never left, though he kept coming back to the same answer; easy money. He had access to drugs via his father, and he had protection from harsh prosecution via his uncle, at least he used to.

"When we get out of here, we're leaving this fucking state!" Martin said toward the end of their stint.

"Where would we go?" Robbie asked. "And with what money?" All three were guilty, not just of pushing and dealing, but of blowing every freaking dollar they ever earned while pushing and dealing. Even Jason, who was already living in the lap of luxury, especially by hillbilly standards, spent most of his money before he even made it. Once his BMW's were six months old, it was time for a new one. He was always turning them in, upside down, loanwise, and never giving a shit about it.

"I know a way," Martin said, but you fuckers will think I'm crazy."

"We already do," Jason said. "Let's hear it."

"Do you think we could do okay on a million dollars?" Martin asked.

"Fuck yea," Robbie and Jason said.

"But how do you plan on us getting a million dollars?" Robbie asked.

"We're gonna kill us one of them there Bigfoots," Martin said.

"What?!?" Jason and Robbie said, incredulous.

"Yeah, man!" Martin said. "I found a fucking guy on the internet, and he really is rich, and he's offered a one million dollar reward for anyone who brings him the body of a real fucking Bigfoot. We're gonna go kill us one, collect the money, then head down to Florida and sit on the beach and drink fucking bear and fuck Cuban bitches."

"Where in the fuck do you expect us to find us a Bigfoot?" Robbie asked.

"Yeah," Jason said. "And you can't trust those fuckers on the internet. It's probably all a joke to get views. Like that one fucker over in Virginia that runs around on his property with fucking sleeping bags over his head when the real Bigfoot Sasquatch organizations start stalking him and his property, because they think they've actually seen a real bigfoot in the background of some of his videos."

"I've seen that ass clown," Martin said. "It's nothing like that. That guy's a class A douchebag, and I hope Bigfoot finds him some day and rips his fucking limbs off of his torso."

"I fucking hate that guy," Robbie said.

"Here's my point," Martin said. "Let's take our fucking deer rifles up to my uncle Roscoe's homeplace. Up there on that old homestead he has just above town. You know where he's got that old apple orchard?"

"Yeah," the other two said.

"Well," Martin continued. "He's seen one of them apple throwing Yowie mother fuckers up there. I say we go up there and wait it out and shoot it in it's mother fucking face, then drag the son of a bitch to that scumbag on the internet and collect our million, then head down to Florida, stay the fuck out of trouble, and live happily ever after."

"If it's so easy," Jason said, "why doesn't everyone do it?"

"You know most people don't believe in this kinda shit," Martin said.

"But how can we trust that your uncle has a Yowie on his property? Isn't he crazy from the war?"

"Hell," Martin said. "He never served. He's just crazy. Makes shit up about having been in Vietnam to look cool."

"Well," Jason said. "It's awfully damn hard to sell product anymore, with the goddam po po following me everywhere I go. I could use a new location. Shed the old rep of being the biggest pusher in my part of the state.

"Fuck it," Robbie said. "Let's do it."

***

"You boys are gonna do what?"

It was uncle Roscoe. He was kicked back in his old recliner, his feet up on the empty wooden beer box he used for such purposes. He'd been on Strohs number whatever the fuck for the afternoon, enjoying some WWE wrestling reruns, when his no better for anything than him potheaded nephew Martin had come in with that thieving friend of his, Robbie. They had some city slicker looking guy with them. Dressed in Banana republic clothing and Sperry deck shoes, Roscoe felt right away this new friend of Martin's might be a little light in said Sperry deck slippers.

"We're gonna kill us that Bigfoot Sasquatch you got living back there in the woods behind your fruit orchard and make us a million dollars and get the fuck out of Appalachiastan," Martin said, reiterating, by way of the short version.

"I knew your brain was fried, boy," Roscoe said, "but this? This is fucking nuts!"

"Do you have a Bigfoot Sasquatch living in the woods behind you, or don't you?" Robbie asked Roscoe.

"Potentially," Roscoe said.

"Have you ever actually seen it?" Jason asked Roscoe.

"Potentially," Roscoe said.

"What's up with this potential bullshit?" Martin asked. "You're sounding like that asshole on YouTube. Either you have or you haven't. It's a yes or no question."

"Hey," Roscoe said, sitting up a bit in his recliner. "I like that guy. He's a few bricks short of a full load, but he makes me laugh. Besides," Roscoe said, pausing for reflection. "I really think I've seen some weird shit in the background of some of his videos."

"Enough," Jason said. "Hook me up with a rifle, and let's get to it. Daylight's wasting."

"They don't hunt deer up in your neck of the woods there, fella?" Roscoe said to Jason, eyeballing him with suspicion, wondering if he was one of those men who enjoyed kissing other men.

"It wasn't our family's thing," Jason said. "But I can shoot. I'm not a virgin."

Roscoe wondered just what in the hell Jason meant by that. Was he offering some sort of service? "I'll getch'ya an ought six," Roscoe said, and then he rose, staggering only a little from the Strohs, before walking into the gunroom and bringing Jason a rifle. "Now what's in this for me?" Roscoe asked, as he handed Jason the weapon.

"You're fucking kidding me," Robbie said.

"Listen, you little thief," Roscoe said. "You ain't stealing from me. If there's a goddamn Bigfoot Sasquatch on my property, and you profit from killing it, I want a cut. Twenty five per cent!"

"Twenty five per cent!" the regional three screamed in unison.

"Twenty five per cent," Roscoe said, "or you go find you someone else who has a Bigfoot Sasquatch on their property. Potentially."

"Okay, okay," Martin said. "Twenty five per cent." He looked at his two buddies who were not looking back at him in a kind way. "Let's go out and get this shit done."

The three younger yet middle aged men left, and Roscoe, now well into drawing social security, sat back down with a fresh Strohs to watch a new match. The classic rerun of Hulk Hogan vs. Andre the giant. The one where Hulk ripped his lower back out slamming the giant. Roscoe, like all true WWE fans, had seen it a hundred times, but it never got old. "Bigfoot Sasquatch reward," he said to himself and then chuckled. "My ass."

***

Three hours and ten beers later, Roscoe's mind was singing a different tune. The more beer he drank, the more likely he thought it was that he did, indeed, have a Bigfoot Sasquatch on his property (*something* had been throwing apples at him out in the orchard last fall), and if anyone was going to make a million dollars off of it, it was going to by God be him.

He clicked the television off with the remote and stood. After gaining all balance he began heading for the gun room, but he tripped over the beer box he'd been resting his feet on and fell to the floor. "Goddamn it!" he said, and then he rose once more to his feet, made it to the gun room without falling again, and took up his Winchester 30/30, a hell of a brush gun that packed a hell of a wallop. He knew these Bigfoot Sasquatch creatures had a tendency to hide behind and blend in with thickets. The Winchester 30/30 would blast right through the cover of any brush or debris and rip a hole right through anything hiding behind it.

With less than an hour of daylight left, Roscoe made his way up the hill behind his house, through his fruit orchard, and about fifty yards into the woods. Then, he heard the loud, thunderous clap of rifle shot. It had come from only one hundred yards away, to his left, so he began making his way to the location of the sound's origin. When he got there he could not believe his eyes. The regional three were standing around an actual, bonafide, and now dead Bigfoot Sasquatch.

"Goddamn," Jason said. "I thought for sure this was all bullshit, but it looks like we're rich."

"I told you mother fuckers," Martin said, taking a bowl out of the inside pocket of his jacket and lighting up in celebration. "Who wants a hit?"

"Me," said Robbie.

"So after we give your drunk uncle his cut," Jason said, declining the weed, "we get a quarter million each. Not rich, like you poor fucks think, but certainly enough to get us out of here and headed for a fresh start in Florida."

"Cuban bitches," Robbie said, exhaling slowly- having taken Martin up on his offer of a toke- a thick white cloud coming out of his mouth, "here we come."

"Literally," Martin said, his not so funny pun an indication that he was already baked.

"Not so fast, you deadbeats!"

The regional three turned, startled, and they saw Roscoe coming toward them, his rifle at the ready.

"What the fuck, uncle Roscoe?" Martin said.

"Thought you could come up here and get rich and famous at my expense?"

"Come on man," Jason said. "We've already agreed to cut you in."

"Yeah," Roscoe said. "Well, maybe I've already decided to cut you out."

"Hold on, man," Robbie said, but he was too high now to think of what to say next.

"Hold on, nothing," Roscoe said. "Now I'm giving you shitbags an option. Walk on down off this hill, get in your beaters and get on out of here, and speak nothing of this, or eat a load of Winchester 30/30 lead."

"You mother fucker," Martin said. "Mom always said you were a piece of shit."

Realizing he'd dropped his marijuana pipe during the excitement, Martin bent over to pick it up, but as it had landed by his rifle, Roscoe did the math in his drunken mind and came up with another number. The number he came up with didn't equal Martin grabbing the pipe, it equalled Martin grabbing the gun.

Bang!

Roscoe blew a hole into the side of Martin's head that left a hole three times the size of that one coming out the other side.

"Mother fucker!" Jason said. "You shot your fucking nephew!" He turned, abruptly, to look at Roscoe, not realizing he was turning his rifle toward Roscoe as well, and in a very threatening manner, so he was the next of the regional three to take one from the business end of Roscoe's Winchester. He went down like a ton of bricks. *A little more weight in them Sperrys than I thought after all*, Roscoe thought as he watched.

Robbie, the last of the regional three standing, didn't waste time with words. He raised his rifle, aiming toward Roscoe as quickly as he could. He squeezed off a shot, but he'd aimed at the Roscoe he'd seen on the right of the three he was seeing (being high will do that to you), instead of the one in the middle, thereby missing, and he didn't get the opportunity for a second shot, as Roscoe put one between his eyes before he could work the action on his rifle.

"Try to steal my Bigfoot Sasquatch, you mother fuckers," Roscoe mumbled. He lowered his weapon and stood in silence as the echoes from all the shooting subsided somewhere far off into the distant mountains. Roscoe wasn't so concerned with hiding the bodies. His property was big. For years he'd been able to hide meth labs in various outbuildings and marijuana patches in various plots around the property. He'd bury these deadbeats, he figured, in shallow graves and let the bears, opossums, racoons and wild pigs that weren't supposed to be in the area, but which he knew were in the area, make meals of them. The only thing Roscoe was thinking about was how to find that guy in Virginia who was offering a million dollars for the carcass of the Bigfoot Sasquatch.

But then he heard a low, guttural growl.

He turned, slowly.

And another Bigfoot Sasquatch who'd been travelling with the one his nephew and his nephew's friends had killed took his head off with one swift slice of a giant paw with razor sharp claws on the end of its fingers.

And just like that...

Roscoe was dead.

The surviving Bigfoot Sasquatch, with tears in its eyes, picked up its fallen friend and draped him over one shoulder and began the long, arduous trek to the Bigfoot Sasquatch burial site, many miles away and hidden under everyone's noses in the middle of a giant thicket in the middle of a set of well marked public trails on land that had been donated to the county by a wealthy individual with no heirs many years ago with the only requirement being that the county name the park filled with trails they'd create after his wife who had passed before him. The trip would take days, so this Bigfoot Sasquatch did not wait.

***

"*Local Repeat Offenders Killed In Drug Feud*," the headline of the local rag read the following week. As it turned out, four dead bodies, those of the regional three and uncle Roscoe, were found by hikers who'd gotten off the trail they'd been on a few days after the incident. They'd crossed onto Roscoe's property and found the bodies. They'd also found a half packed pipe of the sticky stuff that they saw no need in allowing to go to waste and they did partake of the sticky stuff, though they left that out of the details they'd share with law enforcement, because they were on the wrong stateline side of Appalachiastan.

Said local law enforcement, after scouring the place and finding three working meth labs and two patches of marijuanna, and having known all of the men involved, wrote the whole mess off as some sort of drug business arrangement gone awry. They assumed no one would question it, because, they also assumed no one would miss any of the four men now dead- deadbeat, drunken Uncle Roscoe and the regional three.

The assumed correctly.

The End

With Deadly Intent

Recently, and sadly again, there was a shooting tragedy in Smalltown, USA. A lunatic with a firearm shot and killed several innocent people. Please note, at this point, before we go one step further, that as someone raised to understand and respect firearm safety, as someone who formerly hunted regularly, and as someone who hauled multiple firearms around the deserts of the Middle East to protect the free world from the overthrow of radical Islamic Jihadism (though the majority of said free world will *never* understand the danger they were in in the first place, due to blinders set in place by a corruption backed media machine of epic proportions, and further, I'll say, individual members of said free world don't give two fucks for my efforts of keeping them free, for they know not how close they were to losing said freedom), I am here to tell you, guns do not kill people.

People kill people with guns!

And knives...

And cars...

And baseball bats...

And too freely given prescriptions for unneeded deadly medications...

Etc.

I keep most of my personal views in regard to all things politics and religion off of our YouTube channel, and only because I FULLY understand the American social media landscape, but this ain't social media. This is literature. And here, at least still for now, I *do* have the right to freedom of speech that is in no such way hateful or damaging.

Now that I've digressed (but hey, isn't that what I do? Some folks call it rambling), I'll get back to the story.

I had a conversation just this morning (as of this writing) with a lady who actually knew the asshole 'I hope he burns in hell' prick who carried out the recent tragedy I mentioned in my opening, just before going off the rails. She and her partner had gone to high school with this lunatic.

The woman told me a story about the lunatic, her hopes in so doing being that she might find some sort of comfort from my response or my words, and I think I was pretty effective in giving her what she sought by sharing a similar experience I had with a similar lunatic. I'll tell you her story first, and then I'll tell you mine, and yes, be patient with me, deer reader, because there may or may not be a Bigfoot Sasquatch in there somewhere at some point.

Potentially…

So, the lady told me that the piece of shit excuse for a human who'd recently shot and killed innocents at a public place had wrestled in middle school. Her partner was on the wrestling team with him. She said that during their first wrestling tournament, the lunatic lost a match to another kid from another school, and as a response, he quit the team immediately and marched into the locker room where he had a total meltdown, during which he exclaimed, repeatedly, that he was going to kill the kid who'd beaten him.

Mind you, this action might not be all too unexpected from a middle school boy who maybe is undisciplined, or who has not been raised to be respectful, which was obviously the case here, but the lady told me that all who witnessed this could tell that this young shitbag's actions was much more ominous than a typical middle schooler with no respect or discipline. Those in attendance claimed the actions and the words were ominous, and that they honestly believed this young shitbag was, at some point, going to kill someone.

Turns out, they were right.

It appears as if the lady with whom I conversed was suffering from extreme feelings of guilt, because though she knew this shitbag lunatic was unstable, she, nor her partner, ever called anyone to report their fears. She claimed that everyone who knew him felt the same way about him- as if it were merely a matter of time before he did something terrible- yet no one did anything.

One of the beautiful things about our justice system in the U.S. is that if someone has not committed a crime, you really cannot expect them to be tasered, handcuffed, beaten (with or without the knee on the neck) and arrested (or killed) simply for raising a concern. However, one of the *drawbacks* to our American forms of justice is that unless a complete lunatic- a timebomb waiting to go off, such as the lunatic in this case- commits a crime, there is nothing that can be done even if you do voice your concerns. It's a double edged sword that in this case seems to have cut the wrong way.

I told the lady with whom I was having this conversation that I could relate to her feelings of guilt, but I assured her that no one I've met has a crystal ball that actually works well enough to predict the future, and to stop beating herself up. To try to alleviate her feelings to some degree, I shared my similar story with her, and now I'll share it with you.

***

There was this one kid back in school around whom I always felt apprehensive. We'll call him Steve, though that's not his real name. Steve was a bully, and from a young age, I could tell, a complete lunatic.

Steve was one of those 'man children' who was six feet tall and two hundred pounds by middle school. Had he been interested in football, and had he had just a hint of talent and work ethic, there is no doubt in my mind that he could have easily excelled at the sport, and perhaps gone on to play at the college level. However, Steve showed no interest, whatsoever, in *any* sports. His only interest was in being a bully. And he was a terrifying, horrific bully, because due to his size and strength, the teachers had much difficulty pulling him off of the other, extremely smaller students that he would choose as his targets, and he would not stop beating on them until the teachers *did* pull him off (it usually took three male teachers to do so), and every single one of his victims ended up in the hospital. Why no one in the education system blew any whistles on this guy is way beyond me.

Oddly, though I feared Steve and could feel the pit of my stomach drop when he came around, for some reason I'll never be able to explain, he *liked* me. He actually considered me a friend (though I can assure you, I was not), and though my instincts told me to fear the guy, my reasoning told me he was no threat to me.

Until that one night, oddly, in October, so we could say that one "October Night," and that's cool because that's the title of my totally awesome collection of short stories (well, close, it's "October Nights"), but you guys knew that.

Anyway, I'd been turkey hunting at one of my favorite hunting spots. It was up an old forest service road which led to the top of a mountain that I knew like the back of my hand. Remember, I grew up back in Appalachiastan, and in stark contrast to where I now live, in the motherland of Virginia (and fyi, for those who lack a common knowledge of U.S. history, I refer to Virginia as the motherland, because prior to the American Civil War, our states were one in the same- my part of Appalachiastan would split and become its own state during the war) most of the land in Appalachiastan is owned by either private corporations (coal and timber companies) or the Federal Government. As long as you have the proper licenses, you can pretty much hunt anywhere, whereas in Virginia, the majority of the land is private property, and if you try hunting just about anywhere, you're likely to get shot by a disgruntled property owner.

It had gotten dark while I was on my way out of the woods. When I reached my car, parked at the locked gate at the mouth of the road at the foot of the mountain, I was surprised and somewhat frightened to see Steve waiting there, his redneck truck parked beside my car.

"I gut shot a deer," he said, holding up his compound bow, half a dozen arrows quivered on its shaft. "I need you to help me track it."

Now, for those of you reading this who don't know what that means, it means that Steve had shot, or so he was claiming, a deer with an arrow in a non-vital area. Had he hit it in the heart or lungs, more than likely it would have dropped dead within sight of where he'd shot it. However, a gut shot, such as a shot to the stomach, can lead to the animal running and walking for up to a mile before it bleeds out and dies. I have bow hunted, and I have killed deer with arrows, and fortunately, I always hit the vitals and none of the animals suffered more than a minute or two, if they were even aware then what had hit them, but this constant fear of gut shooting any creature is what would eventually lead to me no longer bow hunt.

When a deer was gut shot, the true hunt began. Especially if it was dark, like it was now. Basically, you tried to follow the blood trail by way of a flashlight in order to find the deer. Hopefully it was dead when you did, otherwise, you had to slit its throat with a knife.

Something in *my* gut was telling me that Steve was lying. I felt like he wanted to get me alone in the woods. But didn't he already have me alone in the woods? I mean, technically, we were ten miles out of town. There might be one car, if that, pass through this area all night. This is how I reassured myself that I was safe to venture further into the forest with him. *Besides*, I told myself. *He likes me. Right?*

Steve and I went a short distance up the road before cutting up over a steep incline on the right. Once on top of the ridge, Steve suggested we split up and go in a circle in order to find the blood trail, him circling around from the left, and me from the right. We did so, and even though he was no longer right with me, it made me more nervous, as if I'd felt safer at least knowing where he was and what he was doing.

About halfway through my circle, I stopped. It was then that I realized something was making its way toward me from the left, the direction in which Steve had gone. But the sound was not indicative of something moving in an outward circle a considerable distance from me. It was indicative of something coming straight toward me.

I shined my light in the direction of the sound but I saw nothing. I continued walking the way I'd been going, and when I stopped, I heard it again, and it was much closer. However, I also heard something to my right this time. Shining my light in the direction of this *new* sound, I *did* see something. I saw eye shine!

However, it was obviously not the eye shine from a gutshot deer, as the shine was not three feet off the ground, where the eyes of a deer would be. The eyes I saw glowing in reflection of my flashlight were easily eight feet off the ground.

"What the..." I mumbled, and as I did, whatever was only forty or so yards away from me, to my right, took a step toward me. I instinctively and fearfully took a step backward, and as I did, an arrow came flying at me from my left. It missed my nose by so little that I could feel the wind on my face as it passed. The arrow lodged in a tree right beside my head, its ass-end twinging back and forth, left to right, until it finally settled to a stop. Whatever had been to my right was now gone. At least, I could no longer see its eyes.

"What the fuck!" I said, realizing Steve had nearly shot me in the head with an arrow. Obviously, he'd been aiming for my light, as it was too dark for him to have seen me.

"My bad," Steve said as he made his way to me. "I saw that deer. I shot at it. I missed. I guess I never hit it in the first place. Come on. Let's go."

He didn't even pull his arrow out of the tree. He simply turned, as if nothing had happened, and began making his way down the hill. I followed, keeping a safe distance and making sure not to allow him to get behind me. I was not letting this guy out of my sight.

I would see Steve off and on after that, around town and around school, but I was never alone with him again. I would go off to college the following fall, and after graduating from college years later, I would leave Appalachiastan. I went back, once, for a short stint, thinking I might relocate back (it was after the war, and during the great recession, and I was strung out on drugs via the Army hospital and the Veterans Administration (("here, now we want to you try this one- oh, and *do* keep taking all the others," they'd say month after month, prescription on top of prescription)), and I had no other options), but I was quickly reminded as to the many reasons that I'd left Appalachiastan in the first place. I summarily left again, and I have been living happily ever after, despite any hardships I've endured in the meantime, since leaving.

So here is the part of this story that allowed me to set the lady with whom I'd had the recent conversation with to ease. Ironically, just a couple of weeks before the lunatic she knew carried out his tragedy, I found myself thinking of Steve and wondering where he was and what he was doing. I guess this was because of the fact that I'd recently lost an old friend, and it just put me in the mindset of thinking about some of the people I'd known back in the day.

Thanks to modern technology, I was able to answer my own question about Steve and his whereabouts by way of a quick Google search. What I found was both shocking, but not surprising.

It turns out that about five years ago, Steve seemingly randomly attacked a woman who was pumping gas at a gasoline station back in Appalachiastan. He'd beaten her in the head with a hammer, and though it was quite a brutal beating, to my understanding, she not only survived, but she didn't suffer any long term physical damages, though I'm sure her PTSD levels will be over the top for the rest of her life.

But Steve wasn't finished for the night. After having been detained and taken to a regional holding facility, he attacked another man who'd been locked up while the man was lying in the group lockup cell, sleeping, and nearly strangled him to death.

Due to previous offenses and convictions and a long history of mental illness, Steve was offered a plea agreement, which he accepted. He plead guilty, by way of insanity, and instead of getting sentenced to prison for twenty five years, he was ordered to be institutionalized at a state mental hospital for twenty five years. He's been in for five, he's got twenty more to go. And in my opinion, the world is a safer place with this lunatic finally locked up somewhere. However, I *do* worry about the safety of those with whom Steve is institutionalized.

So, my lady-friend felt a bit better after I shared this story with her, and she had only one follow up question for me. It's the same question I've asked myself, repeatedly, since that night I'd almost been killed by way of Steve's arrow, and it's a question for which to this day I have no answer.

What in the hell had been off to my right that night? Standing, by evidence of the eye shine, nearly eight feet tall? With its instincts, knowing the perfect time to step forward so that I would instinctively and fearfully step back? Thereby avoiding lunatic Steve's arrow and the certain death it would have brought had it hit me in the heat, no doubt, his true inentions?

Was it...

...Bigfoot Sasquatch?

***

Potentially!

The End

Strange Frequencies

*From a letter dated 2-22-2021

Dear Kevin,

I have been a regular viewer of your channel since before you had one thousand subscribers. My, how you've grown. And I don't just mean your channel.

Sure, I was interested in the gardening videos you used to make. They are why I started watching in the first place. I think it was your rose pruning tutorial that YouTube recommended to me. But the reason I kept watching was because of you. I totally get your quirky sense of humor that I believe is way over most people's heads. You remind me of my sister. People either think she's hilarious or abrasive. That's only because they either get her, or they don't, just like I would imagine is the case in your life.

Anyway, what I will say is that I saw strange things in the background of many of your videos long before you ever noticed them or began pointing them out. This is not what shocked me, and when I tell you more about myself you'll understand. What shocked me was two things, the first being that *you* were noticing many of these things, too (but not all- I'm still seeing several things that are alluding you), and secondly, that you were actually pointing them out in your videos.

I can only imagine how many of your original viewers, like myself, felt when this began happening. And I'm talking about those, unlike myself, who do not have the eyes to see nor the ears to hear certain things that you and I and so many others can and do. These viewers must have thought that either you'd lost your mind or that you were playing some sort of games. Trolling them, as I've often read people comment on your videos. I, personally, knew that neither was the case, and I'm happy that you've pushed forward with what some are calling your "shenanigans," actions and statements which I know are your truths.

I will keep my story short, because I have reason to believe you already know it by way of your own. I'd be willing to bet that we share such similar stories that they could be different chapters in the same book.

I could see things when I was a child that others could not. These things- things that some might call ghosts, apparitions, spirits, or even demons- never scared me, because as far back as I can remember, they were there. What *did* scare me, was when they (my parents upon the advice of some public school teachers) sent me to mandatory counselling and began cramming mandatory medications down my throat.

Their efforts did not work, as I continued to see and hear what I saw and heard- things which others could not see and hear- but they were blurry and distorted now due to the synthetic medication I was on. However, so was every damn thing else I was seeing and hearing. The medications were turning my brains to mush, and I knew they'd eventually kill me if I didn't discontinue their use.

What did I do?

I stopped taking them!

Kevin, I am about your age, plus or minus a year or two, and though I know you were raised in a very rural, backwoods setting (I love how you've renamed it "Appalachiastan") and I was raised in the city (go Steelers!), we were coming of age at the same time, during the same era, and one of the trademarks of our era was meds. Remember the movie "Prozac Nation" with Christina Ricci? She was one of my celebrity crushes back in the day (yes, I'm a lesbian, and I know you don't care or judge, and that's another reason I love you and your channel), as she may have been yours. Anyway, I could *so* relate to that movie, because Prozac was just one of the many medications I was on. The only person I knew who was on more meds than me was my mother. Like many boomers, she became obsessed with the meds craze of the 90's, because she viewed it as a way to allow her to excuse her behavior of the 80's. She could now avoid claiming any responsibility for any damages caused by her actions during her decade of decadence.

Anyway, I digress. Another reason, by the way, that I love your YouTube channel. There is only one way to tell a story, in my opinion, and that is the long way!

So, I was sitting in the waiting room of my shrink's office senior year of high school. I couldn't wait to turn eighteen, because my plan was to leave home and get off the meds immediately. I knew it would cost me the relationships I had with many people, mostly my family, but I was willing to take that risk, because I viewed it as worth it. I wanted my mind back.

And that's when *she* walked in!

No, not some ghostly apparition, but the girl of my dreams (and she did bear a strong resemblance to Christina Ricci) who is now my wife of the last ten years. We'd actually run up to Massachuettets to get married about five years before doing so was made legal countrywide. We knew it was coming, but we didn't feel we should have to wait to participate in such a basic human right. Now, we gladly look forward to the day we can smoke the sticky stuff, as you say it in many of your stories, without being deemed as the equivalents of felonious murderers for doing so. I see you can do that now down there in Virginia, and though I know you do not, I envy your ability to do so without life ruining repercussions following.

Did I mention I have a tendency to digress? Like you?

So, Emma- that's my wife- comes into the waiting room and sits down and she looks over at this clown of a ghost that was marching around in the waiting room trying to get everyone's attention with its stupid jokes and silly antics. Yes, just like Beetlejuice, Beetlejuice, Beetlejuice!

I'd been ignoring this vision, really trying to come across as normal in order to get off the meds, though I knew my mother would never allow it. However, I could not ignore the fact that Emma saw it also. She began laughing, but I could tell she was doing her best to hold it in.

I stood and walked over to a table near where Emma was sitting and I took up a magazine and then sat down beside her. "Can you see him?" I said, barely a whisper.

"I can," she said. "Let me guess. Prozac?"

"Oh, but of course," I said. "You?"

"Oh, yes," she said. "They're calling it depression, because my parents are professionals who are friends with the doc, so my family is too good for a diagnosis of schizophrenia, otherwise they'd say I have that."

"Me too," I told her. "I'm convinced my mom was blowing the doctor before she married my dad. Hell, maybe she still is."

And thus our friendship, which would soon become a romantic relationship, began.

Emma and I devised a plan. We wanted to stay under the radar, so instead of just breaking all ties with everyone we knew when we turned eighteen, and flushing all our meds down the toilet and then running away to live happily ever after, we faked it. We acted as if we'd had a sudden change of heart in regard to our treatment. We began talking about how grateful we were to be on such wonderful medications to help us with our afflictions. Oh, what a marvelous time to be alive, these 1990's, we would proclaim. Just look at the stock market!

But in reality, we were planning our escape, and we eventually made it. We convinced our parents we were healthy enough to go to college and be left alone and still take our meds and make arrangements to see counsellors, and that's exactly what we did. We ended up going to Shippensburg University, up in Shippensburg PA, and despite getting off our meds, and not seeing counsellors, and just learning how to handle what we could see and hear that others could not, publicly, instead, we both graduated in four years, with worthless degrees in nothing (it's called a board of regents degree- it's like a general studies with no declared major), and we have been living happily ever after ever since.

Now, here's our secret, which is *not* very complicated. We know that those who cannot see or hear the things that we (and I include you, not so crazy, Crazy Lake, as part of we, here) can see or hear are either going to write us off as insane, delusional, or prankish. That last part, of course, if you're claiming to see and hear these things on social media, as you do, my friend. So what we do, is we simply make no indication or acknowledgement of the things we see and hear that others cannot when we are in the presence of those who cannot. If the blind do not want to see, and if the deaf do not want to hear, yet both want to judge, them fuck them all, is what Emma and I learned to say many years ago, because we intended to remain, as we have, proud lifelong defectors of the Nation of Prozac!

This is what makes me respect you most, Kevin. On your YouTube channel, you do not clam up and act like you cannot see and hear what you're seeing and hearing on your property. You talked about your 'white boy' in a video about a month ago, and I assure you he's there. I've been seeing him in the background of your videos for at least two years. I was wondering who he was, and I'm glad you finally explained. It's so amazing that he visited you first in a dream when you were so young, and it's equally amazing that he's stayed with you, I believe, as a protector for so long.

Now, I know that there's a lot of hubbub about Bigfoot Sasquatch on your channel, and here is my honest opinion on that. Neither Emma nor myself have *ever* seen a Bigfoot Sasquatch. However, we have a good friend, a guy named Vance, who not only *has* seen a Bigfoot Sasquatch, but who, like you, has a *family* of Bigfoot Sasquatch living in the woods behind his house in rural Pennsylvania.

Emma and I met Vance in college, and we knew he was legit, because we met him much the same way we'd met. Not at a shrink's office, but we noticed he was noticing an attention whore of an entity in freshman English one day. We approached him after class, and thus another lifelong friendship was forged.

Emma and I are back in Pittsburgh, but we go out to see Vance several times a year. I want to make sure to make this very clear for the record, especially if you share this story with your readers or viewers, which, by the way, you have my full consent to do, Emma and I have never, I repeat *never* seen or even *heard* any of the Bigfoot Sasquatches that Vance claims is on his property, but we have every reason to believe that he is being honest, and that these creatures do, indeed, exist.

So, if this is the case- the existence of these creatures- and if we believe that our friend, like you, has them on his property, and thirdly, if Emma and I are gifted and have been blessed with the eyes to see and the ears to hear that which so many cannot, why have we not seen or heard our friend Vance's Bigfoot Sasquatch?

Frequencies, dear Watson. Frequencies.

Emma and I have long held a theory that not all messages are meant for all people. I'll use one of your recent videos as an example. You recently made a video in which you told the story of how you were reading a book of Christmas stories to your son this past Christmas season while also listening to Christmas music on YouTube. You told of how when you finished a story and turned the page, which lead to a Christmas carol, at that exact same time that very carol began playing on the YouTube playlist you were listening to.

That, my friend, is called synchronicity, and it was a synchronicity set to *your* frequency, because that was *your* message. You were the one who needed to hear it. You mentioned that you were thinking about your other children who are now adults, and from whom you've been estranged for more than a decade. The synchronicity that you experienced was a message from the great beyond, I believe, and as you stated yourself in your video, that you were exactly where you are supposed to be doing exactly what you're supposed to be doing with exactly whom you're supposed to be doing it.

These things, these synchromatic moments, happen, I believe, in the lives of everyone, though not everyone recognizes them as such.

Yet!

In time, I do believe that most people become tuned with their personal frequencies, though even then, most folks will never acknowledge synchronicity itself, mostly due to religious beliefs that they feel would be compromised if they were to accept things other than whatever is written in their holy book of choice, be it the Bible or the Koran, The Torah or the Book of Mormon, etc.

Still others like to consider themselves too intelligent to believe in such hocus pocus- the smartest guys in the room, I've heard you refer to these types on your channel. These people, in both groups mentioned here, and others not mentioned, will always refer to these events as coincidence. I do not believe in coincidence, but as far as those people receiving their messages on their frequencies goes, it is none of my business and it has nothing to do with me. If they at least note the event as a coincidence, then they have at least acknowledged the event, which means, whether they like it or not, they have received the message. Sometimes, this is the only way the Universe can deliver the message. I refer to it as the frequency of denial. But it is a message receiving frequency nonetheless.

I also believe that there are frequencies in regard to the entities we see. Emma and I have our frequencies set to ghosts, spirits, apparitions and demons. Our friend Vance can see some of these, as well as Bigfoot Sasquatch.

I do believe that though Bigfoot Sasquatch does exist, as do angels and demons and ghosts, etc. there are simply people who will spend a lifetime never seeing them, or any of this stuff, because that is simply not the way their frequencies are set. I do wish, however, so many of them who are so loud in their judgements and criticisms would leave those of us who do have our frequencies set to be able to see and hear these things alone. And for God's sake, I wish the medical establishment would stop trying to medicate our abilities out of us.

Anway, I'll part with a reminder, perhaps, to any of the smartest guys in the room types who may read or hear this, should you choose to share this in one of your books or on your YouTube channel, or both, of a quote of a man one would think they might respect; Albert Einstein.

"Everybody is a genius. But if you judge a fish by its ability to climb a tree, it will live its whole life believing that it is stupid."

Sincerely yours,

Katie

P.

Pittsburgh, PA

4

So Far She's Seen Four (And Not To Mention Ghosts!)

(Originally Titled: Gail's Story)

From a letter received 1 April 2021

Kevin,

Hello, my name is Gail Mayes. I am 47 years old. I found your channel about a month ago and I truly enjoy watching you. Keep up the great work!

I am writing to you to say that I know for a *fact* that Bigfoot Sasquatch exist! I have seen four of them.

The first one that I saw was when I was headed home from a long day of bike (motorcycle) riding. It was a rusty red color.

The second one I saw was once again when I was out riding my bike, and it was on the side of the road. As I was passing it, it reached out for me. The second one was white (dirty white, almost blue). I saw its big eyes and teeth. I was terrified.

The third and fourth ones that I saw were on the side of the road. I was on the way to the grocery store, and they were crouched down. At first I thought that they were round bales of hay, until I came home and they were gone. When I saw them it looked as though they were holding what could possibly be a young one. I'm not sure.

I have seen the X's. I have seen the teepee looking structures too, and I have heard the whoops (howels). I have also heard tree knocks and screams from them. So when you say that he, she, it or they potentially live in the woods behind your home, I believe you.

I lived in Grayson County, Kentucky when I saw them. I now live in Shelby County, Kentucky with my husband and our two Yorkshire terriers. Our home was built in 1812. Our living room is an actual log cabin, the rest of the house was built around it.

I have seen a man pacing back and forth. It looked as though he was wearing a military uniform. He was carrying an old tattered teddy bear. I told my husband that it looked as though he was looking for a child.

We've smelled cigar smoke in the living room and we have heard what sounds to be boots walking across the floor.

I just wanted to share my story with you. You may share it if you would like. The decision is yours.

Sending much love and respect,

Gail Mayes

Shelbyville, KY

P.s.- Thank you for your service!

5

Cease And Desist!

From A Letter Dated 4-04-2021

Comes now, Peter B. Hurt, Esq

To whom it may concern, in this case, concerning you, one Kevin a.k.a. "Crazy" Lake,

It has been brought to the attention of our offices, by our client, that you have publicly slandered our client and his relations in both video and written form, particularly, and of case in this instance, in your not so funny story "The Boy Who Cried Bigfoot Sasquatch" originally titled "The Unfortunate Demise Of Jittery J" in the first volume of your raunchily successful series Bigfoot Sasquatch Files.

Our offices have been informed by our client that with this story, and the main character of this story, one Jittery J, you have based a character tightly on the true persona of our client (name withheld for reading of letter on YouTube and printing in Bigfoot Sasquatch Files Volume 10).

Comes now, by way of our offices, our litany of evidence of your crimes committed:

Whereas in your story "The Boy Who Cried Bigfoot Sasquatch" originally titled "The Unfortunate Demise Of Jittery J" your main character, this so called "Jittery J" lacks the ability to look other people directly in the eyes when speaking with them, because he lacks any form of confidence or self esteem, because he has done nothing of note in life, and he does nothing of note in life, our client, (name withheld for reading of letter on YouTube and printing in Bigfoot Sasquatch Files Volume 10) does not possess the gumption to look other people in the eyes when speaking to them, because he has done nothing of note in life, and he does nothing of note in life.

Whereas in your story "The Boy Who Cried Bigfoot Sasquatch" originally titled "The Unfortunate Demise Of Jittery J" your main character, this so called "Jittery J" knows everything, as you state, for example, "I mean there wasn't a goddamn thing this mother fucker didn't already know about," our client (name withheld for reading of letter on YouTube and print in Bigfoot Sasquatch Files Volume 10) knows everything. He has not one, but *two* degrees from a very prestigious southern University as proof thereof.

Whereas in your story "The Boy Who Cried Bigfoot Sasquatch" originally titled "The Unfortunate Demise Of Jittery J" your main character, this so called "Jittery J" spends the majority of his time in the basement of his home, viewing a specific type of adult video material, our client (name withheld for reading of letter on YouTube and print in Bigfoot Sasquatch Files Volume 10) does spend an unhealthy amount of time in the basement of his home viewing a particular type of adult video material.

Finally, whereas in your story "The Boy Who Cried Bigfoot Sasquatch" originally titled "The Unfortunate Demise Of Jittery J" your main character, this so called "Jittery J" supports himself, financially, by having married a very unattractive woman (on the inside and out) of financial means who supports him, despite spousally abusing him mostly through means of gaslighting, our client (name withheld for reading of letter on YouTube and for print in Bigfoot Sasquatch Files Volume 10) supports himself, financially, by having married a very unattractive woman (on inside and out) of financial means who financially supports him, despite spousally abusing him mostly through means of gaslighting. This last point, further evidenced by a story you wrote in volume three of your raunchily successful Bigfoot Sasquatch Files series titled, "Gaslighting," originally titled "The Unfortunate Demise Of Crazy A," as our client (name withheld for reading on YouTube and print in Bigfoot Sasquatch Files Volume 10) is married to a woman who is bat crap crazy, and whose name begins with the letter 'A,' though no one in our offices can remember what her name actually is, just like in your story, which is case in point number B. And yes, she is an extreme gaslighter. She never tells the same story the same way twice. And it's intentional. To make the listener think they're losing their mind. Classic, textbook gaslighting. So we know you're referencing her!

With this cease and desist letter of communication, our offices are hereby demanding that you cease and desist using our client or our client's persona or image in any way for any characters going forward in any of your printed works, or in any of your videos on social media, which, by the way, our offices have viewed, in length, and have deemed to be fake. However, we do wonder what's up with so many of the faces we see in the background of some of your videos. We want to attribute it to CGI in order to discredit you, because we are paid by your opposition, but you do not appear to be that advanced with your editing skills. Case in point; all those construction paper cutouts you use.

We will provide adequate space at the bottom of this letter, and you can use the blank backs of any of these forms if you need more space, to issue your response to us. You will be given thirty days to respond to this communication before our client may or may not take further action. And please note, our client will know if you discuss this issue on your YouTube channel or if you print it in any upcoming Bigfoot Sasquatch Files volumes, because he watches all of your videos and reads all of your books.

He hates you that much!

Sincerely,

Peter B. Hurt, Esq.

***

*My Response:

Dear Peter B. Hurting,

Sorry to hear about that. Sounds like a personal problem. Take two Advil and don't call me in the morning, because I don't care.

Maybe if you'd spend a little less time in the basement with your client, viewing that smut, you wouldn't be in so much pain. Hey, that's a great idea! You just can't beat it!

Pun intended!

As far as your client goes, and his or her or it or their idle threat. Here's one for you.

Once upon a time, a mean old nasty witch put a curse on the unmarked graves of Jittery J and his bat crap crazy, gaslighting wife Crazy A and she resurrected them both. You see, she was bored, and she knew, potentially, there was a Bigfoot Sasquatch in the area who'd killed them, and who'd had so much fun doing it that he (or she, or it, but definitely not a 'they' because he, she or it had acted alone) wanted to do it again.

Upon the witch's words of hocus pocus, Jittery J and Crazy A did rise up from their graves, just in time for that big 'ol hairy beast of a creature to be passing through, and surprise, surprise, he, she or it (but again, definitely not 'them,' for once again, he, she, or it were acting alone) killed them again.

The end.

There's my response, Peter B. Painful. Put that in your pipe and smoke it, and thank you and your client both for the views and the book sales.

There will be more to come.

Just not in your case.

Pun intended.

Sincerely,

Kevin "Crazy" Lake

Ps- you might want to tell your client (wink, wink) that the next time they place anything in my mailbox, make sure I'm not standing up there in the upper portion of the lower field, hidden just inside the treeline, watching them do it.

Pss- You may also want to inform your client that they are not very photogenic. We have their images saved on several thumb drives (peeking through our windows, trying to figure out where we're at when we were on vacation- walking around various parts of our property to take a closer look at what particular gardening or chores they'd noticed us doing that day before heading into town) to prove it.

Psss-I would tell you to have a great day, but I'm the opposition. However, I don't want to harbor resentment toward you, so I will pray for you.

Dear God,

Please bring Peter B. Hurt, Esq, the same health, wealth and prosperity with which you have so blessed this household.

Pssss- Oh, and please make that thing stop hurting!

The End

Interview With A Killer

(Originally Titled "Bertha's Story")

Though I'm typing madly away, I still feel hesitant to tell this story. Not because it's not worth telling, but because I broke one of my social media cardinal rules in obtaining it.

I hate to reiterate one of my rules as a YouTuber here and now, but it's the only way you'll really understand the full scope of this story. At least the full scope of my obtainment of the story.

Okay, I know you've heard me say this in my videos, or you've read it in my books before, but when you work in social media, as a content creator, and you share a part of your life with potentially millions of viewers, who, remember, are predominately strangers, you must be very, very careful, because many of those strangers are not stable.

When you start out on YouTube, or Fakebook, or TikTok, or whatever flavor of the year new platform is out there, it's only natural to fantasize about going big. Then, once you get a couple thousand subscribers or followers, it's only natural to say to yourself, "wow, wouldn't that be neat if I were out in public one day and someone approached me and said, 'hey, I watch you on (fill in the blank with the social media platform of your choosing).'" And when that finally happens (it happens to us regularly now), it really is a neat feeling. Kind of flattering.

But then you start to think it through…

…and you wonder just how many people around you know so much about you, because they watch you on social media, but they *don't* approach you. Oh, we get the stares and the whispers while we're out in public, and I'm already paranoid (as you know, if you watch my YouTube channel 'Homesteading Off The Grid'), and that starts to get to you. You know the people are talking about how they watch you on the internet, and you can appreciate the fact that they *don't* approach you, but it's still creepy.

But what's even creepier than that, is when you slip up during a morning recording session and say where you're going later that day after you publish your video, and when you get there, there are people waiting on you! Yes, this happened once, and I shared that story in the last volume of Bigfoot Sasquatch Files, so I won't retell it here, but the point is, you learn to become very, very careful about specific times, dates and locations, and (this part is so unfortunate, because I know in my heart that most of our viewers are salt of the earth people who would never cross the line of inappropriateness) you never correspond with people in the comment section of videos. Not only does this hold the potential of an "inappropriate relationship" forming with a viewer (and that concept could go a million different ways), but sadly, it's a must after you get about 50,000 viewers, followers, subscribers, etc. to keep the malicious trolls away. What I mean by that, is that when you reply to a positive comment, in a positive way, the completely malicious sons of a bitches out there who are full of hate, or who are merely bored teenagers looking for cheap, free entertainment, will see that you are reading and responding to comments, and at least a dozen of them will reply to your reply, insulting you, or insulting the viewer who left the original comment. I've said this before, too, and I'll say it again here. Social media is the gutter of the internet. This is so sad, because it could be such a wonderful place to garner free, harassment free entertainment, but there are so many miserable shitbags out there in society who have to muck it up for everyone.

Now that I've had my long winded preface (but hey, you're used to that by now, right?) I think what I'm about to tell you, of how I came to meet Bertha, who, as I know you've guessed by now, is not really named Bertha, in the first place, will hold a lot more water.

Okay, Bertha committed the most blatant red flag raising offense a viewer on social media, at least a viewer of social media posts created by slightly paranoid people like me, can commit. Under a fake user id, she commented on one of my Bigfoot Sasquatch videos, simply, "we need to talk."

I'm thinking, "stalker!" Or, "lunatic!" And who wouldn't, right? I mean, put yourself in my position. You have hundreds of thousands of subscribers. Upwards of five million viewers per month (on a good month) watch your videos, and here's someone you don't know, using a fake profile, letting you know that you "need to talk?"

I prayed for her.

And then I summarily banned her.

Okay, second infraction. She came back at me under a different fake profile and told me I'd banned her old one, and that she didn't know why, and that we needed to talk.

Prayed.

Banned.

Third attempt; she messaged me on one of my online selling platform accounts. Yes, this happens. You'd be amazed at how many 'vertically challenged individuals who live under bridges' will message my Amazon seller's account or my Etsy account just to tell me how much they disagree with a recent video I made or how much of an arrogant narcissist prick I am, and that I needed therapy. Really? You are freaking messaging a YouTube content creator on their Etsy account to insult them and tell them how much you hate them, and someone else needs therapy?

Anyway, this is how it happened.

I reported her to that seller account.

Prayed for her.

And then banned her.

Okay, next, Bertha broke the absolute, beyond a shadow of a doubt, cardinal rule for any social media content creator. The rule that, if broken, usually leads to a visit from the police, restraining order in hand.

She sought me out and confronted me in person.

In the real world.

Well, not really, but kinda.

Alas, you've heard it said that it is a small, small world. Well, this story with Bertha and how we came to meet up in person is proof of that.

Again, as I've said before, many people think that when you create content on social media, you "show your whole life" to complete strangers on the internet. This is so far from true it would blow your mind. You only show a small portion of your life to complete strangers online, but if you are completely open and honest about that small portion, and people can see that you are real, you'll be successful beyond imagination, and it gives the viewers the sense that they know you personally, and it makes them feel as if they know everything about you, even though they really only know a small portion about you.

The rest of the stuff you don't show?

Keep it to yourself!

As I will here, to a great degree.

There are many parts of my life I'll never share on YouTube. Certain hobbies I participate in. Certain places I absolutely love to go to eat, shop, walk, socialize, etc. And the reason I'll never share information about this, is because I am still free to go to these places and simply be Kevin. I don't have to be "Crazy Lake." No one expects it of me, because none of the other people who frequent these specific places and participate in these particular hobbies (and I can assure you they are all legal, and very healthy) know that I'm a YouTuber. Most of them, believe it or not, shun social media, because they know of its extremely damaging negative effects on individuals and society. Did I mention social media was the gutter of the internet?

Anyway, it was only months ago, while I was participating in one such social event, at one of my personal social gatherings, when a lovely woman, about sixty years old, approached me and said, "I know who you are." I smiled wanly (I've always wanted to use that word, wanly, in written format, but I never have. This is a first. Mark it on your calendar.), and asked her please not to share this information with anyone, because I really liked hanging out with this small group of people and doing what it was we did when we got together. I know this has completely piqued your curiosity, but if you're ten volumes into this series, I'm confident you are one of my true, real, probably not mentally unstable followers, and I know you'll respect my privacy. And I can assure you it's nothing sexual. I don't belong to a nudist colony or a secret orgy society.

Bertha smiled, for reals, not wanly, and told me she wouldn't 'rat me out,' as she put it. Then she asked if I'd like to join her for coffee after our group get-together, because she had an amazing story for me she'd like to share. I told her sure, I'd love to get together with her for coffee, and up until that time I had no clue she was Bertha, so all seemed perfectly harmless.

After our little group's get-together, Bertha and I, driving separate cars (hey, I'm no fundamentalist, but some of the best advice I've ever heard came from one, Billy Graham, who said, 'never be alone with a woman who isn't your wife'), met up at one of many local coffee shops (no, not Starbucks). After ordering, taking our seats, and having that first awkward sip, Bertha spoke first, and I nearly got up and left.

"FYI, you've already banned me from your YouTube channel twice, and you got me kicked off of Etsy," she said with a somewhat devious smile.

I felt my blood run cold, as if I were a fly caught in a spider's web. In my mind's eye, I could see this woman, nearing retirement, pulling a derringer out of her pocket and shooting me from under the table, and then running to my house and boiling my inside the house domestic bunny rabbit Winston alive. Oh, why had I not listened to the Reverend Billy Graham in his entirety?

"Calm down," Bertha said, as if reading my mind. "I'm not a creepy stalker. I have no interest in you romantically. I'm a flaming lesbian in a wonderful relationship with a beautiful woman ten years my junior, and I'm not going to stalk you. We've just been needing to talk for a long time."

At this point, I simply continued to stare. I felt a bit reassured after what she'd told me, but still, my not so unhealthy sense of paranoia kicked in. I began looking around the room. As my head turned to the table to my left, the two women sitting there, about my age and not unattractive looked at me. They both smiled. *Oh my God*, I thought. *Have I banned them, too? Have I lost the secretiveness of this coffee shop?* I then looked to my right. There was a man and a woman sitting at this table, early twenties, they stared at me with that blank look of extreme lack of emotion, so typical of the Z generation, and I thought, *Oh, my God! Gen Z stalkers! Are they going to threaten to cancel me?*

"Are you okay?" I heard Bertha say. "Look, if I'm making you uncomfortable, we can leave. And I'll never approach you again. I just thought you'd like to hear my story, because it would be a good one for you to tell on your channel. Or even put in one of your books. You have *got* to be running out of ideas. I mean, how in the hell can one person, someone like you, come up with a different story every freaking day? That's *got* to be *completely* exhausting?"

I don't know how she did it, but Bertha said the most perfect words she could have said in that situation. I sometimes feel that the only other person who understood what I go through as a writer and a content creator on YouTube who loves to provide daily entertainment for his followers (most YouTubers only do a couple videos per week) was Mark Twain, one of my favorite writers. Twain actually wrote about this, at least closely, in his book "Roughing It," when he described how difficult it is as a columnist for a newspaper to come up with something to write every single day, and of how columnists who do this for an entire career, say, like for thirty years, have actually written enough to fill an entire library. Twain got it, I completely understood it, because I live it, and here, across the table from me, Bertha understood, and I felt no more like she was stalking me, preparing to boil my little bunny rabbit who sits on top of his cage all day and only gets exercise when my son, Daniel, grabs him and takes him in the living room and puts him on the rug in front of the wood stove and acts like he's not going to let him hop back into the dining room, where we keep his cage. It's quite funny and good for both of them. I really need to take that rabbit outside more.

"Huh?" I found myself saying, as my thoughts had been all over the globe in the span of less than a minute. I'm with a stalker. Everyone knows me. Gen Z is going to cancel me, because I hurt their feelings. Boiled bunny.

"I killed a Bigfoot Sasquatch," Bertha said. These words brought me to my full attention.

"What!" I said, and it didn't sound like a question. The parties sitting to my left and right looked over, briefly, and even the Gen Z'ers almost showed emotion on their faces when they did.

Almost.

"I killed a Bigfoot Sasquatch," Bertha said, again, but only after the people sitting beside us had gone back to their conversations.

"I'm not proud of it," she said. "And it's haunted me since the time I did it. I was only thirteen years old."

"That's a long time," I said.

"Yeah," she said. "And it's not like I've been able to talk to anyone about it. At least anyone who believes me. So it's been very difficult to shed the weight of the burden. Until April, and now maybe you."

April, Bertha explained, was the name of her partner. April, she also explained, believed every word of Bertha's story from the first time she'd told her about it. Bertha explained it's one of the reasons she quickly fell in love with April. It may come to no surprise to you that the two of them actually met at a Bigfoot Sasquatch retreat in South Carolina.

"It was all about trying to be accepted," Bertha said as she launched right into her story, as if I'd given her my full permission to do so. I guess in a way, by having stayed at the table rather than running away having realized I'd just met up in person with one of my internet stalkers, I had.

"Like I said," she continued. I was only thirteen. I grew up in Georgia. I was a little redneck girl, and I knew I was not like the other girls. I always felt more comfortable around boys, and it was with boys that I did my running around.

"Even though they tolerated me," she continued, "I knew they never fully accepted me, because I had a vah-jay-jay. That's why, when we were out shooting one fall, just before hunting season came in, I told the boys I was going to kill a Bigfoot Sasquatch."

I stared at Bertha, so many questions on my mind, and once again, it was as if she'd read my mind, because without me even speaking, she began answering those questions.

"Oh, sure," she said. "They believed in Bigfoot Sasquatch. They'd seen them. We had quite a few around. Even the adults down in our backwoods neck of the woods believed. Some of them had seen them, and most people had heard the whoops and howls at night. There were certain places down there where one simply did not go at night."

"Why were people scared?" I asked. "I go outside at night all the time," I told her. "And I may, potentially, have some in the woods behind my house."

"And that's why I've been so emphatic about talking to you," she said, and her tone changed. It went from remorseful to warning. "These creatures are not the docile, peace loving, let's all sit around and hold hands and sing kumbaya beings that you portray them as being on your YouTube channel."

"Oh," I said, intrigued.

"No," she said. "They're more like the beasts who take the assholes in your stories in your books to their unfortunate demise."

"Really," I said.

"Yes," she said. "My grandmother on my mother's side was both raped and murdered by one of these mother fuckers, and I'm convinced I killed the one that did it!"

"Wait a minute," I said, sitting up straight and letting go of my coffee cup. "I'm confused. First, you come across as if you're carrying some great weight of shame or guilt because of what you did, and then you claim you killed a rapist murderer. How can you have both feelings about the same incident?"

"Because of my intent," Bertha said. "I didn't set out to shoot the Bigfoot Sasquatch that raped and murdered my grandmother. I simply set out to kill a Bigfoot Sasquatch. To be accepted by the guys I hung out with. It just so happened that I lucked out and killed the Bigfoot Sasquatch, I believe, that raped and killed my grandmother."

"How do you know it was the same one?" I asked.

"Because my aunt had been walking through the woods with my grandmother the afternoon she'd been abducted, and she saw it," Bertha said. "She said it had a white stripe running across the top of it's head, like a skunk. And the one I killed had that stripe. It had to be the same one."

At this point, I was speechless, so Bertha continued with her story.

The boys saw it after I'd killed it, and I don't think they fully accepted me, still, but they certainly held me in higher regard.

"What did you do with the body?" I asked.

"We buried it, of course," she said, her tone making it sound as if she thought I were nuts.

"You didn't call anyone? You could have provided proof of these things existing!"

"Hell no, we didn't call anyone," she said. "All our families were growing weed in that area. It's how we supported ourselves. If the authorities would have come in there, snooping around for Bigfoot Sasqutch, they would have discovered acre upon acre of the sticky stuff, as you call it in your stories, and our whole damn hollow would have been incarcerated.

"Anyway," she went on, "I got a lot of the guilt and shame off my chest with April, though it still comes back in degrees. And that's not why I felt like I needed to talk to you, to the point of losing a couple YouTube accounts and my Etsy privileges."

"Well, what is it you were so persistent about, then?" I asked.

"Like I said," she said. "These creatures are not all friendly. They're not all peaceful trying to live in harmony with the rest of the world. Some of them," she said, pausing, looking around to make sure no one was eavesdropping. They weren't so she continued. "Some of them are as evil and vile as any evil and vile human, like that annoying neighbor you ran off with a crayon, just to give an example. You cannot let that pretty little Asian wife of yours spend too much time alone on that property of yours. I can only imagine what would happen if you had a nasty son of a bitch like Skunk Head- that's what we called the bastard I killed- roaming around your property. If you're not packing heat on your property, because I know you claim you don't kill the wildlife, you should be. If not for your own protection, for your wife's."

We finished our coffee that day and spoke of a few other things; other common interests and of how people who didn't believe in Bigfoot Sasquatch thought that people like Bertha and myself were nuts. We parted ways that day, though we've seen each other many times since, and as I told her that day, I have not and I will not reveal her real identity.

And she's stopped stalking me on the internet, as it's no longer necessary.

And we're packing heat on the homestead now.

So if you want to be that next dick to come poking around leaving gifts at night because you think trolling is funny?

I wouldn't if I were you.

Especially after dark.

When you could too easily be mistaken for 'ol Skunk Head.

The End

7

Skinwalker Potentially?

From a letter received 3-23-2021

Mr. Lake,

My name is S----. I don't care if you tell my story on your YouTube channel, or if you put it in one of your books, which you probably won't (author's note- WRONG!), because it has nothing to do with Bigfoot Sasquatch. Please just don't say my real name or tell anyone the small town I'm from in Texas. I've already done enough damage with this story. My own family hasn't spoken to me in years because of their embarrassment of me, because I continue to believe and talk about what I saw. The reason I'm writing to you about it, is because I fear that you might have something much more terrifying than a Bigfoot Sasquatch on your land. I fear that you, too, might have a skinwalker!

I don't know if you ever saw it or not, but several years ago, there was a guy in Utah that had a big ranch that became known for its skinwalkers. I'd heard about it through some of my friends. My curiosity finally got the better of me, so I watched some of his videos on YouTube. At first I found them somewhat entertaining, though I felt they were fake. Until I watched one that had a very distinct scream coming from, supposedly, a skinwalker, and the sound of the scream made my blood run cold, because I'd heard the exact same scream on our family property here in Texas. The family property, by the way, that I haven't set foot on in five years after having pretty much been excommunicated, shunned and now entirely estranged by my family.

I've tried to comment about this on your YouTube channel, but I think you've blocked me. If so, I'm not angry, and I know it's my fault. I used to comment that your videos were fake, and that you were just doing it to make money on YouTube. I know you can make a lot of money on YouTube if you're good at it. I tried years ago, but I couldn't even get monetized, so I'll admit, that for a while, out of jealousy, I would troll successful channels. Most channels didn't ban me when I called them fake, but I guess you have a zero tolerance policy for people like me, so, here we are. Thank God you finally got a P.O. box so I could mail you this letter.

Even after you banned me from commenting on your channel, I continued to watch, because though I could tell that some of the videos were obviously fake (I'm sorry, Mr. Lake, but I'm just being honest with you), I could also tell that some were not. And what got me, was that the videos I was seeing things in were not the videos where you were proclaiming there were weird things to see in. It's the videos you make where you just tell stories about your life, or when you would read some of your stories from your totally awesome short story collection, "October Nights" (I bought a copy, even though you've banned me from commenting on your channel). These are the videos in which I see things creeping around in the background. Things that many of your viewers claim are Bigfoot Sasquatch, but things which I know to be skinwalkers.

I don't know how I missed it earlier, but I only recently saw the video where your wife was potting oak trees in the garden (she really made a lot of noise doing that, by the way- you should have had the camera farther away from her) and you were splitting wood behind her, just outside the fence. At least you were supposed to be splitting wood. As usual, you just seemed to be doing a lot of talking.

Anyway, I heard the scream in that video, and oh, my God! That is exactly the same scream that I heard in that skinwalker ranch video, and it's the exact same scream I heard on our property here in Texas several years ago. The scream of a skinwalker!

Mr. Lake. These creatures can imitate the sounds of animals around them. I know a lot of people comment on your videos that you have a donkey on a nearby, neighboring property, but I am here to tell you, what I'm hearing over and over in your videos is no donkey. It's a skinwalker mimicking the sounds of a donkey. It's how they communicate with each other, and it's how they lure their prey in.

One of their nastiest tricks is to imitate the sounds of a baby. They can literally sound like infants crying in the woods. They lead people to them this way, and then they eat them.

You must, however, be aware of their most notorious tactic. When they sound like they are close, they are actually far away. And when they sound like they are far away, like in the video of you talking instead of chopping wood, and your wife making all that noise with the pots, that thing was probably within sight of you! I have never been that scared while watching a YouTube video ever!

Mr. Lake. You must proceed with caution. I know you love working on your property, and I know you feel safe working on your property, but you are not safe. You and your family are in danger!

I will share with you briefly my own story.

After seeing the skinwalker ranch video, I couldn't resist my curiosity any longer. The next time I heard that same scream on our property, which was only a few days later, I sought out the creature making the scream, and that decision has ruined my life. It has cost me all communication with my family and it nearly got me killed.

It happened just as the sun was going down. It wasn't dark yet, though it would soon be. I heard the scream coming from a pin-oak thicket down by a creek that was only a hundred yards from our family's old farm house's front porch. It sounded like a donkey, like in so many of your videos, but I knew it wasn't one, because we didn't have any donkeys.

I walked down to the creek, right into the middle of that pin-oak thicket. I stopped, made sure not to make any sounds, and I listened. I then heard it again, but it sounded as if it had moved away while I was moving toward it. I kid you not, it sounded like it was a good mile away.

However, when it screamed, I felt a slight, warm breeze on my right ear, but I distinctly noted not feeling this breeze on any other part of my body. My hair didn't even move. It was as if someone was standing right beside me, blowing on my face. I turned my head to look in that direction, and the skinwalker was right there, its face right in my face!

That's the last thing I remember until I was being shaken by my older brother while lying on the front porch. His wife had thrown him out again for drinking all the time, and he'd moved back in with us. I had just turned eighteen myself. I'm twenty four now.

I had only one physical injury. A cut on my right cheek. It looked like a cat scratch, but it was not an injury made by multiple claws. It was a cut made by only one. As if the skinwalker had reached out with its index finger and given me a little love scratch, so to say, to leave it's mark. Let me know it had paid me a visit.

Well, I did what anyone else would do. At least what I thought anyone else would do. I contacted several different paranormal and cryptozoology groups on social media and I had them come out to our property to investigate. Boy, was this a mistake. It made the local papers, it embarrassed my family, and the rumors began circulating all over the county that my family must be growing some good weed on our property, because I was obviously smoking it. I was kicked out, disowned, and I've not talked to anyone in my family for years. My alcoholic brother who can't keep a job and who really does smoke a lot of weed won't even talk to me.

Mr. Lake. The only advice I can give you is that you need to move. Pack up that pretty wife of yours and that cute little boy and take your cat. Get the hell out of there. Go into town, or even go back to wherever your wife is from. I can't remember if it's Cambodia or VietNam, but either of those two places would probably be safer than where you're living now even though I heard they got ticks the size of mice.

Sincerely yours,

S----

?, Texas

The End

8

It Ain't No Donkey!

As you might imagine, the letter I received from a young woman in Texas recently- the letter you just read, if you're reading these stories in order, piqued my interest, not just because there are so many viewers constantly claiming to hear a donkey in many of our videos, and not just because there are times we hear hideous screams that sound like the screams of a donkey while out and about on our property, but because there are no donkeys in close proximity to us (well, kinda sorta, but I'll get to that), and I know this as fact, because I went investigating, and what I found during that investigation, at the time of the finding seemed insignificant, at least until now, having received aforementioned letter from aforementioned young lady in Texas.

If you follow our channel "Homesteading Off The Grid" on YouTube, then you already know I'm an avid jogger/mountainbiker/walker. I know every road within a five mile radius of our house (I know that doesn't sound like much, but you'd be amazed how many backroads and offshoots of backgrounds there are out here in the country), and I know, by sight, each property. At least the part visible by the road that I can see as I jog, bike or walk by, though I'll admit, many of these estates out here, like one up the road a couple miles that sold only a few years back for $17.5 million, are made up of thousands of acres, most of the property, or course, which cannot be seen from the road.

My point?

No one has any donkeys! (Well, actually, someone does now, but that part comes later).

However, after hearing what clearly sounds like a donkey so many times, and having pinpointed the sound to a particular direction, I finally decided to just stop and ask around about "who has the donkey?"

My findings, to quote the young lady from Texas in the previous story, "made my blood run cold."

So, the first person I asked about a donkey was simply the first person I saw. I was out for a jog one morning, and I saw a woman, a white girl about thirty five years old, loading something into the back of her car. She lived on the side of the road in a small house, on a small property, which bordered one of the very large estates in our area. I simply said, "Hey, do you know if anyone out here has any donkeys?" She looked at me like I was going to rape her, slammed the trunk of her car, and then she ran inside her house.

My first thoughts were, "you're not all that, Karen," but then, as I continued running, thinking about what had just happened, I realized I'd read the situation wrong. I'd never met that woman, but she'd passed me on the road many times while I'd been running, biking or walking and she'd always waved and smiled and she was one of the few drivers out my way who always made sure to slow down and veer away from me as she passed me. She could not have been afraid of me, though she was clearly afraid of something.

A week or so later, I was out on my mountain bike. I happened to be on the opposite side of the large estate that boarded Karen's property. There was an old house sitting by the road, and on the porch sat an old woman who appeared to be as old as the house. I would put both of them at about one hundred.

This was not the first time I'd seen this old woman. I was used to seeing her there. Everytime I biked by and she was there, she always waved and smiled, and I always waved and smiled back and said, "Good morning, young lady." I could always hear her giggle when I did that.

On this day, I stopped.

"Can I ask you a question, young lady?" I said, putting one foot down after stopping my bike only feet away from her rickety old porch.

"Why sure," she said with a smile.

"Do you know if anyone out here has a donkey? I seem to hear one on occasion while I'm out and about on my property. I live right over that hill there."

"I know where's ya live," she said. "Used ta be my cousin's land you bought." This did not surprise me. I live in a place where everyone's related to everyone else except us. We're the outsiders who still after five years here only receive waves from the vast minority of generational locals or other 'outsiders' who've invaded, like Karen down the road. "And you's just 'a hearin' 'ol Cletus," she said, and then she laughed.

"Cletus?" I said. "Is that the donkey's name?"

"Used ta be," she said, and then she leaned forward and spit a mouthful of tobacco juice off the porch, barely missing my foot. It hadn't occurred to me until then that she was chewing tobacco. It was the first time I'd seen a woman chewing tobacco (snuff, actually), since leaving my native Appalachiastan many years ago. But hey, I guess I moved from Appalachia to the South, so it wasn't shocking. "Back when 'ol Cletus was 'a livin'," she added. "'Ol Cletus been dead for fifty years. I know. I was there when he got killed." She spat again. "Well, I showed up right after 'ol Cletus got killed. Happened out there on one my other cousin's property." She pointed in the direction from where I'd always heard the donkey screams.

"What killed him?" I asked.

"Don't know," she said, gnawing on her snuff. "Most folks believe it was a mountain lion. But I think it was somethin' differn't."

"What do you think it was?" I asked.

"Well," she said, thoughtfully. "I think some things are best left unsaid."

I felt entirely let down until she spoke again. When she did, she said, "But I'll tell you this much. Whatever'n't was that killed 'ol Cletus stole 'is voice box. Been going around screaming just like 'ol Cletus used to ever since. And now what in hell lives for fifty years and don't die? Other'n a human? But I'm here to tell ya, what ya'll's hearin' ain't no human. And it ain't no donkey!"

I knew not how to respond to this. Was she putting me on?

"I'll tell you one thing," she said, standing slowly. She moved over to the edge of the porch and cleaned the snuff out of her lower lip with an index finger, throwing it on the ground where I saw she had quite the little pile of snuff balls. "If'n you hear it on your property, better get inside the house."

She turned and walked in her house like I wasn't even there after that.

At the time I was convinced she was putting me on. If she'd been cousins with the woman we bought our property from, then that would mean she was related to the worthless piece of welfare bum shit that used to take the hay off of our land and she probably didn't like me, even though she'd never met me and I'd always been friendly to her in passing. She was probably just trying to scare me off my land so her piece of shit relative could start taking the hay again. Let me tell you, when you get into an area where the same families have lived for generations, you notice that they've developed an odd sort of entitlement mentality. Not that the Government owes them a monthly check, but that they're entitled to have a say in what anyone new to their community does or does not do. They think they own the damn place or something.

But my gut told me this was wrong thinking. This little old lady actually seemed like a really nice woman, and I doubt that she disliked me just because I stopped allowing her piece of shit deadbeat good for nothing annoying welfare bum neighbor to take our hay (should I tell you how I really feel about that guy?).

In time, I would come to believe that she was telling the truth.

Now, as far as Karen goes. And the donkeys that are in our area?

Well, that young lady was no Karen at all. I would end up meeting her for real about a year later. Our kids, it turns out, are in the same grade, though in different classes, at school, and I saw her at a school function. She actually approached me and told me she sees me running and biking all the time and that she loved all the trees my wife and I have planted on our property.

After talking with this lady, whose name is *not* Karen, for several minutes, I reminded her of the morning I'd asked about a donkey. She apologized for having made me feel like a serial rapist. She just said it scared her knowing that I had been hearing the donkey screams, too, because she'd heard the same story the old woman told me, but she'd heard it from someone else. As it turns out, the old piece of shit that used to get my hay used to get the hay off of her family's property until she and her husband bought it a couple years before we bought ours. Just like us, this family had bought their small, five or six acres tract of land for their purposes, not to simply grow free hay for some generational local, and the hay collector took issue with them as well when they told him he could no longer take the hay. I guess he'd passively aggressively stalked them for a while, too, just like he did us, and at one point, he'd told their daughter, who is my son's age, that the "Donkey Man" was going to get her. The woman told me they'd actually called the police on him for that, but the sheriff was his cousin, so nothing was done.

The lady told me that shortly after I'd asked her about the donkey, she and her husband bought a couple of donkeys so that when her daughter heard donkeys she would assume it was hers. The lady told me that in only a few short months, it worked. Though she and her husband hate taking care of the donkeys, and they hate how loud they are, they are glad their daughter no longer fears this so-called "donkey man," and the whole family sleeps better. Though, she admitted, that like myself now, she wonders just what in the hell is out there making the screams of a donkey from far away. Sometimes by day, and sometimes in the dead of night.

Could it be a skinwalker? Like our young lady from Texas suggested in our previous story?

Could it be the ghost of 'ol Cletus?

Or, could it be a Bigfoot Sasquatch, mimicking the sounds of a donkey?

Potentially!

The End

*Author's afterword:

Thanks to all of you who have been fervently following this Bigfoot Sasquatch Files series. I apologize for the later than usual release of volume 10. We'd gotten used to releasing these little jewels, monthly, like clockwork.

The hold up of one month with this release is all the fault of those bastards in Hollywood. Yes, just like the story "A Letter From Hollywood" in a volume several volumes back, we were being "considered" for an online streaming series. It all fell through, not when I refused to rewrite a certain story in a previous volume (when Jane finds out that Dr. (honorary, of course) Drake is her father), but because the funding was never there for the series in the first place.

We'll be moving forward with volume 11 really soon, and there will be no holdups, this time, unless the letter we get from Hollywood next time is actually from a major, bonafide online streaming network like Netflix, Hulu, Amazon, etc.

No more fly by nighters!

Because there's only room for one fly by nighter around here.

And that would be me!

Crazy M F'ing Lake!

See ya next time!